About the Author

I am a Londoner. My father was a master builder. I went to school at St Felix School in Southwold. I worked in the conveyancing department of several London legal firms. My family comprises my son, Julian, his lovely wife, Staci, and two beautiful granddaughters, Lexi and Lois. I went to Tunisia on holiday numerous times and loved the country and its people, which inspired me to write *The Jasmine Flowers* and eventually move to Tunisia when I stopped work, although I go back to England regularly to see my family. In Yasmine Hammamet I have an interest in a beach bar/restaurant but still find time and inspiration to write.

Lindsay Harrison

The Jasmine Flowers

Olympia Publishers
London

www.olympiapublishers.com
OLYMPIA PAPERBACK EDITION

Copyright © Lindsay Harrison 2018

The right of Lindsay Harrison to be identified as author of
this work has been asserted in accordance with sections 77 and 78 of the
Copyright, Designs and Patents Act 1988.

All Rights Reserved

No reproduction, copy or transmission of this publication
may be made without written permission.
No paragraph of this publication may be reproduced,
copied or transmitted save with the written permission of the publisher, or in
accordance with the provisions
of the Copyright Act 1956 (as amended).

Any person who commits any unauthorised act in relation to
this publication may be liable to criminal
prosecution and civil claims for damage.

A CIP catalogue record for this title is
available from the British Library.

ISBN: 978-1-84897-812-6

Names, characters, places and incidents originate from the writer's
imagination. Any resemblance to actual persons, living or dead, is purely
coincidental.

First Published in 2018

Olympia Publishers
60 Cannon Street
London
EC4N 6NP

Printed in Great Britain

Dedication

To my son, Julian, for putting up with me at home while I was clicking away on the computer into the night, for fixing the computer when it went on strike and for his love and acceptance that I wanted to follow my dream and move to Tunisia. To Wassel and Moncef Khsibi, Farhat Gafira, Debbie Hajri, Kate and Riadh Bahri and my other friends in Tunisia who have inspired and advised me.

PROLOGUE

This book is for my son, Julian, for all those who have advised me, for those who have inspired me and for anyone who believes in love. Sometimes dreams do come true.

I can confirm that there was a man, his name was not Farid and there was a woman, her name was not Lucy. This story is a work of fiction but, as with any writer, qualities I have admired or disliked in people have been incorporated into my characters. Others are merely a figment of my imagination. Of course many of the places are real and some incidents actually took place but where truth merges with fiction must remain my secret, and theirs. These two people could be any couple caught up unwillingly in the quagmire of prejudice towards age, race, religion and culture. It must surely be acknowledged that where intolerance on these matters abounds, enhanced by the element of personal jealousy, then broken dreams and tragedy will flourish as surely as night follows day. I am the eternal optimist, a romantic, and I hope, like me, that my reader will believe if the love of two people is strong enough nothing can overcome that love, which in this world and I believe in the next, will defeat anything the human race can dream up to throw at it. The rest is up to God.

CHAPTER ONE

SIMON

The divorce had been easier than she had thought it would be. Simon was reasonable, which in all the circumstances she felt he damn well should be. He had taken a larger mortgage and paid her off so he could keep the big house with its rambling corridors and ancient eaves' cupboards, some of which, in her three years of marriage, Lucy had never even ventured to look inside. She hated spiders. In her fertile imagination there lurked all manner of strange beasties in the dark recesses of the eaves, reached by the four narrow stairs which separated the three bedrooms and bathroom from the two remaining upstairs rooms. The smaller of the two was so tiny it was only really useful for storage but down the corridor, at the far end of the house, was the large and presumably intended to be, master bedroom.

This room was huge, sloping down on both sides to the eaves' cupboards. It was a dark unwelcoming space and Lucy had taken an instant dislike to it, insisting that they used the light pretty bedroom at the top of the stairs with the slightly smaller one next door as a guest room. As such the big bedroom had never been redecorated, the magnolia paint was peeling, the window frames damp and dusty. The floorboards remained bare. It was just a space, bereft of furniture, curtains, pictures or personality, unused and unloved. It was a part of the house which Lucy tried to forget about. On the odd occasion she had been up there she had felt uncomfortable, as though she was being watched by some unknown presence. She knew that in the eaves' cupboards, Simon stored cases of his beloved port wine, which he proudly produced at Christmas and other such occasions. What else he kept in there she had no idea, nor did she care.

"Why did you insist on buying such an enormous house, we've got quite enough space with the two bedrooms we use. We don't need the rest of the upstairs for just the two of us," she had raged at him when she had caught him pouring over magazines for ideas on redecorating the unused part of the house.

His reply shocked her. "I had hoped that one day there would not be just the two of us." Lucy had never really considered having children, it had just never come up between them, but the edge of sorrow in his voice had thrown her off guard. However the subject was never raised again.

When she had finally announced that she was leaving him and his dreadful old house to the next idiot who would put up with him, she already knew the identity of the idiot waiting in the wings.

It had been shortly after their wedding that Simon insisted on buying what she silently referred to as the mausoleum. It was a partially converted gatehouse to a small estate in a smart part of Surrey. The original old house still stood and was occupied by a stockbroker and his model wife but part of the grounds had been sold and there now stood a row of elegant mock-Georgian houses, in complete contrast to the quiet beauty of the original manor house.

The gatehouse conversion had not been carried out very sympathetically and the character in the weathered, soft-grey stone walls, broken only by quaint narrow windows, had to a perfectionist been ruined by a modern porchway and picture windows in the big square living room. The house was by its nature quite dark and although Simon whined about the windows being out of character, Lucy loved the light, bright living room with its huge windows and high ceiling and spent as much of her time as possible there. The dining room, which led directly off the hall, was oak panelled and very dark. If she was honest with herself, it was not so much that she had disliked the house on sight, apart from the living room, but she hated the fact that everyone else on the estate seemed to be about fifteen years older than her. This meant that she had little in common with them and their children were not yet of an age when they could become friends. However, Simon argued it was a convenient drive for him to get to work and manageable for her to get to London where she worked as a secretary.

Simon was a solicitor and she first met him when he defended her cousin's boyfriend, who was up on a fraud charge. He lost the case but gained a wife in Lucy. They had only known each other a few months when he asked her to marry him. Her parents approved and Lucy was swept along on the tide of arrangements, invitations, menus and paraphernalia. Six months later they were man and wife. Lucy wondered on her wedding day if she was making a mistake and whether they should have stayed as friends, but put it down to nerves. She was eight years younger than Simon and impressed by his quiet but forceful personality. He was so much more mature than most of her friends and he treated her with courtesy and respect.

He discussed old cases with her, explaining the reasoning behind the court decisions and on occasion, ventured to ask her opinion and actually listened to her when she gave it. Unfortunately this did not translate into their life together. He saw nothing wrong in making decisions without consulting her. He hurried through the purchase of the house and it had been precisely four weeks from the time they viewed to the day they moved in on the last day of December, he with great delight and she with equally great misgivings.

Simon arranged everything. He chose the decorations and furniture, paying lip service only to her suggestions and eventually deciding for himself. Not that his taste was bad. The cream, lightly patterned wallpaper and toning expensive cream carpet in the living room were elegantly set off by deep wine-red chesterfield settees and mahogany furniture. It would just not have been her usual choice but then when she thought about it, neither was he.

Lucy was five feet, five inches tall and Simon was not much taller than her and quite portly. His mousy, slightly receding hairline, big china blue eyes fringed with amazingly long blond lashes and round serious face put him a million miles from her usual choice of the traditional tall, dark and handsome male. Indeed how many young (and some not so young) women had not in their unspoken dreams been whisked off to a new exciting life by a virile being with jet black hair and glittering brown eyes. Lucy was no exception.

Simon was the opposite, but for once, Lucy's parents had approved her choice. However, within the space of a year, Lucy had met, fallen in love with, married and started to fall out of love with him. It had not taken her long to realise that although she was sure he was fond of her in his way, he saw her more as an extension of himself rather than her own person. He was charming, often amusing, well-mannered but so very different from her.

She was not his first wife. He had been married very young to a vivacious slim redhead who had left him after a couple of years of marriage and run off with an American, but not before cleaning out their joint bank account and stripping their home of everything of any value, and then departing for the airport and a new life in Texas. He divorced her, paid her half the equity in the house, which he really hadn't needed to do but thought it a small price to pay for her to disappear permanently. He spent his share of the proceeds on a shiny red sports car and moved in with an old friend from work where he proceeded to live the life of a carefree bachelor, with varying degrees of success, until he met Lucy.

Simon realised immediately that Lucy was exactly what he needed in a wife. Pretty, blonde, from a respectable family and smaller than him (he had always been conscious of his lack of height. Celine, his first wife had topped him by a good three inches.) Lucy was quite the opposite of Celine. She was also young and malleable. He was fond of her and he was sure she would be useful to him in his business and pleasant to have at home. He knew her parents liked him and he liked them. The only slight problem was of course her job. He did not want his wife to work, but he intended to deal with that situation after they were married. In all it was very satisfactory and filed away neatly in Simon's compartmentalised brain. Lucy had, as he suspected she would, complied with his wishes.

"Lucy, I cannot have you working. I may need you to come with me, to travel or attend a meeting or dinner. If you are working you can't do that," he painstakingly explained and reasoned. "I need you with me, you are my wife." Lucy was flattered that he felt her important and eventually agreed and gave in her notice.

After months of cleaning the house from top to bottom (save for the top two rooms) and never well enough to satisfy Simon's exacting standards, travelling up and down the country at Simon's bidding she was physically exhausted and mentally bored stiff. The people she associated with were often considerably older and she rarely had anything much to say to them or they to her. Lucy was not unaccustomed to conversing with older people as her parents had, from about the age of sixteen, always included her in the various functions they attended and at the London clubs when they were entertaining. With Simon's associates it was different. There was an element of competition which seemed to overtake every social occasion. Lucy found it unnerving and difficult to be her easy-going self when she was forever terrified of saying the wrong thing.

When they were not in Birmingham, Manchester, Norwich or some other part of the country, Simon's idea of an evening out was a quiet meal for two at a good restaurant with a decent bottle of wine or entertaining his friends, most of whom were associated in some way with his professional life. Lucy did not object particularly, but would have liked sometimes to try the local pub on a Saturday night, which she felt would have been a good place to meet other villagers. He would have none of it. When they first moved into the village on the very rare occasions she did persuade him to go for a drink, he stood uncomfortably with his back to the bar clutching his gin and tonic, looking as though it was the last place on earth he wanted to be. Such visits rarely lasted the hour. He found it difficult to relax with her own friends from before her marriage, who drifted slowly into the background as he absorbed her into his own inner circle.

The only people they really knew in the village were Jack and Chloe, a professional couple in their mid-thirties whom Simon felt were on the same level as himself. As Jack and Chloe sometimes used the pub at the weekends, Lucy found that Simon thawed out a bit towards the local hostelry and as such she started to look forward to the end of the week. She had noticed a young couple who seemed to always be sitting up at the bar on high stools, a long haired, skinny chap with glasses and his rather round little carrot haired wife. They were always smiling and seemed to know everyone.

One evening when Simon was sitting with Jack and Chloe discussing the forthcoming local election, Lucy made her way to the bar and stood next to the couple, while waiting to be served. She turned and smiled.

The woman grinned broadly. "Great! I wondered how long it would be before you'd get away from those three!" She peered over her glasses at Simon and his friends and pulled a very serious face.

Lucy stifled a laugh. "I'm not a great one for politics," she admitted, "Especially in the pub on a Saturday night." She held out her hand. "Hello. I'm Lucy."

"Jackie and this is Ewan, my husband."

"Hi." Ewan grinned and gave her a mock salute.

Lucy could not remember an evening she had enjoyed so much for a long time. Simon had taken the best part of an hour to notice her absence and when he came to the bar to replenish the drinks, he gave her a nudge. "Sorry, I was rather engrossed. I apologise."

Lucy beamed at him. "No worries, you know my views or should I say non-views on politics. I'm just chatting to Jackie. We seem to have got similar taste in music and films, not really your thing." She giggled.

"Are you coming back to join our friends."

Lucy noticed the emphasis firmly on 'our friends'. She had, however, managed to put away quite a few bottles of barley wine whilst he had not been looking and put her hand gently on his arm trying very hard to look intelligently meaningful.

"Look, Simon, I'm not remotely interested in politics as well you know. I'm happy with my friends and you are with yours. We can both enjoy ourselves much better if we don't have to talk about stuff that really doesn't interest us. That is if you don't mind."

She leaned forward and placed her bottle gently on the bar keeping her eyes on her husband and smiling graciously. The bottle wobbled where it was half on the beer mat and half on the bar surface before it toppled over. Lucy saw it out of the corner of her eye, made a frantic grab, missed and almost fell off her stool. The bottle dropped and Ewan neatly caught it. The three of them collapsed into laughter. Simon looked at her as though she had grown an extra head. He made one half-hearted attempt to lure her back to his table but to Lucy's relief, Ewan and Jackie resisted his attempts to freeze them out so Simon walked back to his friends, nodding politely to Ewan and Jackie, and Lucy remained happily glued to her bar stool all evening until the last bell sounded.

They spoke little when they got home and the incident was never mentioned. She knew that was Simon's way of expressing his disapproval and found she really couldn't care less. They did not stop going to the pub, although he made sure the visits were less frequent.

After a little gentle prodding, Simon found out that Ewan was involved in the world of electronic data processing which, in the mid-1960s, was definitely business of the future. Jackie was a teacher. He spoke to them once or twice and in his opinion neither held strong views on anything which could influence his wife, so he saw no harm in leaving her to her friends. In truth he was becoming somewhat irritated with Lucy's lack of enthusiasm and involvement in his various interests, particularly politics. He was especially irritated and embarrassed when one of the party members canvassing on behalf of the Tories knocked on the door one evening while he was at work. Lucy, thinking it was her husband and he might have forgotten his key, opened the front door and peaked around it dressed in nothing but a bath towel. Another incident which was referred to only once.

Lucy loved the company of her new friends. They were self-assured, happy with each other and at ease with the world and she looked forward to the comfortable evenings she spent with them.

To celebrate their first wedding anniversary, Simon and Lucy took a Caribbean cruise with Lucy's parents, which even Lucy had to admit was a great success. She loved foreign travel and it was her first cruise. She adored English Harbour in Barbados, the jewellery markets of the American Virgin Islands and lazed happily on the palm fringed beaches of Antigua marvelling at the difference between the islands, so close together and yet each so different.

On board, her parents quickly made friends with a couple from Reigate, who were taking their annual cruise. Richard Handley James was a tubby jovial sweetheart of a man who Lucy immediately likened to Piggy in Marilyn Monroe's *Gentlemen Prefer Blondes*, although he didn't own a diamond mine, merely a chain of estate agencies. His wife, a tall, elegant, cool blonde of indeterminate age, was beautifully and without a doubt very expensively dressed. Lucy found her a little intimidating until she realised that in this case, appearances were indeed deceptive. Elaine Handley James absolutely adored her little fat husband and was just as nice as he was.

Lucy had inherited a passion for gardening from her grandfather and recounted to Elaine stories of the happy hours she had spent in Granddad's greenhouse as a youngster, helping, or perhaps hindering him, in potting up his favoured primulas. He insisted she wore huge plastic gloves in case the sap from the stems irritated her tiny fingers. Granddad had died when she was in her late teens and Lucy missed him dreadfully. She and Elaine developed a strong bond over the three weeks of the cruise and promised to keep in touch on their return to England. What neither of them knew was that this friendship was to be the catalyst that would change Lucy's life.

It had started innocently enough. After the cruise, she and Elaine did keep in touch and Lucy often went to Elaine's home. Together they ambled around the enormous garden and according to the seasons, planting, mulching, picking and pruning. What Lucy enjoyed most was collecting all the fruit and vegetables and sitting at the great oak kitchen table with Elaine, peeling and preparing the produce ready for freezing and bottling for the winter months to come.

Simon took to working late into the evenings, the trips around the country had all but dried up and Lucy was more bored than ever. Her visits to Elaine and her chats with Ewan and Jackie she felt kept her sane. Simon tried to compromise by meeting her every Tuesday and Friday evenings at around 10p.m. for a meal at the local bistro. He was, however, frequently late and often they ended up being the last people to leave. Lucy felt uncomfortable knowing that the staff were waiting to go to their own homes, but too polite and professional to show it.

One particular Tuesday, Simon had turned up really very late. He said he'd been to Birmingham. Lucy was sitting in the bistro for an hour by herself getting more and more embarrassed and angry. It was once too often and when he finally arrived, dishevelled and red faced, they had a heated argument which culminated in Lucy stalking out of the restaurant and going home. She went to bed. She heard his car pull into the driveway an hour or so later and pretended to be asleep. He slept in the spare room.

The next morning she deliberately got up early and sat at the dining table in her nightgown and slippers, sipping her coffee and pointedly taking deep drags on her cigarette, which she knew would annoy him. He stared at her as he came down the stairs, said little and did not stop for breakfast. He curtly announced he would be home late that evening.

"Shame," she said with as much sarcasm as she could muster, "and it's not even Friday yet." Simon glared at her and slammed the door on his way out.

Lucy had, for months, seen her marriage slipping down the drain. Most evenings, when Simon was home, they sat silently in the huge living room, he with his paper and she with her magazine, but not in the comfortable understanding that couples often have which makes constant speech unnecessary. These were awkward silences, with neither party finding anything constructive to talk about. He no longer discussed his work with her and she became more and more miserable and depressed. She approached him about his absences and his obvious unwillingness to discuss the matter had for all her bravado, deeply upset her. She knew she could be difficult sometimes and demanded more of his presence than he was prepared to offer, but she sensed the undercurrent of change and it frightened her.

After he left, she tidied up and hoovered mechanically, her thoughts in turmoil and then she sat down and had a good cry.

She called Elaine and asked if she could come over. She knew Elaine would have been able to tell from her voice that something was wrong but that she would be too polite to comment.

To Lucy's surprise, Elaine seemed very offhand. "You can come if you want. There are some runners and fruit to pick and I suppose I could do with some help." She put the phone down.

Lucy was stunned, but she was so miserable anyway, she felt Elaine couldn't make things any worse than they already were, so she started up her little car and drove to Reigate.

The car ran out of petrol. Lucy sat beside the car on the grass verge at the side of the road and howled. An elderly lady stopped and as soon as she realised Lucy was not about to expire, insisted she give her a lift to the village and back to pick up a gallon of petrol. The car reeked of dogs and a large, hairy King Charles spaniel settled himself on her lap and gazed up at her adoringly as she tickled his chest. For all her misery, Lucy found time to mentally thank Simon for insisting she always carry a can in the boot. As he put it, she had run out of petrol once before and if she didn't have the sense to check the gauge before she left home then she had better carry a can in the boot.

When she finally arrived at Elaine's luxury mansion she was covered in dog hair, her hands were filthy and her hair had partly fallen out of her ponytail as she had wrestled with the petrol cap which was stuck fast. She rang the bell and waited. Elaine opened the door, her pristine cream shirt tucked into khaki, combat style trousers which were in turn tucked into muddy green wellies. Her blonde hair was neatly caught up in a black snood and there was a smudge of dirt on her flushed cheek. She looked wonderful! *God, I must look a sight*, Lucy thought as she smiled weakly at her friend.

Elaine took in her appearance in one quick glance and beckoned her inside. "Hello, my dear. Have you been unwell?"

Lucy was puzzled. "No, not really, just another horrible row with him."

"Ah," said Elaine. "I had rather hoped there was a better excuse for your rudeness."

Lucy had no idea what she was talking about. "Sorry?"

"Yesterday, in the car?"

"I didn't go out yesterday, until I went to corner shop around six for some cigarettes. I was indoors all day, bored to hell."

Elaine's eyebrows went rose slightly and she looked over her glasses at Lucy. "Really."

Lucy was starting to get annoyed. "Yes, Elaine. I was indoors all day."

"Well," said Elaine "Then there must be something wrong with my eyesight."

Lucy felt sick. "Go on."

She sat down at the kitchen table and Elaine put the kettle on. She studied Lucy intently but said nothing.

"Go on," Lucy repeated. "Where was I supposed to be then?"

Elaine regarded her thoughtfully over the top of her spectacles. "Richard and I went shopping in Reigate town centre around lunchtime. We had just finished and were on our way home. We were waiting at the lights and Simon's car drew up next to us. I waved at you and you looked straight at me as though you had never seen me before. I don't know whether you and Simon were having a row, but there was no need for that. It was totally unacceptable and not what I would have expected from you, whatever the circumstances."

She waited. Lucy made no response but shook her head in denial.

"Look, Lucy, I am not that decrepit that I can't recognise Simon's bright red sports car with a personalised number plate. I admit I was surprised to see Simon driving around Reigate in the middle of a weekday afternoon but the car drew up not more than a couple of yards from me and the two of you were definitely in it. I appreciate you may have been upset or something, but you could at least apologise."

She looked at the young woman with undisguised disapproval, but was unprepared for Lucy's bewilderment.

"Elaine. I am not lying. If you must know, I spent the afternoon trying unsuccessfully to tie in that overgrown climbing rose around the front porch. Look." She held out her hands and showed Elaine the evil scratches all over the back of her right hand. "Elaine, I have no idea who you saw but it wasn't me. I don't know who was in the car, but the woman was not me, and Simon told me he was in Birmingham," she added miserably. Elaine stared, unsure what to say. Lucy was obviously telling the truth. She leaned across the table and took Lucy's hands in hers. "Oh my dear, I don't know what to say, I was so sure it was you."

Lucy held back the tears that pricked at the back of her eyes. "It's OK, I should have seen this coming, late evenings, excuses, dinners on his own where I am not included and new people creeping into his tight little circle of friends and acquaintances. Oh shit…"

Elaine pursed her lips and started to say something but thought better of it.

"I have just realised who you must have seen. She's called Carole Jennings. His firm acted on her divorce a few years back before he met me. She's been at a couple of the dos recently and it's been commented on how alike we are. That was who was in the car with him, the bitch." She burst into angry tears.

Elaine did her best to comfort her, interspersed with muttered apologies, but Lucy was resolute.

"Actually, Elaine you've done me a favour. You've given me the escape route and jolted me into actually doing something. I was getting to the point where I didn't know what to do. I tried to make it work, but if I'm honest, I have known my marriage was in trouble for months. Half the time we've been at each other's throats and the rest we've just skirted around each other like a couple of cats. What I need is a job, I need to use my brain again and I need to end this mess once and for all." She smiled. "Do you know, I even considered whether having an affair would help as it seems to be quite usual where we live, but I couldn't find anyone I fancied!"

Elaine frowned her disapproval, but smiled back when she realised Lucy had made a rather feeble attempt at a joke. "Lucy, my love, I'm afraid I can't advise you on this one. You must make up your own mind. I know your life with Simon is comfortable and the future on your own may be uncertain, but you must do what you feel is right. Your head may well argue security, creature comforts and…" she hesitated, "…and your parents' approval."

Lucy laughed. "How well you know me."

"Lucy, look at me. You are young, you have your whole life ahead of you, you must always listen to your heart if you really want to be happy. Everyone advised me against marrying Richard, he was a struggling junior estate agent, nothing to look at and insecure. I was told he'd never amount to anything and I'd ruin my life by marrying him, but I knew I loved him and he loved me. We've been together for over thirty years and that love has become deeper as time has passed. I can't say every day has been wonderful. It hasn't. Like everyone else we've had our ups and downs, but I wake up every morning and know I made the right decision because I followed my heart in spite of everything and everyone."

Lucy listened. She had never heard Elaine talk like this.

"My sweet girl, I can only say to you, when you meet the man you truly love, you will know. It happens only once in your lifetime, and even then not to everyone, only the lucky few."

She sat back in her chair, and snorted. "Sorry my dear, I'm waffling on again."

"No you're not and I love you for it."

Lucy took her friend's hands in her own and they sat, two young hands holding two older, wiser hands. "Thank you, Elaine. I will always remember, follow my heart." Lucy could not know how prophetic those words would be.

She asked him if he would please let her know if he was going to be late so his dinner would not be spoiled. He said of course he would and he was sorry he had been thoughtless. The atmosphere between them lifted and he promised to call her from the office when he was leaving so she'd know what time to expect him. What he did not know was that Lucy had already looked up Carole Jennings address in the phone book. She had known she lived in the Reigate area and found the address in a matter of minutes.

Three times over the next two weeks, when he had called her to say he was leaving the office, she had raced to her car and driven the ten minutes to Carole's house. On each occasion his red car was parked outside. Something in her had hoped she was wrong, and the first time she unwillingly proved herself right, she cried. After that it became easier. "Christ you idiot," she had said aloud to herself as she tore home the last time down the main road to ensure she was home when he got back "If you're going to fuck about so close to home, at least get a car which isn't quite so ostentatious." She sang along with the radio, grimly and out of tune, but the tears at the back of her eyes were held well in check.

She was honest with herself, it was not the affair which hurt, she had long ago realised she had never really been in love with him, just with the idea of being in love. He had been the wrong person at the right time. No, it was not even the betrayal, but her own sense of failure, the hurt that the inevitable divorce would cause her parents who had given her such a fairy-tale wedding and who genuinely liked the husband of their only child. That hurt and for that, she hated him and herself.

She had prepared the dinner before she went out and as she dished up her mind raced as she changed it over and over again. *How should she deal with this? What would he do? Sod it,* she thought, *just get straight to the point, no nastiness, no recriminations and above all no tears. Just announce I am going and go.*

Simon rushed in, full of apologies and kissed her absently on the cheek. He sat down and picked up the paper. She handed him his gin and tonic and he smiled at her and returned to his paper.

"How was Birmingham?"

He looked up, startled. "Birmingham? What do you mean?"

"Oh sorry I thought you were there today."

"No that was last week." Back to the paper.

"My mistake. Did you see Patrick while you were there?"

Simon did not look up from the paper. "Eh, yes, he asked after you." He sensed the conversation was not at an end and gave up on the paper, folding his arms across his middle.

"How's Carole these days?" His eyes met hers and she was pleased to see a slight flush creep up from his neck.

"I've no idea. Why on earth do you ask that? I haven't seen her since that dinner about three weeks ago." He picked up his drink and concentrated on the ice cube floating in the glass.

She smiled sweetly. "Oh that's strange, Elaine saw the two of you in Reigate last week, you know when you were in Birmingham."

She had his attention now. His blue eyes stared widely at her, the muscle in his cheek twitching. "Rubbish. She must have been mistaken." She continued to smile at him and echoed Elaine's words.

"Simon, she's not that decrepit that she can't recognise your car from a couple of yards away. You see, she thought it was me with you and waved at me. She couldn't understand when I just stared through her."

His face had by now turned bright red. "Bullshit. The old bat must be blind as well as stupid."

"Oh, and I suppose I'm stupid and blind as well and that it was not your car parked outside Carole's house three times in the last couple of weeks. Is that bullshit too?" She spat the last few words at him and stood with her hands on her hips waiting.

He looked at her long and hard. "OK. Right I have seen Carole a couple of times. I didn't tell you because I knew you'd react just the way you have. Anyway what do you expect? You've been such a miserable bitch recently, always moaning and frankly I've just had enough of you."

Lucy bristled. "I don't suppose it occurred to you to think that my moaning and misery coincided with your so called working late. How long has this little affair been going on anyway? And don't tell me it isn't an affair, cos I am neither blind nor stupid."

Simon had recovered his composure. He stood up and faced her his fists clenched at his sides.

"Four months."

Lucy glared at him, her mouth slightly open. That she had not expected.

"What are you going to do?"

Lucy's good intentions disappeared. "What the hell do you think I'm going to do," she screamed. "I want a bloody divorce and I'll tell you something else. You can keep this horrible mausoleum if you want, but so far as I am concerned, it is what I want that matters."

"As always," he yelled back.

"No not as always, just for once. I am not going to be your little patsy. I want £5,000 plus the £10,000 my dad gave us which you put into the house I never wanted in the first place." The figures had come from nowhere. She hadn't thought about it, in fact she hadn't even considered the money side of things.

She sat down as far away from him as she could get, the tears streaming down her face.

Simon saw the light in the tunnel. He knew what the house was worth and he had no intention of going through another fleecing as he had with Celine. If the divorce became messy he would lose a lot more than £15,000 and he had no intention of getting rid of the house. He did some quick sums and figured out he could afford that with a bigger mortgage. He sat down opposite her.

"OK. If that's what you want. Agreed."

"That's it?"

"Yes, that's it. The only condition I make is that we deal with this as sensible adults with the least possible expense and trouble."

Lucy nodded bleakly. Is that what her marriage was worth, 'the least possible expense and trouble?' He got up and walked out of the front door and she heard the car roar away up towards the Reigate road.

As she had expected, her parents were devastated. She did not tell them about Carole, just that she and Simon had decided it wasn't working and had decided to separate. Her father, to whom she had always been very close, said very little other than if she were that unhappy then she should do what she needed to. Her mother was less understanding and urged her to work at the marriage, going into long lectures about how marriages were not made in heaven, they needed love and attention and that she should consider her husband and her future above her own whims and fancies. Never at any time did they suspect Simon's unfaithfulness, although her mother did ask once her if she herself had another man.

Rather unkindly she felt her mother was perhaps a bit influenced by the social side of things and in fact they had a good shouting match when Lucy refused point blank to wear her wedding ring when they went out to dinner with family friends. Her mother pleaded with her to say Simon was away on business, but Lucy was adamant and to her surprise, her father backed her up. She was insistent on the divorce and because Simon was as good as his word and the whole matter was dealt with by his firm without recrimination or unpleasantness she actually remained on speaking terms with him. What surprised her most was that when she did attend a dinner and Carole was present, she had no difficulty in speaking civilly to her and in fact was somewhat mollified to find she was actually quite a nice person.

In fact, when Simon died many years later, Carole called her to ask her if she wanted to attend the funeral. With some misgivings she did and was touched when Carole insisted she sit in the front row with the family. Carole also told her that at the time just before Simon and Lucy's divorce, when she herself had been seeing Simon, he had actually told her he and Lucy were no longer together. She assured Lucy that had she known she would never have agreed to see him, having been divorced herself, she would not have wanted anyone else to go through what she had been through. Lucy acknowledged the kindness but decided not to keep contact and closed the book forever on that part of her life.

CHAPTER TWO

THE BOY

After the divorce, Lucy found herself to be a young divorcee with a comfortable bank balance of £20,000, and very much wiser. She secured a local secretarial job at a reasonable salary, nothing too thought provoking for the moment, just a way of keeping busy.

Simon moved back into the gatehouse with Carole, and at Jackie and Ewan's insistence, Lucy moved into the spare room in their quaint little cottage at the top end of the village, a mile or so from the old house. She helped out with the bills, the cooking and shopping and the three of them were always seen around the village together. She had no interest in Ewan other than as a friend nor he in her. The threesome worked well. Her contribution meant everyone had a bit more money to spend. A few months later, the cottage next door came up for sale so Lucy used half of her savings and bought it with a small mortgage, moved in and settled into a comfortable rut.

One warm Saturday in June, they ambled over to the local pub. The air was heavy with the scent of flowers and Jackie's eyes were streaming from hay fever. In between the sneezes she told Lucy that Ewan was being sent on a computer course in September.

After a drink or three she suggested that whilst he was away the two of them should take a holiday together. Lucy had not had a holiday since the cruise and when Jackie suggested they should go abroad, she readily agreed. Jackie's round pink face was wreathed in smiles. Ewan seemed a little less enthusiastic but after a few minutes of his adored wife's wheedling he grudgingly remarked it might do them good.

They sat in Jackie's front room later that evening. "Where d'you fancy going?" she asked.

Lucy grinned. "Somewhere hot and exotic, terribly foreign and away from the usual holiday spots of the Brits."

Lucy had a deep abhorrence of the dreadful reputation the British were rapidly acquiring abroad for their drunken rowdy antics with the consequential upset and insult to the local people. She liked to visit places which gave her a taste of another culture, another way of life and preferably somewhere she could at least speak a little of the language. She had always found languages relatively easy at school. Her French was good, her Italian reasonable. With a bit more effort, she could even make herself understood in Spanish and German.

At the age of seventeen, she announced she had no intention of trying for university and insisted on leaving school. Her disillusioned parents were adamant that if she was not going to university then she go to language college for a year. Unfortunately, in her late teens, Lucy was going through what she later referred to as her "wild time". She was far more interested in the teachers than the languages, and in particular her Italian teacher, Nico. She learned a lot that summer and not all of it in college, but her Italian improved enormously.

Jackie turned up after work with an armful of glossy brochures, each one setting out in great detail the reasons why its offerings were better than everyone else's. As they flicked through the pages they laughed at the impossibly gaudy colours. Shocking pink flowers, the deep azure of the sea and cloudless blue sky. "Not a tourist in sight," observed Lucy, giggling.

They leafed through France, Spain, Italy, Greece.

Jackie stopped. "Canary Islands, that's exotic."

"No it's not, it's just Spain a bit further away and more expensive."

"I can see you're going to be difficult." She grinned at Lucy, who stuck her nose in the air in mock indifference. Jackie flicked through a few more pages. "Hey look at this, what about Morocco. You can't say that's not exotic."

The two girls studied the pictures and picked out a tall, white hotel with Moorish arches over the balconies and a huge marble entrance hallway.

Jackie grinned. "You could really make an entrance there – Oh God, that means new clothes."

"It does not!" Ewan looked up from his paper frowning. "Let's have a look."

Jackie handed him the brochure.

"Bloody hell, that's pricey." He peered at them "Isn't Morocco where they had that earthquake a few years back." He winked at Lucy.

"That's out then," Jackie retorted, "I'm not getting swallowed up by some earthquake and paying for the privilege."

"Jackie, that was years ago," Lucy retorted, glaring at Ewan. But the damage was done. Nothing would persuade Jackie to consider Morocco.

Ewan ambled upstairs announcing that if they were intending to spend lots of money he'd better have a bath whilst they could still afford to pay the heating bills. Jackie stuck her tongue out at his thin back as he went up the stairs. He waggled his bottom at her.

Jackie picked up another brochure and slowly turned the pages. "What about this then. Tunisia?"

Lucy studied the pictures. It certainly looked nice and not as expensive as Morocco.

Jackie's pink face glowed with excitement. "Hang on, haven't they done some filming there recently?

"Yeah, I think they might have done"

"Well that settles it, chirruped Jackie. "If it's good enough for Omar Sharif, it's good enough for me."

Lucy glanced up at her. "What are you talking about, Omar Sharif?"

"Well we might see him!"

Lucy grinned at her. "You idiot. He's not Tunisian, he's Egyptian."

"Oh, that's a drag, still it looks nice."

Lucy studied the page. There was something about the pictures of the old town of Sousse which beckoned to her. The dark, narrow alleyway leading into the old market, the huge sandy blocks of the walls of the Medina and the wide open spaces looking out over the crystal clear blue water. "Yes. I really like this idea," she said softly.

"They speak French there don't they?" Jackie said. "At least if we get lost you'll be able to ask our way out!"

Lucy nodded, already dreaming of the holiday to come. By the time Ewan came back downstairs, swathed in his enormous red bath towel, his hair plastered down and his beard dripping wet, their minds were made up.

"OK, where's it to be then," he asked.

His wife beamed at him. "Tunisia."

He glanced from one to the other. "Are you sure?" He looked concerned. "Why can't the two of you just go and flake out on a Spanish beach somewhere and have done with it. It's also a hell of a lot cheaper. I'm not sure I'm happy about you taking off to some Arab country in Africa on your own."

He glared at Lucy. "I suppose this was your idea?"

"Actually it was Jackie's," she retorted and added wickedly "She wants to meet Omar Sharif."

"Don't be so bloody daft," Ewan grinned. "And anyway…"

"He's Egyptian," both girls chorused, beaming at each other and laughing. Ewan gave up and buried his head in his book.

They chose the hotel, a modest looking, dusty, brown building near to the beach in Sousse. Lucy was quite surprised how reasonably priced it was. They had considered Hammamet which had been popular with the more adventurous bohemian traveller for some time but Lucy opted for Sousse on the basis there seemed to be quite a lot going on there, to her it seemed Hammamet was more beach based but Sousse was a city by the sea.

There was another reason she didn't mention. During her teens she had travelled extensively throughout Europe and had been to the coliseum in Rome. It had been one of the highlights of her travels and she read in the brochure that there was a Roman coliseum in Tunisia at a place called El Djem further down south which appeared to be much nearer Sousse than Hammamet. The brochure said it was wonderfully well preserved and Lucy had every intention of seeing for herself.

A couple of months later, the two friends arrived at the airport, which fortunately was not too far from home. They decided to travel light. As Jackie sensibly pointed out "We've got to lug these cases around ourselves, we don't know what the transfers are like to the hotel and there's no man to carry for us!"

Their flight was called. Lucy's stomach did its customary hop. She adored travelling and particularly flying, most of all the take-off with the noise and being pulled back into the seat as the plane thundered down the runway, striving to get speed and power to lift the huge metal bird into the air. She was not scientifically minded and had often wondered how on earth such an enormous chunk of metal could lift into the air with the grace of a swan. Not for the first time in her life she wished she had been born a boy. She would most definitely have been a pilot.

The flight was uneventful but the food on the plane was dreadful and the landing worse. It was a little after midday and as they stepped out into the blinding sunlight, it was as though an oven door had been flung open. The pilot had mentioned a heat wave, but neither girl expected this. Jackie gasped "Jesus, I didn't realise it would be this hot."

Lucy breathed deeply taking in the dry African heat. She laughed. "Jackie, this is Africa." Even the sound of it made her skin prickle. The first misgivings washed over her. Perhaps Ewan was right and they should have stuck to what they knew. She didn't remember Spain ever being this hot and it was already September. She made a mental note if she was to come again to Tunisia, not to come in mid-summer.

They clambered into the little bus taking them to the terminal building, which seemed to Lucy little more than a large, low, white shack. She was lost in thought. "Africa," she murmured. Even the sound of it was exotic. Land of wild animals, deep forests, surging rivers and hostile natives. She smiled to herself. Twit! This was not deepest Africa but a small country in Northern Africa with hundreds of miles of Mediterranean coastline, all be it that the guidebook said a large part of the country was made up of the Sahara desert. The book had also said it was the most westernised Arab country and the people were by nature very friendly.

The book had however gone on to say that a visitor would have to discourage the numerous street sellers and if you did want to buy anything you had to barter for it to get the price down, but added that bartering was expected and was simply a way of life and not so aggressive as Morocco or Egypt. There had been a small paragraph warning women that they should avoid the predatory native men at all costs!

"Are you coming or not, or have you gone to sleep?" Jackie prodded her.

After what seemed hours of jostling and pushing through the passport control and noise of the airport, the coach took them to the hotel. The journey was uncomfortable and long. They arrived dusty, tired and thirsty. The agent had run through much of the content in the guidebook, beach safety, mosquitoes and don't drink the water. He had added the warning about women travelling alone. Once checked into the hotel he gave them his number in case of emergency, wished them a good holiday and disappeared.

The room was hot, but adequate. The tiny bathroom was not. The toilet was chipped and stained and there was no seat. Neither was there a bath, just a very basic shower head sticking out of the wall, draining into a hole in the ground with a tatty plastic curtain around it.

"There's always the sea," quipped Jackie.

"Daft lump." Lucy threw a pillow at her. "You may end up clean but how do you get the sand and salt off."

"Who cares, we've arrived!" sang Jackie, pulling out one of the drawers in the ancient wardrobe, which fell out with an ominous crack onto the tiled floor.

An hour or so later they headed to the restaurant, clean and refreshed. The meal was a plate of salad, followed by fragrant rice with spicy chunks of meat and a separate stew of large pieces of vegetable, flavoured with a reddish sauce which tasted odd but satisfying. The bread was baked into a round shape about an inch or so thick and served warm cut into slices like a cake. It was the most beautiful bread Lucy had ever tasted. She wondered what was in the dip of crimson red paste next to it, which looked very spicy and when she dipped her finger gingerly into it and licked the thick mixture she thought her tongue would explode. She later found out harissa is a paste made from chillies and is served in or with everything in Tunisia. Lucy loved trying out new foods but sensibly decided that the first night away was not a good time to encourage her stomach to rebel and left the red dip untouched.

After dinner, armed with the basic guidebook map, they took a short walk. The narrow streets were exactly as the brochure had depicted, colourful, noisy and exotic. Many of the shops were still open and from everywhere faces peered out, white teeth beaming a welcome and inviting them into their shops. "Ingleesh, yes? You come see my shop, now." Good natured encouragement and as the book said, no aggression.

The weather remained very hot and they spent the week exploring the town, taking photographs and generally lazing around the beach but Jackie would not go to El Djem. It was the only disagreement they had.

"Lucy, it's just too hot and too far" Jackie complained. "I really am not into trotting around old ruins, the place is inland and the heat will be unbearable."

"How do you know if you don't even try?" Lucy was annoyed.

"You go, I'm quite capable of entertaining myself for an afternoon, but honestly I really don't want to go."

She looked hard at Lucy's pinched face. "Look, you like this place, don't you?"

"Yes, I love it."

"Well then it's likely you'll come back and you can go then. After all let's be honest it's not going anywhere."

"OK point taken." Lucy gave up. She really didn't want to go on her own and Jackie was right. She would be back.

They were catching a night flight and decided to have one last good shopping spree. As they were going to be out for most of the day, Lucy dressed carefully – a long tiered white skirt and a lacy, rose coloured blouse, wide on the neckline and sleeves which fell loose to her elbows. The one thing she didn't want was to get sunburned at the end of her holiday. She brushed her hair until it shone but left it down so it fell around her shoulders in waves of pale blonde and silver where the sun had lightened it.

She looked at her reflection in the mirror. The dark circles under her eyes had all but disappeared and her skin had tanned to a soft honey.

She smirked. She knew she looked good. To hell with Simon! Normally during the daytime she avoided make up but today brushed a grape colour to her lids, enhancing their greenness, a touch of mascara and a slick of pale pink lipstick.

Jackie came out of the bathroom and looked her friend up and down. "Lucy, you look about eighteen. The air certainly agrees with you."

"I feel great, like I could conquer the world and more than anything I feel really contented, better than I've felt for a long time. To be honest, Jack I'm dreading going home."

"Oh come on, we've got all day. Think about that tonight. Anything could happen today. Maybe Ewan will win the pools and we can have another couple of weeks!"

They walked around the Medina, collecting souvenirs and Lucy spotted a silver bracelet set with oval shaped beads in a clear translucent green, flecked with turquoise but which in the sunlight gave off little flashes of colour. "I must have those! They are beautiful. I wonder what they are"

Jackie smiled. "They are probably cheap bits of glass, but they are pretty. Buy them, but watch out for the price. I am sure it will be double for tourists."

Lucy grinned and managed to haggle the price down, although it was more than she would normally pay.

"You got done!"

"They are exactly what I want and will probably last longer than the plates and pictures we've bought."

"You've got a point there," her friend admitted as she fastened the clip around Lucy's wrist.

They stopped for lunch at a tiny restaurant and tried the local food. Some sort of pancake stuffed with everything, tuna-fish, hard boiled eggs, salad, cream cheese, mayonnaise, the spicy dark red chili paste, even chips, and a few things she couldn't place. It was delicious and cost the equivalent of a few pennies.

The two friends walked away from the Medina towards the sea but further than they had been before. It was there they found the café. It was right by the seafront. White tables and chairs curved around the front of the building in a half-circle. Brightly coloured parasols swirled and fluttered like a troop of chorus girls. The place was crowded, mainly local men, some office workers in smart dark trousers and crisp white shirts, others in the ubiquitous uniform of the young, jeans and T-shirts. Most sat in groups in the shade as they sipped from their tiny cups, sheltering from the heat.

They headed for the cool interior of the building, long and thin with a few heavy wooden tables and a couple of benches. All the tables were taken by more men, talking loudly and many playing cards. Lucy stood at the counter and watched whilst the waiter poured out the dark thick coffee into the little cups, topping some of them with a swirl of frothy milk. She stared in amazement as the men heaped spoon after spoon of sugar into their cups. She found it hard to understand how they could fit so much sugar into one small cup and then actually drink it. She noticed that there were large bottles of water on every table and it seemed that the way to drink was to take a sip of coffee and then a drink of water. Maybe that's how they managed the sweet evil looking liquid! She must remember to give it a try, but without the sugar!

As there was no room inside they followed the waiter back into the strong sunlight. Momentarily blinded, Lucy reached into her bag and put her sunglasses back on. The waiter took them to a small table on the edge of the circle, near to the promenade. The table was well shaded and there was a good breeze funnelling around the side of the building, for which they were grateful. With a wide white grin, he put their drinks down on the table, pulled out the two chairs and they sat down. Lucy handed him a note and he explained what he needed before giving her two coins in change. He hovered for a minute in anticipation. She smiled and gave him one of the coins, the grin became even wider. "Merci, madame."

Lucy looked around her. At the table next to them two men were seated, one quietly reading his paper, the other puffing contentedly on the huge floor-standing shisha pipe, as he watched the rings of smoke rising into the air and quickly dispersing in the breeze. She could smell the sweet fruitiness of the tobacco. He looked over his glasses at her and smiled bashfully when he realised she was watching him. Lucy smiled back and turned her attention to the sea as she sipped her ice cold juice.

The brochure had not exaggerated after all. The sky was clear, that electric almost transparent blue that if you see it in a photograph you think it has been enhanced to intensify the colour. The line of the horizon was arrow straight, the sea a darker greener version of the sky, the colour fading as the water reached the beach. There were a few waves topped with white foam which reminded her of the froth on a glass of beer. Her gaze drifted inland to the low line of buildings, a mixture of gleaming white, pale soft sandy beige and pale terracotta fading further back in the shadows to a deeper muddy red colour in the older buildings. Over walls and buildings there were huge bougainvillea trees intermingled with white star-shaped jasmine, the gentle late afternoon breeze wafting the scent everywhere, heady, sweet and romantic. There was a calm harmonious blend of old and new. She felt at peace, as though she belonged in this beautiful country. She smiled to herself, now she was being fanciful.

Her quiet reverie was broken by a group of teenagers playing football, shouting and pushing each other, completely absorbed in their youthful attempts to hit the makeshift net strung between two posts. Their shouts cut across the calm of the café and Lucy marvelled at how loud the Arabic language could sound, almost as if they were arguing. Flashes of white teeth mingled with brown arms waving encouragement to the rest of their team as their thin legs raced over the hard ground. One tall lad took a hearty whack at the ball, which missed the net completely, flew into the air and hit Lucy on the knee, before dropping at her feet. She rubbed her leg but was more surprised than hurt.

The shouting stopped and after a few seconds one of the group broke away and ran towards them. She watched him, his thick wavy black hair cut tight to his head glistening in the sunlight, his strong face already showing signs of the man he would soon become. As he came nearer his lips broke into a beautiful smile. Without thinking, she reached for her camera and quickly took his photo. The smile became a grin.

Suddenly embarrassed, she picked up the other coin on the table and gave it to him. "For the photograph."

"Thank you madame and I'm sorry about the ball. You are not hurt?" he asked her in French.

Lucy smiled at him, shook her head and reached down to pick up the ball. Her sunglasses slid off and he bent down to pick them up. As she raised her head, only inches from his, he looked into the most exquisite face he had ever seen. In a second his memory absorbed the soft green eyes, flawless complexion and gentle curve of her lips as she smiled at him. Lucy sat back in her chair and was about to say something, but seeing his strange expression she handed him the ball and said nothing.

The boy stood up, his lean torso a silhouette against the bright sunlight. He leaned very slightly towards her. "What is your name?"

"Lucy, and you my beau Tunisian?" She was left to wonder afterwards why she had spoken to him in such a familiar way.

He smiled at the compliment and held out his hand to her. Lucy took it and a shock ran through her body. He bent down so his face was very close as his young mind formed the words which were to haunt him for the rest of his life and he spoke in his native tongue. His voice had changed, soft and caressing. Lucy closed her eyes and listened.

Without warning he brushed his lips against her cheek. She smiled.

The moment was gone. The man at the next table who had been watching the boy flung down his pipe, jumped up and aimed a savage slap at his backside. He missed and with a grin the boy ran off back to his friends.

The man clenched his fists in front of him and his face flushed in embarrassment. "Madame I am so sorry. This is very bad. He should not have touched you and he should have never spoken to you in that way. Oh this is very bad." His face was deep red and a trickle of moisture ran down his cheek from his hair.

He was so agitated, Lucy felt sorry for him. "No, I am not angry. But I must know what he said."

The man cleared his throat and looked at the ground, avoiding her eyes and shook his head.

"Please, I must know."

He met her eyes unwillingly. "What he said was actually rather beautiful, but he had no right to speak such words. Oh this is very bad. I know this boy. He is a good boy from a good family, it is not like him. I will tell his father and he will punish him…"

Lucy stopped him. "No don't say anything to his father, he didn't hurt me. I am not upset, but please tell me what he said."

"Yes please do," Jackie prompted excitedly, "but please do speak in English, my French is dreadful."

The man shrugged and spoke in heavily accented English.

"He said that your eyes are the colour of the jasmine leaf flecked with gold from sun and your hair is like the soft Saharan sand."

"Wow," said Jackie. "What a lovely thing to say." She stared intently at the man who shuffled his feet uncomfortably. "Is that all?"

The man looked at Jackie. "No Madame, that is not all." He coughed and shifted his gaze to the space between his feet.

"Please," Lucy prompted.

The man stared hard at her. "You asked his name?"

"Yes, I did," She waited until he continued.

"He replied 'My name is Farid. Remember it beautiful lady and wait for me, for I love you and one day we will meet again, Insh'allah'."

Lucy was stunned. "Insh'allah," she whispered.

"Do you know what this means, Madame?"

Lucy met his eyes. "Yes, it means If it is the will of Allah."

The man nodded miserably. "Oh Madame, I must apologise."

Lucy shook her head amused at his obvious discomfort. "Please, do nothing. I am not offended."

The man shrugged and turned back to his friend, complaining vociferously about how the manners of the young men of good family were fast disappearing, to the nodded agreement of his elderly companion.

Jackie sat with her mouth open. "Bloody hell," she gasped. "That's a turn up for the book."

Lucy sat with her hands clasped together and looked over at the boy, who stood apart from his friends, his arms folded across his chest, still looking at her.

"Lucy? Luceee." Jackie nudged her. "I know he's only a kid but I wish someone would say something like that to me."

Lucy grinned at her. "What would you like them to say to you," she teased. Jackie rubbed her nose which had gone pink from the sun.

"Well, something like this would be nice. My love your eyes are as blue as the sky and your hair is…" she hesitated.

"…the colour of a ginger-nut biscuit!" Lucy finished.

"You cow." Jackie slapped her friend playfully. "Seriously, though what on earth possessed a kid to speak to you like that and more to the point, what about that last bit?"

Lucy hesitated. "I don't know." She stared at her friend with a strange expression that sent a shiver down Jackie's back. "All I know is I've never been so certain of anything as I am sure I will meet him again someday."

"That's it. Come on, the sooner we get you back to England the better. You're bewitched, or he is," Jackie added darkly looking over to where the boy stood staring at them. She hauled Lucy to her feet and led the way out of the café, making sure to take the back way out, away from where the boy still watched them.

Farid was elated and terrified. What had he done and why? And where had the words come from. He brushed the back of his hand over his lips and felt the softness of her cheek. He knew he was really in love for the first, and for what he was sure would be the only time in his life.

Ali watched as his friend stood, arms folded, staring at the two women. He walked over to Farid. "What the hell happened? Who was that woman you spoke to?"

"I truly don't know the answer to either of those questions."

"Look Farid, something just went down and why was old Ahmed yelling at you?"

Farid turned to face his friend and Ali was taken aback by the intensity in his young friend's face.

"Ali. Listen to me. I have just spoken with a woman I have never seen before, in words of love that I never dreamed of before today."

Ali swore quietly. "And Mr A heard you?" Farid nodded.

"Well, you know he's a stickler for tradition and manners and he will most certainly tell your father and your dad is even worse that Mr A in that respect," he added ominously. "Anyway what did you actually say to her?"

Farid repeated the first part and Ali looked slightly happier. "That's not too bad, she'll just think you are a sun-touched teenager paying a compliment to get money out of her. Did she give you any?"

Farid looked away. "Yes," he said quietly as his fingers curled round the coin in his pocket.

Ali peered closely at him. "Then don't be so miserable."

Farid stared back at him, his lips clenched.

"Oh, hell, you said something else. What was it?"

Farid nodded miserably. "You swear you won't repeat this to anyone, ever."

Ali looked hurt. "I'm your best friend," he said simply.

"I told her to remember my name and to wait for me because I loved her and we would meet again, God willing. Then I kissed her cheek."

"You did what! Have gone completely bloody insane. Your father will kill you!" Ali screamed at him. "What did she do? Did she push you away and shout at you?"

"No I spoke in Arabic so she wouldn't have understood. But old Ahmed tried to wallop me and I'm sure he told her what I said."

He stopped and thought for a moment. "Ali, d'you know the strangest thing. Even before Mr A told her, I believe she knew. When she looked at me it was as though she understood and even accepted it."

"Farid, the sun has surely touched your brain, or is it other parts of your body that are responding to a pretty face?"

He waited for his friend to protest or take a swing at him, but Farid looked straight through him.

"No, Ali I mean it. There will be another time, there has to be, because I know that woman is my destiny. I don't want anyone else, ever."

Ali was shocked by his younger friend's calm determination and felt a deep sense of foreboding. "Maybe my friend, maybe, but I fear no good will come of it."

The two girls walked back to the hotel and Lucy said nothing. They finished their packing, then had their dinner with little said between them.

Finally Jackie lost patience. "Look, Lucy, can you please cut this out. You're starting to scare me. That was just a weird kid who took a fancy to you and got a bit out of order. Just think of it as a holiday experience which would never happen at home and if it did you'd just laugh it off and tell the chap he was bonkers. Forget it. Get it out of your system, preferably before we get home."

"I can't. There was more to it than that."

"Lucy I was sitting beside you, it was all over in a matter of a few minutes."

Lucy shook her head. "Not for me it wasn't. When I felt his lips on my cheek I closed my eyes."

She turned and stared at her friend, her face pale under the tan. She hesitated for a moment. "Jackie, I saw a castle in the moonlight. I was on a beach and the boy was there in the shadows. But it wasn't him, he sort of melted into a man in uniform. Jackie, I'm scared, I think I saw into the future." Her voice trembled.

Jackie snorted. "I bloody well hope it is the future you saw and it wasn't a school uniform he was wearing! I don't know what the age of consent is over here, but I am damn certain it's older than he is!"

Lucy's anguished expression disappeared and she laughed as she looked at her friend's indignant face, now a rather unbecoming shade of lobster pink. "OK. You win. I'll never forget what I saw, but I will try and see sense, as you would no doubt put it. Time to go."

"Absolutely and I could murder a hot dog," Jackie retorted.

Lucy grinned. "That's my girl. Always putting her stomach first. Right, first port of call in England. Hot dog stand."

Lucy's tone was light but she was more troubled than she could ever remember. All the problems in her life she had scraped through in one way or another, even in the divorce she had kept an element of control. With what had just happened to her, she felt completely lost, floating in the African heat, with nothing to anchor her feet to the ground.

The flight landed late and of course it was raining. Ewan met them, drenched and grumpy. The ride home was uncomfortable. Lucy listened to the sloshing of the water as the tyres surged through it and watched the rain bouncing off the windscreen. She looked up at the sky, an impermeable smoky battleship grey and watched the dirty brick buildings flying past. Jackie chattered away, Ewan grunted every now and again as if to prove he was still there and Lucy drifted off into a half-sleep, her mind a thousand miles away.

Later that night she lay in bed in the familiar surroundings of her little cottage, looking at the deep gold curtains drawn tightly across the tiny crooked window. She listened to the interminable raindrops still playing their monotonous tune. She turned on her side and wondered why the rain didn't lull her to sleep like it usually did.

"Remember my name…" "Farid," she whispered to the shadows. Could she ever forget it? She closed her eyes and breathed deeply. The air was dry and hot and smelled of jasmine and she felt a feather-light kiss on her cheek. A slight smile played on her lips as she felt sweet breath on her face and then firm lips pressing against her own.

Suddenly she was wide awake. She leapt out of bed as though she had been stung. She slammed on the light and ran trembling into the bathroom. She bent forward so her face was almost touching the mirror. The eyes that stared back at her belonged to someone else, wide, with pupils dilated, the lips moist and parted like a woman awaiting a lover's touch. She ran her tongue over her lips and tasted the sweetness.

Half blinded by the tears streaming down her cheeks she stumbled into the kitchen and switched on the radio. She fell into the chair, her elbows resting on the table, cradling her head in her hands. She screwed up her face, eyes tight shut as she listened to Simon and Garfunkel's haunting melody

Lucy slammed her fists on the table. Why this song, why now, she loved it but even the radio was determined to drive her crazy.

"Don't talk to me about visions in my dreams," she shouted at the radio. "Of course I remember them when I wake up…that is exactly how I feel."

She listened and held her head in her hands until the sweet voices closed, then started to smile, gazed at the radio and muttered to herself, "Important messages in the subway... I don't think so.

She felt relieved. Irrationally she reasoned with herself that so far as she was concerned the word subway meant the tube and that was something she rarely if ever used so she wasn't going to see any messages!

Out loud, Lucy prayed for protection to God, Allah or whichever divine being would listen to her.

CHAPTER THREE

THE COIN

Old Ahmed was as good as his word. When Farid got home late in the afternoon, his father was furious. Farid received a long and intimidating lecture on manners and why he should not approach tourists to beg for money.

"Whilst we may not be rich, we are comfortable and well respected and I will not have you staining the honour of our family by begging for money in the street like a common vagrant, some lower class of person."

"But I..." His father waved his arm in the air to silence him.

This was not the first time Farid had heard his father emphasise the importance of respectability and good manners. Farid knew he put great importance on the family's standing within the community. He rarely answered his father back but meekly pointed out that he had not begged for money. He told his father about the ball rolling under her table and how he had gone to retrieve it. He said he had complimented the lady, not been rude to her or asked her for money.

"Did she give you any money?"

Farid panicked and glanced at his mother who stood quietly by the door. She gave him a little smile, inclined her head and waited. Farid took a deep breath, he realised that if he lied his father would know.

"Yes Baba, but only one coin."

"Give it to me."

Farid's fingers tightened on the coin which was burning a hole in his pocket. "Please Baba, let me keep it. She gave it to me, I didn't ask for it. I swear it. Baba, I will study extra hard and I will help mother and run errands for her and not go out with my friends every day.

Please Baba, please," he babbled as he handed over the offending object.

His father was taken aback by the desperation in his son's voice. He was like a child about to have his favourite toy taken away. He looked at the coin resting in his hand. It was not a fortune. He glanced at his wife who smiled sweetly at him.

"Let him keep it, Hakim, if he is true to his word, works hard and helps me, then I think it we have reached a good bargain. He did not have to tell you," she added. "He is your son and you should be proud he told the truth. And Ahmed did say the lady was not upset by what he said to her."

Farid was allowed to keep the coin. He noted with relief that it would appear Mr A had not told his father everything he had said to the lady. He didn't know why, maybe he had been too embarrassed to say any more. Farid resolved to be more respectful to Mr A in the future. He kept his part of the bargain, helped his mother and worked hard. He would never be a brilliant scholar but he did his best and the improvement did not go unnoticed and his father rewarded him with a couple more coins.

"This is for telling the truth and for keeping your promise."

That afternoon Farid met up with Ali. The two friends wandered down the narrow alleyways in the Medina towards their usual coffee shop. Farid stopped by one of the small stalls where a man sat bent over his work engraving brass plates. He asked how much it would cost to engrave his coin.

"I've never been asked to engrave a coin before, you won't get much on it."

"I don't want much on it, and look here on the back you can put it here." He handed over the coin,

"What do you want engraved?"

"F+L" said Farid. "Nothing else."

A few minutes later he walked away clutching his engraved coin, a few millimes poorer.

Ali nudged him. "You are truly touched in the head my friend. Money is money. I could think of better things to do with it."

"No Ali, believe me I could never spend it. I will keep it with me so she will know me when we meet again."

Ali shrugged his shoulders. "Well it's your money. I'll catch up with you later."

Farid walked deeper into the centre of the Medina and stopped outside a small jewellery shop where the two cobbled roads met. He looked in the window for a few minutes, wondering if he would ever be able to afford one of the beautiful pieces which sparkled under the bright white lights. He puffed out his chest and walked inside. The jeweller looked askance at him.

"What d'you want. If you've not come to buy, be off with you."

"No really, please I want to buy something."

The jeweller grinned, his thick black beard twitching. "What with, the buttons on your shirt?"

"No, with this." Farid regarded him seriously and held out his money. The jeweller stared at him. "I'm not sure what I can sell you for that young man."

"I know I can't afford any of the beautiful things you have on show, perhaps one day, but not now. All I want is a box for this." He held up his prize and the jeweller took it. His eyes twinkled as he saw the engraved initials.

"Your girlfriend?"

"Not exactly, sir."

"What you have more than one lady love."

"No sir, I do not." Farid shuffled uncomfortably. "She's not my girlfriend, just someone close to my heart and this coin is very precious to me."

Surprised by his sincerity the jeweller rummaged under the counter. "Wait a minute." He pulled out a small scruffy cardboard box and held it out to Farid.

The young man looked at him for a moment and stood up very straight. "I am sorry, sir. Thank you but no. My coin needs something better than that."

The jeweller beamed and opened the box. Inside was a small red velvet heart shaped box which he handed to Farid.

"It's perfect," he breathed, stroking the soft velvet.

The jeweller smiled. "Take it, I can't use it with the outer box broken," he added quickly.

"No sir, I must pay you for it." The jeweller took back the heart shaped box and slotted the coin into the creamy satin lining and studied it intently. He glanced seriously at the young man and took the least value coin from his hand.

Farid went home holding his little box safely in his pocket. In the quiet of his room he looked again at the coin, kissed it gently and nestled it into its new home before placing the box carefully inside the tin box in which he kept his treasures.

CHAPTER FOUR

PETER

Lucy went back to work the day after she got back from holiday and buried herself in the pile of paperwork which had built up over the week. She didn't send her photos to be developed and it was only at Jackie's insistence that they were ever sent at all. Lucy reasoned that the longer she left it, the more her memories would fade and the stronger her resistance would be to whatever remained. As a divorced woman in her mid-twenties, she could not understand her own attraction to the boy who she reasoned couldn't have been more than fifteen or sixteen years old, and she had no intention of dwelling on it.

A month later she sat with Jackie, Ewan and a few friends in her living room where they regularly congregated on Friday nights after the pub shut to continue the evening into the small hours. Jackie had brought her photos with her and unwillingly Lucy produced her own. They flicked through the pictures, commenting on the places they had seen and the people they had met.

"Lucy?"

"Yes."

"Who's the lad?" One of the girls held out the photo to her and Jackie's eyes flashed a warning. Neither of them had spoken of the incident in the café, in fact they had never talked of it even between themselves.

"Oh, that one," she replied lightly "Just some local kid, whose football landed under our table."

She girl studied the photo. "He'll be a heart-breaker in a year or so."

They all laughed, Lucy loudest of all.

Lucy put the photos into the bottom draw of her desk, where she kept the various bits and pieces she didn't want to throw away but had no immediately use for. "Out of sight, out of mind," she recited to herself, totally unconvinced. The weeks became months. Christmas came and went and thoughts of the holiday faded. She never mentioned it, not even to Jackie. It was the past. She never again felt his presence the way she had that first night home, although sometimes she woke during the night and she was sure she could smell jasmine. When she drifted off back to sleep her mind was calm and her sleep peaceful.

One bright Sunday morning, Lucy went for a walk over the hills at the back of the cottages. The cold, white, winter sun had warmed into spring and the gardens were awash with dancing daffodils and swaying, elegant, early tulips, their bright colours glorious heralds of the summer to come. Lucy had tied her hair into a tight ponytail in a valiant attempt to prevent it from tangling in the wind but she could feel a few loose strands had escaped as they whipped against her cheeks.

She leaned into the wind, picking her way down the bridle-path towards the Kings Head and found Jackie and Ewan at their usual table. The warmth inside was almost claustrophobic and as she sat down with them, she peeled off her scarf and anorak.

"You look disgustingly healthy," observed Jackie.

"I feel it, nothing like a walk to build up a thirst."

"Point taken." Ewan laughed. "Usual?" She nodded and flopped back into the armchair.

The pub was crowded, as it always was at Sunday lunchtime. She glanced around at the familiar faces and one or two she had not seen before. Her attention was drawn to a scruffy, dark haired young man with a strong stubborn looking face and clear blue eyes, which seemed to reflect the troubles of the world resting on his shoulders. He sat alone, slouched over the table. She'd not seen him before. He caught her looking at him and she smiled. He glared back. Lucy looked away in embarrassment and turned back to listen to Jackie chatting on about her sister's forthcoming wedding.

She laughed at her friend's moans about having to wear lilac as matron of honour. Lucy concurred that lilac would not really do Jackie any favours with her pale freckles and carrot coloured hair. She didn't think about the man again and left at closing time to join her friends for the roast lunch. Every Sunday she and Jackie took it in turns to prepare the meal, after which they spent the afternoons together chatting whilst Ewan slept in his chair, snoring gently.

A few weeks later she saw him again. This time he was sitting with a couple from the far end of the village, whose names she couldn't remember. He looked happier this time, his thick hair neatly combed and the sky-blue sweater over a crisp white shirt reflecting his blue eyes.

He saw Lucy, smiled and came over to their table. "Can I offer you a drink?"

Lucy hesitated. Ewan jumped up and held out his hand. "A pint of best and two glasses of white, please!"

The man glared at him and then with a grin took his hand "I meant the lady."

"Sorry, Peter, we come as a package."

Lucy looked away, but Jackie was smiling broadly. The man grinned, shrugged his shoulders and went to the bar.

"That was out of order, husband dear."

Ewan put his arm around his wife's shoulder. "Sorry girl, but you know me, never one to miss out on a free drink!" Jackie patted his arm affectionately.

"Anyway, Peter owes me a drink. When he was here before I had to lend him the price of a pint."

Peter returned with their drinks and looked at Lucy before sitting down with them. He was taller than she had first thought, with the broad shoulders and slim build of an athlete. He chatted to Ewan for a few minutes and then turned to Lucy, smiling shyly.

"Look I wanted to apologise. Last time I saw you I was pretty rude." Lucy said nothing. "The reason I was uptight was because I had just lost a considerable amount of money on the National, I backed the bloody horse to win and it cantered in second. My wife found out, we had a blazing row and she informed me she was leaving to go and live with the guy I work with."

"Ouch."

He grinned. "Ouch indeed. Good word. Anyway it had just occurred to me that not only had I lost my money and my wife, but also my job. There is no way I can go back. Tom and I work as a team and I can hardly look at him over morning tea knowing he's knocking off my wife. Sorry. That was crude."

"No, I understand, I'm divorced," she added as if that explained everything.

He nodded. "It's a shit isn't it."

"Good word," echoed Lucy. They laughed. She decided he was much better looking when he laughed.

"Basically, now I'm just looking for a job, where to live and what the bitch is going to want off me in the way of cash."

"She might find it difficult if you're not working."

"Don't you believe it; she'll go for everything she can. As far as I am concerned, she can have the lot, except my records. She's bright, but not that clever. She's got no idea what they're worth and hates my taste in music anyway, so I reckon I'll probably get away with them."

He pushed the forelock of hair back from his face.

"Do you mind me asking? Are you Irish by any chance?" she asked.

He laughed again. "No, but you're not the first person to ask. My mum's fair and blue eyed but my dad is dark. I've inherited the combination and although I was brought up in the north, my dad was transferred to Dublin for two years so I picked up a bit of a twang."

He told her he was thirty-one, had two children which no doubt the wife would make it as difficult as possible for him to see. "You got any kids?"

Lucy shook her head.

"Better that way, at least you can draw a line under the whole damn business. Me, I've been told I can see mine every other weekend." He stood up and gave a mock bow. "The earth mother maketh the rules!"

Lucy giggled. She saw Peter a few times in the pub over the weeks that followed. He loved football and ice-skating, but music was his passion. They even liked the same type of music. He told her his parents lived near Darlington and that he was the youngest of three children by some years. "I think I was an afterthought or accident," he confided.

Peter left his job but was lucky in securing work almost immediately in a large sports complex. Lucy's life took on a safe and familiar pattern. She enjoyed her work and now her weekends and most evenings she spent with Peter. Throughout the summer they grew closer. They had much in common from their taste in music to their love of the outdoors and of course each had been through an unhappy relationship. Lucy knew that Peter would ask her to marry him and wondered how she would answer. He was as different from Simon as any two men could be and she convinced herself that she did love him, if perhaps not quite with the passion she had hoped.

His divorce came through just before Christmas and on New Year's Eve Peter asked her to be his wife. Lucy was hesitant at first but agreed. Her parents were unhappy but she pointed out that she had been divorced for some time, that she was convinced Peter would never behave as Simon had done and she was sure he would make her a good husband. He had been promoted, he had good prospects and she knew could be happy with him.

"Do you love him?" her father had asked.

It was a question she couldn't really answer truthfully so she skirted around it. "He's a good man. He won't let me down and he's been through what I have been. We have similar interests, few arguments, we're compatible and most of all we want the same things from our lives. I couldn't ask for any more." Her father said nothing, he knew her too well.

They were married in the late spring, a little over a year after they had first met. He had a bet on the National and this time he won. "You are a good omen," he joked.

The wedding was quiet, very different from her lavish wedding to Simon, for which she was grateful. They were married in the local registry office with family and close friends, regulars from the pub and a sprinkling of workmates on both sides. She wore a pale blue silk dress and jacket and Peter refused to let her pile her hair up on top in the current fashion. I like you just the way you are, he had told her.

Peter's two boys were there. He said Judith, his ex, would be furious, she thought they were just on a visit, but she didn't know so there wasn't a lot she could do after the event. He'd deal with that when it came, which of course it would.

Lucy liked his two sons, Gary and Robin, and she was relieved that they seemed to like her. There had been the initial silent period of resentment but after a few weeks this had lapsed into acceptance, if not yet affection. Lucy felt that it helped that she was quite different from their mother. Judith was tall, well built with short brown hair and an attitude that cleanliness is next to godliness. She didn't work and their home was immaculate even down to the placing of the cushions on the sofa. Within her own domain she was queen. The boys were always well turned out and spotless and kept well under control at home.

Lucy's penchant for mislaying things made them laugh and they loved being allowed to eat chicken with their fingers, licking off the sticky bits, although she made sure they were well washed and clean before they went home. She didn't tell them off, she left that to Peter on the few occasions when they got a bit exuberant or decided to fight with cushions standing on the sofa.

He drew the line at that when Gary hit Robin over the head with a cushion, Robin fell off the sofa and bumped his head on the floor and screamed. Peter shouted at them both and the cushion burst sending feathers flying all over the room. Lucy cuddled Robin, who stopped crying and started laughing when he saw the storm of feathers floating round the room. They spent the rest of the afternoon trying to catch the feathers which turned into a game and the four of them ended up in a giggling heap on the floor.

Peter moved into Lucy's cottage from his rented room after they got engaged. Judith had married Tom precisely six weeks after her divorce was made final. Peter insisted Lucy keep the cottage in her name and they kept their accounts separate. He was still paranoid about Judith "coming back for more" as he so aptly put it. Lucy pointed out that the financial settlement on divorce had been a clean break. Judith got the house and their joint endowment policy had been signed over to her. As soon as she found out that Peter had a new girlfriend she'd opted for that rather than maintenance "So we no longer need to have any contact."

On the one occasion Tom and Peter had sat down and talked, Tom told Peter that Judith was seriously put out he had found someone else so quickly and never actually believed him when Peter said he had only met Lucy after their separation. She stipulated that Tom would deliver and collect the boys as and when required. She made it quite clear she did not want Peter anywhere near their former home and never wanted to set eyes on Lucy if she could avoid it.

Peter was promoted to store manager and got a reasonable salary increase. Lucy still kept her local job and they were comfortably, if not well off. She had successfully persuaded Peter to give up gambling, which he eventually admitted had been one of the main reasons for the marriage break-up, as it was one of the few things about him over which Judith could exercise no control.

Lucy woke up and was sick. She thought she had a tummy bug. When it didn't clear up she went to the doctor. A week later she informed Peter that their family was to expand. After a difficult pregnancy their son was born in the late spring of the following year and they named him Alexander Jonathan after their fathers.

Her only sadness was that after suffering quite badly during the birth the doctor warned her that she might have trouble conceiving again and if she did she may suffer similar complications. Peter hugged her tightly. "That's OK, I've got my family, and you and our son are all I need."

Lucy felt cheated, she would have liked more children, but perhaps it would happen. Alex, as he soon became, was a big strong baby with a mop of dark hair and his father's bright blue eyes. Peter adored him and called him "cherub". Peter's two boys took to him as one of their own and every alternate weekend the little cottage was bursting at the seams in a state of happy and noisy chaos.

Lucy had given up work a month or so before Alex was born and although she did a bit of home typing they now had to watch the pennies. Since their week in Paris after the wedding, they had not been away on holiday but were saving to buy a larger house. She would miss the cottage but Gary and Robin were getting too big now to share Alex's small room and they needed a garden instead of the handkerchief sized patch which belonged to the cottage. They wanted to stay in the village and would have preferred an older house but as the "character" properties commanded a much larger price finally they agreed on a modern house with a big garden. The kitchen opened onto the garden and Lucy found a large Aladdin pot in which she planted a jasmine shrub. By the end of the summer it had spread over the back door and the sweet scent was sometimes overpowering. Jackie constantly complained she was sure it was what started off her hay fever that year.

Shortly after Alex's second birthday, Peter was promoted to area manager. The salary increase was substantial, but it did mean that Peter was expected to travel and would be spending time away from home. He was dubious about accepting the promotion but Lucy said he'd be silly to turn it down and she was quite happy on her own with Alex from time to time. Anyway she could always go and annoy Jackie and Ewan, who although they had no children of their own had bonded with Alex and took their godparent roles very seriously.

Peter's work was hard but the money was good. Although not very often, he was occasionally away for three or four days at a time, and Lucy found she really missed his easy manner and gentle affection. She really looked forward to him coming home. She knew he loved her and she sometimes felt guilty as she had long ago admitted to herself, although never to anyone else, she had probably not loved him in the same way when they were first married. She had great affection for him and could not imagine her life without him. She lived for her family and could not see herself living any other life. What had gone before had for the most part faded to a succession of mixed and distant memories. Save for the boy.

She had thought with her marriage, the birth of her son and her new home that the boy would join her other memories and remain just that. For the most part he did, but some warm summer evenings, when the rosy fingers of the setting sun crept through the windows, if there was a slight breeze the jasmine perfume permeated the whole house and she had only to close her eyes to see him smile. She wondered sometimes what had become of him.

Peter decided they deserved a holiday, a real holiday, two weeks somewhere abroad. Lucy readily agreed. Alex was going to a friendly child-minder two days a week and Lucy was therefore free to work on those days so she knew they could afford a holiday. Peter was away and called her to suggest she collect some brochures so they could look at them when he came home and decided where to go.

Lucy sat in the living room, the brochures spread out in front of her on the low table, the empty coffee cup in front of her. Alex was fast asleep and the room was warm and comfortable and she closed her eyes.

She re-lived the heady days abroad of her teens. Some people are born with the travel bug. Like a butterfly the child grows, the tiny bug becomes a larva until it spreads its wings in whichever direction the child takes it. Once the travel bug bites it never disappears. Lucy missed the excitement of going abroad.

She remembered the cruise and drifted into the reverie of swaying palms, white sand and clear blue Caribbean Sea. Paradise on earth some called it. As she dozed, her spirit soured across the Atlantic to southern Spain, through the mountains of Almeria and north to the elegant gleaming promenades of Alicante, through the forest of Elche to Benidorm, the sleepy fishing that she had loved and over the years had watched turn to a rowdy tourist trap, away across the Pyrenees through the little country of Andorra. Granddad's old Vauxhall had taken her and her friends all over Europe. She smiled to herself and snuggled back into the cushions.

She heard the melodious sound of a Spanish guitar coming from the television and was transported to the bustling intensity of Paris with its bohemian West Bank where she had spent many a balmy summer evening with her student friends listening to Rudi's guitar, his voice softly teasing her with the words of "Au bord de la Tamise".

She smiled, Rudi. Long fair hair which flopped over his pale face, his tight jeans stretched over long skinny legs. An artist, a child of hope and peace. She hadn't thought about him for years. A different world, another time.

Her thoughts strayed to the classical beauty of Rome, the Coliseum and her beloved Sistine chapel where she had lain on a bench and studied the majesty of Michelangelo's incredible creation. Rome, where the car had finally broken down and she, Kevin and Tanya had spent six exciting weeks waiting for the gearbox to arrive from England so it could be repaired, whilst they drank in the beauty of the Eternal City.

Switzerland, where Kevin had taken her photograph, dressed in a bright pink skirt and Swiss cotton blouse, perched on top of rock in the brilliant sunlight with the snow on the mountains behind. She smiled as she remembered the last trip together before they had all gained new interests and families and gone their separate ways. Austria where they had set up camp, crossed to the small bar on the island via a rickety bridge over the stream and got drunk with the locals. Where Kevin had woken up the following morning outside the tent with his feet in the stream and spent the next week sneezing.

Malta where she had spent two or three summers as a youngster with her parents and their friends in the days before Mintoff. She could hear the music of Jimmy's band at the Phoenicia hotel playing her mother's favourite song as they walked into the restaurant. The glamour of the Dance of the August Moon, as a young girl in awe of the beautiful people gliding to the music in fairy-tale surroundings. And the second cruise she had taken with Simon and her parents when she was entranced by the wonders of Greece and Egypt. She giggled as she remembered how her mother had panicked on the journey from Alexandria across miles of desert road to the pyramids, just praying the ancient Mercedes wouldn't break down.

She sighed, it had been so long since her last holiday. Tunisia. In an unguarded moment she found herself once again in the café as real as it had been five years before. She could feel the heat of the sun on her face, hear the swish of the waves and remembered every detail of the panorama. She closed her eyes. She could see him and feel his breath on her cheek, his face was so near she could touch him.

He wasn't smiling. His face had changed. Gone was the boyishness and in its place a young, handsome man with a strong face and arched black eyebrows over the same jewelled eyes. Slowly his lips parted into the beautiful smile still so familiar to her.

"Lucy," he whispered "Remember and wait for me". She stretched out her hands to him and the picture faded.

Lucy opened her eyes. Her arms were outstretched. It wasn't like before, she wasn't frightened. She felt at ease with herself as though this was the most natural thing in the world and with a smile still playing on her lips, she slept, a deep and undisturbed sleep.

She woke the next morning, cold and aching, and realised she was still on the sofa with the brochures scattered around her. She had a quick shower, made a cup of tea and tidied up before Peter got home. She tried to remember her dream, but like so many dreams on waking it had become hazy and confused.

She greeted her husband with great excitement and they had made love in the afternoon whilst Alex slept. She was like a young girl, excited and enthusiastic. He was pleased she was looking forward to the holiday and as she said, planning it was half the fun. They sat on the floor surrounded by brochures. He watched her as she flicked through the pages, her expression distant and dreamy.

"Lucy. Are you here sweetheart?" He laughed. She was completely absorbed.

"Sorry, I was just wondering where to go."

"You looked as though you were already there!"

"I suppose I was a bit," she grinned at him. "Look, you choose. One condition, sun, sea and sand."

He laughed again. "That's three." Peter was not well travelled although he had spent two years in Spain as a child when his father had been posted there. He had gone to school in Santander and was at one time fluent in the language, if a bit rusty now. "OK," he said. "My choice."

Lucy panicked momentarily. Fate could not be that cruel, could it? "Not wholly your choice," she countered. "You choose two alternatives and I'll make the final decision." She knew where it would not be.

Peter studied the brochure intently, flung it to one side and picked up the second one. He was playing with her. He looked up at her "Antarctica!"

"Drop dead." She threw a cushion at him.

"It's got sun, sea and possibly some sort of sand!" he yelled at her.

"Idiot. You know damn well I mean somewhere hot."

It ended up as a toss between Lanzarote and Morocco. Although Morocco was hundreds of miles from Tunisia, Lucy was not sure if she could face another Arab country where so many of the faces would remind her of him. She steered Peter gently towards Lanzarote.

"Come on, Peter, it's Spanish." She prodded him. "You can show off to me and Alex." Lanzarote it was. Lucy was relieved.

CHAPTER FIVE

LANZAROTE

They arrived in Lanzarote in early June. They avoided the peak season both because of the cost and temperature. Alex was still a child and Peter wasn't a sun worshipper as he tended to burn a rather unpleasant shade of lobster. The actual journey went without incident, although Alex had thrown a major tantrum before they left for the airport when she suggested he should pack his teddy bear in his case. He refused absolutely and insisted that the bear should have a label tied around its neck with its name and address. Peter carried his case and Alex carried his bear.

She was pleased at their choice of hotel. It was large and cool, near enough to the town to enjoy and far enough away that they could not hear the night-time entertainment. It was advertised as being child-friendly and Alex loved it. There was a small playground, a children's club and babysitting if required. The food suited her family, being aimed towards the tourists although their attempts to replicate some of the more traditional English dishes, like sausages, did not really work. In fact, they were quite the strangest things Lucy had ever tasted and she decided not to repeat the experience.

Alex decided to live on a diet of chips, a sort of pizza type tart, yoghurt and ice cream. He also discovered calamari although he firmly believed they were onion rings, which he adored. When he found out they were fish, he nodded his head in a very grown up way and pretended he had known all along.

Lucy made sure all of them were covered head to foot in sun lotion but they had a problem with Alex. He refused absolutely to wear his cap. His pale skin left him vulnerable to the sun, but he was a tough little fellow and despite her pleadings each time the cap was put on him, he tore it off, stamped on it and started screaming.

They sat on the beach and watched Alex running about with the other children, still refusing to wear his cap. Lucy saw him stop and wondered what had caught his attention. He ran over to her. "Mum, I want one of those."

She followed his pointing finger to where a large man with an even larger stomach lay sprawled in one of two old fashioned deck chairs, his legs crossed at the ankles and his hands clasped across his middle. He was sound asleep and by the looks of it he had been for some time as his face had gone very pink. His cheeks fluttered as he breathed and with each breath his belly wobbled. The object of Alex's attention was his hat. He wore a large white handkerchief jammed down over his scalp and knotted on each corner.

Peter burst into laughter. "No way is my son going to look like the picture on a 1950s English seaside cartoon!"

"Shhh, Peter, he'll hear you. Don't be so rude."

"He won't he's fast asleep."

Alex looked mutinous and Lucy could see him building up to a tantrum. "OK sweetheart, Daddy will make you a cap just like that one."

"You serious Lucy?"

"Yes," she retorted. "Anything for a bit of peace."

Peter shrugged and disappeared back into the hotel. He came back with the white handkerchief he had brought with him to put in his one smart jacket breast pocket. "Right here goes." Watched intently by his son he carefully knotted the corners to fit Alex and jammed the new 'hat' firmly down on his little head.

"Very fetching," Lucy tried to keep her face serious, and failed.

To her surprise Alex did not go back down towards the sea to play with the other children, but picked up his bear walked solemnly up to the large sleeping gentleman, climbed into the empty deck chair next to him and lay back crossing his chubby legs at the ankles. He placed the bear beside him, clasped his hands in front of him and promptly fell asleep.

Lucy looked at Peter and broke into peals of laughter. Peter put his arm around her and she buried her face against his shoulder to muffle the noise. Unfortunately, Peter was also trying not to laugh and his chest shook, which made Lucy laugh all the more.

A large woman, wearing a huge, pink straw hat and an out-dated sun-dress covered in pink and yellow roses, appeared from the beach kiosk carrying two glasses of juice. She could only belong to their son's adopted role model. The woman walked over to the two deckchairs, side by side and put the drinks down on the sand. A huge smile split her face from ear to ear and she put her hands on her hips. "Oh my goodness, what have we here?"

Lucy could contain herself no longer. She collapsed with a strangled yelp and the tears streamed down her face as she laughed. The woman turned and beamed at her. "As the larger one is mine I assume the smaller one belongs to you."

Lucy nodded not trusting herself to speak immediately. "Yes, I am so sorry. I'm Lucy and this is my husband Peter. The smaller one is Alex."

"Well I'm Alice... and the sleeping beauty is my husband Henry."

Alice turned her attention back to the sleeping duo and after some rummaging around in her enormous beach bag she produced a camera and photographed the pair. Alex shifted in his chair and the bear fell on the sand. Alice picked him up, dusted him off and placed him gently in the crook of her husband's arm. She took another photo and Lucy did likewise. The bear was then returned to his rightful owner.

She pulled up a chair and sat down. "How long are you staying?"

Lucy told her and she nodded.

"We are very lucky, we are both retired and in our forty odd years together we have been pretty much everywhere so we felt it was time to stop. We love this hotel so why change now. They understand our funny ways and take care of us, even down to the deck chairs they keep for us from year to year. I find those other things impossible to get on and off without overturning them and I'm sure if Henry sat on one it would disintegrate. Anyway, enough about me, what about you?"

Before Lucy could reply there was a loud grunting noise from the direction of the deckchairs. Alex had turned over and his flailing arm thumped the side of the older man's ample stomach.

Alice turned to him "Ah, Henry. Good you're awake."

"So it would seem." He sat up, rubbing his forehead and yawned.

"Have you met your new friend?" She pointed to the small child, now sitting upright and staring at the huge person beside him.

Henry regarded him seriously. "No, we have not yet been introduced." He held out one huge paw to the child. Alex's eyes widened and his mouth fell open as he took the outstretched hand.

"I'm Henry. Who are you, and who is your handsome friend?" he said looking at the bear. Alex was speechless.

"Alex and Winnie," said Lucy watching her son with amusement.

"Good afternoon to you both."

Henry leaned forward and gently shut Alex's still open mouth. He hauled himself out of the chair with some effort. He was a giant of a man and looked as though he might have been quite fit in his youth but inactivity and good living had certainly piled on the pounds and muscle had turned to fat as he aged. He raised both hands to his head and adjusted his handkerchief hat so that the front and back were flat and the four corners were at the sides, pirate style. Then he did the same to Alex's.

"Good hat," he nodded to Alex who had by now recovered his speech.

"My dad made it. It's like yours." Solemnly he got up and took Henry by the hand and led him the few feet across the sand to where Alice and his parents were seated. "This is my mum and dad." The three adults were entranced.

"I've never seen him take to anyone so quickly," Alice beamed.

"Do you have any children?"

Alice glanced at her husband. "Yes, we have a daughter, Pat, but she's married and lives in Australia." She smiled. "We've two grandchildren. We have been out there two times but it's such a long way and we're neither of us getting any younger," She looked again at her husband, the pain was etched on her face.

Henry looked down at her with a tired smile. "We had a boy, but we lost our Jamie in a motorbike accident two years ago."

Her face crumpled and Henry hugged her. Oblivious to anyone but themselves, she clutched him round his ample waist and rested her head on his tummy. Then she looked up at him her eyes almost boring into his. "I never saw it, you know. I never saw it."

"I know my love; it wasn't your fault. There was nothing you could have done. It just wasn't a choice, you know that." He stroked her cheek and sat down next to her, still holding her hand.

Peter looked from one to the other and sipped his beer. "Sorry, I don't understand?" Lucy glared at him. Sometimes her husband could be utterly tactless.

Henry glanced at his wife and raised his eyebrows slightly in an unspoken question. She dropped her head in acknowledgement.

"My wife is psychic, she reads cards, objects, she sees things. She can go for months and then something will come to her. She doesn't talk about the gift, if that's what it is. It frightens some folk but it can also attract the wrong sort of people, so she rarely speaks of it. Anyway, Alice felt she should have been able to see our son's death and in some way prevent it. But you know what they say 'Those that have the gift often can't see it in their own'."

Lucy had never heard that, but then hadn't ever encountered anyone to whom it would have applied, so she smiled trying to understand. "I'm so sorry. It must have been terrible for you both. I can't begin to imagine what it must be like to lose a child."

Alice glanced up at her husband who was studying an imaginary spot on the table. "He wasn't planned. I was over forty and I never thought of having another child. Pat was already a teenager and when Jamie arrived our world went upside down. It was one of the most wonderful moments of our lives together, but it wasn't meant to be. God loaned him to us for twenty years and then he took him back." She smiled weakly and Lucy couldn't help but notice the solitary tear which trickled down her round, weathered cheek. There was a short awkward silence which was broken when Alex dumped his bear on Alice's lap. She jumped.

"Can Uncle Henry make my bear a hat like ours?"

Henry rubbed his chin thoughtfully. "Uncle Henry, I like that very much and the answer is yes, of course I can."

They all laughed, glad of the unwitting rescue. Henry obliged with a very small hat for the bear from a tissue which Alice found in her all-encompassing bag. The light faded as evening drew in and Peter pointedly looked upwards. "Anyone for a drink?"

"You've had enough my friend," Lucy chipped in.

Henry glanced at the sky. "No. I agree; the sun is definitely over the yard arm." He grinned broadly at Peter and they headed towards the bar.

The two women chatted amiably whilst Alex played in the sand. The men returned with drinks for all and ice-cream for Alex. Alice did most of the talking, regaling them with tales of their travels and the scrapes and adventures she and Henry had got into as newlyweds.

Suddenly, Peter looked at Alice. "Would you read the cards for us?"

Alice looked surprised Lucy rounded on him. "Peter! No, that's not fair."

Alice glanced from one to the other. "It's all right, I don't mind, if that's what you really want, which one of you?"

Peter was unstoppable. "Yes. Please. But it'll have to be Lucy."

"Why me?" she exclaimed suddenly frightened as to what Alice might see.

Peter smirked "I already know my future. I shall become a boring old man, who wins a fortune on the pools and drinks too much on holiday. My hair will recede and I'll have a long white beard to compensate and I will rely totally on my wife to pander to my every whim."

Lucy said nothing. Alex piped up, "I'll look after you Daddy, but only if you don't have a long white beard."

Alex patted Peter's leg and turned to Alice, his little face very solemn and whispered "If Daddy has a long white beard I won't be able to recognise him." Alice nodded at him seriously.

"We'll all look after each other." Peter put his arm affectionately around his son, and lifted him up onto his knee.

"Well, Lucy, off you go. Let's see what fame and fortune Alice can find for you."

Lucy scowled at him. "Peter it's not like that. And, absolutely not, I'm not sure I want to know what's going to happen to me."

Alex looked as if he was going to cry. "Please Mummy, I want to know if you are going to be a princess in a golden coach like Cinderella."

"I'm afraid that's not very likely sweetheart."

"Come on, Lu, what's the harm, it can't hurt, it's just a bit of fun, isn't it?" He looked at Alice.

"Not exactly," she answered him but looked intently at Lucy. "Have you done this before?"

"No, but…" Her voice faded helplessly.

Alice put her arm round the young woman's shoulder. "It's OK, most people are a bit apprehensive, but what you must never forget is that the future isn't necessarily decided for you, often it's what you make of the choices offered to you. Of course in some things there is no choice. Whatever I see or feel I will tell you"

Two pairs of eyes stared at Lucy. "Absolutely not."

Alex burst into tears and Peter looked cross.

Lucy decided to offer an olive branch. "Look I am not sure if I am going to want to hear what Alice has to say and I don't want to spoil my holiday. What if I promise I will let her tell my fortune on our last day here? Will that keep you two ghouls happy?"

Alex had no idea what a ghoul was but he sniffed and agreed. Peter looked less cross and Alice gazed thoughtfully at her wondering what the dear girl had to hide. The reading was not referred to again. The three of them enjoyed a happy carefree holiday and if Lucy was pre-occupied, she did her best not to show it.

Mostly they went sightseeing with Henry and Alice. They visited the caves at Los Jameos del Agua. Only Peter and Lucy ventured into the caves with the guide. Alex stayed with his adopted uncle and aunt totally absorbed in the ice cream sundae, which was in a glass so tall, he had to stand up to eat it.

Lucy followed Peter and a few others into the dark cave. As they edged their way in crocodile along the rocky pathways the guide told them all to be very careful lest they fall into the inky black depths of the huge cave pools. Lucy hung onto the side rail and couldn't help noticing that the flimsy rope barriers marking the pathway would not be much help if anyone did slip. She grabbed Peter's belt and her heart skipped when some shingle slipped down from under her foot.

They walked into an enormous clearing with a small stage and chairs set out in rows. The guide explained the acoustics were so good it was a natural auditorium and they actually held concerts in the cave. It was hung with tiny lights from the rock face high above which appeared to be black and set with hundreds of stars. It was magical.

They followed the guide through the clearing and into a narrow cavern where the air was cold and the water seemed even darker. Lucy clutched Peter's hand until he complained the blood had stopped flowing and his arm had gone to sleep. They were so near the water's edge that when Lucy looked down into it, she could imagine being swallowed up into the blackness and finding out what was hidden in the silent depths beneath.

"How deep are the pools?" someone asked.

Lucy did not want to know.

The guide stopped, and after him the line of visitors. He rubbed his chin theatrically. "I don't know, let's find out. Alonso?"

A quick grin passed between the two men as the guide gave Alonso a slight shove towards the water. The silence of the cave was ripped apart with gasps and screams of terror. Lucy shut her eyes and grabbed hold of Peter. She opened them to the sound of laughter. Alonso stood in the giant pool, his hands on his hips and a broad grin on his face. The water rippled gently around his ankles and only then Lucy noticed he was wearing high boots. Emotions cascaded over her. She felt sick, exhilarated and angry. It was of course a set-up, another little trick designed to entertain the tourists. The guide pulled Alonso up onto the pathway and turned to the line of people.

"The pools are only inches deep. Just standing water. They look bottomless as there is no breeze down here and the rocks you see disappearing into the "depths" of the pools are in fact reflected off the cave roof. The higher the roof, the deeper the water seems. Watch."

He threw a small piece of rock into the pool and the ripples fanned out wiping away the reflection.

They climbed out of the caves and back into the circular café bar area where Alex was waiting with Henry and Alice.

"Any good?" Henry asked.

"Only if you want the bloody living daylights frightened out of you," Lucy retorted, still a bit shaken by the experience.

Peter recounted tales of bottomless pits, cold dark menacing rocks and monsters lurking in caves, until Alex burst into tears.

"I don't like menaces and monsters," he sobbed. Lucy cuddled him and told Peter to shut up.

The following day the three of them went to Timanfaya national park. Alice and Henry stayed in the hotel bar. As Henry put it, "Alice and I are not built to climb mountains!"

Alex watched intently as the guide poked straw into a hole in the ground, which was surrounded by a low fence. A few second later his little eyes nearly popped out of his head as the flames leapt out of the hole. "How did that happen, Daddy? Is there a man at the bottom of the hole who sends out the fire?"

"Not exactly," Peter explained. "This is a volcano. The fire lives in the mountain under the ground and when the man feeds it straw, the flames come out of the hole."

"Can I feed it, Daddy," Alex shrieked jumping up and down.

Lucy smiled. "No sweetheart, it will burn you. That's why the man stood back so quickly. You must never, ever feed any fire with anything or it will hurt you."

"When I get older then?"

She smiled. "Maybe, when you're as old as Mummy and Daddy."

"Oh, Mum that's not fair. That's forever!"

Peter choked, "Thanks pal."

CHAPTER SIX

THE PREDICTION

Lucy had hoped they would have forgotten about her promise but it was not to be. On their last day as they sat on the bench by the pool Peter gently reminded her and unfortunately Alex overheard. "Yes, come on Mummy, you promised." Lucy smiled at him and remembered her Shakespeare.

"Lead on Macduff," she recited and looked at Alice, who smiled encouragement.

"I don't bite."

"No, but do your cards?"

Alice made no response. Peter put his arm around her and Alex positioned himself on the bench beside her.

Alice produced the cards from the bottomless bag and a small piece of quartz. "She never goes anywhere without them," Henry explained.

"What's the crystal for? Is it like a crystal ball?"

"Peter stop being stupid," Lucy was irritable and scared.

"No, Peter, it helps me concentrate It absorbs and emits positive energy and neutralises negative energy."

Peter looked confused but Alice's tone made it quite plain there would be no further explanation and held out her hands. Lucy took them and waited.

She looked up and smiled at Lucy. "Your bracelet is beautiful. What are the stones?"

"Oh, I am sure they are just cheap beads but I love the deep colours. I bought them on holiday years ago."

Alice stroked the beads and frowned slightly. She turned over both hands and studied the palms. Lucy felt her fingers resting gently on the bracelet. "Don't be scared."

Alice leaned back. She handed Lucy the cards. Lucy shuffled and cut the pack and handed them back. Without any of the flamboyance Lucy expected to accompany fortune-telling Alice gently placed the cards in a line. She turned over the first card. "See here. Three of Swords. You have been married before and you were unhappy. You have suffered betrayal and a period where you felt great loneliness and isolation. Somewhere old and dark."

Lucy thought of the old house when she had first married and inclined her head in acknowledgement.

"Wow," said Peter.

"Shut up," said Lucy.

Alice turned over the next cards, her hand resting for a few moments on each.

"There will be new beginnings. You have many crossroads, you are offered many choices and you must be careful, but there is one road where there is no choice of passage." She stared at Lucy, her eyes compelling Lucy to look at her. Lucy shivered.

"You will experience great love." Peter grinned and Lucy glared at him. He said nothing. Alice took her hands this time so one hand rested on her wedding ring and the other on the simple Tunisian bead bracelet.

"Later in your life you will be offered a choice to live in another country, many miles away, hot and near the sea. The choice you make will affect your life for many years and the lives of those closest to you." She smiled. "You will have another child."

"Brilliant," exclaimed Peter and beamed at his wife.

Lucy smiled for the first time. "That would indeed be wonderful. I was told after the difficulties with Alex that I may never have another child."

"The cards don't lie sweetheart. You will have great happiness in later years."

Peter was fascinated. "You can tell that from the cards?" Alice smiled.

"Yes, and from the bracelet and from Lucy herself."

Peter jumped up. "That's it then. It looks as though an ex-pat retirement beckons, Spain perhaps. I'll have to start collecting loads of those bright patterned shorts, you know the ones you hate. Wonderful! Right, I'm off for a shower before dinner and maybe a swift half at the bar. Coming Henry." He took Alex's hand and the three of them walked together back towards the hotel.

Lucy got up and started to pack up her things.

Alice put her hand on Lucy's. "Stay. There's more," said Alice softly.

Lucy was worried. "What did you see?"

"It's not what I saw, it's what I didn't see. Would you mind it if I did a different type of reading?"

"Why?"

"It's hard to explain. The basic reading really only provides a general picture, but from your hands and from your beads I could visualise times yet to come but with huge gaps and contradictions where there shouldn't have been any." Lucy looked apprehensive.

Alice smiled. "But it is up to you. Unfortunately, I cannot tell you any more at present and of course it could be that you may not want to hear what I have to say. I will not lie to you but how you interpret what I say is of course your choice." Lucy stared at her and nodded.

Alice picked up the pack and placed the cards in a fan shape seven sets of three and one in the centre. As she turned over the sets she nodded to herself, her eyes fixed on the cards, as though the story was becoming clear.

"As I have said your marriage was not happy, you felt isolated and betrayed. Later something happened to you which left you confused and uncertain of your own emotions, but then you found a gentle love and you are content."

She hesitated and met Lucy's eyes. "Lucy my dear child, you will experience great loss but you will also find that which you are looking for. Your choice is hard, very hard and this is a journey you will make alone."

"Alone, you mean without Peter?"

"I believe so. There is nothing in the cards to indicate you will go together and I didn't see him or feel his presence. There are three cards here, The Hermit and the Six and Eight of Swords. These indicate being alone, a regretful but necessary moving on alone and self-imposed isolation."

"But why, when?"

"I don't know," Alice said quietly.

Lucy sat motionless. She could not imagine going into the future without Peter. She started to get up but with strength which surprised her, Alice pressed her hands onto the table and she sat down again.

"Lucy, listen to me. There are some things we must accept and some we can choose. Those we cannot change we must accept and be aware so we can learn from them. Although there are things which happen in our lives which are very hard to bear as they happen, by accepting we can travel on through our lives.

"You will make many journeys, but to somewhere you have been before. She glanced up at Lucy. This card is the most mysterious, it can say many different things and holds many secrets." She frowned. "There is confusion in the next group of cards. You will find something which will become very dear to you, but you will lose it. But you don't look for it. You believe it is not yours to have. You trust your intuition. I see a very bright light, the sun perhaps as I can feel great heat."

She pointed to The Lovers and The Devil. These two together can signify romance, an immense physical attraction, addiction, sexuality, desires are deep and passion intense. The combination can signify an unhealthy obsession. Maybe something is being hidden. Temptation and jealousy. And here, this group reveals great unconditional love which cannot be broken, the birth of a child and with the cards surrounding it, a boy child. The Queen of Cups. Blonde, loving and devoted. She is passionate. She is not bound by the restraints of morality or convention. Her love transcends such restrictions. In this position she signifies that in later years you will have confidence to take risks in love and life.

Lucy was staring at her and Alice hesitated. "Should I go on?" Lucy dropped her eyes but said nothing.

"There is a new beginning and emotional fulfilment and with the Wheel, inevitable change. You will travel, somewhere you feel you are at home, where you are understood."

Alice pointed to the next group. "See, a man tall, dark, young, possibly foreign will enter your life…" She looked up her eyes wide as she looked at Lucy "…he will enter your life – again." She looked away from the cards and held Lucy's wrist feeling the beads. "He stands in the shadows of a small low building beside water, he is smiling and his are eyes bright with love. But there is another man, much younger, a boy perhaps, and in his face burns with the same love. The man and boy have become one."

She stopped searching Lucy's face, which had gone very pale, and smiled. "We have some way to go yet my dear before the full picture is clear." She turned over the next cards and Lucy gasped.

"No, no, Lucy. The Hanged Man and Death do not mean what you might think. It seems that there will be a voluntary sacrifice, a crush or fantasy which cannot be fulfilled. He feels let down and abandoned. But then there is an enforced sacrifice signifying drastic change.

"As I have said, you will have another child, a dark child. Not yet, not in the near future but later. He will change your life forever."

Alice sat with her eyes closed as though in sleep, holding Lucy's hands gently between her own, rocking slightly. When she spoke her voice was hardly audible. "I see a pale shadow behind the child. It is unclear, I cannot make it out except I feel that it is very close to the child. I will try to see more for you."

She turned over the next cards. "There will be major changes, but under your control. Do not ignore the changes and look to the future. One cycle is over, move to the next and you will obtain emotional fulfilment. The Tower signifies upheaval, some problems and sudden change."

Alice tightened her grip around Lucy's wrists so the bracelet cut into her. The beads were hot, almost burning under her fingers and she was tempted to let go, but she knew she had to go on. Her voice had taken on a strange detachment. "Many years from now I see a day drawing to its close and the orange fireball has dipped below the sea, night approaches. There is a narrow ribbon of road leading to an ancient castle but the castle is not a castle and not old but new." Her voice changed "I see a dark building surrounded by tall trees, unloved, deserted, there is much evil in these places. My child, you will experience fear and trauma but you will finally reach your destiny."

She sat back and stretched as though waking from a deep sleep raising anxious eyes to the young woman. What she had seen frightened her.

"Lucy, your reading contained mostly Major Arcana cards which in itself usually signifies life changing events with long term influence and repercussion but the Ten of Cups in its final position indicates eventual harmony, happiness and very possibly marriage."

Lucy's face was completely drained of colour. She stared almost sightlessly at Alice as though she had seen a ghost and tears trickled down her face.

"Oh my dear girl, I am so sorry. I have really upset you." Lucy shook her head wordlessly, her eyes tightly clenched shut as though to shut out the world.

Alice raised her head and gently put her hand under Lucy's chin. "Look at me." Lucy opened her eyes, pleading through her tears. "Ah, I understand. I am not wrong. We have seen the same things you and I."

Lucy nodded, "Yes, the castle I have seen it and the man and boy. That and what you said about a dark building, they scare me," she whispered.

Alice gathered up the cards and put her arm around Lucy as they walked back towards the hotel.

"Sweet girl, the cards are a reflection of the soul or sometimes a mirror into it. Who knows who writes the future, do we do it ourselves by the sum of the choices we make in our lives or is it written by God? The eternal debate, better people than us have argued this for centuries."

Lucy smiled at her. "Thank you, Alice but what do you think?" Alice held her eyes.

"Insh'allah," she whispered.

Lucy gave a little cry, tore into the foyer and ran up the stairs not stopping until she was back in her room. She collapsed against the wall, and curled up on the floor hugging her knees to her chest, shaking.

She tried to reason with herself. Alice was widely travelled and the expression is one often used through the Muslim world. She tried to make sense of everything the old lady had said. Had it been just Alice's way of saying "Only God knows?" Or was it just a terrible coincidence.

Lucy was shocked by Alice's knowledge of her past but more so by her vision of her future. She had never in her life believed in fortune telling in any form be it cards, psychics or indeed gypsy predictions, anything in fact which smacked of deception or charlatanism (save for voodoo, which she was too wary of to discount altogether). In fact, Lucy considered the whole business a heap of money-making mumbo-jumbo; a quick way to make a profit out of some poor soul's pain or ignorance. Too much of what was told could be interpreted in any way the victim wished. It was something other people got involved in, people with problems grasping onto anything which could alleviate their difficulties or those who were looking for a cheap thrill.

The incident in Tunisia years before had indeed concerned her, but she had finally convinced herself that Jackie was right, it was probably a well-rehearsed little act to get money by flattering tourists, or else the boy was touched in the head. She had put to the back of her mind the vision, if that is what it was, that she had experienced on the first night back after the holiday. But Alice's confusion over the man and boy becoming one had dragged her silently screaming back to Tunisia. Were they the same person? Her misgivings were intensified because what it came down to was that Alice had seen practically the same scene as she herself had done before. Something she had only ever mentioned to Jackie in a quiet little cottage room in Surrey years before. And what did it mean a castle but not a castle, not old but new and the dark building. Were they significant, were they all connected? There was a dull ache behind her eyes and her head was thumping from trying to make head or tail of it.

She picked up the bottle of orange drink and walked out onto the balcony. The sun had now disappeared completely and the night sky was thick and velvety. Warm and comforting. She sipped the warm fizzy liquid and screwed up her nose, shame there wasn't a fridge. She lit a cigarette and leaned back in the small plastic chair her mind drifting unwillingly back over Alice's words.

Choices, some very hard. Changing my life and those close to me. Lost and not searched for. What could that be? She thought hard. What could be so important to me that if I lost it I wouldn't look for it because I didn't believe it was mine. That certainly doesn't make sense.

A dark man, possibly foreign and a child. She smiled ruefully to herself. Unless time was to stand still for her, that was certainly not likely to involve the boy.

She recalled Peter's beaming face when Alice had mentioned the child she was to have.

"Of course," she said to herself staring at the bottle. "Peter's got dark hair and so has Alex. Why should another child not be the same?"

She felt as though she had unravelled a small part of the story, only to have it snatched away as she remembered "This is a journey you will take alone."

She was to carry on without Peter beside her, but when and why? How could she not have Peter, they were young, healthy and happy? But things changed. Would one of them fall in love with someone else? Although she cared deeply for him and would never hurt or leave him Lucy knew that deep in her heart she had never shared with him the kind of love where thousands of stars burst when he kissed her, where her whole being was absorbed by him where nothing else in life mattered.

"Which is because, it only exists in fairyland and Mills & Boon," she said emphatically to the bottle. "Peter is solid, reliable, funny and he loves me. What more can any woman ask of her man?"

The air hung empty and silent as though mocking her. "He's a wonderful man and I'll be lost without him, and what about Alex?"

She realised for the first time that Alice had made no reference to her son, simply that whatever choice she made would affect those dearest to her. Surely she could not lose Alex? A tear trickled down her cheek and she wiped it away angrily. What she could not understand was if Alice could tell her all this, why could she not tell her who, how or when. She shivered, suddenly cold. What if one of them should die? It was something she refused to even consider. She went back into the room and dressed carefully for dinner.

They spent the next morning on the beach with their new friends. Neither she nor Alice made any reference to their conversation and when the time came for them to leave Henry hurrumphed a good deal as he picked up Alex and hugged him.

"You never know," Peter yelled from the steps of the coach. "We may even bump into you next year!"

"Look forward to it," shouted Henry, waving.

Alice held Lucy tight, she knew she had to tell her. "Lucy, remember what I said. Stay away from the castle and the old house, there is evil there." Lucy nodded "And the man…"

Lucy pushed her away, a look of horror on her face. Alice smiled and enveloped her in a hug. "No sweet thing, not the same man, a much older man, dark, thick set who smiles with a flash of gold. He is dangerous. If you ever see such a man, stay away from him. Lucy, promise me you'll keep in touch. You've got my number. Use it. I am here if you need me, or you just want to chat" she added lamely. Lucy promised and kissed her friend's cheek.

As Lucy climbed up the steps into the coach, she turned and looked straight into Alice's compassionate face. There was no smile. She felt as though someone had just thrown a bucket of cold water over her. She sat down heavily next to Peter and automatically settled Alex on her lap. Her mind was numb. Was there something else Alice saw but she just didn't tell me.

CHAPTER SEVEN

PETER

The pains started just after the New Year. Peter was quite convinced he had indigestion from the Christmas and New Year excesses.

A couple of days later he was out building a snowman with Alex out of the few inches that had fallen overnight and before it melted. He came into the kitchen holding his arm.

"What's up love," Lucy asked him.

He pulled a face. "Nothing, I must have just bashed it on something or pulled a muscle but I don't remember doing that." He grinned. "But it hurts like hell."

"If it's the same tomorrow, go to the doctor. You're better off getting it seen to."

He protested, but Lucy persisted. Peter was irritated.

"Don't make such a fuss. I've banged my arm, not fallen off a bloody cliff."

The next morning the pain had gone, although he still had indigestion. "See, a lot of fuss about nothing. I told you so. Anyway, what's the matter with you, you've been weird ever since we came back from holiday. It hasn't got anything to do with that card business with Alice, has it? I shouldn't have pushed you into it, you're far too susceptible."

"Of course not, don't be silly," Lucy retorted a bit too quickly. "I just care about you, that's all. Isn't that what wives are supposed to do."

Peter cuddled her. "Well just so long as you're not making something out of nothing. Anyway, sorry I snapped at you, I'm just tetchy. Forget it, I'm sorry"

"Me too" She hugged him back, staring at the wall over his shoulder.

He took her hand and they walked into the living room. He sat down in his big leather chair and pulled her onto his knee. She curled up, her head resting on his shoulder. She sniffed loudly, "I'm tired."

She looked into his pale kind face, pushing the dark lock of hair back of his forehead. "You need a haircut."

"Point taken." They sat curled up around each other in the chair like two contented cats, arms entwined and watched their sleeping son, exhausted from his snowman building.

"I love you both so much" he whispered "I don't know what I'd do without either of you."

"Darling, you'll never have to be without either of us. We'll always be here for you," she replied softly, feeling the tears pricking her eyes.

The niggling indigestion didn't go away and towards the end of January the pains returned, sharp stabbing pains, and pins and needles in his arm, which eased but never completely went away. Peter said nothing to Lucy but made an appointment for the following week to see the doctor. He felt a bit of a fraud going to the doctor with indigestion and a tweaked nerve in his arm, which he had convinced himself was the problem.

He made light of his ailments to the doctor and jokingly told him the only reason he had made the appointment in the first place was because of his wife's nagging.

"Any other problems? No I feel fine, it's just my arm that's niggling me and this bloody indigestion."

"OK, I'll give you something for the indigestion, but tell me do you remember when you twisted or bumped your arm."

"That's the thing doctor, I can't remember actually hitting it on anything." The doctor tapped his pen on the desk.

"Look Peter, it may well be nothing but I'm going to book you in for some tests. Friday OK?"

"So soon?"

"Yes, I'd prefer we cleared this up. You seem to be in good health but better safe than sorry."

The arm certainly felt better and Peter went to work on the Thursday morning. It had been a hard week, he was looking forward to the weekend. He felt tired and needed a good sleep.

The train was delayed. Signal failure at Three Bridges so the tannoy said. When it finally arrived the train was packed. Somehow he managed to get a seat, but they were already about 10 minutes behind schedule. They chugged slowly along and then sat outside East Croydon station for a further 10 minutes, waiting for a slot.

Peter felt himself getting more and more agitated. He had an appointment at 10a.m. and hated being late. He felt his heart thumping and he was sweating profusely, but he felt cold and hoped he was not going to be sick. He clutched his arm, the pain was excruciating, as bad as it had ever been. He could feel the sweat running down his face.

"Christ mate, you OK?" A thickset man with a whiskery beard, thick muffler and a ruddy face leaned over to him from the seat opposite. "Mate?" he repeated.

Peter looked up at him, his face a contorted mixture of pain and confusion. "My chest's on fire." He slumped forwards.

"Bloody hell." The man jumped out of his seat and bellowed down the carriage. "Anyone here a doctor?"

After a few seconds a slight young woman who looked as if she should still be in school pushed her way through the carriage. "I'm a nurse." She looked at Peter and quickly loosened his tie. "Where's the pain?"

"Everywhere." His breath was laboured and ragged and the nurse saw his lips had a bluish tinge.

Peter felt as though a vice had clamped around his chest. He couldn't breathe. His eyes widened in shock as he gasped and exhaled slowly. There was complete silence.

"Oh shit," said the bearded man and sat numbly back in his seat staring at Peter.

The nurse turned on him. "You, give me a hand here, get him onto the floor and get these bloody people out of the way."

He jumped up and turned on the advancing hoard. "Back off you lot. Give the girl some space."

Between them they cleared a space in the corridor and laid Peter on the floor. The man knelt down beside him. The nurse grabbed the muffler from round his neck, rolled it up and pushed it under Peter's neck so his head was tipped back to clear his airway. She knelt on the floor, leaning over him like an avenging angel. She breathed deeply into Peter's mouth and started to count, her hands crossed on his chest as she pushed down on the limp body. One, two, three, four. Another breath. One two three four. No one moved. The only sound was the counting of the young nurse and the gentle purring of the train which had started to pull into the station. After what seemed an eternity the bearded man put his hand on her shoulder. "It's no use, love, he's gone."

"No!" She pushed him away. The man shook his head and stood back.

A man in a brown suit pushed his way through. "I'm a doctor." The nurse sat back on her heels, her face white and the tears bright in her eyes. The doctor knelt down beside Peter.

"What happened? How long has he been like this?"

The nurse looked up at the bearded man.

He pulled at his beard. "About seven or eight minutes I reckon. He started sweating and clutching his arm and chest. He couldn't breathe, his mouth turned blue and then he just… just sort of stopped," he smiled gently at the nurse "She did everything she could."

The doctor examined Peter quickly. He turned to the young woman. "There's nothing more we can do for him I'm afraid." He helped her to her feet.

She looked at Peter, her mouth trembling. "He's so young. Why couldn't I save him? I'm sure I did everything right."

The doctor put his hand on her shoulder. "Look nurse, it may not seem to help much now. I can't be sure of course, but from what you've told me I think he had a massive heart attack, in which case there is nothing anyone could have done. I think that in someone so young there must have been some underlying factor which caused it."

The ambulance carried Peter to the nearest hospital where the orderly went through his belongings, found Lucy's number and made the call every spouse dreads receiving. As she listened to the sympathetic voice asking her to come to the hospital, Lucy sat motionless at her desk, one hand on the receiver and the other clutching the edge of her chair. She said nothing until he had finished speaking. "Mrs Collins?"

"Yes, I understand. I will be there shortly."

So it had finally happened. What Alice had known all along. She felt nothing but a terrible calm. No emotion, no hysteria, no sense of loss. It was simply fate. Over this there had been no choice. She slowly replaced the received, leaned on her desk her hands clasped tightly and stared at the wall.

Ruby James watched her and ground her teeth. She hated private phone calls. The floor manager was a small elegant woman whose delicate appearance concealed a granite interior. The iron hand in the velvet glove had been invented for her. She took no rubbish from those in her department, lateness, untidiness and everything other than 100% commitment received her unqualified disapproval and was suitably rewarded. The perpetual latecomers were made to work late. The untidy ones she paired with those naturally immaculate creatures that every less than perfectly groomed woman hates to be seen near. They soon smartened up. The lazy ones got the rough end of the deal. She was just plain difficult, she made their working lives hell and she was incredibly good at it. But to those whose work corresponded with her idea of good or even acceptable, she was a fair and appreciative manager. Lucy was one such person and Ms James was not happy to see her staring at the wall. It was therefore with some surprise that she watched Lucy rise unsteadily to her feet and walk into her own private space without so much as a knock.

"Lucy? Is everything all right."

Lucy stared through her and shook her head. "I have to go now."

Ruby's eyebrows shot up. "I'm sorry?" No please, no request, just a flat statement.

"Yes, I have to go now," Lucy repeated "I may be in next week, but I don't think so. I'll have to let you know. I'm very sorry."

Ruby's initial inclination was to give her a good dressing down, but instinct told her not to.

"May I ask why?" She pushed her glasses up onto the top of her head and regarded Lucy's pale face dispassionately.

"My husband's dead. I have to go to the hospital now. There will be things to do and my son…" Her voice trailed off.

Ruby wondered if she had heard correctly.

"Oh Lucy, I am so sorry. When?"

"About an hour ago I believe. A heart attack they said."

Ruby remembered Peter. A healthy looking chap with floppy dark hair, a good laugh, she recalled and about the same age as Lucy.

"But, he's so…"

"Young" Lucy finished. "Yes, so young".

"Of course you must go. My dear, I really am so sorry. Let me know when you're ready to come back. Your job will still be here for you," she added unnecessarily and wondering why on earth she's said it.

"Lucy, Lucy…" The girl was staring past her at a dirty mark on the wall above the radiator.

"Yes, Ms James. Sorry."

Ruby detested any show of emotion in her well organised domain, but she walked around her desk and put her arm around Lucy's shoulder. The blank acceptance in Lucy's expression left her cold. This was not normal behaviour in a young woman who has just been told her husband has dropped down dead. Ruby James did not like anything abnormal or which fell outside comfortable categorisation. It made her nervous.

"Did you know there was a problem, was it expected?"

"No and yes," Lucy answered her truthfully.

Ruby felt completely out of her comfort zone. What was the girl talking about? She withdrew her arm self-consciously from Lucy's shoulder and patted her hand. "Off you go now. Leave everything and just call me when you feel up to it. If there is anything I can do in the meantime, let me know."

"Thank you, Ms James." Lucy walked quickly out of her office, closed the door quietly and left the building without a word to anyone.

The orderly replaced the receiver and scratched his head. Strange one that, still it was a call he always hated making and they all reacted differently. You could just never tell. He wondered idly what she would be like. He was quite unprepared for the pretty pale young woman wearing a tailored navy suit and crisp white blouse, with her blonde hair tied neatly back into a snood.

She walked briskly to the desk, looking straight in front of her and quietly asked if she could see her husband. He left her with Peter and waited outside. Some ten minutes later she came out. Her expression never wavered, sadness tinged with acceptance. He dealt with the formalities as compassionately as he knew how and in less than half an hour he walked to the door with her. She promised to call him about the arrangements.

He remained watching her for a moment as she walked away slowly along the gravel pathway her head bowed, clutching the pathetic little bundle of her husbands' belongings. Then she turned and looked back at him and gave a gentle smile. He saw she was crying.

Lucy walked back into the quiet house, made a cup of tea and sat down on the sofa, resting the mug on her tightly clenched knees. She could touch the silence. Numbly she called her parents. Her father answered and listened quietly, trying to think of words which would help. Of course there were none. He agreed to collect Alex from the child-minder and take him to his grandmother. She refused his offer to come to the house but asked that he leave it until the weekend. She needed time to think.

She looked around the room. Her dressing gown lay untidily over the arm of the chair. The carefully folded newspaper was still on the coffee table, where Peter had forgotten to put it in his briefcase, next to his tea mug that she hadn't had time to wash up before she left for work. She sniffed. She could smell his aftershave. One slipper lay under the table and she got up to look under the sofa for its partner, until she realised it really didn't matter. He wouldn't be needing them again.

She sat back on the sofa and looked at the three photos above the fireplace. She and Peter on their wedding day. Smiling and happy, the future awaiting. Her eyes moved to the second. Peter beaming at her, smartly to attention and holding the new expensive briefcase she had bought him when he had been promoted. And finally on to the third. Peter, Alex on his lap and she and Alice one either side of him, the one

Henry had taken last summer; She felt the prickling in her eyes and gritted her teeth, which did nothing except make her jaw ache.

She put her hand to the side of her head and screwed up her face wet with tears. Suddenly with brute force she clenched her fist and slammed it onto the table. The fruit bowl bounced, a tangerine flew into the air and disappeared under the sofa. In slow motion she watched the tall red vase next to it wobble, roll, fall onto the floor and shatter. She looked at the pieces, blood red against the pale laminate and howled until her throat was sore.

"Damn you, Alice, damn you to hell! Why didn't you tell me?" she shrieked at the photograph, the smiling faces mocking her. "I didn't even get the chance to say goodbye."

The half full tea mug followed the vase onto the floor, splattering her skirt. The crash stopped her in mid scream. The bits of patterned china mixed in with the pieces of red glass and the tea was starting to spread out over the floor.

She stood up, stripped off to her bra and pants and left her clothes in a heap by the door. Mechanically she swept up the broken fragments and mopped the floor. She pulled on her dressing gown, gathered up the debris, picked up the heap of clothes and emptied everything into the dustbin, including the clothes. She would never wear them again.

She showered, washed her hair and scrubbed herself until her skin burned. The dreadful contamination of the day was removed from her body if not her mind. Pulling her robe tightly around her she went into the bedroom and lay down on their bed, the bed she would never share with him again.

She found Alice's number in the bedside draw and dialled.

"Hello, 7324... Hello? Is anyone there?"

"Hello Alice, it's Lucy."

"Lucy?" Silence. "When?"

"This morning."

She heard Alice's intake of breath. "Oh, my dear child, I'm so sorry."

Lucy snapped. "Sorry. Jesus Christ, Alice, so am I. Bloody sorry. You knew and you said nothing. Alice, you knew. Why didn't you tell me? I could have done something." She ranted on, alternately shouting and crying until her voice trailed off into muffled sobs.

Alice took a deep breath. She knew this time would come but even so she was not prepared for the anger and aggression in the young woman's voice. "There was nothing you could have done. What could I have told you? All I knew was that your future would not include Peter. Was it really for me to spoil what time you had left. Wouldn't you have been looking over your shoulder all the time wondering and waiting, perhaps for years, feeling resentful against some old woman who read cards for you on holiday?"

Lucy's tired mind registered the sense in this and she started to sob. "But I never said goodbye. We were in such a hurry this morning, I didn't kiss him or tell him I loved him."

"You didn't need too. He knew that. You made him very happy, Lucy, he knew you loved him and he loved you, you and Alex."

Alex. How did a mother tell her young child that he would never see his beloved daddy again?

She listened to Alice's soothing gentle words. "Lucy I can come over now if you want. I know you have things to do and you must be hurt and confused. I have some experience, I can help. I should be there in an hour."

"Oh Alice, I'm really sorry. You've had your own loss so recently; I should never have called you." She started to cry again.

"Look, Lucy, I gave you my number for a reason and at this time you shouldn't be thinking about anyone except yourself, your son and Peter's family. Have you told them yet?"

Lucy's silence answered her.

"Look, just wait until I get there. I'll deal with it."

Alice was wonderful. She called Peter's parents and explained compassionately to the two distraught people everything Lucy had told her. Yes, it had been quick and no his suffering had been short. Yes, Lucy was with her. No, there had been no stress or troubles between them, they were very happy and it was just one of those awful things which happen to some terribly unlucky people.

Her parents collected Alex from the child-minder and took him home with them. Her mum said she would bring him back whenever Lucy was ready.

Alice stayed with her and dealt with the inevitable telephone calls and visits. She left and a short while later Peter's parents arrived. Together they arranged the funeral, and Lucy found it helped having them there. They spent the evening drinking sherry and coffee, talking over all the memories into which those left behind lose themselves.

Lucy's parents brought Alex back with them the following evening. They all agreed that Alex should not be there on the day of the funeral. He spent the day with Lucy's friend who had children of a similar age. With her parents' help, Lucy told her little son that his daddy was gone. He had cried and kept his back turned to them whilst his young mind tried to grasp the reality of life and death. With the strange acceptance without really understanding that young children seem to be able to call on in times of loss, he began to question why daddy had gone and why was he not coming back. Lucy explained that daddy was living in heaven with the angels and that although he could not see him again, he was still there in the photographs and he could talk to daddy if he wanted to. Daddy couldn't answer him like he used to but he would always been in Alex's memories and he would always love him.

The funeral took place on a bright crisp and bitingly cold winter day. Lucy was genuinely moved to see how many of their friends came and some of Peter's school friends she had never met. His parents coped with the strain as best they could. No one expects to bury their own child and at times, Lucy wondered if Peter's mother should stay or go and rest. She was not in perfect health and Lucy worried about her. She had asked people back to the house where there were photographs and little touches which evidenced Peter's presence and also where there was room for Peter's parents to go and sit by themselves if they wanted to.

Alice and Henry proved to be a real treasure. Between them they took charge of everything and whilst Henry dealt with the practicalities Alice sat with Peter's mother offering understanding and sympathy, the two older women sharing loss and memory over tea and sherry. Her own parents stayed close to her offering their support and any help they could offer for the future. In the morning they left only after she assured them she would be fine, she just needed time to adjust as best she could.

In the afternoon, Peter's parents started their journey home to the North but before they left they made arrangements to visit Henry and Alice with whom they had struck up a bond, born initially of mutual grief but which had the promise of becoming a lasting friendship.

Lucy felt closer in those few days to Peter's parents than she probably ever had previously. During their short marriage she had not seen very much of them, if only because of the miles that separated them. She promised to bring Alex to see them and said truthfully they were more than welcome to come to see her whenever they could.

Later she sat with Alice alone in the kitchen late into the evening, with mugs of tea and a plate of chocolate digestives which neither touched. Henry was asleep on the sofa.

She stared at Alice. "Talk to me."

"What do you want to know?"

"Everything."

Alice studied her young friend intently. "You remember when you were sitting at the bench table outside the hotel in Lanzarote when you had Alex on your knee and Peter was beside you before they went back into the hotel."

Lucy nodded.

"As I watched Peter his shadow got up from the bench and went and stood behind you, his hands on your shoulders. He kissed the top of Alex's head and stroked your cheek. The shadow looked straight at me and shook his head. 'Don't tell her Alice, just tell her I love her, I love both of them and I will always be there for them if they need me.' Then it faded away."

Lucy stared at her, her face ashen. "You mean he knew he was… he was going to die?"

"No, I am sure he didn't, at least not his earthly person, only his spirit. I had to do what he asked me. Was I wrong?" Her eyes pleaded with Lucy to understand, to exonerate her from the guilt she felt.

Lucy took her hands. "No, you weren't. Thank you. You were both right. I would have spent the last six months scared of every footstep."

There were more than thirty years between the two women but Lucy had never at any time felt closer to any friend than she did at that moment.

Time chugged along in its usual cruel way, exactly as it always does, one day following the next, oblivious of the pain it had caused to those left behind. Lucy's life moved on, save that Peter was no longer part of it. She went back to work and after the initial embarrassment and uncertainty of what to say, her friends and colleagues also carried on as usual.

A friend at work had a sister who specialised in probate work and Lucy spent an uncomfortable hour going through the procedures that she had never dreamed she would need. The woman was young and considerate. She told Lucy she would need to go through Peter's papers and suggested Lucy bring everything to her and then leave her to deal with it.

A couple of weeks later she went through Peter's desk. When Alex was born they had spent an evening, as he put it "For a serious discussion".

With Peter that was never easy! Lucy recalled fondly that Peter was virtually incapable of a serious discussion. She remembered how they sat either side of the table with a bottle of wine.

"Insurance."

"What about it."

"We need it."

"OK, fire away."

"Well to start with I earn more than you," he grinned "and therefore I am more important and I should have more insurance."

"How do you work that one out?" Lucy took the bait and a good natured and frivolous disagreement followed.

"£100,000 for me and £500 for you!"

"Get stuffed!"

"I can pay the bills without yooooou" he sang. She picked up a cushion and chucked it at him.

"And who is going to take care of Alex, cook, clean and pick up your cheesy socks, wash and iron and generally put up with your idiotic behaviour. Who's going to put you to bed when you're drunk?"

Peter pretended to think deeply "Another wife, I guess," and smirked wickedly.

"Piss off you sod, no one would have you."

She threw another cushion at him and he ducked. It hit the red vase, which wobbled and would have hit the floor if she hadn't caught it. She noted irrationally that it was the same one she had broken the day he died. It was obviously meant to go.

After some discussion, they had compromised £30,000 cover for him and £10,000 for her. Lucy commented that the premiums would be expensive for this type of cover and Peter in an unusually mature manner for him had replied quite seriously that they had a family to consider and if they acted now the premiums would be less than they would later on in life. They had opened another bottle of wine, got enjoyably giggly and made happily sozzled love.

They made their Wills, took out the insurance. The house was owned jointly and if either of them died it passed to the survivor of them. Peter had a few investments and a small savings account but Lucy left that to him and didn't know much about it. Unbeknown to her he had taken out another cheap insurance which only covered him for 10 years but provided a further £10,000 if he died within that time. Because of his age, the premiums were very low and she had no idea the policy existed until she discovered it amongst his papers.

When the formalities were completed, Lucy was surprised to find that she was left with a mortgage-free house and a healthy bank balance. Whilst not being a millionaire she realised that she could certainly be considered very comfortable. Ruby James persuaded her to see a financial adviser and the money was sensibly invested. By the end of that dreadful summer Lucy was as organised as she could be and ready, as Alice had put it, to start the journey alone.

CHAPTER EIGHT

ANTONIO

The weeks became months and Lucy survived. She missed Peter but as he had jokingly said "If I can't support you in luxury during my life, I'll certainly make sure I will afterwards." Lucy had, as usual told him to shut up and stop being morbid, but it was true that without the insurance money she would have struggled. She was financially secure both now and for Alex in the future. Her job was steady, and more interesting and it kept her busy.

Ruby James noticed quickly that although Lucy seemed the same on the outside, reliable and conscientious, she was easily distracted. She promoted her to her own assistant to give her more responsibility and less time to brood. Lucy rose to the challenge and the two formed an unlikely bond.

Alex had started at primary school and was thriving. He sometimes asked her questions about his daddy and once or twice Lucy had heard him in his room, talking in a low voice but she never interfered. That was something between him and his father and if he was happy that was the most important thing. Some children talked to imaginary friends, Alex preferred to talk to his dad and that was fine by her.

Lucy had no particular man in her life, although she had reluctantly agreed to make up a foursome with friends from time to time, and if she was honest with herself, as rarely as possible. She shied away from one to one contact and preferred to have numerous acquaintances, male and female, mostly married but a few singles and one or two close friends. She avoided any situation which could become complicated in that respect. She was always conscious that as a relatively young woman she had already been divorced and widowed.

Later that year she took Alex to Tenerife. She booked the holiday on a whim. It was not her first choice of location, she would have preferred somewhere quieter and it was too close to Lanzarote and her memories. But it was perfect for Alex and at short notice the choice was limited.

The weather was not hot, just pleasant. Not yet ready to tackle the world head on, she kept herself to herself and spent her days with her son by the pool and lazing on the beach or helping him build sandcastles. She had deliberately chosen a 3-star hotel which was child friendly. The entertainment was low key. Early in the evening there was usually bingo and later a quiz in the lounge bar followed by music for all tastes. The bar opened directly onto the swimming pool area and Lucy sat outside next to the pool. She had always enjoyed a quiz and had spent many a happy evening with Peter, Ewan and Jackie going to pub quiz nights, with moderate success.

One evening she sat in her usual spot, sipping her beer and watching the smoke from her cigarette curling up through the still evening air, swirling like a dancer illuminated by the lights around the pool. The quiz had just started. She listened to the booming voice of the DJ, encouraging his noisy audience to come and give him the correct answers, collect their winner's ticket and try to win the bottle of champagne. She whispered the answers to the first three questions to herself, but stayed in her seat. Alex sat beside her, watching.

"Mum do you know the answers?"

"Yes, sweetheart."

"Then why don't you go and tell him."

"No darling, I'm happy here. You go and tell him. I'll tell you and then you can show how clever you are!"

He grinned. "OK, let's go for it."

"Who sang the title song to the Bond film "From Russia with Love?"

"Matt Monroe," she whispered in Alex's ear.

Alex dashed up to the DJ, whizzing past an elderly lady headed in the same direction. A few moments later he ran back to her waving his red ticket, beaming from ear to ear. "We won, Mum."

Lucy smiled. This might even be fun.

"Who was Henry VIII's wife when he died?"

"Katherine Parr." Alex rushed back into the bar and returned with another red ticket.

More questions and a lot more red tickets.

"On which continent do the Tuareg live?" That was a bit more difficult.

"Africa," she told Alex who disappeared like a fox down a hole. This time he didn't come back. She waited.

A few minutes later the booming voice came over the microphone. "While I appreciate that this is one very bright little boy, I think perhaps the person feeding him the answers should perhaps make themselves known and claim the prize."

Lucy stayed where she was. Alex came back with another red ticket, but Lucy stopped answering the questions.

"Why Mum, he's very nice and he gave me an ice cream 'cos he said he wasn't allowed to give me the bottle of champagne."

The quiz finished, Alex went in for a squash and returned with a young woman. She sat down in the empty chair next to Lucy and spoke in English

"Antonio would like to know if you would like to come with us to the café when we close."

"And me?" She smiled at Alex "Of course, and you."

"Sorry, who are you?" Lucy asked more frostily than she meant to.

The woman looked embarrassed. "Forgive me. I'm Sandy. I teach English at the local school, but I help Antonio with the quiz and the music most nights. I'm from Manchester originally, but I came out here about five years ago and met Antonio the first week I was here. He was brilliant, helped me get the teaching job and we've been mates ever since."

She watched Lucy's closed expression and her face cracked into a broad grin. "It can't hurt to have a few drinks together. We're harmless you know. Where are you from?"

Lucy relaxed and felt a bit silly. The woman was only being pleasant and Lucy decided it might actually be nice to talk to someone who saw her just as another woman and didn't know her life history.

"I'm sorry, that was rude of me. We're from Surrey. I'm Lucy and this is Alex."

"Hi Lucy. Hello Alex." Alex put his hand out and the woman shook it, laughing at his solemn little face.

The music finished and Antonio came out to join them. He was a good looking man, about her own age she thought, his dark wavy hair worn long on his shoulders. His brown eyes appraised the newcomer, but he greeted her politely with a grin. The four of them walked down the steps to the café under the hotel. That was the first of a series of pleasant evenings which followed a comfortable pattern. Although she learned a lot about Antonio and Sandy, she talked little about herself, and if they noticed, they didn't try to draw her out.

They were not alone, there were usually four or five other local people in their company. Antonio spoke reasonable English but some of the others didn't. Sandy of course spoke fluent Spanish and Lucy found snippets of Spanish long forgotten from her college days. Encouraged by the flow of wine and beer she became more adventurous and to her amazement people appeared to actually understand her.

Alex loved it. Not only was he having fun but he was allowed to stay up much later than usual. Lucy was not at all sure about keeping a child up so late, but somehow things were coloured differently here. It was almost a lotus eater existence. Long nights, late mornings and lazy dreamy afternoons. They frequently missed the hotel breakfast and more often than not sat with coffee and croissants at the café, which never seemed to close. Everything just moved on about three hours, Lucy reasoned with her conscience. It couldn't hurt.

One evening she sat engrossed in conversation with Antonio, with whom she found she could be herself. She joked with him, laughed with him and relaxed with him. She lost sight of Alex who had disappeared into the café. She spotted him about ten minutes later followed by a pretty little girl with masses of curly brown hair. Each carried a huge strawberry ice cream in one hand and a pain au chocolat on a plate in the other. "What on earth…" Lucy started.

Antonio laid his hand on her arm. "Don't embarrass him in front of his girlfriend," he said softly.

"Oh." Lucy regarded her son from under arched eyebrows. "And who paid for those, may I ask?"

"Ah," said Alex. "I sort of did. Maria said she'd like an ice cream and I wanted one of these." He waved the plate in the air and Antonio caught the pastry as it fell off.

Lucy smiled. "What do you mean, you sort of did?"

"Well, I told the lady what I wanted. She gave them to us and I told her Mummy would pay."

Antonio stifled a chuckle. "Querida, leave him here with me for a year and not only will he be speaking fluent Spanish he'll have learned a few tricks as well."

"I think he already has," she retorted. She reached into her bag, but Antonio quickly gave the money to Maria with a quick stream of Spanish, who scuttled back into the café before Lucy could stop her.

"You didn't need to do that."

"I know, I wanted to."

As he spoke his arm went around the back of her chair. She leaned back and felt his arm around her shoulder. She froze and turned to face him, her eyes wide. Gently he moved his arm, but he looked enquiringly at her.

"You made me jump," she explained quickly.

He shook his head. "Not necessary, I understand."

Another bottle appeared and Lucy gratefully accepted the glass he offered her, and another. Sandy gave him a slight smile and declined. "I'm on my way, early day tomorrow."

They finished the bottle and she noticed Alex had drifted off to sleep. She knew she'd had too much to drink, and it didn't seem to matter, she felt good.

"I must go now." She got up, but her legs wouldn't hold her and she sat down again. She giggled. Concentrating hard, she stood up. "Alex come on, time to go."

She shook the sleeping child, who opened his eyes, grumbled and fell back to sleep. "Alex, Alex."

"Leave him, I'll take him." Antonio scooped him up and Lucy felt a twinge of panic. "It's OK, don't worry."

She walked in front of him up to her room and unlocked the door. Antonio pushed gently past her, took Alex's sandals off and tucked him into bed. He waited. Lucy shuffled uncomfortably, willing him to go. She said nothing.

"May I sit?"

She shrugged. "Look, I'd rather you didn't. I'm really tired." She knew it sounded hollow.

Instead of moving towards the door he moved towards her. She put her hands up, her palms facing towards him. "Antonio, no!"

"Lucy, be calm. I'm not trying to make love with you. I'd be lying if I said I didn't want to, you are a very beautiful woman, but this not now. I know there are many things hurting you. You talk. I listen."

He took her hand and led her out onto the tiny balcony and pulled out a chair. She sat and looked up at him. He sat in the other chair, far enough away not to make her feel threatened.

She got up and poured two glasses of the bottle of champagne he had brought up with him.

Over the next hour, her tongue loosened by the wine, she poured out her heart to a virtual stranger. She told him about her happy childhood, her marriage, the divorce and about meeting Peter. She told him about Alice, her knowledge and predictions and about Peter's death earlier in the year. She left out only the boy.

Antonio's eyes never left her face as he listened to this unwritten autobiography, but he said nothing. She turned to him, suddenly terribly self-conscious.

"Antonio, you must think I am crazy. You must know me now as well as I know myself and I know nothing about you."

He shook his head. "I am honoured that you tell me these things." He made no move to touch her.

She smiled. "Tell me about yourself."

In his wonderfully lilting English he told her about his childhood in Malaga. "I am the middle of three children, my elder brother was my father's pride, quick to follow him into the family business of wine growing. My young sister was not expected and is my mother's delight. I knew that my future was not in Spain. I had always wanted to travel."

Lucy empathised with this. She had often felt if she had not married Simon she might have worked abroad. "What did you do?"

He frowned. "I have thirty-four years. I joined the army, travel without cost, but like for many young men, the army came as a shock. The life was harder than I think but I live it for three years. When I leave I go to India, from there across Asia to Malay where my money is almost gone, but I still have nothing so I decide to go to America, land of opportunity. But it had not much opportunity for me. I stay for two more years, often sleeping, how you say, without roof. I do crop picking, I park cars at hotels and I end up in factory putting food into cans when I decided is not for me. So I return to Spain, but not to Malaga. I go to Costa Brava and as there are now many tourists and I like music my friend he get me job as DJ and entertainer.

"Then I meet man who likes my music and he invite me to Tenerife. I work for him for one season but I am not happy there. It was not nice place, you understand, many fights and I tell him now I go. I got work here and I am here for two years. I am happy here, nice people, families and children." He stopped, embarrassed by that he might be boring her, but Lucy was fascinated. He seemed to have done so much in his short life and begged him to go on.

"Next year I have work in Malta, a new hotel. A client of this hotel tell me about it last year and he books me for next season. You have been to Malta?" Lucy told him how she had been to Malta with her parents as a teenager.

"You travelled a lot."

Lucy nodded "Yes but mostly around Europe. I never had the chance to go to America or India like you."

"Is there anywhere you've been that you would really like to go back to?" he asked.

"Oh yes," he noticed how her eyes sparkled, but her voice tailed off.

"And…" he prompted. "I think this is perhaps what you left out." He leaned towards her and took her hand and she let him. "While you talked to me, I could sense there was something that was not there."

"Oh, it's nothing really." Her voice was light, but her eyes told a different story. "It was just something that happened to me in Tunisia years ago."

She hesitated. He smiled.

"This boy, about fifteen years old for heaven's sake, who I'd never seen in my life before or since, said some beautiful things to me, told me he loved me and that I must remember his name because we were destined to meet again."

"What was his name?"

"Farid."

"So you haven't forgotten him."

"Antonio, how could anyone forget something like that. You've got to admit it's a bit weird."

He looked at her, "No, not weird, as he said, destiny."

"Do you really believe in that sort of thing, seriously?"

"Absolutely. Destiny, she is the most powerful force of all."

He moved his chair nearer to her. "Lucy."

She turned to him and he held her face in his hands, very close. "Time does not change what is in our hearts, but remember what is outside this change. You say this happen years ago. That boy will be man now. Maybe you are in his heart as I think he is still in yours."

He stroked her cheek but kept his distance. She closed her eyes. The night sky disappeared and she felt the heat of the sun, the air was heavy with the scent of jasmine and cinnamon and she felt the touch of soft lips on hers. Her eyes flew open but he was still sitting on his chair just holding her hand. She reasoned she must have drunk more than she thought.

"Have I upset you?" She pushed him away gently. "No my friend, you have just helped me decide what I must do. I can't have my dreams and fears ruled by a boy I met for a few minutes so long ago. I have to go back and lay this demon to rest once and for all."

Antonio nodded. "Maybe the time is right for you now and maybe it will not be demon who greet you. I wish you luck." He stroked her hair and left.

They did not refer to their conversation again and when she left Tenerife, she took with her his little black and gold card. "Call me someday," he had said, knowing she never would. She never did.

Despite her conversation with Antonio, by the time she returned to England at the start of the cool damp English autumn, Lucy had put all thoughts of returning to Tunisia out of her head. She put the whole experience down to alcohol. She went back to work and everyone said how well she looked. Even her mother. Lucy laughed at her.

"What you mean I don't look peaky?" That was her mother's favourite expression insofar as Lucy was concerned. Her mother ignored the jibe.

"No darling, I mean it. The holiday seems to have done you good, exactly what you needed to brush away the cobwebs." She stopped, "No I didn't mean it that way. I'm sorry." She looked so awkward that Lucy actually felt sorry for her.

"It's OK, Mum, I do know what you mean and you're right, it did both of us good. Alex loved it and he even picked up some Spanish."

"Well, he takes after you then. I always said you should have done more with the languages, after all we did send you to language college after you left school." She sniffed "I hoped you would go abroad and work, you know, something like the UN."

Lucy glared at her. "Mum, I did a year studying several languages at the same time and we both know I was a bad student, hardly UN material, and anyway" she added mischievously "Don't kid yourself. We also both know I only got to go to language college because I refused point blank to try for university and you told me it was one or the other!"

"Yes dear, whatever you say, but don't let's argue about it. We'll agree to disagree." That was another or her favourite expressions.

Lucy smiled at her mother. "Don't ever change Mum."

Her mother smiled back. "You always were just like your father!" She looked fondly at her only child. "All I meant sweetheart is that you look much better than you have done for a long time and Alex is positively blooming. You didn't meet anyone did you, a man I mean?" She peered at Lucy over the top of her glasses.

"No, Mum I didn't. I just made friends. It was a lovely break and just what we both needed, a change of air and a world a million miles from home."

"Lucy, I wouldn't dream of suggesting you forget the past, but just remember memories can actually help you move on, so long as you leave them just where they are, as memories."

"Mum, for once you and I completely agree." She linked her arm with her mother's and hugged her. The two women had interpreted her mother's wise words differently.

Christmas came and went. The old year slipped away with a damp foggy whimper and the new year slouched in the much the same way. It was now over a year since Peter had left her and Lucy had become adept at fending off well-meaning friends setting her up with potential partners. As a single and unfortunately attractive woman, a few had initially left her name off their party and dinner lists, but when it became clear she was interested in neither their men nor in fact any man and was not trying to muscle in on their happy homes, she became even more popular. Before long the game was on for her female friends as to who would find Lucy a man. As the long faced miserable woman who had moved in next door said, "You're not getting any younger dear."

CHAPTER NINE

THE RETURN

Lucy thought often about her discussion with Antonio and finally decided to go back to Tunisia on her own, as she said to herself, to put the demons to rest. Peter's parents were more than happy to have Alex and Lucy revelled in the freedom of once again being abroad. She had chosen one of the Hotels near the beach on the edge of Hammamet. Although her first trip had been to Sousse and Hammamet was many miles further north, she was sure that if it was indeed destiny that she would meet Farid again, then it didn't matter where she stayed.

She liked Hammamet immediately. It was very different from Sousse and the hotel was a large modern building, exactly as described in the brochure. The room was adequate and clean. The décor was simple, high white walls, heavy blue patterned curtains which covered the whole of the balcony wall. There were a couple of pictures depicting local scenes and a low dressing table with a small stool. The floor was a covered with white tiles decorated with intricate blue designs. She resisted the temptation to curl upon the large bed and decided to wash away the dust first.

She smiled to herself as she remembered the cramped little room she and Alex had been given in Tenerife. There was just enough room for a chair and she had to push past the beds to get out onto the tiny balcony. Obviously this room was a double for sole use although it had only cost her a few pounds more. There was a lovely view of the pool which was again small, but adequate.

She got dressed and went downstairs to investigate. There were hotel staff everywhere, porters, waiters, receptionists, bar staff and general factotum and occasionally she noticed suited gentlemen, presumably management, walking between the staff and guests to ensure the smooth running of the hotel.

The bar area was crowded and she chose a small table at the back near the pool entrance. She ordered a pastis and sat back inhaling deeply on her cigarette. This was quite perfect. Lucy felt a little out of place being alone as everyone else seemed to be in couples or groups but again she found a table away from the main bustle of people.

The restaurant was large, but made less imposing by partitions creating three smaller rooms. The food was delicious and beautifully presented. Although usually waiter service, on the first night there was a Tunisian buffet in an area to one side off the main seating area. Great plates of salad and fruit, tiny bowls of olives and pickles, hot chicken in a deep red sauce, wedges of golden potato glistening with oil, saffron and herbs, vegetables, braised fennel, mixed fish and what looked like aubergine and courgette fritters, as well as bowls of couscous, rice and pasta and a bewildering array of tiny square cakes and pastries and bowls of what she thought was blancmange. And best of all, she couldn't see a chip or burger anywhere!

Lucy finished her meal and a half a bottle of a delicious local dry rose wine and sat out by the pool listening to the elderly man who played the piano. She had one more glass of wine and went to bed, stuffed and exhausted. She slept for ten hours and just managed to scrape into breakfast with a few minutes to spare. A couple of sweet rolls and a cup of coffee later she was ready to explore a new part of this exotic country.

She wandered around the area nearest the hotel but apart from a couple of shops there was not much there as the hotel was a little was out of the town. Sometimes she would see a slim smiling teenager with glistening black hair and her heart would jump but it was not the person she remembered.

She sat in the bar that evening, wondering whether she should go further afield tomorrow. She glanced over at the door. A woman of about her own age had come in and was looking a little lost. She smiled and the newcomer came over and sat down thankfully. Lucy was glad of the company. She learned Maggie came from Birmingham, she was a hairdresser and was here on her own after a break up with her latest boyfriend.

The women spent the next two days exploring the area when they were not on the beach or beside the pool. Lucy was pleased she had met Maggie. It was much more fun with someone else and she found the constant attention from the men much easier to handle when there were two of them. Once she overcame her initial reserve, she realised Maggie had a wicked sense of humour as well as a winning smile. She poked fun at Lucy because she didn't seem interested in the attention she was receiving. Lucy just smiled and said nothing.

They walked around Hammamet, ate in the narrow roadside cafés away from the big tourist places near the beach, shopped in the tiny shops, some underground and cool which was a blessed relief from the heat of the day. They took a trip up to the pretty village of Sidi Bou Said and took pictures of the charming little houses, all painted blue and white.

One afternoon they set out armed with sun lotion, cameras and sunglasses. It was impossible to do anything but saunter. Even though it was now late in the afternoon, the air which had been slowly warming since eight in the morning had not yet started to cool. The sunlight reflected on the paving, the white shop fronts and tables and on the sea itself. The light blinded her.

As they walked towards the old sandy coloured walls of the Medina, she could see the blocks were smooth where they had been worn by the elements over the years. She could hear the clear voice over the tannoy calling the faithful to prayer and wondered how many thousands of times those ancient walls had heard that call. She had read that the Medina was hundreds of years old and part of an ancient fort. Now the buildings were trapped between times, with little shops and stalls, selling everything from pottery and roughly fashioned jewellery, long embroidered kaftan like garments, souvenirs and toys, all set up for one purpose, to get as much money from the tourist visitor as possible. In the innermost part, where the alleys were at their most narrow there were a few traditional places where local people lived and shopped for their daily needs, but these were few.

They found a beautiful little room set back into the walls. The door was open and as they stepped inside the cool air enveloped them. A young man stood at his easel painting and the walls were covered with his artwork, all local scenes, deep purple hills, the intense blue of the sea and the amazing sunsets. One small picture caught Lucy's eye. It showed a view she remembered. The square outside the big Sousse Medina with its trees providing shade from the midday sun and groups of people seated talking against the backdrop of the soft sandy walls of the ancient building, exactly as she remembered it. She bought the painting.

As they strolled along the narrow alleys she thought how different Hammamet was from Sousse, which seemed to her to be a working city occupied by local people but with a few tourists thrown into the mixing pot for a little seasoning, but not too many as to spoil the overall taste. That had of course been quite a few years ago. Maybe Sousse had altered too, but she doubted it. There had been something proudly everlasting about Sousse, as though it was above such things as change. She hoped so anyway.

They admired the merchandise and ran the usual barrage of over excited traders, many speaking in heavily accented English,

"Here lady, let me ask you one question, how much cost in England?" Lucy was amused to hear one man call out, "Come into my shop, have a butchers."

Someone had learned his English from a Londoner. Maggie for once was unhappy with the attention. "D'you know, if they would leave us alone to just look I'm quite sure I would actually buy something. At the moment I just want to get away."

They stayed only a short while, bought a couple of postcards and walked back to the hotel.

They changed for dinner, had a couple of drinks at the bar and then a light meal. Neither of them were particularly hungry.

"Lucy would you mind very much if I went to bed. I've got a filthy headache and I'd rather get rid of it now that end up being more crotchety than usual tomorrow."

"Go ahead, Maggie. I'm going to have a look round and see what there is to do tomorrow."

Her new friend disappeared towards the lifts and Lucy headed out towards the pool area. As it was summer, the pool bar was still open and the guests crowded around it, chattering, reminding Lucy of the pigeons in Trafalgar Square when a child throws down some seed. She stopped long enough to have another pastis but as most of the people were in couples or groups she felt awkward and decided to try a beach bar to see if she could find a solitary chair to sit and look out at the sea.

CHAPTER TEN

THE MAN

She walked slowly past the huge hedges of bougainvillea and some trailing orange flowered creeper she had never seen before. As always the air was heavy with scent of the jasmine. It was a scent she remembered and would always remind her of Tunisia. She took the neat flower edged path out of the back gate which led to the beach and saw a low building gently lit by candlelight. She walked under the narrow archway, ducking her head to avoid the trails of jasmine and along a row of wooden slats laid crossways to form an access across the sand. She could see some stools surrounding the bar itself and a few dark wood tables with benches either side. Tiny candles inside glasses flickered on each table. There was little other light, just a couple of wrought iron lamps hanging from either end of the bar, casting long weird shadows across the sand.

One or two of the tables were occupied but most of the noise was coming from the bar itself where she could see a group of youths, all still wearing their long shorts, some with t-shirts or vests and some with their bronzed chests bare. They all seemed to be talking at once in loud guttural Arabic. She smiled grimly. So much for a peaceful chair looking out over the sea. As she approached the voices quietened and a few heads turned. She had no idea what was being said but was sure she was the subject matter.

Lucy was not unaccustomed to male attention but was completely surrounded and within minutes the language had changed to German. "Hello lady. What is your name?" was followed by a stream of other unsophisticated quickly to the point beach boy chat.

She let them talk for a few minutes and then smiled sweetly. "I am not German. I don't understand you," she said in that language.

There were a few puzzled looks and then one bare chested man with greased back hair and a pair of particularly vile crimson patterned shorts, who seemed to be their leader spoke to her in English. Lucy ignored him and turned to the barman and ordered her drink in French. Immediately everyone was speaking in French. It was not so much the attention which was overwhelming but the noise and sheer numbers were starting to irritate her.

The same bare chested man put his hand on her shoulder and suggested they went for a swim. Lucy pointed out sharply she was hardly dressed for the occasion. He gave a lewd smirk and sensing what was coming next Lucy shook his arm from around her and turned her back on him to lean on the bar. He shrugged and walked over to a couple of girls seated at of the tables away from the bar and most of the others followed him.

The barman grinned at Lucy. "Well handled, Madame," he said in French. Lucy grinned back.

"Thanks, but I am actually English." He raised both hands, "Sorry, my English she not good." They both laughed and the other three lads still at the bar joined in. Lucy got out her camera.

"May I take a photo, so my friends at home will be jealous? So many handsome men together!"

The barman came out from his post and the four men jostled for position and stood together, their arms resting on each other's shoulders like a football team as she took the photo.

The barman took the camera from her. "Now you Madame." She stood between the men and waited, facing the bar. There was a slight movement in the shadow at the side of the bar and she noticed a man standing on his own. He wore dark trousers and a short sleeved white shirt. She couldn't see his face. The barman called out to him but he shook his head.

Lucy held out her hand towards him. "Please come for my photograph." She was rewarded with a flash of white teeth. The barman laughed loudly and the man walked forward out of the shadows.

"Quiet Ahmed." His voice was deep and commanding.

He was young, quite tall, his strong shoulders emphasised by the epaulettes designating him as security. She noticed the trousers fitted closely over slim hips. He was a handsome man, high cheek bones, strong chin and a slight smile under his narrow moustache but without the trace of softness which too often accompanies male beauty. His eyes never left hers. She was helpless, as a moth being drawn too near to the candle flame. She shivered.

As he reached the line-up waiting for the photograph instead of joining the end of the line, he waited, looking from one man to the next and the line parted. He took his place next to Lucy and another photograph was taken. The barman beamed. "Now my friend, one of just you and the lady."

The man put his arm round her holding her gently as they stood side by side, so differently from the crushing oppression of him of the crimson shorts. Unconsciously Lucy inclined her head towards his shoulder and he held her closer, almost possessively. She felt his head resting very lightly against her hair and she sighed.

The camera flashed. "Very good, very good. I take very good picture," grinned Ahmed.

The tall man didn't remove his arm and Lucy didn't try to move away.

"You will sit with me?" He spoke in French.

Lucy nodded and mutely followed him to the table furthest from the bar, lit only by a single candle. He sat on the bench next to her.

Ahmed brought them two beers and she noticed he gave his friend a strange look but neither man spoke.

Lucy took the offered cigarette. As he cupped his hands around the lighter, she leaned towards him and put her own lightly over his, their faces so close. His eyes glittered in the candlelight. He smiled at her, a beautiful smile, his teeth white against his dark face. Lucy's eyes widened. "Once, many years ago, a boy smiled at me like that, I took his photograph and gave him a coin," she murmured, half to herself. The man said nothing. She looked up at him, a little embarrassed.

"What's your name?" she asked. He answered her in Arabic, not guttural like the lads at the bar, but soft like a caress.

"Please, I don't speak Arabic. What did you say?"

He spoke in French. "My name is Farid. Remember it, beautiful lady and wait for me for I love you and one day we will meet again, insh'allah"

Lucy gasped and felt the blood drain from her face as though a ghost had walked though her. She knocked over her glass as she pulled away from him. "Farid? No Farid, you cannot be the same person. It's not possible." He leaned towards her and took her shaking hands in his.

It had never occurred to Farid that she wouldn't know him. He recognised her as she came under the archway onto the beach, which is when he stepped back into the shadow of the building to give his pounding heart time to recover.

He watched as she defended herself against the chatter and remarks of his young friends and was glad to see the attention was unwanted. He was particularly pleased by the way she rebuffed the particularly suggestive approach made by Moez whom he regarded as an offensive creature.

He studied her pale face. The years hadn't changed her. She was just as he remembered. He smiled to himself. It may have been true, but how had he ever found the courage to say what he had said to her? It was a question he had asked himself many times without ever finding the answer.

Lucy was frightened. The eyes so close to hers were half-closed beneath arched brows. His lips, slightly hidden by his moustache and full enough to be sensuous without being feminine, were slightly parted. She felt the intimacy of his hip resting against hers. Thoroughly disconcerted, she saw the flicker of a smile and dropped her gaze to his chest, open at the neck revealing a light covering of body hair and she watched the muscles in his arms tighten as he reached for his glass. He drank deeply and as he put the glass down he ran his tongue slowly over his lips, savouring the taste.

Lucy held her breath. She closed her eyes and experienced a sensation of warmth radiating out from the centre of her body to every finger, toe, pore and nerve ending. She trembled. Farid felt her move and held her closer. He could feel her breath on his chest and saw the quick rise and fall of her bosom.

"But I don't understand. The Farid I saw was a boy, and you…!"

He laughed. "…are a man, but in my country, as I think in yours, boys become men, and as you say it was many years ago."

Suddenly Lucy's mind flew back to Alice's words. "The boy becomes a man and appears out from the shadows." It was suddenly so clear. She swayed and Farid held her close his arm tightly round her. She rested her head on his chest and he saw the tears bright in her eyes.

"And you remembered me?"

"I could never forget you" he replied quietly.

She stared at him, bewildered. How could the slim adolescent that she remembered have become this formidable man sitting next to her? She sensed rather than saw him watching her and felt his lips brush her cheek so softly as they had once before. She breathed in his scent, his nearness intoxicated her with sheer maleness and she was sure he felt the sensations that rippled through her. She had nursed the picture of the beautiful boy for so long she was unprepared for the man he had become. She tried to calm herself and came out with the first thing she could think of to say. "I gave you money, what did you spend it on".

Farid put his hand in his breast pocket and pulled out his wallet. He opened it and handed her a coin. "This coin you mean."

Lucy stared at him. "That can't be the same coin, surely not." Farid smiled.

"Take it and look closely."

"What am I looking for?"

"There on the back." She held the coin towards the candle and clapped her hand over her mouth.

"F+L. Oh Farid, is it the same coin?" He nodded. "When did you have it engraved?"

"Shortly after you gave it to me. I bought a small box to put it in and then when I became older I moved it to my wallet so it could be close to my heart."

Ahmed watched as his friend sat in the darkness, his arm around the English woman. He rarely saw Farid with a girl and he had certainly never seen him smile at any woman that way. It was almost as though they knew each other, this woman and his young friend but that was impossible. It was clear the woman didn't know Farid when he took their photograph. Anyway the woman was obviously a tourist and quite a lot older. He shrugged. No, it was impossible but to his amazement he saw Farid cup the woman's face in his hands and kiss her gently. He watched as she put her arm around his neck. He took them another two beers. Neither noticed him. Lucy remembered little of that evening. The feeling this man evoked in her she had never experienced before.

They sat close, side by side and then she spoke to him in English.
"I'm sorry I speak no English."
"What none at all?" He shook his head. "You speak in French you are in my country now." He teased her about her inability to find the right words in the French she had rarely used since her college days. She learned that his home was in Sousse where was born, with his parents and siblings, when he was not working in Hammamet, but that with the long working hours he spent little time there.

She told him about her marriage to Peter and that she had a son, but that Peter had died. He stroked her cheek.

"It must be very hard for you now, but you have a man in England now?" She kissed him gently. "I have no man."

The bar closed and Ahmed came over to them. Farid handed him some coins, but Ahmed grinned at him and just took one of them. Farid nodded his thanks. He walked back with her to the back of her hotel, his arm close around her waist. In the dark shadows he pulled her close to him, kissed her feeling the softness of her lips and probed the sweetness of her mouth as her lips parted. He moved quickly away but not before she felt the pressure of him against her. She didn't know whether to be elated that he was affected by her in the same way she was by him, or frightened of what the future held.

When he spoke his voice caressed her. "Good night my Lucy, dream of me. You will see me here tomorrow evening, eight o'clock?" It was a question, but one Lucy could not have declined. She nodded and hoped he could not guess what her dreams would be.

"Good night my beau Tunisian." The words spoken long ago took on a new meaning. He smiled broadly.

"Thank you," he whispered in her ear. He turned and walked away from her, his hands in his pockets, the blood coursing through him and his mind in turmoil.

Lucy sat on the balcony for a long time watching the moonlight dancing on the waves. Her thoughts of strong arms around her naked body did nothing to encourage her sleep and when she finally drifted into a sort of disturbed rest she was haunted by the image of a handsome face and a smile that enveloped her soul.

Farid lay awake. This was the woman he had dreamed of since boyhood and by the way she felt in his arms he knew his life had changed. He was scared by the emotions she had drawn from him and Ahmed's surprise had not gone unnoticed. He knew that his friends regarded him as strange. He had always preferred the company of his friends and tourists he regarded as potential trouble. He had been aware in the past of the interest he created in some of them but rarely had he followed it through. With Lucy he realised there was unlikely to be a future, he knew from their first meeting that she must be years older than him. He remembered the rush of unwarranted jealousy as she told him she had been married, but her husband had died and she had a son. The vision of another man's hands on her and she bearing his child left a sour taste in his mouth.

He was no monk. There had been women in his life, a few, but he had never felt close to any of them. He smiled to himself as he recalled his first experience with a blonde German woman, older than he by many years, but very experienced in the ways that mattered. It had been around his seventeenth birthday and she had broken him in, so to speak. He had known at the time that he was only attracted to her because in a coarse way she reminded him of Lucy.

He could not shake off the niggle which told him that nothing good could come of this relationship but a stronger feeling as old as time itself would not be banished. With a ferocity that surprised him, he realised that no matter what the future held for them he must have Lucy next to him for as long and as often as he could. He dozed, a smile playing on his lips as in his mind he felt her softness underneath him and her breasts against his chest. His body would not allow him to sleep and the dawn light was visible through the curtains before he finally drifted into sleep, his arms clasped tightly around his pillow.

The following day when Lucy woke she could see the sunlight under the curtains and rubbed her eyes. Her watch read 11.45a.m. She leapt out of bed in disbelief. She could not remember the last time she had slept this late. She showered quickly and tied her hair up in a knot before making her way to the dining room for lunch where she found Maggie munching her way through a huge plate of salad.

After their meal the two girls lay by the pool. Lucy lay on her back staring at the sky from under her glasses thinking about the evening to come. Maggie knew something had happened to her new friend as she watched Lucy's face which had taken on a glow which had little to do with the sun.

"Am I right in thinking something happened to you last night?"

Lucy turned over and Maggie was amused to see her face was flushed.

"Ah, I think a man has come into your life." She grinned, savouring her companion's embarrassment. "Come on Lucy, isn't that what holidays are all about!"

"Yes, I did meet a man and he wants to see me again tonight."

"Bloody hell. One meeting and you've got a man in tow. Not that I'm annoyed, I was starting to get concerned about your apparent lack of interest in the opposite sex, I don't suppose you…"

"No I did not!" Lucy slapped her leg playfully "But I refuse to say whether I will or not!"

"Am I to meet this paragon of perfection?"

"I thought the expression was paragon of virtue," Lucy quipped.

"Oh Lord, I hope not that would make him really boring, virtue is not what I would have in mind."

Maggie's grin was infectious and Lucy laughed but felt herself blush to the roots of her hair.

"I'm meeting him at eight o'clock."

"Hell that's not fair. I'm on the night flight and the bus is picking us up at eight-thirty!"

They spent the remainder of the day lazing by the poolside and Lucy watched enviously as Maggie's olive skin turned deeper brown.

She knew that unless she was very careful her own fair skin would burn but it didn't stop her being envious of the beautiful tan which some women seemed to obtain with little effort.

That evening, Lucy showered, washed her hair and brushed it until it shone in a pale halo round her face. She pulled the sides back into tiny silver clips, made up her eyes with a sparkling mauve eye-shadow and deep purple liner. She knew without false modesty that her eyes were her best feature and that the mauve brought out their unusual colour. She had hunted everywhere for the eye-liner and eventually found it in a shop in one of the side streets off Oxford Circus which catered for theatre people, but having found what she was looking for rarely had the need to use it.

She agonised over what to wear. The clothes she had brought with her were for a happy-go-lucky holiday. In her heart she never dreamed she would actually meet Farid again and she had not considered he would be a man not a boy.

She sat on the bed and wondered if she was doing the right thing by meeting Farid. She poured herself a large vodka and tonic and then pulled most of her clothes out onto the bed before deciding on what to wear. She surveyed the array of swimwear, shorts, one or two pairs of light trousers, a couple of vests and t-shirts and a pale pinky-lilac top with narrow straps, as well as her travelling clothes.

She thought carefully and poured herself another drink. She was worried. The previous evening Farid had sent her senses on self-destruct and she knew she would need every ounce of her mental strength to resist what she knew they both wanted. It was all moving just too quickly and she did not want him to think that she would let him make love to her within hours of meeting. She admitted to herself she was terrified of the thought of having sex. No man had touched her since Peter died and instinct told her that Peter's gentle lovemaking would be very different from the intense passion she sensed in this young Arab man.

She jumped as Maggie arrived. "Just come to say goodbye and see how you're doing." She burst into peals of laughter. Lucy stood in her bra and pants, her bed covered with clothes, most of them inside out where she had tried them on, changed her mind and flung them in a heap onto the bed.

"You've really got it bad, haven't you!"

Lucy glared at her. "Shut up, Maggie, I'm trying to think. What the hell do I wear? I don't want to be boring," she pointed to a high necked orange t-shirt lying on top of the discarded heap. "And most of all, I don't want to be provocative or tarty."

"Why not?"

Lucy eyed her distastefully. "Because I don't want him jumping on me the second we meet thinking he's got an open invitation."

"Why not?" Maggie repeated grinning broadly.

Lucy looked exasperated. "Grow up," she snapped and sat down on the bed, taking a swig from the glass beside her.

Maggie went over to the bed and picked up the white trousers and the lilac top. Lucy was a bit worried that the top was quite deep cut at the front, but agreed with Maggie it was still better than the vests and plain T-shirts. She looked at herself in the mirror and added a little pale gloss lipstick and a small silver necklace and bracelet. She thought about her flat comfortable flip-flops, but Maggie suggested the delicate pair of silver sandals with a wedge heel would be much nicer. She fiddled with her hair, adjusted her top and jigged from one foot to the other. Maggie found it quite amusing. As her bus didn't leave until 8.30p.m. she walked with her to the back gate. She was quite determined to catch sight of the man who had turned her new friend into a quivering jelly.

Farid was standing next to the security box chatting to guard. As they came down the path Maggie clutched her arm. "Don't tell me your chap is that gorgeous man who looks like a movie-star with a body made for one thing only."

Lucy felt a surge of pride. "I most certainly do."

"You lucky cow! And you don't want to…"

Lucy cut in quickly. "Maggie. Shut up!"

Farid certainly did look handsome. His hair shone in the evening sunlight and his tight blue jeans fitted like a glove. He wore a white shirt with the sleeves rolled up, open at the neck which showed just enough to be interesting. As the girls approached he turned to face them and his face broke into a smile. He kissed Lucy gently on both cheeks.

Maggie held out her hand. "Hi, I'm Maggie, Lucy's friend."

Farid smiled and shook her hand but said nothing.

Lucy laughed. "I forgot to tell you he doesn't speak English!"

She explained to Farid that Maggie had said he looked like a movie-star (but omitted the bit about his body). He raised his eyebrows and in heavily accented English said "Thank you." He then bestowed on Maggie a little half smile.

Lucy turned quickly to her friend. "And now Maggie it's time to say goodbye."

She took her friend's arm and walked her reluctantly back to the gate.

"Bloody hell. You lucky cow!" exclaimed Maggie. "He is absolutely gorgeous."

Lucy nudged her hoping that Farid hadn't heard. "Maggie, I'm going to thump you in a minute! Now go. I'll give you a call when I get back to England." Maggie grinned and walked back towards the hotel.

Lucy turned back to Farid. He watched her as she walked back towards him and what he saw pleased him. She noticed his eyes lingered on the neckline of her top. She wished she had worn the orange t-shirt. They only stayed a short while at the bar and had a couple of beers each. Then they walked hand in hand down the beach road. Lucy felt decidedly under-dressed and Farid noticed how other men's eyes followed her. He slid his arm protectively around her, resting his hand just above her bottom, enjoying the gentle sway of her hips as she moved.

Farid had asked around that afternoon in advance to find out if there was anything he could take her to see. He knew he couldn't go into her hotel. He settled on a local Tunisian dancing display which was being held outside one of the larger hotels. They walked through the narrow access way and came out into a large open terrace. The show was just starting and they sat down. Lucy was entranced and he watched her animated face following the twirling swaying dancers with their brightly coloured national costume. The waiter came over and Farid ordered for them both.

She sipped her drink, her savouring the sweet heady liquid. "What is it?"

He smiled. "It's Thibarine, it's made from dates and herbs, although the recipe is secret - do you like it?"

She nodded although she found the sweetness cloying and wasn't at all sure how strong it was. She decided to stick to beer as she had no intention of becoming inebriated. As the tempo hotted up he was amused to see her feet tapping with the music, her fingers drumming out the rhythm on the table top.

"I think you like our dancing?" She turned to him, her face pink with excitement and her eyes sparkling.

"It's wonderful, loud, colourful and a beat you could dance to all night. D'you dance?"

He shook his head. "Never, if I can help it. I can't dance, although I have been known to get up and shuffle from side to side with my friends, but only when we I am so drunk I won't remember!" She laughed at him, quietly pleased that there was at least one thing he admitted he wasn't good at.

Farid wondered why she flushed and looked away from him, obviously embarrassed. Lucy's mind had gone beyond the dancing and unbidden wicked thoughts of what he might be good at had surfaced.

The dancing finished and he ordered a coffee. The waiter brought a large cup of cappuccino for her and a tiny cup of what looked like white froth for him into which he emptied two sachets of sugar.

"What's that?"

"Cappucin. It's Tunisian coffee, black with a top of milk froth." She noticed he also had a glass of water and he drank from each alternately, in the same way she remembered the men had done in the café at Sousse. When he ordered a second, she stopped him. "I'll have the same as you." The waiter showed a little polite surprise and returned with two tiny cups.

"What's the problem? Have I done something wrong?"

"Not at all, it's just that most women tourists stick to cappuccino. D'you like it."

Lucy sipped the tepid liquid, it was very strong and quite delicious. She took a quick drink of water and another drink of coffee. She looked at him over the top of the cup, her eyes sparkling. "I love it!"

By the time they went back to the beach bar, Lucy was feeling a little light-headed. The alcohol had kicked in and the coffee had acted as a stimulant. She felt wide awake and very happy. They sat back down at their table and had another beer each.

When the bar closed he led her down onto the beach. They sat on the sand with their backs against the stack of beach chairs away from the lights of the road. The moon was the only light. Lucy was suddenly very frightened, not of him, but of herself and how she felt about him. Farid put his arm loosely round her shoulders and they talked. He held her closer and turned her so she faced him, his hand dropped and stroked the swell of her breast as he kissed her. This was not the kiss of yesterday, but a deep, searching kiss. A promise of things to come. Lucy didn't fight the feelings rising inside her.

His fingers teased her as he pushed the narrow straps from her shoulders. She felt him tense as he looked at the mounds of her breasts pale in the moonlight. As stroked and kissed the soft skin Lucy felt the yearning transfer itself to the depth of her femininity and was sure he could hear her heart pounding.

She felt his hand on her tummy. His eyes were half closed and screamed sensuality. His hand slid under her t-shirt and stroked the soft skin. Lucy gasped and pulled away from him, knowing that if she didn't stop him now she would not be able to.

"I can't."

Farid froze. "Why, I can feel that you want me."

He rested his head on her chest and listened to the pounding of her heart.

"Oh God, of course I want you, you must be crazy if you don't know that."

"Then why?"

She raised his head and looked at him, her eyes wide and lips parted in a gesture of sensuality which made him want to take her at that moment.

"Because I am frightened. It's been a long time since I made love and because no man has ever made me feel the way you do."

"I'll be gentle with you." He spoke because he was expected to, but doubted whether he could be gentle. His body would not obey him.

She smiled shyly. "I need time."

"We don't have time, you go tomorrow. I need you. I have needed you for 8 years."

Lucy took a deep breath. "I promise, next time."

"Will there be a next time?" he asked whispered as he stroked her breast. A ripple of delight ran through her body.

"Oh yes, my love, there will be a next time." With a light gesture she stroked his stomach where the shirt buttons had come undone. He cursed and pushed her hand away. Lucy shrank away from him. Immediately he pulled her to her feet, the bulge in his trousers obvious in the soft light. He held her close so she could feel every part of him.

"No, no, it's just if you touch me, I…" his voice trailed off.

"I'm sorry." He brushed her lips with his and slid her straps back onto her shoulders, fumbling in his urgency.

Farid turned away and closed his eyes as he buttoned his shirt, his body screaming for release. After what seemed to Lucy a very long time he turned to face her, cupped her face in his hands and kissed her, deeply but undemanding.

"I expect a promise to be kept."

"I keep my promises. I will be back in two or three months' time."

"Then I will wait a little longer."

He tore off the top of the cigarette packet and asked her to write her phone number on it, which he put carefully in the back of his wallet. Then he walked with her to the promenade and watched as she walked back up the narrow pathway to the hotel.

Lucy was shaken by the sheer masculinity of this man and knew that if he had pressed her she would have succumbed to him. She also knew she would be back.

CHAPTER ELEVEN

FARID

Two days after she returned home, Farid called her. The conversation was awkward. It was strange hearing his soft deep voice sounding so clear and yet over a thousand miles away. He told her he loved her and was counting the days until she returned. They spoke often on the telephone and he asked her each time when she was coming back.

Her colleagues at work were immediately aware that something had happened to Lucy since her holiday. She glowed, she laughed and she was as happy as they had ever seen her. Her eyes shone and she was often seen staring out of the window with a funny little smile on her lips. She kept her counsel and said nothing. Not even to Marie.

Lucy had known Marie since she first started work at Jacksons, but they had not really known each other well, as Marie was in a different department and they saw little of each other. However, after Peter's death, Marie had taken Lucy under her wing and the two had become firm friends. As there was another Marie in Lucy's department, she always referred to her friend as M to save confusion.

M was like Lucy in that she had been bitten by the travel bug as a teenager. Before Lucy had taken off by herself for her holiday in Tunisia the two women had already agreed they would holiday together later in the year.

M arrived at Lucy's house one Saturday morning with an armful of brochures. As they flicked through them, Lucy remembered the time she had done the same thing with Jackie and then with Peter. She got a lump in her throat as she thought of her husband. Why had God seen fit to take someone so fit and well, not long married with a small child and his whole life in front of him? As Peter had died suddenly, the death was of course investigated and as it turned out, Peter did have a heart problem. He had probably been born with it but as the doctor explained to her, sometimes these things can take years and then strike without notice at any time. It was just so unfair.

Marie made a couple of suggestions and Lucy turned to her. "M, I'd like to go to back to Tunisia."

M knew that something had happened to Lucy on that last holiday but Lucy had not volunteered anything and M had not asked. Now it would appear she was about to find out.

"That's a brilliant idea" she said excitedly. "When do you want to go? Late August, early September would suit me."

"That suits me fine because Alex is going to the seaside with his grandparents for a couple of weeks before he starts school. But, there is just one thing I must tell you which might change your mind. When I was there in June I met someone and I would like to see him again."

So she was right, it was a man. M was pleased as she knew Lucy had been devastated by Peter's death and so far as she knew had never even been on a serious date since.

"That's fine, but how do you know he will be there again?"

"He's not a tourist. He's Tunisian."

M frowned. "OK, just so long as you don't expect me to tag along as a gooseberry and for God's sake don't try and fix me up with one of his friends. You know my choice in men doesn't run to tall, dark and handsome!"

Lucy grinned. "I promise."

They agreed on their dates and the booking was made. As the departure date became ever closer Lucy's emotions went into overdrive, nervous anticipation, fear and excitement.

They stayed at the same hotel as Lucy had been in before. Farid had told her there was no point her staying at the hotel where he worked because his contract finished just before she arrived.

"It is good you come then, because I have only part time work and I can see you every day. My new hotel contract does not start until October."

The plane arrived late and they reached the hotel shortly before midnight. They fell into bed without unpacking.

M was however surprised to see her friend still asleep at nine o'clock. Lucy was always an early bird. She peered her friend over her glasses. Lucy lay on her back, her arms outside the sheet. A ghost of a smile played on her lips and her hair was flung out over the pillow in a tangled mess. M knew there could not have been a man in the room but Lucy certainly gave the impression that a man had been involved, if only in her dreams. She shook her.

"Come on brat. We'll miss breakfast."

Lucy stretched and sighed, her dream gone. M shook her again and she sat up with a jolt, her eyes focusing on the cup of tea being held out to her.

She grinned. "Thanks M, you're a star."

After breakfast she called Farid. "When did you arrive?"

"Last night, about midnight."

"Why didn't you call me then? Now you make me wait again until morning." Lucy laughed

"I thought you might be asleep."

"You think I sleep, knowing you are here!"

This was totally true. Farid had lain awake much of the night, his thoughts full of the promise she had made to him and as usual his body would not obey his mind's desire to sleep.

"You will meet me after lunch for coffee at the bar just outside the hotel and then again tonight."

"I will, Farid. I have missed you."

"And I have missed you. You disturb my days and my nights and I long to hold you again."

She said nothing to M but privately she was a bit worried about what M would make of Farid. His dark foreign masculinity would not appeal to M. She liked her men pale and large and as she put it "teddy-bearish". She had a penchant for Australians since visiting that country several years ago and left Lucy in little doubt before they came away that relations with Tunisians were not on her holiday agenda. Lucy was sure M would not approve of Farid. Her fears were not unfounded.

Farid was disappointed to see that Lucy had brought her friend with her. He had not expected to have to entertain the two of them, particularly when Lucy explained to him that M spoke no French. The three sat just inside the coffee bar, Lucy next to Farid on the sofa and M in the chair opposite watching them. Lucy worried that Farid might decide this was not a good idea. He didn't. He did his best to hide his feelings. He tried to be pleasant but all he wanted to do was to kiss his woman and be alone with her. The conversation was difficult with Lucy stuck in the middle having to translate between the two of them and conscious every second of the warm firm body so close to her.

M was concerned at the way Farid had his arm around Lucy, holding her tightly resting his hand loosely just above her breast. The intimacy between the two was obvious. This relationship was far more dangerous than she had expected and she was seriously worried about her friend. Because Farid's type did not attract her personally, it did not stop her being well aware that he would definitely appeal to other women.

After a short while, M disappeared in the direction of the ladies' room and didn't come back for some time. Lucy went up to the bar and found her in deep conversation with a large man with a mop of blonde hair, whom M simperingly introduced as Pieter. "Pieter with an "I" she explained." It transpired her new friend was South African, on a golfing holiday with friends and staying in their hotel. Lucy beamed with undisguised delight. M adored golf and Lucy could see that there would be few more times when she needed to entertain her friend.

M made her excuses and went off with her Pieter back into the hotel to watch the afternoon entertainment leaving Lucy and Farid alone. Farid took her hand and they walked up to the beach bar where they had been on her last visit, and as before sat away from the bar and other people.

"Tell me more about you and your family," she asked.

He hesitated. "I have had a brother, Saleem and two sisters, Meriam and Fatma. I am the eldest son and I am responsible for them. Saleem wants to be an engineer, he has done well at college. Fatma is very young still and sometimes I worry for her, she is, how you would say, a little wild." Lucy noticed the shadow flash across his face at the mention of his sister, but he said nothing more.

"My family live together, except for my sister Meriam who is now married. I help my family and send money to them. It is the custom here." She smiled in acknowledgement.

"A lot of money was spent on my sister's marriage. A wedding in Tunisia goes on for many days and is very important." He grinned and promised to show her photographs of the wedding.

Lucy noticed how he kept the conversation general and away from his own life.

"My sister's husband is in agriculture, which is an important industry in Tunisia. He and his family have a lot of farm equipment and she has married a good man who treats her well and she has her own home."

Lucy told him a little about herself and felt comfortable and at ease with him. Later in the afternoon she went back to the hotel to change for dinner leaving Farid with a promise to meet him at the back gate at 8p.m. as before.

M was waiting for her in the room and said little. They sat on the balcony with a glass of wine and Lucy drew heavily on her cigarette, waiting. Finally she looked at M defensively. "Well, I can tell you want to say something."

M stared at her. "Lucy, he's dangerous. I am scared for you. The way he looks at you, he's already in bed with you. Sure he's devastatingly good looking and he's got one hell of a body. Even I can appreciate that but as you know he's not my cup of tea. There's just something about him. There's a physical presence about the man which alarms me." She glared at her friend. "And you, young lady are like a bitch on heat. You can't keep your eyes off him. My point is, Lucy, is he just one of these young men you read about who target tourists for what they can get, be it money or sex. You're too good for him, for Christ's sake he's a security guard and I'm worried you're going to get in way over your head."

Lucy was angry. "What d'you mean I'm too good for him," she shouted. "What d'you know about him. Let me tell you he's the eldest son of four children. His father has been unwell. He gives money to his family and goes home every week on his day off, and I can tell you they don't earn that much anyway. He left school and didn't go to college so that his brother could go and learn mechanical engineering and didn't have to go to work. He works all the overtime he can get so keep his family and I admire him for it."

She glared at M. "And no, before you ask he hasn't asked me for any money and I haven't given him any and yes, you're bloody right, I do intend to go to bed with him. Frankly, I'd regret it for the rest of my life if I didn't and yes before you say anything, I'll be careful."

Lucy caught her breath and stood with her hands on her hips waiting for her friend to speak.

M looked crestfallen and Lucy was sorry she had shouted at her.

"I'm sorry M, I shouldn't have yelled like that, I know you only look out for me."

M smiled sheepishly. "I'm sorry too. I was out of order, it's none of my business, you're a grown woman and if you fancy a devilishly handsome toy-boy, it's your decision."

M had hit on the one itch she couldn't scratch. Quietly she hugged her friend. "Yes, that is the only thing that worries me, the number of years between us." M said nothing.

M went out to meet Pieter and left Lucy to get ready. She was absolutely terrified at the thought of making love with Farid. She had told the truth when she said no man had touched her since Peter died, which seemed like a lifetime ago. She had seen his reaction to her when he stood up was afraid of what she saw. She felt physically sick with apprehension and wondered whether simply not to turn up.

She was worried he would find her inadequate in comparison with other women he must have had. There was no way a man like that had got to his age without having had a number of lovers. And was M right? Lucy argued with herself that he was one of the local men she read about in the book, who prey on older or single women looking for sex and cash. Her heart told her that it was not as if there were twenty or more years between them but her head pointed out that even in England twelve years was still a big difference and in Tunisia men who were serious about a woman virtually always went with younger girls, or at least no more than a year older. It just wasn't accepted. In fact if he had not been the Farid she saw as a boy she might have convinced herself that M was right. But this was the man she had dreamed of, the boy who became a man. The man Alice had told her about. Was this one of the choices that she had to make, and whichever way she went would change her life?

She could not believe she had promised to have sex with a man she had really only known for a couple of days. She went downstairs to clear her head and bought a couple of decorative plates in the shop to take home. She went into the hotel bar and ordered a cappucin and a half bottle of water. The waiter brought her a cappuccino. Normally she would have drunk it, but she told him quite sharply that was not what she had ordered. Surprised, he brought back a small cup of the strong liquid.

"This is bloody ridiculous," she snapped silently. "Think about something else." but her heart raced and her stomach was awash with butterflies.

By late afternoon, Lucy felt ill. She went back to the hotel and fell asleep, half hoping she wouldn't wake up in time. It was not to be. She woke around 7p.m. She was relieved that M was still out. She had a shower and as she rubbed in the gently perfumed body cream she made a decision. She was going to enjoy the inevitable. Having made the decision she felt better.

She left her hair loose and brushed it until it shone, she wore little make-up, just enough to cover what she thought of as her older bits. Her skin which was just starting to tan was soft and silky. She wore a cream dress with narrow straps. Her white strappy sandals had a low heel. She had harboured an unwelcome twinge of conscience all day. She wondered if in his mind he still saw as she had been before and not the thirty-something she now was. She glanced critically at her reflection in the mirror. Surely she could pass for a woman in her twenties. Exactly what she had hoped. She felt better but she was still scared witless.

CHAPTER TWELVE

THE PROMISE

Farid watched her as she walked towards him. Lucy was not the only one who was apprehensive, but as she was fearful of him, he was also fearful of himself and being unable to control his desire for her. He knew above everything that he mustn't give her cause not to keep her promise.

They went to a small bar outside one of the hotels, overlooking the sea. He noticed she drank three or four glasses of wine. They sat close together but he forced himself not to gaze into her beautiful eyes for too long or touch her in any way that would spook her. She looked like a child in her simple cotton dress, but the glances she stole at him confused him, sometimes like a frightened child and sometimes quite differently.

As they walked back to the beach bar, he put his arm round her shoulders and she put her arm round his waist and hooked her thumb into his belt. They sat at their table, side by side, their faces close. They talked about their lives, their families and themselves. He kissed her once or twice, gentle and undemanding. She turned and looked out to sea. The night was clear and the stars were bright. It was a night for love. The moon was almost full and he noticed how it lit up her beautiful face. How he wanted her.

"Are you happy?" It was a strange question and he wondered why he had asked it.

"I'm happy."

"Do you remember?" she turned to him and put her hand on his thigh. "I remember."

She couldn't see his eyes, but she felt the muscle in his leg tense.

The bar had closed and Ahmed stood alone. Farid went over and spoke to him but seemed agitated. Ahmed looked at Lucy, shook his head and walked away up the narrow pathway under the arch and sat on the wall, his back to the beach.

Farid motioned to Lucy and she went over to him. "I am so sorry," he said softly. "We have nowhere to go, I can find no place for us tonight." He looked keenly at her. "Will you stay here?"

Lucy took his hand and gently placed it on her breast. "I will stay anywhere with you." He held her close. His hands cupped her face and she felt his tongue stroking her parted lips. He kissed her and felt her tremble.

"Come." She took his hand and he led her to a small room at the back of the bar. His kisses were now quite different, urgent, searching. His hands fumbled as he undressed her and she lay back naked on rough matting, one arm behind her head and her knees slightly raised. He stood looking down at her, an alabaster statue in the moonlight shining in through the small window. As he removed his own clothes he saw her shiver. He knew she was frightened.

Lucy gazed at his strong brown body, glistening in the warm night air. He took off his trousers and stood looking down at her. Her eyes went unconsciously to his lower body. He needed no encouragement from her.

He knelt down beside her and kissed her passionately, his hand tangled around her hair as he held her prisoner, his lips sucked hard on her nipples and within seconds his fingers found the warm dampness between her legs. He lowered himself onto her, murmuring in his own language. The sound of his voice relaxed her. He stroked the soft skin, consciously holding back the desire held in check for so long. She felt strong hands pulling her hips towards him as he entered her gently but his restraint left him and months of celibacy were smashed in a single thrust. Lucy screamed and immediately his mouth covered hers. The pain was unbelievable, she was being split in two.

He held her tightly moving her roughly to his own desperate rhythm until he came with a muffled cry. It was over in minutes. She felt violated, the weight of him crushing her chest and she struggled for breath. He rolled off her and lay beside her the sweat running down his sides.

"My darling, Lucy. I am so sorry. It is your fault. I have dreamed of this since I saw you again. I have thought of nothing but you. For months I have struggled to control my body but it will not obey me. Today I have been all day with… I am sorry I don't know the word in French."

Despite her pain Lucy smiled weakly. "I understand." Her face was wet with tears.

"But I have hurt you, my darling."

She forced a smile. "No, it's my fault not yours. I spoke the truth when I said it has been a long time since a man has touched me."

Lucy reached for her dress but his arm gently restrained her.

"Not yet, my darling." She saw the flash of white as he smiled. He bent his head and kissed her feet, as his fingers stroked her ankles and moved slowly up her body. He raised her leg and stroked the back of her knee. Lucy held her breath as his hand moved to her inner thigh. She felt his breath warm and shuddered with pleasure as he nipped the back of her neck. She felt the roughness of his hair on her breast as his tongue traced circles around it, moving ever inwards until he took the nipple between his lips and caressed her as only a lover can. She stroked the back of his neck and he pulled her towards him again. They moved together and Lucy forgot the pain as waves of pleasure coursed through her body. He bent to kiss her and she flicked her tongue over his nipple. "Es tu Ange ou Demon," he cried as he came again and as she held him close she felt the throbbing heat of him inside her.

"Am I Angel or Devil," she murmured in English. "My darling, I don't know, but I think that is question I should be asking you."

When they had dressed, he held her close. "Lucy, I must ask you something." She waited.

"My darling you are tight like virgin and yet you say you have a son." Lucy took his hand, lifted her dress and traced his fingers over the scar. "My son was born by operation." He bent his head and kissed the scar. "I am pleased!" He grinned at her and she blushed.

As they walked back towards the road, he stopped and put his arms round her.

"My lady, my Lucy. Now finally you are mine."

Lucy was horrified to see Ahmed walking towards them from where he had been sitting on the wall. He must know! She turned to Farid, her anguish all too obvious to him. He stroked her cheek. "Ahmed is my friend. He knows of my love for you. He keeps watch. Did you want anyone to find us together? There would be much trouble for us both."

Ahmed shook his friend's hand. Lucy turned her head away in embarrassment, but Ahmed took her hand and gently kissed her on both cheeks. He spoke in English. "Madame, you are very beautiful. It isn't hard to see why my friend is so much in love with you." He lowered his voice to a whisper, although Farid couldn't understand what he said, "he is indeed a lucky man."

Farid barked something at is friend she did not understand. Ahmed shrugged his shoulders and said nothing, but he smiled at Lucy.

When Lucy got back to the room, M was already in bed. She sat up as Lucy came in.

"Oh boy, don't tell me. I can see it written all over your face and incidentally you've got sand in your hair."

Lucy smiled and rested her index finger against her lips. "Tomorrow." M grinned, turned over and went to sleep.

Lucy decided against having a shower, she preferred to sleep with the scent of him close to her and her last thoughts that night were of glittering eyes and a beautiful smile which somehow lessened the pain.

The following morning, Lucy felt as though she had been kicked in the stomach by a mule. Her thigh muscles ached and the lower part of her body was on fire. She found blood on her sheet and when M was in the shower she tried unsuccessfully to remove it. Quickly she made a cup of coffee and deliberately split a little over the stain.

As she showered she inspected the damage. Her bottom was bruised from the hard ground and her chin still flushed where his stubble had rubbed her skin. Her mouth was swollen and her eyes bright. She looked like a woman who had spent all night making love.

Lucy had been with men before but had never experienced the strength of a man's body as she had with Farid. The pain had dulled but her body still throbbed as she went down for breakfast. M pulled daintily at her croissant and watched in astonishment as Lucy wolfed down a salad and selection of cold sausage and cheeses, a slice of warm bread, a plate of tomatoes and black olives, followed by two croissants with honey, a large bowl of yoghurt and three cups of milky coffee.

"Have you finished?"

Lucy nodded, her mouth full of croissant. M raised one eyebrow and Lucy choked as she stifled a giggle.

"I wish you wouldn't do that, at least not when I've got my mouth full."

"Well it's just as well I didn't do it at any time in the last half hour, isn't it."

"Oh Lord, I'm sorry. I was starving." She blushed and M raised the other eyebrow.

"Are you fit to go out today? When you came down the stairs just now you were walking as though you'd been on horseback for a week."

Lucy glared at her. "I am quite fit thank you. If I remember we are supposed to be going on the coach to El Djem in about half an hour."

CHAPTER THIRTEEN

EL DJEM

The coach was hot. All the people on the tour were English, save for a couple of French men and one woman and the guide talked continuously, if not completely accurately in both languages, about the country in general, how not to get overcharged and finally about the sights they were about to see. The first was the Roman amphitheatre at El Djem and the second the city of Kairouan, the fourth holiest city in the Muslim world.

Although Lucy usually found the continuous tour guide chatter irritating, on this occasion she was pleased. It didn't give M the opportunity to ask questions.

The coach parked a little down the road at an allocated parking area and they walked slowly up a slight incline, following the guide. There were a few souvenir shops but Lucy didn't notice them. She had wanted to see El Djem since she read about it before her first visit with Jackie. She had seen pictures but nothing prepared her for the silent majesty of this massive ancient ruin. It was hard to believe, as Mohamed the guide told them, that it dated back to around 230AD. Parts of the structure were so well preserved they appeared almost as they would have done when it was built.

As they walked under the huge archway Mohamed told them at one time it held up to 30,000 people who came from all parts of North Africa to watch the gladiators and the games which were held there. The two women climbed up the stone steps inside the main structure of the building. Several sets of steps were roped off, presumably designated unsafe. They wandered along the narrow passageways under huge arches supported by solid tall columns. One section had been rebuilt with a reconstructed seating area showing how it would have probably looked originally. Lucy thought it didn't seem to fit, but it allowed a view of the surrounding countryside and the arrow straight road leading away from the ancient ruin. They stood silently on the far side looking down into the arena below.

"You can almost hear the screams, people shouting and clash of swords as they fought."

M nodded. "It's magnificent, isn't it?" Nothing more needed to be said.

They climbed carefully down the steps and went into the two tunnels which used to house the poor victims waiting to be killed or torn apart by lions, those about to die. Lucy shivered. The underground passageways were cold and dank and as they came back up into the arena, the magnificence of the huge creamy weathered stones was the more intense in the blinding sunlight.

Mohamed was standing nearby with some of their party, pointing up to the ruined top of one of the walls where two young boys had climbed up over the ropes. Lucy heard an agitated man, presumably their father, yelling at them to get down or they would fall. The whole party watched spellbound as the two boys tried to climb down but the smaller of the two missed his footing and slid about ten feet down the column onto a narrow ledge where he seemed to be hanging by his fingertips. The father ran over and climbed up towards the boy. He caught him as he slid the last few feet and the two of them fell on to the ground. The man got up and grabbed his son by his collar, marched him back through the main archway to where a woman stood. He shouted at the woman and then turned and yelled again at the boy, then strode off in the opposite direction still muttering under his breath.

Mohamed gave a wry smile.

"He won't do that again in a hurry, I think," he said to the French women standing next to Lucy. Lucy agreed with him. Mohamed grinned broadly at her.

"Madame I didn't know you spoke French."

"You never asked me," she grinned back as she walked back to join M. Mohamed was not so easily ignored. As they walked around the monument, he insisted she walk with him. He told her he was pleased to be able to speak to someone who not only spoke his language but was actually interested in what he was saying. He explained how the monument had never been finished and how much of it was built to impress and had little practical purpose. He told her proudly how it was the largest monument in Africa.

"Mohamed, why is there a huge hole there where the walls have fallen down."

Mohamed was not happy, he took her by the arm and pointed. "It did not fall down Madame. Some hundreds years ago the Ottomans used cannon to blow a hole to suppress our people." Lucy then received a short lecture on the struggles experienced by the Tunisian people at the hands of the Ottoman Empire. When Mohamed slowly moved the conversation towards more modern day politics, Lucy excused herself and scurried back to join M.

They walked up to the far end of the arena and took some photographs. Lucy looked up towards the sun, partly hidden behind the structure. With the clear blue sky behind it the ruins appeared dark and saturnine against the fierce light which filtered through the gaps between the stones. Farid's face against the moonlight jumped into her mind. Are you Angel or Devil he had cried, she wondered which he would turn out to be. She pushed the thoughts out of her mind, took out her camera and lined up a photograph directly into the sun.

"You're mad, there was no way those pictures will come out. You're taking them straight into the sun."

"Exactly, I'm not looking for an exact photograph, I'm trying to get the effect of the brilliance, the colour of the sky and the way the stones look black with the specks of light coming through them. The effect is amazing. Anyway, if they don't come out, so be it but it's worth a try." As it happened the photos did come out and gave Lucy exactly the ethereal quality she wanted. The coach rumbled on towards Kairouan. Mohamed gave another of his well-practised speeches and then attached himself to her and M. Even M agreed he was a good at his job.

Lucy found the Great Mosque fascinating and was pleased she had remembered her shawl, because of course to go into the mosque arms and shoulders must be covered. Mohamed explained it was the oldest mosque in North Africa and the minaret was the oldest in the whole world because originally mosques didn't have minarets, although he admitted it had been partially destroyed and rebuilt several times but the base was believed to be original.

"The muezzin calls believers to prayer, you see the people are going now to pray, but I am sorry you are not allowed inside. That is only for Muslims, but here, if you come to this corner you can see." It was dark and Lucy could see what appeared to be hundreds of columns, there was rough carpeting on the floor and even from outside she could see it was beautiful.

As Kairouan is renowned for its carpet making, there followed the inevitable visit to a carpet factory. Despite all attempts to change their minds the two women managed to escape without being inveigled into making a purchase, although Lucy noticed with amusement one or two of their company had not been so lucky.

That evening they got back to the hotel in time to shower and get to the bar before dinner. Lucy knew M now had the time to ask questions and decided to head her off.

"What were you up to yesterday then?"

M looked surprised and then grinned. "I know what you're up to but I'll play along! I went out with Pieter, had a game of golf, I bought a new pair of trousers and then we went to a barbecue on the beach and back to his friend's house for a few drinks and then he drove me back. OK now what happened to you? Somehow I don't think you were playing golf."

Lucy pulled a face. "I wasn't. We went to the Oceania bar up the road underneath the other hotel and then back to the beach bar where we were yesterday. We just sat and talked."

"You don't get sand in your hair from talking"

"OK. You want the truth," or at least part of it she thought.

"That would be nice."

"We made love in a little room behind the bar on the beach it was the most amazing thing that ever happened to me and that's all I'm prepared to say, even to you M."

"It doesn't surprise me. I should think anyone looking at the two of you the other night would have placed an evens bet on that. What worries me is that you hardly know him and it just isn't like you."

I've known him eight years Lucy said silently to herself. "He's different," she replied.

"Yes, I agree, he's certainly different. He's so different from anyone you've known, he's also from a completely different way of life and I hope to God you don't think you're in love with him, because if you think you may be, just remember one thing. Keep your feet on the ground. When you've gone home, he's still here in this resort with warm balmy nights, moonlight, sea and sand and a hell of a lot of other women on holiday who are going to think he's just as bloody gorgeous as you do. And before you say anything, I'm only thinking of you."

"I agree with everything you say, and I promise I'll keep my feet just where they are now." On cloud nine she added to herself.

After dinner, Lucy could sense M was reluctant to leave her, but she had promised to meet Pieter and Lucy desperately wanted to be alone with Farid. She persuaded M she would be fine.

CHAPTER FOURTEEN

A MISUNDERSTANDING

She met Farid a little while later and they walked fingers entwined. She felt as though they had known each other for ever. He had dressed carefully. His hair was newly cut and glistened. She could see he had shaved and trimmed his moustache and when he kissed her she smelt a delicious musk with a hint of sandalwood. His shirt was again open at the neck and she yearned to stroke the soft dark skin. She noticed one or two women sneak a glance at him as they walked along and she felt proud to be the one with him.

They walked quite a way down the promenade and Lucy heard music coming from a small bar at the foot of a hotel set back off the road. She asked if they could stop. Farid hesitated a moment and then led her to a table on the edge of the covered terrace. He thought quickly. He wanted so much to impress her, he wanted to hire a car and show her everything about his country. He couldn't. He had virtually no money until the weekend. Since his father's illness, which he had made little of when talking to Lucy, his father been unable to work and most of the money Farid earned he sent home to his family. The little money he had saved had gone for the tests his father needed in the private clinic so he would not have wait for an appointment. The tests had shown that his father needed an operation and although his condition was not life threatening as yet, the operation should not be left any longer than necessary.

The waiter came over and Farid was deeply relieved when Lucy asked for coffee. He was already trying to work out if he could afford drinks, if he cut back on his cigarettes.

"I absolutely love this coffee but how can you put so much sugar in such a tiny cup?"

"We Tunisians have a sweet tooth, but you are sweet enough." She blushed. He started to speak but was interrupted by a small plump man with receding hair and huge brown eyes, who tapped him on the shoulder. Farid stood up and greeted the man, she noticed they shook hands and kissed on either cheek. There followed a steam of unintelligible conversation and then the newcomer turned to her and shook her hand.

"Hello, I am Abdul-Aziz, and you can only be Lucy. Farid has spoken of you many times." He spoke excellent English and invited both of them to join him and his friends. Farid glanced at Lucy, who nodded.

They walked down to the beach and she was disconcerted to see two tables pushed together and half a dozen men sitting round them. They walked over and Farid introduced her to each one. At first she felt awkward being the only woman, but they were all friendly in an easy inoffensive sort of way and most of them either spoke English or slowed down when speaking to her in French and after an initial shyness, Lucy found she was thoroughly enjoying herself. There were several bottles on the table, water, some sort of fizzy orange drink and a few of bottles of beer. Everyone just helped themselves to whatever they wanted. The table was also littered with boxes of cigarettes. It seemed everyone in Tunisia smoked.

Farid was in deep conversation with Abdul-Aziz and although sometimes he looked over at her and smiled reassuringly, she thought he looked worried.

Abdul-Aziz explained to Lucy that he worked at the hotel opposite and he would be happy if they would both come over. Lucy remembered it was not acceptable for local people to use the hotels, but Farid seemed happy so they followed his friend. They sat in a small annexe off the main bar, it was quite dark, lit only by two table lamps. She was bewildered when Abdul-Aziz brought them two beers because she was quite sure Farid didn't have a lot of money. She had noticed when he paid for the coffees there were only a few coins in the little pouch he carried. They talked a little and he kissed and stroked her hair. He held her hand in his and gently ran his fingers across her palm until she gave a little shudder and he kissed her again.

"Tell me of your life at in England and when you will come back to me?"

Lucy smiled, thankful for the time to gather herself together. Being near to him was electrifying. She knew that whatever he asked she was powerless to refuse him.

"I have my son, Alex, and my job. I don't have much time for much else. Alex starts school when I get back and I have to juggle my job and my life at home. Sometimes it isn't easy, but I am lucky because although his father's parents live in the North of England, especially as they have lost their son, they are more than happy to have their grandson to stay sometimes. Of course in the future that will have to be in the school holidays."

"So you will only come in the school holidays then," Farid asked miserably.

Lucy grinned. "Farid, they have about thirteen weeks holiday each year, and I will not be able to afford to come here for all that time anyway, so I will try to come three or four times a year."

"And what must I do when you are away?"

"I hope you will wait for me, as I will for you."

He held her close but wondered what had happened to Abdul-Aziz. A few minutes later his friend re-appeared and Lucy wondered what was being said in such urgent tones.

"Look my brother can you get me the room or not."

Abdul-Aziz nodded. "Yes, but you must hurry because the director has just gone out to the Beau Rivage but he will be back in about half an hour and although you are my good friend I will not lose my job for you. If you are caught you will be in serious trouble as well. Is she worth it?"

Farid glared at him. "Have I ever asked you before to get me a room, or have you ever known me ask anyone else?" Abdul-Aziz shook his head.

"Then you have your answer."

Farid turned back to Lucy and took her roughly by the hand. "Come, Cherie."

Lucy was now quite confused and followed him across the bar down a corridor at the far end of the reception hall. Abdul-Aziz opened a door and Lucy found herself in a bedroom. Farid turned on the side light and put his put his arms round her. "We must be quick. The director is out but he will be back soon."

Lucy stared at him as he started to take off his clothes. Mutely she did the same and stood facing him in her underclothes. She was pleased she had chosen a white lace ensemble instead of the comfortable alternatives she often wore. Inside she felt excited, but cheap. This was not quite how she had imagined it would be. She had dreamed of a beautiful room, perhaps with flickering candlelight and flowers giving off their heady perfume, with her beloved slowly undressing her before making love all night. The reality was to be a plain whitewashed hotel room with a rather unpleasant pink satin bed cover and a quick tumble with one ear open in case the director returned unexpectedly. She wondered gloomily how many times he had done this before with other tourists.

"Lucy?" She slowly removed her underclothes and looked at him. He stood naked in front of her, making no attempt to hide any part of himself. His strongly muscled chest with its soft covering of hair glistened in the low light. As Maggie had said, he was truly gorgeous.

Farid stared at her. Her skin gleamed and her hair fell loosely over her shoulders. Her breasts were full and all the more prominent as the pale skin stood out against the rest of her lightly tanned body. He wished with all his heart he could stay all night with her, but there was no time.

Despite her embarrassment she watched, fascinated, as his body moved as he looked at her. Her mind recalled the pain of the previous night and she prayed he wouldn't hurt her again. She raised her eyes to his face like a frightened hare and caught her breath. There was no softness in the eyes which burned her through to the core, just raw passion. He kissed her deeply and traced his hands gently over her skin, down her back stroking her and moving down her belly as he turned her so her back was to him. Lucy was kneeling on the satin coverlet and when he touched her she uttered a little moan. Farid could wait no longer and gripped her hips, pulling her towards him and with what she could only assume was a muttered curse drove himself deeply inside her. Lucy let out an expletive she rarely used and it was over.

Lucy tried to get up but he pulled her back. "I thought you said we must be quick," she snapped.

"Not that quick."

It couldn't have been much quicker, she thought peevishly, feeling cheated. She felt nothing but pain after their animal coupling.

She stared at him and tried to move but he held her firmly. He pulled her back so she lay on top of him. She wriggled but he was too strong. He stroked her back, running his fingers lightly down her spine and she sighed luxuriating under the practised touch of a man who knew a woman's body. For a moment she thought she saw his expression change and started to pull away, but the moment passed.

Farid knew he must be careful. He knew he had only a few minutes, but he would have to take the risk. They lay together and he stroked, kissed and caressed her until Lucy felt herself respond as the violin to the maestro who plays it. He knelt on the bed in front of her and raised her so her legs wrapped around his waist. He clamped his teeth and knew that he must wait. He stroked and teased her until he felt her breathing quicken and he felt the treacherous waves flooding through her. She gave a little gasp as she gripped his hips pulling him deeply inside her. He held both her hands prisoner behind her head and Lucy gasped as his lips parted in a smile but it was the smile of a wolf. He crashed his body down onto hers and pounded into her with a ferocity which left her fighting for breath. His head tilted backwards and his eyes closed as he exploded inside her with a hoarse cry and collapsed onto her chest. She lay stunned waiting with him while his body subsided, feeling every breath he took. His eyes opened and the wolf had gone. Lucy buried her face against his soft chest hair breathing in the intoxication of sweet enveloping scent. When he finally lay beside her he simply gazed at her so his memory would hold forever her flushed cheeks, parted lips and half-closed eyes, her hair spread out on the pillow. His Lucy.

He heard the gentle tap on the door. "Now my love, we must go." He spoke in his own language and Lucy thought again how much more beautiful was the Arab language for words of love.

As they walked back to the reception, Abdul-Aziz waited for them. Farid looked at the floor.

"We must pay for the beers." He waited, wishing with all his heart it could be different. Stunned Lucy took a note out of her purse and handed it to him. He nodded and gave it to Abdul-Aziz, who pushed it in his pocket without offering change.

Lucy felt sick. She wished she was a whore, she would prefer that but it was he who was the whore and that made it worse. They walked silently back to the hotel. Lucy savoured the thought that for the first time in her life she felt she had paid for sex. She felt old and dirty. It would never happen again.

Farid knew exactly what she was thinking, but what could he do. The money he earned was not enough to pay for a hotel room, or even to pay his friend to find one for him, as Abdul-Aziz had done. He would have to explain, but he had no idea how to. By her expression he could see that Lucy had never done anything like this before. They walked in silence. He kissed her gently and she pulled away.

"May I see you tomorrow," She shook her head.

"I don't think so," she whispered sadly.

Farid panicked. "But I must talk with you."

"I think it's too late for talking, don't you?"

"My Lucy, you don't understand. I must be able to explain. I can't leave you like this."

She stared him straight in the face and was momentarily taken aback by the fear she saw there. Against everything she had felt at that moment, she nodded. By her expression he wondered if he would ever see her again.

In the morning, M was concerned to see her friend was very unhappy. It was obvious all had not gone well with Farid. She didn't know whether to be sorry or relieved.

"Tell me friend, what happened."

"We went to a bar, had a coffee then sat on the beach with some of his friends and I had a really good time."

"So what's with the expression as if someone's just died?"

"I suppose they have in a way. It seems you were right and I think I found out what he's really like."

"Oh Lord, I don't like the sound of this. Go on."

Lucy took a deep breath and stared at her friend, her expression flat, her voice harsh.

"The truth? OK. After we left the beach we went with his friend to the hotel where the friend works, had a drink and then Farid took me into one of the hotel bedrooms, where he fucked the living hell out of me then he asked me to pay the friend a hell of a lot of money for two beers."

"Oh sweet Jesus. Bloody hell, Lucy." This was about as strong as M's language ever got.

"Bloody hell," she repeated, taking in Lucy's anguished face. "That's beyond belief."

Lucy said nothing.

M was getting more angry by the second. She grabbed Lucy's hand. "Well girl, I hope you don't intend to see him again and I hope you told him to stick it where the sun don't shine!"

Lucy stared at her and a slight smile tinged her lips. M went beetroot red.

"Oh Christ, Lucy, that's not at all what I meant." Lucy grinned.

"Actually no, thank heavens that didn't come into it!" She giggled and silently thanked her friend as the two of them collapsed onto the bed in fits of laughter.

"Was it worth it… in the hotel?" she asked as Lucy wiped away the tears, still grinning.

Lucy's smile faded. "Put it like this, part of it I never want to repeat in my life and part I'd move heaven and earth to have again."

"I see," she didn't, but it was plain Lucy wasn't about to expand on what she'd said.

"I never really warmed to him you know. I never completely trust a man who won't look me in the eye, and he wouldn't."

"Actually, M I think that has more to do with the fact that neither of you speak the other's language."

"You may be right, let's hope so. Are you going to see him again?"

Lucy nodded. "He said he needed to explain and I have to find out or I will regret it the rest of my life."

M shook her head. "I think you're crazy, but I can see that nothing I'm going to say will change your mind, so do what you have to do."

They spent the day peacefully on the beach, and that evening as they sat having a coffee after dinner, M spoke quietly as Lucy got up to go.

"Have a lovely time, Luce and remember if he upsets you or tries that again, just walk away."

Lucy smiled sadly. "I wish I could, the man is like a drug. You don't know whether to take it to relieve the symptoms or worry about what the side effects might be."

M watched her as she walked away. "I don't like it," she thought, "I don't like it one little bit, this is only going to end in tears. I just hope it's sooner, not later."

CHAPTER FIFTEEN

COMMITMENT

After the embarrassment of the previous evening, Farid had managed to borrow some money from a friend, at least enough for taxis and drinks for the rest of Lucy's holiday. He knew he would have to work as much overtime as he could get when his contract started in October so he could pay it back.

He noticed the closed expression on her face as she walked up to him. He kissed her gently and led her towards the taxi rank. He opened the taxi door and spoke quickly to the driver.

"Where are we going?" He heard the apprehension in her voice.

"Somewhere nice, you will love it." There was no suggestion in his voice and the smile he gave her was affectionate, but not intimate.

The taxi took them a little way out of the main town to a place which looked like a secluded private house. There was a narrow archway festooned with purple bougainvillea twining up through its ironwork. The pathway led quickly to another arch, this time covered with highly scented white jasmine and onward down a winding path edged by high oleander bushes in every shade of pink intermingled with more jasmine. Tiny lights were hidden in the bushes. The effect was magical, a pathway of intoxicating scent and tiny star shaped flowers which glowed in the moonlight. Farid was captured by her soft smile as she brushed her hand against the jasmine and held it to her nose.

She smiled. "The smell is exquisite and it will always remind me of your country. I wonder why is it that no matter how expensive the perfume it can never completely capture the true essence of the jasmine flower."

"The flowers are exquisite as you say, but their beauty cannot match your own."

He held her close for a moment and wondered what he would do when she left, and what he could do or say that would make her come back to him. He turned away knowing that if she had guessed the vision his overheated mind was seeing she would have quickly returned to the calm of her hotel room. He noticed the corners of her mouth twitched upwards as she looked at him and he flushed. He felt her shiver as he pulled her close to him and felt her warmth against his chest.

At the end of the pathway was a small blue door which had been left ajar. He pushed it and Lucy walked into Aladdin's cave. The courtyard was partly enclosed, draped with loose swirls of dark fabric and in part open to the sky.

It was one of the most beautiful places Lucy had ever seen, dark and full of secret corners. The walls were covered in tapestries and paintings, depicting Arabic scenes, Bedouin tents, the desert, palm trees and the ancient Medina. The depth of the colours, deep blues, cream, warm brown and crimson invited the observer inside the heart of the paintings. The seating was mainly rough benches and one or two huge chairs, all heaped with cushions covered with similar tapestry-like material in similar shades of olive, brown and gold.

There were small round tables of gleaming beaten brass. Subdued half-light came from stained glass wall lamps and hanging wrought iron candelabra and cast strange shadows into the corners and angles of the room. A tinkling sound came from water spilling over a small fountain, overhung by a huge potted palm and surrounded by pots of smaller palms and geraniums and everywhere the heavy scent of the jasmine. From somewhere there was soft Arabian music.

He led her to one of the dark alcoves and they sat down. Lucy took his hands, her eyes shining. "It's absolutely beautiful, I never knew places like this existed here."

"There are one or two, but the tourists prefer the hotels and noisier public places. Only those who appreciate beauty come here. I knew you would like it."

"I love it," she whispered feeling as though she had stumbled into someone's private space created with deep sensibility and reserved for pleasure and lovemaking, intensified by the seductive warm evening air stealing in through the shuttered windows. The waiter appeared from nowhere, dressed in national costume, his soft slippered feet making no noise on the woven rugs.

He watched her as she drank in her surroundings, every glance revealing some little ornament or tiny lamp she hadn't noticed before. There were a few other couples but no-one had looked up as they came in. This was indeed a place where people came to be alone with each other, oblivious of the world outside.

In one corner a couple sat facing, leaning towards each other so their faces almost touched. She saw the man whisper something and the girl rested her hand lightly on his thigh as she gazed at him and he cupped her face in his hands as he kissed her gently. Lucy longed for Farid to do the same.

She sipped her coffee, tasting the bitterness of the thick tepid liquid and drank a little from the water, intensely conscious of the closeness of him. She watched as he emptied all the sugar provided into the tiny cup. She passed him her sugar and he caught her expression and smiled at her, his teeth white against his face with seemed even darker in the dim light.

She leaned back against the rough wall, half facing him, her hair framed in a halo of light from the lantern in the corner shone a pale gold. The softness of her skin appeared almost luminous. How he wanted her. In an unguarded moment his glittering eyes held hers and he heard her soft intake of her breath. She saw the strange predatory expression she had seen the night before. She shivered and the shadow disappeared.

"Are you cold?" He asked unnecessarily. He cursed himself. Be careful, this is a woman not a young girl, she sees things and will look straight into your mind if you let her.

"No, I'm not cold, just a little nervous. You seemed different for a moment."

He forced a smile. He wanted desperately to explain what had happened the night before, he knew he must do so now because there could be no love between them without trust. He held her face in his hands.

"Lucy I need to explain. My family are not poor. My father earns a good wage, and our family home is big enough that we have our own private spaces, but as you know I prefer to earn my own money and also to send a little home to help my family support my younger brother and sister. My needs are few as the hotel provides me with food and lodgings to sleep in."

She looked at the floor. "I understand, there is no need to explain."

He cupped her chin in his hand and forced her to look at him. "Yes, there is every need. Last month my father was taken ill suddenly and was taken to hospital for tests. I sent some money home so my father could go to a private clinic for immediate treatment. He has a heart condition and has not been able to work since then. This is why I had nothing left yesterday as my money is not paid until the first weekend of my new contract." He waited but she said nothing.

His voice caught in his throat. "You did not need to tell me what you thought yesterday. I should not have done what I did but I wanted you so badly nothing else mattered, not even my pride." He handed her a note and she looked up at him questioningly.

"How can you give me this now?"

"I would rather borrow money from a friend and pay him back than I would have you think badly of me. Only a certain type of Tunisian man will take money from a woman, and I am not one of these men."

"I am happy you said that." She was pleased at how wrong M had been and angry with herself for doubting him.

He lay back against the cushions and she snuggled into him, conscious of his arm loosely round her shoulder and she put her arm around his waist and his muscles tensed at her touch. He stroked her hair, kissed her eyelids and tried to fill his mind with thoughts of anything but her. She was too close and he could not trust himself. It had been wrong to bring her here, however beautiful it was, this was a place for lovers. He felt the familiar yearning and the only thoughts which his mind would permit was of her naked body in the moonlight. He gave up the fight and looked down at her cradled like a child beside him, wanting nothing more than to feel his skin against hers again. That could not be, he had nowhere to take her.

"Lucy, are you afraid of me?" She hesitated. "Cherie, this is me, your Farid. I mean you no harm, I want only to love you."

"That is what I'm afraid of."

"Lucy, what is it you are really afraid of. Is it my lovemaking or is it that you are frightened to love me?"

"Both." He waited. When she spoke her voice was soft and uncertain. "I am afraid to love you because the strength of what I feel for you I have never felt before and I hardly know you. There are so many things which stand in our way. We come from different worlds, different cultures, everything. I am older than you and I have a child. In my country that would be difficult, but in yours it's impossible."

"Nothing is impossible, insh'allah."

She smiled in spite of herself. That word seems to cover everything and there is no answer to it. He sensed her embarrassment but he knew he had to ask. "But go on, and the other thing you are afraid of."

Lucy looked away. She had no idea how to explain what she felt, the sensations she had experienced, the strength of his body and the fear that he would grow tired of her.

"Farid. Have you known many women? You are still a young man, but you have made me feel like no man has ever done. You are so strong and you seem to know what a woman wants."

"My sweet Lucy. I have known women, yes, but not so many as you may think. And my darling, a man's strength and the way his body behaves is reflected in the desire he has for the woman he makes love to. With you I am strong. What I do with you is natural to me, not from my own experience. Your body talks to me, she tells me what she wants and she is talking to me now."

His voice was deep and melodious. Lucy felt herself falling, weightless and waiting for strong arms to catch her. As though reading her thoughts he held her close and she raised her face to receive his kiss.

They left the little villa and walked back towards the town. Her mind on other things Lucy only half noticed the road running along the beach side stretching away wide and straight flanked by twin lines of palms, their frond swaying seductively in the gentle breeze. The pale walkways glistened in the soft light. It was a mild Mediterranean evening, warm and pleasant, the only sounds floating in the darkness coming from the swishing of the waves.

The bustle of scantily dressed summer holidaymakers, their colourful plumage loud and tawdry against the cool cream paving, were blissfully gone. Most had flown home for another year, migrating north until once again they shook out their wings with the first glimmer of summer sunshine and headed south once more.

A few couples passed them and smiled a greeting. An elderly gentleman in a cream linen suit raised his panama hat to Lucy and she nodded in acknowledgement. She felt as ease as though she belonged with this formidable man in his beautiful country. Farid linked her fingers through his, his thumb stroking her palm as led her down a narrow sandy path towards the beach. Here there were no lights and she could just make out the outline of the small cove and rows of dense bushes. As they walked in the sand, she stumbled and he caught her and pressed her close to him. In the darkness they found a small patch of beach surrounded completely by bushes.

He pulled her down onto the sand. There was no urgency, time had no meaning. He lay beside her and stroked her into complete submission, playing her body like an instrument, bringing her to a crescendo until she could take no more, and stopping until she begged for more. He guided her hands onto his own body and her instinct took over. She played the same game, touching, kissing and pulling back. "Mon Ange ou Demon," he whispered. She never knew who won that game or whether they both gave in together but when he finally lifted her onto his body there was no pain and as they moved together as one she knew that whatever the future held for them, he would be her true and last love.

They lay together in the sand throughout the night, touching and learning about each other until they slept, one behind the other like a pair of spoons as he cradled her in his arms. Lucy awoke as the first rosy fingers snaked across the dawn sky through the morning haze over the sea. Farid stirred as she moved and suddenly he jumped up and she gazed at him marvelling at the splendour of his naked form, a silhouette against the rising sun.

"The time, what is the time?" She looked at her watch.

"It's just gone 5a.m." He muttered an oath and scrambled back into his clothes.

"My darling, please hurry. They will be coming to clean the beach, as you know it is against the law for us to be here on the beach."

"And tomorrow I go home."

Farid hauled her to her feet. "You can't go, please, Lucy. You can't go, not now when I've just found you again."

"I must, but I will come back."

"When?"

"In a few months."

"You swear it."

"I swear it."

He sat down in the sand and once again he tore the top off his cigarette packet and wrote on it. "Here, my address, now write yours on this. He gave her the packet. She wrote on it and handed it back to him. "Good, I have your telephone number and your address. I have no phone, but I will call you from the box. I must ask you this, you must know I have very little money, but sometimes you will call me back?"

Lucy smiled. "Of course, and you must write to me."

They walked back towards her hotel. She was surprised how many people were out so early in the morning, but of course hotel people probably all changed shifts around the same time. He kissed her deeply a short way from the hotel. "Bon voyage, my Lucy. I wait for your return."

He turned away and walked quickly back towards his lodgings wondering if she would indeed come back to him, and what he would do if she didn't.

M heard her come in. Lucy's smile, flushed face and obvious happiness left questions unnecessary. She climbed into bed and fell immediately asleep until M shook her.

"Come on, I'm not missing breakfast for you!"

In the morning after breakfast they sat by the pool drinking coffee. "Have you decided the drug is worth the side effects?"

Lucy nodded. "Yes, I have. I'm coming back."

"No matter what the consequences or difficulties."

"In spite of those," she replied with conviction. "D'you know M. I remember a quote from a film years ago about an English army officer in India who fell in love with a girl who was half Indian, half English. When they talked about how the world would view their love he said: 'Why didn't God make all people the same on the outside as they are on the inside' and d'you know what she answered." M shook her head. "'Because even if he did, they'd change it once his back was turned'."

M looked at her. "That's one of the truest things I've ever heard, but the problem is, Lucy that God hasn't made everyone the same. Whether you like it or not, you may think you love him and he may even love you. Some things you could probably overcome but the brutal fact is that you are years older than him and there is Alex to consider. You have different cultures and religion. Even I know that over here that adds up to a pretty insurmountable problem. Lucy, it's his right to have his own family, a young wife and children, the children you probably can't give him. Have you told him that?"

Lucy shook her head. "It never came up. M I've only known him a short while, we simply want to be together for as long as we can."

"And what worries me is that the longer it does go on, if he really loves you then the question of marriage and children will come up. If you agree to marry him, you will both be ostracised from his family. If you marry him regardless and if you don't tell him that you probably can't have children, he'll hate you for it."

"M, I was only told I probably can't have any more children, and that it wasn't likely and I shouldn't anyway for my own health."

"Lucy, don't clutch at straws. If you want to be with him, then fine, come back. Let this thing run its course but don't bog the two of you down so deeply you can't get out. Just enjoy it while you can. See it for what it is, a holiday romance."

"Thanks, M. I know you mean well and I do take on board what you're saying. I'll take each day as it comes and deal with every obstacle as it comes up."

"Good, now let's get another cheap drink before we get home and pay through the nose again!"

Lucy meant exactly what she said, but what M didn't know was that Alice had told her that she would have another child, although she knew this was unlikely, clutching at straws was exactly what she was doing. She would deal with each problem as it arose. The only question she faced was whether Farid was a choice or whether he was predestined. As Farid would say Insh'allah.

Lucy gazed out of the coach window as it sped her away from Hammamet and her love. M left her to her thoughts. She listened to the chatter of holiday makers comparing the virtues and one or two disasters of their holiday. She wore her sunglasses to hide the tears which refused to stop trickling down her cheeks. She wanted him so badly she ached but something whispered to her and wouldn't stop. The passion she felt for him was completely alien and terrified her and if this was only the beginning could she control what was to come.

She watched the passing landscape. The coach took the main road and there were few buildings and fewer villages. The terrain was not unlike Spain in parts, although greener. Huge bushes of bougainvillea and oleander clothed the low buildings, deep pink, purple and orange intense against the sunlight which was bright to the point of being blinding, even through her sunglasses. The coach rolled on past fields of olive trees in neat lines, each field separated by a low hedge of prickly pear. Goats and the odd sheep grazed on the verges between the road and the fields under the watchful eye of their shepherd, often little more than a boy. Here and there a donkey wandered, picking its way delicately through the stones which lined the roadside. The landscape was flat with the only shadow on the horizon being some misty grey hills which appeared to rise out a purple nothingness as though they hung from a cloudless sky. The sun streamed in through the windows and she pulled the little curtain across to shut out what promised to be a beautiful day in her own idea of paradise, knowing she would not be a part of it.

That night, Farid lay on his bed in the small lodgings he shared with three other hotel workers. Where was this leading? She had responded to him but he knew in his heart that she had more to give, even if she was not aware of it herself. The question which burning him was would she be able to give more. He sensed the intensity of his lovemaking had shocked her. He knew he loved her and felt that he had known her for years. In truth he had spent only a few weeks with her. How well did he really know her? She was, after all, whether he liked it or not just a tourist. He'd been with a couple of tourists before and thought sadly that none had ever matched his passion and he never followed it through after they left.

A few of his friends had gone abroad at the invitation of girls they had met. One or two had remained, but most had returned some years later, considerably richer. He despised the men who went with girls for money or the visa to Europe to seek their fortune, although he knew it was one way to get enough money to come home and find a Tunisian girl to marry. Unfortunately, most of these girls were not impressed by a handsome face, they also wanted money, a man with a home to take them to, a car and sufficient wealth to provide them with the lifestyle they wanted and to impress their friends and relatives, without having to work themselves, although it was accepted that if a woman did work, her money was her own.

He had never been tempted to take that route. He wanted no Tunisian wife. He loved Lucy for herself, not what she could give him, but was he deluded by the years of dreaming of the young woman he had first seen. Had he built her up into something she could never be? The Arab fire of passion lay deeply embedded in his soul and he knew that if he was to remain faithful to a woman she would have to meet that passion.

The main thing which worried him was whether she had told him the truth about having no man friend at home. He could not see how a woman who was as pretty as Lucy would not have someone at home. He argued with himself that on each occasion he had phoned her, she had always been happy to talk with him in such a way that it was obvious there was no-one else with her and the always picked up the phone immediately, she was always at home. He trusted Lucy, and he knew that he would wait for her until she returned to him. Above all he was sure the passion he needed was there in Lucy and it was up to him to bring it from her. He brushed all the troubled thoughts from his mind and fell into a deep sleep.

CHAPTER SIXTEEN

LUCY AND FARID

Lucy's life took on a different pattern. Every three months she returned to Tunisia. By now, Farid was established in one of the larger hotels. His first year had expired but he was kept on and she became a regular guest at the hotel. He had explained to her from the outset that relations between staff and guests were strictly forbidden and if he were discovered he would be dismissed. As he was on shift work he was obliged to work sometimes at night, but he usually managed to find someone who would change shifts, for a small payment, so he could work during the daytime during the times Lucy was there. On the few times he was not able to do so he managed to come to her room at midnight each day during his break.

Although Lucy welcomed the times they could make love in the comfort of her room, it was never quite the same as he always listened for the beep of his communicator.

On one such occasion, Lucy had arrived during the daytime and Farid was furious to be on night duty but he had not been able to find anyone to change shifts with him. Lucy had not seen him since the Easter holidays and Farid was desperate. He had over the months unleashed in Lucy a sexuality neither had believed was possible. She met his every needs, their lovemaking was intense, gentle, aggressive and sometimes almost violent. She was a different woman each time they came together and on occasion she exhibited a dominance he had not dreamed of. At first he rejected it until he saw the sparkle in her eyes and the tell-tale little smile which told him it was all part of the game of love. He had kept his trust with her and although he saw many very pretty girls, some of whom were quite blatant in their appreciation of him, he waited only for Lucy. His woman played many parts and he did not need any other.

He had spent the evening standing at reception watching his darling seated demurely so close to him and yet untouchable, sipping her pastis and reading her book. Sometimes she glanced over at him with a flicker of a smile. He was sure he could smell her perfume. Lucy was wearing a low scoop neck T-shirt which moulded to her body and each time she reached for her drink he glimpsed the soft rise of her breasts.

Once she looked up at him as she bent forward and gave him a sensual slow smile. As she sat back she leaned right back in the chair and crossed her legs at the knee exposing her bare thigh. She ran her hands down her thighs as she smoothed the soft fabric. Farid was embarrassed at his own reaction. She smiled wickedly at his obvious discomfort and he cursed softly as he realised she was doing this on purpose to torment him. He vowed to make her pay for her tricks. After several tantalising hours he was free to go for his break.

At exactly midnight he knocked softly on her door. She answered wearing only a tiny silk nightdress which finished just below her knees. Farid glared, scooped her up and threw her on the bed, tearing off his clothes, almost before the door had closed. She lay on the bed her hands behind her head admiring him, his arms and face darkly tanned from the sun contrasting with the honey of the rest of his skin, the line of his mouth thin and his eyes alight with undisguised desire.

He lowered himself on top of her and muttered roughly, "There will be no foreplay, you have tormented me for three hours. If you are not ready now you should be." He pulled her nightdress up around her neck, nipped her breast with his teeth as he pushed her legs apart, stroked her for a few seconds. Lucy gasped and Farid held her prisoner under him as he moved. She wrapped her legs round him and within seconds he gasped as his aching body reached its climax and he sank his full weight on top of her.

It was exactly then the beeping started. Farid swore loudly and Lucy couldn't stifle her giggle. The weather was particularly hot. Both of them were drenched in sweat and as he lifted himself from her and tried to get up to answer the communicator, he slid off the bed onto the floor. Lucy collapsed into peals of laughter. If she had not known him so well she would have cringed at the look he gave her.

He reached for the offending object and answered, barking harshly at the intruder. Then he turned back to Lucy who was attempting a serious expression, without success.

"Tonight my love you are truly a demon."

She reached out her arms to him, but he scowled at her, turned away and reached for his trousers. Then with a grin he threw them on the floor and lay down again next to her.

"What was that about?"

"Absolutely nothing. Just to tell me to go to the pool door after my break for the remainder of the evening as they expect there may be a little trouble from a crowd of lads who have gone to the beach bar and will probably make a lot of noise when they come back."

"How long do you have?"

"Long enough to make you pay!"

He kissed her lightly and teased her nipples with his tongue, he caressed her and she sighed and pulled him towards her. He turned away from her and reached for his cigarettes. Lucy slapped him hard on the back and pulled on his shoulders until he lay under her. She slid her body so she lay half on top of him her back to him and took him in her hands moving them up and down stroking him to the point of detonation before taking him in her mouth. She felt his body shudder and his hands cupped her breasts as he came.

She lit a cigarette and handed it to him and they lay together watching the curls of smoke rise up to the ceiling. She cuddled into his body tracing her hand tantalisingly up and down his stomach, his chest and his neck, her fingers teasing him. He felt her hand slip down between his legs and cup him. The gentle pressure of her fingers sent shivers through him and he felt himself harden. To his own amazement when he thought he could give no more, she mounted him and rocked back and forth until he once again came with a shudder of pleasure.

Farid was completely exhausted and felt his legs would give way as he hurried down the back stairs to the rear pool door. He used every ounce of his strength not to fall asleep and when the group of young people came back from their drinking around 3a.m. in the morning, making a great deal of noise, was in no mood to be polite. As they approached he stood up, went outside the box and told them in a jumbled mixture of French and Arabic to bloody well shut up and go to bed.

One man opened his mouth to reply but seeing the tall man glaring at them, hands on hips, his mouth set in a hard line and his eyes glittering in anger, decided against it and the group made their way quietly back to the hotel.

The following night, Farid again managed to go to her room and in the early morning he fell asleep on the bus back to his lodgings and slept until late afternoon.

His shift had now changed to days and he met Lucy after her dinner. They spent a quiet evening with his friends on the beach, but this time there was another woman with them, a tiny elegant Italian woman who was a friend of one of the older men, Ibrahim. She told Lucy the two had been lovers many years ago, but although that side of their relationship has gradually faded, their friendship had remained. Lucy was surprised and although she said nothing, the little woman's eyes crinkled in amusement.

"It is possible, no, for man and woman to remain friends after the loving, she runs away?" She asked in a soft low voice.

Lucy smiled. "I'm sorry was I that obvious?"

The other woman leaned towards her and whispered.

"There are two parts of each person. One the sex and the other the friend. For us, the sex she is not good but the friend she is perfect!" Lucy said she thought the explanation was an excellent philosophy and the two women laughed together. Farid turned to watch her and was pleased she had mixed so effortlessly with his friends.

They sat on the beach together after the others had gone, side by side. They had been there most of the night. She gazed at the sea as they shared a cigarette. The night was clear and she watched the stars twinkling like a million diamonds. They waited. Slowly the night sky faded and the stars disappeared. The velvety blackness gave way to a clear grey blue and the first signs of the new day appeared. A single rosy finger shot across the horizon, reflected on the sea followed by more in every direction as the sun rose throwing a deep orange blanket across the skyline. Lucy shaded her eyes from its splendour. The sunlight shone on the gently rippling waves and Lucy thought it was as though the stars from the night sky had fallen into the sea.

Farid watched her face, illuminated in the morning light. She closed her eyes.

"Isn't it wonderful how at night the moon holds the stars, the jewels of the universe but at daybreak she surrenders her treasures to the sun. As she sleeps he guards them for her until she wakes and then he returns her jewels to her. It's a cycle they have continued since time began."

He watched her intense little face, his beautiful dreaming girl and kissed her gently.

She turned to him, a little embarrassed. "How silly you must think me."

"No my darling, I was thinking that I have only one jewel, that shines brighter than any star in the sky and I will give her to no-one, not even to the sun himself.

He walked her back to the hotel, kissed her and watched her hurry back down the winding pathway until he could see her no longer.

On their last night, Farid took a chance. Although there was a rule that once the shift finished the staff left the hotel, he made the excuse that he did not want the bus back to his lodgings and disappeared unnoticed into Lucy's room. They spent the night together and he slipped silently back into his shift in the morning. This time he had been lucky.

Lucy sat in the reception area with the three other people waiting for the coach, trying her best not to look at the man standing only a few feet from her in whose arms she had been only hours before. As she sat on the coach she looked out of the window at him. He stood impassively watching her, his face expressionless and his arms folded. As the coach pulled away, Lucy saw him place his fingers on his lips. She did the same and the tears streamed down her face.

It was early morning and the red dawn sky was melting into clear blue. They travelled the same route as usual and she watched the countryside flying by from the windows of the bus taking her away from her love. The hills to the right, greyish purple merging with the grey blue of the sky, groves of olive trees in parallel rows no matter from which way you looked at them, the scrubby grass immediately beneath their branches dirty green melting into the reddish ochre of the dry earth. The coach sped past the flat landscape and its checkerboard of wobbly lines of prickly pear. It had been a hot summer and there were dry steam beds where no water had flowed for months.

Lucy was lost in her dreams when suddenly the bus screeched to a halt swerving into the side of the road. A similar bus going had also stopped. The driver got out carrying a small case and ran across the road, narrowly avoiding an open back truck, whose driver leaned out of the rolled down window shouting and leaving the offender in doubt of his feelings. Lucy's driver got down and there was a good deal more shouting and waving of arms. Eventually, the case changed hands and the second man ran back across the road. Their driver got back in the bus and chucked the case on a spare seat, muttering to himself. Lucy learned that a passenger had left the case behind. At least the little scene had served as a welcome diversion.

They continued towards the airport and the scrub-land gave way to scattered rough grey block buildings, many of them just basic structures without roofs or windows, homes which had been started and abandoned for one reason or another, she presumed. As the bus reached Sousse there was a huge unfinished structure, six or more storeys high which looked as though it had been there for years, and more square unfinished buildings intermingled with small blocks of apartments, cream, terracotta, beige and grey. Gaily coloured washing hung on lines on the balconies enclosed with green coloured railings. A narrow minaret rose high behind the flat roofs the cream stone sparkling in the sunlight. The bus sped past more unfinished buildings, across the railway line, past a body of water to the right and into the airport. Lucy wiped the tears away from behind her sunglasses.

As the plane sped down the runway taking her away, she started counting the days before she could come back.

CHAPTER SEVENTEEN

ALEX

In the late spring, Lucy took Alex with her to Tunisia. She longed for her times with Farid but missed her son. Reluctantly his grandparents agreed to part with him for the fortnight, with a promise from Lucy that he could stay with them over the next half term. When he called her, Lucy told Farid she was bringing her son and to her delight he seemed genuinely pleased. On this occasion Lucy decided to stay at a different hotel. Alex was old enough to understand that his mother had a friend she came to see in Tunisia when he stayed with Nanny and Granddad but he was too young for Lucy to explain to him that the relationship was not a public one.

"But how am I to be with you?" Farid's disappointment was plain.

"If I stay at your hotel, say we are out for the day with Alex and you are on duty in the evening, Alex will run to you as his new friend. How are we to explain that?" Farid saw the sense in this, although he did not want to think of Lucy being so close to him and yet so far that he could not touch her. He thought hard.

"I will arrange something for us, I'll call you next week."

Farid was at a loss. In the evening after work he went to the small café in Hammamet that they often used and sat alone wondering what to do. He wanted to see Lucy but he couldn't jeopardise his job if Alex was there.

Cathy watched him closely. She had grown fond of the couple who often sat together, hand in hand, unnoticed by the guests most of whom were tourists, and interested only in each other. She knew how difficult such relationships could be with the restrictions and problems they faced.

"Hello, Farid. No Lucy today."

Farid started, he had not heard her approach him. "No, Cathy, not this time. She is coming back in a month or so with her young son. It will be difficult for her to stay with her son in my hotel and I must find a different hotel for them."

Cathy understood. "Ah, I can see your problem." Without quite knowing why she said gently, "look, I only work now in the afternoon. My husband takes over around 5p.m. If you would like me to sit with the boy sometimes in the evening I would be happy to do so."

Farid's face lit up and he grasped her hands. "Cathy, that would be wonderful. I am happy for the boy to be with us in the daytime, but I see Lucy so little, I would like to be able to spend a little time with her by myself."

"That's settled then. Just let me know when and you can drop him off here when I finish and I'll take him home with me. Actually you would be doing me a favour as well. Someone new will keep my boy entertained and out from under my feet. The lad can even stay overnight if you're going to be really late." Her eyes met Farid's in silent understanding.

"Thank you, Cathy," he murmured sincerely.

The following week Farid called Lucy and she noticed immediately he seemed much happier.

"I think you should stay at the Olive Grove hotel."

Lucy knew this was one of the newer hotels which catered for families. Farid knew it was also close enough to his place of work and Cathy café bar. He told her of Cathy offer and Lucy offered a silent prayer of thanks for Cathy's sweet understanding. She had been worried about leaving Alex with a sitter arranged by the hotel. Although the service was offered, it was really a checking up service and not beyond 11p.m. She liked Cathy immensely and during the time she had been going to Tunisia, Cathy was the nearest she had to a close friend.

She knew the Olive Grove was a noisy bustling hotel, the food was aimed, in so far as it could be, towards the English tourists and guests found no problems in finding enough for their children to eat. There was a large shallow pool with inflatables and toys and the hotel provided daytime pool and garden entertainment for the children. In the evening there were shows, again family orientated and Lucy thought it would be quite perfect for Alex.

The weeks passed quickly and soon, Lucy arrived again in Hammamet, bringing with her a very excited little boy. The days whilst Farid worked she spent curled up by the pool watching Alex having the time of his life. He was a happy child, tall for his age, who mixed well with other children and had learned to swim the year before. Within a few days he became one of the leaders and to the amusement of the animation team insisted on helping them with the younger children. The evenings she spent with Farid.

Alex took to Farid immediately. "Are you my Mummy's friend?" he asked.

He seemed oblivious of the fact Farid could not talk to him but Farid realised what was being said to him and nodded.

"Then you will be my friend too and can I have an ice cream?" he asked with childish impudence.

Lucy burst out laughing and explained. Farid regarded the child's upturned face. "I am happy," he replied seriously in English. When he returned with the ice cream, Alex jumped up to claim his prize. Farid sat down and Alex snuggled in next to him.

Lucy watched her son as he sat next to Farid and a wave of nostalgia overtook her as she remembered how he used to do the same thing with Peter. She looked around at the other families and back at her son and this young man whom she loved. How she wished the three of them could be one of those families, but that could never be.

Some evenings she left him with Cathy and spent the evenings with Farid, but other times they sat together, the three of them, watching one of the public entertainment shows in the town centre. Alex usually fell asleep as the time passed and Lucy and Farid sat happily their arms around each other as the child slept. He would walk her back to the hotel, carrying the child and reluctantly left her to spend the nights apart, save for the times when Alex stayed with Cathy overnight. One night they spent at his friend's house, but she was embarrassed because the man was there with his family and she left as soon as possible the next day, explaining she must get back to her son. She did not miss the look which passed between husband and wife at the mention of her child. They spent a night on the beach in the little cove away from the main road, but she longed for a bed and to wake in the comfort of quiet room, her arms around her love.

The day before she was due to go home was Farid's day off. He drove them down the coast to a small marina. Alex was fascinated by the rows of yachts and the silvery coloured fish which swam in the harbour so close to the quayside you felt you could touch them.

They wandered amongst the little shops, waving away the insistence of the shop keepers to come in and have a look until Farid shouted at them to leave her alone, exasperated at his countrymen.

They walked to down the narrow streets Alex spotted a woman eating calamari. He had first tasted these in Tenerife when he thought they were onion rings, but even after Antonio had explained it was fish the dish had remained once of his favourites.

"Mum, look it's those calmar things. Can we stop here so I can have some?"

Farid objected, but Lucy insisted, knowing it was only the money which stopped him and handed him some money to avoid his embarrassment. Alex munched happily on his squid rings, and Lucy had the same. Farid opted for a thick dark lamb and vegetable stew and Alex watched him intently as he dipped the chunks of soft warm bread.

"Can I have some?" Farid obliged and dipped a small piece of the bread into the gravy, handed it to the boy and waited. Alex popped the whole thing into his mouth and his little face turned bright red.

"Mummy! I'm on fire!" He grabbed his glass and drained it. Lucy glared at Farid.

"Harissa," he explained, patting the astonished boy gently on the back.

"You idiot!"

Alex put down his glass and grinned from one to the other. "More!"

Farid raised his eyebrows at Lucy and she shook her head.

"Absolutely not. He'll be up all night and you won't be there. I'll be the one who has to sort him out."

"Mum, can he stay over with us tonight." Lucy choked on her meal.

"No my love, he has his own home to go to."

Farid waited for her to explain and laughed. "The boy is a mind reader!"

Later as they walked arm in arm along the key, Alex's attention was drawn by one of the yachts.

"Can we go on one of the boats, Mummy?"

"No darling, these belong to other people."

"But they're not using them now. I'm sure they wouldn't mind." His little face pleaded with Lucy and she explained to Farid, who shook his head smiling at the child.

"Well can we play make believe then?" Alex ran over to the largest yacht, a beautiful white vessel with tall masts and gleaming gold and black paintwork. He leaned against the railing and shouted happily "This is the one I want. Can you take my photograph?" Lucy obliged.

Alex looked around and to her embarrassment he ran over to an elderly woman sitting by herself enjoying the sunshine, who had been watching them. "Will you take our photograph?" The woman beamed at him and stood up. "Of course young man."

Lucy handed her the camera with a muttered apology. "I'm sorry. That was rude of him." The woman smiled. "Don't worry yourself, my grandson does just the same sort of thing."

She turned to Alex. "Now young man, you go and stand with Mummy and Daddy."

Lucy flushed and Farid immediately asked her what the woman had said. Lucy told him.

He grinned broadly and his arm around her waist, putting the other round Alex's shoulder.

It was one of many photographs Lucy would treasure.

As it was their last day and Lucy was due to return home the following evening, Cathy agreed to have Alex overnight. By the time they got back to Hammamet he was asleep and Farid carried him to Cathy car.

One of Farid's friends had offered him his small apartment on the far side of Hammamet for the night as he would be away that weekend. Before going to the apartment they sat on the beach, as they often did, and watched the waves lapping gently on the sand, white in the moonlight.

Although he had been concerned at first about Alex's visit, Farid had accepted that the boy was part of Lucy's life and that if Lucy was to be part of his life then Alex would be too. He knew there would be some problems for them, not only because of Lucy's child but because she was much older than him. His family would be disappointed but there would be more children and he was sure they would eventually come to accept her. In his youthful enthusiasm and love for his lady, Farid put aside the implications of what he was about to do.

She gazed up at the stars in the inky blackness and he kissed her cheek. "Lucy. Could you ever live here, in Tunisia?"

"Of course, it is such a beautiful place. I could spend the rest of my life here."

"No, Lucy, I mean with me, as my wife."

Lucy's eyes were huge as she looked at him, the shock all too apparent. "Farid, I never dreamed…"

He stared at her, his mouth set in a hard line. "So you don't love me," he said flatly.

"Oh, no, that's not it. I love you more than I have ever loved anyone. My life with you is perfect but it is not just us, is it. There is Alex, his grandparents and your own family. So many people to consider. You know your own family couldn't accept me." She knew she was babbling but didn't know how to stop. "I don't know very much about your culture but enough to know that an older woman with a child is not want they want for you and how would we live…" she added lamely. Her voice tailed off at his expression, a confused mixture of hurt, disappointment and anger.

"I could deal with that, if you could, but obviously you are not the woman I thought you were. You do not want to be my wife, to have my children and to love me for the rest of our lives together, as I love you now."

"I can think of nothing I want more, but it can never be," she hesitated but knew she must be honest with him.

"Farid, what you say is right, we could possibly cope with all those things which are against us, but I must tell you that when Alex was born I was told I might not be able to have any more children."

Farid was confused.

"But…"

"Yes, I still take precautions as you know but I suppose at the back of my mind it is because it at least makes me feel that perhaps one day I might have another child. It makes me feel… that I am still a woman."

Her distress was open to him, as though she expected his rejection, and he held her close.

"Lucy, my darling, you are my woman. If there will be no more children, then I can accept that. But if it is the will of Allah that you have another child, then it will be."

Lucy's mind flew back to Alice's words. "You will have another child, a dark child. The child will be a boy. He will change your life forever."

She hugged him tightly, "Oh my darling, I love you so much."

He put his arms around her, his mind trying to absorb the enormity of her words. Of course he wanted children of his own, he had just never considered any alternative.

They spent the night at the apartment. Their lovemaking was tender and passionate and when she awoke in the morning and drew back the shutters to let in the morning light, Lucy imagined herself in this little home with her family, Farid and Alex and god willing, another child.

Later in the morning, she went back to her hotel and packed their things. She collected Alex from Cathy's house and spent the day by the pool, her thoughts in turmoil.

Farid met them at the café bar after work and sat with them until it was time for them to leave. He was pensive as he walked back with them to her hotel to wait for the coach. As the coach arrived, he took Lucy's hands.

"Lucy, think on what I have said. I mean it. I want you as my wife. I know we have not spent much time together, but you are all I have ever wanted, as you know, since I was a boy. I know what you have told me and I can accept that because I must. I want to spend the rest of my life with you."

Alex chattered non-stop most of the way home, at the airport and on the plane. Lucy answered him mechanically but the child was happy and didn't notice. He was looking forward to seeing his friends again and telling them about his adventures.

The spring turned into summer. They spoke often on the phone but neither referred to the conversation again. The weeks turned to months and finally it was time once again for Lucy to return. Alex had gone to his grandparents and she had another day to wait before her flight. She did not know how to feel, the nervous anticipation was almost as it had been the first time she went back. Would he still feel the same? She knew how important children are to the Arab men, they believe it proves he is a man. Would Farid eventually grow tired of her and of having no children of his own? She convinced herself it would be better to walk away and let him have the life she was sure he wanted, but when she saw him again and felt his arms around her all her misgivings melted into nothing.

CHAPTER EIGHTEEN

SALEEM

Saleem was tired. The work which Farid had found for him was not at all to his taste. The hours were long and the pay was bad. He had no wish to be a hotel porter, but he acknowledged that it was good experience after college and a way of earning something. At least he was in Hammamet and away from the eyes of his family for the first time. The freedom to come and go as he pleased was new and exciting.

He finished work and walked purposefully towards the Medina for a coffee before going back to his lodgings. He was meeting his girlfriend and knew he didn't have time to go to his usual haunts away from the main town. The Medina cafés were more expensive and were full of tourists but there was one small place tucked under the back wall of the Medina which had retained its traditionally male clientèle, the prices weren't too steep and it was directly on his way. He sat outside idling watching the people strolling across the square. His gaze rested on a tall figure, which he was sure was his brother. The man was standing on the other side of the road looking towards the row of shops as though he was waiting for someone.

He saw the girl come out of the shop and to his surprise his brother walked towards her. He watched her, as did most of the others in the café. He could see she was European, her creamy skin only slightly tanned. She wore cropped white trousers and a bright orange vest top with a little frill softening the low V neck line. She certainly would have made a more than acceptable picture in any event, but it was her hair which made her stand out, almost white blonde swirling around her shoulders like a cloud and reaching almost to her waist.

He had been about to call to his brother, but his voice died in his throat as the girl slipped her arm around Farid's waist. His brother's arm went around the girl's shoulder. Saleem was speechless, he'd go so far as to say he couldn't remember been more surprised. The girl kissed Farid on the lips and he watched as Farid gently chided her. She pouted and pulled a face at him and Farid smiled in a way that Saleem had never seen him do before. The pair linked hands and walked towards him.

He hunched himself back into his chair. They were going to walk right past the café, not more than a few feet from where he was seated. He could see she was not as young as he had first thought, late-twenties he reckoned, but she was certainly beautiful. As they passed, Farid glanced automatically into the café and Saleem saw the shock register on his face, obviously deciding whether to pretend he hadn't seen his brother.

Saleem was not about to be ignored. He stood up, his arm outstretched. "Farid."

Farid took the outstretched hand as if it were a stick of dynamite. They kissed on both cheeks and exchanged the usual greetings. He noticed with amusement that Farid avoided looking at the woman and waited. She glanced at Farid, who bore all the markings of a cornered rabbit, then he smiled down at her.

"Lucy, this is my brother Saleem."

Lucy put out her hand and Saleem took it. Despite the late afternoon heat, her hand was cool and her grasp firm.

"Hi," she said. "I'm pleased to meet you." Her voice was deeper that he had expected, soft and musical. Saleem was a little taller than Farid and she had to look up at him. Her eyes were amazing. Green, but with amber flecks like sunlight and the corners crinkled slightly as she smiled at him.

He moved towards an empty table at the edge of the terrace and she took Farid's hand and followed him. Farid gave up any hope of escape although he was acutely aware of the attention Lucy was creating in this male dominated environment. Much of the conversation had ceased as she came into the café and Farid felt uncomfortably conspicuous. Lucy however seemed completely oblivious, or if she had noticed she ignored it and a lower murmur of conversation spread through the café. Farid thought glumly, "I'll bet they've got a new subject and it isn't politics!"

Saleem found Lucy entertaining and he loved her funny accent. She spoke quite good French, although her grammar would probably have sent her back to school.

"I'm sorry about my dreadful grammar," she explained at the outset. "I never really speak French unless I'm over here. By the time I go home, I'm just starting to get a bit better."

She stopped and smiled at Farid. "He's very good. He can at least understand me and he tries to correct me. It's even more difficult when I go home because when we speak on the phone, I have to start all over again remembering."

He glanced at his brother who gave him a watery smile. So she'd been here before, from the way she spoke, probably several times before.

"It's easy for you two, I've noticed almost everyone here speaks French as well as Arabic." She used the English word and Farid gently stroked her hand.

"It's Arab, not Arabic."

She beamed at him. "J m'excuse mon Professeur. You see, he teaches me many things."

"I'm sure he does," replied Saleem, before he realised what he had said. Farid flushed and told him to mind his mouth. He watched as Farid took Lucy's hand and raised it to his lips. His eyes locked with hers and despite the heat Saleem felt a cold shiver run down his back.

"God help him," he thought. "He's in love with her."

Farid caught his brother's expression and made his excuses and disappeared into the café, with a look that left Saleem in no doubt that he was to shut up.

Lucy however had no such inhibitions. "What do you do?" she asked him.

"I have just finished my final year in college and Farid found me this portering work in Hammamet as a way of earning some money before I move to my real work, as an engineer," he added proudly. Lucy found his youthful enthusiasm refreshing and asked him questions about his course. He was pleased she seemed genuinely interested, but decided to satisfy his curiosity before his brother returned.

"How long have you known Farid?

He sensed her hesitation. But she replied with a smile. "Over two years now. I try to come over every three months, whenever I can get away from work."

Saleem tried not show his surprise. Farid had said nothing to any of his family and Saleem could not remember him staying with any one girl for more than a few months. Farid came back and made announced it was time they left. He shook his brother's hand and said to him in his native language. "Say nothing, you understand." Saleem nodded, but he turned to Lucy and suggested they meet up a few days later. Farid was furious, but there was little he could do but to agree.

Lucy was thrilled and they met again a few evenings later, but at a much larger establishment, more frequented by tourists where Farid felt they would be less conspicuous. Saleem immediately noticed the rather handsome leather jacket his brother wore. Farid had not wanted to wear the jacket because he knew what would happen, but Lucy had insisted.

"Brother, you look very well and I admire your beautiful new jacket."

To Farid's annoyance he spoke in French and he was forced to explain to his brother that Lucy had given it to him.

Saleem inspected the jacket and asked if he could borrow it. Lucy was delighted. They all laughed and Farid told him to keep his thieving hands to himself. Saleem noticed that he never wore the jacket when he came home.

Lucy was happy and her bubbling laughter made him smile. To Farid's acute embarrassment she showed Saleem the slim gold bangle Farid had given her. Saleem became even more concerned, he had never known Farid give anything to a woman who wasn't within his own family and of course gold was what a man gives a woman when he intends to marry her. Farid was eternally grateful that Lucy made no mention of the inscription inside the bracelet, F+L.

By now they were at ease in each other's company. Farid was content that his brother would say nothing at home. They had always been close and he trusted him. When they left, Saleem held out his hand to Lucy. To his embarrassment she kissed him on both cheeks. Her skin was soft and smooth and her touch cool. Lucy was not to know that unless people were really close or related, it was something only people of the same sex did with each other. It was not really acceptable in this case, but he was pleased nonetheless. Farid jokingly warned him off, to cover his embarrassment.

Saleem had noticed the scent she wore and to her surprise asked her about it.

"Chanel No.5. I always wear it."

"Sensual and delicate, like you," he thought "Brother, you're a lucky man," he said aloud, in his own language.

Farid smiled, his eyes holding his brother's. "I know," he replied softly.

Saleem cornered his brother some weeks later over a coffee. Farid thanked him for not speaking out. "I don't want our parents upset by this and you can imagine what would happen if Fatma got wind of it. She's quite determined to marry me off to that Sarra."

Saleem raised his eyebrows and grinned. "You've noticed then."

Farid started to laugh. "Don't be stupid. I'd have to be blind and daft not to. Every time I breathe she's there with Sarra in tow, doe eyes gaping at me. Not that it's her fault, poor kid, Fatma's put her up to it. She's just pushed at me, she's always in the next seat and if I step backwards I'll fall over her. Frankly sometimes Fatma takes it right to the wire. I'm bloody certain half my mates in Sousse think I'm at it with her and they're just waiting for the announcement. I've never been anywhere near the girl and I don't want to. Don't get me wrong, there's nothing wrong with her, she's just not for me."

Saleem thought of little Sarra and how different she was from the pale elegant blonde his brother was in love with. "I'm not surprised."

Farid caught his implication. "Would you be interested in Sarra?"

"Normally yes, she is a lovely person, but not in your position I wouldn't." Saleem held out his hand and Farid took it, certain that his secret was safe with his brother.

"I'll tell you another thing, brother. If that sister of mine thinks I'm ever going to agree to her marrying that bloody Hama, with Sarra as my wife offering gentle persuasion on her behalf, she can think again."

Farid's voice was harsh and Saleem caught the aggression behind it. "Look, I know he's an arse, but what have you got against him personally?"

Farid stared at him. "He's years older than her. Hell brother. She's still a kid. I also think he's already married. I hate to admit it but I'm sure he's screwing her although if I knew for certain I'd kill them both. Has he ever indicated commitment, has he ever mentioned marriage? No, because if he had you can bet your sweet life she'd tell the world."

Saleem was shocked at the anger in his brother's voice but sensed there was something more.

"Go on."

"You want the truth? OK. I've heard he's into drug running and other stuff and mixed up with some syndicate. Although I don't know how deeply involved he is and I don't want to know, provided I can keep him away from my sister. If she won't leave him alone then I'll have to go into it further. And as you know he's been known to mouth off on the political front and I certainly don't want our family involved in that sort of trouble."

"You're right of course."

Saleem was intrigued how his brother was so well informed. "It's my business to be" was the only curt reply he got.

"Look brother, I know this is asking a lot, but no mention of Lucy to anyone, ever. The trouble it would cause would be catastrophic. In fact it's probably better if you don't even say you've seen me. That might be a mistake, especially with that nosey sister of ours. If you haven't seen me, you can't be tricked into saying something you shouldn't." He hesitated, wondering whether to go on. "Saleem, I have said this to no one but Lucy. I intend to marry her. I know she is older than me and she already has a child, but this is what I want."

Saleem said nothing. So there was a child as well. He was horrified. It was worse than he thought, his brother was obsessed with the woman. Even at his young age he knew the relationship was difficult and with the child it would be impossible.

"Well, it's bound to get out sooner or later. Anyone could have seen you together."

"It's possible and if you're ever asked, just play it down. She was a tourist I showed how to get to the Medina, or some such rubbish. Just make sure it's plausible, invent, use your imagination."

"I'd be surprised if you haven't already been spotted," Saleem thought grimly. "Walking around a place like Hammamet like a pair of love-struck teenagers doesn't help much." But he said nothing and as Farid had asked, never mentioned Lucy to anyone.

CHAPTER NINETEEN

THE JOURNEY HOME

Farid had changed in the three years she had been with him but he was still young. At first when they talked, he had told her it was expected of him as the eldest son to marry, produce children and tend his parents in their later life. That was his culture, his responsibility but it was something now they never talked about. What he didn't tell her was that to please his father he was always pleasant enough to the young girls who were introduced to him by his hopeful parents, but to him they were as dates on a bunch. Dark and luscious but all the same. All he wanted in his arms was the pale beauty that was his Lucy.

Lucy was always desperately unhappy when she left him, but it got harder every time. She knew that he was and always would be the real true love of her life. She had loved Peter dearly. He had been a good husband and of course he had given her beloved son. But she had never experienced before anything as strong as the emotions this man created in her. More than anything she hated the last day of her holiday.

This time was no exception her heart pounded as it always did. She felt sick. The journey home was the worst because it was the time furthest away from seeing him again. She sat in the café next to the hotel entrance waiting for the bus. Her bags were packed and stored in the baggage room. The music blared and she wished they would turn down the volume. She wondered whether to drink the whole bottle of water, if she didn't she would probably be thirsty on the coach, but if she took it with her by the time they reached the airport she would be bursting for the toilet. It was only 10a.m. but already the heat was oppressive. It promised to be a hot, humid day and there was little breeze to cool her. She felt sticky and miserable.

Farid was not there. He had worked the previous night and was by now asleep. Even if he worked by day he hated seeing her onto the coach, preferring to say goodbye the night before, properly, as he put it, rather than a formal handshake in front of the hotel. Lucy looked at her watch. 10.15a.m., the bus was late. Her hands shook and she felt like she was waiting for her own execution because that is what it was, only it was not her head she was losing it was her heart. The bus arrived and Mussa lifted her case onto the coach. He smiled sadly at her and although she tried, Lucy could not return his smile.

Poor lady, he thought. Although Farid made every effort to keep their relationship low key some of the porters and door security sensed the depth of feeling between their friend and the lovely English woman. They knew in advance when Lucy was due to arrive because Farid's attitude changed. He was happy and unusually chatty. He arranged his days off to coincide with Lucy's visits and most of them were happy to take on an extra night duty to help him. Similarly, when Lucy had gone, Farid's mood darkened. Some wondered how long they would last together, there were so many things against them, but that they were at this moment obviously in love was undisputed. This was no one off holiday romance but most believed it could only end in tears, the question was simply when.

Mussa shook hands with Lucy. "A bientot, Madame."

"A la prochaine, Mussa," she replied, impulsively kissing him on both cheeks. He blushed.

"Farid is a lucky man, Madame." It was Lucy's turn to blush as he put out his hand to help her up the steep stairs onto the bus.

The hotel was the last stop for the bus before it started back to the airport and Lucy sat down on one of the only free seats next to a plump elderly English woman who she noticed frowned at the familiarity between herself and young Mussa. Lucy gave her a wide artificial smile and the woman in polite response had little option but to return the smile.

"A friend of yours?" Lucy caught the disapproval in her tone. She looked straight at the stern face.

"Yes, actually he is. I have known Mussa for some time, since he came to the hotel, a shy boy out of school but willing to work hard for little reward, and be polite and helpful regardless of how the clients treat them, as most of them are," she added.

The woman's expression softened. "I'm sorry, I was being very rude and I must agree with you there. I suppose to a certain extent I am shy with them. It's my fault, not theirs. I am in their country but I don't speak any French you see, beyond the usual 'thank you'. What does it mean 'A bientot'?"

"Roughly translated it means 'see you soon' and I answered him 'until the next time'."

"So have you been here a lot, when are you coming back?"

"In three months I hope, or whenever my boss will let me."

As the coach sped along the long straight road, Lucy was thankful for the companionable chatter, although it was obvious to the woman that she was upset.

"You have a special friend here?"

Lucy nodded wordlessly. The older woman patted her knee. "I understand."

The kind gesture was all it took for the tears to trickle down Lucy's cheeks.

"Oh my dear, I didn't mean to upset you."

Lucy shook her head. "No, please, it's just that leaving is always so difficult."

To her surprise the woman put her arm round her shoulders, "believe me I do understand." She sighed and hesitated. "Many years ago I fell in love with an American GI stationed in England during the war. Each time he went away a part of me died. So many young men never came home and although every woman told herself it would never happen to her, we all knew that it could. But I was one of the lucky ones, Jack and I were married in London just before the end of the war and within a year we were back in the States. It was very difficult, the difference and sheer speed of life in New York, the enormity of the country and of course the animosity of his family." She stopped and looked at Lucy wondering whether to go on.

Lucy smiled at her "What happened?"

"I come from a very ordinary middle class family. My father was a country vicar and I had never been out of England before. Jack's family were very rich, he was an only child of elderly parents and they had high hopes of him marrying well, but then he comes back from the war with a mousy English wife who has little money and no prospects. I thought sometimes about what I had done, leaving behind my family and everything I knew, but I loved him so much nothing else mattered." She glanced at Lucy, embarrassed by her disclosures.

Lucy smiled encouragingly. "Did it work out for you in the end?"

The woman stared out of the window. "Yes and no, I suppose you could say. We wanted to travel and see the world. Jack told me about all the wonderful places he had read about and now the war was over he wanted to go and find out for himself. We had no chance. In all the time we were together we never left America. His family made sure he was held closely within their circle, he worked with his father and the hours were long and tiring. The idea of course was that he would take over from his father when the time came. Holidays were spent with one or another group of his relations at the summer home in Florida. But at least when our son, Harry, was born, the family thawed a bit towards me. I had done my part and the family line was safe.

Her grey eyes misted over. "But my Jack was never a strong man and when the 'flu epidemic came at the 50s he died, along with our son."

"Oh how awful. That must have been dreadful for you." Lucy hesitated, "so you came back to England?"

The woman's expression changed. "Not immediately. Their initial hostility towards me had strengthened me as a person and although I knew I would return to England I was determined it would be in my own time, not theirs. I expected them to try to shut me out completely and pack me off as quickly as possible."

She smiled wistfully. "It was strange, but when Jack and Harry died, they insisted I should live with them. It was as though I was all they had left of their family. I stayed with them for over a year, but I longed for my own parents and my sisters and the cool autumn rain of England. The summers there are so hot and the winters so cold, it is as though everything is one extreme or another. England is so gentle in comparison."

"I am so very sorry." Lucy wondered how she would have coped had she lost Alex as well as Peter.

The woman held both Lucy's hands in her own and peered over her glasses. "Oh no, my dear, my time with Jack was the happiest of my whole life. When I left, Jack's parents insisted that I took with me the money they had put aside for our son and the other children they hoped we would have."

"Did you never think of marrying again?"

The woman studied her intently. "Never. I wouldn't, no I couldn't even dream of burdening another man with the knowledge he was second best. It is true that real love only comes once in a lifetime and even then not everyone is that lucky. No, my dear, what I did was what Jack and I always wanted to do together. I travelled the world. I can remember standing in front of the Coliseum in Rome and I am quite sure that as I gazed up I heard Jack say 'It's wonderful Babs, I told you it would be'. Even now I sometimes feel him with me…"

She patted Lucy's knee. "It may seem hard now, during the times you are separated. Sometimes you will feel so lonely. There are so many mixed emotions, in the darkest times suspicion creeps in. You are alone, but who is he with? Does he still love me or will I get that letter telling me he has found someone else? It can all seem so hopeless but I am sure that if God means it to be, then it will be."

"Another woman once said that to me," Lucy murmured Babs smiled, "then she was a very wise woman."

For the rest of the journey, Babs regaled Lucy with tales of the places she had been and the people she had met on her travels. Both agreed that Rome and Egypt were the places they would like to go back to and Babs was adamant that Lucy should visit America. "It is a truly amazing place, a world on its own. You can travel within one continent from the icy beauty of Alaska, the spectacle that is Niagara and the great lakes, through mountains and vast grasslands to the Cajun colour and bustle of New Orleans, and everything in between, but if you do go, make sure you book a long trip. You need months to appreciate it, not weeks."

Lucy was surprised when the bus pulled into the airport. Babs had succeeded in taking her mind off her own misery. The airport was not particularly busy but the incoming plane had been delayed due to a dispute at Gatwick between the baggage handlers and the management.

The two women checked in their bags and sat down over a cup of coffee, watching the other travellers coming and going. Babs's attention was drawn to an elderly couple who were obviously worrying about how the delay was going to affect their journey home from the airport.

"You can learn so much about people from just their clothes, their expressions and the way they interact with other people around them."

Lucy agreed "And by their reaction to unforeseen situations like this," she added.

They watched a middle aged Tunisian man trying to comfort his wife. From what Lucy could make out she was concerned about her parents who were on the incoming flight. She was much younger than him and her pale face was streaked with tears. She held a sleeping baby but her two other children were in competition to see who could cry the loudest. Failing to succeed in comforting either his wife or his children the man gave up and walked away to sit with his friend, leaving her to cope with their offspring.

"Typical bloody Tune," Lucy muttered. Babs grinned and nudged Lucy who followed her gaze to where a couple sat side by side, a few feet from them seeming utterly oblivious of the noise.

The man epitomised elegant French couture from the top of his perfectly oiled hair and fine cream shirt down to his immaculately pressed trousers and brown suede loafers. His manicured hands held a book and he read without raising his eyes once as she looked at him.

His companion looked bored. Her narrow strapped dress, beautifully cut on the bias, screamed money. Unfortunately, it had a very low neckline exposing her décolletage and Lucy thought was more suited to an evening at the Ritz than an airport lounge. She was also vastly over made-up. Her face was set like a plaster caste with thick foundation which because of the heat had lodged in the fine lines around her eyes and mouth, drawing attention to rather than disguising them. She had a rather flat face but her cheek bones were cleverly sculpted with blusher. Her eyes outlined heavily in black liner and lashings of mascara, glanced contemptuously at her fellow passengers.

Her lips were carefully shaped with pencil and filled in with pearly almost white lipstick. It may have been a look she might have got away with at home, but with her deep tan she appeared theatrical rather than attractive.

Lucy noticed with amusement that whatever effect she was trying to create, was in any event rather spoiled by dark roots clearly visible under the platinum blonde plait coiled around her head. She doubted very much the woman was French. They seemed an unlikely couple.

The man put down his book, stretched out his legs and closed his eyes without glancing at his companion. She sat tapping her elegantly shod toes on the marbled floor. He took no notice and she asked him the time although there was a huge round clock on the wall. Without opening his eyes, the man pointed in the direction of the clock. She pursed her lips, rummaged in her handbag and pulled out a large silver purse containing her make-up.

Lucy and Babs watched spellbound as she pouted in the mirror and applied a further layer of pencil and lipstick. Finally she checked her appearance, holding the mirror at arm's length and then blotted her lips, from what Lucy could see, removing most of the goo that she had just put on. She stared at her snoozing companion, and with a practised toss of her head smoothed down her skirt and stood up, her feet slightly apart balancing precariously on high stilettos. She placed her hands on her hips, fixed her lips into a slight bored smile, pushed out her chest and fluttered her eyelashes as though waiting to be photographed for Vogue.

Lucy was mesmerised but Babs started to giggle. For an elderly respectable widow, she had the most infectious laugh, Lucy had ever heard. Babs had her hand over her mouth trying to stifle her laughter but it bubbled over and she went red with embarrassment as she rocked back and forth in her seat.

Quite unaware she was the cause of Babs's present condition the woman turned to Lucy and in very broken and unfortunately comical English enquired, "Your vrend, she ees unvell."

Lucy shook her head, the tears pricking the back of her eyes. Her mouth twitched and she leaned towards the unsuspecting woman. "Actually no, I think she is on something," she whispered wickedly.

The woman's eyes widened. She stared at Babs's bright red face topped by a shock of iron grey hair scraped untidily into a loose knot on the back of her head. Her eyes travelled down taking in the baggy creased trousers and sensible walking shoes. She looked back at Lucy.

"Oh, zees ees not gut, really ees not gut."

Babs was finished. The tears streamed down her face, her rocking became faster and her whole face was split by a huge grin. She let out great gasps of air and knotted her shirt in her hands which were clenched into fists as she tried to control her laughter.

The woman tottered back to her companion and sat down shaking her head. The man was sitting up watching them and from the twinkle in his rather attractive brown eyes, Lucy was sure he was aware of the source of Babs's consternation.

Fortunately the loudspeaker announced the plane was now ready to board and the Frenchman led his lady to the front of the queue. Babs sat for a moment recovering her equilibrium and by the time they were seated on the plane was back to her old formidable self.

"Sorry about that. I've always had rather a problem. Once I start giggling I can't stop and watching that daft female was just too much. Honestly, Lucy I haven't laughed like that in years. My God, you're good for me my girl, you really are."

The rest of the journey was uneventful. The two women exchanged phone numbers and when Lucy arrived home, for a change she was still smiling.

CHAPTER TWENTY

FATMA

Farid hated that week immediately after Lucy left for England. He was ill tempered, sullen and was barely civil to the various females his ever hopeful father thrust in his direction. His mother chided her husband when he complained Farid seemed totally disinterested in seeking out a suitable partner.

"He knows his responsibilities Hakim, but give him time. He will find a wife when he is ready. And my husband, how old were you when we married?"

"You know quite well, and yes, I agree I was older than Farid."

"Exactly, Farid is young. Let him be." Ryma was a quiet and gentle woman, the soft persuasion behind her husband, but she had a steeliness of character and wisdom which held her family together with a strong bond of unity.

Neither Farid nor any of his family were aware, but his mother was ill. She had been tired for some months and had an unhealthy pallor. Her cheeks which had before been full and rounded were sunken and she had lost a lot of weight. She laughed when they commented on it and said what could they expect with her advancing years and a such troublesome family. Her response was met with gentle protest and loving concern. The end was quick. She collapsed, was taken to hospital and three days later she died with her family around her, leaving a grieving husband, two strong sons, a happily married daughter and one untamed girl as yet unmarried. One of her last thoughts was how she worried about her youngest child.

The death of his mother caused Farid deep pain. They had been very close and it had been to her that he turned in his moments of trauma, anxiety and fear and she had been the guiding factor throughout his life. He had often wished he could have discussed with her his relationship with Lucy but this would have been unacceptable and placed on her a heavy burden. He knew that on her death the pressure would be on him to marry and bring to the family home a young healthy bride. He was aware of the problems in that he worked 40 miles away from Sousse, his married sister lived in another town further south and his brother was starting out in his chosen field of engineering. It was his youngest sister who was the real problem. His mother had been a steadying influence on Fatma and now that she was gone he didn't even want to think about the scrapes in which she was likely to find herself.

His sister was a headstrong girl, far too self-opinionated for Farid's liking. He had known for some time that she was seeing that man, Hama, a person Farid knew to be completely unsuitable, but his sister had no intention of waiting for her man until she was twenty-seven like her sister. She wanted to get married and she wanted to marry Hama and refused to listen to anything said against him.

Fatma was not stupid and she realised that with her father's ill health and his growing dependence on his eldest son, her brother's approval in her choice of husband would count strongly. If she were to achieve her goal of marriage to Hama, she needed her gentle friend, Sarra, married to her brother and to be the voice of persuasion in her favour. She lost no opportunity of making certain that everywhere Farid turned, Sarra was there.

At first he had viewed the whole scenario with amusement. Sarra was often in the house when he came home and he soon realised this was at his sister's instigation. It was not that he had any particular objection to Sarra. She was about the same age as his sister, small, quite dark skinned and her gentle chocolate brown eyes followed him everywhere. He knew quite quickly without any element of self-importance that if he asked Sarra to be his wife, she would agree.

The girl was an unusual choice of friend for his strong minded sister, but to a certain extent they were well matched as they bounced off each other. Sarra somehow curbed his sister's more outrageous antics and Fatma managed to draw out of Sarra a sense of fun which would probably have never surfaced without her influence.

Fatma had often wondered about her brother, why he never had a regular girlfriend, or indeed even a stream of non-regular girlfriends. She had pushed her concerns to the back of her mind and kept to the main objective of marrying him off to her friend.

Now with the death of her mother, everything had changed. It was now essential and more than that, it needed to be as soon as possible. As the only woman in the house, Fatma could see herself being expected to take on more and more female responsibility and she had no intention of burying herself into family life. Yes she had to do something and she had to do it soon. At every family gathering, she made sure Sarra was present, each time she knew Farid would be at home, Sarra was there. In so far as propriety would permit, and she pushed that to the limit, she shoved her friend under her brother's nose at every opportunity.

Farid's amusement turned quickly to irritation and he began to ignore the two of them. It was not that he paid any attention to other women either. Fatma was now very worried. She wondered for a moment whether her brother actually liked girls at all or whether… She didn't even consider the alternative. If it were true that would be a complete disaster, not only for her, but for her whole family if it ever became known.

She banished the thought from her mind. Farid had been a normal young man and she was aware he had girlfriends a few years ago. Of course she had no idea if he was seeing anyone in Hammamet where he worked. It was quite possible. Men had so much freedom. Not for the first time, Fatma wished jealously that she had been born a boy.

One evening, a month or so after her mother died, she sat in the large living room watching her brother slyly from under her fringe. He was in a particularly foul mood. He had arrived home the day before, but had said little, eaten less and she knew he didn't sleep well because she had heard him walking around during the night.

He told her he was off work as he had hurt his leg quite badly when a ladder slipped and he had fallen. He had been hospitalised overnight and told to stay at home for the week and it meant from her point of view that he was constantly under her feet and when he did speak it was usually to criticise.

He sat reading his newspaper, his eyes darting across the page under heavy brows drawn together in a permanent frown. His mouth was tight and straight and set in an unattractive thin line. He was edgy as though he was waiting for something or someone and he had checked his watch two or three times. His cheeks moved constantly as he clenched his teeth. He ran his hand irritably through his sleek black hair. Sarra for once was elsewhere and Hakim was dozing in the armchair.

Farid checked his watch again. "I'm going out." He let the paper drop to the floor and stood up.

"Your dinner will be ready in a minute."

He swung round and glared at her. "I said I'm going out. I'll eat when I get back."

He kicked the paper on the way out and swore under his breath. Fatma looked at the clock. It was just before 9p.m. She had had enough of his moods. She waited until she heard the door close, pulled her shawl around her shoulders and followed him. He walked quickly to the corner shop to the public phone and she watched as he put the coins into the box and dialled. To her amazement his face completely changed. Gone was the miserable angry man and he was wearing the beautiful smile that she rarely saw.

She made sure he could not see her, but she watched how much money he had put into the box. This promised to be a long call. She leaned against the wall and waited. She could see he was talking and the smile never left his face. A few minutes later he put the phone down. "Well that was short and sweet," she muttered to herself. "What a waste of money."

She waited for him to move but he stayed still. She was confused. A couple of seconds later the phone rang. He grabbed it. The smile returned. He had his back to her and she edged closer to him, keeping herself tight to the wall in the shadows, just out his sight. The night air was still and she could just hear him. He was speaking in French.

Fatma gasped. The only explanation was that he was speaking to someone who didn't speak their language. The call must be to someone abroad judging by the money he had put in the box and by the expression of happiness on his face, the person at the other end was a woman.

Fatma felt sick. She slid back along the wall and ran into the house. If Farid was caught up with some woman she didn't know, all her plans would be ruined and she would end up an old maid or married to some conventional idiot where she was tied to the house and other boring wives. She had no intention of letting some foreign stranger wreck her life.

Farid came in about five minutes later. Mechanically she produced the dinner, rice, lamb stewed with large pieces of vegetable well spiced with cumin and harissa. He sat down and smiled at her. Not the beautiful smile she had seen while he had been on the phone, but a pleasant smile for his sister. He looked at her quizzically when she failed to acknowledge him.

"I'm sorry I've been such a brute. I know I've been impossible today but my leg is really hurting me. Food's good, thanks."

"It didn't seem to hurt when you hurried to the phone," she thought bitchily.

"That's OK, we all get bad days sometimes" she muttered. She noticed he cleaned his plate.

The next couple of days passed without incident, she could tell he was trying to be pleasant but he was edgy. "Like he's waiting again," she thought. Then the performance repeated itself. He kept checking the time and exactly at 9p.m. he got up and went out. He came back about fifteen minutes later.

Fatma lay in bed that night wondering what to do. "How do I deal with this whole rotten business? I need to know more." She resolved to speak with him tomorrow before he left, she needed to be alone with him, to draw him out. It was not going to be easy with her father there and also Saleem was down for the weekend.

They finished their midday meal and the time ticked on mercilessly. Farid was due to leave in the early evening. They sat and talked and Fatma grew more agitated. To her relief Hakim decided to go to bed rather than fall asleep in the chair as he usually did and Saleem went off to meet his friends.

Farid was in a reasonably affable state of mind and smiled at her over his paper.

She smiled back sweetly. "How's the leg?"

"It's fine now thanks. I'll just take it easy when I get back to work."

"How is work?"

"Good, I enjoy it. It's a hard graft sometimes. Actually the trade's dying down now so it should get easier."

That was the opening she had been waiting for and she took a deep breath.

"What are the tourists like, you know the clients?"

He looked at her in surprise, usually she showed no interest at all in his work. "They're all right for the most part. You get good ones and bad ones. You know, a necessary evil of the hotel trade."

She grinned. "What all nationalities?"

"Well, mainly English, French and German and a smattering of others."

"Any girlfriend in Hammamet?"

Farid stared at her. "No. No time for that. I'm there to work. Why d'you ask anyway?"

"No particular reason." She smiled again affectionately. "Can't I be concerned for my brother's welfare?"

"Sorry Sis, it's just you've never asked me anything like that before."

Fatma pressed on. She was not about to give up now.

"Don't you ever get to go out with any of the tourists? There must be a lot of nice looking girls around."

His eyebrows shot up and she saw he had reddened slightly. "No. I told you no. That's enough, Fatma."

She realised she had gone too far. "Sorry, I was just winding you up."

He glared at her "Then don't."

She thought quickly and changed track. "What do you think of Sarra?"

Ah, so this is where it was leading. Farid relaxed. "She's a nice enough kid, why?" As if he didn't already know the answer.

"Nothing, just asked. She's a good friend and she really fancies you."

That remark he did not expect. "Quiet," he warned softly. She said no more.

When Hakim came back from his sleep, he was pleased to see his two children chatting amicably. Too often there was friction between those two, he thought.

In the evening after Farid had gone back to Hammamet, Fatma sat herself down to think. Hakim was dozing in his chair and Saleem was still out.

"Right, what have we got," she said to no-one in particular. Hakim grunted. "Sorry Baba, I was just thinking aloud."

Hakim dozed. Fatma's sharp analytical brain clicked into action as she slowly picked through that she had seen and heard and what her brother had said.

First. She's a tourist. She doesn't live here and she doesn't speak Arabic.

Two. Why did he say the tourists are English, French and German? There are many more French tourists than any other, not many English come here. Why say English first. She must be English. Another mental tick.

Three. If she is English as I believe, she speaks good French. If it were only the basic French learned at school that wouldn't be enough. Tick

Four. Sara's twenty-two and he called her a kid. This woman with whom he is obviously besotted must be older, possibly older than him. Married perhaps? She thought hard. It was unlikely as she didn't believe Farid would get involved in anything like that.

Five. Her brother had one day off a week and he had almost always come home on that day. Almost always. A couple of weeks ago he had missed two weeks in a row without explanation and then recently he had been really miserable. The woman must have been in Tunisia for those two weeks and then gone home. Tick.

Six. How often had he been doing this? She thought back over the year. Yes, he had definitely done this before. Last April. She remembered because it had been her birthday the week before and he had apologised and said he had to work for the next two weeks. And then there was last New Year. He always came home at New Year, but again he had told them at Eid not to expect him over the two weeks around New Year because he had to work.

Seven. How long has he known her? He had known in advance she was coming at New Year so he must have met her before that. This meant he had known her for at least a year and probably longer. That worried her as it was very unlike her brother. But if he was so serious about her, why had he said nothing to any of his family.

Fatma was seriously concerned. Her brother had never kept girlfriends very long, sure he had quite a few when he was younger, but always one after the other, in fact she had quite lost track of them and that was only the ones she knew about. She had often thought it was though he had each girl on trial, as though he was looking for something and that the girl was discarded for the next while he searched for some important part that was lacking in all of them. But how long had this woman been around. Surely it couldn't be longer than a year or at the most, eighteen months, could it?

Quietly she crept out to her room and dug deep into the large chest which stood in the corner. Her old diary. She idolised her oldest brother and looked forward to his visits, she admitted partly because he usually brought her something. Never anything expensive as she knew he didn't have much money, sweets, a cheap bangle or something similar.

She was sure she would have written it down if he had missed two weeks together. She found the little book and sat down to study it. Flicking through the pages she soon realised that there was a pattern emerging. Two or three times he had been missing for two weeks, including last New Year.

A cold shiver ran down Fatma's back. This person could have been on the scene for two years or more. Of course, it was all falling into place. That was about the time he had given up on the string of casual girlfriends.

Fatma was not at all sure she wanted to draw her conclusions, but it had to be done. She needed to understand exactly what was going on if she was to do anything about it. That she certainly intended to do. No foreign bitch was going to ruin her chance of capturing Hama.

She put the diary back in the chest and went back into the living room. Her father had gone to bed. She sat at the table with her hands clasped in front of her and thought.

She must be someone older, possibly older than Farid although not by much as that would be ridiculous. I think she is English but she speaks reasonable French so is probably well educated. She comes here at least three or four times a year. She must have money to do that. She stays in Hammamet where he works. If she was in Sousse at some time over the years someone would have seen them and told me, or Dad or at least Saleem. Is he going to marry her and if not why not?

Her head was spinning. When she had first sat down to analyse her information whatever conclusion she expected to reach, it was not this one.

Saleem came in. He was obviously surprised to see her sitting alone deep in thought.

"What you up to?"

"Nothing, just thinking."

"Does it hurt?"

He looked as though he had had a beer or two. She ignored him. Their father did not approve.

"Sorry Sis, just kidding. It's just you've normally got your head in a book, if Sarra's not here. She isn't is she?"

"Yes dear brother, she's hiding under the table," she snapped and then a crazy thought entered her head. Her brother would know. The two men were very close and Saleem had worked for some months in Hammamet. Farid had got him the job.

She grinned at her brother. "That was unnecessary. I apologise. As I said I was just thinking."

He smirked at her. "What d'you want. I know that calculating little grin. You want something."

Fatma took the bull by the horns. It was now or never.

"Actually I was thinking about Farid. I am worried about him. He seems to be distracted and he doesn't seem very happy at the moment.

I wondered what was upsetting him. Does he have a girlfriend who is messing him about?"

"How the hell would I know? I'm down here and he's away up in Hammamet. Anyway if he wanted you to know, he'd tell you himself, miss nosey. Worried are we about matchmaking with Sarra and that you might get your nose put out of joint."

He picked up the paper. Fatma bit her tongue. "Seriously Saleem, I am worried about him. I'm sure he has got some girl and she's obviously making him miserable."

Saleem put down his paper. "I can see you're not going to let this lie are you? So tell me, what's eating you."

Fatma knew she had his attention and plunged in. "OK. He misses two weeks about every three months. Just before he is really happy and immediately afterwards he is miserable and moody. I'm sure he must have a tourist as a girlfriend. You know someone who comes over here regularly so he's looking forward to seeing her and then miserable when she goes home. It seems to have started a couple of years ago."

She expected her brother to make some crack about her imagination going haywire, but he didn't. His face was serious, which for him was unusual. Fatma felt exhilarated. She knew she was onto something, it was now just a matter of finding out exactly what.

Saleem's brain was spinning. "It couldn't be," he thought. "Surely not the woman he met who his brother had obviously been crazy about. The same one with the child he had said he wanted to marry. But, all that was well over a year ago and he had not spoken about her.

God Almighty, was he still seeing Lucy. He thought back over the times Farid had been home. Neither brother had ever mentioned it but he had noticed Farid no longer chucked his wallet and keys on the little table as he came into the family home, as he had always done. Now the wallet stayed in his pocket all the time as though he was determined no-one should see what was in it. A photograph perhaps? So was it Lucy, or indeed was there anyone at all or had his sister's imagination just gone into overdrive?"

Fatma watched him intently. She could see he was wrestling with something in his head.

"Saleem. Saleem. Are you listening to me? You've said nothing for ages."

Her wheedling little words cut through his thoughts and involuntarily he his mind went back to Lucy's soft melodious voice. In the comparison, his sister lost.

He decided to do what Farid had suggested. Invent, imagine, but make it plausible. He knew his sister would not be satisfied until she had some information.

"Look, there was a woman, that summer I was up in Hammamet, but it was nothing. You know Farid, the usual short run and then probably on to the next one." The beer was making his head thump and he just wanted to go to bed.

"And."

"And I've never met her again. That's it."

"You met her!"

Saleem realised immediately he had made a terrible mistake, but it was too late. His sister's eyes were sparkling and he could see her desperate for more information. This was better than she had hoped for. Saleem had met the meddling bitch.

"Well go on. What did she look like?"

"How like a woman," he thought irritably. "Not was she nice or amusing or a decent person. Just what did she look like?"

"I can't remember it was ages ago."

"Don't give me that rubbish. You're an ordinary healthy male. Of course you remember what she looked like. Tell me."

His mind started to clear. Farid had said, if you get stuck, invent. He grinned. "OK you want to know, I'll tell you.

"She was English, thirtyish I should think, stunningly beautiful with a neat figure and waist length silver blonde hair. She was intelligent, fun to be with and she had a voice as sweet as honey… and she wore Chanel No.5 perfume," he added for good measure. Actually he felt he had described Lucy pretty well, and it was the one thing his sister would not believe. He thought he had been rather clever.

He was right. Fatma was livid. "You are a real beast and how would you know what perfume she wore anyway," she yelled at him. He was playing with her. She doubted he had ever seen this mystery woman of Farid's, if there even was one. She stomped off to bed, feeling a bit silly to have been made a fool of by her brother. Saleem relaxed and congratulated himself on his quick thinking.

But Fatma was no fool. As she lay in bed she sifted through what he had said. An unpleasant smirk started to form like a slow malignant growth. Evil and boding no good. Saleem had tripped up, trying to defuse the situation with too much information which she wouldn't believe. He had almost succeeded.

Fatma recapped on what she had said to her brother. She had never mentioned the woman's nationality or that she thought she was older than Farid. Yet Saleem had confirmed her suspicions. Her brother didn't speak English either so when they met they must have spoken in French. It was as she had thought, a French speaking English woman, who was not only as old as Farid but it would appear a good bit older. Her brother said she was "stunningly beautiful" and if he thought she was thirtyish she was probably older. The smirk grew. Saleem had tried to be too clever for his own good.

What worried her was that if Saleem had thought he had got away with spinning a story she wouldn't believe, had he also lied about her appearance. But why would he? If what he said was true, then this was a hell of a lot worse than she thought. She would have to get rid of a woman who was not only well off, but beautiful and with her claws firmly embedded in Farid. That was a tricky combination.

Now all she had to do was wait until the next time. Farid always told the family when he was not going to be coming home. It would be hard to wait a couple of months but Hama would understand. He had to.

CHAPTER TWENTY-ONE

THE RING

Lucy had noticed Farid was very quiet. They sat in the dark café. The room was long and narrow and the seating laid out to represent the interior of an old aeroplane; porthole windows looked out through the fuselage to a smaller room with more luxurious seating to signify first class. Everything was designed to be intimate, from the bucket-type seats to the small decorative lamps on each table. But in the late afternoon as the sun dropped in the sky it shone in through the front of the café and Lucy could see the dark paintwork was shabby and the edges of the tables worn. The imitation leather of the seats was patchy with the odd rip.

Pictures of planes lined the walls and a propeller was suspended from the low ceiling. Part of the nose cone and cockpit of a plane took centre stage and while Lucy could see that at night with clever lighting it would probably be very attractive; the place reminded her of the exotic dancer, whose blood tingling sensuality should only be viewed at night and in the daytime should be left to sleep.

They sat opposite each other and the interior of the 'first class' was cool but the eyes which met Lucy's were not. He was troubled.

"My darling, I must tell you now I will not be able to see you very much this time and I am so sorry."

Lucy felt her stomach turn, had he tired of her already?

"My father is ill and needs constant care. This is my responsibility. I will only be able to get out sometimes in the mornings when my uncle can sit with my father."

"But why you?" she asked petulantly. She had spent longer away than usual as Alex had come down with measles over the spring half term and she had not been able to get away. It had been more than four months since she had seen him and now he was to be taken from her.

He looked sadly at her. "My sister is married and has her own problems, as she was pregnant and has just lost the baby last week. My brother is working and my younger sister is irresponsible and so tied up with herself that I could not rely on her, and to be honest my love, as I am not working right now, what excuse can I offer?"

Lucy was feeling irritable. Her period had arrived early and her back was aching. She felt fat and ugly. Had he got another girl he wanted to see instead of her?

Although she knew the answer and the reason for it, she was determined to provoke him.

"Have you said anything about me to your family?"

Farid avoided her eyes "No, only my brother. My father would not understand and I can't trouble him at the moment. Believe me, I promise I will speak to them when the time is right."

If we are not both dead first, or hell freezes over, Lucy thought uncharitably, but said nothing. She stole a quick look at his face which was clouded with disappointment but she felt he was uneasy. What was it he was not telling her?

Farid was worried about his father. He had a history of heart trouble and desperately needed another operation and he could not afford private care. He caught Lucy's concerned expression and smiled at her. The shadows disappeared. He took her hand. "Lucy, do you really think I want to be away from you?"

He held her hand tightly and she frowned. "I do understand. I am sorry I was just being selfish. I want you all to myself but I know you have the responsibility of your father. It is only right, he has cared for you during your childhood and now it is your turn to care for him."

"Lucy, I was not completely honest with you. My father is very ill, he has a heart problem."

Lucy felt very small for having doubted him. "When do you have to go?"

"I must be home before my uncle leaves at two o'clock. We can go for a walk around the market and eat at the fish restaurant."

Lucy looked happier and agreed but only on the condition she paid. She knew as he wasn't working he couldn't really afford to eat out, particularly if he was looking after his father. After their meal she suggested that he take the hired car so he could stay longer with her and come back to her more quickly. He dropped her back at the hotel and she watched as the little Renault turned right at the roundabout on its way to Sousse. Lucy spent a solitary afternoon reading and went to bed early.

The following morning she was surprised when the phone beside her bed woke her and glanced at the clock. It had just gone 7a.m.

Farid's voice was excited. "My father is feeling much better and my uncle has a day off so he has agreed to stay with him. I think he knows I have a girl because when he told me he grinned and instructed me to enjoy myself. Can I pick you up in an hour? - and bring a swimsuit and towel."

Lucy wondered what was so urgent, and scrambled to be ready when he called. She pulled on her white trousers and a brief turquoise top. She had little time to put her make-up on and made do with a flick of lipstick. She pushed her mascara along with the lipstick into her bag. She was in such a hurry she forgot her sun lotion and had to run back up the stairs to get it.

She wolfed down a couple of croissants and a coffee and ran down the long driveway to the front entrance. He was already there, leaning against the front of the little car, smoking. A couple of girls glanced at him appreciatively as they walked past, swinging their hips. Lucy knew he attracted attention wherever he went and suffered alternate pangs of pride, anxiety and sheer undiluted jealousy about what he might be getting up to when she wasn't there. Unfortunately that was the nature of the relationship but she realised if it wasn't based on trust, it might as well not exist.

"Where are we off to then?"

He grinned. "Wait and see."

He drove north for about half an hour and then down a narrow bumpy track towards the beach where they stayed alone in a secluded tiny bay. They swam, and laughed their arms entwined alone in the sea as though the rest of the world did not exist. The bay was hidden from the road by a row of trees. The sand was clean and untouched as though no feet had trodden it for many days. A row of flat rocks ran along either side separating a small part of the beach from the rest of the bay. They lay on the sand with no thoughts but of each other, and Lucy felt that nothing in her life would ever be more beautiful.

Later, Farid drove back past the Hammamet turn off and continued south. She wondered where he was going, perhaps to one of the villages, but to her surprise he continued on towards Sousse. Lucy was surprised, he didn't like going into the town and usually they stayed away from the centre, but this time he drove straight to the main square and parked the car in one of the side streets.

They walked hand in hand across the square. It was midday and the heat was intense. They sat down together, side by side on one of the few vacant seats and he offered her a cigarette. She shook her head and gazed around the huge open space which was thronging with people. The elders sat, watching the endless cabaret of passers-by, gently fanning themselves with a paper or whatever came to hand as they rested from the sun on long benches which lined sides of the square, protected from the sun by gently swaying trees.

There were tourists, and a group of about twenty students, noisy and animated, couples and older women with their bags of shopping from the nearly Medina, their loose clothing keeping out the sun's rays but their faces damp from the heat. Men sat in little huddles in the shade of the trees, chatting and smoking.

Lucy noticed one group of three old men deep in conversation. Another very old man sat with them but Lucy noticed he said little. He looked around him contented in his own company. Occasionally his deep-set black eyes fixed on a group of children or a young couple wrapped up in each other. His weathered face was heavily lined and she thought he had probably spent his younger days outdoors, a shepherd or farm worker perhaps, maybe even a soldier. She wondered at the thoughts of a life drawing to its close, hidden behind his expressionless face. What tales he would be able to tell of times long past. Was he seeing in his mind the changes which had taken place since his boyhood, the French rule of his youth, political unrest, war, the rebirth of his country or was he thinking of his own loves and dreams. Only his eyes moved, his body motionless, suspended in time as he relived his days in the warmth and beauty of his native country.

What a wonderful picture he would make, but Lucy didn't reach for her camera. To trap such a life forever on soulless paper would be an intrusion. Such scenes are best captured in the mind. The old man watched her and nodded to himself as though he had read her thoughts and to her surprise he smiled at her, then closed his eyes and dozed in the shade of his tree.

Farid had been watching her. He noticed the old man smile as he looked at her. He thought to himself, even the very old can appreciate the gentle beauty of this woman. He leaned towards her and whispered. Lucy blushed and stroked his cheek.

They walked across the square towards the Medina, his arm loosely around her waist and he dropped a furtive kiss on her nose. Public displays of affection were unacceptable. He led her into the dark belly of the Medina which was alive with people. His arm tightened around her as if to ward off unwanted attention. The narrow streets were cobbled and uneven, the ancient high walls festooned with carpets and long swathes of material, glorious peacock colours shot with gold and silver thread, but their beauty darkened by the walls that were so high they seemed to meet over the top of the narrow passageways and blocked out much of the sunlight. It was not a place she would want to be on her own as every street looked the same and she was sure she would get lost, but with Farid she felt safe.

He led her to a small square within the market area. There was a large open stall which sold meat and the carcasses hung on hooks in the cool of the interior. The gentle eyes of a cow stared lifelessly into the bustle of humanity. A little further along on the corner there was a small jewellers shop and he stopped outside. Lucy looked at the array of gold laid out in trays of deep red and royal blue velvet and marvelled at ornate filigree necklaces hung from tiny hooks.

Farid took her hand and bewildered, she followed him up the steps into the shop. The inside was lined with glass cabinets full of gold and silver jewellery on three sides and the fourth side there was a long serving area with a small room at the back. She could see a desk with a couple of machines where she assumed the jeweller made some of the jewellery. There was little room to move in the shop which was lit only by spot lights picking out the precious stones and the soft gleam of the metals in which they were set. It was magical.

An old man with a thick grey curly beard sat on a stool behind the desk, half hidden by the scales on which he weighed the objects before pricing them. He smiled as they came in and peered at Lucy as she moved from cabinet to cabinet, admiring and sometimes gasping softly at the delicate intricate beauty of the design, so different from the classical rigid settings of English jewellery. His dark eyes under heavy black brows missed nothing and he watched the young man, his arm around his girl's waist as he too watched her.

Farid led Lucy over to the old man who handed her a small heart shaped box. Lucy opened it and looked questioningly at Farid. Slowly she smiled in understanding and picked up the coin which nestled in the box. She turned it over. F+L engraved on the back.

"Now there are two," whispered Farid. Lucy put her arm around him.

"What a wonderful present. Does anyone else know about the coins?"

"I have told no one about this one. And the one you gave to me, only my friend Ali. He was there when I had it engraved. He said I was mad. I should have spent it!"

She laughed and put the box in her bag then turned towards the door but Farid held her back.

"Wait, there is something else."

The jeweller gave her a toothless grin and placed two boxes on the counter each containing a gold ring. Lucy looked up at Farid, her face a mixture of wonder and surprise.

"Which do you like?" he asked softly.

The old man beamed and reverently removed the rings from their boxes and laid them on the glass. The first was a heavy wide gold band, set deep with tiny diamonds with a lightly fluted edge to the shank. She tried it on her right hand. Farid could see it looked wrong and it was too big. She held her hand out to look and then took the ring off and handed it back to the old man. He looked at Farid.

Lucy picked up the second ring. It was a narrow gold band curved on one side, the other side curving in the opposite direction. Both sides were set with very tiny stones and the two halves met in a long oval shaped diamond in the centre. She slipped the ring onto her finger, a perfect fit.

"It's beautiful," she breathed.

Farid laughed. "That is my choice too." She looked up at him adoringly.

"My darling, somehow I knew it would fit you."

Lucy stared at him. "Oh, no. Please I couldn't. I mean the money…"

Her voice trailed off as his eyes darkened. "Please wait outside while I speak to the jeweller."

As Lucy waited she could hear the two men talking. She saw the old man weigh the ring. He said something to Farid and they appeared to be arguing but some minutes later Farid appeared, grinning broadly. He slipped the ring onto her finger, cupped her face in his hands and without caring who saw him he kissed her deeply. The old man had often seen the boy from long ago who had bought from him a red velvet box, and watched him grow to manhood. Farid had been to the shop the afternoon before and asked to see some rings.

"Do you still have your coin?" he had asked.

"Yes, this one," Farid took out little pouch out of his wallet and showed the coin to the jeweller.

"And the lady?" Farid blushed.

"The same one," he murmured, "and now I would like another coin for her engraved with the same inscription."

The jeweller cursed himself for being a sentimental old fool. He had dropped the price of the ring so much he thought he had probably made a profit, but only just. As he watched the young man place the ring on his lady's finger he knew it was worth it.

CHAPTER TWENTY-TWO

HAMA

Fatma was unhappy. Hama was late. She had been sitting in the square for a good ten minutes. It was terribly hot and although she sat in the shade she was perspiring heavily. She peered over the top of her sunglasses and watched irritably as a couple walked past her, the man's arm loosely around his partner's waist.

As she looked around the square Fatma was surprised to see her brother get out of a car. She wondered what he was doing in Sousse and so far as she knew he didn't own a car. She waited. The passenger door opened and a girl got out, a pale girl with long white blonde hair.

Fatma sank back into the shadow of the tree and gaped as her brother put his arm around the girl's shoulder and hers slid round his waist. They walked over to bench a little way from Fatma and she stared at the girl. She was not a girl, she was a woman. Her throat tightened. She had to be the one Saleem had spoken about. She wore narrow trousers and a top which Fatma thought might as well not have been there. The straps were little more than ribbons and the neckline was cut low to reveal the curve of her breast. Fatma felt frumpy in her loose trousers and simple cotton blouse.

She hoped her brother would not see her, and particularly if Hama arrived. She knew he disapproved of what he considered her wayward ways but she needn't have worried. Her brother had eyes for no one but the woman, the way he looked at her he was bewitched. She saw him lean forward and whisper in her ear. She blushed and kissed his cheek. Fatma was incredibly jealous. Why did Hama never look at her that way?

She turned and watched them walk towards the Medina, arms around each other.

"Hello gorgeous, remember me?" She turned and glared at Hama, who sat down heavily beside her. He was not a tall man, but thick set with a mop of gleaming oiled black hair. He was dark skinned, a legacy of his heritage with sharp almost black eyes. There was something menacing about Hama and if Fatma was honest with herself, she found that terribly attractive.

"You're late," she muttered irritably.

He frowned. "I had business to attend to. Well, I'm here now so what do you want to do?" Fatma caught the warning in his voice and turned her attention to him, giving him an appealing smile. She took his hand.

"I'd like to go to the Medina, and you can buy me a present for being late."

Hama grinned. "As a matter of fact, that is exactly what I intend to do. I've come into a bit of money and who better to spend it on than my girl."

Fatma glowed. "My girl," she repeated to herself and for a moment forgot her brother and his dreadful woman. She jumped up.

"Come on, let's go then!" They walked towards the Medina entrance and Fatma could see the cloud of blonde hair a little way in front of her. Each time the pair in front of her stopped, Fatma found a reason to look terribly interested in the wares laid out in front of the small shops. She didn't want to lose them but had no intention of being seen.

When they stopped outside the jewellers she eyed Lucy with malice as she pointed out things in the window to Farid.

"You've got no chance there," she smirked to herself, waiting to savour the disappointment on the insipid face. To her astonishment she saw her brother take the woman by the hand and lead her into the shop. Fatma was furious. She had never been into a jewellers shop with a man.

She pretended to look closely at the rows of beads and ornate silver necklaces.

Hama was watching her closely. He missed nothing. He followed her gaze and smiled to himself as he recognised Farid. His smile broadened at Fatma's expression as Farid took Lucy into the jewellers.

That's interesting, he thought, so young Farid is enamoured by a tourist, very enamoured if he is buying her gold. His eyes rested on Lucy for a moment, mind you, I think I would even do the same for that one.

Hama filed the information in his head. He distrusted Farid, the man was a nuisance and he had heard was asking questions about him. He needed to be careful and if he had to ditch Fatma to get her brother off his back, then so be it. There was too much at stake. He liked Fatma, she was fun to be with and was a good lay, but there were plenty of others.

"So what do you want then?" Fatma started as though she had forgotten he was there. As she turned her face to him he was surprised at the naked animosity he saw there. Hama rethought the situation. Perhaps Fatma would prove useful to him and not a hindrance. Time would tell.

She glanced back towards the jewellers. Hama took her hand.

"Oh no, my love. I'm sorry I am a traditional man. Gold is not on the agenda, not yet anyway…" he murmured in her ear to mollify her. Fatma beamed. She knew as well as he that proper jewellery was something you bought a girl if you were really serious about her, your intended.

Fatma smiled and picked up a pretty necklace and matching bracelet set in silver with tiny stones in different shades of pink. She watched as Lucy came out of shop alone and stood waiting.

Fatma turned her attention back to the jewellery. There was no price but she could see it was probably expensive. She looked at Hama expectantly. He sneered. He could run to that

Hama barked out an order to the small thin man standing next to them, his hands clasped subserviently in front of him. The man carefully took the items from the card they were pinned to and handed them to Fatma. He waited.

"They're lovely."

"How much?" The man hesitated, he knew Hama by reputation and if he was buying then it was one of the times he was awash with cash. He named his price and Fatma's eyes widened. She handed the jewellery back to the man. Hama said nothing but unrolled several notes from a wad in his pocket and handed them over.

"That's what I'll pay." The man counted the money and gave a crooked smirk. It was not what he had asked, but it was more than he expected to get. His eyes met the shrewd black gaze and he shuffled uncomfortably, aware that his customer had read his thoughts.

"Thank you, sir." He wrapped the parcel and handed it to Hama, who put his arm around Fatma and gave her the present. Her eyes shining, she leaned over and kissed his cheek, just as she had seen Lucy with Farid, she thought.

Hama stepped back angrily, he had no wish to be seen buying jewellery, even the cheaper stuff, which is why he hadn't haggled on the price. He certainly did not want to be seen by anyone who mattered getting kissed by Fatma. She realised her mistake immediately and flushed to the roots of her hair.

"Hama, I am so sorry. I was just so happy at the beautiful present, I forgot where we are."

Her face was fearful and her mouth parted appealingly. As he had pulled away the top button on her blouse had come undone and his eyes dropped to her ample bosom which fluttered in her confusion. Hama felt his body twinge in anticipation. He enjoyed screwing Fatma, she was a willing partner and would do pretty well anything he asked of her, although there were one or two little tricks she had yet to experience. As Hama admitted to himself, he had some more unusual requirements from time to time. He ran his tongue over his lips. He looked at his watch, he had time and he could use the room above the bakery again. It wasn't far. Hama took Fatma's hand and stroked the palm. He was gratified to feel her tremble.

"Come, we have better things to do than stand here."

He started walking further into the Medina but Fatma stood rooted to the spot as her brother came out of the jewellers, and she watched as he slipped the ring on Lucy's finger. Hama turned and followed her gaze as Farid kissed her full on the lips. He saw Fatma's face burning in anger. He licked his thick lips in anticipation. From anger followed passion.

He watched as Farid and Lucy walked away from them, their arms around each other. He watched Farid's arms close around her slim waist. His eyes followed the woman. She was certainly a stunner. His eyes moved down her body and he felt a tingle of anticipation. He wondered if she too would be a willing partner and his thoughts strayed to what he would like to do to her.

Fatma was livid, she could see her plans evaporating. She followed Hama into the bakery and up the back stairs. As the door closed behind them he threw her onto the bed and pulled off her trousers. He tore at her blouse. A button popped off and she lay there panting. He lay down beside her and closed his eyes. In his mind he saw the pale skin and soft blonde hair of the unknown tourist. He rubbed his face against her breasts and sucked until she groaned with pleasure. He stroked the soft skin between her thighs and moved his hand across her until he brought her gasping to climax. Smiling to himself, he mounted her. Hama felt slim white thighs tighten around him and he came in a haze of pleasure. As he opened his eyes, he looked into Fatma's dark face glistening with sweat and her black hair spread out in a tangled mass over the pillow.

Angrily he gave her a shove and turned away. He lit a cigarette and sat with his back to her as he puffed on the foul smelling tobacco he favoured. His mind had deceived him. He looked back at Fatma and clenched his teeth.

She lay quietly and said nothing. She had done nothing wrong and he had shown a tenderness he had never done before. Now he seemed distant and angry. Sometime later he seemed to remember she was there. He turned back, his face inches from hers. His lips were curled back over his teeth in a strange cold smile. She shivered.

He bent down, picked up his tie up off the floor and wrapped it tightly around her wrists and anchored her to the bedstead. Her eyes widened in surprise. He tweaked her nipples and she flinched. He nipped her breast with his teeth and flipped the struggling girl roughly onto her belly lifting her up by her hips as he positioned himself behind her. She had deceived him and now she would learn some of his more intimate desires. With his fat hands clamped tightly around her he forced himself into her bottom. Fatma screamed in agony and he laughed. He pushed her head into the pillow to silence her so she could hardly breathe, his enjoyment increasing as she writhed under him, desperate to free herself from the terrible pain. He continued to dig himself into her until finally he came with an animal grunt and a crude expletive, collapsing on top of her.

Half an hour later the pair came back down the stairs. The baker watched as Fatma held her blouse closely round her chest. She looked terrified, her hair was a mess, her face streaked with tears and her eyes wide in her flushed face. He stared at Hama, who threw a note onto the glass counter. The baker stuffed it into his pocket.

The baker watched him as he strode out of the shop. He noticed there was blood on Fatma's trousers. The baker shook his head.

"That is one evil man," he muttered to no one in particular.

CHAPTER TWENTY-THREE

THE DILEMMA

The plane landed mid-afternoon so Lucy decided to get the train home rather than a taxi. She had hoped it would be raining to match her mood, but for once the sky was a brilliant clear blue and the sun shone. She thought the airport looked cold and sterile as the characterless buildings and bare trees flashed past, she felt as though she was returning to her cell. No, that's not fair she reasoned. I love my little house with its big bright kitchen, comfy sitting room with soft leather seats, my pictures and family photos. She spent the evening watching television until she went to her bed. She couldn't sleep and the tears which trickled down her face seemed endless.

Two months later, Lucy thought she had picked up a bug. She felt sick, she ached and she was irritable. She burst into tears after shouting at Alex over nothing. He disappeared next door to his friend's house as he put it, to get some peace. As she cradled her tea, her feet tucked up under her on the sofa, she studied the photos. There were none of Farid. She wanted no questions about her other life, as she saw it. Those photos she kept in her bedroom.

She smiled at her mum and dad resplendent in evening wear, side by side for the formal photo. Her mother's soft smile, so like her own, shining out of the oval face and her grey eyes hidden by the huge unflattering round glasses she always wore. Her classic cream chiffon dress set off her enviable slim figure. Her father was resplendent in his dinner jacket grinning from ear to ear, his white hair slicked neatly back in the traditional short back and sides. He had made one feeble attempt to "get with it", as he had said to his wife. He grew his hair and stopped using grease. The result was a thick thatch of untamed white hair which stuck out over his ears. He endured his wife's giggles for a few months and then to her relief abandoned the experiment and went back to simply being himself. They must have been in their late forties when the photograph was taken. Her mother looked years younger and not for the first time Lucy thanked her silently for her inherited genes.

Her eyes drifted to the photograph of herself and Peter with Alex as a baby. She suddenly felt ashamed. She had not long come from the embrace of her lover and a now she was looking into her late husband's honest happy face. It seemed a lifetime since his death, as though she had slipped unnoticed from one existence into another and morphed into a different person.

She thought of her comfortable settled married life with a loving husband and small child, a pretty home, friends and family. Now she was a single mum with a young Arab lover and a growing fatherless boy. Her own mother had died two years ago and whilst it was a shock it was not altogether unexpected. She had always been fragile and Lucy felt guilty that she had not been able to remarry and present her very conventional Mum with another Peter. She knew her mother worried about her daughter and, of course, knew nothing of Farid. Lucy had kept her relationship away from her parents, which she knew would have upset both of them.

Her father, the ever present rock in her life, had remarried a little over a year later. He was not designed to live alone, as her mother told her before she died. Not that he thought he needed looking after (which he did) but that he needed someone to look after. Then he found Emily, a plump little Welsh woman, quite a bit younger than him, but with short iron grey permed hair and an infectious laugh. Lucy had been horrified to begin with. Shortly after the wedding they moved to a bungalow just inside the Welsh border. Her stepmother had longed to return to the Welsh countryside where she had been born and her father had of course obliged her by selling the house in which Lucy had grown up, and moved to Wales.

She remembered the conversation they had just before his marriage and she had gaily informed him, through gritted teeth, that she wished him every happiness. He however knew his daughter well enough to see through the façade. Her initial reaction to her stepmother was fairly normal in the circumstances. Distrust. Her father just asked her to give his new wife a chance and recently she had been forced to admit both to her father and herself that she had been wrong.

They were indeed good for each other. Emily mothered, cooked cleaned and cared for him. He fussed over her and bought her little gifts for which she scolded him and told him not to waste his money, but beamed with happiness. She learned from her father that Emily had endured a violent marriage with a husband who drank most of his money, but it had taken her twenty years and a lot of courage before she had taken the plunge and divorced her husband. She had remained single and raised her son alone, who now lived in America with his own wife and daughter.

If Lucy was completely honest, she just missed her Dad. There was however the truth which many children will not admit to anyone, often not even themselves. An element of relief that she would not have to restructure her own life and that of her son around caring for an aged, lonely and increasingly infirm parent. She would always remember her Dad as he was in the photograph. Bright, happy and forever cracking bad jokes. She had no doubt Emily would look after him. He had his truculent moods and he sulked, but he was essentially a kind loving man. Emily could cope with the moods. She ignored him, her back turned and her short grey curls bristling. Shortly afterwards he would creep up behind her and tickle her. All would be forgotten. But her dad wasn't there. She couldn't just hop in the car and be with him in half an hour. Yes, she missed him.

She had a little cry which made her feel a bit better, pulled herself back from her melancholy and switched on the television. She squirmed uncomfortably. Her tummy had been playing up all week which was unusual. She rarely suffered from such inconveniences. Like many people she found that in the first couple of days of her holiday her stomach always felt a bit light as she adjusted to the different food and the heat, but that was different. She had long ago learned what to avoid, in particular, for the first few days, the extra strong, spicy harissa which she adored, but an excess of which had kept her ingloriously glued to the toilet on one of her earlier visits. Her stomach churned at the thought of it and she rushed to the loo.

"I must have picked up a bug," she confided to Ruby over coffee, "but it seems to come and go." Ruby clucked over her and insisted she go to the doctor if it didn't get better, but Lucy recovered a couple of days later and hoped the bug had run its course.

Lucy woke up on the Monday morning and was violently sick. She knew she had been overdoing it at work. They were very busy and Ruby unloaded a lot of her own work onto Lucy as there was no way she could cope and the firm couldn't afford another senior staff member at the moment. Lucy called in sick and went to bed with an insipid drink of warm milk mixed with water.

"Forget the pills," her mother used to say. "A nice warm drink and give the tum a rest for twenty-four hours. If it clears up all well and good. If not give it an extra day and if it doesn't get better get yourself to the doctor." Mum was, as usual, right. By the next day she felt a bit better and dragged herself into work.

"I don't have time to get sick," she joked with Ruby. But the sickness returned and this time left her feeling weak. As she walked in through her front door after work, she collapsed on the sofa and burst into tears.

It was Wednesday and she waited for Farid to call. It had become a ritual, every Wednesday and Sunday as near to 9p.m. as he could manage. If he was at work, he was sometimes late, as he had to find a moment when he could get to the phone, but she always waited. She would talk for a minute and then called him back. She knew his money was limited and tried to ignore her own huge phone bill. It was worth every penny to hear his voice telling her how much he missed and loved her.

She sat and waited. He was fifteen minutes late. "My darling, I am late. I am so sorry." She scolded him playfully and her spirit soared. "A client would not stop talking to me," he joked, " I think she wants to make love with me."

Lucy burst into tears and sobbed down the phone "You have forgotten me already."

Farid was astonished, he was only teasing her. "I could never forget you, I love you so much, always remember I waited many years for you. Nothing will ever change. My Lucy, there will never be anyone else."

Lucy blew her nose and snuffled down the phone. "I haven't been well, forgive me."

"You are not well, you must see your doctor. I cannot have my darling crying." The phone went dead.

Lucy waited a five minutes to collect herself before calling him back.

"My love, I thought you would not call me."

She could tell he was unhappy as he thought he had upset her. She reassured him and lied that someone had called her so she could not return his call immediately. Her voice was husky.

"Oh my love, I want to be with you so much. My life is dead without you. Can you feel me kissing you?" She closed her eyes and remembered his kisses.

"Lucy, we will be together at New Year. I will make love to you so that you will never leave me again. You have made the reservation?"

"I will do it tomorrow, and yes I will stay at your hotel." She answered the unasked question.

The last time she had again stayed in the hotel where he worked and when he could he would creep upstairs to her room where they made hurried, urgent love. If he was caught, it would be instant dismissal. Relations between staff and clients was absolutely forbidden. They used to meet at Cathy's café bar an hour or so before or after his shift depending whether he was working nights or days. When she stayed in his hotel it meant they could at least make love in a bed instead of on the beach or some other hidden place, but she hated the night work.

Farid explained to her that work in the tourist industry was fiercely contested. The industry was relatively new and to keep his job he had to work the hours he was told, within reason. "I promise you I will offer to work at night as much as I can before you come back, then I can ask for two weeks of day work when you are here again and we can spend all our time together. You must be here for the New Year, so we can celebrate the start of another wonderful year together."

"I hope next year I can come for longer. I have been promoted at work and I have an extra two weeks' holiday. I must spend them with you." He kissed her loudly over the phone.

"You must spend your life with me," he whispered, his voice like liquid honey and her skin tingled. Afterwards she made herself a cup of tea, took a sip and was sick. She called Ruby in the morning and told her she was going to the doctor as she didn't seem able to shake off the bug.

The doctor was sympathetic and listened intently. "I think you may just be a bit run down, but I am going to make you an appointment at the hospital. Just routine, to make sure it's nothing," he added seeing her worried face.

Lucy sat in the waiting room. She was due for an X-ray and the young nurse took some details from her.

"Age? General health?" Question, answer, Question answer. Lucy just wished the whole thing was over so she could go home. She was feeling sick again.

"Any chance you might be pregnant?"

"No," Lucy responded automatically but her world stopped turning. She thought frantically. When was her last period? She remembered, it finished about a week before her holiday, she recalled being grateful her visitor would not muscle in on her time with Farid.

She stood up, rushed past the astonished nurse and threw up in the toilet. She wiped her face on the paper towel and gazed long and hard into the mirror. She noticed for the first time the shadows under her eyes and down the sides of her nose. She felt her breasts, they were tender. She slammed her hand against the wall. Of course she had not had a period since she'd been back. Of course she had taken precautions. She thought hard and admitted to herself that she had forgotten once, the night on the beach… Of course, it would explain everything – the sickness, tiredness and the moods.

"Dear Christ," she stormed at the mirror. "I am unmarried with a good job and a young son to care for. I am pregnant by a man years younger than me who lives 1,000 miles away. It might as well be a million miles, because that is how far his life is from mine in England. What the hell am I going to do?"

She couldn't relate to the face in the mirror, which mocked her like some alien being and she wanted to put her fist through it. Even in her shock Lucy realised that her life could not carry on in the same way. Everything had changed. She walked slowly back to the waiting room and sat down, oblivious to the curious stares of the other patients.

"Mrs Collins?"

Lucy took a deep breath. "Look, there is a possibility I might be pregnant." The nurse smiled widely.

"Don't worry. I'll arrange a scan. You don't want to have an X-ray if there is any chance of pregnancy. I'll need a sample please." Lucy nodded.

She waited for what seemed a lifetime until her name was called. She followed another nurse to the small side room, a lamb to the slaughter. As she sat on the hard chair, she prayed. The trouble was she wasn't absolutely sure what she was praying for. The possibility that she was carrying Farid's child horrified and excited her at the same time, and her memory recalled the teenage boy she had first known and she smiled to herself. Would her child look like that?

Alice had said she would have a boy. The thought entered her head like a spear. She sat bolt upright. "Oh dear god, it's happened!" she spoke out loud.

"Mrs Collins? Are you all right?"

"It's nothing, I'm sorry." She listened to her own heart beating frantically. The nurse looked at her out of the corner of her eye.

She must think I'm crazy, thought Lucy. A young doctor came into the room, and Lucy thought he should still be in school. He studied her notes, smiling at her. "Yes, Mrs Collins, congratulations, I can confirm that you are indeed pregnant."

Her stomach suitably prepared, the little machine moved across her stomach, backwards and forwards guided by the young doctor as he watched the monitor. Lucy fixed her eyes on his gleaming white coat.

"They're coming to take me away away, they're coming to take me away." Lucy giggled.

The man smiled indulgently at her, the practised smile of a doctor.

"Ah, here we are." He grinned broadly at Lucy. "Well Mrs Collins. You are about eleven weeks pregnant. Have you got any other children?"

Lucy nodded again. He waited. "Yes, I have a boy."

"That's nice. From your notes, I take it this wasn't planned. Well, your husband will be thrilled," he added somewhat naively.

"I doubt it, he's dead."

The nurse stared intently at something on the wall and the young doctor coughed. "Oh, I do apologise, I am so sorry. When did this happen?"

"Quite a few years ago," said Lucy relentlessly, looking him straight in the eyes.

"Ah. Ah, I see, my apologies." Before he could dig himself in any deeper, the young man left the room, muttering he'd be back in a moment.

Lucy smiled at the nurse. The nurse grinned back. "I suppose I should say sorry to him, that was unkind."

The nurse's eyes danced in amusement.

"Don't you dare. He's won't be so quick to make assumptions in future!"

Lucy drove home, the scan photograph beside her. She glanced down at it and narrowly missed a bus pulling out. Ignoring the driver's abuse, she slowed down and pulled into her driveway, left the car where it was and forgot to lock it. She sat curled up on the settee, her thoughts in chaos. "A baby, what on earth am I going to do with a baby! I'm approaching middle age, I've got a job, an organised comfortable life, a son to consider, and a young lover, who doesn't know he's going to be a father," she added as an afterthought.

Alex. She thought of her firstborn with her own pale skin and his dad's blue eyes.

Her hands rubbed her stomach gently, closed her eyes and lay back on the sofa.

"Mum, oh Mum, where are you when I need you", but Mum had gone. Self-pity crept up. She indulged herself in half an hour's gentle sobbing and a few more cups of tea.

"You have to make this journey alone. There are choices, in almost everything there are choices." Alice's voice echoed through her head.

She couldn't even talk to her friend. Dear wise Alice. Henry had died and Alice had gone to Australia to live near her daughter. They met to say a tearful goodbye and Alice reminded her never to forget what she had told her on the holiday. "There is what is considered right, acceptable and sensible, but if it is not going to make you happy, don't make that choice, it's the easy way out. Always follow your own heart; only then will you be truly happy."

They spoke regularly on the phone, but the last time she called, Alice's daughter had answered. Alice had suffered a stroke and wasn't able to talk to her. She sounded terribly upset and Lucy learned that the old lady was not likely to recover and had never really got over Henry's death. She was just waiting to join him.

One half of her brain asked her why didn't she feel happy. She was carrying the child of the man she loved. The other half taunted her. "You have a choice." Everything could be as it was before. A choice. She put both hands on her tummy, fingers spread and thumbs upwards in the way pregnant women have done since life began.

She started to doze and her face felt hot and the light was very bright, like the sun. As she drifted towards sleep she saw a boy with gleaming black hair and jewel bright eyes, his face illuminated by a beautiful smile. She smiled back. As he walked towards her he became Farid. He put his arm round her shoulder and kissed her lips. Then he bent over her and very gently kissed the head of the sleeping child cradled in her lap.

Lucy opened her eyes and smiled. A choice? Yes, but no longer hers, the child's father had just made that choice. There was of course another, a much harder one, what of the father himself and that choice only she could make.

Lucy said nothing to anyone about her pregnancy. This responsibility she intended to carry alone for as long as she could and she decided it was one could never ask Farid to share. To go to him with a child, outside marriage would be impossible. To marry him would be equally as impossible. His life was to include a young

Tunisian girl half her age who would present him with a clutch of happy healthy children who would be raised in the confines of a loving Muslim household. With a grim smile she imagined herself married to Farid, seated with his family, nearer to his mother's age than his own, his father expressionless. His brother, sisters, aunts, uncles and their families all traditionally present to see the newborn and to sneak a glance at the middle-aged Englishwoman who had ruined Hakim's son's life, and on a mat in the middle of the floor, a tiny honey coloured infant.

She had no place in his family, she was completely different from them in every way possible and she didn't even speak a word of their language. Her decision was made. Farid would never know. She would not go to Tunisia for the New Year. How could she? Her pregnancy would be obvious, if not with her clothes on, then certainly without them.

Lucy wrestled with the idea of simply never seeing him again. This she couldn't bear. She decided to plead an unavoidable family commitment at New Year and that she would need to come earlier instead. To see him just one more time and then disappear out of his life forever. She would change her phone number and if he called work she wouldn't be there any more so it wouldn't matter.

She remembered with a start that she had given him M's phone number when they were both there together. Just in case. She reasoned he had probably lost it. All she had to do was change her home phone number and let him think she had moved when she marked his letters as gone away. Let him just think she had dropped off the face of earth. It was actually so easy. He had no other way of finding her. He would never come to England. He couldn't afford it and she reasoned that he probably wouldn't be able to get a visa. No, he would never be able to search for her, even if he wanted to.

Lucy lay back on the sofa and put her feet up, her hands resting on her stomach. She studied the Tunisian pictures of a world so different from her own. Looking down at her still flat stomach, she made a promise to the living being inside her.

"I will raise you myself and love you enough for both of us. I will never remarry. No other man will ever be able to call you his son. I will teach you as much of your heritage as I can. But I swear to you my son, when you are a young man and you can understand, I will take you there so you can see for yourself the country where we could all have been happy, had the world we live in been more tolerant and the circumstances different. One day perhaps you may meet your father and then the choice of what to do will be his and yours to make."

The bouts of sickness eased as she entered the second trimester. She gave her notice in at work. She had enough in the bank, Peter's money had been well invested. She didn't spend much on herself and vowed she would live for her sons. She never doubted for an instant that her unborn child would be a boy.

She decided to tell Jackie. She was feeling really down and really wanted to speak with her old friend, but Jackie and Ewan had moved from the village and bought a bigger house in town many miles away after Ewan got a job offer; as he put it, "I couldn't turn down." She hadn't seen her very often but now she really needed someone to talk to.

As soon as she called, Jackie knew something was wrong, but when Lucy told her she was horrified. She knew Lucy had gone back to Tunisia and met a man there, but she never dreamed it was the boy from the café so many years before. That Lucy had never mentioned until now.

Jackie screamed at her. "You are totally crazy. He's just a kid, and how the hell did you meet up with him again?" Lucy ignored part of the question.

"Don't be bloody stupid. He was a kid then. He's a man now."

"A very young man," retorted Jackie "And you are a good bit older. Lucy what are you going to do? How the hell did you get pregnant?"

"Do you want me to draw you a picture?" Lucy snapped.

"You know perfectly well what I mean. You take precautions, don't you? You have haven't you?"

"Of course, but as you well know there is a chance they don't always work, and I was unlucky."

"You can't have a child like that. Lucy, you must be crazy. No one need even know if you have an abortion. You know you were told after Alex there could be complications and at your age..."

"Shut up, Jackie, I'm not exactly fifty yet!" Jackie ignored her.

"What are you going to do about work? Lucy, for God's sake think. You can't go through with this. Does he know?"

"No, he does not, and he never will."

The phone went silent, then she heard Jackie sigh. "You mean you're going to have the baby and never tell the man that he has a child? Lucy, your baby will grow up. He or she will want to know about their father, you know that."

"Of course. I've got years to think about how to deal with that."

That was of course the one thing which really troubled her. Did she have the right to deny a child a father and a father his child?

"Look, Jackie, what this all boils down to is this. Are you with me, or do you want nothing to do with me?"

"You fool, you're my friend, whatever madcap scrapes you get yourself into. Of course - just let me know what you need or what you want me to do, so long as it doesn't involve the boy."

Lucy ignored the jibe. "I'm not asking you for anything. Just be there, I think I'm going to need someone to talk to over the next few months."

"You know I always will be."

Lucy hugged the cushion. At least she had one real friend in the midst of the mess she had created.

Ruby was upset.

"What d'you mean you're leaving! You can't. Why? What am I going to do without you? Is this an April Fool or something?"

"Ruby, it's autumn not spring."

"Lucy, you are kidding. You're not really leaving, are you?"

Ruby tried to convince her to stay. She had no idea Lucy was pregnant and Lucy made the excuse she wanted to see more of Alex and have a chance to visit her Dad. Ruby knew her financial situation was sound and Lucy told her she just wanted a break. Eventually, Ruby had no option but to accept her resignation but made it plain her job was open for her. Privately she thought Lucy was being a bit silly and would get so bored she's be back within the year.

And then of course there was M. M, who knew her better than anyone and with Jackie was the only person she felt she could really trust.

When M's parents died she inherited a sizeable sum and their beautiful Lincolnshire cottage. She left work and moved to the country where she quickly became part of the local community and involved herself happily in village life. She was delighted when Lucy asked if she could stay for a week. Alex was spending the half-term holiday with her father and Emily and Lucy did not want to be alone with her thoughts.

M had gone with her on that momentous holiday when her commitment to Farid had been made but she didn't know Lucy had met him years before. Lucy knew she did not approve of Farid, in fact she didn't approve of anything at all about him! She had an inbuilt distrust of foreigners who didn't speak English. She herself spoke not a word of any other language and saw absolutely no reason to learn any. She had no time for the "Latin look" as she put it. "Arab," Lucy had said.

"Same difference," said M disparagingly.

Most of all however she disapproved of Lucy paying for anything when she was with Farid. Lucy explained she earned more in one month than he did in six and as they needed to stay in the tourist zones some of the time, she had to pay.

"His problem," M said. M's men-friends paid for her company.

The two women sat curled up on the huge old sofa in M's four hundred-year-old cottage.

"You are what?"

"You heard. I'm pregnant."

"I never knew you were seeing anyone."

"Well, I'm not really seeing anyone, at least now how you would usually think of it."

M grinned. "Immaculate conception was it?" Lucy pulled a face.

M poured herself a glass of wine. Lucy declined.

"God, you really are pregnant, aren't you?" She lifted the glass to her lips and regarded Lucy over the rim.

Suddenly she slammed the glass down on the table. "Oh you frigging lunatic. Please tell me it's not his, that…" Her voice tailed off.

"Arab," Lucy finished and nodded.

"Lu, you bloody stupid… Twit. How long, I mean how far gone are you?"

"Thirteen weeks."

"Thank heavens, you've still got time."

"There is no way I am having an abortion."

Her quiet determination surprised M. "Lucy, you can't have the baby. Who's going to support it? - he can't," she snorted.

"M don't be a bitch. You know perfectly well I don't need his money, or anyone else's for that matter."

"Lucy, think about this. What is your Dad going to say? What about Alex, and Peter's family?

"M with respect I think Peter's family, however nice they are, are in my past. They are Alex's grandparents but that is all. I can't let their feelings influence this. Alex won't suffer, in fact he will have the brother, or sister he's always wanted," she added quickly.

"And your Dad?"

Lucy smiled to herself. "Believe it or not, my Dad will be fine with it. I'm not sure my mum would have been, but Dad, yes."

"And his, the boy's family?"

Lucy looked at her friend, her green eyes strangely cold. "They won't know."

M stayed silent for a moment. She took the other woman's hand and squeezed it.

"Yes, I think you're right. We can deal with this by ourselves." Lucy hugged her, she had not missed the word "we".

Lucy changed the subject and then chatted about M's involvement with the cricket club, the village hall committee and her cake stall at the Christmas fair.

Inevitable however the conversation came back to Lucy.

M went out to the kitchen after dinner, came back and handed Lucy a steaming cup of coffee.

"Sorry, can you have coffee?"

Lucy laughed, "Of course I can."

"Lucy, I've never had any children and as you know I don't feel particularly comfortable with them, but there is nothing wrong with my maths. If you're thirteen weeks gone, then by New Year when you go back, you are going to be showing, particularly if you… You know get it together with him."

Lucy smiled. "I'm not going at new year. I've already told him I can't."

"What then?"

"Soon."

"Okay, but then you would normally go back about four months after that and by then you'll be like a tank."

"Thanks for that!"

"You know what I mean," M laughed in spite of herself.

"Look M, when I said his family won't know, I should have said he and his family. I mean none of them will ever know."

M thought hard. She neither liked nor approved of Farid, but she knew how much he meant to Lucy and uncomfortably she felt it was mutual between them. She had seen them together and if ever two people were in love, then these two were, despite the obvious differences between them. She had hoped it was a passing whim but as the years passed, she was forced to admit it was more than that. She watched Lucy's pale face, her green eyes brimming with tears.

"Oh Lucy, do you mean you'll go next time and then never go back after that?"

"I can't, can I? If I did it would tear me apart and for him, it would mean complete disaster. Things aren't the same over there as they are here and a baby changes everything."

"So you'll never go back?"

"Yes, but when the baby is a young man. That country is after all half his heritage. I owe him that."

Lucy snuffled and showed every sign of dissolving into tears. M hated tears, her own or anyone else's. She had always been good at making Lucy laugh and now was certainly the time to try.

She sat on the edge of her seat and pulled her glasses down to the end of her nose and surveyed Lucy over the top of the rims. She pulled the end of her nose and scratched her head. Lucy watched her. M crossed her arms in front of her, frowned and pursed her lips.

"Well, well, well. What have we here? I shall have to find you a nice rich English speaking man. Someone who can support you and the infant. No more of this frog talk which I can't understand. For all I know you could have been telling him I'm an old toad!" Lucy sniffed and smiled weakly.

"Let's see who can we write to."

Lucy looked puzzled.

"Let's sit down and make a list." She patted the seat beside her. Lucy stood up and flopped down next to her. "What are you talking about?"

"First, Clint Eastwood. He's wealthy." Lucy smiled. She realised what M was doing and silently thanked her for it. "No, on second thoughts going bald and too old."

"Agreed," said Lucy.

M frowned. "Who do you fancy then?"

Lucy smiled. "Gregory Peck!"

M let out a hoot of laughter. "Lucy, have you no shame. Now you say you fancy a man old enough to be your father!"

"That's as maybe but I must admit my dear mother, who was not prone to making such comments about men always said he could put his slippers under her bed any day. Did you see him in *Roman Holiday* and *The Guns of Navarone*? God, anyone in their right mind would fall for him."

M took off her glasses and peered through them in mock disapproval. "Lucy. I am trying to be sensible, please concentrate."

"Yes Ma'am. What about Sean Connery? He's certainly well off, but I hate golf."

"Connery. Well I suppose you could call him English speaking."

Lucy wrinkled her nose. "No, on second thoughts, although I must say I do fancy him but I think he's married anyway."

"Ah," said M, "I was forgetting you like the young ones. Sorry!" Lucy stuck her tongue out.

"I have just the man. Harrison Ford."

"Yeah, put him at the top of the list!"

M ran through her hit list and wrote each one down, with her comments and Lucy's beside the names.

"M."

"Yup"

"There's one small problem. If you are going to write to all these people to try and raffle off my baby and I, have you got any addresses?"

"Ah," said M and put her pen down. "That is a small problem."

She looked at Lucy. "Lucy, I have to ask you this. Weren't you on something, you know?"

"Yes, I've taken the pill but I may have forgotten once, but it's only 95% safe apparently."

M glared at her. "Well instead of going at it like bloody rabbits, perhaps you should have stopped at 94!"

Lucy choked. "M, behave."

"No girl, I think I should be saying that to you. Why didn't he use a thingummy?"

"He hates them, so do I. Whenever I see one I tend to dissolve into hysterical laughter."

M laughed. "They're not that funny."

"They are, ever since some bloke told me years ago it was like having a bath with your wellies on. And believe me laughing at the wrong time tends to defeat the object of wearing one in the first place."

M let out a hoot. "I love it! Turns the whole business into a bit of a flop, you mean."

Lucy knew she had come to the right place. M had a way of making even the worst problems seem less dreadful.

"Seriously though, I thought I might take a job, only part time, you know, school dinners or even take in home typing or become an Avon lady."

M regarded her friend seriously. "I think you'd make a very good Avon lady, or you could do those Tupperware parties, or even Ann Summers," she added mischievously.

Lucy laughed. "I can't see myself flogging Tupperware and I don't think I'd have the courage to sell Ann Summers stuff. Maybe ten years ago, but certainly not now."

M poured herself another glass of wine. Lucy had a lemonade and relaxed for the first time that day.

M regarded her friend intently. "Lu, when you were talking about the baby you called it 'him'. Why did you do that?"

Lucy was caught completely off balance. "Did I?" Her smile was wide and transparently artificial.

"You know you did."

"The hospital must have told me."

"Lucy, tell me the truth. There are bits of this that don't make sense and they involve him."

Only Jackie knew the whole truth but she was hundreds of miles away. Dear Alice would never be able to tell.

M poured another glass of wine and waited, her bare feet curled up under her. She could see the battle going on in Lucy's head, the uncertainty was pathetic, like a child who isn't sure whether to lie about cutting the heads of the neighbour's daffodils and possibly get found out, or to tell the truth and face the likely consequences. She knew if she put pressure on Lucy she would say nothing but if she waited Lucy would find a way to wriggle out.

"Lucy, there's a lot obviously worrying you; have you talked it over with anyone?"

"Only my next door neighbour, who moved away. We were very close at one time and I did speak to her on the phone."

"But you can't tell me," M felt hurt.

"M, she was there when the whole thing started."

"When was that?"

Lucy stared at her. "When I was twenty-six," she said slowly

M hesitated. "Twenty-six. What, before you even met Peter?"

"Yes, the year before."

"But Lucy, that's impossible. How can that involve Farid? - he would have been at school."

"You think I don't know that?"

"Come on, Lucy, that's not what I meant and you know it. He could only have been a kid, so what's this all about. How can it involve him?" Lucy said nothing.

"How long have we known each other?"

"Donkey's years."

"Lucy, be serious. You know, I met you at work before you met Peter. And you've never said a word."

"Sorry. Look, M, it was the thing fantasy is made of and you know what you're like about that."

M shrugged. "Well, sometimes truth is stranger than fiction, as they say."

Lucy looked over at M curled up on the chair, her cat on her lap. Two pairs of eyes focused on her.

"Okay, are you sitting comfortably? Then I'll begin!"

She told M about the holiday with Jackie, about the strange youth and what he had said, his kiss on her cheek and the coin she'd given him.

M stared at her silently. Finally, she smiled. "That's weird."

Lucy smiled back, "That's what Jackie said."

She told her about the experience she'd had the first night back from that holiday. She told her about Alice's predictions of Peter's death, the man in the shadows and the boy child she would have. She told her about the dream she herself had when she found out she was pregnant, about the boy with the football becoming Farid the man, kissing her and their child. "So you see, M, whether or not to have the child is not my choice. His father made that decision."

"Bloody hell, Lucy. Am I reading this right? Are you saying that you'd met Farid before and that he was the same boy?"

Lucy nodded.

"And you said absolutely nothing?"

"Would you have believed me?"

M thought for a second "Probably not, I'd have recommended a shrink."

"Exactly, I know I would if anyone had told me the same thing."

This was far beyond anything M had imagined. "And you've decided not to tell him, but you're going back, effectively to say goodbye, only he won't know that."

"Yes. I waited for my boy to become a man, I have lived every minute of the years I have been with him and I have never been so happy in my life. Now I will simply walk away and not look for what I have lost, just as Alice predicted, but I shall hold dear the rest of her prediction, that one day I will be happy again. In the meantime, I've got my memories and my photos."

"Do you resent the baby?"

M's perception surprised her.

Lucy picked her words carefully. "To start with yes, because he has cost me my love. But now I know that every time I look at him, I will see his father and I will love him the more for it."

"What will you call him?"

"Farid told me one of his family names is Ben. I asked him at the time where the Ben came from and he said it was from his mother's side. So I will call him Ben, for his father and grandmother he will never know."

"You know he'll ask about his father. Every time he looks in the mirror when he's older he will see how different he is from Alex."

"I've got plenty of time to think on that one."

"Look, M there could be one other small problem, Farid may still have your phone number. He might just get someone to call you if he can't get through to me. He knows you don't speak French, so whoever does call will speak English. If you ever get that call, I'll write something down so you can read it to him."

"I don't like the idea."

"Neither do I particularly but I can't think of anything else. If I write down what to say, you can simply read what I've written and you won't need to tell lies or say anything else."

M nodded. "Okay, let's hope it never comes to that." But she had a dreadful feeling it would.

M could see the conversation turning maudlin and she could see Lucy was tired, but she wanted to make sure her friend was not going to spend the night crying.

Theatrically she swivelled her upper body to face Lucy.

"Who's got the film rights to *The Lucy Collins Story*?"

"Idiot," Lucy said affectionately.

She watched as M stood up and executed a very regency mock curtsey. She spread her arms, palms to the ceiling and stuck her nose in the air with her eyes shut in an exaggerated gesture. Lucy giggled.

"To sleep, perchance to dream. Come on girl, time we both turned in."

For the following weeks, Lucy did not know which way to turn. She reasoned with herself the course of action she was about to take was the only possible one. But as she lay in her bed and tried to find sleep, in her subconscious mind she could sense the heat of him close to her, feel his arm loosely across her breast and hear his gentle breathing as he slept. Her dreams told her she was about to make the biggest mistake of her life in leaving him and not telling him about the baby, but when she awoke alone in the cold wet English morning common sense won the battle and her dreams were banished to the night.

Lucy thought how strange it would be not going to work and having so much time to herself. It wasn't a good thing because she would also have time to think far too much. Work had always been there as a crutch to keep her mind off her problems. After her son was born there would be no more foreign holidays, she would take her children to Bognor, like her parents had done when she was a small child. She remembered her days at Bognor with affection. Yes, Bognor, Swanage or some such south coast English family resort would do nicely for her boys, save for the journey she had promised her unborn child at some uncertain time in the future.

She was sure her son would not have the problems in England he would have faced if he had been raised in Tunisia, born to an unmarried much older mother. The stigma of illegitimacy there still existed. This was England. Many children were now born to unmarried parents, and many more lived with only one parent. Nor was she worried that her son would be half-Arab. Again such prejudices were no longer a factor in the west. Once again she thought how different her culture was from Farid's and how different their lives would have been in North Africa.

For herself, she would let no man get close to her. Her son's father was her true love and she would not sully his memory with another man. She would go back to Tunisia, say goodbye and take herself out of his life forever. He would forget her in time.

She had seen the young women in his country, sleek, doe eyed, slim and pretty. She had read somewhere that the Tunisian people were amongst the most beautiful in the world. Whoever had written that was right. She smiled. Farid had matured from the attractive boy into a very handsome man. And now she must let him go, her beau Tunisian. She fought back the tears, It was the first thing she had ever said to Farid. Only now she understood what Alice had meant when she told her she would lose something very precious, but she would not seek to find it again, because she believed it was not hers to have.

CHAPTER TWENTY-FOUR

THE LAST TIME

On a chill winter's day Lucy arrived in Hammamet. Farid was surprised when she refused a glass of wine, but she told him she'd had a stomach upset and alcohol seemed to aggravate the problem. He commented she had given up smoking and she pleaded the same excuse.

"So you have no vices left?"

"Only you my love." He kissed her.

"Farid, can we go to Sousse?"

"Of course, we take the car tomorrow. Why do you want to go?"

"I want to go to the café where we first met."

"You mean where I fell in love with you and my life changed forever? You stole my heart and my life."

He held her close. She closed her eyes and listened to his heartbeat. "I love you so much."

He kissed her eyelids and tasted salty tears. "Why the tears, my darling?"

"Because the thought of being without you is unbearable."

"Lucy we have another two weeks. Think about leaving only when you have to." He held her away from him and studied every aspect of her anxious pale face.

"My princess, you will never be without me, I waited too long for you."

Lucy looked away. She must try now to break the bond which held them.

"My love, you will marry one day, a young and pretty Tunisian girl who will be welcomed into your family and give you children. I have no place in that life. You told me yourself that your father expects you to marry a Tunisian girl, someone the family approves of."

He looked angry. "That was at the beginning before you became real and I fell in love with you all over again, but this time as a man. I fell in love with you because of who you are, not just a boy's dream."

He took her hands and held them tightly. "Lucy, remember I only said what was expected of me, not what I would do." He looked militant. "I do not always do what is expected of me. I will choose my own wife, not one of my family's choosing. It is you I want to marry, I told you this more than a year ago, you remember. I know you said you may not be able to have children, but I believe it will not be so. Allah could not be that cruel."

She nodded trying to shield him from her despair.

"Then we will be together and our child will be born. It will be a boy. His hair will be dark like mine but he will have my beloved's beautiful green eyes."

Lucy thought her heart had stopped. She gasped and pulled away from him.

He stared at her.

"You do not want to marry me and have my child?"

Lucy flung her arms round his neck and kissed him. "I want your child more than I have ever wanted anything in my life."

Farid once more gave her that wonderful smile. "Then it will be. Insh'allah."

"Insh'allah," she echoed.

The time passed quickly; although they made love, Lucy tried to make sure the lights were low in case he should notice the change in her body. Farid commented that she had put on weight, but she joked that it was the comfort food she ate during the English winter and he said it suited her.

The following Sunday he drove her to the airport. She did her best to keep the conversation light and her abject misery to herself. Farid held her as close as the public place permitted then they sat opposite each other holding hands, a foot apart. *It might as well be at the other side of the universe*, she thought.

He stroked the little ring which she wore on her right hand. "Wear it always, my love."

Lucy held his face between her hands and stared at him, memorising every line, every feature. She kissed him, oblivious of the stares.

"I will never take it off. You will always be with me. Farid whatever happens to us in our lives, I need you to know that I have never loved anyone the way I love you and I never will again. There will never be anyone else."

He held her tightly and wondered why she spoke as though she were going away for a long time.

"Beautiful lady, it is only a few months until the spring when you come here again. I will speak with my family and tell them I am going to marry you. There are many arrangements to make and formalities we will have to go through here."

She winced at his words and held his arm tightly.

"No, Farid. Please don't speak with your family yet. We need to talk about this more together and then speak with your family."

He let go of her hands and sat back in his chair.

"As you wish." His voice was cold.

Lucy turned his face to her own. "No my love, you must not think like that. I swear if things were different and I could marry you tomorrow I would, but as you say there are many things to deal with both here and in England. I too have my family. We will make our arrangements when I come back."

Farid looked uncertain and a slight smile touched his lips. "You are right of course my darling, I have waited so many years for you, I can wait a few months more."

The cool impersonal voice on the loud-speaker broke through. Her flight was called. Lucy walked away, somehow managing to put one foot in front of the other. She turned just once and looked at him.

Farid waited until she boarded the plane and watched her as she walked towards the aeroplane steps. He saw her hesitate and turn as though looking for him, although he knew she could not see him. To his surprise, she seemed to stumble and buried her head in her hands. The stewardess helped her up the steps. He thought she looked so lost and alone and he was powerless to help her. As he walked back to the car, Farid was very uneasy. He waited until the evening and called her. She told him how much she loved him and was just miserable they were apart again.

They spoke often throughout December. On New Year's Eve he dashed out to the phone box.

"My dearest angel. This year will be the start of our new life together. I love you so much."

Across the miles, he could hear her ragged breathing, but when she spoke her voice was clear and calm.

"My darling, be happy now and forever. When we are apart always know I love you. Nothing will ever change my love for you."

On the third of January, Lucy changed her phone number.

CHAPTER TWENTY-FIVE

DESERTION

Farid stood by the phone. He was back at work but slipped out to make his Wednesday call. He dialled the number and heard the long dead tone. He dialled again and a third time. He didn't understand. Perhaps her phone wasn't working. He would try again tomorrow. He tried every day that week. He was frightened. He called the operator. The phone had been disconnected. Not out of order. Disconnected. Had she moved? She had said nothing. Had something happened to her, but if it had why had her phone been disconnected so quickly? It didn't make sense.

He walked dispassionately back to the hotel and had a huge row with the director. He spent the night wondering what to do. He couldn't even go to find her, he had no passport, no money and it would take months to get a visa, if indeed he could get one. That morning when his shift ended he went back to his lodgings and searched for the piece of paper Lucy had given him years ago to see if there were any other phone numbers he could try.

The next day he waited outside the hotel after his shift ended instead of returning to his lodgings. He needed Kassem's help and waited for his friend to arrive and open up his shop.

"Kassem. I need you to do something for me urgently."

"Of course, Farid. What is it? Why are you here and not in bed sleeping?"

"Who can sleep when their world has ended?"

Kassem was surprised. He knew his friend to be a calm sensible man and not given to dramatic pronouncements, but now he was certainly agitated.

"Your English is good, isn't it?"

"It's okay, why?"

"I need you to make a call for me, to England, please now."

"England!"

"Yes, to this number. Ask to speak with Mrs Collins."

Farid handed him a dog-eared piece of paper. On it Lucy had written her home number and her work number.

Kassem dialled and within seconds a cool crisp voice answered. Kassem hesitated.

"Good morning. I want speak with Mrs Collins please."

"I am very sorry but Mrs Collins no longer works here. She left last year."

"Why?" asked Kassem.

After a slight pause the voice replied, "I am afraid I have no idea, but she's not here. Can anyone else help you?"

"Wait," said Kassem and repeated what had been said to Farid.

Farid sat down on the wall and stared at his friend. He shook his head and waived him away with one hand.

"No thank you, madame." Kassem replaced the phone.

"Farid, what's wrong?"

"Wait a minute Kassem, let me think."

He took out his wallet and carefully pulled out Lucy's photograph. He remembered that behind it was a scrap of paper with a number on it. Lucy had given it to him when she had bought her friend Marie to Tunisia with her. "For emergencies only," she had smiled and added, "don't you go chatting up my friend."

He handed the paper to Kassem with a couple of coins.

"Try this number."

Kassem protested. "Farid this is crazy, who are you trying to speak with?"

"Her friend, Marie."

"Whose friend?"

"Kassem, please, just dial the bloody number, please I can't lose her again."

Kassem didn't understood. "D'you mean the blonde, your woman?"

Farid's expression said everything.

Kassem made the call "Hello, Miss Marie."

"This is Marie. Who is this?"

"My name is Kassem. I have Farid with me. He wishes to get speak with Lucy but her phone is no good and she works none." Kassem was struggling with the language and when M made no reply he thought she had not understood. "Madame?"

"Please tell Farid I have a message for him."

M pulled the piece of paper out of the draw and opened the envelope. Her hand was shaking.

She glanced at the paper and clenched her eyes tightly shut. She took a deep breath, this was not going to be easy.

"It reads, 'My darling. Our dream is ended. I cannot…'"

"Wait Madame, I must tell Farid."

As M read out each sentence, she could hear Kassem speaking in Arabic. "'I cannot speak with or see you again. I cannot explain why but trust me it is for the best. My love for you will never change but please do not try to contact me. Live your life and be happy. Forget me, my darling. As you said to me many years ago, one day we may meet again, inshell…' Sorry, I don't know that word."

"Insh'allah," said Kassem "Thank you, madame."

He put down the phone.

Farid sat silently without moving as he said the words over and over to himself. Kassem watched him and suddenly Farid leapt to his feet like a man possessed.

"Why?" he screamed. "Why?"

A few people turned and stared at them. Quickly Kassem pulled his friend away from the phone and dragged him inside his shop. He pulled down the curtain at the shop front and pushed his friend onto a stool.

"Kassem. What is she doing? Is she ill? Is she dying and she doesn't want me to know? What has happened that is so bad for us? I cannot lose her all over again, I can't, I can't…"

Farid started to cry. This was a Farid that Kassem had never seen and he didn't know what to do. "Farid, explain to me. What do you mean, lose her again? You have never lost her. From the time you met her, you have been in love with each other. Any fool could see that. When did you lose her before? I don't understand."

Farid had told no one about his first meeting with Lucy. Only Ali was with him and he had not seen Ali for years. He was a year or so older than Farid and when he came out of the Army he went to work in Tunis and they had lost touch.

He glanced up at Kassem, standing uncomfortably beside him. "Come. I need a good strong coffee." Kassem closed up the shop and they walked in silence to a café well away from the hotel in the old part of town.

They sipped the strong sweet brew. "Kassem, I must trust you with this. Please tell no one."

Kassem nodded.

"I met her in Sousse just before I turned fifteen." Kassem gasped. "No, no, my friend it was not like that!"

Farid smiled in spite of his misery. "I spoke with her only once for a moment and I never forgot her."

"You were bewitched by a Djinn," muttered Kassem glancing up at the Hand of Fatima amulet on the wall.

"No, my friend, I was in love."

"And then?"

"I never saw her for many years and then by the will of Allah against all odds I met her again, here in Hammamet."

Kassem swore. "It must indeed have been the will of Allah." He glanced again at the amulet.

"It's true, I swear it. Kassem I told her I want to marry her."

"Farid you are crazy. Make love with her, but marry her, no. She is English, she is Christian? She knows nothing of our ways, our life. She has her work and her son also, I think."

Farid nodded.

"Farid, she lives in her own world and you in your world. She has her own culture. She is beautiful, yes, but by your own admission she many years older than you, and your family…" His voice tailed off.

Farid swung furiously round to face him. "You think these things matter. I have loved her half my life."

"Of course these things matter. What about children? You are not thinking with your head my friend." He thought for a minute. "When did you tell her you want to marry her?"

"I told her many times, but it was last time she was here about two months ago that I said I would speak to my family."

"What did she say?"

"She told me to wait until she comes back in April. But she is not coming now, is she?" He said the words almost like a prayer.

"So she knew you were serious about this marriage."

"Yes."

"Farid, look at me. Think man, think." Farid's eyes welled with tears, his voice was harsh.

"She was happy enough to be with me on her holidays but she doesn't love me enough to marry me and spend her life with me. I know that now."

Kassem put his hand on his friend's shoulder.

"You fool. She loves you, a blind man could see that. The trouble is she loves you too much to marry you. She knows all the things I have just said are true. Oh, Farid, remember your lady as the dream she once was, but do as she says, live your own life."

"She is my life."

"No, Farid. Marry a good Tunisian girl who understands our ways. There are several I think who might have you."

Farid glared at him. "Are you quite mad? I don't want any other wife. Who would you suggest?" he muttered sarcastically.

Kassem knew he had his friend's attention and tried to steer his thoughts away from Lucy.

"Faiza, perhaps." Farid pictured her. A tall, rounded girl with a broad smile, a big chest and a come-to-bed expression.

"I don't think so."

Kassem grinned. "No, perhaps you're right, not really your type. What about Sarra? She obviously adores you."

Farid snorted. Kassem ignored him. "Yes, Sarra would be a good choice," Farid admitted. "Okay, I get your point. She's a nice enough person, but do I want to be tied to my sister's best friend for the rest of my life. We have nothing in common and I don't love her, she is like a younger sister to me." And, he added ominously "She is not Lucy. I would be utterly untruthful with her and that would be wrong. Each time I make love with her, I will see only my Lucy."

He caught Kassem's exasperated expression.

"Yes, my friend I know what you are thinking. I am sure Sarra would give me children, children with soft brown eyes and shiny black hair…"

"And what the hell is wrong with that? Isn't that what we all really want when it comes down to it? A good wife to keep our house and warm our bed and many healthy happy children."

"Yes, my friend, for most men I agree, but for me there is only Lucy. I want my English rose and I would settle for one child, the child of our love and the child I will now never have."

Later that day he went back to his lodgings but slept little. He went back to work in the evening, tired, with his shirt unpressed and his eyes red. As he went in through the back door of the hotel to get ready for his shift he walked past Mahmood, who had just finished the day shift. He disliked Mahmood. He had always been the one who refused to change shifts with Farid which would have allowed Farid to work the day shift whilst Lucy was there.

Mahmood was several years older than Farid with a thin weaselly face, lanky hair and small dark eyes that missed nothing. Lucy didn't like him, she said he gave her the creeps. Although only a few of the hotel staff suspected a relationship between Lucy and Farid, she had made no secret of the fact that she had a Tunisian boyfriend. It was a very good way of keeping away the would be suitors. She had refused Mahmood's advances, curtly declined his suggestions and saying her boyfriend would not approve.

Mahmood however did not miss the glances which passed between Farid and Lucy, nor the way Farid held her hand a little too long when she wished him good evening. He knew Farid disappeared sometimes during the nights when he was on night shift and he also noticed that when Lucy was not in the hotel, Farid also went to the phone, always around the same time, because he saw him checking his watch. Putting two and two together was not difficult for Mahmood. The ammunition was useful, but as yet he had not been quite sure how to use it to his best advantage and Mahmood never did anything that would not benefit himself. He didn't like Farid, for no other reason that he was delusional enough to think that if Farid was out of the way, the he was sure Lucy's shapely legs would be wrapped around him and not Farid.

He was actually thinking about her when he saw Farid walking towards him. The other man's distress was plain and his heart leapt. Gleefully he touched Farid's arm as he passed.

"What's the matter mate?" he said with mock concern.

Farid shook his head. "Nothing," he muttered.

Mahmood grasped the arm tightly. "What, blondie fucked you off then?"

The moment he uttered the words he knew his mistake. Farid swung round, and pulled his arm away. The expression on his face was pure venom. He swore at Mahmood and did something he had never done before. He swung his elbow back and hit the other man as hard as he could. Mahmood turned sideways, but the blow caught him just below his right eye and he screamed. Farid grabbed him, pinning his arms to his sides and leaned over him until their faces were almost touching.

"If you ever speak of her again or I hear that you have said one word to anyone, there will be no corner dark enough for you to hide in. Get it?"

Mahmood nodded his head up and down very fast his face damp with fear. "Yes, Farid. The swing door hit me."

"Good," his assailant said softly and patted the damaged cheek. "Good, let's keep it that way. Get some ice."

Mahmood was shaken; he thought Farid was an easy target. He was normally amiable and although never friendly, he had never thought of him as dangerous. Now he wasn't quite so confident. He touched his cheek and wondered if the bone was broken. He vowed silently if ever the chance came he would get even with Farid.

Farid walked through to the front of the hotel, his hand throbbed, but he felt an awful lot better.

The days melted into weeks and Farid lived in grey fog. He went through the motions of life but always at the back of his mind he thought Lucy would relent and contact him. He reasoned that although he had no phone at home or in his lodgings, she would find some way of telling him she still loved him, some encrypted message perhaps. He even asked once at the hotel reception desk if there had been any message for him, but by the quizzical look he got, he decided it was too risky to ask again. And she had his address. He checked his box regularly, but there was nothing. It never happened. It was as though she had never existed. All he had of her were his memories, an old engraved coin and a couple of photographs.

Many times when he was alone he studied the tiny photograph he always carried with him. The two of them together. She had kept the same one in her purse and he kept his in his wallet next to his heart. He looked at it again. Two happy people, sitting side by side, her head on his shoulder and he inclined towards her, his cheek resting on the top of her head. A time past, another life.

One afternoon in early summer he was feeling particularly low. He saw a woman who looked from a distance like Lucy and his heart jumped and he started towards her. When she came closer to him he saw it was not her and he sat on the beach for an hour away from the crowd and cried until he thought he would never be able to shed another tear.

Eventually he went to Cathy's cafe bar on the edge of town, where they often used to pass time together. Farid reasoned that if she had contacted anyone, it would probably be Cathy as they had become good friends over the years. Cathy smiled at him and he asked her if she had seen Lucy.

She shook her head.

"Sorry, I haven't seen Lucy since she left last year. Funny, I thought she'd have been back by now. We used to speak sometimes on the phone. I got a call from her just after she went home last time and I thought she sounded a bit odd then and I haven't heard from her since. I tried her once, but the number was disconnected and I thought she must have moved. Due back soon, is she?" She stared at Farid and saw with amazement he had been crying.

"I don't know," he replied flatly and turned his head away.

She watched him wander back out of the bar, his eyes fixed on the dusty road. She shrugged. *Shame*, she thought. *Of all the couples I've seen, that was one I thought would last and I've seen a few come and go.*

She told her husband. "Shame," she said again. "Nice couple they were, often used to come in here and sit quietly together. I liked both of them and her little boy was a real treasure. I had many a good chat with the two of them and I thought she and I had become friends. I can't understand it. Just by watching him you can tell she's dumped him, but she adored him. You didn't need to be Einstein to figure that one out."

Her husband couldn't see the logic in that. "Probably the age difference didn't help," he said.

"Don't be daft, there is no more than a few years between them. What does that matter if they love each other? It's not the end of the world."

"About eleven or twelve years actually." Cathy nearly dropped the plate.

"Good God, I'd have put her early thirties."

Her husband put his arm round her waist. "I thought you women could suss these things out, maybe I'm wrong. I only know because I went to school with Farid, he's a year younger than me and Kassem from the shop told me when they first started to come in here that she was in her mid-thirties then."

"Have you seen Kassem recently?"

"Yes, last week, strangely enough we were talking about Farid and how he's changed."

"And what did Kassem say?"

"Not a lot, he was unwilling to say very much, but he did say she'd completely disappeared, changed her phone number apparently, the lot, simply disappeared off the face of the earth without a word to anyone."

"You gossipy old men," she quipped. "I thought it was only women who gossiped," she nudged him playfully. He glared at her.

"Seriously though it does surprise me. Lucy was crazy about him, never stopped talking about him and how happy she was. I even heard them talking the last time they were here about getting married."

"Maybe that's why she ran," her husband answered quietly .

"What are you getting at?"

"Look sweetheart, you know what families are like out here. Would my family have accepted you if you had been years older than me, even without the other husband and child?" She looked up at him.

"No, I suppose they wouldn't, it wasn't that easy anyway." They smiled at each other. "I do feel so sorry for them, though." Another couple of customers strolled into the café. Cathy shrugged, smiled at her husband and went out to greet them.

CHAPTER TWENTY-SIX

AND THEN THERE WERE THREE

Lucy felt guilty. After the initial sickness had passed she had sailed through her pregnancy and if she was honest with herself she had not attended the classes as she should. She felt she had been through one pregnancy and had a fair idea of what was expected of her. She ate sensibly, although was somewhat amused how the rules, if you could call them that, had changed in ten years. The fact that women had been giving birth since time began seemed to have been forgotten. There were so many things to remember, what you should eat, what you should not eat, get enough exercise but not too much of the wrong sort – so much to think about.

The doctor chastised her gently and told her it was high time she went for another scan and it would not be long before she was due, but he had to admit she seemed in fine health. Her blood pressure was good, although her weight had increased a bit too much, and he pointed out she did seem quite large.

The young doctor at the hospital had moved on and in his place she found an avuncular middle aged man. As he ran the machine over her stomach, she noticed he hesitated and peered at the screen for some time, moving the image back and forth. She was fascinated and scared at the same time.

"What's the matter?"

He beamed at her. "Absolutely nothing my dear, nothing at all. You are very well and so are your children."

Lucy froze. "My children?"

"Yes children. I wasn't sure to start with but I could hear a second heartbeat. There is another child but in such a position that he or she is hidden behind the first one. My dear, you are carrying twins."

Lucy didn't know whether to laugh or pass out. She giggled as she remembered Alice's comment about a shadow behind the child. Even Alice hadn't foreseen twins.

"Can you see what they are, I mean are they boys or girls?"

"The larger of the two is a boy, the smaller as I said is hidden and I can't see. You'll just have to wait and see."

Lucy decided to tell no one about the twins.

Ben Collins was born a healthy baby boy with a sheen of dark downy hair who screamed in protest at being removed from his warm comfortable existence. Shortly after he arrived, another much smaller child followed, a little girl. She whimpered softly and the midwife whisked her off, just to make sure she was quite healthy. Just as a precaution, Lucy was assured.

It was a surprisingly easy labour, during which she opted to be alone. There were none of the traumas which had accompanied Alex's birth. When M arrived to inspect the newborn she found her friend sitting up in bed cuddling her new son, who suckled greedily. Lucy kissed the soft dark downy head and whispered "And now there is another beau Tunisian. Welcome to the world, my love."

M admired the infant but declined to hold him. She watched Lucy intently.

"I can appreciate you are very pleased with yourself and of course you have every right to be but why the huge grin?"

"I have a little surprise for you."

M groaned. "I am not sure I can take any more surprises at the moment."

The door opened and the nurse appeared. Lucy's grin widened threatening to split her face in two.

"Oh, M, you're going to love this"

M's mouth fell open as the nurse handed the baby to her mother, a tiny pale infant, hairless and quiet.

"Sweet Jesus. Two of them. Twins!"

"Twins," Lucy repeated, her arms around each child.

M stood up and stared down at the smaller baby. "A girl? One of each?" Lucy nodded happily.

"Bloody hell. When did you know?"

"Only a few weeks ago, I didn't want to say anything in case, well you know I told you about the trouble I had before. I couldn't bear the thought I might lose one or even both of them."

M nodded in understanding. "Have you thought what you're going to call them?"

"I knew the child would be a boy and I have already decided on Ben, but I do admit I had not bargained on having to choose another name. Of course I had no idea if she would be boy or girl so I'm not sure yet what to call her. I've tossed over a few names, but no decision as yet."

Her friend gazed at the sleeping child, her cheek resting on her mother's breast and her tiny mouth puckered.

"She's so tiny and delicate, like a little rosebud," M whispered as she stroked the child's face.

Lucy beamed. "M you are a genius. That's what I'll call her."

M glared at her. "Don't be daft. You can't saddle the poor little darling with a name like Rosebud."

"You idiot, I'm not that cruel. No, Rose, it's a perfect name for her, thank you so much."

M was thrilled to think she had named the baby and she couldn't take her eyes away from the tiny child. She knew she would never now have children of her own, but this was as close as she would ever hope to get to having her own baby girl. The child woke up and immediately clutched M's finger which she held onto whilst her mother fed her.

Lucy stayed in hospital for a few days but as mother and babies were both trouble free she was soon back in her own home. M decided to stay for a week or so.

"Mind you, I'm here to look after you, not the infants. That's your sphere of influence, not mine. You know my views on the small people."

As M regarded all babies as machines which produced mess at both ends and a vast amount of noise she was secretly surprised at how quiet they were. Ben cried lustily but only when he was hungry, and Rose rarely gave more than a kitten-like mew and never really cried at all. Once Ben was fed and changed he slept but Rose would lie on her back gurgling. One evening when Lucy came downstairs, she found

M sitting on the sofa beside the little basket peering closely at her daughter. She stood motionless behind the door and watched. M stroked the little cheek and jumped as the baby held onto her finger. Fascinated, she murmured to her under her breath and although Lucy could not hear what she was saying her voice was gentle and she didn't try to move the tiny hand. "I see you are making friends."

M sat back as though embarrassed at having been caught.

"They're mesmeric, aren't they?" she said. "Sometimes I just sit and watch them. They are just so different." What she meant was that whilst Ben was darker and more like his father, Rose was most definitely her mother's child. Lucy did not catch her meaning and M did not expand on it.

"I know. They are so different from us. It is almost impossible to imagine what they will be like in ten years' time. It was the same with Alex, there's something about babies which just makes you want to watch and see what they do next. Although at that age there's not much they actually do except sleep, cry, feed and pee."

"Charming," said M, "but I do understand what you mean. I've just never really had anything to do with babies. I've never had my own and I was an only child. So were my parents and they were both in their forties when I was born, so I didn't really have much to do with young children." Lucy cradled Ben and M was bold enough to hold Rose, but drew the line at nappy changing.

When M left, she kissed both children. "She's like a little doll, she's quite beautiful." She looked at Ben and grinned at her friend. "And I think this one will be a heartbreaker like his dad when he's older."

After she had gone as Lucy rocked her babies to sleep she whispered to Rose. "My beautiful little girl, you my little love are a bonus I never expected, my rosebud." She studied the tiny face with pale soft skin and smooth head and kissed her. The child gurgled and burped. Lucy smiled and gently wiped away the milk which trickled down her chin.

She looked down at her son and her face changed. "In M you've made your first female conquest today, probably the first of many."

She smiled sadly at the sleeping child and wondered how long it would be before he broke her heart when she looked at him and saw his father.

Alex was fascinated by his new siblings. He insisted on having one hand on the pram as he walked proudly beside his mother. At home it was usually Rose who sat quietly on his lap, because Ben tended to wriggle and Lucy was terrified Alex might drop the squirming infant.

Rose was as different from her twin both in appearance and temperament as two children could be. From babyhood she gurgled and cooed her way into the hearts of every man, woman and animal she encountered. Even the large rabbit which belonged to their neighbour's daughter allowed Rose to stroke his long silky ears, but if anyone else tried, including his crestfallen owner, his ears flattened against his back and he thumped his feet angrily on the ground.

By the time Rose turned a year old, her baby blue eyes had darkened to her father's strange golden brown. The contrast with her paleness and almost white blonde hair was stunning. She remained small and although not thin enough to cause concern she fed little, taking only what she required and refusing more. She was a gentle child, preferring to watch what was happening around her rather than try to be part of it.

In complete contrast, Ben made it clear he had no intention of failing to make his opinions heard. Sometimes Lucy caught Rose watching him, an expression of wonderment on her tiny face as though questioning why such a vast amount of noise was necessary when a burp or gurgle could bring a better outcome.

Ben ate everything offered to him and gained weight quickly. His baby hair remained almost black and with his honey coloured skin there was little doubt of his foreign heritage. Unlike his sister he had inherited his mother's flecked green eyes which regularly sparkled in anger when his whims and wishes were not immediately catered for.

Lucy never ceased to be amused by the looks of surprise when she informed onlookers that the two were twins. She resisted all attempts to gain information, some hinted at and some more direct, as to who was their father.

CHAPTER TWENTY-SEVEN

FATMA AND MICHELLE

Fatma had forgiven Hama for the dreadful experience above the bakery. It had taken a lot of wheedling and several gifts before she relented. He knew he had made a serious mistake and not for the first time cursed the memory of the blonde tourist who had very nearly ruined a comfortable and sexually rewarding relationship with Fatma. What finally made up her mind was when Hama cleverly took her to the same jewellers where she had seen Farid buy Lucy's ring. Fatma was ecstatic and although she had hoped she too would receive a ring, she willingly settled for a beautiful gold bracelet, which cost Hama more money than he cared to think about, but she ensured he received adequate reward.

Farid had started to resent the weekly trips back home to Sousse. For some time, his sister had made his life a misery dropping more and more hints about Sarra, even so far as to tell him that Asim down the road was interested in her and he'd better get in quick or he'd miss out.

"Unless that is you've got someone else in mind," she'd added watching him carefully. He kept his face expressionless as he shook his head. He couldn't be bothered to fight with her. Still, recently she seemed to have eased up a bit and last time he had been surprised that she had never mentioned Sarra once.

Fatma noticed that Farid had stopped his trips to the phone. For all her pressuring and sparring she actually cared deeply for her brother. She was just too obsessed with Hama to really see anything else. Even Saleem couldn't shake him out of it. Fatma was convinced that it was something to do with that English bitch she had seen him with in the Medina. Hopefully the woman had dumped him, although she couldn't understand why. Apart from the fact she couldn't understand anyway why anyone would want to separate from her brother, there was the question of the ring. She had seen him put it on the woman's finger. They were so obviously in love with each other – no she didn't understand it, but whatever had happened it was a good thing. He'd get over it but she hated to see how obviously miserable Farid had become and hated the English woman even more because of it.

If the truth be known, Fatma had pretty much given up on Sarra. She had done everything she could to push them together, but the girl said very little, which Fatma knew would not impress her brother who would be bored to death.

"If I wanted a man, I'd make damn certain he knew it, why can't she actually do anything instead of just gazing at him." Her thoughts strayed to Hama. He was a strange man, other than the one experience she preferred to forget, he was usually quite kind. He scared her a little and she knew he had a reputation and a lot of people were fearful of him but she never knew why and thought it better not to ask.

She was thinking about Farid when she noticed some new people moving into the next apartment block. Fatma immediately noticed the daughter. Even with a woman's viewpoint she could see she would be very attractive to a man. She was tall, but quite well rounded with wide almond eyes and dark brown hair with a hint of chestnut, which Fatma was sure owed more to the bottle than Mother Nature and she had a generous mouth which always seemed to be smiling. A glimmer of an idea entered her mind.

Ayesha was a bit brash with her choice of clothes, which worried Fatma a bit. But then she thought of the blonde, who had worn a top which exposed her shoulders and part of her breast. Fatima thought it odd because her brother was actually quite conservative over what he approved of in women. However, Fatma felt confident he would like Ayesha and decided to make it her business to befriend the girl.

The first time she was invited into the apartment there was another girl there, who Ayesha told her was her sister, Michelle. She was surprised because the two girls were quite different but it was all she could do not to clap her hands with delight. She completely forgot about Ayesha. This one was absolutely perfect. She was smaller than her sister, slim to the point of being thin and she looked European. Her hair was long and a soft honey colour. She was just on her way out when Fatma arrived, but Fatma decided she would definitely need to see more of her.

She asked her friend if they were indeed sisters. Ayesha smiled mysteriously. "We are half-sisters. Our father married my mother and then unfortunately she died when I was only a year old." Fatma murmured her sympathy. "And Michelle's mother?"

"She lives in Paris," was the only answer she received.

On making a few somewhat less than discrete enquiries, Fatma learned that their father got mixed up with an eighteen-year-old French girl on holiday, got her pregnant and married her about three months before Michelle was born. As could be expected the new wife couldn't cope with two young children and the male-dominated culture when she was not much more than a child herself and had been used to the freedom of Paris. She disappeared back to France just after Michelle's second birthday, so the girls were brought up together by their father and his family.

This was better than Fatma could have dreamed of. A young beautiful blonde who was half-Arab, used to the culture and what was expected of her, and of course with Arabic as her native language. Quite perfect!

Within a very short time Fatma had ingratiated herself with both sisters. Michelle turned out to be a very pleasant girl; she jokingly told Fatma that she was quite used to being bossed about by her elder sister and didn't mind a bit.

"I am very lucky really; when I turned thirteen my mother wrote to my father asking if I could come to Paris. I pleaded to be allowed to go but my father of course refused. It was only after my aunt intervened and told him that Paris was a good place for a girl to learn how to become a proper young lady that he agreed. I think she pointed out to him that I would be much more likely to make a good match if I learned polished manners and culture. Fortunately my father had never seen the other side of Paris and after some persuasion agreed.

After a few months when I had received my passport, I made my first trip to Paris."

Fatma listened enthralled and wished she could spend several months a year in Paris like Michelle. The Paris influence gave her an intriguing European difference which set her apart from her sister and the other girls, but she was gentle and unassuming and never tried to push herself forward and was therefore popular with the other girls as well as the men, in whom she showed little interest.

Fatma was ecstatic, with one or two tweaks she could see her brother's and her own problems solved by one unsuspecting girl.

She persuaded Michelle to tie her blonde hair back at the sides with clips, saying how it suited her. She bought her friend a turquoise V-neck top. Michelle was a little concerned about the neckline but said nothing because it had been a present from her new friend. Fatma said it would look wonderful with her white trousers. She remembered everything Saleem had said and for good measure bought a bottle of Chanel No.5 spray from the shop in the Medina. Michelle didn't like the scent particularly and from her days in Paris she knew it was a fake but wore it to please her friend.

Fatma doubted very much if Farid had ever seen Michelle. He didn't spent much time in Sousse and when he was there he was either out with Saleem or one of his friends or with his head buried in the newspaper indoors. She knew Farid would be back on Wednesday for his day off and she felt Michelle was now ready for the task she had in mind.

"I'd like you to come over to us for a change this Wednesday, to meet my family?"

"I'd love to, but Wednesday is a bit difficult for me."

Fatma panicked. "No it has to be Wednesday because I want you to meet all my family and you can wear your new outfit." Michelle didn't want to offend her new friend and agreed.

Fatma was like a cat on hot bricks. She wriggled about, couldn't sit still for more than a few minutes and generally drove Saleem crazy. He was concerned. He'd seen this before. He knew his sister well and was certain she had some scheme or another which probably didn't bode well for anyone except herself.

Almost two years had passed since Lucy disappeared from Farid's life. The ache was as bad as ever and time had not lessened it. As he walked from the *louage* towards his home, he passed a café and saw a woman with long blonde hair. Although he knew it was not Lucy, seeing the woman had given him enough of a jolt so that his mind was full of her as he opened the front door. As usual he flung his keys on the table. His wallet stayed in his pocket.

He greeted his father and family and sat down in his usual chair. Fatma had moved it slightly so it directly faced the door, but he didn't seem to notice. It was early evening and only two small lamps were lit. There was a gentle knock on the door.

Farid looked up. "Expecting anyone?"

Fatma jumped to her feet and opened the door. She had left the corridor light on. As the door opened Farid saw the figure of a woman, her hair drawn back at the sides and fanned out around her shoulders, and with the light shining behind her, white blonde. She wore a deep V-necked turquoise blouse and slim white trousers, set off by a pair of jewelled white sandals. She smiled.

Before she could speak Farid shot out of his chair. "Lucy!" he shouted as he ran across the room, his heart so full of love he saw only what he wanted to see.

He flung his arms around the astonished girl and kissed her. Slowly he drew back. Her lips were soft but he realised in a second she was not Lucy and her perfume was sickly sweet. He stared into a pair of shocked brown eyes.

Hakim leapt to his feet. "Have you taken leave of your senses, you animal? Apologise immediately," he bellowed at the top of his voice.

Farid took no notice, he looked from his brother to his sister and finally at the unknown girl, picked up his keys and walked out of the door without a word.

Hakim tried to placate the frightened girl who burst into tears. He wished not for the first time that his dear wife was there. She would know what to do. He sat the girl down and then motioned to Fatma to deal with the situation. He stalked off into his room shocked and bewildered.

Fatma stood completely still. Without thinking she muttered to herself, "What is wrong with him? She's perfect."

Saleem heard her. He had been as horrified as his father, but watching his sister's smiling face as the door had opened he knew instantly what had just happened. He had immediately seen the resemblance to Lucy. He walked slowly over to his sister his face twisted in anger.

"Stay here and don't move," he commanded her. Fatma flinched. He motioned to Michelle who followed him like a lamb out of the door. He walked her back the short distance to her apartment.

A few minutes later he came back. His sister was sitting in the chair.

"Get up." She did. He stood a foot or so away from her looking down at her with such a look of fury that she shrank away from him.

"You filthy rotten little bitch! Don't deny you set that up." He had never spoken to her like that and Fatma was scared.

"I was only trying to help him," she stammered. "He's been so miserable since that dreadful English woman left."

She realised what she had said, but it was too late. Saleem came as near as he ever had done to striking his sister. He was shaking with fury.

"So you thought you'd create a clone."

"No, no I didn't."

She was really frightened now.

He sneered. "Fatma, I am neither blind nor stupid. You gave up with Sarra and when Michelle and her family moved in you saw your chance to get another malleable young girl to marry off to your brother. What beats me is how you knew how Lucy wore her hair and how she dressed. I never told you and when Michelle moved in, she never dressed like that. You tried to recreate Lucy and all you've done is devastate your brother, caused our father great pain and ruined our family's reputation. Not to mention frightening an innocent young girl out of her wits who thought you were her friend. All I can hope for is that she is either too much of a lady or too embarrassed to ever repeat what happened."

Fatma started to cry. "It's too late for that," he snapped angrily. He took her by the shoulders and shook her. "What I want to know, and I want to know now, is how did you know? You hardly ever leave Sousse and I don't remember the last time you went to Hammamet. Farid told me he only came once or twice to Sousse with Lucy."

Fatma shrugged, her mind desperately trying to work out a way to wriggle out.

Saleem stared at her, his disgust evident. "Oh Fatma are there no depths you won't sink to? Did you follow them?"

"It wasn't like that," she protested. "How would I know where to find them to follow them? You know I go to the Medina square quite often. I meet my... friends there. Well, I saw Farid and that woman..."

"Lucy," cut in her brother.

"Alright, Lucy. I saw them walking hand in hand across the square towards the Medina." Saleem frowned.

"And yes, okay, I followed them, but you have to believe me I was there anyway, you know I often go there," she repeated to emphasise the point. "It was just coincidence."

Saleem acknowledged to himself that in that part she probably was telling the truth. She was always hanging around the square, more often than not looking for Hama.

"Go on."

"I was frantic. Don't you know brother, that she would have ruined him and our family? You talk about me ruining our reputation. What would she have done? She's one of those older women who come here on holiday just looking for a man." Saleem decided not to labour the point that they had known each other for a lot more than just one holiday.

Fatma was babbling. "They were speaking in French so she doesn't even speak our language. She doesn't know our culture, our religion or our ways and she's so old! Can you see Baba accepting her into our family, or our aunt for that matter?" Her confidence was rising.

"Anyway, it's obvious she's not around anymore, or he wouldn't behave the way he does. Mind you I don't know why she's gone because she was all over him. I even watched them go into the jewellers and when they came out he put a ring on her finger and he kissed her in front of everybody. It was awful, anyone could have seen them."

Saleem's eyebrows shot up. "That I didn't know," he muttered to himself.

He put his hands on his sister's shoulders, holding her at arm's length. He could feel her trembling. "Look. I will give you the benefit of the doubt that it was a coincidence you seeing them. I will also try to accept that you were trying to help Farid, but don't you realise Fatma, while you may have made Michelle look a bit like Lucy…" He thought for a moment for the right words. "Farid was in love with Lucy, he undoubtedly still is and you can't replace that with a clone."

"Or Chanel perfume with cheap cologne." Farid walked back into the room, his face pale. He smiled at his brother.

"Come, I need to talk to you. Let's get out of here."

He ignored Fatma completely, but as the two men were leaving Farid turned and stared at his sister as if he were seeing her for the first time and he didn't like what he saw.

"I don't know why you did this, but know something. You can stop throwing your friends at me. My wife will be of my own choosing, not yours or indeed anyone else's."

His voice was hard. "And Fatma, you will never marry Hama because he is already married with a child." He slammed the door.

Fatma felt the room spin and slumped into a chair. "You're making it up," she screamed at the closed door. "He can't be married. He's going to marry me."

"I don't think so my child." Hakim had come back unnoticed into the room and heard the conversation between his children. He sat down heavily next to his daughter and thought how young she looked with her tear streaked face and wild eyes. "Farid is right. He told me of this some weeks ago. Do you want me to go on?" She looked at the floor and nodded.

"Very well. Hama is married. He has been married for several years. He has a son and his wife is pregnant with their second child. The family live near Nabeul. I always knew that you were seeing someone but until Farid told me, I didn't know who. When I learned it was that Hama I was worried for you. Then I asked around my friends and learned more than I wanted to know. I was going to forbid you from speaking with him again, but now there is no need for me to do that. You have had a very lucky escape my daughter. He is in deep trouble with the police, drug smuggling, people trafficking and prostitution and there is talk he is even mixed up in arms dealing. He was arrested this morning and they will probably throw away the key."

Fatma sat completely still. She didn't believe it, but then tiny fingers of doubt crept in. The times when he wasn't there, times when he had to go away quickly, meetings with people she didn't know, talking in hushed voices and of course the times when he had so much money he couldn't spend it quickly enough.

Her father watched her. "Fatma let this be a lesson to you. Our culture is the way it is for a reason. I and your brothers will respect your wishes to choose your own husband, as we did with your sister, but only we are in a position to ensure he is an honourable and respectable man who will care for you, simply because we love you." He put his arms round her in an unaccustomed gesture of comfort and affection and she hugged him.

"Thank you, Baba, and I am sorry I have hurt you." Her remorse was genuine. Fatma deeply loved her father, but how could Hama have deceived her so? - and how she hated that awful English woman who had caused all the trouble from the beginning.

CHAPTER TWENTY-EIGHT

AFTERMATH

The brothers stopped first at a café they knew well a short way from their home.

"Saleem, thank you for what you said to Fatma." He regarded his brother intently. "I know you have not told anyone about meeting me in Hammamet a couple of years ago."

"You asked me not to."

Farid nodded in acknowledgement. "I think I owe you an explanation. I started seeing Lucy over five years ago."

"That long! I had no idea, or even that you were still seeing her."

"I'm not."

Saleem looked keenly at his brother and he could see he was telling the truth.

"I am sorry, Saleem, but it wasn't fair to involve you. I said nothing because I knew the problems it could cause, particularly if our father got wind of it. That's why we rarely came to Sousse, in case anyone saw us together."

"But you saw her in Hammamet?"

"Yes, as often as was possible, she stayed in the hotel."

"That must have been difficult for you."

Farid grimaced. "Believe me it was. Do you have any idea what it's like pretending you don't know a woman you have been with all afternoon? I used to watch her in that huge reception bar and the men looking at her in such a way I wanted to punch them."

Saleem laughed at his indignation. "Did she ever make you angry and encourage them?"

"No, she was polite and clever enough to let people know she had a boyfriend here and it worked. They left her alone after that."

"And no one suspected?" Remove line break

Farid frowned, "I think one or two may have done, but there was nothing definite and nothing was ever said." He ignored the incident with Mahmood. "But it was very difficult when all I wanted to do was throw her on the nearest sofa and make love to her!"

Saleem grinned at him. "Yes, I can see that might have been a problem! But tell me about her. Do you really love her that much? I don't need to spell out for you the problems you would face."

An inscrutable smile appeared on Farid's face. "Come brother, I think we need a change of scenery."

Saleem had no idea where they were going; they walked out of the town centre, through the narrow streets towards the promenade. He was surprised, Farid rarely went to the *zones touristiques*. Eventually they came to the seafront café on the corner. The place was quite full, but where it had once been a meeting place for local people, since the new seafront hotels had gone up it was patronised mainly by tourists The atmosphere was noisy bright and alive. Farid led him to a table on the edge nearest the sea.

They sat with their coffees. Saleem had no idea why there were here.

"Do you remember when I used to go out and play football with my friends?"

Saleem nodded. "Ali, Mustafa and that crowd, you mean?"

"Yes, that's right. Do you also remember the time old Ahmed came to our apartment? He was very angry and he and our father locked themselves away in Baba's room."

"Oh yes, I remember that day. I was only a kid but I can remember Baba was furious about something and it was about you because mother made me come away. She was very worried."

"That is the day I fell in love."

Saleem stared at him.

"We were playing over there, it was much more open back then. She was sitting at this table with her friend and the ball hit her on the leg. I went to pick it up and apologise. She smiled at me and I fell in love with her."

"Farid, you were a kid!"

"I was nearly fifteen," he corrected, "and I fell in love with her. It was a like a bomb had detonated in my chest."

"You are quite mad!"

"Brother, that's exactly what Ali said!"

"She gave me a coin."

"And old Ahmed saw you?"

Farid nodded.

"Is that all?" Saleem thought that was no reason for his father to get so cross.

"No, brother. Every ounce of common sense left me. I told her she was beautiful. She asked me my name. I told her and to remember it and to wait for me because I loved her and we would meet again… and I kissed her cheek."

Saleem choked on his coffee.

"I knew then this was the only woman I would ever want. Old Ahmed saw everything and tried to slap me, but I ran away. He was purple in the face and his moustache bristled, you know how it does." His brother smiled.

"I watched Mr A talking to her and her friend and when she smiled at me, I knew he had told her what I had said." Saleem swore quietly.

"I'm not surprised Baba was livid."

Farid's expression softened. "You know, Saleem, I've often wondered if old Ahmed told him everything because father seemed more angry when he thought I'd been tapping tourists for money."

"And father let you keep the money?"

"Yes."

"Are you telling me that woman was Lucy."

"Yes and I kept the memory of her in my heart and the moment I saw her on the beach in Hammamet five summers years ago, I knew it was her."

"Did she recognise you?"

"Not immediately. I smiled at her. She looked wistfully at me and said something like, "A boy smiled at me once like that many years ago in Sousse. I gave him a coin." Then she looked embarrassed."

"Go on, this is like something out of one of Fatma's books!"

"I said to her the same words I spoke to her the day I met her. She went white and held my arm for support. I thought she was going to faint. 'Farid', she said, 'It can't be you, but you're a man', and she sat down and just stared at me. She was silent for a few moments and asked me if I spent my money."

"Did you?"

"Would you give away the first present you ever got from the woman you love?"

"You still have it?"

Farid opened the little pouch inside his wallet and handed his brother the coin.

"How did she know it was the same one she gave you?"

"Look closer." Saleem turned over the coin and read the inscription, 'F+L'.

"I had it engraved and bought a little box for it."

"The red heart-shaped box."

Farid stared at him. "How the hell do you know that?" he asked, his voice cutting.

"I'm sorry, Farid, I was a real brat when I was a kid. One day when you were out, I went through your treasure box. I wondered what a coin was doing in a love box. I didn't see the inscription."

Farid's face flushed with anger, "But you didn't take it."

"Our mother caught me looking at it. She took it away from me and the box as well. She looked at the coin and I watched her turn it over and then she smiled that slow sweet smile of hers. She rubbed the coin gently on her skirt and put it back in the box. She told me never ever to touch it again."

Farid's heart turned a somersault. "So Mama knew," he said quietly.

"She knew many things," answered his brother, "but she kept them to herself. I miss her."

"Me too," said Farid. They were silent for a few moments, each with their memories.

"Who knows about this, Farid?"

"The whole story, no one except you. As I said, Ali was there when I met her, but I haven't seen Ali since he went into the Army.

There is no way that he would know she came back. Kassem knows that I have been seeing Lucy for a long time and I told him I had seen her once before many years ago."

"Why Kassem?" Farid explained about the phone calls.

"I was distraught, he was the only person I could think of who spoke good enough English, who I felt I could trust."

"Remember, I speak English now."

"You weren't there."

"Okay, but I will be if you need me again."

Michelle refused to speak to Fatma again. She had been humiliated and embarrassed. Fortunately she was a sensible and kind enough person not to repeat the incident to anyone. Saleem explained to her that Fatma thought she was trying to help her brother by finding someone who looked like the girl who had left him, but she decided she would stay away from Fatma.

Michelle had been shocked by the passion in Farid's kiss. She was woman enough to admit to herself that she had enjoyed his strong masculine embrace and the look of unguarded love when he thought she was someone else. She hoped one day a man would look at her like that. She felt it was a shame she could not have met him differently as herself and not as the lookalike Fatma had encouraged her unwittingly to become.

She went back to wearing her hair the way she had always done and threw away the turquoise top, but the damage was done. When their paths crossed, Farid acknowledged her politely, but never went out of his way to speak with her or seek out her company. What she couldn't know was it was not that Farid was disinterested in her, he simply wasn't interested in anyone who wasn't Lucy. His lady, his Lucy was somewhere in the world and he was not ready to give up the hope that she would come back to him.

Farid's birthday come and went. Although in Tunisia, birthdays are not celebrated in the same way as weddings and births, each year he secretly hoped that perhaps Lucy would remember, but there was no word from her. In the past she had always tried to be in Tunisia on his birthday and given him some little gift, but this time there was nothing. The pain would never leave him but it had dulled to an ever present ache.

He knew his father's health was not improving and that he hoped Farid would marry and also take up his responsibilities as the eldest son. At least his sister had got over her infatuation with Hama, who was not spoken of or seen again. Within months she had been introduced to another young man, whose father was a surgeon and who hoped to follow him into the medical business. The family were respectable and by most standards, quite comfortably well off. She seemed genuinely to care for her new boyfriend. He had been concerned that Fatma's forthright manner would leave her unattractive to decent men, but Ahmed told him he rather liked it, it made her different from most of the other girls he knew. Farid approved of Ahmed and he knew his father was happy with the match. He was particularly grateful that now someone else could share the responsibility for his often wayward sister.

He had no worries about Saleem, who was making good progress in his employment. Saleem had matured into a clever, interesting young man and was intent on doing well for himself. Farid had no doubt he would succeed. Although he had always been close to his brother, the evening they had spent together after his sister's dreadful charade had brought them even closer.

CHAPTER TWENTY-NINE

FARID

The season was coming to an end before the couple of months' lull until the Christmas and New Year rush. He was still working in Hammamet and was now in charge of the security staff of the hotel. He had filled out a bit, his shoulders broadened and although he hated to admit it, his waistline had gained an inch or two. He had a few close friends but had lost the general camaraderie which had made him so approachable in the past. His face had changed little, save that he rarely smiled. He absorbed himself in his work, had no objection to long hours and the money he did not spend on his family he put away, but for what he did not know.

He remained without female company for almost a year after Lucy disappeared and on one occasion paid for his relief in the back streets of Hammamet, but resolved never to repeat the experience. Later none of his girlfriends had lasted. He used them simply as a physical release to try and convince himself he was still alive. He had little time for personal relationships and he preferred it that way.

Farid didn't much like the tourists. As he said "They are a necessary evil of my employment," which usually caused amusement to the listener, who of course thought the words were said in jest.

He did acknowledge that most of the visitors were pleasant and polite, if a little self-obsessed, which of course they were entitled to be. They had paid for their couple of week's holiday and felt they deserved to be waited on. There were he noticed a few creeping in who caused trouble. Much of it was light hearted and almost always the result of too much to drink. These he called the good-timers, teens and twenties looking for a Costa-type holiday and frequently finding they had come to the wrong place.

Sousse had its bars and nightclubs and a pretty good night-life but Hammamet had for the most part retained its dignity. The bohemian era of the sixties had all but disappeared and the nightlife was essentially hotel based, save for the scattering of bars and nightclubs frequented by locals and tourists alike. This of course meant the hotels also took the brunt of the problems. These were rarely serious, but were a continuous irritation. Revellers intent on using the pool after dark which was dangerous so far as the hotels were concerned, if disaster struck, the hotel would very probably be held responsible. Then there were the disturbances during the night, again usually caused by inebriated guests shouting or arguing in and outside the rooms, which had to be dealt with swiftly but diplomatically.

Particularly in the season when the night air was warm, couples could be seen walking in the sand. Trysts and lovemaking were not uncommon, particularly with the determined Tunisian male and his tourist partner, and of course amongst the Costa crowd who forgot that Tunisia was not Spain but those indulging could find themselves in a good deal of trouble.

Although Tunisia was acknowledged to have adopted many of the customs of Europe and as such alcohol was served in hotels and tourist areas, a moderate display of affection was frowned upon, tolerated but kept under control. Suggestive behaviour anywhere and certainly on the beach was forbidden. As such the security presence employed by the hotels was ever present. Every entrance, the reception, bars, disco and pool as well as the beach were constantly watched and patrolled.

The tourist industry was doing its best to expand, with the new purpose built town Port El Kantaoui several miles north of Sousse. There was already talk of another being created to the south of Hammamet, Farid was keeping his eyes open for the opportunity of employment at one of the numerous modern seafront hotels due for completion in a few years' time. The French influence was still ever present, although Tunisia had won its independence from France in the 1950s. The economy was now relatively stable and although there would always be the pockets of unrest on the political front and the rumblings had grown louder in recent years, however for the tourist, it was a safe and comfortable place to be. The crime rate was minimal with much less of the thieving and muggings which were happening more and more often in Europe.

The wages were low, but then so was the cost of living outside the tourist zones, where it was usual for a couple of tourists to spend as much on one meal as their waiter earned in a week. However, they felt they got good value for money and for the most part tipped well although the resentment bubbled under the surface at the level of wages and hours of work for little reward.

Extra money and perks were available for the men. European women were fair game. As they shopped the men walked alongside, chatting, never too close and rarely aggressive. Their athletic build, shiny black hair, soft brown eyes and gleaming smiles attracted the women. Of course many told them to disappear, often rudely but there were enough who didn't to make it profitable and the knockbacks were taken in good humour as they moved on to the next victim.

A particular target for the men were the older women with money to spend, divorced, single or just on holiday with their friends. These were the ones who were happy to receive the attentions of a good looking younger man. A trophy with photos to show their envious friends at home. The fact that were they expected to pay for everything from a cup of coffee to dinner and presents didn't matter. The money was there to be spent and it was more fun to pass the time, days and nights, with an attractive and flattering companion.

The women played their part. They preened, pampered and paid. The men accepted, flattered and looked good. These relationships almost always involved sex, some men had lodgings and apartments where they took their women. Getting into the hotels was difficult so quite a few assignations took place on the beach, on the scrub land or in the shadows, in fact anywhere away from prying eyes.

For the hotel based man it was easier to get into a guest's room but to be caught was instant loss of employment and a lot of other problems besides. Tunisia protects its tourists, they are an important part of the economy. Security was tight and the management vigilant. Only the animation teams who often lived in the hotel flourished. It was pretty easy to worm their ways into guests' rooms and they moved from one to the next as the season progressed. However, competition for jobs was fierce and it was not unheard of for one man to report another and to recommend his friend for the swiftly vacated job, for a sweetener naturally.

Farid had himself once been a victim of this unpleasant practice. He had been on the beach on night duty and Lucy had walked down to see him. An overzealous informant had gone to the director and accused Farid of being on the beach all night with a woman whilst he was on duty. Unfortunately for the informant, for a large part of the night Farid had actually been in the hotel with the director. No action was taken.

Many of these relationships ended with the holiday; a few women returned the next year, and even fewer of these May and September relationships ended in marriage. Some lasted but these were rare. The marriages almost always broke down because the man simply wanted gifts, money and a passage to Europe and after a few years he walked away and came home, usually considerably better off.

Where the woman stayed in Tunisia after marriage, the relationships sometimes floundered because the woman could not accept the male dominated society and found to her cost that what was acceptable in a tourist was quite unacceptable in a wife.

From the man's side the failure was frequently caused, as Lucy's friend Cathy so aptly put it, when there was just one woman too many. Tunisian law permits a man only one wife, but sometimes no-one reminded the man. After divorce a few of the women stayed in their adopted country but most licked their wounds, put it down to experience and slunk home sadder, wiser and almost always a lot poorer.

Farid was by his standards comfortably off. He knew his colleagues regarded him as strange. With his few true friends he was as he had always been, if a little more serious and subdued. A few knew of his love who had disappeared without trace years ago and some had heard the rumour but would never ask him. He was rarely seen with a woman, preferring the comfortable friendship of his own kind.

Farid stood at the main door of the hotel. It was early evening and it was drizzling. There were few people about. A couple stood in the shadow of the café next door waiting for the rain to stop and he watched as the man put his arm around his partner's shoulder and kissed her. He mulled over his own monastic existence. His mind strayed to the Spanish girl, on holiday with her grandparents. He had found her innocence refreshingly interesting. The elderly couple spent much of their time in the hotel lounge reading, and left her to herself. A couple of the hotel staff had asked her to go with them, but he himself had never approached her. He could see she was bored and she used to smile shyly as she passed him and once or twice sat down on the low wall talking with him. She was childishly pretty with dark brown hair which curled around her neck. She seemed very young. He laughed when she tried to talk to him in French and she smiled a lot.

Farid found himself attracted to the girl, which surprised him a little. He remembered the night he walked with her on the beach. She was due to leave the next morning and he noticed she had been drinking. He had chided her about her age and was surprised to learn she was twenty. After much kissing and persuasion, she allowed him to make love to her. He held back and was very gentle. Afterwards she was terribly embarrassed. He had put his arm round her and told her not to worry, it was just between them. When he came on duty the next day she had gone.

His lip curled as he remembered the Russian woman who was exactly the opposite. Tall, middle aged and bottle blonde. She was holidaying alone and she had pursued him unmercifully until eventually he capitulated. She showered him with presents and made passionate and sometimes violent love. Her Slavic features, heavy body and huge pendulous breasts did not particularly excite him but he welcomed her as a short-term diversion and the raunchy sex gave him momentary freedom from the frustration of his self-imposed celibacy. She gave him her phone number and tipped him extremely well when she left. He never called her and she never came back.

The rain stopped and he watched as the couple left the café, the man's arm around her waist and his hand resting loosely on her bottom. He felt resentful.

CHAPTER THIRTY

DEBBIE

Farid was standing outside the hotel and he watched her as she walked up from the beach. He thought she must be in her early twenties. She had a short yellow shirt dress, open at the front over a white bikini, her red hair swung in waves around her shoulders as she walked. She was wearing huge sunglasses but the way her head moved from side to side it was fairly obvious she was looking around her as though she expected attention. And she got it. She strolled towards the hotel next door but stopped a few feet away from him idly looking into one of the shops. Although she wore sunglasses he could see she was looking in his direction. He thought nothing of it as he presumed she was waiting for someone and he ignored her.

The next day instead of walking directly across the road from the beach, she made a deliberate detour passed the reception area where he stood talking with one of the older security guards. She had her sunglasses on top of her head and he noticed her eyes were large and cornflower blue. She didn't look at the other man, but kept her gaze fixed on him. As soon as she saw she had his attention, she smiled broadly, but continued walking towards the neighbouring hotel.

"There's one for your pot," his colleague commented crudely with a smirk. Farid made no response but noticed the girl walked on straight past the other hotel towards the Medina. Debbie had noticed Farid the previous day, mainly because he had seemed completely disinterested and that intrigued her. For her that was a novelty and certainly made him all the more interesting.

She got back to the villa she and her two girlfriends were renting. Both of them were stretched out on sunbeds. Ellen sat up. She looked at Sharon whose back was starting to tan beautifully. She stared at her own skin which had gone pale pink but nothing more. She was a gentle girl whose impression of elegance belied her natural shyness.

Debbie looked flushed and very pleased with herself. "Hi kids. How about we have a little party tomorrow before we go home at the weekend?"

Ellen looked puzzled. "How can we do that, we don't know anyone?"

Debbie grinned. "I said a little party."

Sharon turned over, suddenly interested. "Come on Debs, what are you up to now?" Her white teeth gleamed against her olive skin and her huge brown eyes sparkled.

"Well, let's be truthful here, none of us have found it difficult to get male attention!"

The three girls were well aware that individually they could all be described as pretty, but as a trio they were so different from each other, they were stunning and attracted a lot of attention.

"And?"

Debbie smirked conspiratorially from one to the other. "Ladies, we've come to an Arab country for a reason. What I mean is there are three of us and before we leave we need to have a nice intimate little party for sex. Oh, sorry, I meant six!"

Debbie and Sharon collapsed into girlish giggles. Ellen looked the other way, but she could see Debbie was up to something and it made her nervous.

Sharon grinned. "Hang on a sec, Debs, I know you. You've got someone in mind, haven't you?"

"Well as a matter of fact I have."

"Tell me about him."

"No, wait and see. You go and find your own fellas. I suggest we all meet back here around nine tomorrow night. We've already got loads of booze all we need now are the blokes."

"You're on." Sharon leapt off her lounger and danced a little jig. "See you tomorrow night." She was already sifting through her likely victims.

Ellen was not so sure, to her it sounded as though it might be a recipe for disaster. She was the eldest of the three. She knew the other two were intent on sampling the delights of this new country, but she was a born romantic and had come on holiday with certain misgivings. She had her fair share of boyfriends, but never became too attached to any of them. She had wondered if perhaps she might find a sweet holiday romance, so she kept her reservations to herself and agreed to come with them.

Debbie made sure the next day she wore her tiniest bikini, gold with metallic rings holding two small bits of material around her hips and a third ring holding even smaller pieces which barely covered her bust. She deliberately left her beach wrap open.

Farid saw her coming and turned away to speak with Kassem in the shop. However, this time she didn't walk past, but stopped immediately in front of him and pulled out her cigarettes which were tucked in her bikini bottoms. She slid a cigarette between her fingers and smiled expectantly without speaking, waiting for him to offer a light. Farid obliged without comment but her hands closed around his as he lit the cigarette and stayed there for more than a fraction too long.

She managed to stroke his hand lightly before he pulled away. "I've seen you here every day, do you always work days?"

Farid did not speak English. He had picked up one or two words from Lucy but it was never necessary because they always spoke in French.

He just shrugged when she spoke to him. "No English."

Debbie had not taken into account that he might not speak her language. At a loss for a moment she continued in broken French and Farid had little option but to acknowledge her. As security they were not encouraged to chat to either guests or the public in general, save for the usual civilities.

Her voice was light and frothy. "I am here with my friends, but I don't know my way around. Please tell me a nice place to go for coffee."

"There are plenty in the Medina and by the seafront over there." He pointed and turned back to Kassem who watched with interest.

"I have tried some of them but it is very difficult," she hesitated, "being a girl alone, it is very difficult over here and there is too much attention. Will you go with me?"

Farid was quite sure she was well used to the attention. Unfortunately, Kassem had spotted a potential customer and to Farid's dismay disappeared back into his shop.

"I'm sorry I am working and we are not encouraged to socialise with guests. I apologise," he added politely.

She smiled slyly at him, her eyes half closed.

"I think you don't work all day and all night, and I will always meet you away from this hotel if you like."

Farid knew he was being singled out with no effort on his part. She was making it clear in the most blatant way she would like to know him better. His eyes rested on the swell of her breasts, the thin strip of material left little to his imagination. She was certainly pretty. He saw the director approaching and made a quick decision

"Where are you staying, which hotel?"

"Oh, we're not in a hotel, we are renting a friend's villa just past the Medina." She smiled broadly displaying even white, almost predatory teeth, he thought. He felt inexplicably uneasy.

"You know the large café in front of the Medina."

"Yes."

"I will be there around seven." She smirked and stroked his arm. He watched her hips swinging as she walked away and wondered whether he had just made a decision he would come to regret.

The director walked up to Farid.

"Farid?"

"She wanted to know how to get to the Medina," Farid explained. The director nodded and walked on.

When he finished his shift Farid debated whether or not to meet the girl but he was quite sure that if he didn't turn up, she would be here again tomorrow and he certainly couldn't afford a scene of any sort. He had no intention of putting his job in jeopardy over some over-sexed female.

He showered and changed quickly taking little trouble over his appearance. He didn't bother to shave. He saw no point; he was not trying to impress her. He arrived at the café early and found an empty table. He did not know what to expect but his instinct told him to keep her at arm's length and this table had two small benches, one on either side. He sat down and waited.

Debbie dashed back to the villa, her heart thumping. She loved a challenge and it seemed she was going to have to work a bit on this chap if she was going to get him to the villa by nine tonight. She was pleased that both the others were out. "Still searching," she grinned to herself as she poured herself a vodka with a dash of lemonade and ransacked her wardrobe.

"Perfect," she breathed to herself, picking up a white dress. She dressed carefully, lined her eyes with black, applied too much mascara, slicked on a double layer of lipstick and poured another vodka.

As she left the villa, she grabbed a last drink and made it a large one. She knew she was late but fortified with alcohol she made her way quickly towards the Medina. She felt good and by the looks she was attracting, she was sure she looked good.

The woman was tired. It had been a long day. She hurried toward her home wondering if her husband was waiting for his meal. She realised happily he would not be home until late. He was going to Mehdi's house to celebrate his engagement. She breathed a deep sigh. Whilst she loved her husband dearly she had little time for herself these days and since the children had been born she had come to realise just how hard a woman's life could be in this male dominated country. Still, tonight the boys were with their grandmother and she could steal a few precious hours of peace and tranquillity.

On impulse she stopped at the beach side cafe next to the old Medina. The place was full and she sank gratefully into one of the few spare seats. She glanced around her at the usual eclectic mix of local men, one or two girls, mostly foreign as she was. She had come to Tunisia many years before and although much had changed she knew few Tunisian women would ever venture alone into such a place. Liberation had not reached quite that far yet.

There were groups of tourists intermingled with the others and a contented buzz around the place. The woman indulged in her favour occupation of people watching. Her gaze rested on the young man sitting alone. She recognised him immediately. He seemed to be waiting for someone, but what was Farid doing here alone? He seemed ill at ease. She started to her feet but suddenly the buzz of conversation dried up and she followed the eyes of every person in the cafe.

The girl wore a white, almost see-through dress, her red curls shone like a beacon and her wide eyes swept across the hushed assembly. A huge smile indicated she had located her prey. To the woman's amazement she swayed across to Farid. The woman held her breath as a gust of breeze swept the girl's skirt up round her hips. She glanced at Farid. He stared at the girl, his face set and his discomfort obvious as his hands gripped the bench. As she approached Farid, the girl's smile broadened and she bent to kiss his cheek, displaying her ample cleavage and positioned herself next to him

Farid had seen her as soon as she entered the cafe. He wished he hadn't come at all. The narrow straps of her dress held up a tiny bodice from which her bosom was struggling to escape. She was obviously not wearing a bra, as her breasts bounced as she walked. The material was partly transparent and the outline of her body was clearly visible. At first he thought she wasn't wearing any underwear at all. He thought even from a distance she was wearing too much make up. She looked like a tart. He wanted to go.

He held his breath as the slight breeze blew her full skirt which filled out like a parachute and rose up around her hips for a moment, revealing minute white knickers tied with a tiny bow at the side. Farid looked away. Her laughter tinkled as she clutched at the skirt and completely unashamedly smoothed it down.

Farid could see the other people in the café, men and women alike, staring at her as she walked over to him and he wished he was invisible. Her bright carmine lips were stretched into a well practised artificial smile. He put his hands down at his sides on either side of the bench. To his dismay, rather than sit opposite she walked around the table. She leaned forward and he could clearly see her bare breasts as she kissed him lightly on the cheek. She had been drinking. She sat down very close to him he felt her bare thigh on his hand. She made no attempt to move and he pulled his hand sharply from under her.

The woman was stunned. What was Farid doing with a mantrap like that? She watched mesmerised as the girl flirted with her old friend.

Debbie realised immediately she was going too fast. The one thing she didn't want was for him to get up and leave.

"Sorry," she whispered and gave him her sweetest smile.

Farid relaxed a little. She drank cola and he ordered a coffee. He asked her about her holiday and kept the conversation simple but he made no move towards her. Debbie started to get worried. Time was moving on and she sensed no particular commitment from him.

The alcohol was really starting to kick in and she slipped her hand onto his thigh, far too far up for Farid's comfort. She leaned close to him and her breast brushed his arm. "I'm so pleased you arrived." He wondered with her unaccustomed use of French whether she realised what she had said, but her half closed eyes and smile invited him and he was sure she knew. Her hot breath was like a caress on his neck. Her strong perfume enveloped him.

Farid had not been with a woman for longer than he cared to remember and to his embarrassment he felt his body respond. Unfortunately, she was immediately aware of his discomfort and she pulled away embarrassed.

He ordered another coffee his eyes steely and his expression set, cursing himself for his reaction to her. A short while later he suggested they leave, they were still attracting stares from other clientèle and Farid wanted to be anywhere other than where he was.

The woman read a bit more of her book, then paid for her drink and hoped he had not seen her. She stood up to go. Unfortunately the pair rose at the same time.

As they left the café Debbie linked her arm possessively through his. "Where are we going?" she asked.

"Wherever you want to, but I can't stay long, I have to work early tomorrow and I must go soon." He spoke abruptly, by now quite convinced he should have gone straight back to his lodgings.

She bestowed on him her sexiest smile. "You will go only over my dead body," she whispered in English to herself. Farid gave her a half-smile. He had not understood.

The night was drawing in quickly and already it was quite dark. As they walked she continued to tease him, little almost accidental touches of her hand on his thigh, her hips bumping against him, once her hand even brushed the front of his trousers. She murmured "sorry", although her saw by her expression she wasn't.

The woman was worried. Something was definitely not right. She feared for her friend. It would take a strong man to resist such an open invitation. Against her better judgment she followed them.

They turned from the main street into a side road and girl stopped and kissed his cheek, this time moulding her body against him. She bit his ear gently and nuzzled his neck. Farid's control was fast disappearing. He disentangled himself but Debbie sensed that the gesture was somewhat reluctant. She allowed herself a little smile.

As they walked, she hooked her thumb into his belt. She kept her step in time with his so that her breast kept brushing against him. Farid found himself walking very uncomfortably. He could see the road disappeared into a dark narrow dirt track with a high wall running alongside it which led up to a development of four new villas with. There were few lights.

As they turned onto the track he turned to speak to her. She stopped and pulled him towards her, her tongue on his lips and her hand stroking the nape of his neck. He kissed her back and felt her hand slide down his body as she stroked him. Farid's restraint left him.

The woman watched from behind the dense bushes and waited, dreading what she knew would follow but hoping with all her heart it would not.

She gasped as Farid pinned the girl against the wall, feeling every part of her body through the thin material. He and put his hand inside her dress freeing one of her breasts, teasing the soft skin. He heard her sharp intake of breath and his mouth stretched into a thin line. He bent his head and sucked on her nipple until it was firm and hard. He slid his hand down inside her knickers and stroked her. She moaned. His body was bursting and he pushed himself against her.

"Is this what you want?"

He put his hand under her chin and forced her eyes to meet his.

"We'll be at the villa in a few minutes," she whispered hotly in his ear, enjoying the control she felt over him.

"That's not what I asked."

"Yes, of course this is what I want, but not here, not like this…"

Farid wasn't interested in conversation. 'Yes' was good enough.

The woman saw him hold the girl against the wall with one arm across her chest as he undid his trousers.

Debbie gasped; she had only been teasing him to get him to the villa. Too late she realised she had pushed him too far, she was no longer the one in control, if she ever had been. Suddenly she was frightened and she struggled against him.

The woman clapped her hand over her mouth as Farid pulled the girl's skirt up around her waist.

Debbie felt his hot throbbing hardness against her thigh as he leaned his weight against her. He pulled angrily at the tiny bow of her knickers then pushed his knee between her legs and with an expletive lifted her up, wedging her between himself and the cold stone wall as he pulled her legs up around his hips. She flinched as the rough stone ground into her bare back. He pulled her hard down onto his body and she screamed as the tortured organ rammed into her. Farid clamped his free hand over her mouth keeping the other across her chest. She was pinned against the wall like a butterfly on a card. He was too far committed to even notice her pain, and with a couple of fierce upward thrusts he felt the pulsating spurts offering his body the relief it craved. "Oh, Lucy, God help me!" he muttered.

The woman felt sick. That the girl had invited sex was never in question but she knew she had witnessed a rape.

With a grunt, Farid let her drop to the ground. The girl sat there for a few moments whimpering like a puppy and watched as he wiped their combined wetness from his body with a handkerchief, which he threw away.

"Have you got another one?" she whispered. He stared at her, as if seeing her for the first time.

"Use your knickers," he said roughly. "Where were you taking me anyway?"

Her eyes were wet with tears. "Only up that track, the villa's just there. We just decided to have a little party but now it's all spoiled."

"Who's we?"

"My two girlfriends and I. We're leaving on Sunday. We just wanted to have some fun, you know just a few of us," she added lamely.

"I thought you said you didn't know anyone."

"We don't, not really."

"Oh, so your friends have been out on the prowl as well have they? You're playing a dangerous game girl. How old are you anyway?"

"Eighteen. And it's not like that."

"What is it like then?" Debbie hung her head, not looking at him.

"Go on, I want to know, speak to me."

"Well, we've never been here before and we just wanted to know if well… you know if what they say about…"

"About what?" he snapped, fast losing patience.

"Well you know, about Arab men."

Farid didn't know, but he could guess. He stared at her in disbelief and swore loudly. Debbie looked up at him. His face was contorted, his lip curled in a derisive sneer.

"Well, now you know."

She nodded miserably.

"Let me tell you something for your own good. If you carry on like you did with me tonight, you will find yourself passed around the men like a bag of sweets. If you want to be a whore so be it, but if you just want to play with fire, make sure you can stand the heat or you will get burned again."

He spoke quickly and some of the words Debbie didn't understand, but the gist of it was crystal clear.

Now the pressure on his body had been released, Farid just wanted to get her back to her villa so he could get away as quickly as possible.

"You're sure that's where you are staying?" his voice slightly more gentle. Debbie nodded miserably.

"Yes, it's only a two minute walk." Some forlorn hope wondered if perhaps he would still come with her.

"Right, go back there."

He turned and walked away, leaving her sitting on the ground with her back to the wall, her knickers beside her and her dress torn and dirty. The woman crouched down on the ground as he passed. She saw his cheeks were wet with tears.

"Oh Lucy, my darling, forgive me," he whispered.

As she stood up Debbie winced from pain in her back and felt the semen trickle down her leg. She felt cheap, but then that was probably what he'd called her, a cheap tart.

Farid stood in the shadow of the wall and watched her until she got to the door of the villa and went in. He was worried; although it was obvious sex was what she wanted from the start, he knew he shouldn't have taken her the way he had. He turned away and walked quickly to the nearest place he could get alcohol, wanting only a strong drink and never to set eyes on her again. He realised with a wry smile he didn't even know her name.

The woman waited until he disappeared and watched the girl close the door of the villa behind her. She stayed a few moments longer then hurried home, hoping in time she would forget what she had witnessed but knowing she never would.

CHAPTER THIRTY-ONE

ELLEN

Debbie shut the door behind her and leaned back against it. She threw her knickers in the trash and quickly pulled on her wrap which was hung on the back of the door. She could hear voices from the other room, male and female and the music was loud and thumping.

"Debs, is that you?"

"Yeah," she called out. "I'll be down in a sec."

She ran up the stairs into the bathroom and looked in the mirror. Her face was a mess. The black around her eyes had run into rivulets down her cheeks and her lipstick was smudged into a wide gash across her face. Her hair was a mass of straw-like knots and she picked out pieces of grit from the wall. She turned and looked at her back in the mirror. It was scuffed and scratched and an angry red colour. She noticed her dress was torn and one of the straps at back hung loose where it had been ripped off.

She flung the dress onto the floor, stepped into the shower and closed her eyes, feeling the cool water easing her aching back. In her haste she had forgotten to lock the door and didn't hear the gentle knock. Getting no reply Sharon opened the door.

"Good God almighty! What happened to you?"

Debbie turned off the shower and glared at the intruder. "I got fucked, that's what happened."

"Bloody raped more likely." It was more a question than a statement.

Debbie decided to bluff it out, she had no intention of letting her friends know what a fool she had made of herself.

"Actually you're wrong." She smiled languidly patting her skin dry with the towel. "I got my man, but we just couldn't wait until we got back here. He walked all the way here with a hard-on and I could see he wanted me desperately."

"So?"

"Sharon, he's absolutely gorgeous, so I just let him. I mean let's be honest, I was going to let him anyway and it seemed so much more romantic in the open air," she added lamely.

"Romantic!" Sharon snorted "I don't buy it. Look at the state of you. Your back is raw, your cheeks are patchy as though someone's taken a rasp to them, your boobs are bruised and as for your hair, it looks as though you've been dragged through a hedge."

Debbie smirked. "I pretty much was. Unfortunately where I lay down was all stony and with all the heaving and thrusting, my back got a bit scratched up. Frankly I didn't even notice until it was all over."

Sharon didn't believe her but she could see Debbie was sticking to her story.

"Was it worth it, and why isn't he here now?"

Debbie thought quickly.

"Oh, yes," she breathed, "it was worth it, and if he's typical, then Arab men are every bit as passionate as they're cracked up to be." That part at least was true, she thought.

Sharon opened her mouth but Debbie cut in quickly. "He decided it would be better not to come back here when I told him we wouldn't be on our own. He doesn't speak English anyway and he was embarrassed at what my friends would think of how messed up we were."

"He was certainly right there." Sharon was still not convinced.

"So you're seeing him again tomorrow before we go?"

"Oh, I should think so. He said to come by the hotel where he works," Debbie ad-libbed gaily, grinning at her friend.

"Fine, we'll come with you. I think I need to see this wonder guy. I'll see you downstairs in a sec." She turned and walked back down the stairs.

Debbie dressed in a loose tunic dress, tried to brush the tangles out of her hair and gave up, pulling it back into a ponytail. She splashed on some cologne, smeared foundation on her cheeks. She gazed into the mirror. Sharon was right, she was bright pink where his stubble had rubbed against her face and her lips were bruised.

Her friends had overdone it. The room stunk of booze and cigarettes. It was in darkness save for one table lamp, but Debbie could see there were several men and another woman she recognised from the next door villa. She was wrapped around one of the men like a python. Debbie guessed she was in her forties, her tight skirt was up round her thighs. His hand was inside her blouse. The woman's lips were parted and her eyes closed. The man was a lot younger, but neither cared and it was clear they would be a lot closer in a very short time. She whispered something to him and he smiled broadly and kissed her. A few minutes later they left and Debbie saw through the window that a light went on in the bedroom of the villa next to theirs, and off a few moments later.

A well-dressed man sat on the sofa, his arm draped casually round Sharon's shoulder and his other hand resting on her knee. They were talking animatedly and he seemed to Debbie to be quite pleasant. His English was perfect and he smiled at her as she poured herself a vodka and then turned his attention back to Sharon who was gazing at him, enthralled.

Two men sat one each side of Ellen. Debbie noticed how pretty she looked, her white skin glowing in the soft light against the loose dark dress, but noticed she seemed a bit drunk and still had a full glass in her hand. She talked to each man in turn, her grey eyes sparking as they always did when she was happy.

The two men looked at Debbie as she came into the room. Both she reckoned were in their late twenties, although she could see that one was a much bigger and heavier man than the other, the muscles in his arms standing out in the half-light. The smaller one introduced himself as Sharif and the bigger man as Ali. She acknowledged them with a slight smile but didn't reply. After her experience, she felt uncomfortable.

Another man got up and was pouring himself a scotch. Debbie sat down in the empty chair gratefully. The man came back and sat on the arm of her chair his arm along the back to support himself. To her relief he made no move towards her.

"Your boyfriend, he has go? " She smiled at his broken English.

"Yes, he had to go back. He works in a hotel and starts very early in the morning."

"Ah, hotel work. It has very long hours. I too in hotel. Start at six." Debbie nodded.

She wished she had gone straight to bed, her thighs were bruised, and even the soft leather of the chair was hurting her back. Her cheeks were sore where Farid had taken her so forcefully, and her lower body was throbbing in pain. She kept up the conversation for a short while and then made her excuses and went to bed. She heard the front door close and assumed he had also gone.

She turned on the light and started to read. A short while later, she heard Sharon whispering. Her bedroom door closed softly and she heard a man's muffled voice and Sharon's giggle. Then she fell asleep.

The living room was empty save for Ellen and the remaining two men. Sharif turned the music down and handed a scotch to his friend. Eileen already had a full glass and she drained half of it. Whisky? She didn't like whisky, did she? She couldn't remember.

The two men spoke quietly together. Ellen didn't understand them and was drunk enough not to care. She had gone along with her two friends' idea of a party but the more she thought about it the more scared she became. She was not a heavy drinker but in her nervousness had drunk a lot more than usual. She lay back on the sofa her legs splayed out in front of her and her head thrown back. Ali sat very close to her and had his big arm draped over her shoulder. She smiled lazily as his hand slid down and rested loosely just above her breast.

He moved his fingers and gently stroked her nipple through the thin material. Ellen felt a pleasant warmth flow over her. He kissed the hollow in her neck and smiled as she quivered. His touch and his soft voice excited her.

Ali said something sharply to Sharif in Arabic, who looked at Ellen for a moment and shrugged his shoulders. He picked up his coat and left.

Ali continued whispering softly to Ellen. She thought it sounded so romantic. Her eyes closed and she listened to the music.

She could feel the heat of his body against her skin. Her lips parted. He traced his fingers slowly along the inside of her thigh under her dress and found the softness of her. His fingers teased and stroked her. Waves of pleasure flooded over her. She felt her dress slipping off and he lifted her gently onto the deep pile rug. She was naked. She didn't care, this was as it should be. Ali's lips caressed and stroked her. She arched herself against him.

Very gently he moved, so his body was over her and slipped himself gently inside her. He moved rhythmically. She was dreaming. She stroked his hair as she responded to him. She opened her eyes. He smiled, leant forward and kissed her. She wrapped her legs around his hips holding him tightly. She felt the tempo increase and she matched him stroke for stroke. She felt the flood of warmth as he shuddered and sighed deeply. He had been gentle with her. He slid off her damp body and lay beside her on the rug for a moment watching her. Then he sat up, lit two cigarettes and handed her one.

Ellen lay back, one arm behind her head watching the smoke drifting up lazily towards the ceiling, hanging in the still air. Her body shone with sweat, luminous against the dark rug and her lips were full and parted. She bent her knees up and wiggled her toes against the soft pile. The picture was one of unconscious sensuality.

Ellen felt no remorse or embarrassment. She had wanted everything which was done to her. She had enjoyed every minute and if the truth be known she was sorry it was over. It wasn't. All night they talked and made love, in ways Ellen had only dreamed of. When Debbie came down in the morning she found them sleeping on the sofa, covered only by a loose sheet. It was obvious they were naked. Ellen lay with her head against Ali's chest. She was smiling, even in her sleep.

Debbie felt a quick rush of jealousy. Her own body ached and although she had another shower, her wounds both physical and mental still smarted. She picked up the glasses and started clearing up. Ellen stretched out and opened her eyes. Debbie watched her as, still half asleep she reached up and her fingers stroked the muscles of her companion's chest. She noticed Debbie watching her. She looked quickly at the sleeping man beside her and smiled at her friend, her expression one of satisfaction and total happiness. *Like the bloody cat that got the bloody cream*, Debbie thought enviously.

Ellen had changed. She had always been the quiet one, the one who was not sure about the antics of her two more adventurous friends. She had never flirted overtly the way Debbie and Sharon did, but now it seemed to Debbie that Ellen had blossomed in one night. She thought of her own sordid encounter and wondered grimly how she was going to get round the lie she had told Sharon yesterday that she was to meet the man again. She hoped Sharon would have forgotten.

She disappeared into the kitchen and attacked the washing up. When she came out Ellen had on her dress and her new friend sat bare chested beside her, his black trousers tight over his thighs. He had a magnificent physique. He had his arm draped around Ellen's shoulder his huge paw resting just above her breast. His eyes never left her, he seemed completely captivated. Debbie wished her own chosen partner had been the same.

Sharon surfaced with her man about an hour later. Debbie was even more dejected when she saw them come down the stairs hand in hand. At that moment she didn't know who she hated most, that man or herself.

She watched as Ali and Ellen exchanged phone numbers and addresses. It was then that she realised that she didn't even know that man's name and probably never would.

There was a knock on the door and Sharif came in. He and Ali left together a few minutes later. Sharon kissed her man goodbye and he followed them. Debbie felt ghastly, she ached all over and she felt sick. Cattily she asked Sharon why she hadn't got her man's phone number.

Sharon grinned "He's actually not Tunisian. He's an Egyptian businessman and only here for a two day conference. He told me straight out it was a one off, but believe me it was worth it! Anyway, enough about me, when are we going to see this man of yours?" She hadn't forgotten.

"Later."

To avoid any further questions, Debbie walked back upstairs, got back into bed and promptly fell asleep. When she woke a little after two, she was ravenous. Fortunately the girls had finished the clearing up and made lunch. There was enough left for her. After she had eaten, Debbie realised she had to think how she was going to get around her own problem. An idea came into her head.

She took another shower, washed her hair and tied it back into a ponytail. She put on a pair of jeans and a soft pale blue blouse with loose sleeves. She wore flat sandals, little make-up and just one elegant gold bracelet. She looked as different from yesterday's vamp as she knew how.

"Debbie, you look lovely!" Ellen actually meant it. She had always thought Debbie looked and dressed far too obviously and she hadn't seen this side of Debbie before. It suited her. Debbie felt better. Sharon came in from the kitchen and stared at Debbie.

"You'll knock him for six. You should always look like that," she exclaimed. Debbie felt her confidence rising. *I can do this*, she thought.

The three girls walked together, in no particular hurry. They were for the most part already packed and ready to leave the following day. They walked happily around the Medina, smiling at all the remarks directed at them, buying a few bits and pieces to take home. They sipped mint tea at the big café and Debbie was quite sure that if anyone was there who had been there the night before they wouldn't associate her with the vamp from yesterday evening. She was right.

Finally they made their way towards the hotel where Farid worked. He stood outside talking to Kassem. He saw the three girls walking towards him and thought how nice they looked. He didn't recognise Debbie until she was a few feet away from him.

"Oh shit, she's back," he said to Kassem and turned away.

"That's not the same girl."

"Oh yes, it is, my friend, but I admit I didn't see it until just now, believe me this is probably another of her little tricks."

Farid had not told Kassem what had happened, just said she had been a nuisance. He would never tell anyone, but he realised the one thing. He could not afford to ignore her or be rude in case she decided to take the whole matter further. He knew that if she chose to report his behaviour, he could be in very deep trouble.

She tapped him on the arm.

"Hello," she said softly. "I'm pleased you're here, I just wanted to say sorry about yesterday."

Farid thought he must have misunderstood her.

He turned and she smiled sweetly at him her hand outstretched. Bemused he took it and gave her a slight smile in response. "Yes, I'm sorry too."

Encouraged Debbie continued the charade. Like her, both her friends knew a little bit of basic French but Debbie knew only she and Farid would understand the true meaning of what she said.

"No harm done?"

She looked him straight in the face. Farid shook his head.

"No harm done," he repeated.

"Nor me." The relief Farid felt was tangible.

The two girls watched him with undisguised interest but no animosity. Quickly he realised that they must have been the two staying in the villa last night and probably seen the mess their friend had got into. He assumed Debbie had made up some story about them making passionate love behind a bush or some other such romantic rubbish. He wasn't of course far wrong. And as they hadn't seen their friend's mystery man, now they were here to vet him.

Her eyes pleaded with him not to let her down. Quickly he glanced around. The director was nowhere to be seen. He motioned to her to move away from the hotel entrance so he was not visible from the reception area.

Making sure her friends could see, Farid put his hand on her shoulder and she flinched slightly.

"My back," she whispered.

For a moment he almost felt sorry for her. He let his arm rest loosely, he was not prepared to move closer to her even to save her embarrassment. She put one arm round his waist and laid her head gently against his chest.

"Thank you." He gave her a weak smile.

"We leave tomorrow; I don't suppose I could see you again?" she whispered close to his ear.

"I don't think that would be a good idea," he whispered back, just wishing she would go.

He pulled away and said loudly so her friends could hear.

"I'm sorry. I can't see you tonight, they've put me on a double shift." The girls heard but only she understood. He lifted her hand and kissed it. She turned to him, her back to her friends.

"One last question," she said quietly.

He waited. "Who's Lucy?"

Farid paled and he tried to keep his voice steady.

"Why do you ask?"

She whispered softly. "Last night when you came you said the name Lucy."

He said nothing and watched her silently as she walked away with her friends.

If only I'd played it differently, she wondered *but then that was probably the trouble, I played it instead of just being nice. That's a mistake I won't make again, not with a man like that. I wonder who she is, that Lucy.* She felt a wave of intense jealousy towards the unknown woman.

Ellen, ever the romantic, had thought how gentlemanly he had been.

"He's very nice and ever so handsome," she said.

Debbie smiled gratefully. Sharon was still not sure, she couldn't get out of her mind how her friend had looked in the bathroom. That didn't sit right with what she had just seen, but she put it out of her mind as it appeared no lasting harm had been done.

"What's his name?"

Debbie smirked. "Farid," she replied. She had heard Kassem call him that.

Farid could not remember when he had felt more relieved. He hadn't slept at all. He knew he could have had his life completely ruined if it came to her word against his. Although he reasoned that she had said yes, when he thought about it in the solitude of his own bed he realised it the whole situation could have been interpreted very differently if she had told her side of the truth to anyone else. It would have been all too easy for her to report he had invited her to the café and when she wanted to leave he had followed her and raped her. He too decided it was a mistake he would never make again.

Kassem smirked. "What was all that about? Are you going to see her again?"

Farid put his arm around his friend. "Would you take tea with the Devil, because she came disguised as an angel! "

"But I thought…"

"My friend, that subject is closed."

"Got her number? I might call her myself."

"I haven't got her number and I don't even know her name, and before you say a word, she doesn't know mine either." He put his hand in his pocket and felt the piece of paper Debbie had slipped there as he had held her.

"I only asked. She's the first woman I've seen you with since the Russian last year. At least she took your mind off the other one for a short time." His voice tailed off as Farid turned on him, his face dark with anger.

"That subject is also closed."

Farid stormed back into the hotel kicking open the glass door. Kassem watched him in astonishment. "So he's still hung up on the English woman after all this time," he muttered and he walked back inside his shop, shaking his head.

CHAPTER THIRTY-TWO

ELLEN AND ALI

Ali turned up in the evening at the villa and he and Ellen went for a walk together. He was absolutely besotted with her and she with him.

"I must see you again." He tried to kiss her but she pushed him away with a giggle.

"Ali, there's more to life than this." She wondered if there was!

"I've been thinking about you all day. Why do you have to go back to England?"

She laughed. "I have work to do, I have to work so I can save up my money to come back."

He sat up. "You will come back?"

"Of course I will." He enveloped her in a bear like hug.

"Habibi, I will be waiting. When?"

She thought carefully. "In three months' time."

"So long."

"Ali, I am a teacher, I must work."

"I will phone you every day."

"No, it's too expensive, phone me sometimes, but write to me so I can read your letters and think about you often."

Ali hesitated. Although he spoke reasonably good English, writing was something different.

"Yes, I will write," he answered simply.

"And now I must go back. We leave soon."

He rolled on top of her pinning her to the ground and grinned.

She got back to the villa half an hour later, her hair tangled and full of grass. Sharon burst out laughing and even Debbie had smiled. Ellen had definitely made a conquest.

Ellen said goodbye to her friends at the airport and caught a taxi home. She left her case inside the door, went straight to bed and thought about her big bear. She missed him. She had only known him for two days but when she had told him she would be back, she meant it. Ellen had had a couple of boyfriends before, but had never experienced anyone like Ali and to her surprise she realised anyone else would now be insignificant in her life.

When she went back to school, she told her friends about her new love. Jackie, one of the other teachers laughingly asked her if she had liked Tunisia, as opposed simply to her new man. Ellen was intrigued to learn that Jackie had been to Tunisia many years before.

Ellen's telephone bills turned into a nightmare but to compensate she stopped going out and spent most of her time at home when she wasn't doing school work, writing long loving letters to Ali or speaking with him on the phone. She was quite surprised to find out that they actually had a lot in common, both loved music and dancing and had an interest in history and historical sights and old ruins. Ali was intrigued to know Ellen also loved football. Being passionate about the subject himself this sealed the pact between them. But once the novelty of Ellen's new love had died down at school, the only colleague who Ellen really talked to was Jackie.

As Jackie listened to Ellen's growing love for her man, she hoped with all her heart that Ellen would be luckier with her Tunisian romance than her old friend Lucy had been.

True to her word, Ellen went back to Tunisia in the autumn half term and for new year and again at Easter, the whole summer holiday and in the new year Ali asked her to be his wife and she accepted him.

Jackie was surprised to receive the invitation to their wedding. Although she and Ellen had become quite good friends she had not thought the relationship with Ali had developed into marriage.

"Ellen, that's wonderful." She congratulated her friend "But do you really think you are doing the right thing? You may have known each other for eighteen months but how long have you actually spent together? Are you sure you're not just wrapped up in romantic dreams and this isn't just a holiday romance, and he's using you as a ticket to England. They do that some of them, you know."

Ellen expected this, "Jackie, I know what I'm doing. I agree we haven't spent that much time together but I have a stack of letters and so has he. We have got to know each other on the phone and I actually feel I know him better than any other man I've ever been with." She gave a happy smile. "Anyway, he has never asked me for anything except myself and we are going to live in Tunisia after we are married. He doesn't want to come to England. He has a good job and his family are quite well off and we will have our own home."

"You don't have to sell him to me, you know. You are the one who is getting married!"

"Sorry, I'm just excited. Anyway, my mind is quite made up, so are you coming to the wedding or not?"

"I wouldn't miss it for the world. Although it was more years ago than I care to remember I absolutely loved the place. It must be something in the air! My friend Lucy took it one further, she kept coming back for some years."

Lucy had never returned after the twins were born and without thinking of the possible consequences, Jackie asked quickly, "Would you mind very much if I asked her to come with me to the wedding?"

Ellen beamed at her. "Absolutely, the more girls from England the happier I will be. From what I understand, Tunisian weddings celebrations go on for days and there will be loads of people. Ali tells me the couple getting married ask pretty much everyone they've ever known, and those they forget the family will remember! One more won't matter, but make sure you book up because it gets quite busy in the summer."

CHAPTER THIRTY-THREE

HAKIM

Hakim had never really seen the need for his eldest son to work so far away from home and did not really understand why he chose to do so. Although he did not know what his son did whilst he was not working, he kept in regular touch with family, if not in person by phone or message as is usual in Tunisian society, so Hakim knew where he worked and a little of his daily life. Years ago when he asked him, Farid replied that with the twelve-hour shifts, getting to and from lodgings, eating and sleeping there was little time for a social life. Hakim had not worried too much, his boy was sensible and whilst he liked the companionship of his friends and enjoyed himself like any young person, he had never been one to get involved in crazy stunts like the children of some of his friends and neighbours.

He sat on his balcony. His back hurt and he stretched in the old wooden chair, clutching at his side as the muscles rebelled. He felt old this morning, the heat was already mounting and from the clear azure of the sky promised to be intense in a matter of hours. Although the balcony faced away from the morning sun, even in the shadows the heat hung like a curtain pressing down on him. His grey hair, still thick and springy was cropped close to his head and his shaggy moustache was peppered with white.

He had been a handsome man in his day but at sixty-five, his face was heavily lined and particularly now the furrows on his forehead were deep as he lost himself in thought. He had gone to the doctor about his aching back and all the wretch could do was tell him it was to be expected at his age, which was no help at all. "That is something I could have worked out for myself," he muttered irritably to himself. Still it was nothing like the pain in his chest a few years before, but after the operation he was told his heart was sound although he should give up the smoking. To hell with the issues of advancing years. He yawned, he had not slept well. He felt comforted that there was nothing medically wrong with him, this was just because there were too many problems in his life for someone of his age, then settled back into his chair and reached mutinously for his cigarettes.

Hakim watched the people hurrying to and fro. A colony of bees, mostly workers, but one or two drones and queens who did not work but relied on others to work for them, all simply wanting to complete the daily chores before the heat became oppressive, when they could retire to the relative cool of their homes. He noticed a few of the older men still favoured the loose comfortable robes of their youth, which are still worn extensively in the south of the country, but with the influx of tourism in the north, particularly in the towns and cities, most of the men there had now adopted the European dress.

He thought of the European influence which had crept in, stealthily, one foot at a time testing the water, first one modern hotel, bar and nightclub and then another and now even a casino was planned. He knew it would of course be only for tourists as Muslims are not permitted to gamble. Not that gambling had ever appealed to Hakim, life was enough of a gamble in itself. He felt quite strongly that all any man could do is care for his family, keep the respect of the community, follow the teachings of his religion and try to ensure that his children did the same. He was uneasy about the confusion which the tourists caused, exhibiting to the young people their hedonistic lifestyle.

They came seeking fun and love and wreaked their havoc during their brief holidays, after which each returned to his or her mundane lifestyle. He smiled, they were no doubt seated in grey clothes behind an office desk for another eleven and a half months before shaking out the moths from their Hawaiian shirts, baggy shorts and tiny short dresses, to once again drink and party the night away under the warm night skies of his homeland.

Unfortunately as there were so many of them, these invaders took over a good part of the year and their influence was widely felt, particularly amongst the young. For the young Tunisian, Hakim mused, it must seem that these Europeans lived like this all year round, without the restrictions of moral code, appearance or family concern, a life of abandonment and selfish indulgence. Hakim felt that the ways of their ancestors were often pushed to the back of young men's minds and now this was spilling over into political unrest. He could understand why many of his young countrymen tried to go to Europe and knew there were many ways to achieve the necessary visa, not all of them honourable.

He had never heard any tales of his son being in any sort of trouble or doing anything which would in any way shame his family. He was now in his thirties and old enough to make his own decisions. Hakim acknowledged that Farid was a dutiful son, giving a proportion of his income to his family and causing him no particular distress, other than the usual teenage moods, squabbles and problems which any parent should expect and take as a part of everyday life.

Hakim was aware that Farid had a presence about him. His firstborn son was a handsome man, his thick black hair was well cared for, and with high cheek bones and strong chin defined by a narrow moustache which sat above a sensual but not over generous mouth he would have passed as good looking anyway. But it was his mesmeric golden eyes which held attention. Hakim could see a woman would find it hard to break away from his gaze if he didn't want her to. He was not sure whether Farid was aware of the power he could exercise. If he was Hakim had never seen him use it. He was not overconfident or brash like some of the young men, but came across as pleasant and well mannered.

Hakim knew that the employment situation in Tunisia was uncertain but the hotel and tourist trade was certainly one of the most secure. Tourism had really taken off in the past ten years or so with new hotels and facilities going up every year.

He thought of Port El Kantaoui, to the north of his home town, a session of luxury hotels and a new marina for the wealthy tourists to park their yachts. It was an elegant purpose built tourist resort, all the pseudo-Moorish Andalusian architecture, smart white buildings and narrow cobbled walkways with cafés and shops selling mainly tourist paraphernalia. And the restaurants... He smiled to himself, even a very simple meal would set you back more than half a week's wages; still they didn't seem to mind, these visitors.

He admitted that Sousse had its hotels but for the most part they were kept on the coastal areas out of the main town, which retained its old comfortable environment. Those in the town were designed to blend in and some had been there for years, old dusty buildings fronting directly onto the streets, the interiors revamped in a desperate bid to keep up with the new young generation springing up in clutches along the coast.

Farid had told him about the planned development to the south of Hammamet which was due to be completed around the millennium. It was to include a shopping and entertainment centre in the form of a Medina - expensive apartments and the obligatory marina for the yachts of the rich and famous. There would be a long coastal roadway lined with palms and numerous luxury hotels to be lined up like sentries overlooking the wide road running parallel to the beach. All very Mediterranean and in his quiet opinion more suited to Spain or France. But progress was exactly that. Tourism was increasing year by year and with it the job market in all things associated, providing security for men and their families, but bringing with it the temptations of Europe.

Yasmine Hammamet the new resort was to be called. *Clever name*, Hakim thought. Jasmine, the flower of happiness and love, releasing its perfume more strongly after sunset and symbolising welcome, a bringer of peace. Some even consider it an aphrodisiac.

Hakim's mind wandered, he loved the smell of jasmine, it reminded him of when he had been a young man walking near the beach and in the countryside around Hammamet, nearly fifty years before , his heart full of hope and love and at peace with himself. And now several kilometres of that coastline and rolling countryside dotted with sheep, goats and olive trees was to be given over to the new *zone touristique*.

Hakim felt a bit guilty about his eldest son. When Farid left school instead of going to college he had gone straight to work to help support his family. Hakim knew his own health a year or so back had caused his eldest son great distress and he often wondered how Farid had managed to find the money so quickly for his operation. He had never asked and Farid had never mentioned it. He himself worked a few hours for his friend in the shop for a few dinar, but he could not put in the long hours which had once provided his family with a comfortable home and existence.

Farid had worked in the security side of the tourist industry most of his adult life, mainly in the Hammamet area. This his father did not altogether understand because Sousse and later Port El Kantaoui were equally as important tourist zones, but Farid brushed this aside and explained that he had contacts in the Hammamet area who were more likely to be able to help him stay permanently employed. Employment was uncertain. Many employers either decided not to keep on their workers on for too long to avoid giving them a contract of employment or alternatively laid them off for a few months over the winter and took them on again in the next season. It was therefore necessary to be somewhere it was possible to get quickly back into another job.

Hakim raised the subject occasionally, but Farid pointed out that particularly now with the new hotels there would be work for all who were on the spot and ready to jump in quickly. Hakim did not labour the point any further.

He had wondered for some years whether his son had any thoughts on marriage, he knew he had several girlfriends in the past and he was sure there had been a woman a few years back but Farid had never mentioned anything so it was unlikely to have been a serious relationship. There were of course the sisters and cousins of his friends but Hakim did not think there was anyone he was considering as a wife. It was quite usual in his country for a man to marry a relative and he had hoped for some time that Farid might be interested in his cousin's youngest daughter, Sarra. He chuckled to himself as he recalled his own younger daughter's ingenious and sometimes almost reckless attempts to interest her brother in the girl.

Hakim knew the problems which young men experienced. At the time of their lives when their hormones burned and mating instincts were strongest, their religion and culture taught that sexual and indeed close social association with a girl outside marriage was wrong. He reasoned that the young men of today most likely had relationships with tourists and a certain type of local girl, but not the type they would marry. Every man wanted to marry a virgin, a modest girl without experience who they could introduce to the world and delights of womanhood and mould around their own ideals. But this did not solve the problem of the natural desires of a testosterone fuelled young man and so more often than not, tourists became the obvious target. Whether they were virgins or not was of no importance to the man, he was not going to marry one of them. Most of the women, young and old, paraded in clothes (or often lack of them) which exposed pretty much everything and for those working in the tourist industry the sexual honey pot was ever open.

He watched idly as a young woman walked up the slight incline away from him towards the sea. She wore her hair in a knot high on her head. Hakim noticed the angry flush across her shoulders and the top part of her back where her pale skin had already burned. She leaned forward, as she hurried up the dusty uneven pathway, her shorts exposing the lower part of her buttocks. *'At least that bit's not burned!'* he thought smiling to himself.

He watched until she disappeared. He found himself strangely unmoved by the expanse of exposed female body. People and places around him were changing far too quickly for his liking. "But then I am not as young as I was," adding dourly to himself ,"but was I ever that young?"

Hakim was aware of what was referred to as 'le bezness' which had sneaked into in his country just as it had in many other places as far afield as Southern Europe, across other African, Asian and Caribbean countries. Wherever women go and men were available, there are those who were happy to oblige with whatever the woman wants, in return for gifts, clothes and money or a passage to Europe, and le bezness flourished. Many women are aware of it, they just don't think it will ever happen to them.

Hakim was also aware that the type of man who indulges in le bezness is usually the poorer and not so well educated man, one with little or no training and who as a result earns little money. The holiday industry makes it easy for him to meet the tourists so he tries for employment in the discos, shops or hotels, particularly in the animation team, bar or restaurant where he is in constant contact with the guests. Unfortunately in such cases the man's family can also be involved. They accept the gifts he brings, use the money he obtains, assist him whenever they can. They will smile at the woman and accept her into their home as his friend, knowing full well their son's relationship is almost always based on how much he can get from whichever woman he is with at the time.

He shook his head as he remembered the pretty young French girl a couple of years before whose boyfriend was called to military service. Although not formally engaged she had already obtained her right to stay card. He persuaded her to open a bank account so they could save jointly for their wedding. His family took her into their home for a year while he was away. She worked and saved hard for their wedding. Her family sent her money and the bank account grew. Her boyfriend always found reasons not to pay into the account and made little contribution. She went home to visit her parents for a month and when she returned her young man had cleaned out the account and disappeared. The family of course said they knew absolutely nothing about it or his present whereabouts. As Fadil had said if the girl doesn't want to get fleeced she should keep her legs together and her money in her own country.

Hakim mused over the implications of such relationships. Any woman could find herself a target and the more successful man can work two or three relationships at the same time. He professes attraction followed quickly by the immortal words "I love you", which of course he will know in many languages. He will make it known how bad the wages are and ask for small gifts such as cigarettes, taxi fares or a coffee. The woman will not mind, because he has told her how little money he has, and of course because he finds her so attractive and never stops telling her. If she follows this up with larger gifts such as money, restaurant meals, a visit to a nightclub, the man is very happy, if they are not immediately forthcoming, he will hint at them. If she comes back for a second helping she will be asked to bring with her a bottle of whisky, designer clothes or a mobile phone for which he will probably even specify the brand, label or make he wants.

He will ask her to send money, small sums to start with, he has lost his job and has no money for food or to call her and already enamoured, she takes pity on him and sends the required funds. She may even be asked for another mobile phone because the one she gave him has been stolen, is broken or even gets bad reception so he finds it hard to call her. The second phone will more than likely end up with one of his friends or relatives. He will suggest she rents a flat during her holiday rather than stay in a hotel so they can be together, and he will make sure she provides drinks for him and his friends.

The whole business, for that is of course what it is, will usually include requests for a large sum of money, the most common and obvious reasons given are to extricate himself from military service because of course my darling that will mean I cannot see you for a whole year, which is of course untrue. There is the desperate plea for money because a close member of his family is ill and needs urgent medical attention, which can run into thousands of dinar. The plea is almost always accompanied by the apology that he has tried every other possible alternative to raise the money, and that he would never dream of asking her, but he has no option and he will of course pay it back, but never does. On occasion of course the reason may be true but in the vast majority of cases, it is simply a ploy to obtain money, all just part of le bezness. He will hint at starting a business venture or even buying a flat for them to live in, and she will of course pay for it. The venture, if it ever existed at all will most likely fail and the money will arrive in the man's own pocket. If the woman is stupid enough to buy a flat, it will more than likely end up as his and his Tunisian wife's home.

If his chosen victim turns out to be poor by his standards he will not necessarily cast her aside but will continue the relationship if only for the free sex. Then of course he can then move it forward by promises of marriage and a longing to visit her country, in short he wants to go to Europe to seek a better life. Whether with her, another woman or just to earn some money and then go home a wealthier man, is another matter.

The Government and the police in tourist zones are well aware of the problem. It does not matter that the laws of the country and those of general acceptable behaviour made illicit associations quite difficult. Here in Tunisia, Hakim knew that local men were not allowed into the hotels without consent of the management if they were not guests and once inside were never allowed on the upstairs floors. Behaviour which could in any way be considered sexual was forbidden but of course if two parties want the same thing, nature will find a way and where sex, money or other benefit are concerned the Tunisian man is nothing if not inventive.

Hakim pushed his thoughts to the back of his mind and got unsteadily to his feet. His back hurt and he cursed himself for sitting so long.

"I am becoming old," he said to no one in particular and slipped his feet into his comfortable old shoes, smiling as he remembered how he had rescued them from the rubbish bin years before after his dear wife had decided they had seen better days.

He made his way slowly along up the hill keeping in the shade of the buildings. His friends sat around the table in their usual place and he lowered himself thankfully into a chair. They sat together in a huddle, sipping their coffee and smoking, chewing over the things that old men talk about, the bubbling political unrest, problems in their country, social and otherwise, the lives and loves of their families and what they should be doing to guide their children in the right direction through the whirlpool of life without allowing them to sink into the quagmire.

Hakim noticed that Fadil seemed angry.

"What ails you my friend?"

"Oh, it is just Moufid again. He is working as a waiter at that new Hannibal hotel and he's got himself caught up with a German woman older than his own mother. He came in yesterday and I caught the wretch showing off to his brother. He's wearing an expensive watch and waving around a new phone which this woman has given him."

Hakim shook his head in sympathy. "What did you say?"

Fadil's face flushed. "I shouted at him that he was nothing more than a whore to get picked up by such a woman."

Hakim tried to placate him but succeeded in making matters worse. "Look, Fadil, these relationships mean nothing to our young men. They think they are providing a service to these women which they believe they are obviously not getting at home. The men are gaining things from the relationship and scratching their own itch at the same time. I am sure there is no personal involvement and provided they protect themselves I suppose there are worse things which could happen."

Hakim was surprised as Fadil leapt to his feet and the near violent altercation which followed.

"Of course there are other things to consider. How would you feel if it was your Farid?"

Hakim was angry. He too leapt to his feet and shouted back. "Farid would not put himself in such a position. He has no interest in such women. Moufid has never been too choosy, as well you know. This German woman is not the first."

"How do you know Farid is not involved? Do you ever see him with a woman? Does he ever bring one home with him? Do you think he is a monk or do you think perhaps he has no interest in women?"

Hakim was furious at the implication and the two men faced each other over the table and were finally persuaded to sit down before they were forcibly ejected Fadil was finally mollified when Hakim had been forced in the end to concede that he would probably feel the same if it were Farid and not Moufid who was involved.

What both men agreed on was that the problem started when the woman believed herself in love with her young man and wanted to take it further. This, they agreed, nodding their heads in unison, could then definitely become a problem. They refused to consider that the situation could, all be it on rare occasions, be reversed or worse still mutual. Both intensely disapproved of foreign marriages where the language, religion and culture were completely different. They were adamant in their agreement that these rarely worked and invariably disrupted the family. Where the woman was more than a year or two older they agreed it was quite out of the question.

CHAPTER THIRTY-FOUR

CONFESSIONS

Over the next few days Hakim thought a lot about what Fadil had said. He had never considered that his son could be a part of what he considered that rather sordid situation and something which only affected other families. Moufid had always had an eye open for a new woman and it was well known he was not discriminatory. Young or old, provided they had money Moufid would try to bed them and relieve them of whatever other benefits he could worm out of them.

Hakim reasoned with himself that Farid was quite different. But he had to admit to himself that his son rarely showed anything other than polite interest in any girl he had put in his path, so Hakim thought perhaps he might have a few girlfriends in Hammamet. He quickly dismissed as ludicrous the thought that his treasured eldest son might have been at any time the temporary plaything of some middle-aged half-dressed woman, providing sex in return for money and gifts. How he hoped Farid would decide to settle down.

A few days later he thought his hopes had been realised. To Hakim's surprise, Farid finally decided to ask sweet natured Sarra, his cousin's youngest daughter, to be his wife. Hakim was relieved and sure she would make him a good wife. He admitted to himself that he had rather pushed his son towards choosing a partner but he was the eldest son of the family and Hakim felt that the time was right. Farid has made numerous excuses but finally after two or three years of increasing pressure he told his father that he had decided to marry.

"You have asked her?"

"No Baba, but I think she will be a suitable wife and I believe she will accept me."

Hakim was happy although "suitable" was not quite the word he had hoped to hear from his son, but he banished the uneasiness as a show of nerves, although whether on his part or his son's he was not sure. It was not unusual for marriages to be agreed upon where the two people were not in love, just where the union was sensible and approved of by the families and often for the benefit of everyone.

The formalities with her family were duly observed and Sarra accepted Farid's proposal. The preparations for their marriage began. The initial celebration of formal engagement was to be in a month or so with the marriage in the following summer.

Hakim was worried. He had witnessed what he had though was every mood and disappointment that his eldest son had shown since his birth. There had only been one unexplained outburst that he could recall, when Farid in his mid-teens had apparently said things he should not have done to a woman tourist. Their neighbour who had witnessed the altercation in the cafe had scurried home to tell Hakim but when he tackled Farid about it, Farid refused to explain. Hakim always believed there was more to the story but neither Farid nor Ahmed had been forthcoming and against his better judgment and his wife's gentle pleading he had let the matter lie and even allowed Farid to keep the single coin the woman had given him.

Farid's behaviour was now something new and it troubled him deeply as the days went by. His son seemed to have shrunk into himself and lived behind an invisible barrier through which no one could reach him. Even his own sister, commented on it, so he knew it was not just his imagination.

"I think he is just concerned at the responsibility he has now decided to take on, but he will be able to deal with it. He is a good boy," Hakim told her sternly.

His sister agreed, although neither were convinced. Hend had moved into the family home after his beloved wife died. As Farid was not married it had been a good arrangement for both herself and Hakim. She had been married at twenty to a man some fifteen years older than herself. Her husband was a good man but they were not blessed with children and when he died she found herself alone and lonely. When her brother suggested she move in with his family she was happy to do so and take care of him for as long as she could, although she admitted to herself she was not a youngster anymore!

Hakim sat in his old comfortable chair. There was a peaceful silence throughout the home. Hend was spending the night with her cousin who lived in a nearby village. Saleem was working away and Fatma was holidaying with a friend down in the south. He dozed off and when he awoke his back had started to ache. He pulled himself up and shuffled across the floor to his room. A muffled sobbing came from his son's room. He stood transfixed, suddenly wide awake but completely at a loss at what to do. He listened for a few minutes but the weeping did not stop and Hakim's world disintegrated as he unwillingly relived the last weeks.

He was finally forced to admit to himself Farid was simply being carried along on the rolling tide of wedding preparation and had no real wish to marry. The sobbing spoke more loudly to Hakim than words ever could. Weeping was not the action of a man looking forward to his wedding but of a lonely man fulfilling a duty. The only reason Hakim could see for his despair was that he was in love with another woman, but a woman he could not have. But what other woman? He knew of none. He raised a silent prayer to Allah for guidance.

Hakim sat down in his bedroom his head in his hands and went through the possibilities, as calmly as he could. It must be someone Farid could not marry for reasons he did not want to begin to conceive. Images raced through his brain and he threw them out, but they sneaked back in and began to fester like a wound. He swore. A woman already married to another man? He thought about that, but even in his anguished state he thought it impossible. Farid was not that sort of man. Perhaps a woman whose own husband had died, or worse still divorced, with a child he did not want to take on as his own. To accept the child of another man was not an easy thing as it would put a strain on his own family and affect his standing within the community. He shook his head. Fadil's crude comment came to his mind but Farid had never, praise be to Allah, shown any interest in men. Again he put it out of his mind as impossible.

He cast his mind back over the years. It came to him that once his son had been happy, there were weeks when his eyes sparkled and he walked on clouds, he smiled and he loved the world. Sometimes he was deeply miserable for a few weeks but then the shadows lifted and the happiness returned, as though the source of this joy came and went with the seasons. He concluded there had definitely been a woman then.

Hakim thought about this. Some years ago everything changed. He remembered because it was just after the New Year. Farid told them he would not be home, but then his plans changed and he spent the celebrations in the family home and with his friends in Sousse. He seemed happy and content but immediately after the New Year his happiness disappeared, he was haunted and desperate, he did not eat and Hakim knew his son was drinking heavily. Eventually he seemed to simply give up. Thankfully, the drinking stopped and Farid came and went as before but he was a changed man. To someone who did not know him well he looked the same, but to Hakim it was though he viewed life through a shroud. He seldom laughed and when he did the sound was hollow.

Hakim felt a cold sweat across his back. The alternative he had tried not to consider kept edging back into his mind. His beloved son had fallen in love with a tourist and for the first time it occurred to Hakim that it might not always be the girl who fell in love. Perhaps she did not want him. That was it! Farid had got in over his head, the woman had not returned his love, or got bored or nervous about making a commitment and run back to her own country. And Hakim was sure whoever she was, she had disappeared from his son's life years ago.

He felt a little better. The explanation fitted and a broken heart could eventually be cured and brought back to life by ministrations of a good woman, like the one his son was to marry very soon. That will solve the problem, he told himself. Just give him time. In a couple of years when he cradles his own child, he will not even remember this girl's name. He felt more at ease having convinced himself the problem would eventually go away by itself.

Farid was not pleased to be at home, it gave him too much time to think. He had not been feeling well, just sick and scared. He knew that he was doing the wrong thing in marrying Sarra, but years had passed and it was as though Lucy had ceased to exist. No one had heard from her at all, not even Cathy. He had no wish to go through life alone and Sarra was a pleasant undemanding person and as different as anyone could be from the one he had tried for so long to forget.

Farid knew his father suspected that something was wrong but he had not broached the matter and neither had Farid. He sat in the chair in his room and only when he thought his father was asleep did he allow his tears to fall. He had tried to forget, he really had, he knew he had gone a bit wild when Lucy disappeared and he finally accepted she did not intend to come back. The whisky had helped initially but it left him feeling sick and he couldn't work. He had bedded a few willing females including the dreadful English girl with whom he could have got into serious trouble, but the experiences were always a one-off physical relief and no one ever touched his heart. He had taken a chance on the beach and sneaked into a couple of hotel rooms. He took risks he would not have taken before, but he was past caring as though tempting destiny to intervene. She had not.

He knew it was unfair to marry Sarra. He was aware without any self-importance, that she adored him. Frankly he had given up. He had no wish to marry and couldn't be bothered to look for a wife when the woman he wanted to marry was out there somewhere. Farid was a decent enough man to make a promise to himself. When he married Sarra he would make sure he cared for his wife and he hoped that Allah would grant them the children he knew she would want.

He moved across to look out of the open window into the silent darkness and spoke softly as he made his vow.

"I will try to forget the past and be a good husband. Above all things I will do everything in my power to ensure she never knows or has reason to doubt me."

He swallowed feeling the tears running down his cheeks. He clutched the window frame and raised his eyes and said aloud to the night sky. "I will do all I can to hide my true love from her so that she will never know it will not be her sweet face I see in my dreams, but yours my darling, the pale shadow whom I have loved for nearly twenty years."

He gripped the frame and his breath came in ragged stifled gasps. "My darling, why? What did I do, what happened and where in the name of Allah are you?"

Hakim sat on his balcony basking in the stillness of the night. Although he could not hear every word his son said, he was now certain that the problem was a woman he had loved deeply and could not forget. He thought he must have misheard, how could Farid have loved a woman for nearly twenty years, he would have been only a boy. Hakim shivered in the warm night air.

He felt guilty he had overheard something not for his ears. But Farid was his son, his beloved eldest on and he was not about to leave him to deal with his pain alone. He raised himself awkwardly from his chair and went inside.

"How great are the problems of youth," he murmured to himself as he knocked softly on the door to his son's room.

He waited and knocked again.

"Yes."

"May I come in?" Again a hesitation,

"Of course, Baba." He pushed open the door. The room was in darkness and he shuffled in his slippers towards the bed where his son now sat, his head turned away.

"Talk to me, my son."

"About what, Baba?"

"What happened nearly twenty years ago that has caused you so much pain." Farid's eyes widened. "Yes, my son, I heard you. I was sitting on my balcony."

Farid dropped his chin to his chest, his hands clasped tightly together resting on his thighs. Hakim waited. Very slowly, Farid raised his head and stared straight at his father, tortured eyes in a tear streaked face. Hakim stepped back. He hoped he would never again have to witness such anguished desperation in the eyes of another living soul.

He sat down uncomfortably on the bed beside his son and in an unaccustomed gesture put his arm round his hunched shoulders. "Speak to me, I am your father."

To his amazement Farid rested his head on his father's chest and cried like a baby. His own voice trembling Hakim tried to comfort him.

"Baba, how can I marry one woman when I am in love with another?"

"Farid, you said you have known this woman for twenty years. How can that be?"

Farid poured out his heart. He told his father about the first meeting with Lucy, how he had found her again so many years later, their years together, how happy they were and that she was to return in the spring when they intended to speak with the family about their marriage, and finally how she had never returned and disappeared from his life forever without a word.

The words tumbled out of him like a river where the dam has finally been breached. Hakim listened, but he held his counsel and when Farid finally looked up at him he said simply, "Tell me about her."

"She lives in England, a place called Surrey. I fell in love with her at our first chance meeting when I was only a boy and I never forgot her. She went back to England and got married, but her husband died leaving her alone with an infant child. Some years later she returned to Tunisia for a holiday and we met again. It was strange Baba, our first meeting was in Sousse but our second in Hammamet. In a country of millions of people, it must surely have been the will of Allah." His father nodded encouragingly.

"Go on." Farid's face took on a glow of pure happiness.

"Baba, her hair is like the soft sand of the desert and her eyes the colour of the jasmine leaf kissed by the sun." Unconsciously he had repeated his words to Lucy when they first met. "Her voice is gentle and when she smiles I feel alive like I have never felt at any other time. When she left me my life ended."

Hakim's blood grew colder with every second. He had never heard his son speak that way, but he reasoned if Farid had met her when he was only a boy, it followed that the woman must be much older than his son, and she had a child.

"This was not part of le bezness then," he said harshly. Farid stared at him.

"Baba, I love her. When I met her I knew little of such things and that was never part of our love."

"You never took from her gifts or money, so that when you spoke of marriage she ran away believing you wanted more, or a ticket to England?"

Farid gave a flicker of a smile. "Yes Baba, she gave me money. She gave me one coin the day I met her, the one you wanted to take from me but my beautiful mother stopped you. She brought me little gifts from England, but I bought her gifts as well, and I bought her a ring."

"A ring!" Hakim was horrified.

"Yes, Baba, a ring. Of gold and diamonds - and Baba…"

"Yes, I am listening."

"Do you remember when you were rushed to hospital with your heart problem and the family paid for your operation?"

Hakim waited, although he knew to his dismay what was coming next, he shook his head from side to side in denial. "Yes, Baba. I told her you were ill and she asked if she could help. I refused, but she knew we couldn't raise the money in time and she sent me the rest, so you could have your operation within days instead of waiting until your health got much worse, or you died," he added pointedly. "She told me that because she loved me so much, my father was as dear to her as her own."

"And the money?" Hakim spoke more harshly than he intended.

"I kept money back from my wages and tips each month and gave it to her. It would have taken many years to repay it all, but she never asked me for it. I just used to give her money from time to time and we never spoke of it."

"And the child?"

"The child is a boy, her dead husband's child. She brought him with her once and we went out together. He is a good son, I liked him."

Hakim closed his eyes, so his son had been going around with this woman and her child. How had he not heard of it?

"Baba, I know what you are thinking. She is older than me. I was not quite fifteen when we met. Illness and death can strike at any age, but can the woman or the child be blamed because the husband died suddenly." Hakim frowned. "And before you ask, she knew I didn't want to go to England. She knows about the trickery that exists. She was happy to stay here with me, in Tunisia. When I took her to the airport the last time, I felt that something was wrong. Yet the last words she ever said to me were to say how much she loved me. Then she changed her telephone number and my letters were never answered. I swear I have no idea why."

"Is this why you have never wanted to marry?"

Farid nodded silently. "It would never be my wife's head on the pillow beside me, or her arms around me and I don't know if I can trust myself enough not to say her name at a time when I should say my wife's name."

A shadow passed across Farid's face. "I know this, Baba because not long ago I went with a girl, just once. She asked me the next day, 'Who is Lucy?'. I had called her name whilst being with another woman and I didn't know I had done it. Can I do that to my wife?"

"Lucy." The name Farid had called out to his neighbour's daughter in that awful night at their home a few years back. "How old is she, my son?"

"She is twelve years older than me." Hakim closed his eyes tightly. It was an impossible situation.

"Farid, how can you want to marry a woman who will probably never give you children, who knows nothing of our customs and how people think in our country?"

"We talked of children. If we had married when we had planned, I am sure I would now have my own child, with the woman I love and Baba, you know me well, do you think I would sacrifice my love because of the murmurings of a few old people. I would have loved her child and cared for them both as my own family, and I had hoped in time my family would come to love them too."

Hakim felt as though he had lived every one of his years twice over. It had been more than five years since the woman disappeared. If the wound was still as raw now, his son was right, he needed to think carefully before marrying and possibly ruining his new wife's life as well. People do marry without love, but in this case the families were close and he knew Sarra was in love with his son. He was fond of his cousin's child and did not want a rift caused within the family.

Unfortunately only Farid could make the decision, although if any hint of this became known what Sarra's family and indeed his own would think or say he didn't want to think about.

The two men spoke long into the night. "Baba, I must ask you. Please promise to me you will never speak of this conversation."

"I will not, but Farid, what do you intend to do?"

"I must tell Sarra. I do not think the whole truth is a very good idea but I will tell her in a way which will hurt her the least." Hakim acknowledged it was for the best, but he slept little that night wondering what how his cousin would take the news if Sarra refused to marry Farid.

The following day Farid kept his promise but he was in no way prepared for the way Sarra took his confession.

They sat alone as took her hands in his. "Sarra. If we are to be married there is something I must tell you. Many years ago I met an English woman. I loved her very deeply and I wanted to marry her but she left without explanation and never returned. If we are to be married I must be truthful with you. I am still in love with her and I am not sure I can ever love anyone in the same way again. I cannot start my married life on a lie, but if you will still have me I will make you a good husband."

She sat silently listening to him, her hands clasped loosely in front of her nodding occasionally. Farid was disconcerted. He had expected some sort of reaction, tears or anger, but not her quiet acceptance. When he finished she smiled at him, a gentle sad smile.

"Farid, I was honoured when you asked me to marry you as I have loved you since I was a child, but do not take me for a fool. I always knew there was someone in your life, and you forget Fatma is my friend. She also knew and she told me what happened with Michelle, when you called her Lucy and embraced her, thinking she was someone else."

Farid was taken aback, he had thought Sarra to be no more than an infatuated young girl and he was amazed Fatma had told her about the sordid business with Michelle. "Why did you accept me?"

"Because I hoped after so long that perhaps time had dulled the pain of your lost love. It would be easy for us to marry, I love you and would make you a good and faithful wife, our families are close and everyone approves of the match and I believe that in your own way you are fond of me and as we both know our ways are not those of the western world. Love is not an essential part of marriage, respect, family, good prospects and mutual religion and culture are more so. If love follows then it is a bonus."

"Sarra, if I were to marry anyone else, it would be you. You are right of course and I misjudged you. I think because I have watched you grow from the girl I knew into a beautiful woman I felt it would be good for us all, and you know I would have cared for you, but I realise it would be utterly unfair to you. You are one of the kindest people I have ever met and I would make you so unhappy."

"Farid, if I thought you could one day love me the way you love your Lucy, I would marry you, but until now I didn't know the depth of your love for this woman. I need a man who belongs to me, not to a dream. You were right to tell me before we locked ourselves into a kind of companionable hell." Farid stared at her.

She stopped and looked at him. He said nothing. "What I mean is that I would be looking for something you could never give and I have no way of knowing whether I would become so bitter that I would spoil the friendship we now have. For your part you would simply be living a terrible lie."

She paused and breathed deeply before continuing. "We will tell our families together that we have changed our minds, that we decided to marry because we had grown up together, but we both realise that it is not what either of us really wants. If we present ourselves together, there can be no argument or trouble with either family. Only we will know the reasons and I hope we can be friends, as we have always been."

Farid was shocked; he had never realised Sarra's inner strength. She had made it easy for him and with a united front there could be no disgrace on either family. They stood up and he hugged her close. Sarra trembled. She hoped desperately that he would release her before she broke down. What she had said was true. She had always loved him, firstly with the adoration of a child and later with the passion of a woman which is why she could never marry him whilst he was in love with someone else. Sarra was a romantic. Not for her the necessity of jewellery, presents, big house and car. She needed a man who would love her the same way, and if it was not to be Farid, then she would wait until she found such a man. Allah willing she would find her own dream.

CHAPTER THIRTY-FIVE

DEBBIE AND FATMA

Ellen's months before her wedding were chaotic, she was backwards and forwards to Tunisia until she felt she should be entitled to a season ticket. She knew it was customary for the women to congregate together and Ali's sister made sure she was introduced to his friends' sisters and other female friends so she would not feel left out.

The arrangements made, Ellen gave in her notice at work and went at the end of the spring term to start the wedding preparations. Now she was seated with a group of women discussing weddings and associated topics. She got the distinct impression that marriage was uppermost in everyone's minds. Although a few of them spoke English, her own knowledge of French had improved dramatically and she had even picked up a little Arabic.

Fatma was bored. She had hoped to meet up with some friends that day but they were going to some pre-wedding women's gathering. Reluctantly she agreed to go with them; it wasn't really her scene at all, but it was better than doing nothing.

Ellen found herself in conversation with a girl around her own age. She seemed different from the others, more animated and unconventional. She talked of history, politics and education. Although Ellen was looking forward to her wedding, she was getting somewhat overwhelmed by the conversation never moving from that subject and found Fatma's conversation a refreshing relief.

"Can I ask how you are so well informed about these things? - it seems quite unusual here."

"No, not really, a lot of girls go to university now and although we have to juggle home life with employment, a good many girls carry on working after they are married. I certainly would," she added.

"Fortunately my future husband is happy to indulge me, although for how long, I am not sure. Like all men he wants children and then I will be forced to give up." Ellen caught the thread of rebellion and felt that whoever this woman was married to would have their hands full.

"You say you have siblings - how many in your family?"

"Four - two boys and two girls. I'm the youngest. My sister's married with a baby, Saleem is a mechanical engineer and my eldest brother, Farid, works in security at one of the hotels in Hammamet."

"That's a coincidence. My friend Debbie met a chap called Farid in Hammamet the year before last, at the same time I met Ali. He was part of the hotel security. She only went out with him once, so far as I know, but she was really keen on him. She tried to bluff it out to us at the time and pretend he was totally enamoured with her, but thinking about it afterwards I got the impression he wasn't really interested and it was just a one-off. She's never mentioned him again and I never asked."

Fatma was extremely interested. "That sounds like my brother!" She stopped, seeing Ellen's surprised expression.

"It's just that my brother got tied up with some dreadful English woman years ago, no offence to the English," she added quickly, "and he's never really showed much interest in anyone since, Tunisian or visitor."

"And your friend Debbie, is she coming to your wedding."

"Oh yes, she arrives next month; she's going to spend some time with me before the wedding to help me with all the bits and pieces, as she put it, that I'm likely to forget."

"With all the people who get involved, I doubt there'll be much chance of that," Fatma laughed.

"Anyway, I must go now, but I look forward to meeting you again, and your friend."

Fatma got her wish a couple of weeks before the wedding. Ellen brought Debbie with her to the next gathering. Fatma could immediately tell what a man would see in her. She was slim and pretty. Her red hair was a little bit too fiery to be real but made an attractive contrast with her blue eyes, which seemed to Fatma to miss nothing. She was dressed casually in light trousers and t-shirt but she wore a lot of jewellery and too much make up. She looked very pretty and young, but Fatma sensed something predatory, which made her uneasy. She wondered if Farid was the person Ellen had spoken of, because she couldn't see her brother being interested in someone like this. But then her brother had changed so much since the English woman, she had no idea of his life away from home, but now she needed to find out.

Ellen had told Debbie about Fatma and at first she was horrified at the possibility of meeting Farid's sister, but looking at the scenario sensibly, even if it was Farid's sister, she couldn't see that he would have told his sister, or indeed anyone else, about the nature of their encounter.

Debbie was not used to being ignored by a man and she had been sure he would call her or at least write to her after she pushed the piece of paper with her address and phone number into his pocket, but there had been no word from him. To her, he still represented a challenge, one she was determined to win, and now she saw her opportunity.

Ellen introduced them and Fatma was surprised by the immediate warmth in the girl's face. She smiled broadly and put out her hand. Her touch was light and friendly and Fatma wondered if she had perhaps misjudged her on first impression.

Debbie sat and chatted as though she had known Fatma for years. She had a knack of being extremely pleasant if she wanted something.

Fatma took the plunge. "I understand from Ellen you might have met my brother?"

"Your brother?" Debbie replied coyly.

"Farid?"

Debbie smiled prettily. "I do know a Farid - does he work at the Palace Hotel?"

Fatma smiled to herself. "Yes, he does. What a coincidence. What do you think of him?" She waited expectantly, watching the other girl's face for any trace of emotion.

Debbie dropped her eyes, modestly she hoped. "I think he's wonderful," she breathed.

"How long have you known him?"

"I met him two years ago when I was here with Ellen, we talked outside the hotel and I saw him a couple of times." She left the interpretation deliberately vague.

"Have you heard from him recently?"

"Not for some time now, but I've been away a lot, so I may have missed his calls." Debbie smiled sweetly at her new friend.

Fatma was surprised, this was not quite how Ellen had told the story.

"He's so handsome and attentive, I'm surprised he hasn't been snapped up already. He's not married or anything, is he?" Debbie laughed, as though the thought was unthinkable.

"No, he's not married. He nearly got married last year but they called it off."

Debbie took a deep breath. "Who is Lucy?"

Fatma stared at her as if she had sprouted horns.

Good, thought Debbie, whoever she is she has no friend in Fatma.

"Why d'you ask?"

Debbie leaned towards her and lowered her voice. "Can I speak frankly, with no offence intended to you or your brother?"

Fatma clenched her teeth. "Please do."

"I always felt that your brother was holding back on me, as though there was something he wasn't saying and he mentioned the name Lucy. I wondered if she is his girlfriend or something."

She could see she had Fatma's attention. She gazed at Fatma as innocently as she knew how.

"You see, I always thought there was a spark between your brother and I, but this Lucy seemed to come between us and I am sure if she wasn't around we could have had something. I could sort of feel her, like an ever-present spectre."

Fatma frowned. "Lucy was some English tourist he met, his girlfriend six or seven years ago. I hesitate to use the word girlfriend as she was hardly a girl. When they met he was only about twenty-three. She was certainly much older and I am sure she has a child. I don't know whether she was still married, divorced or what, but he was smitten with her."

Debbie held her breath "What happened?"

"I've no idea. He knew her for several years and then she simply disappeared out of his life and frankly broke his heart."

"How awful. Did you know her?"

Fatma hesitated. "No I didn't know her, he kept her secret from us, he used to see her in Hammamet where he works and of course our family live in Sousse." She sneered to Debbie. "As you can imagine, he could hardly have brought her back to our house and introduced her to our father and the rest of the family, could he, although my brother met her a couple of times I believe."

"So you never saw her?"

"I didn't say that, I said I didn't know her."

"So you did see her, what is she like?"

"Nothing spectacular," Fatma lied through her teeth. "She wore tight trousers and a little strappy top which was so low at the front it left little to the imagination, a bit tarty on a woman of that age, don't you think?" Debbie nodded her agreement.

"What did she look like?"

"Very pale, you know the sort that goes a rather unattractive pink at the first sign of sun, typical English tourist, no offence," she added quickly.

Debbie smiled. "None taken, go on."

"She had very long blonde hair, probably out of a bottle, which I always thought was wrong on an older woman."

Debbie nodded sympathetically, patting her hand.

Fatma remembered what Saleem had said "And she has green eyes... like a cat," she added herself.

"Oh, how nasty," exclaimed Debbie.

"Quite. I can tell you I was very relieved when she disappeared."

"And you have no idea what became of her?"

"No, hopefully she dropped off the edge of the earth."

They grinned at each other, united in their cause.

CHAPTER THIRTY-SIX

SOUSSE

Lucy was not at all sure about going to the wedding. She didn't know Ellen or Ali. The wedding was in Sousse, which at least held only a few memories. Had it been Hammamet she would never have considered going. She remembered Farid saying he would never work in Sousse, he liked to keep his work separate from his home life so she was not likely to run into him. Sousse was a big place and there was equally little likelihood that Ali would know Farid.

Jackie could see she was uncertain and helped to convince her that after much consideration this was one chance she could take. Lucy privately thought it would also solve the problem of some of Ben's questions, which now came quite regularly, about his father, why he and his brother and sister were so different and why did his father not live with the family, if his father lived in another country why could he not go there? Lucy never forgot the promise she made to her son the day he was born. She knew she would take him to Tunisia when he was old enough to understand so he could discover for himself the country where he had begun his life but that would be many years in the future. But she reasoned that if the twins went with her in the summer, she could at least answer some of Ben's demands.

The two women decided to book into one of the newer hotels and have a holiday at the same time. Jackie's husband Ewan refused the invitation on the basis of workload and Alex declined saying if it was all right with his mother he would prefer to remain at home. He didn't know why his mother was so edgy but his instinct told him it was something to do with Ben, Rose and their father.

Alex remembered his holiday but he had been very young and the memory was sketchy. He remembered his mother's friend who bought him an ice cream and a nice lady with whom he had stayed on a couple of occasions.

He remembered his mother being happy when the twins were born and he was introduced to his new siblings, but he also remembered hearing her crying in the quiet of her own room when she thought he was asleep. When they were small he asked about their father and whether he had died like his own father. She shook her head and just told him that their daddy lived thousands of miles away. She had let him believe what he wanted. Now he wondered if it was all connected and if the man who had bought him the ice cream could be their father. He asked her once about it and she said that yes, the twins' father was a Tunisian, but he saw that his questions upset her and as Alex adored his mother, he let the matter lie and they never spoke of it again.

This time, he felt it better he left the trip to the twins and his mother and anyway, he admitted to himself the main reason was it would give him time to spend alone with his new girlfriend.

Ben was ecstatic. He had overheard his mother talking with Alex. He wondered why she said she was worried about meeting his father in some place he had never heard of. He wondered if it was nearby. He had been to France once on an aeroplane. Perhaps it was in France. Perhaps he would meet his father. He asked his mother, but she said not to worry, they were just going to Jackie's friend's wedding and for a little holiday. Rose had never shown much interest in her father and couldn't really understand the fuss Ben made, although she was excited about going on an aeroplane again.

M was a regular visitor since the twins' birth, and as the year's passed she and Rose became close. M never showed favouritism between the youngsters, but Lucy knew that from the moment she first saw the little girl, she simply adored her. Sometimes Lucy wondered if Rose regarded M as a second mother. As it happened a week or so before she was due to fly to Tunisia, Rose came down with chickenpox. Lucy was in a quandary as to whether she should go at all. That Ben loved his twin sister was without question but on this occasion he was furious.

"She's gone and done it on purpose!" he shrieked at his mother. "She's got that chicken thing so we can't go!" Lucy tried to pacify him and explained that Rose hadn't asked to get chickenpox.

"Yes she did. She went to Mattie's house when she knew she had it."

"Look, Ben, Rosie isn't infectious any more, she just doesn't feel very well and I can't leave her on her own. Anyway, you're lucky you didn't get it as well."

"Of course I didn't get it. I couldn't get it when I am going to meet my father, could I? He won't like me if I'm covered in spots!"

Lucy ignored the reference to his father. "Rosie is not covered in spots, they've nearly gone."

M smiled to herself as she watched the young boy square up to his mother, his hands on his hips, his small face flushed with annoyance and his green eyes blazing. She took a deep breath, wondering as soon as she had finished whether she had said the right thing.

"Lucy, I'm quite happy to stay with Rose. I can look after her for a week, and if I stay here at your house I can keep an eye on Alex as well."

Lucy frowned. "M, I'm not sure that's a good idea, I mean I know how you feel about children."

M pulled herself up to her full 5 feet 2. "Rose is not children, as you put it. She is Rose and that is quite different. Anyway I want to…" Her voice tailed off and Lucy smiled at her.

"Okay, I know you want to have the chance to spoil her unmercifully and I do admit I'd feel a bit happier if I knew there was someone to keep an eye on Alex, although I doubt he will see it that way," she added with a grin.

"Fine, if you think you can handle a little minx and a truculent teenager for a week, so be it, but for heaven's sake, if either of them give you any trouble, don't stand for it."

Alex ambled into the kitchen, followed closely by Rose. "Don't stand for what?"

"You behaving like a brute and Rose like a brat."

Alex frowned. "What do you mean?"

"Marie is going to stay here for a week, to look after Rose," she added quickly seeing Alex's mutinous expression. "I just said she wasn't to put up with any rubbish from either of you."

Rose whooped with delight and rushed over to M, knocking her back onto the chair and jumped on her lap. "Oh good, so Auntie M is going to look after me. I promise I'll be good."

"You're dead right you will, sweetie," M said ruffling her curls affectionately. The little girl looked up at her adoringly and M thought not for the first time how like her mother she was, save that her hair had darkened to a deep honey and of course her captivating golden brown eyes which were her sole inheritance from her father. She looked up at Alex.

"Anyway, Alex will be the man of the house and he will look after both of us."

Alex looked mollified and rested his hand on Ben's shoulder. "Okay, Mum, you get this little wretch out of the house for a week and I'll take care of Auntie M and the brat." Ben grinned and Rose stuck her tongue out at him.

The following week as Lucy got off the plane at Monastir, she was unprepared for the rush of emotion but was given little time to brood. When they got into the terminal building the porter rushed up to carry their cases and Ben told him excitedly that he was going to meet his daddy. Fortunately the porter didn't understand and Lucy quickly shoved a bag of sweets into her son's hand to distract him.

The new hotel was on the edge of Sousse, a few minutes' walk from the beach. It stood large and white, a very elegant building standing on its own at the centre of lush gardens ablaze with summer colour. As they went through the glass swing doors the air conditioning felt almost cold. The reception area was awash with white marble, low bench seats covered with woven cushions amidst potted palms. The hallway was huge and she could see through the floor to ceiling windows at the back an enormous pool with the sun sparkling on the gentle movement of the water. Jackie turned to her, a mischievous smile lighting up her flushed face.

"Wow, this is a bit different from last time. I wonder if they pulled the other one down!"

Lucy laughed but had to agree it was certainly different. Their room was large, there were two beds pushed close together each with a table. Wrought iron wall lights gave each occupant sufficient light to be independent of the other. There was a small day bed for Ben in one corner of the room. The walls were white and bedcovers, cushions and floor to ceiling curtains all deep green edged with cream. There were two roughly painted pictures, one on each side of the room, both depicting Tunisian scenes. The dressing table was large enough to take both all their female paraphernalia and the large inbuilt wardrobe more than adequate for their clothes and the rest of their belongings. To Jackie's delight the bathroom was spotless with a modern shower unit over the bath.

"D'you remember that other hotel?" she giggled "I was quite convinced that the shower was going to spout sand rather than water."

They washed off the dust and changed for dinner. Lucy was relieved to see that tourism had not yet completely taken over the country and that although some of the food had been prepared with the European tourist in mind, there were still Tunisian specialties and a wonderful salads with dips and bowls filled with things she had long forgotten. After dinner they had a few drinks at the bar, then Lucy carried a sleeping Ben to his little bed. She and Jackie sat long into the night on their balcony chatting quietly over a bottle of wine.

Lucy gazed out over the blackness of the sea. There was no moon and the only light came from the street lamps along the promenade. The heavy scent of the jasmine was strongest in the early part of the evening, but she could still smell its perfume. She closed her eyes and breathed in the familiar scent as the breeze touched her face in a soft caress. She felt a tightness in her chest and prickling behind her eyes as the memories flooded back. She opened her eyes and watched a couple strolled up from the beach, their arms wrapped tightly around each other. She watched as they walked slowly until they stood in the shadows of the hotel building and kissed. She felt the warmth of tears on her cheeks.

"You okay, Luce?" Jackie had seen how her eyes followed the couple and needed no words to know the feelings which must be bottling up inside her friend. Lucy dragged her eyes away.

"Yeah, I'm okay. Just a few old memories sliding into my head. God, Jackie, it seems so long ago."

"It was bound to open up some old wounds, kiddo. Everything must be so familiar it is bound to bring back memories, some good and some not so good. I know you try to hide it but you're only human. There's no shame in letting your feelings show."

"That's as may be, but the thing I don't want to do is mope around the place feeling sorry for myself, I think it was a mistake to come. I must have been crazy."

"Crazy perhaps, but a mistake no. You needed to come back. Lucy there is only so far you can run before you trip over your own feet. Let's just enjoy the wedding and be happy for Ellen. She's going to need some support from us Brits with all the noise and excitement which I understand is a traditional accompaniment to weddings in this country."

Lucy nodded, smiling broadly. "You haven't seen half of it yet. The weddings over here go on for days, there are traditions to follow and I feel sorry for the youngsters who try to get out of some of them. The older members of the family come down on them so hard the unhappy couple normally capitulate to keep the peace. Still, it brings a family unity which we don't see so much of at home anymore."

They finished the bottle of wine and Jackie felt her head dropping gradually onto her chest.

"Come my friend, tomorrow is another day."

Lucy slept soundly, thankful for the gentle numbing effect of the wine, and only woke when Jackie shook her reminding her that breakfast finished at ten.

"What time is it?"

"Just gone nine, you've slept for hours."

"It's those curtains," Lucy complained. "They've got that blackout stuff at the back so you can't see any light at all. I'm used to being woken at dawn. My curtains at home are useless, I could do with these." Jackie surveyed the eight foot high curtains, which covered the whole of one wall of the room.

"They won't fit in the case." Lucy threw a pillow at her.

They spent the morning by the pool and slept in the afternoon. Lucy started to relax. So long as she stayed in the hotel she was safe, safe from what she was not sure, but unfortunately not from her own thoughts. They watched the evening entertainment, music and dancing and games earlier in the evening for the children. Ben was captivated. He met up with another English family and formed an immediate bond with a boy about his own age.

There was another day before the wedding celebrations started and Lucy was determined to do two things. Firstly to try to drive away the ghosts and secondly to go nowhere near that café, whether it was still there or not, she had no intention of finding out. She comforted herself that she was unlikely to be able to find it again even if she wanted to, although in her heart she felt that if given the opportunity her feet would take her there.

Ben whined about going shopping and Lucy agreed he could stay with his new friend by the pool. The mother had promised she would watch him like a hawk and Lucy agreed.

They browsed around the main square in front of the Medina in the late afternoon, after the heat of the midday sun had died down a little. The air was still warm and away from the seafront there was little cooling breeze. They sat down on one of the benches, as far away from where she once sat with Farid as she could find.

Jackie wanted to explore the Medina and although Lucy was happy to take in the little shops and stalls on the edge, she persuaded Jackie not to go into its deep dark heart. It held too many memories. Sub-consciously she twisted the little ring on her right hand.

Later they met with Ellen and Ali for a coffee. The morning was hot and there was little air so Lucy wore a light cotton dress and piled her hair into neat knot on top of her head held with a pink bandanna. She had a slight headache and kept her sunglasses on. She liked Ali immediately and was in no doubt that he absolutely adored his quiet English wife to be.

"Would you ladies like some mint tea?" Jackie and Ellen nodded but he was surprised when Lucy declined.

"Sorry, Ali. I don't like mint tea. Could I have a cappucin and some water, if that's okay?"

Ali grinned. "Two mint tea, two cappucin and one large bottle of water." He poured out two glasses of water and, as he heaped the sugar into his tiny cup, was amused to see Lucy ignore the sugar and took alternate sips of coffee and water.

"You are unusual, Lucy. I know few people who drink that without sugar."

She smiled. "I don't have the Tunisian sweet tooth."

"Yes, but you also order water. That is very Tunisian." He was surprised to see Lucy's smile fade.

"Oh, someone I knew years ago told me it was the best way."

Ali noticed Lucy looked over at Jackie and the silent understanding between the two women. So Lucy had a history in Tunisia. He didn't press the subject, her expression asked him not to.

As they walked back to their hotel, Jackie put her arm around her friend's shoulder. "It was never going to be easy, you knew that." Lucy smiled. "I know."

Jackie noticed a scruffy man with lanky hair and a thin face watching them intently. She realised he had been following them and nudged Lucy. "There's some guy following us, he has been for some time." Lucy hesitated. "There's only one way to deal with that," she muttered. She stopped dead, took a photograph of nothing in particular and the man came within a few yards of them.

Lucy turned towards him, smiling broadly. She hesitated, there was something familiar about him but he wore large dark glasses which hid part of his thin face. She removed her own and stared straight at him. "Can I help you, is there something you want?" she asked him in French.

The man smirked and pushed his lank hair back from his forehead. "No madame, I apologise, I just wondered if you needed a guide."

"No thank you," she replied "We are quite all right, but thank you for your concern." She turned her back on him and the man shrugged his shoulders and walked away.

Mahmood had thought he recognised her as soon as he saw them leave the café. At first he was not sure but when she took off her glasses, he knew he was right. It had been some time ago but there could not be two women with that pale blonde hair and stunning green eyes, the woman he still thought about sometimes when he couldn't sleep. When she spoke her voice held the same dismissive tone it had always done when he had tried to worm his way into her affections. Yes, it was definitely Farid's woman. He knew she had disappeared but he wondered what had brought her back and why to Sousse. Life was suddenly more interesting.

CHAPTER THIRTY-SEVEN

THE WEDDING

Lucy often felt guilty that she lost contact with Cathy, they had spent so many happy hours together during her time with Farid, just sitting chatting outside Cathy's café, but she simply couldn't at the time face keeping any ties at all with Tunisia. She was amazed to bump into her old friend in the market in Sousse, but Cathy explained she had moved from Hammamet some years before.

"And you, why are you here after all this time?"

"I'm over for a wedding with a friend from England. Her mate Ellen is marrying a Tunisian guy who she met on holiday a couple of years ago. We had coffee with them yesterday. He seems a really nice chap, huge but gentle."

"Oh, I heard about that. It must be Ali's wedding. I thought you might know him, he was one of Farid's friends from school but then I think they lost touch over the years. I haven't seen him for ages. I think he worked in Tunis for some years. To be honest I haven't really seen anyone from Hammamet since we've been down here."

Lucy shook her head numbly. So Ellen's Ali knew Farid. It was a shock to hear his name mentioned after so long. Surely Farid would not be at the wedding?

Cathy gave Lucy her number and insisted she call her to arrange to meet up. Lucy was worried about meeting someone she had known before, someone who knew Farid, but she hoped that unless she brought up the subject, Cathy would be tactful enough not to. Even so, she wasn't sure if it was a good thing to arrange another meeting.

The wedding preparations were almost complete. It was to be a mixture of English and Tunisian culture. Ellen was determined not to miss the entertainment and fun of the final day. In Tunisia the bride often does not arrive until well into the evening, misses all the entertainment and then sits on her throne and dances for an hour before the party ends. The days leading up to the final day were to be traditional but the last day's party was to be English with everyone mixing together and a huge marquee to keep the sun out.

Debbie went with the other women to the first of the four day celebrations. She gazed in amazement at the beautiful things which Ellen had accumulated for her future life. Following tradition these were laid out for the women to view. She went with her friend to the women's day at the Hammam and watched as Ellen's hands and feet were painted with henna in readiness for her marriage. She declined Ellen's suggestion that she too should be so decorated. It wasn't she objected in principle, she just knew it would ruin her outfit.

The final day of celebration was as beautiful as any English bride could hope for. The sun blazed down, the sky was rich delft blue with not a cloud in sight.

Ben was looking forward to the wedding. When the day arrived, unfortunately he followed his hastily gobbled breakfast with a huge ice cream, several glasses of lemonade and half an hour in the pool. Lucy was concerned to see him rush out of the pool to the toilet. He came back, but his face was pale and he said he had been sick.

"Mum, do I have to go with you? I want to go to bed. My tummy hurts and I think I'm going to be sick again." Lucy wrapped him up in the towel, took him upstairs and tucked him up in bed. He fell asleep immediately.

Jackie was obviously disappointed. "Look Luce, it doesn't matter, I don't want to go on my own, but I don't really know Ellen that well and we won't be missed with all the other people."

"Thanks Jackie, but I can see from your expression that you are telling fibs and you want to go."

Jackie looked at her quizzically. "You used to come here a lot. You must know someone. Isn't there anyone you could ask to watch Ben for an hour or so? We don't have to stay long at the wedding."

Lucy hesitated, she knew it was unfair to ruin Jackie's day and she knew she was excited about going to the wedding. With certain misgivings, she called Cathy.

"Cathy, I am so sorry to ask you but you know I told you we are here to go to Ellen's wedding; now my stupid boy has filled himself full of sun and ice cream and is confined to bed. Do you know anyone who could sit with him for an hour or so, just so we can make an appearance? It won't be for long."

"I'd be happy to sit with him myself. I only live a few minutes' walk from the hotel." Lucy protested but Cathy insisted. "To be honest I miss having my own boys under my feet. What time do you need me?"

Cathy put down the phone and thought about the conversation. She was surprised. She knew from before that Lucy had a son but she couldn't remember there being two boys. Maybe she had a younger boy as well, otherwise it would be a bit odd that Lucy needed a babysitter. Surely the boy she knew would by now be much too old to need a sitter. However, if that is what Lucy wanted, she would help out her old friend.

Debbie dressed carefully. She brushed her hair vigorously and took it back off her face into a mass of red curls, with a large bow at one side. Her apple green two-piece was chic and expensive, if cut a little lower than was really suitable. She cringed when she thought how much it had cost her. She wore cream leather wedge heels and carried a matching clutch bag. She felt very French and sophisticated. She realised too late the heels were a mistake and wished she had worn something looser and a lot cooler. The weather was stifling hot and she was perspiring under the foundation she had pasted on her face to hide her freckles.

She hailed the taxi and when she arrived was totally unprepared for the bustling scene which greeted her. She searched in vain for Fatma, but there was no sign. The place was packed with people all talking at the same time. After a while she managed to muscle her way through the crowds to Ellen, resplendent in a traditional white English bridal gown, her hair gently curled around her little face and her grey eyes shining with happiness.

"Ellen, you look gorgeous," she exclaimed quickly. "I don't suppose you have seen Fatma?"

"Fatma? Oh, you mean the girl you got to know last week. No, she won't be here. Ali heard that her uncle died on Thursday. He knew the family well as a teenager but lost touch years ago. They were invited of course, but he had heard they are now in mourning anyway I'm sorry, you seemed to get on well with her. Let me introduce you to some of the others."

Debbie abruptly declined the offer. She was furious. Fatma had told her she would try to get Farid to come to the wedding party, but if the family was in mourning, then as Ellen had said, presumably so was he.

She sat down by herself in the shade, an unattractive scowl on her face. "What a total waste of time and money," she muttered to no one in particular and pulled at her skirt which had started to ride up. Unfortunately the lining was too tight and clung to her thighs. She could feel the sweat trickling down her neck, inside her collar and tickling her back. She thought quickly. She was only here another week and she was quite determined to meet Farid again. She wondered how long mourning lasted.

She thought again of Farid and pictured him standing outside the hotel the first time she had really stood close to him when he lit her cigarette. She imagined his magnetic gaze lusting after her. For the thousandth time she wished she had handled that day differently. She comforted herself with the knowledge that two years had passed and time would hopefully have dulled the edges of his memory, although it certainly hadn't her own.

Debbie watched the woman as she walked towards her. She noticed irritably that several of the men also watched her. She wore a pale shell pink dress, almost to her ankles. The sleeves were wings of floating silk. She wore a single string of creamy pearls and delicate drop pearl earrings. Her sandals were decorated with pearl beads and she wore her long blonde hair in loose waves with just the sides held back by pearl flower-shaped clips, framing her oval face. Her translucent skin showed she was wearing hardly any make up. She looked cool and beautiful. Although she was wearing a pair of lightly tinted sunglasses, she held her hand up to her face, shielding her eyes against the sun. She reminded Debbie of Cinderella at the ball. Debbie felt like the ugly sister, over-dressed and frumpy.

The woman reached the table where Debbie was sitting and asked in French if she could sit down. Debbie nodded, relieved to have someone to talk to, even if it was her. She sat down with a sigh. Debbie noticed that close up she was not as young as she had first thought, in fact quite a bit older, a woman in her mid-thirties, she reckoned.

"Oh it is so hot today," the woman smiled. Debbie answered her.

"You're English aren't you?" Debbie nodded.

"Good, so am I."

She took off her sunglasses and Debbie stared into a pair of flecked green eyes. She gasped in shock. It had to be her, but what was she doing here? Inwardly she cursed Ellen, she hadn't mentioned Lucy would be at the wedding, but then why should she.

Lucy's smile faded as she saw Debbie's expression. "I'm sorry, do we know each other? - it's just you're looking at me as if you've seen a ghost."

Debbie thought she was going to be sick. So this was Farid's Lucy. She was beautiful, even now. God, how she hated her.

"I'm so sorry," she muttered. "You reminded me for a minute of someone I used to know." It was a weak excuse but the only one she could think of. There was a short silence as she studied her rival.

The woman smiled again, even her teeth were perfect.

"Well anyway, I'm Lucy, and you are?"

"Debbie."

Debbie was functioning on automatic. "Are you a friend of Ellen's?" she muttered.

"No actually, I'm really a gatecrasher, I suppose. I came with Jackie, my friend who's a teacher, and worked with Ellen in England. Jackie and I came here on holiday years ago so she asked Ellen if it was okay for me to come along. Ellen said it was and here I am."

Lucy chatted amiably about the wedding, how lovely it was and how fabulous Ellen looked.

Debbie tried her best to respond. After a short while she realised that this was getting her nowhere, she had to make sure there was nothing left between the woman and Farid.

"Is your husband with you?" Lucy shook her head. "No, my husband died some years ago."

"Oh, I am so sorry." Debbie put on her most sympathetic expression.

"Thank you, but it was a long time ago and it is true that time heals although of course you never forget."

"Do you have any children?"

Lucy's face lit up, "Yes, I have three."

"Oh, you are so lucky, I would love to have children, when I'm married and older of course," gushed Debbie making a mental note that if the husband had died some years before the children must be quite old.

Lucy smiled to herself at the childish response.

"What was he like, your husband?" It was a strange question and Debbie instantly regretted it but she needed as much information as possible. Lucy stared at her, but put the rather personal question down to youthful inquisitiveness. She replied quietly.

"Peter was a lovely man, tall and slim with dark hair and clear blue eyes. He was typically English., very pale, you know the type that burns in the sun," her voice tailed off as she remembered gently dabbling lotion on Peter's inflamed back after he fell asleep on the sand in Lanzarote. Debbie reached over and patted her hand. "I am sorry, I shouldn't have asked."

So the woman had a dead husband and three children. She couldn't figure out in her young mind how Farid could have fallen for a someone like that with so much baggage. She stared at the woman; she must have been absolutely stunning in her twenties and of course men don't really think with their brains she thought cattily.

"Do you like Tunisia?" Debbie changed the subject quickly and Lucy quietly acknowledged her tact.

"After my holiday with Jackie, I came quite often, although I haven't been back for a few years. But yes, I love the country. It's beautiful and quite unlike anywhere else I've ever been and of course the people are so friendly."

Debbie saw she looked sad and grinned conspiratorially. "As one woman to another, what do you think of the Tunisian men? Aren't they just gorgeous?" She noticed immediately a flicker of uncertainty in the older woman's face and waited.

Lucy remembered what she had read years before. "It is said the Tunisian people are amongst the most beautiful in the world, and I can't argue with that." She felt a non-committal answer was the safest, but Debbie was not going to be put off.

"I completely agree. I met some gorgeous chaps when I was here with Ellen, one in particular. I fell head over heels for him. We had a great time if you know what I mean." She smirked. "But I got the impression I was one of many. At least he wasn't married then. Trouble is, a lot of them are married, which they sometimes forget to mention and I don't agree with dating a married man, don't you agree?"

This was complete rubbish. In her short career Debbie had made no differentiation between single, married or in between. If she wanted a man, then she let nothing stand in her way.

Lucy nodded her agreement. "I agree. It can cause so much harm to everyone, not only the two people but to their families as well. That sort of betrayal makes you cynical and the damage takes years to fade, if it ever really does." She thought of Simon.

"You say you used to come here quite often. Did you have a special man?"

"Yes I did," Lucy replied simply.

"But it didn't work out?"

Lucy stared at her and hesitated wondering why the girl seemed so interested. She looked at the young face smiling at her and saw no malice in the question.

"Yes, it worked out. I loved him very much and I know he loved me, but sometimes things happen over which you have no control, which is what happened with us and we lost touch," she added lamely.

"But you still love him?"

"Oh yes, I still love him. I always will."

Debbie saw the strange green eyes were full of tears and held her breath.

"What was his name?"

Lucy held back for a moment. For years she had tried to block him from her mind to allow herself to live from day to day. But as soon as she got off the plane, the memories had flooded back and never a moment passed when she didn't think of him. The girl was watching her, her expression open and sympathetic. Lucy reasoned that she didn't know this girl and there was no way the girl could know her, so what harm was there in replying.

Debbie felt a flood of jealousy as she saw the unashamed love in Lucy's face.

"His name was Farid."

She caressed the name and Debbie clenched her teeth. She smiled broadly.

"Well what a coincidence; that chap I fell for was called Farid as well. He works on security up in Hammamet. He was beautiful," she sighed, "thick black hair, a really strong face with a little moustache and a really great body, but d'you know what really set him apart, he had the most unusual eyes, they weren't brown but a sort of dark gold. Just made you melt when he looked at you."

She watched Lucy intently. The woman sat completely still, as though in shock, her face ashen. Debbie felt triumphant. She went for the kill.

"Trouble is," she went on relentlessly, "there's no future there. I heard the brute went and got married. Still I suppose you can't win 'em all."

She stood up and smiled at Lucy. "Look, it's been nice talking to you. But I must be going, I promised to meet my friend. Have a great day." She held out her hand and Lucy took it wordlessly. Debbie noted irritably that even her hand was soft and cool.

She got up, smiled and walked away towards the marquee where she stood in the shadow of the awning, watching her adversary.

Lucy made no move. There could be no mistake. This girl had described Farid as she remembered him. "We had a great time… one of many… married." Debbie's words hammered in Lucy's brain, her cheeks were wet and she thought she would pass out.

Jackie came out of the marquee and saw Lucy sitting alone at the table, her head bowed resting on her clenched hands. She had put her sunglasses back on but as Jackie got nearer, she could see Lucy had been crying.

"Dear God, woman, what on earth's the matter?"

She put her arms around Lucy, who buried her face in her friend's shoulder, oblivious of the curious stares.

Jackie pulled her to her feet and led her away to a spare table at the side of the awning sheltered from the heat of the sun and away from the rest of the gathering as she had seen one or two people were looking over at them.

Debbie watched the two women and as they sat down she moved closer and strained to listen.

"Lucy, tell me please. What is it? You look as if someone's just walked over your grave. Oh shit, he's not here is he?"

"No, he's not here. It's worse. You saw that girl I was talking to?"

"Yes, the bottle redhead with too much make-up. What about her?" Debbie winced.

"She knows Farid, at least used to."

"How could you possibly know that?

"She described him in detail, d'you know I could see him as she talked. I wasn't sure to start with and then she said he worked in security and I knew it was the same person."

"Lucy there could be loads of people called Farid who work in security."

"Maybe, but not with dark golden eyes that made you melt when he looked at you. You know she even used those words."

Even Jackie remembered the boy's eyes from long ago, when she had seen him they seemed to draw you in like a magnet.

"Oh, Lucy, it must have been a horrible shock to hear someone else talking about him like that, but he's bound to know a lot of people."

"Jackie, it was the way she talked about him, said they'd had a great time and left me in no doubt they'd been more than friends. She even said she thought she was one of many."

"Lucy, I'm sorry, but what d'you expect? You left Farid years ago and he's not a monk, he's bound to have had girlfriends."

"She told me he's married," Lucy said flatly.

"Oh shit. I am so sorry, but it had to happen sooner or later. He couldn't wait forever and you never contacted him. You really do still love him, don't you?"

Debbie held her breath. "Jackie, I will love Farid all my life and beyond. There is never a day that goes past I don't think about him. In the morning when I wake up, I can smell the scent of him on the pillow and feel his arms round me. The last thing I remember at night is his body pressed close to mine and his warm breath on my neck as he tells me how much he loves me."

Debbie could hear her sobbing as she listened. In her short life she had never felt about anyone the way this unknown woman felt about the man she loved. She wondered if she had done the right thing and wished for a moment she'd said nothing.

"Jackie, I hurt him so badly. I know I must never see him again. That's my punishment for leaving him because of Ben and Rose."

Debbie started. Ben and Rose! So that was it. She had broken up someone else's marriage, She had left Farid for a married man and now she was regretting it. Debbie felt better. If that's what it was, then it was all her own fault. There was still a chance. She really must try and root out Farid. She moved away and started chatting to Sharon.

Jackie took her friend's hand. "Talking of Ben, we'd better go and see how he is. It was good of Cathy to sit with him, but if we've told him once we've told him a hundred times, ice cream, fizzy drinks, sun and swimming all at the same time don't mix."

Gratefully, Lucy wiped her face and made sure her sunglasses were firmly in place. She had taken a careful look around the guests when she arrived, but saw no sign of Farid. It must have been as Cathy said, they had lost touch over the years.

They said goodbye to Ellen explaining that Lucy was feeling unwell and they really had to go. Lucy kept well away from Debbie as they walked through the crowds of people.

CHAPTER THIRTY-EIGHT

CATHY

Lucy was still shaken by the encounter with Debbie when she reached the hotel. She left Jackie in the bar and went to check on Ben. Before Cathy arrived she had made sure Ben was already tucked up in bed asleep and the curtains were drawn. Lucy had asked her not to wake him because hopefully he would sleep off whatever had upset him.

Now when she quietly opened the door she saw Ben was still asleep and Cathy she sat out on the balcony engrossed in her book. She could hear Ben snoring gently as she crept out onto the balcony.

"Hi."

Cathy looked up surprised. "Hello, Lucy. Sorry, I was deep in this daft book, I never used to get much time to read at home when the boys were small but now I am never seen without a book. I'm surprised you're back so early. Was everything okay?

"Yes, it was lovely, but I was worried about Ben," Lucy half-lied.

"You didn't need to be. I have looked after children before you know, and I knew where you were if I needed you. Are you okay Lucy? - You look... well frankly, a bit washed out. Oh heavens, you didn't see Farid did you?"

"No. He wasn't there. I'm fine. Really I am. It must be the heat."

She changed the subject quickly. "How's Ben been?"

"He's fine now. I thought he was going to throw up again just after you left but he just heaved a bit and went back to sleep. I kept the curtains drawn and he's been out like a light ever since. You were right, too much of a good thing."

They both laughed and looked over at the sleeping boy, his head turned to the wall and one arm flung across the pillow.

"I didn't know you had another boy, I do admit I thought it a bit odd when you asked me to babysit." She noticed her friend blushed.

"Sorry I never thought to mention it."

"Well you couldn't really could you? I haven't heard from you for years."

Cathy's tone caught her off guard and Lucy felt embarrassed. She looked at the floor. "It's been seven years and all I can do is say I am sorry."

"I'm sorry too. That came out wrong I was just surprised when I didn't hear from you. What happened, Lucy?"

Lucy didn't reply.

"Lucy, what happened between you and Farid?"

Lucy was trapped. "It just didn't work out."

Cathy stared at her. "But you adored each other and then you just disappeared. I called you a couple of times but the number had been disconnected."

"Yes, I'm sorry, I should have called you. It was bad of me, but after we split up I just couldn't face any connection with Tunisia." That at least was true.

Cathy nodded. "That I can understand. You know Farid went to pieces. He asked everyone if they had heard from you, then he started drinking and went a bit crazy. Thank heavens that was short lived, but he really changed. He became cynical and morose and seemed to lose that sparkle he always had. You really hurt him you know."

Lucy's eyes welled up with tears. "I know, what I did was unforgivable, but it had to be done, everything changed and I had to go. Anyway, I understand he's okay now, he's got his own life."

Cathy wasn't sure what she meant, but had the sense not to pry.

"What about you?" asked Lucy.

"We moved to Sousse not long after you disappeared. Farid still works in Hammamet so far as I know, so we never see him. His brother Saleem is working in Tunis, the elder sister was married and the younger one I never had much time for anyway. So none of us have any contact with the family now."

Lucy felt relieved, then there was only a very slim chance that Cathy would see Farid, but now she must ask her friend to go, she didn't want any more questions.

"Cathy, thanks ever so much for stepping in. I would have been lost without you. We'll have to meet up again before I go back to England." She walked towards the door hoping Cathy would follow. She didn't.

Lucy turned back to her. "Look, I'd better get the little monster up. If he's been asleep all afternoon, I'd prefer he's awake now or none of us will get any sleep tonight." She smiled broadly and waited. Cathy made no move to go, but got up and drew back the curtains.

Ben turned over and grunted, then propped himself up on one elbow, rubbing his eyes. His colour had returned and he looked much more himself. On seeing his mum, he looked sheepishly at her. "Hi, Mum. Sorry I messed up really I am. You were right as usual. Too much ice cream, sun and swimming."

Lucy smiled at him. "Don't forget the lemonade, but no harm done, sweetheart."

He glanced at Cathy. Reluctantly Lucy explained. "This is my friend. She agreed to sit with you while we went to the wedding." He smiled.

Cathy noticed immediately the closeness between mother and son. She watched Ben as he sat up and leaned against the bedhead, his chest bare. He yawned and ran his hand through his black hair, in a gesture she thought was reminiscently familiar. He turned to face her and the light caught his face as he grinned broadly. "Thank you for sitting with me."

Cathy felt the blood drain from her face. "Oh my God!"

Lucy spun round. Her friend was staring at Ben, her hand over her mouth, her face pale. Cathy's gaze moved quickly from Ben to Lucy and back to Ben, her eyes wide in amazement. "Oh my God!" she repeated.

Lucy understood. She sank down onto the bed her head in her hands. Ben jumped out of bed and ran over to her, his body dark against his white shorts.

"Mum, are you alright?" He put his arm round his mother. Lucy's eyes pleaded with her friend. Ben was still quite small for his age and she had hoped in vain her friend would not add up the years.

"Yes, darling I'm fine, honestly. I just had a bit too much sun today, like you." She smiled weakly at him. He smiled back, his father's smile.

"How are you feeling?" she whispered.

"Great. Mum, can I go and see Aunty Jackie?"

"Of course you can, she's in her room or if not she's already gone to the bar, but put your T-shirt on." He beamed at her and pulled on his T-shirt and sandals on his way out of the door, which slammed behind him.

Lucy turned slowly towards Cathy, who sat motionless, her hand still over her mouth.

"Lucy, please tell me that's not Farid's son."

"What do you want me to say?"

"Oh dear God, and he doesn't know."

Lucy's voice broke. "No, he doesn't know and he mustn't know."

"But why?"

Lucy stood up and poured two glasses of wine. She handed one to Cathy, drank her own quickly and refilled it, then sat down on the bed beside her friend.

"Cathy. Have some sense. I am years old than him, his family would never accept me and Alex, another man's son. He couldn't see any of the problems and I loved him so much I didn't want to. In Hammamet we were miles away from his family, we were safe in a dream world and then when I went home in the summer I found out I was pregnant. Suddenly the dream became a harsh reality."

"So that's why you came back early instead of at New Year like you used to?"

Lucy nodded. "I shouldn't have come back at all, but selfishly I had to see him one last time. It was dreadful, he was so happy. He talked about us getting married. He even bought me a beautiful silk dress which must have cost him a fortune. I pleaded with him not to buy it but he said I must take it home so I could have it altered if necessary and remember to bring it back for our wedding."

She felt the tears pricking as she remembered. "He wanted to speak to his father and I had to persuade him to wait until I came back in the spring."

Cathy watched as Lucy twisted the ring on her right hand until it cut into her skin. She put her hand over her friend's. "And he bought you that?"

She nodded and gave a wistful smile. "He was like a child, he was so pleased. Again must have cost him much more than he could afford and I felt awful. I've never taken it off."

"And Ben?"

"Cathy, how could I have come back to Tunisia and presented myself to his family, with Alex in one hand and the other on my expanding stomach? I know Farid would have been overjoyed, he even talked about the son we would have. He described Ben before he was born. It scared the daylights out of me."

Cathy started to speak, but Lucy cut her dead. "Please say nothing. Cathy, think sensibly for a minute. Farid's family is the centre piece of his life, parents, brother, sisters, uncles, aunts cousins and all. He would alienate himself from them all if he had married me and taken on Alex. It was a no-win situation for him. He could marry an old woman and take on another man's child as well as his own, and you know what the feelings are here about that. I couldn't live in his family home but he couldn't support us and as you know the man is expected to support the wife and if he can't the families step in to help. Can you see that?

"His status amongst his community would be ruined. We would have been outcasts and I could not put him through that. Eventually he would have wished he had never met me."

Lucy was rambling trying to justify everything she had done. "The alternative was that if he didn't marry me I couldn't come here to live, that would be too awful for us both and the prejudice would still have been there. I would have had to stay in England and Farid would have a bastard son living a thousand miles away in another country, whom he could not see or support. That would alienate his family and it would break his heart. Either way he would have grown to hate me. I took the only way out." She didn't mention Rose, there was no point in adding to the problem.

"Does Ben know?"

"Fortunately he's young. He knows Alex and he have different fathers. He knows Alex's father is in heaven and when he was very young he assumed his father was as well. In the last couple of years he's been asking questions and I told him his father lived in Tunisia, but I didn't know where. I know I will have to tell him eventually, but not yet."

"And Farid?"

"As I said, I did the right thing and…"

Cathy watched her friend as she wrung her hands together, still twisting the little ring, "And what?"

"And anyway I found out today I had done the right thing. I learned Farid got married."

"Who told you that?" Cathy sounded surprised.

"Some over-made up girl at the wedding young enough to be my daughter said she'd met him in Hammamet and had a fling with him a couple of years back, I knew it was him because not only did she refer to him as Farid, she described him to me. She had a moan because I think she still fancied him and then found out he'd got married. Glibly told me 'You can't win them all', and then waltzed off to meet her friend with a smile on her face. It obviously wasn't a relationship based on love." she added sarcastically.

Cathy hesitated. "I do see where you're coming from Lucy and I remember there was talk about him marrying a cousin or something, but I thought they called it off. I didn't know he was actually married now. It is quite a close community and I am surprised I didn't hear about it, but as I said, I haven't seen him or the family for ages."

"Well, he is married so I know I was right in what I did. I will go back to England and raise my children. I will tell Ben about his father when the time is right. Farid has his future with his wife and I am sure in time will raise his own children. Everything is as it must be."

Cathy nodded. "I suppose you're right, but it must have been a nightmare for you."

"It was and it still is. No other man has been near me since Farid. He was the love of my life as the saying goes, but in my case it is absolutely true. Now, my friend, I want your word on whatever is dearest to you that you will say nothing to anyone, not even your husband."

Cathy smiled. "I promise I won't. I wouldn't hurt either of you, and it would serve no purpose. Your secret is safe with me."

"I do trust you, Cathy. You're the only person here who knows. And now, tell me about your family and all the terrible things you've all been up to since we last saw each other." She forced a smile but Cathy ignored the ploy.

"Lucy, will you come back to Tunisia again?"

"Honestly, I don't know. When Ben was born I made him a promise I would come back when he is older. I meant a lot older. But when Jackie mentioned Ellen's wedding I just had to come. Come back again? I must, for my son, although at this moment I cannot think of anything worse."

"If you do and Ben is with you, be prepared. I haven't seen Farid for more than five years, but I recognised his son immediately. In ten years' time, Ben will look exactly like his father and anyone who knows Farid will see it. Be careful."

"I thought of that. Now let's talk about something else."

Cathy's mind was racing and Lucy noticed she avoided looking at her. There was obviously something worrying her beyond the shock of seeing Farid's son.

"Cathy, what is it, what are you not telling me?" Cathy forced herself to look at her old friend.

"Lucy, the girl at the wedding, did she have bright red hair?" Lucy stared at her and nodded.

"Oh God, I am so sorry."

A cold shiver ran down Lucy's back. "Tell me whatever it is. I need to know."

"I saw him with her once in a cafe in Hammamet. She was dressed like a tart, see-through dress, far too much make-up. She was all over him and making a terrible spectacle of herself. He was really embarrassed and I remember wondering what on earth he was doing with her."

"So she did go out with him then," Lucy murmured more to herself.

Cathy looked at the floor. "So it would seem."

"Cathy, come on. Spit it out, something's obviously bothering you."

"Nothing, really nothing." Lucy knew her too well. "I don't believe you," she said harshly.

Cathy refused to look at her. "Cathy you have to tell me. More depends on this than you can possibly realise. The truth, please. What can be so awful? - so he bedded the little tart. It was years after we separated, he had every right."

Cathy was forced to picture the terrible night. How could she kill the love she knew her friend still held for Farid.

"Lucy, it was ghastly. You know how you just feel something is really wrong? When they left the cafe I followed a little way behind them. She was such a predator I honestly felt scared for Farid."

Lucy smiled. "I thought it was the other way around – it is the girl you should fear for."

Her smile faded at Cathy's distraught face.

"Lucy she was holding him, touching him and rubbing against him. He's not a saint." Her eyes pleaded for understanding. Lucy felt icy cold, a terrible picture building in her mind.

"They were walking towards the new villas at the far end of the town. There were no lights and the road was just a dirt track at the time. It was pretty obvious to me she was leading up to one of the villas for a night of sex, but it backfired on her."

She watched anxiously as her friend's face turned white. "Go on," she whispered.

Cathy panicked. "Lucy, you have to realise Farid probably had not had a woman for months, even years. He was utterly loyal to you, but any man would have struggled to refuse her. For God's sake she wrapped herself round him like a python, touching him everywhere."

"And…"

Cathy held her eyes. "Do you really want to know?"

"Yes, I must, whatever it is."

Cathy took a deep breath and the words tumbled out. She just wanted to get it over with.

"He spoke to her and I saw her smirk and whisper something. I looked away. It all happened so quickly. When I looked up the girl was imprisoned against the wall. She struggled but he simply pulled up her skirt and I heard her scream. It was over in seconds. Lucy, he forced her."

"You mean raped her?" Cathy looked away. Lucy stood up and fled past her to the bathroom. Cathy heard her retching. Her face ghostly pale she came back a few minutes later. Cathy tried to put her arm around her but Lucy pushed her away.

"It seems I was right to leave him, but not for the reason I thought. The man I loved would never have done that. It seems I never knew him at all."

"Lucy, you don't know what happened, what caused it and what had gone before. When he walked past me he was crying. I heard him say 'Lucy, forgive me'."

Lucy shook her head. "I never will. Cathy I know how difficult it must have been for you to tell me this, but you have closed a chapter in my life. I no longer feel any guilt for running away."

She forced a weak smile. "I wonder if his wife knows."

"I doubt it ever came up in conversation," Cathy answered drily.

"No, I suppose not. Come on, let's both go down to the bar and get smashed!"

CHAPTER THIRTY-NINE

THE CAFÉ

The encounter with Cathy had left her stunned. She tried to put out of her mind the awful picture of Farid and the girl. It had happened, it was past and there was nothing she could do about it but the numbness in her brain refused to go away.

That Cathy had recognised Ben as Farid's son scared her. She knew Ben looked like his father but as he was so young she hadn't realised it would be so obvious to anyone else. Even though the two had never met, he had inherited some of Farid's ways. She saw it every time he ran his fingers through his hair and when he sat at the table waiting for his dinner he always clasped his hands in front of him, his thumbs pointing upwards side by side, exactly like his father. For the rest of it, she just wanted to forget.

The following evening she told Jackie how Cathy had recognised Ben as Farid's son, but not about the girl.

Jackie could see that the incident had upset her more than she was saying.

"It's a good thing we're leaving soon." Lucy said nothing, but Jackie noticed she was very quiet and seemed to have withdrawn inside herself.

After breakfast the next day she was still worried about her friend.

"Luce, will you be okay? I promised Ellen I'd go over and say goodbye before we leave. I'll only be gone an hour or so."

"Yes, I'm fine. I promised Ben I'd take him down to the beach. I'll meet you back here around six."

Lucy showered quickly, washed her hair and left it loose to dry. She pulled on her trousers and a pale pink blouse with a wide deep pink belt. She looked at herself in the mirror. Washed out and middle aged. She smiled so the corners of her mouth turned down. I needn't worry about meeting Farid she thought, he wouldn't know me now. Then, for reasons best known to herself, she opened her bag and carefully applied her lipstick and a little mascara.

Farid was unhappy. It was his own fault, he should never have agreed to accompany his sister on their walk along the promenade. He was due back to work in the morning and would have liked to seen a couple of his old friends. He rarely had time nowadays to see anyone in Sousse as he worked every hour he could. But he was very fond of his eldest sister and she had been very close to their uncle. When she said she wanted to take the baby out, she could hardly go alone and her husband had gone back South on a business trip.

It was extremely hot and his vest clung to him. Farid wished Meriam would have waited until late in the afternoon when the air was cooler and the breeze stronger. They walked slowly back towards the main town and the café which held so many memories for him. He tried to avoid this area and found little reason to stray into the more tourist parts of the town, preferring the narrow dusty streets away from the coast where his own people lived.

His sister had always loved the sea and he watched her as she looked dreamily out over the ripples, her lips curved into a contented smile. The wheels of the buggy made only a slight purring sound on the even paving and the baby slept soundly. They reached the cafe. There was a little breeze and he noticed the umbrellas fluttering like multi-coloured butterflies. Meriam turned to him.

"Farid, can we stop, I really need a rest and tea would be most welcome."

Again, there was little he could do but agree.

They walked over to the shadier part of the café which was sheltered by the overhang of the building and sat down at the back by the wall. As they sipped their drinks he looked around him. He had been back to the café only once a year, on the anniversary of the day he had first seen Lucy and never at any other time. The place had been here for as long as he could remember, long before the main bustle of tourism invaded his home town. Only the waiters changed, and he was sure even some of those had been there years. To him the old cafe was part of the ancient part of the structure of the town.

It was a beautiful day. Lucy pulled her sunglasses down from her head to cover her eyes. Even the sunshine seemed to mock at her misery.

Ben ran alongside her, urging her to hurry. He couldn't decide whether he wanted an ice cream first or to go straight to the beach. Lucy couldn't remember which street to take and found herself walking up a shady narrow lane. She reasoned she must be going in the right direction because they were walking towards the sea. She could see an open area in front and at the far side the low wall separating the promenade from the beach.

As they came out of the shadow of the buildings into the bright sunlight she put her hand up to shade her eyes. Ben decided he wanted an ice cream first. "Come on, Mum, there's a place over here and I can see the ice cream sign!" He pointed to the far side of the open ground.

Lucy looked over. Ben was running towards the café, their café. She yelled at him but he was already rushing across the rough ground, his brown legs flying and his black hair shining in the sunlight, exactly as another boy had done so long ago. She had no option but to follow.

She sat down. The café had not changed, it was just as she remembered it. The day she had met him, the first time they had come here together when they found each other again, and the time when they sat together holding hands at the table by the pillar in the shade, the day he bought her the ring. She could see the white tables were still arranged in a semi-circle around the main body of the café, as they always had been, umbrellas still fluttered in the breeze. Time had passed it by and she hoped it always would.

Farid watched the people coming and going and his attention was caught by a young boy as he dashed along. He remembered how once he too had run across the open ground, all flying arms and legs, hot and sticky and not a care in the world. He was surprised when the boy sat down at one of the far tables nearest the sea. He had taken him for a local lad, but realised he must be with his family. The woman appeared flustered as she sat down next to the boy looking out towards the sea and his heart missed a beat. The way she was dressed and her long blonde hair reminded him of the first time he had seen Lucy, in what seemed another life time. But he was used to the sensation. He had given up counting the times he thought he had seen Lucy. At first he used to start towards the woman, his heart pounding, only to stop when he realised yet again he was mistaken. He looked away.

The baby woke up and started grizzling. Meriam picked him up and rocked him.

Lucy felt uncomfortable. She did not want to be here, of all places. Why had she missed the turning and ended up here instead of further down the road where she had been heading. The waiter was young, black haired, handsome and smiling. *Why do Tunisians always smile?* she thought irrationally. She ordered for them both. A huge ice cream in a tall glass for Ben and her usual cappucin and a bottle of water.

Ben had to stand up to eat his ice cream and Lucy lovingly watched his young face, flushed with excitement and hoped he was not going to get sick again. However he quickly devoured his treat and sat happily looking out to sea.

"Can we go to the beach now?" Lucy laughed.

"Give me a minute young man, I would like to finish my coffee."

"Sorry, Mum." He grinned at her.

Lucy looked around her as she sipped the dark tepid liquid. She lit a cigarette. The place was crowded as always, there were few spare tables. The usual eclectic mix of tourists, families and young people of all nationalities mingled with Tunisian business men looking strangely out of place in their smart trousers and white shirts. Other than as a meeting place, the local people rarely used the café now; since the tourist invasion, there were many cheaper places in the town. The air was alive with chatter in numerous different languages.

Farid turned his attention back to the woman. Although she had her back half to him and he could not see her face, he noticed the glances she was receiving from one or two of the more appreciative male clientèle, but there was something else about her. The way she rested her chin in the palm of her hand as she looked around, the way she held her cigarette with her hand tilted backwards. But it was as always wishful thinking, Lucy was thousands of miles away where he couldn't find her.

Lucy watched a couple of children playing with a beach ball. A baby started to cry and she looked towards the sound. A pretty Tunisian woman sat in the shadows near the café building. She had the baby on her lap and rocked it gently to hush the crying. A man sat with her.

The baby would not be quieted and Meriam was hot and flustered. "Farid, you are always good with him, would you hold him while I go and splash some water on my face?" He put out his cigarette and held out his arms to receive the fractious infant.

Lucy saw the man lean forward to take the child. She watched as he gently stroked the child's cheek, his face clear in the sunlight. She gasped. Her cup clattered down onto the saucer and the man looked up. For the first time in more than seven years Lucy looked into the face of her beloved.

Farid stared at her. This time surely there could be no mistake. Lucy watched the familiar smile light up his face. She looked at the now quieted infant nestled in the crook of his arm and thought her heart would break. He was so close and yet as lost to her as if she had been on the other side of the universe. She took off her sunglasses to wipe away the tears that trickled down her cheeks and despite everything, she smiled back.

Now Farid was sure. He started to his feet, still clutching the baby and looking around him wildly as if he didn't know what to do with it. Meriam came out of the café. Her brother was half out of his chair staring at one of the tourists as if he had seen a ghost, a blonde woman with her arm around a young boy.

"Meriam, take the baby, please, quickly." He held the child out to her, his arms outstretched.

"Farid what is it?"

"Please sister, now!" His voice was desperate and she was caught off balance as he pushed the table to get out. She sat down hard on the seat and he had no option but turn to her until she was settled otherwise he would have dropped the infant.

The moment was gone. Lucy left the money on the table, grabbed Ben by the hand and ran with the startled child as quickly as she could. She disappeared around the back of the café and leaned against the wall, her heart pounding, the tears streaming down her face.

Farid pushed his way between the tables but she had gone. He reached the table where she had been sitting. The sunglasses lay next to the half empty coffee cup, beside it a small bottle of water and a heap of unopened sugar sachets. A packet of cigarettes lay beside the cup, the ones Lucy smoked. He picked up the packet and opened it. There neatly tucked inside was the tiny lighter, exactly as Lucy had always done. Without thinking, he put the cigarettes and sunglasses in his pocket and looked around him. She had disappeared.

Farid walked slowly back to the table where his sister sat, stunned by what she had just seen.

"Farid, what just happened?" Meriam was obviously upset and it was too late anyway, Lucy had gone. He sat down heavily.

"Farid, who was that woman, do you know her?" He knew his sister well and could see that she demanded an explanation and was not about to move until she had one. He took a deep breath.

"Some years ago I met an English woman in Hammamet. Her name was Lucy. I was very much in love with her and I thought she loved me, but then she disappeared out of my life and if you want the truth I have been looking for her ever since."

"Is that why you and Sarra never married?"

Farid was astonished. "You don't miss a lot do you, sister?"

"Not much where my brother is concerned. Tell me."

"Sarra knew I was in love with someone else. She told me that she is not the type of girl to marry unless that man returns her love and she knows he will be happy with her. She knew I could never be that man and so like the sweet person she is she decided that we should tell our families it was a mutual decision and that we had mistaken friendship over many years for love. She saved us both embarrassment and the anger of our respective families."

"She is indeed a good woman. But how is this to do with today?"

"The person in the café was Lucy."

His sister stared at him. "You mean the girl who left you?" He nodded.

"And now she has come back again," Meriam said flatly. "Does our family know about her?"

"Yes, although not at first. Saleem bumped into us in Hammamet that summer he worked there in the college holiday and I told Baba just before Sarra and I decided not to get married."

"And Fatma, she doesn't know does she?"

"Some things happened at home that made me wonder that myself."

Farid told his sister about the dreadful encounter with Michelle and how he had run across the floor of the apartment calling out Lucy's name. She was horrified.

"It came out that meeting was engineered by Fatma, she had tried to recreate Lucy in Michelle, but what I couldn't understand was how she knew what Lucy looked like. Then Saleem told me Fatma had seen us together in Sousse. He tells me she admitted to him that she followed and saw us hand in hand."

"Here, in Sousse!"

He nodded. "Yes, we used to avoid Sousse. I didn't want to draw attention to us. As we had the car there were lots of other places to go."

"The car, you don't have one!"

"Lucy used to hire a car sometimes when she came over. She loves the countryside and the old towns, Kairouan, Dougga, El Djem even up to Tunis and Sidi Bou Said, we drove everywhere," he added simply.

"I don't understand." She stared at him. "Farid, how long did you know her?"

Farid smiled "Three and a half years." His sister tried to hide her astonishment.

"Farid, then if you avoided Sousse why in heavens name were you here the day Fatma saw you?"

Farid hesitated. His sister's expression gave nothing away. She appeared calm, if a little flushed. "I came to buy Lucy a ring, Fatma saw us in the jewellery shop."

"A ring!" Meriam cursed silently. The tale was starting to make sense.

"Now I see why Fatma was concerned and it's a great pity that she saw you. As I am sure you know she was doing everything she could to get you to marry Sarra so she could have a friend to plead for her in her own quest to marry that Hama she was keen on at the time. She was extremely lucky that his true nature came out and he was arrested before she was drawn into something from which she would not have escaped. But Farid, but she is indeed a vengeful person and she had her heart set on that man, she probably blamed your Lucy for everything."

Farid saw his sister in a new light. She was a quiet gentle person, but it occurred to him that she was indeed very like his mother, she saw a lot but kept her own counsel.

"That occurred to me as well and I think it's very important that if the person I saw was indeed Lucy that Fatma knows nothing about her being here. She may now be settled, but she has a long memory. What I don't understand is why Lucy is here now, and why she ran when she saw me. I don't know but I intend to find out."

His sister looked thoughtful.

"The wedding a few days ago. Your old friend Ali married an English girl."

"Ali? Ali from school? I knew there was a wedding because the girls were all talking about it. I didn't take much notice. But I hadn't realised it was that Ali who was getting married."

"The same. I believe by some coincidence she may have come over for the wedding."

Once again, Farid's mind was drawn back to the first day he met Lucy and how he told Ali he what he had said to Lucy. He smiled as he remembered Ali's reaction and how he had yelled at him.

"So, Ali married an English girl, but how did you know? You live miles away."

"Farid, I am an old married woman with a child." She emphasised the word old and grinned. "We women sit and chat, while our children play. I know much of what goes on around here. Ali brought Ellen along several times so sit with the women and I know there was talk of a lot of English people coming over for the wedding. Fatma asked me if I would go to one of those gatherings with her, which I admit surprised me. Gatherings of women are not normally her sort of thing." Farid nodded his agreement.

"There were also a couple of friends of the bride, although I am certain I didn't see your… Lucy." Farid noticed the hesitation. "It is possible Fatma got talking to people and names may have been mentioned. She spent most of the time talking to a friend of the bride and I didn't see much of her. On the way home she seemed very chirpy and I suppose she may have learned something, put two and two together and come up with the right answer, so I think Fatma may already know your Lucy is here, but Farid I am not sure I understand. Apart from spoiling her plan so far as Sarra was concerned, what is it that Fatma has got against this English girl? For all her wildness she loves you and would want you to be happy."

Farid hesitated. He knew Meriam loved him very much, but she valued family very highly as he did. She saw his discomfort.

"Farid? I am here to help you, not to judge you."

"Lucy has been married twice before." He heard his sister's sharp intake of breath and wondered whether to go on.

"I'm sorry, Farid, you just surprised me, that's all. Go on."

"She was married young, she found out her husband was unfaithful and she divorced him. She married again and her husband died."

"He was much older than her?

"No, he died very young, just dropped down dead from a heart attack. He left her with a young child."

"She had a child." He nodded, noticing that she had not added up the years. The child his sister had just seen was obviously young, about five or six he reckoned and he realised that the other child whom she had brought with her years before must be in his teens by now. So now Lucy had two children. She obviously hadn't wasted any time. She had not waited for him as he had for her, but why should she; it was she who had left him. He felt angry.

His sister thought for a moment. "Yes, I can see that this would be a problem for our family, but it isn't the end of the world, if she is an honest and decent girl and the family like her they may come to accept her. After all it is not her fault her husband has died. We remarry after death and sometimes there are children. And of course you could have more children…"

Her voice trailed off as she noticed her brother's strange expression.

"What is it?"

"Sister, Lucy is not a girl. She was not a girl when I met her."

She stared at him. "Farid, how old is she?"

"She is twelve years older than me."

His sister's distress was obvious.

"Farid you could not marry a woman of this age. It's ridiculous, it's awful." She stopped and glared at him. "Is she rich?"

"I think she has enough money to live on, if that's what you mean. She told me her husband left her comfortably provided for, as he should."

"That's not what I mean and you know it."

Farid glared back at her. "If you mean what I think you do, then no I was not looking for money, sex or a ticket to England!" His sister was shocked at his bluntness.

"But people will think this." He ignored her.

She looked confused for a moment, as though something had just occurred to her. "But that was not the woman I saw in the café, the pretty pale woman with the blonde hair?"

"That was Lucy," he replied emphatically. Meriam tried to hide her surprise. From what he had said the woman must be in her forties.

His expression had changed and he pleaded silently for her approval. Meriam adored her eldest brother, she couldn't hurt him.

"I know you need me to understand, and I can understand love. I can also see why you would love her, she must have been an exceptionally beautiful woman, and indeed she still is, but Farid why can you not remember as she was. Remember your time with her forever if you will, but don't spend the rest of your life chasing a dream that can never be. If this woman is as beautiful a person in her heart as she is in her skin, then you must know why she left. You are a young man with your life in front of you; she has her children, she has moved on and she wants the same for you. Farid, don't make her sacrifice worthless."

"What d'you mean, sacrifice?"

"Farid, however much she once loved you, she knows she can only bring you heartbreak. She is giving you her blessing to love again." He said nothing.

That night, Farid thought on this as he lay in bed, but he couldn't believe that this was the reason. He knew Lucy had loved him and he had seen in her face today that she still loved him. He returned to Hammamet the next day, a troubled man.

CHAPTER FORTY

YASSINE

Lucy got back to the hotel and was determined to say nothing to Jackie about seeing Farid. She saw no reason to spoil her friend's holiday. By the time Jackie got back she had positioned herself in the far corner of the pool bar and pretended to read a book, although she couldn't see through unshed tears. Jackie could see her friend was deeply upset. Her cheeks flushed by alcohol sat unnaturally in her pale face. On seeing her friend, Lucy smiled broadly and launched into a tirade of aimless chatter. Jackie knew her too well.

"Lu, just shut up for a minute. What happened? You look as though someone just spat on your grave."

Lucy's voice tailed off into a whisper. "Oh, Jackie it was horrible, it seems I've been a right fool. I've been chasing a dream that never was." She whimpered out her story and Jackie put her arm round her friend's shoulder.

"It is for the best. Now at least you know that he has moved on, he has a family. Lucy just think of your time with him as a wonderful part of your life that you will never forget , but a part that is over, and always remember that he gave you two beautiful children. You have your own family to think about."

Ben was still confused about the incident in the café, but was more upset about being whisked off in the opposite direction from the beach on the basis that Mummy was not feeling well. He had been placated with another ice cream and sat quietly licking the last drops off his fingers.

Cathy was worried about her friend and arrived the next morning. Lucy made Jackie promise she would say nothing about her seeing Farid. The three women chatted over coffee and Cathy told them about the festival in Hammamet that evening. One of her friends had invited her to stay. Ben thought it was a wonderful idea. Jackie felt it would be good for Lucy to get away from Sousse and a pleasant end to their holiday, so she readily agreed. Lucy tried to think of a way out of going. She was still shaken with the raw emotion of seeing Farid with his wife and child. She couldn't face the thought of spending the evening with a crowd of happy people at a festival. She knew she would only spoil the evening.

She spoke quietly to Jackie when Cathy went with Ben to get some lemonade.

"Jackie, I would much rather just stay here, sit by the pool until the sun goes down, have a couple of drinks and go to bed. I'm sorry I'm such a misery guts but all this has really thrown me."

Jackie nodded her head in understanding. "Yes, I'm sorry I'm being selfish. We won't go."

"Oh, no, please not on account of me. Look, Jackie, if I am truthful, I would rather be on my own."

Cathy came back with Ben and Lucy said she really didn't feel up to going out.

Cathy looked hurt. "Oh, Lucy, you are only here for another couple of days. Don't miss out on this, it's a brilliant evening and to save us travelling back, Asma says she has room for all of us to stay in Hammamet tonight."

Jackie helped her out. "Come on, Cathy, Lucy knows how she wants to deal with this. Being here has obviously brought back memories. Leave her be, and anyway now we've told Ben we can hardly not go. I think Lucy may well be better by herself, it will give her time to get things in perspective."

Cathy nodded, but she was still worried about her friend. Ben cuddled his Mum and she kissed him, a little smile on her face as she watched him disappear back into the hotel, Cathy in one hand and Jackie in the other.

Lucy sat reading, trying to put Farid and his new family out of her mind, until slowly one by one the guests abandoned the pool to change for dinner. The sun dipped behind the hotel and Lucy gathered up her bits and pieces and went back to her room. She didn't much feel like eating so she ordered a sandwich from room service and ate it thoughtfully as she sat on the balcony watching the couples strolling arm in arm along the wide straight promenade. A slight breeze moved the palm fronds which swayed seductively. She listened to the sound of the crickets and the gentle swishing movement of the trees.

It was a perfect Mediterranean summer's evening. Lucy brushed her hand across her eyes. So it was done, her dream was ended. She had seen him with her own eyes and there would be no more wondering about what the future held. Whatever it was it could never include Farid. Now the choice was hers. She could spend the rest of her life moping or start to live again, as he had done. She tried not to think of the red-haired girl.

She picked up her plate and went back into the room, pulling the heavy door shut behind her. The gentle hum of the air conditioning was the only sound in the room. Without thinking she went into the bathroom and washed the plate. It slipped out of her hands, fell on the ground and broke.

"Shit!" She picked up the pieces and threw them in the waste-bin. She stared at her reflection.

She looked like a clown with dark circles under her eyes and patches of pink on her cheeks from the unaccustomed abundance of daytime alcohol. Her fringe stood on end from being under her sunhat and as she tried to straighten it a streak of red appeared on her forehead. "Shit," she said again and sucked her finger where a sliver of the plate had cut her.

She thought of the pretty young woman she had seen with Farid. She closed her eyes and his mocking face watched her as he cuddled his baby. She thought about the red haired girl and burst into tears. She tore of her clothes and flung them on the floor in a heap and got under the shower, trying to wash away the picture of Farid with his wife and baby and Farid forcing himself on the girl. She scrubbed her body until it tingled then washed her hair kneading in the conditioner until her head hurt, rinsed it off and got out of the shower.

Without a glance in the mirror she towel dried her hair and bundled part up onto her crown in a clip, leaving the rest loose. Where she had not combed it through it fell in waves and tangles around her shoulders like a gypsy. She grinned broadly at her reflection and made a decision. She was not going to sit in her room like an abandoned wife, bemoaning what might have been. She was going to get dressed, get drunk and enjoy herself like everyone else. She was on holiday.

Lucy dressed without thinking, cream trousers, a plain shirt and her usual sandals. She looked at herself in the long mirror. The same old Lucy. Angrily she undressed and threw all her clothes on the bed. She hunted at the back of the draw and pulled out a pair of tiny red lace knickers and matching bra. She put them on, struck a pose with her hands behind her head, smirked at the mirror and felt better. She went back to the wardrobe and took out a cherry red skirt and white blouse with a wide scooped neck. She pulled the blouse down so it lay low over her bosom and off her shoulders. She poured herself another drink. She felt very lightheaded.

She skipped back into the bathroom and put on her makeup. She slipped on her comfortable sandals and then at the back of the wardrobe she noticed Jackie's high heeled gold sandals. She kicked off her own and tried them on. Perfect!

She rummaged in her jewellery case and found the heavy gold earrings she had pushed in there as a last minute decision before leaving England, although she never thought she would wear them.

She smiled broadly at the strange being who looked back at her. The old Lucy had disappeared and the miseries had gone. Her eyes seemed very green against the mauve eye-shadow and liner and her teeth very white set off by bright red lipstick. She frowned and added a little touch of foundation to hide her pink cheeks and the dark circles. Her arms looked bare. She went back to the jewellery case and added a thick plain gold bangle. Suddenly the world felt a better place. She poured herself a pastis and topped it up with water. She downed the cloudy liquid in one gulp, took a deep breath and closed the room door firmly behind her.

The bar was crowded, almost every seat was taken. She was aware of the admiring glances and swung her hips as she walked outside to the patio and sat down at one of the few empty tables. In seconds the waiter arrived and she ordered her drink

Lucy listened to the gentle music drifting across the water, mingling with the ever present scent of jasmine and she relaxed. She lit a cigarette, sipped her pastis. There wasn't much water added and it seemed strong. Even with the sweetness of the added touch of grenadine it burned her throat and she added more water watching the pale pink cloudy liquid lapping with the movement of her hand as she swirled it around in the glass. She took a deep drag on her cigarette and looked around her.

Two men sat at the next table. One was dark. He was a lot older than his companion, his sky blue T-shirt clung to his muscular torso and he frowned as he reached into his jeans pocket. The other man reminded her of Farid, but she realised that at the moment every man who even looked a little like Farid would seem that way. He could easily have been European, but she heard the familiar Arabic. The darker man got up and left. His friend lit a cigarette, leaned back in his chair and tilted his head back as he exhaled. He sat sideways to Lucy and she studied his aquiline profile. She noticed irrelevantly that his thickly waved hair was lightly gelled at the front, like Farid.

The older man came back and stood by the table. He seemed agitated. The younger one noticed Lucy watching them. He turned to her and his smile took her by surprise.

He spoke in French. "My friend, he has lost his room key, he can get another from reception, I think?"

Lucy returned the smile. "I believe so, but he will have to pay for it."

He grinned. "That will upset him." He said something to his friend who looked even more annoyed and disappeared back into the hotel.

The waiter asked him if he would like another drink. The young man looked at Lucy.

"You will have one with me, of course only if you do not mind if I sit with you?"

Lucy hesitated but she had forgotten her book. As well as feeling lightheaded she was starting to feel conspicuous sitting alone, and felt she would be glad of the company of someone who did not know her or her problems.

"Of course, I'd be happy for you to sit with me." The man got up and sat down opposite her, leaning his forearms on the table watching her.

"I am Yassine, and you?"

"Lucy."

"May I ask why such a beautiful lady sits alone?" Lucy found herself staring into a pair of soft hazel eyes and shook her head. "You shake your head to say you are not alone or that you are not beautiful? You are wrong, you sit alone and you are beautiful, but I think you are also sad."

Lucy said nothing and was relieved when the waiter appeared noiselessly with their drinks. She thanked him in English. The young man looked surprised. "You are English."

Lucy nodded.

"But you speak in French."

His English was good. "Yes, I am English but here it is easier to speak in French." He agreed but continued in her own language. He told her he worked for a bank in Tunis but he came originally from the south where his parents still lived. His voice was mellow and calming and Lucy warmed to his easy manner. He offered her a cigarette, she shook her head. The alcohol and lack of a proper meal was making her head swim.

He watched her as she sipped her drink. "I notice you also drink a French drink. This is unusual for an English girl." Lucy was flattered at being called a girl and laughed.

"I first tried this in Paris as a teenager. I spent some months there and I learned to love the city and its people. I also grew to love its pastis and cuisine."

He looked puzzled. "What is teenager?" She laughed again and thought to herself, *that is what you were not all that long ago!* She explained.

"That is a good word. I will remember it. Thank you. It is also good to see you laugh, you are even more beautiful when you are not sad. Why are you sad?"

His expression was serious and he seemed genuinely interested. As she leaned forward to reach her drink his hand closed over hers, it was warm and gentle. She tried to withdraw her hand and Yassine noticed immediately the tension flood through her.

"Ah, I see, a man has hurt you. I am sorry, and for this I apologise."

He hesitated wondering whether to continue. "I too am hurt by a woman. I tell you something. It is not her fault. She is my love but she comes from Mexico. She wants to be with me but it is a problem. She wants me to go and live in her country but I cannot see myself living and working there. I know not the language. I have my work, my family and I too love my country. We try to be apart but it not work either. She is a wonderful and happy person, my Elena, but I think she not loves me enough to come to me."

"Perhaps she just feels as you do." She hesitated and added thoughtfully. "It seems so strange, the world is now so small we can go across it in a day but in so many ways were are still as far from each other as we have ever been."

Yassine listened to her "You are so right, you are very *sympatique*, I think."

Lucy smiled. "No, just a woman." His hand closed over hers and this time she did not pull away.

They talked for a long time, sometimes in English, sometimes in French, about Tunisia, its history, its future and its people. Yassine was surprised she knew so much about his culture. "I think perhaps you have lived here at some time."

Lucy shook her head, "Not quite, but almost."

The alcohol had loosened her tongue and she found it easy to talk to him about Farid. He did not judge her or advise her, he just listened.

"Why did you leave him if you love him?"

"There were reasons." He didn't ask her to explain, but Lucy told him about the wedding and about seeing Farid with his family.

Yassine nodded and stroked her hand. Lucy felt a tingle long forgotten.

"So now he does not want you?"

"It seems that way." Yassine muttered something under his breath in Arabic.

"I'm sorry, I don't understand."

He smiled at her. "I said he is a stupid man." She looked at the two hands that now held hers and said nothing.

The bar closed and Yassine suggested they go to the nightclub. The club was almost in darkness, the only light from the few dim wrought iron wall lamps casting eerie shadows. The loud Algerian music throbbed through the room and as they danced he held her gently. "When do you go to England?"

"Tomorrow evening."

"Me, I leave after lunch tomorrow for the south. My friend and I we stay here just two days and now we go to his cousin's wedding."

"You are coming back to Sousse?"

"No we go straight back to Tunis and then in September I go to Paris with my work for one year. I must find somewhere to live, just a studio I think. Paris, she is expensive?"

"I haven't been to Paris for many years, but yes, when I was there it was expensive."

She rested her head against his shoulder and felt his arms tighten around her. They swayed to the music and he kissed her hair. Lucy closed her eyes remembering other times, another life.

Finally the music stopped and it was late when they walked to the lift. As the doors closed he kissed her, without pressure or condition. "You want to be with me?" The lift stopped, it was not her floor but she did not resist when he led her out. She looked up at him, his mouth was curved into a slight smile, his eyes invited her and she followed him.

As he closed the door behind them the room was in shadow save only for one bedside lamp. He poured her a drink and Lucy felt the smoothness of the wine. She was definitely well on the way to being drunk.

"You are so beautiful."

"And you are so young."

He held her at arm's length, his hands resting loosely on her shoulders. "I am not so young, I am twenty-eight. I have seen many things in my life and I know that if we wish to be together then age is no barrier." He kissed her again, this time deeply, searching out the softness of her mouth and the gently pulsating hollow of her neck.

"And now we are together, you and I. I think we need to be together tonight. Perhaps it is good for us both to feel loved again. Perhaps it is the will of God that we comfort each other."

"Insh'allah," Lucy whispered. She saw the flash of a smile.

"Insh'allah," he echoed.

Gently and without force as none was needed he pushed her blouse down and teased her flesh with soft movements of his tongue. Lucy moaned and felt a warmth stealing over her.

Yassine undressed her slowly, stroking and lifting her into desire she had not felt since Farid had made love to her the day before she went out of his life forever. He lowered her onto the bed and she lay on her side watching him remove his clothes.

When he lay beside her stroking her back, his body tense and pressed tightly against her, she felt his featherlight kisses on her face, her hair, her neck and listened as he whispered to her. "You want me to make love with you?"

"It has been a long time, there has been no man since…" She felt the gentle pressure of his fingers against her lips.

"Since Elena, for me also, but now I wait for you to come to me."

Shutting her mind to thoughts of anyone but the man whose lean strong body now ran the length of her own, Lucy gave herself completely to this stranger. His gentleness as he touched her, his moans of pleasure as she touched him were his alone. The time belonged to the two of them and to no-one else. They made love throughout the night, sometimes gently, sometimes with passion, until finally when the sunlight peeped through the dark curtains and shimmered on the polished floor they fell asleep, his arms around her. Lucy's last thought before her eyes closed was of another man's kisses and a contented smile played on her lips as he cradled her head against his shoulder and she slept.

When she woke, Lucy could hear the even breathing of her companion. She moved and he pulled her towards him. "You are so beautiful," he whispered.

"What, even in the morning?"

He kissed her, his lips just brushing hers "More so this morning my lovely English, because you are no longer sad." It was true.

He held her close. Lucy felt as though a new door had opened for her in the darkness offering her a breathtaking view to the edge of the world. He was not the reason, only the catalyst. She no longer felt alone. Love had not been part of their night together, only loving. She felt desirable and alive thanks to a young man she knew she would never see again. Although Farid would always he her one true love she believed for the first time that there could be a life after the empty years of loneliness and waiting for something she now knew could never be.

When Jackie and Ben came back around midday, Lucy was fast asleep in her own bed. Jackie shook her and she smiled and stretched her arms over her head.

"How do you feel?"

"I feel fine, and I am hungry." Jackie frowned, but said nothing. Lucy dressed quickly and they went down for lunch. As they came out of the restaurant, Lucy saw Yassine checking out at reception. He was dressed in jeans and T-shirt and had a travel bag slung over his shoulder. He turned and saw her and a smile lit up his face.

Lucy stood rooted to the spot as he came over to her and kissed her on both cheeks.

"And now I say goodbye, my Lucy and I thank you for a truly enjoyable evening. I will think of you when I am Paris." Lucy smiled. He had been tactful. She wished him well and watched as he walked away.

Jackie gaped at her. "Lucy, what the hell have you been up to?"

Ben tugged her arm. "Mummy, who was that man?"

Lucy laughed at the two pairs of eyes watching her. "He was someone I had a drink with last night, we walked about life, about Paris and about everything. He took my mind off my own troubles and for that I will forever be grateful."

Jackie coughed. Ben ignored them both and headed off towards the pool

"Is that all?" Jackie asked pointedly.

"That's all," her friend replied. Her night with Yassine was not something she would forget, but it was not to be shared with anyone.

Two people who came together at the right time for them both, but ships that pass in the night.

Mahmood asked around but no one seemed to know anything about the two English women and the child who had been staying at the hotel. He was not allowed into the hotel so he spent the evening sitting on the wall outside until he saw one of the chambermaids he knew leaving after her shift. He asked her and she looked at him dubiously.

Mahmood beamed at her. "I was only asking because I am sure one of them I knew many years ago, I just wondered if it was the same woman." He fixed his expression into one of friendly interest.

"They have gone now. I heard one of the porters say they were just here for a wedding. Anyway they checked out earlier today." Mahmood cursed inwardly, he had rather hoped he could renew his acquaintance with Lucy, still it could not be helped.

CHAPTER FORTY-ONE

DEBBIE RETURNS

Debbie decided that she would not stay in Sousse for what was left of her holiday, if Farid was in Hammamet then that is where she should be. She checked her money, she had just enough. She called the Palace and booked in for a week.

Farid went on duty that evening, his mind still full of Lucy. He was surprised to feel a gentle tug on his sleeve. He turned and stared at the girl who had just come out of the hotel.

"Hello, remember me?"

He could hardly forget. Of all the people in world he did not want to see at this moment it was Debbie. She was dressed as she had been the last time he saw her, pretty and demure. Debbie of course had the advantage. She had met Lucy and thought that she now knew what he wanted in a woman. She had even tried to change her voice. Farid thought she sounded as if she had a cold.

"Yes, I remember you. You are welcome. I hope you are well, and your family," he said formally, in the words that he would to any returning client of the hotel. He wished she was anywhere but here. She smiled prettily.

"Yes, thank you, we are all well. I was very sorry to hear about your uncle, please accept my condolences."

"How did you know about that?" he snapped rudely.

"Oh, I was in Sousse for the wedding of a friend." For once she had Farid's undivided attention. She soon confirmed his worst fears. "…and I met your sister, Fatma. I like her enormously."

"My sister was not at the wedding, if it is the one I think you mean."

"No, but I have been here for a couple of weeks and as I am the bride's best friend, I was invited to some of the women's gatherings before the wedding. Your sister was there. Fatma and I found we had much in common."

So it had been Debbie, Meriam had seen talking with his sister. He noted her French had improved considerably since their first meeting, as indeed it had. When Debbie had a goal, or a trophy dependent on which way you viewed it, she put her soul into it and had taken French lessons.

Farid was now very worried. He wanted this person to have nothing at all to do with his family, and particularly Fatma. He silently agreed with what Meriam had said; unfortunately he thought this girl and his younger sister probably did have a lot in common. He didn't trust either of them.

He sat down on the low wall. Debbie sat down beside him, far enough away not to be invasive. She talked for a few minutes about nothing in particular. Then of her own accord she got up and went back into the hotel. Farid was confused. The irritating little flirt had disappeared and been replaced by a pleasant girl who appeared in no way threatening, save that she knew Fatma.

Debbie went and sat down at one of the tables where she knew he could still see her. She ordered a drink and took out her book and started to read. A couple came and sat next to her and Farid noticed she spoke mainly to the woman and only to the man when he spoke to her.

Debbie dressed carefully every evening, long floating skirts, feminine tops with just a hint of cleavage, but never anything suggestive. She ingratiated herself with both guests and staff alike who thought her an attractive agreeable young girl. She received several offers but turned them down with a pretty smile using the well-used excuse that her boyfriend would not approve.

She made a point of chatting to Farid a few times during each evening, but only for short periods at a time. She had no wish to cause him any trouble but wanted to make sure she was never out of his sight. She made herself sweet and available. He started to feel he may have misjudged her. Perhaps in two years she had grown up, it certainly seemed that way, although he still didn't trust her.

On Thursday his shift changed to days and just before he finished he saw her sitting at the bar next door. She came over to him. "When you finish, will you have a coffee with me. Please don't think of me badly. I was going through a very bad patch when we first met, but that's all over now."

He thought she looked very appealing. She wore little make up, and the freckles which scattered around her nose made her look even younger. Her red hair fell gently onto her shoulders and the pale green top was ruffled and feminine. Her cream linen skirt finished just above her ankles and as she sat down on the wall beside him when she crossed her legs he could see enough tanned calf to be attractive without provocative. She put her hand on his and he flinched. "Please, let me buy you a coffee if only to say sorry for my awful behaviour before."

Everything in the sensible side of his brain screamed "Run" but the demon on his shoulder argued against it, whispering to him, "Don't you want to find out what she and your sister talked about? Remember they might have mentioned Lucy."

Farid agreed to meet her at a small coffee bar on the edge of the Medina. He arrived first and she a few moments later. He was pleased to see she had changed and did not seem to be trying to impress him. In fact she was simply being friendly.

Debbie was happy. She was thrilled he had agreed to meet her. Perhaps they could put everything that had passed behind them. As they talked, she drew Fatma's name into the conversation and led cleverly on to the wedding. Farid let her talk. For all her appearance, he was still very wary of her.

He asked her "Did you meet Ali, the bridegroom? I used to know him well as a child, but I haven't seen him for years."

"Yes, I met him briefly, but as I said I know Ellen very well."

She omitted to say that Ellen was one of the two girls he had seen her with after their first disastrous encounter. "She's a really nice girl. They are very lucky to have found each other and I wish them both every happiness," she gushed.

Debbie had the opening she needed. She had to make sure Farid knew it was Lucy she had met. If she could paint her in bad and inaccessible light, perhaps she would have a better chance of making him stop dreaming about the wretched woman. She mentioned a few other people she had spoken to at the wedding and since she had been in Sousse, then she turned to him and smiled widely. Farid noticed with some discomfort that although certain things about her appeared to have changed, the predatory smile had not.

Debbie took a deep breath.

"I was quite lucky actually, I hardly knew anyone at the wedding and I was pleased when an English woman came and sat down at my table. She was really sweet to talk to. We chatted for ages. She was about my mum's age," she added pointedly, "but I suppose she must have been attractive when she was younger, long blonde hair and green eyes."

Farid's breath stuck in his throat. Could she be talking about Lucy?

"The woman told me she'd been here before some years ago and had a Tunisian boyfriend at that time, but it just fizzled out." Farid tried to hide the shock he felt.

He said nothing and waited. Debbie realised she had to make her conversation sound plausible. She knew Farid's feelings for Lucy and she was sure from what she'd seen and heard that Lucy had felt the same.

"She didn't actually say it but I think she was quite sad and I could see she had loved him once, but she said it was just one of those things that hadn't worked out and that was that."

The pain in Farid's face was tangible and Debbie realised it was going to be a long road for him to forget that woman. But she had wanted him for two years and wasn't about to give up now. She had to say something that would sever the bond between him and the woman forever. She smiled softly and inclined her body towards him. "Still it all turned out right for her; she's married again now."

Farid felt as though he had been kicked. So he was right, she had married someone else and had his baby, the boy he had seen. She certainly hadn't waited very long. He looked at Debbie. She was watching him intently and he felt uneasy.

He was not a stupid man and he wondered why was she telling him all this? Why should she go into a detailed description of some woman she'd met once at a wedding? He suddenly remembered what she had said to him after their encounter in the dark alleyway that first time. "Who's Lucy?" she'd whispered in his ear… and she had been talking to Fatma who obviously knew Lucy's name and what she looked like after the Michelle incident.

He felt sick. The bitch was leading him, and he would let her. He needed to know the truth.

"Was her husband at the wedding?" he asked innocently.

"No, I assume he stayed back home with the children. She was there with another woman with carrot coloured hair, you know carrot, not like mine," she stroked her own deep bottle-red waves as though inviting him to do the same. He ignored her.

Farid decided to draw her out, he had to find out exactly what she did know. He knew she was toying with him but he could play the same game. He gave her what he hoped was his sexiest grin and patted her hand affectionately, putting her completely off her guard.

"Oh well, as you said, it all turned out right for her in the end," he said. "You seem to have had a good chat and their men are what women talk about, aren't they?" He looked at her his eyes smouldering. Debbie was captivated.

Farid gave her a slow sensual smile. "Go on, tell me, what did you talk about, you and the English woman?"

Debbie did not have the sense to realise that men rarely ask that sort of question but she was so surprised by the ardent attention Farid was lavishing on her she didn't intend to lose the advantage. She thought quickly and remembered Lucy's description of Peter and the conversation she had overheard between Lucy and Jackie.

"We talked about her husband. I think she said his name is Ben. She told me about him. He doesn't sound anything special, you know the sort, typically pale blue eyed English, she said he goes bright pink as soon as he sees the sun."

She laughed and Farid laughed with her. "She seems quite happy with him. Not like me, I like dark handsome men." She returned Farid's gaze and he held her eyes. She sat back and smiled at him very sweetly. She had done her work she had told him Lucy was married and therefore inaccessible.

Farid smiled back. A different sort of smile that didn't reach his eyes. He wondered how women can be so stupid as to trip themselves up by talking too much. The bitch knew it was his Lucy she had described but she had no way of knowing he had seen the child, a young boy, obviously born since he had last seen Lucy. There was no way the black haired brown-skinned child was the product of the man Debbie had said was her husband. She was playing with him. But what was true and what had she invented? He knew he would get nothing more out of her.

"I think we should go now," he murmured quietly. "Do you have any money?"

She stared at him. "Yes."

He beckoned the waiter. "Would you pay the man then?"

Stunned, Debbie reached into her handbag and handed over a note. Farid took it and said something to the man, who grinned and the two shook hands. The waiter kept the change and smirked at Debbie.

As they came out of the Medina Farid turned to her. "Goodbye then, it was nice seeing you again. Have a good journey home."

"But I don't go for another two days."

"No but I've got two days off and I will not be spending them with you."

Farid walked away in the opposite direction from the hotel so she would have no excuse to follow him. His mind was in turmoil. It was quite feasible that Fatma had told her about Lucy if they were as friendly as Debbie had said, she may even have seen Lucy at the wedding, but the story didn't add up, and certainly not the child. There was much more he needed to know and above all he was going to find Lucy.

CHAPTER FORTY-TWO

TROUBLE

Farid noticed the English women when they first arrived and registered trouble. Both large ladies, well into their forties he thought. They came into the foyer, flushed and sweating profusely in the late afternoon heat, Munir took their cases and the smaller of the two flashed him a lopsided smirk, brushing her damp hair back from her face with a coquettish gesture. Munir ignored her and looked at the floor. He was young but not so naïve that he didn't immediately recognise a potential problem looming.

Farid smiled at him encouragingly, having experience the same confusion sometimes himself when he first started in the tourist trade. The larger woman immediately grinned back and swayed towards him. Her damp dyed hair, the same bottle-red as Debbie's, was stuck to her cheeks, clashing horribly with the pink face. Farid found himself comparing her with Debbie and for once, Debbie came out the winner. He grimaced.

Two shrewd eyes, half lost in the podgy face, met his and her lips parted in a feral smile again not unlike Debbie's. Farid felt a shiver run down his back in spite of the heat. No woman should wear that expression. This was certainly one client he intended to avoid. She offered her hand and waited until he took it reluctantly. The smile widened exposing a row of small perfect white teeth which looked completely out of place nestled in her course features.

"Hello. I'm Tracey and this is my friend Daisy. So you're the security are you? I am so pleased; I shall feel very safe here with you."

Farid stared blankly at her and shrugged, but the small sticky hand still held his firmly. He pulled away from her and resisted the urge to wipe his hand on his trousers. She laughed loudly and her enormous bosom wobbled.

She turned to her friend. "Just how I like them," she whispered, "young, shy and very pretty!"

Daisy let out a raucous screech of laughter and dug her friend in the ribs. *How revolting they are*, Farid thought, as Munir led them to the check in desk. He turned his back and faced out towards the sea, his hands clasped behind his back, but feeling the sharp little eyes firmly fixed on him. Tracey watched him, his broad shoulders firmly set and his legs slightly apart. She studied the long muscular frame and firm bottom and licked her lips involuntarily.

Daisy patted her arm. "Cool it girl! There's plenty of time for that. Let's have a look round first and see what else is on offer."

"No way. I've picked out mine, you carry on looking." She lowered her voice and whispered, "I'm going to get a fuck out of that one if it kills me."

"More like you'll kill him!" Tracey slapped her hard on the shoulder.

"Don't worry babe, I'll make sure he's on top so I can hang onto that gorgeous arse."

The women's crude laughter echoed around the elegant marble foyer and to Farid's relief they were allocated their keys and disappeared into the lift, the crude sound still ringing in his ears. He noticed they had opted for separate adjoining rooms rather than the usual twin. That in itself did not bode well, he hoped that they were not expecting visitors.

Farid was pleased his shift was almost finished, but he was more concerned that later in the week his shift changed. He had no wish to work nights with those two around. That sort were always trouble in the evening, probably drinking all day and causing problems at night with drunken behaviour, which he or some other unlucky security guard would have to sort out.

Tracey looked for him the next day, but Farid had allocated himself to one of the outer gate security boxes and the only time he heard, rather than saw Tracey coming, he pulled well back into the box and she missed him.

Farid was correct. By the evening the two women were getting steadily more inebriated. They flirted, smiled and giggled at everyone, regardless of whether they were with partners or not, and the hotel staff from the most junior porter to the night manager.

Tracey's huge bosom strained under her long tight orange vest, exposing her flabby arms and wrinkled chest. Her legs were encased in white leggings and her huge thighs danced along for the ride as she walked. Her lips were painted orange and clashed with her cheeks which were pink from the sun. Her false eyelashes gave her the look of a startled clown.

Daisy was a little thinner than her friend and appeared almost acceptable in her knee-length green smock which successfully hid most of her wobbly bits, if the observer chose to look beyond the dreadful bright pink lipstick. Unfortunately, as she became more drunk, the lipstick smudged into an ugly gash and her smock rode up when she sat down exposing rather more than was necessary to all who unhappily looked in her direction.

Eventually, having embarrassed at least half the people in the bar and been ignored by the other half they fell into the lift around midnight, drunk and dishevelled. This façade continued during the week. A couple of days before they were due to leave, Daisy hooked up with a heavily built strong looking German about half her age, who had been watching her with interest and who now kept feeding her more and more drinks. Eventually the two disappeared upstairs.

Tracey went looking for Farid who had so far managed to avoid her by keeping himself around the pool and rear gate security posts. That evening he was horrified to learn that neither of the reception staff had turned up and had no option but to stay at the front of the hotel. He had so far managed to stay around the corner out of sight of the bar, seated on the low wall. He knew his luck couldn't hold out for much longer and sure enough a heavily perspiring nightmare in shocking pink zoomed in on him.

Again the proffered hand, again resisting the urge to wipe his hands on his trousers after contact with a wet fish. She whispered something to him as she forced her ample backside into the space on the wall beside him. He had no idea what she said and deliberately avoided eye contact. Unfortunately as he dropped his eyes his gaze rested on her huge bosom. Tracey watched him shrewdly and ran her little pink tongue over her lips. To his intense discomfort she ran her hand from her shoulder down to her bosom. Farid stared at the long nails resting on the heaving flesh and felt the blood rush to his face as she leered at him.

"You like?" she whispered. "Come to room 2011 at midnight, and I'll give you the fuck of your life."

Farid did not understand but he knew well enough the word fuck, which is universal. He dragged his eyes away and gazed fixedly out to sea. She opened her bag and took out a small notepad and pen and wrote on a sheet of paper which she tore off and pushed in his shirt pocket before he could stop her. "Just in case you forget," she wheezed in her best attempt at a sexy voice.

He could have kissed Abdul when his colleague appeared and seeing Farid's obvious distress informed him the director wanted to speak with him. "*Excusez moi,*" he muttered at Tracey and almost ran into the hotel.

"Sexy accent," she said watching his disappearing form. Abdul quickly followed Farid.

Farid needed no interpretation of her words and when he looked at the piece of paper she had written simply her room number – midnight. The sweat glistened on his face. He could not imagine a worse fate than being alone in a room with Tracey.

Tracey continued to simper at him most of the evening until about 11.30p.m., when she made her way to the lift, her face wreathed in smiles. The night manager was relieved. The two women had been relatively quiet and at least they had caused no further embarrassment to other guests that evening.

Tracey almost ran to her room and stripped off her clothes which she kicked in a heap behind the chair, her heart pounding, whether in anticipation or from the alcohol she didn't care. She checked her makeup and added a bit more for good measure and then eased her huge body into a black babydoll night-set. Looking in the mirror she saw only the full glistening lips, sparkling eyes and the delicate lace of her specially and expensively purchased seduction kit.

Unfortunately the reflected image told a different story of copious amounts of white flesh bulging out from the black lace which stretched unattractively across her chest, now sagging heavily without its usual daytime support.

She ran her hands over her breasts and teased the nipples into stiff peaks feeling the tingle of sexual anticipation and gave a small sigh as she sprayed herself with the sickly sweet smelling perfume she loved, not realising it could not mask the smell of sweat or drink.

She poured herself a large gin and sat down on the bed to wait. The clock ticked ominously on passed midnight and it was only half an hour later when she finally accepted all her efforts were to go unrewarded. Angrily she pulled off the black lace and flung it on top of the heap of other clothes. "You will pay for this," she muttered as she clambered into bed and fell sleep almost immediately. She didn't hear Daisy's door slam much later.

Daisy was furious with the German, who had taken her to his room. He offered her a large glass of some strong white fiery liquid and a funny smelling cigarette, which they shared. He stroked her breasts and ran his fingers up the inside of her thighs and she lay back and closed her eyes luxuriating in the unaccustomed attention. He explained he was a poor student and being stoned and drunk she gave him quite a large amount of money, which he had pushed quickly into the bedside draw.

Daisy knew she was drunk, but she couldn't care. She started to giggle and stroked his leg. She saw him give a satisfied little smile as he pulled her to her feet. He told her to undress and when she stood naked in front of him and he called her his *dickbauchig hure*, which she took as an expression of affection. He pulled off his trousers. She put her arms out to him and closed her eyes and the room started to spin. From what she remembered in the strange fog which engulfed her, he had screwed hell out of her, on top, underneath, from behind, over a chair and every which way he could think of, while she struggled feebly against him. Her breasts were bruised and one had teeth marks. There was a nasty mark on her thigh and her bottom was so sore she couldn't sit down without pain. "Please God, not that as well," she muttered to herself.

She vaguely recalled that when he had finished with her he curtly told her to get dressed and pushed her out of the door, shoes in hand, closing the door firmly behind her and leaving her to find her own way back to her room on the floor below. She was furious to learn that what she had taken as an expression of affection was the opposite. He had simply called her a fat whore. To add to her anger and embarrassment she learned he had checked out of the hotel first thing in the morning, with her money.

Both women decided against telling each other the humiliating truth, but pretended they had had a wonderful time. Both were equally determined to enjoy their last full day. To the profound relief of staff and guest alike, the duo ignored the hotel and went drinking elsewhere. Around three in the morning they staggered back. Daisy was very unsteady, but Tracey had reached the destructive stage of 'I feel wonderful and anything I want is possible.'

Although she was still angry at Farid, she had not totally given up on him and convinced herself there must have been a good reason why had had not turned up. As he was unfortunately again on front duty, he could not avoid them. There was nowhere to hide. She leered at him. "Hello Darling!"

He acknowledged her with a nod of the head and a curt "*bonsoir*".

As they walked into the lift their cackling was still audible at reception. Stepping out of the lift on the second floor, Daisy missed her footing and fell heavily onto the big settee in the window alcove. "I'm pissed," she shrieked.

"No you're not, you're drunk."

"Okay, so I'm drunk, whoopee," she yelled.

Tracey flopped down beside her. "That guy tonight was a bloody laugh, he lives near me and I got his number. I'll call him when I get home."

Daisy glared at her. "He had hairy feet."

"So what? Provided nothing important is hairy, who cares?" Both women dissolved into peals of crude laughter which got louder and louder as they compared notes of their evening's entertainment.

A door opened and a skinny middle-aged man leaned out. "Can you two shut up please and go to bed? Some of us want to get some sleep."

Daisy sat bolt upright and screamed at him "fuck you" in perfect Arabic, which other than 'thank you' was the only other word she knew in that language.

"That means fuck you," yelled Tracey and slapped Daisy on the shoulder as they both started cackling again.

The night manager was not surprised to receive several phone calls complaining about the noise and motioned to Farid and Abdul to go and sort it out. Farid hung back but had no option. As the lift door opened he saw the two women splayed out on the sofa arms around each other laughing hysterically.

Tracey beamed at him. "Come to join the party," she slurred.

Farid stared revolted at the lump of blubber, a lurid mixture of tanned and pink flesh bulging out of a strapless dress which had slipped down to almost completely reveal her huge white breasts. "In your dreams," he muttered.

Daisy stopped laughing and was lying back on the settee her eyes closed, her legs apart and her dress almost up around her hips. Farid turned to Abdul, whose eyes were fixed on Daisy, his expression a mixture of disgust and fascination. Farid could see that her skimpy black knickers were in full view, revealing a mound of curling dark hair and much more.

He pulled his friend by the arm. "Right let's get this sorted out as quickly as possible and get out of here."

Abdul went to the settee and shook Daisy trying to reason with her. She stretched her arms out towards him and he took her hands to help her up. Abdul was quite a small man and Farid watched helplessly as Daisy grinned, and pulled him down. Abdul fell on top of her. She kissed him full on the lips with a throaty chuckle. "Come to Mama."

Farid moved forward to help his friend but Tracey with a speed which caught him by surprise leaned forward and grabbed his arm. Farid tried to push her away but Tracey used his weight to haul herself to her feet so her face was inches from his. Farid felt a wave of nausea well up in his throat as the revolting mixture of sweet perfume, alcohol and stale sweat encased him.

He pushed her away as she attempted to kiss him but she fell backwards against the wall and pulled him with her. Her dress was up around her hips. One of her breasts fell out of her dress and she dragged his head down so it was buried in the sagging flesh and he could hardly breathe. She had her feet apart to support herself and he felt her huge body pressing against him. He winced with pain as she grabbed at him He tried to pull away but she held him in an iron grip. He spat out an obscenity.

Tracey at last realised it was completely futile and that Farid had no intention of succumbing to her charms. She bared her teeth in like a snarling dog and screamed "Get off me you fucking pervert!" She looked over at Daisy, who grinned and started shouting.

A door opened and a couple of male guests ran out in their pyjamas. What they saw was Daisy on the settee with Abdul lying across her and Farid pinning Tracey to the wall, her legs apart and his head buried in her chest. They yelled at the guards to let go of the women.

Daisy released Abdul and he scrambled to his feet, his face covered in lipstick. Tracey relinquished her hold on Farid and leaned back against the wall smirking, her breast completely exposed. Her smirk faded. The eyes which met hers were pools of molten gold, blazing in undisguised fury and revulsion. She cowered away from him and knew she would never forget that look.

Farid remembered little of the chaos that followed save that one of the guests escorted the two women to Tracey's room. The other called Mohamed, the night manager, who came running up the back stairs.

Mohamed listened to what the man said he had seen. Abdul tried to explain what had happened but Farid remained silent. Mohamed had never seen Farid so angry. He told them both to go and wait in the anteroom downstairs.

The two women sat on Tracey's bed sniggering, quickly collating their story. They stopped as Mohamed came in. He insisted that Daisy went back to her room as he needed to speak separately with them.

What he noticed was that for all the commotion neither woman seemed particularly upset or traumatised by the experience.

He followed Daisy and sat on the chair watching her.

"Are you able to tell me what happened?"

"We were sitting on the settee and the two men came out of the lift. They sat down with us and chatted. They were very nice but it got out of hand. The smaller man leaned across me and started kissing me. I was terrified. I could see my friend pinned against the wall. Her dress had been pulled up, and the other man had his head buried in her breast. It was awful, her legs were apart and I think he was trying to have sex with her."

Mohamed was horrified. This was virtually what the guest said he had seen.

He went next door and spoke with Tracey, who had by then sobered up a little. She had already agreed with Daisy what they should say. She had no intention of allowing Farid to escape in view of the humiliating rejection he had given her. She knew his name by his hotel identity badge.

She smiled at Mohamed. "Do you know, even when I first arrived I was aware Farid was interested in me? He shook my hand and held it too long." Mohamed nodded wisely which Tracey took as encouragement. As she warmed to her story she couldn't help adding little embellishments here and there.

"He has been chatting me up all week you know, making little suggestive comments, but I never thought he would attack me."

Mohamed raised an eyebrow.

"Did he ask you for your room number?"

Tracey nodded.

"Did he ever come to your room?"

"Oh, no! If he had I would have immediately made a complaint."

Mohamed nodded again. "Of course." He listened to the tale of woe and violation. Tracey warmed to her story.

"Tonight he sat down next to me and put his arm around me, stroking my breast telling me he wanted to…" she hesitated "well, you know, he wanted to…"

Mohamed held up his hand, "I understand, madame."

Tracey watched Mohamed carefully, but his sympathetic expression gave away nothing. "And of course you pushed him away."

"Of course I did, but he hauled me up off the settee and pushed me up against the wall. He put his mouth on my breast. Then he put pushed my dress up and touched me intimately, you know." Her story matched Daisy's almost word for word. She batted her eyelashes at Mohamed who in spite of the gravity of the circumstances had to stifle a smile as he noticed one eyelash had come partly unglued and looked like a spider trying to escape.

"So he pinned you against the wall and forced himself on you?" Tracey tried to look horrified.

"Yes, only he didn't get the chance because I started screaming and those men came out."

"Ah, yes of course," said Mohamed.

He had watched the two women all week flirting and drinking. It occurred to him that if they were frightened why hadn't they started screaming earlier as soon as the men approached them and made their intentions clear. He didn't believe any of it, but that still didn't explain what the two guests said they had seen, unless it had been the other way around and the two men were trying to fend off the attention of two out of control drunks.

He studied the woman sitting in front of him. She was huge. Although Farid was tall and strong, for him to pull this struggling half-drunk woman upwards from a settee and keep her pinned against a wall against her will, with only the weight of his own body and one hand to restrain her while he tried to ravage her would take some doing. Whilst he suspected there were a few of his staff who might try to press their luck with some of female guests, Farid was not in his opinion one of them. He was a good looking man and Mohamed was not so naïve to think that he could not have had his pick of other women had he wanted it, without chasing after someone like Tracey.

He smiled sweetly at Tracey who sat snuffling as she realised she ought perhaps to show that she was upset by her experience. Changing the subject completely Mohamed spoke gently to her.

"I am sorry you have had such a traumatic experience but apart from this dreadful incident I hope you have no complaint against the hotel and your holiday has been enjoyable."

Tracey sniffed and nodded.

"Thank you, yes, which is why this upsets me so much," More sniffing.

Mohamed stared at her. "So in general you like it here and you find our people pleasant and easy to talk with?"

"Oh yes, they are very nice, most of them," she added remembering her situation.

Mohamed took a deep breath. "Do you speak any Arabic or French?" he added almost as an afterthought. Tracey grinned at him.

"No way, I don't need to. Pretty much everyone here speaks English, which is great."

Mohamed sat back and studied the smirking pink face. Then he smiled broadly. He had seen Tracey hanging around Farid several times and noticed his discomfort.

"Well madame, you are right, almost everyone does speak English. Of course there are one or two who have no knowledge of your language at all. I am confused Madame. The man you accuse of, how did you put it, chatting you up all week and making suggestive remarks, the man who asked you for your room number and who talked to you on the settee this evening unfortunately speaks absolutely no English at all."

Tracey was stunned. *You stupid cow!*, she thought. Her still befuddled mind flew back over the week, of course he had never actually spoken to her save for a couple of polite phrases in French. How could she have been so silly.

"You're wrong," she whispered. Mohamed shook his head.

"No madame, I know my own staff. Perhaps it is you who are mistaken." He was angry. "Perhaps Abdul, the other one, perhaps he translated whilst he was violating your friend, although from my memory his English is pretty limited as well."

He stood up. "Madame, may I suggest that you and your friend get some sleep after your terrible ordeal. Your complaint has been made, my report will be filed and the matter dealt with following the hotel's protocol in such incidents. The two security men will of course be suspended and sent for disciplinary action whilst the matter is fully investigated at our head office. We must protect our guests and take all such allegations of harassment very seriously."

His words were mechanical and impersonal. He thought to himself it was a shame we cannot also investigate sexual harassment by guests in the same way.

Tracey went red. "Thank you," she muttered and held out her hand.

Mohamed stared at her before taking the limp paw as though being presented with a live grenade and snatched his hand back quickly. "And Madame, please make yourself available tomorrow morning as I am quite sure your tour representative will want to speak with you." Tracey nodded miserably.

On hearing what Mohamed had said, to Tracey's annoyance, Daisy changed her mind and said she had been really too drunk to remember much at all.

By late morning the tour representative already had a copy of the statements which Mohamed had ensured were ready for her. After reading the reports and speaking with both women, Sally agreed with him that there was little or no truth in the alleged assault. In her opinion the two men had done what they were asked and tried to persuade the women to go to their rooms after complaints of noise had been made. She too had observed Tracey's unrequited advances towards Farid, but like Mohamed, she was obliged to follow up the report with her superiors.

Sally was a sensible woman of indeterminable age, married herself to a Tunisian. She had been in the job a long time and knew that occasionally some of the staff did get out of hand with the guests, unfortunately sometimes without the encouragement of the men who simply took up the invitation. She could recall only having one complaint over the years, when she believed the man had been invited to the woman's room, done his business and the woman had later regretted the incident because she had too much to drink and was scared her husband might find out. With Sally's motherly encouragement this was admitted and the subject was dropped without Sally needing to take it further.

In this instance she knew the report must be made and was sorry because she knew the men would be suspended until the matter was fully investigated. From what she could see there were far too many differences and retractions in the stories the women had offered and of course Farid's inability to speak English held a lot of weight in his defence.

After she had spoken with the women she watched them go out to the poolside, behaving as though nothing had happened, although the story had circulated and they were given a wide berth by all the staff. Everyone was pleased when they retired to their rooms to make their arrangements to leave.

Later that evening, Sally sat with Judy, the rep from another hotel. "I doubt they will even take the matter further when they get home. Their version of the story will just get bandied around their friends, if they have any, and treated as an adventure from which they had a lucky escape. There will almost certainly be no thought of the men who could quite possibly lose their jobs and most definitely no consideration for the families they help to support. With that accusation hanging over them, even if the men are believed, if the story gets out which of course it will, they may have trouble finding other employment. You know, no smoke without fire."

"I don't suppose the hotel can refuse to accommodate those two tarts in the future?"

"I doubt it, unfortunately and I'd like to wring their bloody necks." She slammed her cup down on the saucer.

"Give it a break, Sally. You can only do your job and you can't right every wrong in the book."

"I know it just pisses me off. These people work long hours for peanuts. I know there is good and bad in every country and there is always a bad apple somewhere. I know a lot of shenanigans go on over here, but let's be honest that is what some of the women come here for, a holiday romance with a handsome Arab and a tale to tell when they get home."

Judy grinned at her and added, "And some of the romances survive!"

Sally smiled. "Okay, so mine did. But I didn't come looking for it, it just happened and I'll have you know my lovely husband was not in the hotel trade, he is a well-respected businessman who happened to be in the hotel at a conference, so you can leave that one alone!" Sally was happy to admit that hers was a success story and she knew there were many who were not so lucky.

The two men were suspended and sent to head office. The evidence against them was confused and sketchy. Mohamed made a statement that the women had been making a dreadful noise and on receiving a complaint he had despatched the two security men to sort out the problem. He confirmed that the women had caused trouble all week and he was aware Tracey had been annoying Farid since the day she arrived.

When Farid entered the office there were three men sitting behind the desk. He sat down nervously. They came straight to the point.

"You know why you are here?" More a statement than a question. He nodded.

"Did you arrange to meet the women or did you have relations with either of them prior to the incident?"

"No sir, I did not. I was told by the night manager to go with Abdul to sort out the noise they were making. There is no way I would have gone near either of them if I hadn't been instructed to do so."

"Did you find the woman, Ms Jackson, attractive?"

Farid stared at the impassive man in the dark suit who spoke. "No, I did not. She is one of the most revolting women I have ever seen. She was drunk and she attacked me, not the other way around."

"But she is a woman, could you not control her?"

"Sir, with respect, that is not a woman, that is a huge tub of fat who stunk of sweat, alcohol and cheap perfume. She is crude, ugly and an abomination of womanhood." His eyes blazed in anger and the director had no doubt he was telling the truth.

He was exonerated, as was Abdul. What the men were not told was that Sally also made a statement that Tracey had been in other hotels within the group on two previous holidays and had caused trouble on both occasions.

CHAPTER FORTY THREE

ESCAPE

Farid's life had for many months settled into an uneventful routine. On his return to the Palace Hotel after his suspension, he had kept his head down and simply done his job without incident. There was only one hiccup and this he had dealt with, he hoped for the last time. It had been early afternoon when the weekly coach arrived with the next lot of guests.

Farid stared. He felt as though a lead weight was crushing his chest. He had seen her get down from the bus and watched the familiar swaying step, fixed wide smile and eyes hidden by huge sunglasses. Debbie. Farid was angry. Extremely angry. As always, the last person he wanted to see was Debbie.

The porter took her case and she walked slowly towards the main doors. Farid held his breath and looked away but she stopped directly in front of him. He took the outstretched hand mechanically and muttered his customary greeting, *"Bienvenue en Tunisie"*. His words were spoken quietly and without emotion. She smiled broadly, her white feral teeth exactly as he remembered.

"So formal, my dear friend." She spoke in French and he made no response. The other guard's face was expressionless but Farid knew he would raise the point later. "Damn the bitch, damn her to hell. Hasn't she caused me enough trouble?"

He spoke roughly to his colleague and strode quickly away towards the reception desk.

"I'll catch up with you later." He heard the staged whisper which followed him like an evil wraith and the inference was unquestionable. He was livid. After the problems of the previous summer which saw him suspended but from which he had finally been exonerated he wanted no trouble, no involvement and, above all, no Debbie.

He thought carefully. When he had returned to work after his suspension he had learned that a girl had arrived for a week while he had been away and had been asking at the hotel after him. He had been told she had questioned not only the other security as to his whereabouts but even the pool bar staff and the reception manager. Whilst not actually accusing him of being in a relationship with her the girl had made it plain by hints and innuendo. His immediate thought was that perhaps it had been Lucy, but he knew in his heart that after everything that had passed between them, Lucy would never have behaved that way. Now after the embarrassment of his suspension, his character would again be under scrutiny.

At the time he had stated emphatically he had no idea who the girl might be and thought it might be a friend of one of the women who had accused him in the summer come to cause trouble, which was the truth as he saw it. It had never occurred to him for one moment that Debbie had resurfaced, but now seeing her, he realised it could only have been her, come again to torment him.

Without proof of his involvement, coupled with the fact he had been cleared of any wrongdoing in the summer, there was little the management could do save to inform him that he was now on probation, he must remain in the foyer at the front of the hotel and that conversation with guests was forbidden. Farid had been happy to agree, he wanted no more problems, just to get on with his job within the comfort zone of his colleagues and without involvement in any way at all with any female, either in work time or outside it.

However, the atmosphere was uncomfortable, he felt constantly under surveillance and after due consideration and to the relief of management, he had asked to be transferred to another hotel within the chain and the request had immediately been granted. He was due to move shortly.

His thoughts returned unwillingly to Debbie. Short of slapping her he could not have been much ruder at their last encounter. Why had she come back? The question remained unanswered and he had not the slightest intention of asking her and hoped the opportunity would never arise.

He was absolutely determined he would not give her any reason to involve him in her life again. He learned from a colleague that she had booked only for one week. The same evening he walked from the back gate of the hotel after his break in the early hours of the morning, past the swimming pool and noticed a patch of wet ground where the pool was being refilled. Gritting his teeth he deliberately walked onto it and turned in such a way that he slipped on the wet ground, the pain shot through his leg as he felt the tendon in his ankle give out. Pulling himself to his feet he hobbled back to the main building and shortly afterwards left the hotel for hospital. By the time he returned to work his transfer to the Regale had been completed, Debbie had gone and so for the most part had the pain in his leg.

Some months later, Farid stood on duty in the foyer at the Regale. The evening was quiet and as it had been raining few guests came and went but remained inside the hotel. He was lost in thought. Were all women truly like Debbie, or that dreadful Tracey, they just hid it better? He smiled and Lucy's face became as clear as the daylight. His Lucy. The smile faded. Yes they were all like this, even Lucy had betrayed him in the end. Not for the first time in his life Farid swore to himself he would remain single.

Since the Debbie incident and his move, life had been blissfully uneventful for Farid. He was the model employee. Together with his usual shift of night duty, he worked his time off where possible. He worked, ate, slept and worked again. He made himself pleasant to all. He rarely spoke to the guests, and only when asked he directed them to the various places of interest, the Medina, the harbour, the shops and where to find the best bargains. Always with a smile, but nothing more. He pocketed his tips with quiet appreciation and spent nothing, save for the small contribution which as always went to his family. He opened a bank account and the balance grew slowly but steadily.

Every year since his very first meeting with Lucy he spent an hour at the café in Sousse on the anniversary of the day they met. During the brief years they were together they sat together but now he always sat alone. He never missed a year. He never explained his reasons for having this day off, nor the coin he carried with him always. Those who knew him best assumed it must be to do with a woman, but he never offered an explanation and the one or two who had ventured to ask him never did so again.

CHAPTER FORTY-FOUR

BEN

Ben was starting to ask more questions. It started one afternoon after Alex collected him from school. He had obviously been crying. Lucy cuddled him.

"What's the matter sweetheart?" He refused to tell her. Alex answered for him.

"Forget it Mum, just some bloody kids who were taunting him saying that I couldn't be his brother and his mother must have fucked with some foreigner."

"Alex!" Lucy yelled at him "How dare you?"

"You asked! I'm only telling you what they said."

Bed stared at her. "Mum, why do I look different from you and Alex? I even look different from Rosie."

Lucy swallowed, her throat dry. The time had come quicker than she thought it would. Although he mentioned his father just before they went to the wedding she thought once they came back he would forget about it again.

"You see darling, Alex's father died when Alex was only very small and I didn't meet your father until a long time afterwards."

"Where is he? Why doesn't he come and see us?"

"Because he lives a long way away in North Africa."

"Africa! Is he black?"

Lucy laughed. "Ben, Africa is an enormous continent. There are all sorts of different people there, different races, cultures and colours - black, white, brown and every colour in between. Your father is not black, he's an Arab."

"What's Arab?" He looked worried.

"Arab is just a different race of people. There are a lot of different races of people in the world. Arabs come from North Africa and right the way around into Asia, which is another huge place. They speak Arabic and have their own customs and way of life, just the same as we do."

Ben went off thinking about this. Every now and again he asked questions about Arabs and Africa but Lucy managed to keep her replies general and avoid talking actually about his father. Some months later he pressed her to tell him about his father. They were sitting alone in the living room, Alex was out with his girlfriend. But this time Ben cornered her and demanded information. Lucy tried to head him off but this time he was not giving in.

"It's my right to know," he screamed at her. She had never seen him so upset. "I want to go there."

"Where?"

"Where he lives. Africa."

Without thinking Lucy yelled at him "You've already been to Africa, to Tunisia where he comes from."

Ben froze "Tunisia is in Africa? You mean when you took me to Jackie's friend's wedding and I got sick with the ice cream? That is where my father lives, in Africa?"

"Yes," Lucy answered, her voice flat.

"Then why didn't we see him?"

Lucy didn't know how to answer. "Aren't you happy here with me, and Alex?"

"Of course I am, but I see other children with their fathers, although I know with some of them the first one doesn't live with them any more so they've got a second one, but not a real one." Lucy couldn't help but be amused. Ben made it sound a bit like trading in an old car for a new one, which in a way it was. She tried to stop herself being so cynical.

"Alex and I can't see our fathers, can we?" His mouth puckered and she thought he was going to cry.

"No, you can't, darling. You see Alex's father and your father were the most wonderful fathers any children could ever have, and so important that I could never hope to find another father for you even half as good - so what you have is a mother who loves you enough for both parents."

Ben considered this. "Good," he said. "I wouldn't want a father I didn't like; some of my friends at school have, you know," he said seriously.

"Mum. What do Arabs look like?"

She felt like saying, why don't you go and look in the mirror, but didn't.

"Well, as you know English people can look very different from each other. Think about your friends, James and Terry at school. It is much the same with Arab people. Some of them have very dark skin and black hair, and some are as pale as us, with lighter hair. It all depends on parents and their parents, going back over lots of years." Lucy realised of course that this was a very wide generalisation and not altogether accurate, but it would have to do for the moment. Ben seemed to accept it which is what mattered.

"Why aren't Rosie and I the same?"

Lucy smiled. "Well, you see, Rosie takes after me and you take after your father."

"What does my father look like?" Lucy thought she had bone stuck in her throat. The struggled to speak.

"You look very like him, and you're going to be as handsome as him when you get older."

She described Farid, and on looking back, she was sure this was what developed Ben's way of dressing and how he told her he couldn't wait to grow a moustache.

"Do they speak English?"

"Some do and others only speak Arabic and some French, it all depends…"

"Does my father speak English?"

"No, sweetheart. Your father never learned English - he speaks Arabic and French"

"I want to learn to speak Arabic."

"Why?"

"So when I meet him, we can talk together."

Lucy stared at him and felt the ground was starting to slide from under her feet and wished she could finish this discussion

"If that is what you want, then I will see what I can do when you're older. Now can we have some dinner, otherwise we will both go to bed hungry?"

She go up and went into the kitchen. She hoped her agreement would end the conversation and to her relief he turned his attention to his food.

Ben never mentioned their conversation, however he had not forgotten her promise and when she went to the end of school year parents' meeting, she was approached by a tall thin man who looked down gravely from soft grey eyes, the sort of man she thought you could instinctively trust. She had seen him before and knew him to be one of the teachers, although he taught the older boys, in the year before they left for secondary school.

"Mrs Collins, might I have a word with you?"

"Of course, is there something the matter?" He motioned to her to sit down next to him.

"No, not at all; it's just that your son told his head of year he wants to learn Arabic."

"Oh, good heavens, I thought he'd forgotten all about that." She felt the rosy flush rising from her neck into her cheeks.

"So he has mentioned this to you? I'm glad because he told us that he had your agreement."

"Yes, he does, if that is what he wants," she acknowledged.

"Mrs Collins, may I ask you a personal question?"

Lucy knew what was coming and looked at the floor. "You don't need to," she replied. "As you have probably guessed, Ben's father isn't English and Ben is determined to learn his language, although his father doesn't live with us," she added quickly. She avoided looking at the teacher.

"Mrs Collins, I think is an excellent idea, but unfortunately the primary school doesn't actually have the facility to teach Arabic as a language." Lucy nodded,

"I sort of expected that, well perhaps he can start when he gets older."

She looked up at the teacher who was grinning broadly. "The school doesn't but I do. My father was in the consulate in Cairo and I spent several years teaching English there as a second language and later in Tunis, where I met my wife, Hana. As you may know, spoken Arabic varies from country to country, and the only really pure Arabic is the written word. I can teach Ben the basics, but unfortunately it may well be peppered with my wife's North African dialect. May I ask where Ben's father is from?"

"Tunisia." Lucy grinned.

"Tunisia! My wife will be in heaven and I will tell her not to use the dialect, although I feel my plea may fall on deaf ears. There is of course a lot of French in the Tunisian language."

Lucy tried to detach herself from the conversation through her own embarrassment but appreciated the teacher's interest in helping Ben achieve his goal.

"Yes, I know, I found after a few visits I could understand a few words of what was being said."

"So you met Ben's father in Tunisia?"

Lucy hesitated, she wondered if he was now judging her. The holiday romance, pregnant and ran home, which if she was honest was pretty much how it had been. As though he read her mind he smiled at her.

"I'm not prying Mrs Collins, I'm merely interested, and I admire Ben terrifically for wanting to learn. And must tell you he is determined that he wants to learn. He's very young, and I think if he starts now it will be much easier for him. If he is willing I would be happy for him to come to our house. I believe we live only a little way from you. My daughter has been brought up to speak English and Arabic equally, as well as French. If you are happy for your son to learn, then I would be honoured to teach him."

Lucy smile back, touched by his tactful approach. "I'd be more than happy Mr…"

"Clark, John Clark."

"Mr Clark, thank you."

Ben watched them but stayed at the other side of the room. She called him over and the two adults explained to him that although he couldn't study Arabic in school, he could go to Mr Clark's house once or twice a week after school and he could learn there. Ben was unsure, he had expected to be in a class with other children and felt uncomfortable about going to Mr Clark's house. He knew he had a daughter, but she was now in big school and he was at the age when he didn't much like girls anyway!

Lucy took his hand. "Mr Clark's wife is from Tunisia, like your father."

Ben beamed. That sealed the matter. Ben would go with Mr Clark after school every Monday and Thursday where he would study, and then have dinner with the family, then Lucy would collect him afterwards.

True to his word, at the beginning of the next term, Mr Clark took Lucy and Ben to meet his family. Hana Clark met her at the door wearing wide trousers, an embroidered smock top and an apron. The sweet spicy smells emanating from the kitchen transported Lucy immediately back to the Cathy's café in Hammamet where she used to wait for Farid to finish his shift. Another friend she had been forced to forget after her flight. The dark eyes which greeted her were friendly and although she should have remembered, Lucy made the basic error of commenting on the wonderful smell of cooking. Immediately she spoke she realised but it was too late. As was Hana's custom, she was of course invited to stay for dinner, and neither Hana nor her husband heard her protests.

The dinner consisted of couscous with chicken and saffron potatoes, and a vegetable stew spiced with harissa. It was hot, but tastily hot and so unlike the burning curries which flooded English takeaways. Ben ate as though he had been starved, Ben who until a year ago had turned his nose up at anything more highly spiced than a sausage! He broke off large chunks of the thick warm bread and dipped it in the gravy and grinned sheepishly at his mother. Lucy could have sworn his eyes actually rolled upwards with delight when Hana proudly served delicate little flaked pastries flavoured with cinnamon, honey and almonds. There were no lessons that evening and the pair of them went home stuffed with food and bonhomie.

Ben blossomed under Mr Clark's teaching, although Lucy rather thought that Hana also had a hand in it because Ben was also gaining an interest in cooking, North African style! By the time Ben left school to move up to the seniors, he was fluent in Arabic although Mr Clark was apologetic in that he had not managed to stop his wife injecting her native dialect into Ben's teaching. He admitted that Ben had found the writing difficult, but he was a determined child and no doubt would master it later on. Mr Clark said the boy had also picked up some French but also the Arabic accent and she noted with amusement that this would cause the French teacher in his next school some consternation.

This was proved correct when the twins moved to the higher school. Rose was unimpressed by Ben's fascination with learning Arabic. But, not to be outdone when she had been told that she was to be taught French in her next school, she had thrown herself into learning that language and was soon top of her class. Ben was crestfallen. He still found French difficult and to Rose's amusement often found himself in trouble when he muddled the Tunisian Arabic with the pure French which his exasperated teacher attempted to instil into him. But Rose adored her twin and Lucy was happy to see them bent over the book while Rose tutored Ben with his French.

Rose had always been a shy child but she had developed a complete fascination with old movies. If she did not have her head in a book, she was at the pictures or glued to the television screen. Her idol was Elizabeth Taylor. Lucy was sure she had seen every one of her films at least three times, including some of the ones she shouldn't have been watching at her age. One evening she walked in to find Rose lying on the floor her face in her hands completely enthralled. She was watching *Who's Afraid of Virginia Woolf?*.

"Rose turn it off. That's going too far."

"No, Mum, please watch. Isn't she wonderful?"

Despite her disapproval, Lucy sat down beside her daughter and listen to Elizabeth's drunken character, hands on hips screaming insults at her mild mannered husband, history teacher, Richard Burton.

"Yes, sweetie she is a wonderful, but I don't really think the film is right for you yet." Lucy moved to turn off the set.

"Mum, how can a beautiful woman suddenly turn into a screaming madwoman? She's fantastic, I mean she is so fabulous, to demean herself on screen for the whole world to see her like that."

Lucy grinned. "Rosie, it's called acting, and if I remember she won an Oscar for it, that is a prize for acting. As an actress, she can be anyone she wants. It isn't really her, just the part she's playing."

Rose thought about this and her pretty face lit up. "Mum, when I get older I want to be an actress like Elizabeth Taylor."

Lucy giggled. "I hope you make it my love, at least none of our family would ever need to work again if you made that kind of money!"

"Mum, don't be horrible, you know what I mean."

"Of course I do, I was only playing."

Rose's fascination with the movies never left her, and Elizabeth was never superseded as her idea of the perfect actress.

CHAPTER FORTY-FIVE

JANE

Summertime always saw the once a year visitors on package deals, the families with their children who rarely strayed from their hotel except to go to the beach. There were the couples who came for romance and spent their evenings walking hand in hand and their days curled up on sun loungers. Then there were the groups of friends who tried to fit in a bit of everything into their two weeks. A few history buffs who used the hotels solely as a base to explore the countryside and kept the local tour operators in business, although these were fewer than they would have hoped.

It was the times out of the high season which Farid enjoyed most and which for him were the most profitable. Particularly in the winter months regulars often returned, retired people with money to spare who came to escape the harsh northern weather. These were the people who looked out for a familiar face and as many of the flights arrived in the evening, Farid was one of the first people they saw. He greeted them with a smile and a few chosen words of welcome. They tipped well and one or two even brought him gifts, usually English cigarettes. An elderly gentleman brought him two bottles of whisky. Farid sold one of them and paid the money into his account.

One such visitor was a shy elderly lady who had arrived at the Regale the previous night. The flight had been delayed and it was about midnight when the bus dropped her at the hotel. The porter was assisting another couple and Farid carried her case for her to reception. She had thanked him, and he noticed the small face upturned to his was pinched and drawn with tiredness and the deep shadows under her eyes made her seem to him very old.

Farid had one of his rare days off. He had stopped for coffee and noticed the lady as he walked past the Medina. She was attempting to buy some of the cheap pottery on display at the small stalls which line the Medina entrance. Unfortunately as there was little trade out of season, she was unmercifully harassed by each seller trying to draw the confused woman into their own shop. Farid was annoyed. She was almost in tears by the constant pestering. He wondered why these people were so stupid. It was obvious she intended to buy and they were simply frightening her away.

Without realising why he moved across to her. She turned to face him and her doe eyes widened in recognition. Farid gently took her arm and with a few harsh words to his compatriots he led her to a small fixed price shop around the corner. She accepted his help gracefully, her birdlike hand clutching his arm in grip which belied her build. She stepped into the shop and spoke softly in perfect French.

"I don't suppose you would wait for me, please?"

Farid hesitated for a moment and then nodded and stood guard whilst she collected her souvenirs. He walked with her to the taxi rank and put her into a waiting car with a curt remark to the driver not to deviate or overcharge. She pressed a coin into his hand with her thanks.

The following evening he saw her sitting alone in the lounge. In common with many of the older guests, she had changed for dinner. Her beige trouser suit was exquisitely tailored over a cream silk blouse, her jewellery was expensive but understated and her mousey hair liberally streaked with grey was neatly arranged waved her tiny face. She sipped her drink and her eyes met his over the rim of her glass. She smiled. Farid smiled back.

Later in the evening he watched her as she left the hotel and walked over to sit on one of the benches looking out to sea. She sat motionless, gazing out over the dark sea, drinking in the coolness of the night air and listening to the lapping of the waves against the sand. A short while later she returned, her pale face flushed from the breeze.

She stopped and held out her hand to him. He took it with a smile. "Thank you; had it not been for you I would have taken nothing home with me, I could not have faced those people again. I know they have a living to earn, but they confuse me so. Thanks to you I will leave this country with my souvenirs and my memory of a very kind man." Farid murmured a protest. "No, young man, you had no reason to come to my assistance, that was an act of kindness, for which I thank you. I know your free time is limited and you all work very hard and long hours, but you gave up your own time to help someone you didn't know and didn't need to. Thank you."

She turned to the porter standing at the door and beckoned to him, as he came over, she handed him her camera.

"Please, I would like you to take my photograph with my saviour here." The porter grinned, Farid blushed, and the photograph was taken.

He chatted with her a few times after that. There were no objections raised by the management. The elderly lady was obviously no threat to the reputation of the hotel and she indicated she was very happy with the comfort and service she had received and would definitely return. When she left at the end of the week Farid made a point of carrying her case to the coach.

She gave him a soft smile "I hope to see you when I return in a few months' time."

He nodded. "I will be here, madame,"

As he helped her up the steep stairs onto the bus she pressed a note into his hand. He watched her as she waved from the window and smiling went back to his post, pushing the note into his pocket.

If only all our clients could be as sweet as that one, he thought.

Later when he took off his jacket at the end of his shift, Farid took the money out of his pocket. It was not one note, but three tightly folded and he stood astonished as he stared at a week's wages.

The lady was true to her word, she returned a few months later and it seemed to Farid that if it were possible she was even smaller, thinner and more frail than he remembered.

They shook hands. "It is so good to see you again. I hope life has been kind to you." She spoke clearly but softly.

Farid replied, but wondered about the strange greeting as he watched her walk into the lift with the porter. After dinner she came out, sat down beside him and asked him how he had been since she last saw him. Farid glanced over at the night manager, who gave a small nod and turned back to greet another guest.

The little lady smiled uncertainly at Farid. "I hope you don't mind me asking this, but I am hoping to do a little more shopping, for myself this time, and I would be very pleased if you would help me."

Farid hesitated, he had not had a day off in several weeks and his bank balance was growing. The twinge of uncertainty was clear to her. She nodded as she read his thoughts.

"Please, if you agree, I will only permit this if you allow me to make up the money you will lose and if it too much trouble of course I understand."

Guilt washed across Farid's face as he remembered the huge tip she had given him before.

She smiled. "My friend, if I may call you that, I want nothing from you but your company and your assistance. However independent one's spirit may be, one's body does not understand and there comes a time when another person's help and companionship is both wanted and needed."

Farid felt cheap. "I shall be honoured," he replied.

On his day off she hired a car. He was surprised to see how good a driver she was. The weather was quite warm for the time of year and they stopped at one of the smaller hotels with an outside terrace.

"Would you like coffee?"

She shook her head. "I would much prefer tea, but tea with milk please." He laughed and motioned to the waiter.

"One English tea please." The waiter smiled.

"I think the lady does not like our tea."

She beamed at him. "Young man, I like mint with my lamb and nuts in my cake, but neither in my tea." The waiter chuckled and disappeared to fetch English tea for the nice English lady.

She told Farid that her name was Jane. Pushing aside his protests she insisted that he call her by that name. She told him she came from a comfortable family background which had enabled her to follow her desires as a young woman, she had travelled extensively throughout Europe with friends. He watched as she smiled, lost in her memories.

"My parents disapproved of course, it was not what was expected of young ladies in my day you know."

"What did they want you to do?" She beamed at him and the gesture took years from her.

"Why, of course they wanted me to marry a rich man, behave as a good wife should and produce children, what else?" They both laughed.

"That is what is still what is expected of most young women here today," he added.

"And do they all follow their parents' wishes?"

Farid thought of his sister. "Most do, but there are of course the exceptions."

Jane studied his expression and but did not press him on the subject.

"I did of course marry in the end, he was not particularly rich, but he had good prospects and my parents approved. I was never a beauty, a true plain Jane, but I suited his purpose. I had children, just the two, but my daughter died as a baby."

Farid murmured his sympathy.

"Thank you, but it was many many years ago and the heart finds a way in time to mend itself."

"And your husband?"

She stared at him. "My husband was a clever man; as was anticipated he made a fortune in business although sometimes I am sure in a not altogether honest way, but after twenty-five years of marriage, keeping his house, entertaining his questionable friends, he left me for a younger model."

Her gentle eyes shone with a conspiratorial gleam. "The defection cost him dearly. I am not a stupid woman. For most of our married life he had his other interests, if you understand what I mean. I saw divorce as inevitable in the end and so I made myself aware of his business interests and his assets and bided my time until circumstances made it easy for me to get my divorce. He found to his dismay that his little mouse of a wife was not an idiot and could make life extremely uncomfortable for him."

She smiled sadly deep in thought. "Oh, yes it cost him dearly, but sometimes I wonder if it was all worth it. The divorce was messy and vicious and it was only because he could not find anything that I had done wrong that I finally won my case and came away with almost half of his fortune, which was unusual for a woman in those days." Jane's voice was guarded.

"Our lives are never easy and sometimes from one disaster another rises like a phoenix from the ashes."

Her expression darkened and Farid saw there was no room for further explanation and remained silent.

"Enough about me, tell me of yourself," she asked.

To his own surprise, Farid told her of his childhood, his family, the problems of the summer at the other hotel and finally of Lucy. She listened intently, never probing, never questioning. She leaned towards him and took his hands in hers.

"I am a great believer in destiny. What is written for us at our birth will come to pass, but it is how we use the gifts we are given and deal with the adversities thrown at us which forms us into the people we become. I truly believe that our deeds and thoughts will be weighed at judgment. And where our kindnesses will not go unrewarded our self-importance and selfishness will serve us badly."

"You are a philosopher, I think."

"No, my young friend, I am just an old woman who has seen and experienced much in her life. I have travelled widely, both as a young woman as I said, and later with the benefit of my husband's money, throughout the world. I have learned a lot about people. We have all made mistakes, some more than others. For me…" Jane hesitated as though unsure whether to continue.

She signed. "For me, my greatest mistake was my son, Nicholas. He was the older child and when little Emma was born he was five years old. He became impossible because he was no longer the centre of attention, and had to share his parents with his sister. But my sweet daughter died when she was only two and all the attention was once again on him. He grew up pampered and selfish. He watched his father and took his ways. He had many girlfriends, but never married. I still think the one girl he actually cared for realised he would always be the most important person in his own life and left him.

"After the divorce, seeing I had been left quite comfortably off Nicholas decided to come back and live with me. Because I was emotionally drained and vulnerable, I agreed, which was a huge mistake. He has only ever worked when he feels like it, which isn't often and believes the world, and particularly me, owes him a living. After a year or so I found the courage to tell him to leave. He agreed on the basis that I make him an allowance, which when at forty years old he should be looking after his mother and not the other way around, is still never enough. I now only see him when he wants more money. It's awful but I can truthfully say I actually dislike my son."

Farid listened. From his own childhood and close family he found it hard to understand the way of life and mind of her son.

"And now you, my young friend, you are so very different. We do not know much about each other, but I believe you have been honest with me and I know that what you have you share with your family. I know it is your culture, your way of life and it is a good one but I think even in your world there are some who do not follow that path. You have suffered from the misdeeds of others and the loss of your loved one, but it has not changed your ability to see good in people and you are at heart I believe a kind man. From what you have told me of your Lucy, I am sure she must have had good reason to leave. What may not now be apparent to you I am sure will be clear in the future. If it is written, then you will meet your love again. You should never lose faith."

"I never have," Farid muttered and she patted his hand, her wistful smile reaching out to him with an understanding that no-one had for a very long time. Farid found himself deeply drawn to this frail English woman.

She watched him closely. "And tell me, how do you look after yourself?" The question surprised him.

"I don't understand."

"Do you save your money or do you spend it? How do you live? Indulge me, I am an inquisitive old woman."

Farid smiled at her and explained how he shared lodgings with other hotel employees some way out of town and most of his food was free in the hotel. Before he realised it he had told her how he had opened his account at the local bank and put all his tips and as much of his wages as he could into the account.

"Why do you save?" she asked bluntly.

"I want someday to be able to make more of my life, perhaps even to finish the education I had to leave to help my father support the younger members of our family. I would like to have a business of my own, to marry and have my own children, but it will take a lot of saving." He laughed, openly and without guile Jane noticed.

"Well, Farid, I hope you succeed and I am of course sure that your savings are with a good and reputable bank."

Farid regarded her solemnly. "Jane, when I have worked as hard as I have for my money I investigated many options for my small savings and I thought it best to choose the largest bank in the centre of town."

"Very sensible, you have a good head on your shoulders as well as a kind heart."

She regarded him seriously and he smiled. "Farid, what is your full name? I will write to you when I return to England."

Farid told her. A flicker of a smile crossed her lips and she handed him a little notebook and pen. "Please write it for me; I am afraid some of the names here have me very confused."

Farid carefully printed out his name. "I am sorry, my writing in your language is not good." She grinned mischievously "Please don't apologise; my writing in your language doesn't exist!"

At the end of the day she was tired so he drove her back to the hotel. As they passed quietly through the flat countryside, green after the recent rains, he looked over at her. Her head had dropped and her eyes were closed. Farid felt suddenly protective of this tiny person who had come unwanted and unbidden into his life, but who was the only person he had spoken openly to outside his own family for many years and who actually seemed to care about him as a person.

The following week he again took his day off and this time he drove her to see the ancient ruins at Dougga and watched fascinated as she clambered over the rocks and perched herself precariously at exactly the right spot to take her photographs. To his embarrassment she insisted on taking more photographs of him, waving away his protests.

"Why should I not have photographs of my handsome young guide, my friend? My old cronies at home will never believe me otherwise!"

When she left she gave him money. This time, Farid tried to refuse. "No, please, Jane, I do not want paying, I do this because I enjoy talking to you, showing you my country. You have allowed me to be your friend."

"Thank you, Farid, but this is not payment for your services. This is because you are my friend and if I am quite honest, the money means little to me at this stage in my life. I am simply helping you in a way that I can, in the same way you have helped me in the way that you can, more than you know. The time I spend with you is the release I need from the person I have become. With you I can dream and be for a short time the person I was, that I want to be again, but know I never will."

As he lay in the privacy of his own bed, Farid again considered her words and after much thought concluded that for someone who had seen and done so much the burden of advancing years was an unwelcome inevitability, nothing more. He had never really before considered what it was like to be old.

She did write to him from England. A postcard showing the Tower of London. There were only a few words in a spidery script telling him she had not been very well but hoped to be back later in the year.

She did return in the early autumn when high season was drawing to a close. She booked a month this time. It was hot for the time of year and the heat seemed to affect her. They spent time together on his days off, but she seemed distracted and easily tired. He drove this time and took her to see the mountains at her request. She spent a long time in silence lost the beauty of her surroundings. Farid was worried about her, she had become an integral part of his life.

On a warm day at the end of October, Jane was due to return to England. They sat outside in a café under the shade of the parasols looking out over the sea. She tried to give him a small blue envelope and this time he refused adamantly. A shadow passed across her face.

"My dear friend, I doubt we will ever meet again, take it."

Farid frowned. "Why are you not happy here, have I upset you?"

Jane shook her head and avoided his eyes. "Farid, listen to me. My friendship with you during our short time together in your beautiful country has given me more pleasure than anything else in as many years as I can remember. Your gentleness, the companionship we have shared, your willingness to listen and to trust your secrets to me has renewed my faith in human nature."

She tried to smile but her eyes were sad and he was startled to see a tear trickle down her wrinkled cheek.

"Then why will you not come back?"

"Farid, you of all men know that life does not always give us what we want most."

Farid stayed silent. She handed him the envelope, making him promise not to open it until she had gone. Then she kissed him softly on both cheeks and as she hugged him for a moment he felt a tremor pass through her. He said nothing and put the envelope in his inside pocket, his emotions in turmoil. Back at his lodgings that night he opened the envelope. It contained more money than he had ever seen at one time, with a short note written in shaky elegant hand telling him to keep faith and wishing him every happiness in his future life. When he came on duty the following evening she had gone.

He sent some of the money to his family, bought for himself a small pottery dish to remind himself of his first meeting with Jane and put the rest into his bank account. He never saw her again.

Many months later he was summoned to the director's office. His immediate thought was of more trouble, surely not Debbie. He felt sick. Surely the whole round of problems was not going to start all over again.

The expression on the director's face was inscrutable. "Sit down, Farid." Farid obeyed.

"I have a message for you from the Amen bank, the bank manager wishes to see you on a matter of urgency." Farid looked astonished.

"Look, Farid," he continued, "I have no idea what this is about, but I must ask you, are you in any sort of trouble."

Farid shook his head emphatically. "Absolutely not."

"Do you know why they want to see you? Do you have any association with the bank?"

"Only that I have a small savings account with them."

The director's eyebrows raised slightly, he knew that very few of the young single men saved anything. What did not go to their families, they spent.

"So you have no financial worries?"

"No, I do not. As you know I work as much overtime as I can and I have been able to save a little in the time I have been here. Working at the front of the hotel I sometimes get tips, and I save as much as I can. I hope one day to have enough to be able to have my own family."

"I am pleased to hear this, Farid, but you do realise this is somewhat unusual and I did have to ask you?"

"I understand. I had arranged to work my free day tomorrow, but may I change my mind and take it as I think I should go to the bank."

"In the circumstances, I think you should."

As Farid left the room the director rubbed his chin. He was a strange one, that Farid. He knew there had been some trouble at the previous hotel from which he had been cleared of involvement and had asked to be transferred. But Farid had certainly been an exemplary employee in the time he had been at the Regale and had caused him personally no problems. He liked the young man and was impressed by his quiet demeanour and the replies he had been given.

The next day, Farid put on his only decent pair of non-uniform trousers and a clean shirt and made his way to the Bank. He waited nervously for about fifteen minutes and to his surprise was greeted by a portly gentleman in an expensive grey suit who announced himself as the bank manager. He was ushered through to a large cool office at the back of the bank. He took the seat offered to him and waited.

"Are you Farid Ben Mohamed Khalifa, who is employed at the Regale Hotel?"

Farid nodded, his mouth dry.

"Do you have identification?"

"Yes, of course." He pulled out his identity card and for good measure his hotel identification. The bank manager carefully studied each document, then got up and took a photocopy of each, half turning to Farid.

"You have no objection?" Farid shook his head.

"I have received a communication from England with precise instructions that this envelope is to be given only to you and not to anyone purporting to act on your behalf. I am personally to check your identification and compare it with the photograph that was enclosed. I am to offer no advice or direction before you have considered the content of the letter, following which you may or may not decide to discuss the matter with me. I can tell you that your identification checks out."

"May I see the photograph?" The director hesitated and smiled.

"I see no reason why not."

Farid stared at the photograph of himself standing in front of the ruins at Dougga; he recognised it as one of the photographs Jane had taken the previous year.

The director handed to Farid the open envelope with a logo in the top corner and the stamped address of an organisation in England. On it was typed his name, care of The Director, Amen Bank… Inside the envelope was a smaller sealed blue envelope, the same as the ones which Jane used. On it was written in sloping spidery writing which he immediately recognised. 'Farid. To be opened only by him in the event of my death'.

Farid stared at the director, who immediately noted his obvious distress. Farid's hands shook as the bank manager watched him intently. Their eyes met. The older man smiled encouragingly. "Go on, open it, it is addressed to you."

Farid pulled out the single sheet of thick blue paper, and read.

'*My dear friend, and I am once again honoured to call you this. As I explained we would not meet again. It seems that God, or Allah as you wish, has other plans for me and has decided that my stay in this life is over. I will not dwell on unnecessary explanation. I knew that my time was limited last time we met but I decided not to spoil our* last few days in each other's company. When you read this I shall be gone.

'Above everything I wish you happiness and the love in your life which you so deserve. Remember what I told you when we last met. Keep faith. I hope you find your lost love.

'My gift to you is made in memory of a kind and sweet-natured man, whom I wish I had been given a chance to hold in my life for longer. I know my gift will change your life forever, but I also know in my heart that the use to which you put this will be good.

'Follow your dream, dear friend, and if I can be at least partly instrumental in helping you achieve it, I will be happy.

'I am tired now and I must rest. Goodbye dearest Farid, the world is a better place when men like you live in it.

'Always your friend, Jane.'

Farid sat motionless and stared blankly at the bank manager, who watched him carefully.

Finally he spoke. "I received a letter from a London firm of solicitors acting in the estate of Mrs Jane Beaumont, who died in December last year and who was known to you."

Farid nodded wordlessly. So Jane had died only weeks after returning to England. He felt an unaccustomed pricking behind his eyes and his lips quivered. It did not go unnoticed by the man opposite him.

"Farid, may I call you that? The letter stated that a bequest had been made to Farid Khalifa. I was informed that you had a savings account at this bank and worked at the Regale Hotel, but Mrs Beaumont had no further information. My instructions were to contact the hotel director and verify your identity. You will appreciate therefore that this is why I was obliged to contact your employer."

Farid nodded again.

"Mrs Beaumont stated that the young man was her friend and indeed more than this, she regarded him as the son she had never been fortunate enough to have by blood, whose kindness and trust had made the last part of her life not only bearable but happy.

"The reason for the delay in contacting you is that the will was challenged by her son on the basis of her incapacity. But it would appear Mrs Beaumont was a very astute lady and the will had been witnessed by her lawyer and doctor. I understand that after much unpleasantness the will was found to be sound and the objection overruled. The bequest is yours. The money will be paid into your account once you sign this acknowledgement." Farid scribbled on the piece of paper in front of him.

"Don't you want to read what it says?"

Farid shook his head, "No, you are the man of words, not me. I have had my account with you now for a couple of years. If you say this is what I should do, then I shall. I am just sorry about Jane…" His voice tailed off and he stared at the man seated opposite him.

The bank manager regarded the silent figure over the top of his glasses. He beamed at Farid. "Do you want to know how much Mrs Beaumont has given you?" Farid blinked and said nothing. "£100,000." Farid stared blankly at him. The director regarded him seriously and confirmed the amount in dinar.

"She's gone crazy," Farid squeaked.

The director smiled. "No, Farid. I understand Mrs Beaumont was an extremely wealthy woman; this bequest was a fraction of her estate, but she was well aware it would change your life. Now, we must talk about what you intend to do with this amazing good fortune. I think perhaps tea would be a good idea!"

Farid sat quietly as the older man's words washed over him. He was sure he would never have seen half of that if he had worked for fifty years. What had he done to deserve this, befriended an old lady whom he had genuinely come to care for, but this was impossible.

"Farid?"

"I am sorry, I just don't know what to think."

"I'm sorry, I am rushing you. I will of course be happy to keep the money here in the bank until you have had time to consider your future. You must have some idea though, every man dreams of having enough money to do everything he desires. You have a young lady perhaps?"

Farid smiled for the first time. "No sir, I don't, but I do know two things I want to do." The older man watched him, wondering what was coming next.

"I would like a regular payment made to my father each month."

The director nodded. "We can discuss the details later. And for yourself?"

"I am going back to school. I told Jane, Mrs Beaumont..." he added quickly, "that I wanted to finish my education and better my life and that is what I will do. I want to learn English and take a course in hotel management when I finish the necessary education and later possibly start my own business. Do you think this would be possible?" he added uncertainly.

"I am sure it will be, but don't you want to buy anything for yourself?"

Farid shook his head, "Not yet; I need to sort out my life first, there are some things I must do because I need to know which way my life will go before deciding what to do with such a huge sum of money."

"I am pleased you have a good head on your shoulders, I am confident Mrs Beaumont knew exactly what she was doing in leaving you money."

Farid held his eyes. "I do not intend to disappoint her."

CHAPTER FORTY-SIX

A NEW BEGINNING

He said nothing when he went back to the hotel and it was two weeks later that the director asked to see him.

"I just wanted to ensure that your business went well and there are no problems which would affect your work here." It was a lame excuse and both were aware of that.

"Yes, thank you." Farid could see the older man was more than interested so he decided to tell the truth but be economical with it, if that was the right word in the circumstances.

"I have been left some money and the bank needed to verify my identity before paying it into my account, that was all. I do however need to ask you if I can finish my contract with the Hotel at the end of this month, as I want to go to college."

"College? - but Farid you are…"

"Old!" Farid laughed. "Yes, I know and that worried me too, but I have found a place where I can learn enough English so that I can enter a hotel management course and I have made my reservation for next year, but there are certain educational standards I much reach before they will accept me. I must leave my work so I can study and my English is good enough to enter the course."

The director was surprised as jobs were still jealously guarded and unemployment was high. He was also disappointed that Farid gave no further information but could hardly in all decency press the matter further. As there was still considerable unemployment it would not be hard to replace Farid and he gave his permission that his contract would be terminated by mutual agreement.

Hakim was extremely proud and Saleem was one of the first to congratulate him. But he told no one the amount of money which Jane had left him.

"Brother, such good fortune could not happen to a nicer person. You have had some hardship in your life and I know you left school to work so you could help Baba pay for my education. If there is anything I can do to help you, please tell me."

"There is, you can help me with my English and when I am able to carry on any sort of conversation then you must speak to me only in English!"

"You are really serious about this, aren't you?" His brother's expression needed no reply.

Farid studied hard and played little. This was no hardship to him as his hours in hotel work had been long and with the overtime he worked he had little free time anyway. As an older student he found the English hard but he knew he must have a reasonable command of the language in order to take up his place on the course.

With his college diploma he would be able to take up an under-manager's job in one of the smaller hotels, provided his results were good enough. He knew he had the ability to deal with the clientèle and the presence which came with age which would not be the case with most of the other students. He felt this would be an advantage when seeking employment. He had ideas of what he wanted to do but knew that experience would be essential. As he studied he wished Lucy was with him. He knew that she too would have been proud of him, but she was not here and he must, for the sake of his education, put her out of his mind as much as humanly possible.

His brother helped him enormously. He now had a new girlfriend who worked in the offices of one of the more expensive hotels in Sousse. She came to Hammamet sometimes for the weekend and as she had studied in England she was able to help Farid not only with his English but to explain some of the management side of the business of which Farid was essentially ignorant.

Although he could have afforded better accommodation, he chose to rent a simple room near to the college. The bank manager had assisted him in investing some of his money and Farid had thankfully taken his advice. He had in his account only what he needed to survive on a day to day basis and a small reserve for emergencies.

One evening, at around the time the shifts changed, he went back to the Regale. As he walked into the hotel he felt a pang of loneliness. He missed the companionship of his colleagues and had few friends in Tunis where he studied. To his surprise he was greeted by the director who had first told him about his appointment with the bank. He was ushered him into the back room like an old friend. The man appeared genuinely pleased to see him and Farid told him of his experiences over the past year. In English he asked Farid how his studies were progressing and Farid responded. The director listened intently.

"Farid, I can only congratulate you. You have worked in the hotel trade for many years and never bothered to learn English and yet you have made amazing progress in one year. If I can be of any help please let me know, and you can of course look to me for any reference or recommendation you need in the future." Farid thanked him, both surprised and embarrassed and asked politely about life generally within the hotel.

"Let us just say that I wish some of my older employees were still here. The younger ones do not have the ability to deal with the guests in a friendly but formal manner and one or two of them are causing me a headache." Farid smiled.

"I am afraid I too must have caused one or two headaches from time to time." The director held his gaze.

"Farid, I am aware of the problems you had and I believe none of them were of your own making, as so often happens you were in the wrong place at the wrong time. We are all aware of the trouble that the more persistent of our clientèle can cause." Farid's embarrassment was obvious, but he ignored it. "I am pleased for you and your good fortune and you appear to have used your time well. Now please assure me that when you complete your college work, as I am sure you will meet the standard to enter the course, that you will let me know if there is anything I can do to help you."

Whatever Farid had expected when he entered the hotel, this was not it. As he left, he held his head high. The support of his family had been welcomed, but the support of this avuncular man who had once been his boss, encouraged him not to fail in his intent and he fully intended to go back with his diploma in hand. He passed his exams and a year later started on his hotel management course.

The year that followed was difficult. At first, Farid found it hard to deal with the fact that many of the students could almost have been his own children and he made few friends. The students found it strange that someone of his age should wish to be at college. There were few girls on the course. One or two of them showed an interest in him and then backed away when he made it plain he was there to study not enter into any relationship. The men found him hard to get to know, but eventually came to realise that he was totally honest with them, he was not interested in their girlfriends and simply enjoyed a chat, a drink and perhaps a night out here and there. He had his own small circle of close friends mainly among the older students who found it easier to ignore his age and saw him for what he was. The only thing he told no-one was of his good fortune. He stayed in simple lodgings as they did and spent little.

One evening as he sat in a café with his two closest friends, a girl quietly approached their table. He saw her and was surprised when she put her finger to her lips and grinned at him. He said nothing and smiled when she crept up behind his friend and put her hands over his eyes from behind. Aymen sat quite still and then laughed.

"There is only one person who would dare approach me from behind like that." He laughed, turned and swung the girl onto the empty seat beside him. "Khawla, you minx." The girl collapsed into peals of laughter and hugged him.

"Hello little brother. Still drinking coffee instead of studying?" Aymen introduced his sister and her eyes rested momentarily on Farid. He returned the smile. She reminded him of a china doll. When he stood up to greet her, she didn't reach his shoulder. Her long black hair hung loose and as she sat down with them her wide almond eyes danced as she looked from one to the other. She was absolutely tiny. She looked directly at him, a stern expression on her face.

"You must be a desperate man to keep such bad company!"

"Oh, they're not that bad, and I suppose these two are the best of a bad bunch."

Aymen punched him lightly. "Bloody cheek, old man."

"That hurt," said Farid, trying to look injured.

"What the tap I gave you or the remark about your advanced years?"

"I see your manners have not improved Aymen," his sister commented dryly.

He learned that Khawla had been at the college a few years before. She had graduated with a first class diploma and was now working in one of the hotels in Tunis. Over the next few months, Khawla joined them on several occasions and Farid found that he truly enjoyed the company of a young woman who seemed genuinely interested in him simply as a friend. It was a new experience and one he cherished.

Aymen had gone out with his girlfriend and Farid sat with Khawla in a local cafe. It was the first time they had sat alone together.

"You look happy tonight." She beamed at him.

"I am very happy. Mehdi is coming home."

Farid waited.

"I haven't had a chance to tell you before. Aymen has always been with us and he does not approve of Mehdi."

"And so who is this mysterious Mehdi?"

"Mehdi is the love of my life. We knew each other as children, then we lost touch and then when I went to college he was there a year above me. He is a very ambitious man and decided when he left college he wanted to work in London. He now works at the London Hilton as a trainee manager. He wants to put in about five years in London and then for us both to go and live in Paris. Aymen disapproves strongly and believes that Mehdi will break my heart when he finds a girl in England and even if he doesn't, Aymen is convinced that I should stay here with my family and not go gadding off to Paris, as he put it."

"He has got a point, you know. I wouldn't approve if my sister went to live with a man, here or in Paris."

"Oh, no. I have told him I must be married before I agree to go with him to France. Aymen says he won't marry me, but Mehdi told me he is going to ask my father if we can be married when he comes back next week."

"Have you told Aymen?"

"No, you are the only person I have told."

Farid smiled slowly. "Why?"

"Because you are my friend. You have seen me for who I am, not as a sister, a child or even as a woman, just as a friend. I am completely fed up with being treated like a kid. I may be small but there is nothing childish about my brain. I have the same feelings that any woman of my age has, but Aymen although he is younger than me, treats me like a baby that has to be protected from the world and everyone in it."

She stopped and gazed thoughtfully at Farid. "Why is that? Why have you never seen me as a woman? In fact come to think of it, I've never seen you with a girl." Her almond eyes narrowed for a second. "You do like women don't you?" Farid glared at her.

"If you must know, you are not the only one with a love of your life. I just lost mine along the way, but I intend to find her again, now I have the education, the prospect of a good job and the means to do so." He hesitated, he had said more than he should. Khawla frowned.

"What do you mean, the means to do so? I thought you were as skint as the rest of the students?"

"I was lucky enough to be left some money, so now I will be able to go England and try and find her again."

"When did you last see her? What happened?"

Farid regarded her thoughtfully. "Khawla, I have no idea what happened and it was a lot of years ago."

"Farid, do you know how many people live in England? The population of London itself is only a little smaller than in the whole of this country."

"I admit, that I didn't know, but I do have some leads. People we both knew here, the wife of a friend of mine and the number of an old friend of Lucy's. I just didn't have the money to do it before. I may even have to hire someone to find her if I can't do it by myself."

"That takes a lot of money." Farid regarded her seriously.

"Khawla, I have enough if I need it." He felt he had said enough, but he could see he had her attention.

Khawla stared at him. "Why did she leave you?"

Farid met her gaze. "That is what I have to find out. You see Khawla, after she left I went a bit crazy, did some stupid things and met some stupider women. Then completely by chance I saw her in Sousse some years ago and although I never got to speak to her, I knew by her expression that she still felt the same way about me. If you really love someone, you know that," he added unnecessarily.

Khawla said nothing for a moment. "I do understand. Mehdi has been gone for three years and although he has been back a few times, we have still been separated. Nothing in my feelings for him has changed, so believe me I do understand."

Farid thought privately that the situation was a bit different and three years was not that long, but to Khawla of course it must seem like a lifetime.

The following summer, Mehdi and Khawla were married. Farid went to the wedding with Aymen, who if not altogether approving of the match had been pacified when Mehdi agreed not to go immediately to Paris but to spent time working at home before taking such a huge step.

Farid's time at college ended and finally clutching his diploma, he went, as he had promised himself, back to the Regale. The director was genuinely pleased to see him and took Farid to one of the good restaurants in Hammamet to celebrate. True to his word he gave Farid a glowing reference and within a few months, Farid started work as assistant manager in one of the new hotels in Hammamet.

CHAPTER FORTY-SEVEN

A BUSINESS AND A HOUSE

Unfortunately, Farid found management monotonous and became disillusioned with the complaints from the tourists, everything from the basics that there was no English television, the fridge, the shower or the air conditioning didn't work properly and there was nothing they could find to eat in the restaurants. They objected to the meal times saying they were inconvenient and there were some complaints about the facilities and the décor in the rooms and the hotel catered too much for business people and not enough for them. The business clientèle in turn complained of lack of facilities and that the rooms allocated were inappropriate and too far from the conference areas. Their wives didn't like the rowdiness of the tourists and the new idea of buffet style breakfast. They wanted serving and disliked having to queue up with the tourists and serve themselves. Farid thought that most of these complaints could be dealt with easily.

After a year he had listened carefully and learned that many of the complaints concerned facilities and other things provided by suppliers. With the number of hotels being opened and others being refurbished to compete, he realised there was an opening for hotel supplies of the best quality and decided to start his own business in the not too distant future. He used his time at the hotel to make contacts and to learn what it was people wanted. He learned quickly that whilst variety and quality were essential, to deliver on time and to charge a fair price were equally so. Reputation was everything.

He made his contacts amongst the clientèle, other hotel managers and suppliers and after a further year he quit his employment and with the assistance of Jane's money he started his business. He rented an office in the centre of Hammamet and employed one person to help him, Sami, a friend of Saleem who had recently qualified as an accountant but was willing to turn his hand to most things and he proved more than up to the task. He complied in every respect with Farid's strict code of honesty, reliability and quality of supplies as well as keeping his books in order.

Farid travelled, staying in and learning from other hotels. He ordered linen from Egypt, glassware from Italy and food supplies from France. His business grew and his reputation as an honest man and reliable supplier of good quality merchandise spread. On the occasion when something he supplied was not up to the standard required, it was changed without question and if it happened more than once, the supplier was removed from his list. When the newest luxury hotel, the Sahara Oasis opened, he won the contract for supplying the hotel. His money made more money and Farid became a very rich man.

Unfortunately the drawback was that he had no time to go to England and now he was established in business he was determined to go there, find his love and present her and her son with a comfortable future. Next year, he promised himself. In the spring I will go to England.

Farid's only real personal extravagance was his house. He purchased a plot of land on the coast some way south of Hammamet. He employed an architect recommended by the manager at the Sahara Oasis and drew up the plans for his new home. The architect was surprised that his obviously wealthy client did not want a huge house, but just a good sized family home with four bedrooms and a pool. Unlike most Tunisians Farid also wanted a large garden, not simply a good area of land but a proper garden.

When the finished plans were presented to him, Farid was overjoyed. He had particularly asked for artist's impressions of the finished building so he could ensure before mistakes were made that everything was as he wanted it. The drawings were exactly those of the home which he and Lucy had talked of one day having for themselves. Smooth white walls with wrought iron balconies, one on the east to catch the morning sun and one on the west to watch the sun go down.

The interior was white. The floors were soft creamy marble tiles. From the small hallway a curved open wrought iron staircase led to the four bedrooms, all leading off the central landing. Two had their own bathrooms and the third bathroom was to serve the remaining two rooms. Downstairs there was a square kitchen with a wide door opening onto the garden. He had already chosen the huge terracotta pot in which to plant the jasmine which was to overhang the door, something Lucy had insisted upon. There was a small dining area which opened on to a larger living space, but not so large it became impersonal, with two recesses in which to place items of furniture or freestanding ornaments. Farid already knew how Lucy wanted to decorate their home.

Outside there was to be a patio area around the pool leading onto a smaller area with a built in barbecue, intimate, low white walls like a courtyard with raised beds which he would fill with geraniums and all the bright colours Lucy loved. Grassy areas surrounded the house on the other two sides separated by a short driveway leading from the white gates to the house. He insisted that the whole garden should be walled and planted with bougainvillea and jasmine.

Farid knew that he paid too much to the builders, but he insisted that the house be finished quickly and everything had to be exactly as he planned. If he was to go to England he wanted to be able to bring Lucy back to the home of her dreams. That she might indeed be married was pushed to the back of his mind, he convinced himself this was one of Debbie's fabrications. The child he could not explain to himself, so he didn't try.

Finally the house was finished. The furniture was delivered. Farid was adamant he wanted to see his home only when it was completed and decorated, ready for him to move in. The architect and builder were somewhat surprised but organised the delivery, and with Meriam's help arranged for the contractors to place the furniture as their client had specified, the curtains hung and everything just as he wanted.

When Farid saw into his completed project for the first time, he was stunned. It was beautiful.

He walked up the driveway listening to the click of his shoes on the cobbles. Lucy had been very definite in that she did not want gravel, which she complained got dirty quickly and spread everywhere. He smiled as he remembered how she had said that apart from that gravel sneaked into her sandals and got stuck between her toes. He unlocked the door and turned the brass handle.

He took off his shoes and stepped gingerly across the tiles into the living room and raised the shutters. Two long white settees lay at right angles to each other, a low white wrought iron glass topped table linking the two. The television was set into the wall with a sliding front to hide the black screen when it was not in use. The floor to ceiling curtains were heavy cream brocade, mottled to match the tiles and edged with gold. A chandelier hung from the centre of the room, the crystal droplets reflecting the sunlight and sending rainbow patterns around the walls. There were two matching wall lights and all could be dimmed to a gentle glow.

In the centre of the floor was one huge rug which leant its colours to the cool whiteness of the room. The silky pile gleamed a mixture of amber, white, gold and deep rose pink, the colours picked up again in the painting which dominated the long wall. He had commissioned the painting from an artist in the Sousse Medina and now he gazed at it. It was the view from their café, over the low sandstone wall looking out to sea. The scene was evening and the rosy glow of the setting sun formed patterns over the water, which seemed alive. Farid wondered if it had been a good idea to ask for that view. The tears pricked his eyes and he fought them back. He remembered the time they had sat together watching the sunset and how Lucy had said she wished she could capture it forever. Well now he had, but she was not there to see it.

He turned away and went to the shorter wall which backed onto the kitchen. There were the two hooks, as he had asked. He unwrapped the parcel he was carrying and gently placed the first of the photographs its new home. He stood back and looked at it. It was an enlargement of the photo of himself and Lucy sitting with their backs to the sea, their hands clasped together, looking at each other and not at the camera. A little smile played on her face and her hair spread like a silk curtain around her shoulders. He look the smaller picture and placed it on its hook. Lucy's heart shaped face gazed back at him and she smiled, her lips slightly apart. He moved to one side and her green eyes seemed to follow him. His tears fell unchecked and he made no move to stop them.

Slowly he turned down the lights and made his way upstairs.

Three of the bedrooms were painted off white, each with a different tint. In the guest rooms the walls were tinted peach and pale green, each with curtains in a deeper colour. The second bedroom, a little smaller than the main bedroom, was covered with a pale blue wash, for the boy he would now never have. He slammed the door to shut out the memory of what could never be and wondered why he had asked for this.

Finally he opened the door to the main bedroom, which was completely furnished. This was pure white with deep rose curtains held back with gold brackets. The double bed was made up and the matching spread which covered it was edged with gold. Several plump cushions sat upright against the ornate white headboard. A small pale pink crystal chandelier hung from the centre of the ceiling, matching the lamps on the bedside tables. The furniture was fitted into the walls with small gold handles. He opened the doors to the left and looked at the rails and shelves arranged for himself. He turned to the second set of doors and hesitated before he opened them. There was a long rail with narrow drawers down one side and a shoe rack at the bottom, arranged for a lady.

He took a long final look at the room and softly closed the door and walked slowly down the stairs, lost in thought. He locked the door, set the alarm and turned and looked back at the house. Yes it was a house built for a woman, a woman who didn't know it existed. It was to be another month before Farid could bring himself to move into his new home, and only then because Meriam told him he was crazy and agreed to stay with him for a week, as she put it, to help him sort himself out.

CHAPTER FORTY-EIGHT

THE CHARADE

Lucy enjoyed her work as a senior manager. She loved the bustle of the noisy office and although she said little herself there was always someone with something to say. It was sometimes difficult to concentrate but after a while she had got used to it. Far better a happy noisy office than a miserable silence. The general rule was that management kept themselves inconspicuous until needed, and Lucy had been told to crack down on the younger more exuberant members of staff only when the chatter got so bad it was disrupting output.

She took little notice of the men around her, the office mainly employed women but one or two of the other senior staff were men. She had known with the instinct present in most women that Jonathan was attracted to her and it was obvious too to some of the more observant staff. He was a pleasant enough man, a year or so younger than her. The floppy lock of hair that fell over his forehead reminded her a little of Peter but she offered him no encouragement, any more than she did any other man. She was happy to have them as friends but wanted no more.

Lucy sometimes wondered how different her life would have been had Peter lived. Would she have had more children? For a certainty there would be no Ben and no Rose. She thought of her handsome son, already exhibiting signs of becoming a serious threat to the hearts of women in a year or so. And of course, Rose, the daughter she never thought she would have, a small pretty girl with a pale oval face and shy gentle nature. She could not imagine being without her children.

She wondered if her life would have been easy and regulated, she would probably have gone back to work anyway but Peter would most likely have wanted that to be part time or at least something which did not pose a challenge, and certainly not the career job she now enjoyed.

She thought of the round of coffee mornings, village committees and a middle-class existence with much of the conversation revolving around family as is often the case with comfortably off women who don't need or don't choose to work. Her smile faded. Could she have gone along with that, would they have survived together, she and Peter? She realised with a pang of guilt that she thought of Peter less and less as the years passed. She supposed it was only natural, although she had long ago admitted to herself that although she had loved Peter it was never with same soul destroying intensity that she had felt for Farid.

There was a strange sweet smell in the room. "Lucy, wakey wakey, are you by chance drifting off to sleep?" Lucy opened her eyes and took a moment to adjust to Jonathan's tall shadow blocking the sunlight from the open window. She laughed. What she could smell was his somewhat overpowering cologne.

"No, Jonathan just resting my eyes, I'm a bit tired."

"What's so funny?"

"Nothing Jonathan, just thoughts."

He looked annoyed. He had asked Lucy out a couple of times but she always found a polite reason to decline and eventually he gave up. His only complaint about her was that she insisted on using his full name. Jon, he thought, made him sound more youthful, and he was very well aware of his middle aged status amongst a staff mostly comprised of twenty-somethings. He tried to compensate with bright ties and used expressions much more suited to teenagers which unfortunately simply served to make him look pathetic. Midlife crisis was what the younger members of staff said behind his back. It was shame really, Lucy liked him and thought how much nicer he would be if he could only just be himself.

No one in the office knew very much about Lucy. She had worked there for many years and was quietly popular. She was kind, professional, never criticised unless it was deserved and was pleasant to everyone in a reserved sort of way. The general estimation was that she was about forty and being flattered she never corrected them. She wore her hair in a neat coil and always her own unofficial uniform of narrow dark pencil skirt and pastel or white blouse. She used little makeup and tended to just blend in, which was her intention.

Of course she came to the Christmas party and the summer barbecue but always alone. There was no scandal surrounding Lucy and in fact the longer serving members of staff could only recall her being out of sorts on one occasion, when she came back from a foreign holiday years before when something had obviously upset her deeply. Once she was seen to be crying in the restroom but she never spoke of it and it was thought better not to ask. They knew she was a widow and that she had children, whom no-one had ever seen.

"Lucy?"

"Sorry, Jonathan, I was miles away, did you want me for anything?" He bit back the retort which sprang to mind.

"No, I just wondered if you were coming to the barbecue."

The office barbecue was an annual event held at the chairman's country house. It was split into two halves. The barbecue and games from midday and it was acknowledged that the younger ones would go home around 5p.m. and then the house staff set up for the party following for the adults in the huge conservatory, which opened out through wide sliding doors onto the rear lawn of the large garden. It was always fancy dress, there had been Hawaiian, Wild West, James Bond, and last year a 1960s theme. Everyone entered into the spirit of this and rooms were provided for anyone who wanted to change. Lucy always kept her outfits non-controversial, usually something just added to the jeans and shirt she wore in the afternoon.

"Oh, course. I wouldn't miss it. I'll see you there no doubt, Jon." He was pleased for once she had used the name he preferred.

Lucy had a headache. She crept away quietly and sat in the restroom away from the door behind the magazine racks. She heard the door open and a stream of chatter. She recognised the voices. Laura, a fresh-faced girl who had arrived straight from school two years earlier, the other was most definitely the brash voice of Jose Butcher, who fancied Jonathan dreadfully but he showed no interest in her at all. She was not an unattractive woman but insisted on wearing her hair curling round her face in a style too young for a middle aged woman and her clothes were always just a bit too tight. Her worst fault however was the way she screwed up her eyes and nose when she tried to listen in on other people's conversations and then she resembled a piglet squealing when its tail was pulled.

"Did you see Jon, he was trying to chat up Lucy again?"

"She encourages him," retorted Jose, "and I bet she monopolises him at the barbecue," she whined.

"Don't be daft, you're just jealous. It's the other way around if you ask me. He just won't leave her alone. Anyway if the barbecue is as good as it was last year, I'll be happy."

Jose sniffed. Lucy knew that Jose didn't like her but she was equally sure the reason was because Jonathan did. Lucy had always found a reason to come alone and not to bring her children in the afternoon as most of the staff did. She had no intention of parading her children and leaving herself open to the inevitable speculation. She just wished to maintain her comfortable anonymity.

She heard Jose's voice again. "Yes and I suppose Miss Perfect will keep it toned down as usual, boring. Frankly I cannot see what Jon sees in her."

Laura peered at her. "Don't be stupid, Jose, you know bloody well what he sees in her. Anyway what's the theme this year?"

"Africa," giggled Jose. You can imagine some of the costumes that will throw up. "Perhaps Miss Perfect will turn up with her face blacked wearing an orange and purple jungle frock with a basket on her head."

"Jose, that's not fair." Laura giggled and Jose found herself enjoying the attention.

"I bet she doesn't bring the kids, as usual. They must have something wrong with them, what do you think? Stunted growth, buck teeth and a lisp or just plain ugly. No wonder she's ashamed of them."

"That's wicked. You're going too far," but Laura laughed anyway.

Lucy heard the door slam and sat motionless. She had smiled at the orange and purple jungle frock but her anger mounted when Jose bad mouthed her children. She was furious. She went back to her desk when she had regained her composure, ignoring Jose completely. Laura just thought she was in a bad mood.

Lucy sat looking out of the window. It was a beautiful hot day and she basked in the warmth of the sun. A small smile started playing on her mouth and Jon was astonished to see her beaming out of the window like the Cheshire cat. She caught him staring at her.

"Yes, Jonathan, anything wrong?" Jon caught his breath. He hardly recognised her. Miss Perfect (as he knew some of them called her) was grinning manically from ear to ear with what could only be described as an evil twinkle in her eye. Lucy was still smiling when the time came to go home.

Alex came over in the evening and the two boys were playing cards. Rose was reading a book. Lucy finished the washing up.

"Children, will you do me the honour of accompanying me to the summer barbecue this year?"

Their three surprised faces looked up at her.

Alex grimaced, "I can't, Mum, Sadie's got her hands full of Amy at the moment and she doesn't do that sort of thing anyway, not that wretched barbecue with kids screaming everywhere."

"I'm not talking about the midday session, you are all too old for that anyway. I meant the party after the kids have gone."

"Oh well, I can probably manage that. Sadie will probably appreciate getting me out of the house for a few hours after Amy's gone to bed. She is always complaining that when Amy is asleep she's then got to deal with me."

Ben was thoughtful. "What's brought all this on Mum? You've never taken us before."

Lucy repeated the comments Jose had made about them and about her turning up in a purple and orange jungle frock with a basket on her head. Ben grinned at his brother.

"Oh boy, I have a ghastly feeling our mother is up to something."

"You're damn right I am." Lucy smirked.

"Mum, no." Rose yelled. "I refuse point blank to become a hunchback with a lisp and trundle after you in a purple and orange frock with a basket stuck on my head!" Lucy giggled.

"You moron," squealed Ben. "It's Mum whose wearing the frock, not you."

Alex punched his brother playfully. "Shut up, short arse."

Ben grabbed at him "Okay Lurch."

The two of them grappled until Alex tripped his brother up and he sat down hard on the floor.

Lucy watched them happily. Ben got to his feet rubbing his backside, his face flushed with exertion. "Anyway less of the jungle frock, what exactly is the actual theme this year?"

"Africa." There was silence and slowly Ben started to grin.

"Brilliant," he muttered and looked intently at his mother.

Alex glared at him, misunderstanding completely. "What do you mean brilliant? How can I pass for an African, I refuse to black my face and Rose would need to be dipped in a pot of black paint. Anyway, nowadays we'd get done for racism."

Rose giggled. She got up and jammed Lucy's shopping basket on her head. Alex wrapped a towel round her waist and she pranced around the room.

"Will you two sit down please, I need to talk to you, and Rose get my basket off your head! Listen to me you crazy idiots. Ben understood. There are parts of Africa where people aren't black."

Alex eventually realised what she meant. "God, you are really going for it this time."

"Yes, my children, I am. Miss Perfect is about to announce that leopards can change their spots and there is absolutely sod all wrong with my beautiful children."

The four of them sat around the kitchen table discussing tactics. Alex left later in the evening and when she was alone with the twins Rose raised the subject of fancy dress.

"Mum, what are we going to wear?"

"Well I'll have to part-make and part-buy your outfits, but I already have mine." Her voice was low and Ben saw her eyes glistening. He stretched his hand out to her but she shook her head.

"Ignore me, sweetheart, I'm just a sentimental old fool."

"Can I see it?" Rose asked.

"No, not yet, darling."

Her colleagues at work noticed a slight change in Lucy. She seemed happier and chatted a bit more. Jose tried to sound her out by asking what she had decided to wear for the barbecue. To her surprise Lucy smiled at her.

"I have absolutely no idea, but I am sure something will come to me."

Encouraged by the unaccustomed friendliness Jose ploughed on, "Are you bringing your kids this year?" Lucy looked her straight in the eyes.

"Probably not, they have their own friends and they wouldn't want to come out with boring old Mum, now would they?"

"Shame. No one has ever seen them." Jose sniggered and Lucy looked up from her computer thoughtfully.

"No I don't suppose you have," and looked back at the screen. Jose gave up.

To Lucy's delight the day of the summer barbecue was in the middle of a heat wave. The temperature had reached 25 degrees by midday, and the forecaster said it was going to get hotter, which suited her plans admirably. To save changing at the house, Lucy had booked them a room at the hotel in the village which backed onto the rear lawn of the chairman's estate where the guests congregated.

They checked in early as soon as the room was available to avoid bumping into other guests who might also be going to the party. It was actually a suite, two rooms, one good sized room and a smaller one annexed to it with a shared bathroom. They sat together watching television. Alex was his usual quietly confident self, but Ben was strung out like an elastic bank about to snap. Rose was ecstatic. Her costume was the most beautiful thing she had ever seen but after she was sure it would fit, Lucy had refused to let her wear it again until the party. She sat squirming with excitement.

Ben heard the door open softly and saw a small dark woman hurry into the smaller room. He said nothing. He was desperate to get into his costume and assumed the woman was a chambermaid.

Their childish enthusiasm infected Lucy who still adamantly refused to show them her outfit. Ben gave up asking her and noticed that the chambermaid had not left the suite.

He turned to Lucy. "Mum, who is that lady who went into the other room?

"Mind your own business, nosy, she'll be in to see you all shortly." She disappeared into the small room.

Ben admitted defeat and turned his attention to the buffet lunch Lucy had ordered. "I wish I knew what she is up to," he sighed looking at Alex.

"I don't know any more than you, but knowing Mum when she gets a bee in her bonnet it will all have to be dead right, and we, little brother, will take our lead from her. This is her party."

Ben held up his hand, palm facing his brother. Alex slapped it with his own.

"Mum!" they said in unison.

Amal sat down next to Lucy on the bed. She was a tiny woman of about fifty, recommended to her by Hana Clark for the purpose. Lucy had met with her a few times to chat and discuss what she wanted. "I want to be correct in every detail, not for other people but for myself. With Rose I think the costume will be enough. The boys you can bend the rules a bit and turn them into Omar Sharif in Lawrence of Arabia if you like. So long as they look as if they're Arabs, no-one will be any the wiser."

Amal grinned. "Unfortunately I think Alex is more likely to look like Peter O'Toole as Lawrence than Omar Sharif. Rose, you will not recognise and Ben, well Ben is another matter completely." Her dark eyes sparkled and Lucy hugged her.

"Amal, you're an angel." The little woman beamed. "Shush, this is great fun, now fetch me Alex."

Amal fussed around him arranging his outfit. He felt wonderful in his long white robes and headdress with the square golden band keeping it firmly on his head. The Lawrence costume suited his tall lean frame and his blue eyes were brighter than ever next to the fake tan that Amal had sprayed all over the bits that showed, assuring him it would come off easily when he protested. He sat down adjusting his sword, or cutlass, he didn't know which and waited for the others.

Amal beamed at Rose. This she was going to love. The costume was that of a traditional Tunisian dancer. She sprayed the upper part of Rose's body with tan and helped her into the tight red bodice embroidered with small gold discs. Her midriff was bare and the baggy trousers in shades of maroon, gold and black clung to her hips and flared out to be gathered around her slim ankles. The gold tassels swung as she moved. Her deep blonde curls cascaded over her shoulders. The veil was fine red voile held by a thick band of gold braid from which more gold discs hung over her forehead. Her eyes were blackened with pencil and her lips painted deep red to match the amazing false nails which Amal had painstakingly attached. Amal handed her the huge gold coloured bracelets with Lucy had found in a junk shop and the picture was complete.

She turned to view her creation and beamed. All the girl needed now was a clay pot on her head. Rose had drawn the line at this and Lucy agreed it was unlikely to stay there for more than a minute. Amal shrugged in defeat. Rose pranced into the other room and Alex solemnly bowed to her. "Little sister, you look amazing." Rose beamed at him and they sat down side by side to wait.

Amal worked her magic on Ben. She studied the handsome face, at fifteen still not a man but no longer a child. He waited while she adjusted his white ceremonial embroidered jebba and sash with baggy trousers and traditional shoes. She shaded his face and darkened around his eyes with shadow, added emphasis to his chin and a stuck on a narrow moustache, which he complained itched. She slicked his hair and oiled it so that the tight curls glistened under the lights. He twirled his robes and turned to face her, his expression stern. Amal stared at him. In the matter of ten minutes Ben had changed from a teenager to a handsome young Arab of wealth and family. Amal muttered something under her breath. Ben bowed deeply from the waist and thanked her.

Amal flushed deep red. "Oh, Ben, I apologise, I had forgotten you spoke my language."

Ben grinned. "Don't mention it. I just hope all the girls think the same."

"Unfortunately, of that there is little doubt," Amal replied dubiously. Ben's grin spread from ear to ear and she slapped him gently.

He followed Amal into the room where Alex and Rose were watching television. Rose shrieked with delight and jumped up to hug him. Alex turned and stared at his brother, who stood hands on hips frowning at him.

"Shit," was all he said.

Amal disappeared into the other room. They waited and Ben went into the bathroom to adjust his moustache in the mirror, still complaining it itched. After about half an hour Lucy walked through the door. Alex gaped at her open-mouthed.

Lucy was dressed from head to toe in traditional costume. The dress was silver and covered with gold and silver embroidery. It fell from the shoulders into wide straps over the upper arms and only a thick band of embroidery joined the bodice and wide skirt which flared from the hips, leaving her middle and lower back bare. She wore tiny embroidered slippers. Her lips were painted deep rose and numerous bangles and gold chains covered her neck arms and ankles. Her hands and feet had been decorated with traditional henna designs. Her eyes were heavily lined with black and sparkled like emeralds, too brightly Alex thought. The headdress fell away revealing tumbling waves held back from her face. Alex could just remember how she used to wear her hair like that when she was younger. He thought how beautiful she was and how proud of her he felt.

"Mum, you look beautiful. That is a fantastic dress. When did you get it, I've never seen it before?"

Lucy hesitated and her voice broke as the spoke. "It was bought for me any years ago in Tunisia before the twins were born but I never had the chance to wear it."

Only Amal knew this was a dress which a woman would wear during part of her wedding celebrations. She looked at Lucy and smiled to herself, nodding as she understood.

Ben came out of the bathroom and crept up behind his mother, circling her with his arms. Lucy smiled, turned round and gazed at him, the narrow moustache setting off his broad smile, his teeth white against his darkened face. She gave a little cry, her feet unable to move. He was Farid. He was smiling at her exactly as he had done two decades before when he walked out of the shadows of the beach bar in Hammamet. She leaned towards him and buried her face against his chest. Instinctively he put his arms round her and she him.

Amal swore, she knew this would happen. Lucy was holding the bridegroom she never had. Amal hustled her into the other room and sat beside her on the bed, talking softly as she wiped away the tears. When the door reopened, Lucy put held out her arms to her son.

"I am sorry my darling, for a second I thought you were your father." Ben looked worried and hugged her. Seeing how upset she was he said lightly "I bet he doesn't have green eyes." Lucy shook her head, thankful for his tact. "No he doesn't. You get your cat's eyes from me!"

She put the shock of seeing him to the back of her mind, as far as she was able, but her heart still pounded as she glanced at his handsome profile, so like his father.

Lucy walked between her children out of the hotel across the lawn to the back gate of the mansion. She wore her veil, a wisp of silk embroidered with gold and silver. She pushed her hair back and her eyes were hidden by her veil.

Sounds of music and voices wafted across the hot still air and they were greeted by a sea of colour. Most people had taken the traditional African theme and there were colourful long tunics, heads and bodies draped in brightly coloured materials and a few Zulu costumes with just one or two Moroccan fez hats visible. The chairman was dressed as an African Chief complete with enormous headdress. Alex noted another Laurence whose robes, he noted happily, were far inferior to his own and the chap didn't even have a sword.

They walked slowly, his mother's hand rested lightly on Ben's forearm with Alex on her other side, his hand on his sword. Rose walked in front. Ben's face was impassive but he winked at Alex. The chatter hushed to a whisper and gentle murmur went around the guests, the same question on everyone's lips. "Who are they?"

The chairman was as intrigued as his guests as to the identity of the little party. As they walked slowly towards him, Ben spotted Laura looking very pretty in a sky blue two piece costume. She stood next to another girl and Jose Butcher. He pulled slightly on his mother's arm and she stopped for a moment. He bent his head and whispered to Laura, "I hope you will keep one dance for me."

She stared at him. Ben half closed his eyes and smiled. "I am sorry I speak to you in Arabic." He repeated the invitation in heavily accented English. Laura nodded, speechless. Ben bowed deeply in acknowledgement. The family walked on. Lucy nudged him and stifled a giggle.

Laura stood watching him, her mouth open. Her friend nudged her. "What language was that?"

"He said it was Arabic," whispered the stunned girl.

"Fucking hell. He's a real fucking Arab, but who is he and what the fuck is he doing here?"

The two girls eyes remained glued to the four figures. Jose snapped at them.

"Jenny stop swearing and Laura shut your mouth, you'll catch flies."

"He's gorgeous, but who is he?" Laura persisted.

Jose looked at her. "I haven't the faintest idea, I've never seen any of them in my life and he was probably talking gobbledegook anyway."

As the little party reached the chairman, Lucy spoke in a clear but soft voice.

"Mr Bartholomew, I am Yasmine and may I present to you my children."

The chairman took the outstretched hand and the two boys bowed stiffly from the waist. Rose bent into a deep curtsey. As Lucy raised her veil and looked at him the chairman stared into a pair of laughing green eyes. Only one person he knew had eyes that colour. Entering into the spirit of the occasion the chairman said loudly, "Madame Yasmine, you and your children are most welcome."

Lucy grinned and Robin Bartholomew kissed her cheek and whispered, "Lucy, you look gorgeous. Are they really your children?" She nodded proudly.

The chairman looked from one boy to the other and despite the make-up, he could see the obvious difference between them and understood why Lucy had kept her private life to herself. Although the elder boy and the girl resembled their mother, the younger boy was an enigma. That he was Lucy's child was clear as the strange green eyes they shared but his profile and dark complexion left no doubt in his mind that a different man was his father.

He was aware how hurtful office gossip can be, particularly with disagreeable Jose Butcher involved. What he did not understand was why Miss Perfect had chosen this occasion to blow her cover. When she did explain to him later on in the evening about the conversation she had overheard, he laughed out-loud. "Good for you my girl, Good for you."

He looked around the lawn and said loudly.

"Lucy shall we dance?" and led her onto the floor. A buzz went round the guests.

"It's Lucy, Lucy Collins! You know Lucy - Miss Perfect."

"She bloody is too…" said Jonathan to the fury of Jose Butcher.

Rose had a wonderful time. She had learned a few dance moves from Hana Clark and aided by a glass of wine when her mother's back was turned, overcame her natural shyness enough to show off her skills to her enchanted audience.

Alex and Ben thoroughly enjoyed themselves. Every woman under the age of thirty, and one or two older ones who should have known better, flirted with one or both of them.

Laura, having got over the initial shock couldn't resist throwing a loud comment in Jose's direction.

"What was it you said, stunted growth, buck teeth and a lisp or just plain ugly? Get your glasses checked woman."

"Fuck off," was all the reply she received. She was even more annoyed when the Egyptian accountant confirmed Ben's Arabic was faultless.

Jonathan was amazed. He couldn't get over the transformation in Lucy. She was positively stunning, but being Jonathan he couldn't quite get his head around Ben. That Ben was her son was obvious but the fact that he spoke Arabic and looked foreign did not sit quite right with Jonathan's conventional upbringing. From that day Miss Perfect fell off her perch in Jon's eyes and although no less friendly towards her he did stop pursuing her, which suited Lucy admirably. She was quite happy to have him as a friend.

Lucy also found that most of her other colleagues who had kept their distance became more friendly now she had undoubtedly proved that not only was human after all, but she also had a good sense of humour and brilliant timing.

CHAPTER FORTY-NINE

BEN

Ben kept contact with Mr Clark and his family throughout his school life, but he knew few people who spoke Arabic outside that fraternity and so frequented a café in town owned by a Moroccan family.

The first time Lucy saw him there was when she was out shopping. She heard a burst of laughter and glanced over at a group of young men sitting around a table outside the cafe in the summer sunshine. Her gaze drifted from one to another and rested on her son's face. She hardly recognised him. He was completely at ease and definitely one of the crowd in his blue jeans and open necked white shirt, his close cropped black hair lightly gelled and glistening in the sunshine. She could hear the conversation was in Arabic.

That evening Lucy mentioned that she had seen him.

"Oh that. Yeah I go there sometimes. I like to keep up my Arabic. I may need it someday."

He grinned, nothing his mother's concern. "Mum don't worry, they're ordinary students, Algerians, Moroccans and Tunisians, not terrorists!"

"I didn't think they were!" Lucy felt old and middle aged but she relaxed

"I was just surprised to see you there and to be honest I didn't recognise you at first, you looked so…" she hesitated, "at home with them."

"Why shouldn't I be, I'm half Tune." Lucy looked up sharply. "Where did you hear that expression?"

"From a girl over here on holiday to visit family." Lucy shrugged in acknowledgement.

"What do you talk about?"

Ben looked surprised. "What do people of my age normally talk about? – music, girls, football, you know and there's a bit of politics chucked in as well. There's a bit of rumbling unrest over there at the moment so I'm told. Bad working conditions, low wages, no proper contract of employment and people at the top have a finger in too many pies taking a lot out and not giving much back. Anything they can they get their claws into and get richer while a lot of the ordinary people stay poor."

Lucy could see he was warming to the subject.

"Sweetheart, don't get too involved in the politics of another country, there's a lot going on in the world generally, not just there."

He glared at her. "Sorry, Mum." His eyes locked with hers. "I just said, I'm as much Tunisian as English, don't you remember?" She looked away and ignored the jibe although he could see she was hurt.

"Of course, I'm sorry it's just that I worry."

He smiled sheepishly. "I'm sorry too. That was unfair. But anyway I have to concentrate on my studies and Pierre's helping me with my French. As you know it was never my strongest point. His Mum is French. He's a nice guy, he's studying medicine and hopes to get into Bart's. Anyway he takes the piss out of my accent and told me to stick to Arabic."

"And the others?" she probed gently.

"Ahmed and Hamdi are still at school, but a year above me, and Azziz has just started a business course."

"Have you thought about what you want to do?"

"I quite fancy the idea of a business management course myself, if I get the exams I need."

"That's interesting, there are a lot of good courses around and where do you think you will go from there?"

"I would like to try for a place in hotel management… In Tunis," he added levelly.

"But why? Surely you'd be better off going for a job in one of the London hotels. There must be an opening for a bright, presentable young man with the languages and qualifications you will have."

Ben caught the edge of panic in her voice and tried to defuse the conversation. "You asked me if I had any idea what I wanted to do and

I've told you. But that is years away and I'll probably change my mind again."

He beamed at her. "Is there anything to eat around here?" She got up and went back into the kitchen, her mind uneasy. She had known that as Ben grew older she would no longer be able to push Tunisia to the back of her mind, but she had tried to convince herself she could deal with that as and when it arose.

CHAPTER FIFTY

DESTINY

It was an exceptionally cold day in April as Lucy hurried to the tube station. She hated the underground, but had business to attend to. After Peter died she invested wisely and made an annual pilgrimage to the City and her financial adviser to discuss matters generally. She hadn't slept well and her head was pounding. She was late which was unlike her and she had been in two minds as to whether to call and change her appointment. Her mood was not helped by Ben's attitude of late which was entering into the typical stage of a teenager convinced he knew everything and she hadn't forgotten his comment about working in Tunisia.

With Rose, life was so much easier. She was a stunningly beautiful teenager. Over the years her hair had darkened to a rich tawny blonde. Her deep golden eyes held the same mesmeric magnetism as her father's. She shared her mother's clear porcelain skin with only a tint of olive. Her generous mouth curved upwards and when she smiled, which was most of the time, her face lit up and her eyes sparkled. Save for her obsession with becoming an actress, Rose had no idea what she wanted to do after her school years and was happy to drift through her life, enjoying her studies and in her spare time her activities were much the same as any young person of her age. Although she rarely spoke of it, Lucy knew her daughter still held onto her acting dream. She had caused her mother no particularly anguish over her fifteen years which was a relief in that Lucy had found as the weeks passed that she needed regularly to draw on her reserves of strength to cope with the problem that was Ben.

The boy had matured quickly and the shadow of a moustache made him appear older beyond his years. He was already too popular in her opinion with the girls at school who found him fascinating, particularly the way his silky black lashes half veiled his eyes under high arched browns and the little half smile which promised things way beyond his years.

Lucy listened to the monotonous rumbling of the tube as she thought over the particularly disturbing conversation she had with her younger son a week or so earlier. The whole thing had started over nothing.

Lucy was suffering from one of those evenings when the past kept flooding back. The house was in darkness when she arrived back from work. Rose was staying with a friend overnight so she made herself a sandwich, took the half-full bottle of wine out of the fridge and watched a hopelessly romantic film on the television, which had not helped at all. After a good cry she opened her photo album and flicked through the pages, the details of each picture as clear in her mind as the day it was taken. She opened another bottle and sat quietly thinking as she waited for Ben.

As the clock marched on relentlessly towards midnight her concern mixed with fear. She poured herself another glass. She felt a bit light-headed. He was still only fifteen, but she found it hard to accept that her beloved child was fast approaching manhood. As she heard the door open softly she glanced up at the clock.

Ben crept into the kitchen and she waited but said nothing. He was quite obviously surprised and then annoyed to see her.

"You couldn't sleep then?" he muttered defensively. She nodded.

He sat down opposite her, his eyes glittering. "Well no words of recrimination, you surprise me, Mother."

His lips curled in a derisory smile. Something had obviously upset him as he was rarely unkind or rude to her.

"Ben, you may think you are already a man but you are of an age when you could make some terrible mistakes which could alter the rest of your life and I could not bear that. I love you too much."

Her son's eyes softened and as he leaned forward to take her hands in his. He smiled. "And beautiful lady, I love you," he whispered.

Lucy snatched her hands back as though she had been bitten. To Ben's amazement the tears welled up in his mother's eyes as the years fell away and she remembered the words another boy had whispered to her. She clenched her eyes tightly shut.

"Sweet Jesus, Mum, what the hell did I say?" He stood bending over her, his arms tightly around he and she wept as she tried to bury her face against his chest. "Oh Farid, where are you my love?" she breathed.

Ben stiffened and pulled away. "What did you say?"

He sat down heavily opposite her and looked searchingly at his mother. Lucy shook her head wordlessly and closed her eyes again.

"Mum, look at me, Mum please." A shudder racked through her as she forced herself to look at him. His expression was a mixture of confusion and anger.

"It's him, isn't it? My father? Why is it you always refuse to speak to me about him?"

Lucy tried frantically to gather her senses. Damn the bloody wine, how could she have been so stupid but his smile and words had been a mirror to her soul.

Ben took her hands again, his grip firm. "You will speak to me. And don't do what you always do and tell me it's late and we'll talk tomorrow because we never do. Do you realise I'll be sixteen this year. I could be married soon. How do you think it feels to know I will have to produce a birth certificate stating Father unknown?" He stopped as he saw the hurt in her face. "You still love him, don't you?" It was more a statement than a question.

"Yes, Ben I still love him, I have never stopped loving him and I will always love him."

"Then why did you split up?"

"I left him because I love him."

"That doesn't make sense," he muttered.

Her voice gained momentum as she tried to defend herself. "You think you know it all, you know nothing. Your father is from a different world and a culture so alien to our own that you could never start to understand. His are a proud people to whom family is the cornerstone." The words flowed unchecked. "Marriage to a much older woman already with a child by someone else and who is pregnant as well was unacceptable. He would have married me and ruined his whole life. My son, love was never the problem, only prejudice."

Ben's face had paled and his grip tightened on her wrists so that she felt the thick gold ring he wore cutting into her skin. "You're hurting me."

His grip loosened, but only slightly. "And have you ever thought what you are doing to us? I know it doesn't seem to worry Rose but it sure as hell worries me. I have a father I have never met and who has never once tried to contact me. Has he?" he added uncertainly.

Lucy shook her head angrily and squirmed in the chair trying to free herself from his hold.

"So in other words he couldn't give a shit."

Angrily she pulled against him. "No Ben, you're wrong! He was distraught when I left. It was only when I stupidly went back for Ellen's wedding that I learned he had done well for himself and had recently married, as he should, to a young Tunisian girl who has given him a child. It broke my heart but finally I knew that in leaving I had done the right thing."

Ben sat impassively waiting. She glared at him. His hands were tight around her wrists and she was held prisoner. Suddenly she pulled hard against him, caution thrown to the wind as alcohol and emotion took over.

She shrieked at him. "You are totally wrong Ben, the reason he didn't try to find you is that he doesn't know you and Rose exist."

The room was suddenly completely silent then Ben exploded.

"He doesn't know we exist! What sort of shit is that! What the fucking hell about me? It's okay for Rose, she looks like you but the taunts I went through as a child, the times I needed a father to talk to and all you ever thought about was him and yourself. God almighty, you have hardly ever spoken his name. I know nothing about him and now you tell me he doesn't even know I exist. Christ, Mum, I've never even seen a photo of him. Any normal woman who loved someone would at least have a photograph of him."

Lucy was furious, angry at herself for being so stupid, angry with Ben for asking the questions to which she had no answer and most of all angry with him for being the image of his father, reminding her every day of what she had lost.

"Don't you dare shout at me," she screamed "I have my photographs, I have just never shown them to you. Oh yes, I have suffered leaving the man I loved and watching the product of that love grow into the man I lost." Her voice had risen to a hysterical scream, she snatched her hands away and jumped to her feet. She clenched her fists and banged them on the table.

"You want to know what your father looks like? - look in the mirror and you will see your father. You are his image. Don't you realise how deeply I love you? I love you twice, first because you are my son and again because you are all I have left of the love I can never have."

Ben's expression changed to fear as he digested his mother's words. Slowly he stood up.

"Mum, you said 'marriage to a much older woman'. How old were you when you met him?"

"I was twenty-six," she shouted without thinking.

"Well you can't have been that much older than him," he yelled back.

He was totally unprepared for his mother's reaction. Lucy stared at him, hands on hips, a slight smile on her face. "I am nearly twelve years older than him."

Ben gasped in horror, his brain trying to make some sense of the figures and failing. "That makes it years before Alex was born. My father must have been about my age."

The expression of disgust on his young face shocked her but Lucy felt a detached calm as she spoke, although the words seemed to come from someone else.

"Two and two do not always make four." He stared at her. She fixed her eyes on a spot on the wall over his head as she prepared herself for the time she had always known would come.

"I met your father for the first time for only a few minutes when he was a teenager. It was my first holiday to Tunisia, but I never forgot him. There was something about him which frightened me. The words he said to me at that first meeting were the words you said when you came in tonight. After the holiday I returned to England and a year later I met and eventually married Alex's father, Peter. It was only after Peter died I met your father again, years later."

She glanced up at her son, who seemed to have recovered his composure slightly. She turned from him and went to her bedroom. At the back of the wardrobe she pulled out the little basket in which she kept her treasures, her magic box. When she was a child she heard a young actress say that she kept all her most important treasures in one box, her magic box. Lucy had bought the wicker basket the next day and had since that time kept a souvenir of all the things which had mattered in her life. She pulled out some photographs, look a deep breath and returned to the kitchen. With a strange expression she handed one of them to Ben.

He stared at a picture of his mother next to a tall young man in uniform with a wide smile, his arm loosely around his mother's shoulders, taken at night.

"The evening we met for the second time."

Mutely, Ben took the second photograph she handed to him. It was a picture of a smiling boy approaching manhood, silhouetted against a brilliant blue sky. It could have been him. He stared at his mother.

"That was the first time I saw Farid."

Ben closed his eyes and whispered, "Now I understand."

Finally Lucy gave him the last photograph. It showed an elderly couple, a large man with a ruddy face and an elderly woman in a floral dress with a big hat. Peter sat beside them beaming at the camera and a young Alex sat on his knee. Ben looked puzzled.

"Will you tell me about it?"

She nodded, "Yes, I think it is time, you have a right to know and I hope you will now be able to properly understand. That last photo is of Alex and his father with Alice and Henry. We met them in Lanzarote on holiday shortly before Peter died." She explained about Alice's prediction. "Of course I was sceptical; I have never been one for fortune telling but there were some things she said which made me think. After Peter died something drew me back to Tunisia and by an incredible coincidence I met your father again."

"You went back to the same place where you first saw him?"

She smiled at him. "No, Ben, we met in a completely different part of the country. It was pure chance."

It was Ben's turn to smile. "No, Mum, it was destiny. Insh'allah, as Allah willed it, Mrs Clark explained that some things are like that." He was perfectly serious. "And so that is the end of the story. It is just a shame that your friend Alice could not see further into the future for a happy ending for us all."

Lucy ran her tongue over her dry lips, avoiding his gaze.

"There is more, Mum?"

"Alice said one day I would go back."

"When?"

"She didn't say, but she said I would know when the time was right."

"But not yet?" Lucy saw the hope in her child's face and smiled at him.

"No my love, not yet, but someday. I made you a promise the day you were born that when you became a young man and able to understand that I would take you back, both of you."

Ben smiled. "Then I will wait." He got up, kissed her cheek and silently walked off to his bedroom.

Lucy made herself a coffee and sat quietly, her hands clasped around the mug. The silence was broken only by the steady ticking of the clock. Eventually she dragged herself wearily up the stairs feeling totally drained. She slept little that night and her dreams transported her back to the quiet beauty of the warm sandy beach and to Farid. He stood alone, his arms outstretched towards her and then he faded away.

The train rumbled on but Lucy's mind was still on her conversation with Ben. She pulled her scarf tightly around her neck. Even inside the tunnels the cold reached its nasty prying fingers into her bones. Inside the train was reasonably warm but each time the doors opened, the cold rushed in again.

She shivered and longed for the sweet breeze and clear sunshine of springtime. It was late this year. Lucy loved England in in the spring, the soft light rain keeping everything fresh. She loved the opulent pink cherry blossom and the gaiety of the spring tulips, life emerging from the ground after winter's cold. She loved flowers and May was the herald of the summertime medley of freesia, roses and lilies. Most of all she loved the pale pink droplets which would become the sweetly scented white star-shaped jasmine flowers of summer. The jasmine she had planted when she came back from Tunisia the year the twins was born, that now spread lazily over the arch outside her kitchen window permeating the house with its perfume and reminding her of the bitter sweetness of a life long ago she had thought would never end.

She glanced out of the window and jumped to her feet, having nearly missed her stop. As she stood in line with the commuters she felt every one of her fifty-plus years. The altercation with Ben had left her drained and she knew there would be more questions when he had fully considered the impact of what she had told him, although so far he had not raised the matter again.

As the escalator carried its passengers on its never-ending mechanical journey Lucy studied the advertisements. Adverts for perfume, cosmetics, London theatre shows, exhibitions and travel, set in neat rectangular blocks, each leading to the next, often repeated as though in harmony with the monotony of life. The escalator discharged her into the rush hour crush.

Lucy's eyes continued to flick idly from one advert to the next as she was carried along the river of humanity following the other lemmings along the tunnel. Suddenly she felt as though she had been kicked in the stomach.

She stopped and stared at the wall, her breath caught in her throat. Completely oblivious to the vociferous comments of the commuters bottling up behind her, Lucy stood motionless staring at the brightly coloured picture which came at her in third dimension.

In large letters arched over the top of the poster 'TUNISIA' against a background of the desert. Beneath the words merging into the scenes she knew so well, the majesty of El Djem and the blue and white buildings of Sidi Bou Said, in smaller letters she read

'A land of ancient history, majestic ruins, amazing desert and luxury hotels. All this, warm sunshine and the clear blue Mediterranean sea.' She stared at the words along the bottom of the poster

"Come to Tunisia, the land where dreams come true."

"Words written on subway walls…".

How Lucy got through the day she had no idea. A dense fog enveloped her and she was unable to register anything beyond the enormity of what she had decided to do. That evening before going home and before she could change her mind, she handed in her notice to the amazement of her department manager, who long ago had decided that nice Mrs Collins was a totally reliable, pleasant employee who lived for her children and her job, and who would eventually need to be forced into retirement.

"You are going to do what?"

"I am taking a long holiday."

"Where?" he asked unnecessarily.

"Tunisia." He repeated the name unconvinced.

"But why hand in your notice, especially now when we are so busy?"

Lucy hesitated. "Well, I can stay for three months, if that is all right with you." He smiled at her, noting the hesitation.

"Look, Lucy, I am sure with your exemplary record we could come to some arrangement, if you want to take a long holiday."

He was astonished when his trusty employee smiled in a way he had never seen her smile in all the years she had worked for him. The smile which lit up her face in what was clearly, even to the cynical man watching her, the look of a woman in love. Surely the middle aged, but undoubtedly still very attractive, Mrs Collins had not fallen in love.

He realised for the first time that he actually knew very little about her, only that she lived alone with her daughter and two sons, who by their appearance obviously had different fathers. He had been at the barbecue in the summer but thought little of it. If the truth be known he never really took much interest in the lives of his employees outside the office. So long as their work was up to scratch they could live in trees with monkeys for all he cared. He knew from her records she was a widow but Lucy had never spoken of her life and he had never asked.

Tunisia, he thought quickly, could that be something to do with the younger boy's father?

"Pardon me, Lucy. Are you sure what you are doing?"

"Yes, Donald, for the first time in my life I am following my destiny."

Whatever reply he had expected, it was not that one. Completely out of his depth, he muttered, "Well if you change your mind, you know where to find us."

Lucy flashed him one beaming smile. "Thank you, Donald, but I will not change my mind, not this time."

On her way home that evening, Lucy called into the local travel agency and picked up a brochure. The hand that unlocked the front door was unsteady and she was pleased to see the house was in darkness. By the jacket flung carelessly across the arm of the settee and the shoes discarded under the table, Lucy knew Ben had been in, changed and gone out again and then she remembered, the twins had gone ice skating.

There had been a row the previous evening when Rose informed him she was going with her boyfriend and Ben had been adamant she was not going alone. He didn't like Jason Berry and didn't trust him. The boy was at least two years older than Rose and already had a reputation Ben did not care for. Lucy was thankful for the silence which gave her time to think. Whatever she felt, there were other people to consider. Her children.

That evening, she called Alex and asked him if he would come over. Although she tried to keep her voice steady, her son knew that whatever it was his mother had to say, he needed to be there. An hour later, mother and son sat in Lucy's comfortable kitchen at the table where only a short while ago, which now seemed a light year away, she had sat with his brother.

"Well, Mum, come on. Whatever it is I know it is important. Don't keep me in suspense, spit it out."

He grinned and Lucy smiled back indulgently. Not for the first time she congratulated herself on having two handsome sons, so close to each other and yet so different. Alex, 6 foot 4 of lanky Englishman, his pale face and blue eyes so like his father, cheerful and happy go lucky but with an underlying sense of responsibility which had only surfaced since his marriage.

She felt a pang of loneliness as she remembered the short but happy years she had spent with Peter. She was pleased Peter had left a legacy, not only in her son, but in Alex's baby girl, Amy, whom he worshipped. At the thought of her granddaughter, Lucy felt a pang of guilt. If she followed her dream, would she lose her family? There was so much to consider.

And Ben. The opposite of his brother, an inch or two shorter, his honey brown skin and curly black hair so different from his brother, moody and quick to anger. Although ten years separated them the two had been close since Ben was born. Alex fought the youngster's battles for him and Ben worshipped his big brother. As they matured the sibling love between them grew ever stronger and when Alex married Ben immediately took Alex's little plump wife to his heart.

Again Lucy was troubled. Could she in her own selfishness jeopardise the bond between the brothers and if her dream came true, move her younger children a thousand miles away, or would it all come to nothing anyway. Her head ached.

Alex watched her face as her expression changed with her thoughts.

"Mum, I'm still here. Hello! What is it you want to tell me?"

"I've quit my job. I leave in three months."

"Is that all. Why?"

"Because I've decided to take a long holiday."

Alex waited. "And?" She was silent. "Does this have anything to do with Ben's strange mood over the last week or so?"

"You've spoken to Ben?"

"Yes. I saw him at lunchtime. He was waffling on about some woman's prediction and you going off to seek your fortune. It didn't make an awful lot of sense."

Lucy smiled. "It isn't exactly like that." She explained the exchange between herself and Ben. Alex was incredulous.

"Bloody hell! No wonder Ben is wandering around in a daze. I admit Mum, I think I'd be pretty pissed off too if I had just found out my father didn't even know I'd been born."

"That's very easy to say and a lot harder to have dealt with at the time," she snapped.

Alex ignored the remark. "Anyway, how does all that affect us and why have you suddenly decided to up sticks? From what Ben said you can't go yet 'cos you're waiting for a sign or some such mumbo-jumbo.' Anyway, with respect, Mum, sometimes I think you forget you are no spring chicken to go gadding off around the world on a whim."

The tension broken, Lucy grinned. "Thank you for that vote of confidence, my dear!"

"No, Mum, I'm serious. If you were waiting for a sign, God that sounds ludicrous… then how come you have suddenly chucked in your job and are ready to travel?"

"Quite simple. I saw something today which made me realise that the time is now."

Before Alex could press the point, Lucy hurried on.

"The reason I asked you to come over, before I speak to Ben and Rose, is that I need to know how you feel about it."

"What, about you taking a long holiday travelling – fine, you deserve it. You've worked your butt off for years and you rarely take much of a holiday, so as far as I am concerned, go for it!"

"And what if I should find what I am looking for?"

"Shit, you mean their father?" She nodded. Alex's face was a mixture of fear and exasperation.

"Mum, have some sense. In any case, how can you find one man after so many years in a country of millions? And…" he added ominously, "Ben tells me you think he is already married with a child."

"That's the part I don't understand. Everything else Alice said was right. It doesn't make sense, but it is one of the choices I have to make and I have a nagging feeling that if I ignore this I will regret it for the rest of my life. I know that sounds melodramatic but I have to know."

She stopped for a moment and took a sip of wine. "Actually, Alex, the whole thing has been hanging over me like a shroud ever since some friend of Ellen's I have never met before told me at her wedding years ago she'd been out with him. She seemed terribly interested in me and I got the impression that she knew who I was, which is when she told me he was married."

Alex stared at her. "Doesn't that seem to you to be an enormous coincidence? Are you sure she wasn't simply jealous because he'd given her the push? You were a very beautiful woman and you still are, or so my friends tell me."

He grinned and Lucy blushed. "Alex, behave!" Lucy slapped him playfully but the more she thought about it, the more possible it seemed. She recalled how the girl was so eager to push the fact that it was the same Farid who was now married. But again, she had herself seen him with the girl and baby. No this was not a straw she could clutch in all common sense. She must accept that he was now a father, and attached to another woman. She could play no part in his future.

But there was Ben and for his sake she needed to find Farid. She had no doubt in her mind that essentially Tunisian family values would have remained unaltered, but times must surely have changed a little. She reasoned that acceptance or at least recognition of grown up children would not be as hard to deal with as accepting a pregnant older woman and her child by another man would have been some sixteen years before. No, her mind was made up. What she must do is find him and let him meet his children on his own terms, without her involvement. She owed that to all three of them and the decision as to what to do with their relationship must be theirs not hers.

Alex's cheery voice cut into her thoughts. "Maybe this omen or whatever it is means that you are destined to find someone else there."

"Don't be so bloody daft!" *Anyway I don't want to meet anyone else*, she added to herself.

"Mum listen to me. You have taken care of me for all of my life. I have my own family now, my own home and I am happy. If by some miracle you do find him and things work out for you, if you do want to live abroad, and thousands of people do you know, then that's fine by me. So long as you promise we can visit you and vice versa I can live with that, but have you thought about how this will affect Ben? I know he is a wretched know-all sometimes, but the fact is he is still only sixteen."

"Not quite…" she murmured.

He ignored her. "And Rose, what of poor Rose? You know she is not like Ben, she has never taken much interest in her father and you plan to uproot her from everything she knows and dump her in a foreign country?"

"Darling, I am quite sure that their father will want nothing to do with me and as you said he is married with his own family. I behaved badly and I am sure he does not want to be reminded of that time in his life. But I cannot escape the fact that my children have a right to know their father. When, and if being a very big word, I do find Farid, it will be up to them.

"Farid is a good man at heart and whatever else, I am convinced I owe them all a chance to decide for themselves. He will not blame his children for their mother's mistakes. At least I can hope that he will allow both of them to visit him sometimes if they so wish."

Privately, Alex thought the whole sorry business would end in tears. His poor mother was blatantly still crazy about this man, whoever he was, and Alex could see no happy ending for her but he kept his thoughts to himself. There was also the point to consider that Ben and almost certainly Rose might not want to go. Whatever decisions they made, Alex knew he had to offer his support and just be there when they needed him, as they always had for been him.

"When are you thinking of going?"

"I've said I'll work three months' notice and I thought about September. Ben and Rose will have finished exams and it will give us all time to think."

"So all you have to do now is talk to them."

God help us all, she thought.

"Will you stay until they come home? I'd rather talk about it with you beside me."

Alex nodded his agreement.

The front door slammed to announce the arrival of her younger children. Ben strode in first carrying his skates, a deep frown on his face and his mouth set in anger. He left the door open and flung his jacket on the back of the chair and his skates on the floor. Rose crept in a minute later and Lucy could see she was upset. She started to speak but the word's died on her lips as Ben glared at her.

"Don't even ask. That sodding thug tried it on with Rose. He asked her to go with him to get a Coke and instead took her round the back of the rink in those bushes. It was only 'cos I hate the sight of him that I followed them."

Lucy put her arms out to her daughter. Rose clung to her mother sobbing. For all her beauty she was a gentle child, small for her age and with her soft golden eyes looked more like a fawn than a teenage girl, but Lucy felt she had to ask the question.

"Rose, sweetheart, look at me." Rose raised her tear-stained face. "Did you know what Jason was going to do and has he ever done it before?" Rose burst into loud sobs and Lucy saw Ben clench his fists. Lucy stroked her daughter's hair and waited until she spoke.

"No, honestly, Mum, I didn't know. Yes he has kissed me and he did try to put his hand inside my T-shirt at that party last weekend, but he stopped when I told him not to."

"Did he hurt you?"

"No, he did not. I got there before he could!" Lucy smiled gratefully at Ben.

"And I can tell you I don't think he will be back," Ben added with an ugly smirk. Lucy's smile faded.

"What did you do?"

"I kicked him in the balls and from the state of him at the time, I think it will be a long time before he tries it on with another girl."

"Ben!" Lucy spluttered. Alex grinned.

"And you hit him, there was blood everywhere," Rose added with a snuffle.

"Go on, Ben."

The boy stared at her unrepentant. "Yes, Rosie's right, I did hit him, twice in the face right where it is going to show. Now people know what will happen if they mess with my sister."

Rose went over and hugged him. Ben kissed the top of her head and pushed her away from him gently, clearly embarrassed. "It's okay Rosie, no harm done, just be more careful in future."

He turned back to Alex. "Anyway Lurch, what have you and Mum been cooking up? When we came in you looked involved in some sort of plot."

"Sit down, Ben." The words seemed to Lucy to come from another person. Ben frowned. "What have I done now?"

Lucy smiled. "Nothing, well other than what you have just told me. We just need to talk."

Ben pulled up a chair and sat resting his elbows on the table. "Do you remember what we were talking about before?"

"I can hardly forget it," he replied curtly.

Rose looked puzzled. "What were you talking about with Ben?"

"I believe the time has come for us to go to Tunisia."

Ben's stared at her. "But I thought…"

Lucy cut him short. "That aside, do you want to go?"

"Bloody hell, Mum, that's all a bit sudden isn't it? When are you thinking of going? Anyway what about exams?" he added.

"When the exams are finished, in September."

Rose let out a wail. "I don't want to go, why do I have to go?"

"Don't you want to go on holiday to a lovely place with a huge swimming pool, beautiful warm sea and a long beach? You will be able to see the girls dancing, you know like that lovely outfit you wore to the barbecue."

Rose broke into a huge smile. "Oh, that's different. Would I be able to dance with them?"

Alex put his arm around her. "Only if you can balance the clay pot on your head!"

He winked at his mother over the top of Rose's head and she returned the gesture.

Rose jumped up and thumped Alex. "Oh you are horrible, you are making fun of me, I only wanted to dance."

"Sweetpea, I am sure if you are good enough you will be able to dance with them. I saw you at the barbecue and you were really good."

Rose smiled tentatively at him. "Do you really mean that?"

"Yes I do," replied Alex seriously.

"Then I will go!" She sat down and crossed her arms in front of her. "Can I have some new clothes?"

The family stayed long into the night talking and weighing up the options and possibilities. Rose fell asleep on the chair. Lucy was impressed by the maturity of her two sons. Finally, Ben asked the question she had been waiting for.

"What if we do find my father and he doesn't want to know me?"

Lucy looked at him for a moment and grinned. "How could he not want to know you, how could he not accept a mirror image of himself? He will definitely want to know you." Her words were strong and said with a total conviction that unfortunately Alex did not share.

Ben couldn't wait to tell his friends. With youthful enthusiasm he told everyone. Lucy had forgotten to ask him to omit the fact he was going to hopefully meet his father.

Her embarrassment was compounded by the knowing looks and nudges which came from one or two of her acquaintances. She could almost hear the whispers.

"So, Mrs Collins is finally going off to find her children's father. I suppose he left her in the lurch, probably some holiday romance. What makes her think he'll want either her or his kids now? Silly cow!"

Lucy didn't care. They could assume what they wanted. Few people knew the truth and they were the ones who mattered.

M of course thought she was quite mad.

"You can't go back. It's taken you years to get over him and now you want to open up Pandora's Box. You tried it once before when you went to that bloody wedding and you came back a quivering wreck. Now you want to do it again."

"This has nothing to do with Pandora," Lucy quipped feebly. "I'm doing this for Ben. He has learned the language here from an Englishman and the culture from a book. He has the right to know a country of which he is as much a part as England."

"Lucy, you are a romantic and a dangerously stupid one, I might add. Ben has come to terms with who he is, an Englishman who happens to have a foreign father. You must be off your head," she added bluntly.

"Quite probably," said Lucy and listened to every possible reason her friend could conjure up as to why she shouldn't go, which culminated in a rather lame, "You should let sleeping dogs lie."

"Unfortunately, M, this dog has a pup and the pup wants his dad."

"And what about the other pup?"

"She isn't too bothered and thinks Ben makes a huge fuss. Her best friend from school doesn't have her dad living with her. As I understand it she was the product of a one night stand with a Spanish guy so Rosie has never thought it a big deal. She is happy to go because she thinks she is going for a nice holiday and can join the dancers. And of course she has been promised new clothes."

"I still think you are bonkers and unfortunately I am quite sure that if you do ever find him, he'll only break your heart, again," she added with emphasis.

"M, if you remember I left him."

"Okay, so you broke each other's hearts. Anyway what makes you think he'll even agree to see you, particularly if as you say he now has a family?" M hoped that this would be the killer blow to make her dearest friend see sense.

Lucy thought for a moment. "Actually, I don't need to meet him."

"What d'you mean, isn't that why you're going, and anyway why now after all this time?"

"I am going for my children and I am going now because I know this is the right time for me to go."

M's eyebrows shot up. "How?"

Lucy explained quickly about the advert on the tube and expected to be told she had completely lost her marbles, but to her surprise her friend just smiled.

"Maybe this is the right time. This whole charade has been eating away at you for too long, but tell me, Lucy, because I know you as well as anyone, are you serious when you say if you do find him you don't need to meet him."

The mask of fierce resolve did not hide the pain M could see so clearly. "Oh, Lucy, why drag yourself through hell and back? You've been there once already. You don't fool me, I know you would give ten years of your life to see him again."

Lucy bowed her head. "Of course you are right and I am certain he would cut me dead after the trouble I have caused him, but it would honestly be worth any pain if I could just see him one more time."

"Lucy think, do you really want to see him? He's no longer the boy you met, or even the man you left behind sixteen years ago. Why not remember him as he was. By now he's probably fat and bald with a double chin and minus half his teeth."

Lucy gave a watery grin. "M, he's in his forties, he's not that old."

"Agreed, but Lucy you are and you need to accept it. There is an awful lot of difference between a woman in her thirties and her fifties. I hate to say it because you have weathered advancing years a lot better than most of us lesser mortals, but the fact remains you are still a woman the wrong side of fifty. Don't you want him to hold onto his own dream of the beautiful woman he loved so much?"

"That is a chance I have to take."

Marie realised she couldn't persuade her friend this was the craziest thing she had ever done and gave up.

"D'you want me to come with you?".

To her relief Lucy shook her head. "No, but thanks. This is something I have to do by myself."

CHAPTER FIFTY-ONE

A DECISION MADE

It seemed strange asking the travel agent for a holiday in Tunisia after so many years. The young woman smiled her professional white toothed smile, reciting standard phrases, her voice on automatic pilot expounding the virtues of Tunisia. Lucy let her speak and when she stopped for breath Lucy said quietly, "I have been before, just not for a number of years."

"Oh, I'm sorry, do you know where you want to stay?"

Lucy had tossed this over in her mind. She didn't want to stay in Tunis or in the south, she had thought of Sousse or Hammamet. She had no idea where Farid would be or even if he still worked in the tourist industry for that matter. She was quite confused and had eventually decided on the new resort a few miles south of the old town of Hammamet. If Farid was still in tourism she felt it would be the likeliest place to look, although the words 'needle' and 'haystack' came to mind.

"There has been some recent building between the old town of Hammamet and the new resort which is in the course of construction, Yasmine Hammamet. Would that interest you?"

Lucy smiled. "That is exactly what I was thinking. When I was there it hadn't been built."

The girl reverted to professional mode. "Oh, I understand it is very elegant, quite European in fact. They are still building at one end of the resort but there are some good hotels. What type of hotel do you prefer, modern, traditional, luxury or family? All the ones we deal with cater for the holidaymaker, lovely swimming pools, enough English food to be comfortable and some English speaking staff."

Lucy looked at her thoughtfully, of course that was what a lot of tourists wanted nowadays, little England abroad, none of this nasty foreign food and people who understood them without having to make the effort of making yourself understood in another language.

She wondered how long it would be before Tunisia fell victim to the all-inclusive bug which had ravaged Spain and other popular destinations. In her opinion there was little point in going somewhere like Tunisia if you just wanted to eat three meals per day in the hotel, drink as much as you could, lie by the pool and never venture further than a few yards from the hotel entrance. What about the beauty of the countryside, the local people, local food, the fascinating history of the country itself. The spirit of adventure had deserted most people.

The girl was fidgeting and wondered if this woman actually intended to make a booking or not. Lucy looked back at her and immediately the plastic smile reappeared. Lucy wondered whether she bleached her teeth as well as her hair.

"I am travelling with my son and daughter and we don't really mind about the English side of things. We eat everything, we all speak French and my son also speaks Arabic." Lucy couldn't resist adding the last part and the girl looked suitable impressed.

"Oh, well in that case I think you might like the Palms. It's quite traditional and on the end of the main promenade just over the road from the sea, about ten minutes to the Medina and about the same again to the harbour." Lucy looked surprised.

"If the resort is just being built, how is there a Medina?"

The girl beamed indulgently. "People who go to North Africa nowadays like to visit the markets so when they decided to build the new resort they included a Medina. Very smart I understand with little souvenir shops, courtyards with cafés and restaurants, and even a theatre." Lucy forced a smile, remembering the ancient majesty of the soft stone walls of the Hammamet Medina with its central narrow winding passageways and little studios and shops set back into the walls. She winced.

"A new Medina, so they thought of everything." She spoke softly, half to herself.

The girl missed her meaning completely. "Oh, absolutely, but of course there is the old Medina at Hammamet a few miles away, if you prefer that sort of thing, and the cabs are cheap and cheerful."

Lucy chose the Palms and booked for a month. If she couldn't sort out her problems in that time then she felt it was not meant to be. She paid the full price in advance, just in case she decided to change her mind. The salesgirl looked thrilled; this was indeed a good booking she had closed. To say the parties concerned had mixed emotions was an understatement. Ben was ecstatic, Rose excited, Alex deeply concerned and Lucy plain terrified.

The children's exams were over and the arrangements were made. It was warm day in September when Lucy and her children boarded the plane.

Lucy had chosen the hotel because it was on the edge of the resort centre. She convinced herself that she would be less likely to meet anyone knew. It was completely illogical reasoning. In a country of millions of people it was in any event a remote possibility, ignoring the fact she had only been back for a week in sixteen years. She was still nervous that one day she might bump into Farid unprepared. Although part of her yearned to see his beloved face once again, she knew that many years had passed, and would there be, as the saying goes 'too much water under the bridge'.

To have made the decision to come back based solely on the poster in the underground and a prediction made more than twenty years before had been crazy. She thought of Alice and words spoken long ago. But this was her choice and now she was here.

For the first few days they stayed in or near the hotel but Lucy grew restless and one afternoon she left the children by the pool saying she wanted to look around the shops. She took a taxi to Hammamet old town. She followed the pathway which led between the sea and the large cafe next to the Medina. The sea was calm, its colours blending in shades of deep azure and pale turquoise where the sand was close to the surface. Here and there a line of deep black shadows indicated the ancient rocks lurking just below the water. She watched as a group of boys played in the shallows, diving from the rocks and smiled at their whoops of delight as they disappeared into the clear depths before rising like seals, their lithe tanned bodies glistening in the bright sunlight.

The path was wide and wound along the rise of the low banks down to the sea, the brownish yellow cobbles intermixed with dirty grey sand. It meandered aimlessly separating the sea from the graveyard which lay silent behind high rough walls.

Lucy walked slowly, the heat of the sun strong on her bare shoulders and she was relieved when the pathway met the road back towards the Medina. She noticed a cafe opposite the Medina, which she was sure had not been there before. It looked new and welcoming, raised as it was from the road, the large square orange sunshades offering blessed cool from the midday heat.

She sat sipping her water, her eyes taking in the uneven mottled stones of the old building with the minaret rising awkwardly from behind the palisade, incongruous in its comparative newness, a gleaming creamy white obelisk with a single band of neat sandy bricks linking it to the soft worn beige of the ancient Medina.

Her eyes were drawn to the little cafe opposite, nestled into the protection of the walls, overhung by dense trees, dark and comforting. She remembered sitting there with Farid and Saleem so many summers ago. It had not changed. Its old white furniture had seen better days but somehow its very shabbiness made the memory more real. She wondered idly if the chairs were the same ones and dismissed the thought as ridiculous. How the mind conjured up such idiocies.

She wondered what he was doing. Was he perhaps at home with his wife and family, or did he now live in Sousse or was he asleep at his lodgings after a long shift. Was he so close she could almost touch him or was he perhaps he was now thousands of miles away in another country to seek his fortune like so many others? She smiled. No she was sure he would never leave his beloved Tunisia. He was here. She could feel him. She closed her eyes.

"Madame, you would like something else?"

The waiter's soft deep voice shook her back to the present. She shook her head.

"No thank you, I was just dreaming."

Lucy smiled and rose to leave. He held out his hand and she took it. She looked up into a gentle intelligent face. He nodded his head. "I understand Madame, Tunisia she is a land of dreams, and sometimes they come true." Lucy stared at him.

CHAPTER FIFTY-TWO

THE CASTLE AND AN OLD FRIEND

The children were happy to stay near the hotel and bask in the sun near the pool and beach. Ben, with the optimism of the young was quite convinced he would meet his father and as they were on holiday for a month saw no reason not to enjoy himself. Lucy went out alone a couple of times to have a look around the small shops set into the base of the hotel. As she walked back into the hotel she passed one of the smaller cafés. A man sat by himself at the table nearest to the roadway and was staring at her with a mixture of interest and surprise. As she passed he stood up and followed her a short distance behind. She turned and looked at him and then suddenly remembered the man who had followed her and Jackie that day in Sousse after Ali's wedding, but that would surely be too much of a coincidence.

This man wore big dark glasses but she simply couldn't place him. As before, there was a niggle that she knew him but more than that she couldn't remember. He was small and wiry with a weasel like face and oily complexion. He ran his hand through lank greying hair and smirked at her. She shuddered and walked quickly back into the hotel. To her dismay he followed her inside and started talking to the same reception clerk who had checked her into the hotel. The clerk retrieved some papers and she saw the weasel faced man run his finger down the page and nod. Instead of going outside where Rose and Ben were in the pool Lucy went directly to the lift and her room.

The children came up later in the afternoon and Lucy had already showered and changed for dinner. She was relieved to see them but said nothing. The evening passed without incident and Lucy was pleased to see the man was nowhere to be seen.

On impulse she phoned Alex and during the conversation she mentioned the man she had seen. He made no response.

"Alex? Are you still there?"

"Yes Mum, of course, who was that man? Do you know him?"

"I am sure I have seen him before, more than once and he certainly seemed to know me, which is surprising considering how long it is since I was there."

"Was he a friend of Farid perhaps?"

"No, I am sure not. He seemed a furtive sort of person, in fact he quite gave me the creeps. No, definitely he is not the sort of person to be friends with Farid."

"Well just be careful. If you are worried about it or anything else, call me and I'll be on the next plane."

Lucy felt better after their conversation. Alex was so reliable. She didn't mention the incident to the twins, she reasoned it would have served no purpose.

Alex was unhappy. He didn't like the sound of this man, particularly as it would appear he was no stranger to his mother. He discussed the matter with Sadie.

"Alex, I can see you are concerned. I was thinking of visiting my mum anyway for a couple of weeks, so why don't you tell work you have a family emergency and get over there. "

Alex kissed her. How well she knew him.

Ben had made friends with a couple of lads his own age and that evening Lucy sat with Rose in the reception bar and left them by themselves at the next table.

"So you're here with your family?"

"Yeah, my Mum and my sister."

"Where are they?"

"Over there." Lucy smiled and noticed one of the boys' eyes lingered on Rose. She decided she would need to keep an eye on her young daughter.

Lucy noticed Ben was drinking beer but it was a holiday and provided he didn't get stupid there was no harm in it. He was talking a lot which he always did when he'd made new friends. Chattering like a lot of old women, she thought. She noticed to her discomfort that the weasel faced man had appeared and sat down with another man quite near to her. She felt inexplicably frightened and decided to go in for dinner a little earlier than usual. Ben saw them walking towards the restaurant and bade a hasty farewell to his new friends.

"Ben, if it's okay with you, I'd rather you didn't talk about our personal life to people you don't know, or even with people that you do know," she added quickly. "And apart from anything else I think you've had enough to drink."

Ben realised she was upset. "Sorry, Mum, I'd didn't think, that was rude of me. Look I'll take Rose down to the pool bar after we've finished dinner to see whether there is any entertainment. We'll meet you back upstairs later."

"Okay, but please keep your eye on Rose. She is already attracting too much attention."

Ben grinned. "You don't think I noticed. Remember what happened before, no one gets near my sister!"

As they left the restaurant she noticed the two men had gone. Ben and Rose disappeared out of the back door towards the pool area where the outdoor entertainment had just started and Lucy went straight to her room. The children arrived about an hour later. Ben was talking rapidly about the girl he had just met, Rose ribbed him unmercifully and started tickling him. The two of them rolled about on her bed laughing. Lucy forgot about the two men as she tried to quiet them before someone complained to the management.

The next day, Lucy left the two of them by the pool. Ben was suffering a little from the excesses of the previous evening and Rose wanted to sunbathe. Although she loved them dearly, at this moment she welcomed the solitude. She walked along the promenade towards the centre of the resort. "Why am I here?" she asked herself.

As she wandered slowly along the paved walkway, glittering in the sunlight she was lost in her own daydreams. The sun was clear and white in the afternoon sky. The light breeze was exceptionally warm for the time of year, stifling almost from its long journey from the great desert in the south. Lucy was hot and she wished she'd put her hair up, it was sticking to her neck.

Couples and families strolled lazily along the arrow straight road. There were a few odd shaped trees that she didn't recognise, needles spaced out along horizontal branches facing upwards in a smart salute to the sun. The clip-clop of horses hooves broke the tranquillity as a caleche clattered past, its open seating framed by gaudy plastic brightly coloured flowers. As she reached the roundabout which led down the main road towards the Marina she looked around her and thought how different this was from the first time she came to the narrow dusty streets of Sousse.

The resort was a collection of low rise hotels, a recent addition to the full and ancient history of Tunisia. The fringed palms, symmetrically placed by human hand swayed from right to left and back, whispering their welcome. This could quite easily be any modern resort in Europe, save for the rows of little shops sheltering beneath the hotel colonnades, offering cheaply made clothes and handbags bearing the fake insignia of French couture houses, plates, bowls and ornaments in brightly coloured pottery, pictures of Tunisian scenes, souvenirs and of course the ubiquitous furry camels in different sizes.

Lucy stopped to look at the array of postcards and smiled. In amongst the vista of old Hammamet, the new resort and the tourist pirate galleons, there were also pictures of Berber tents, the desert, salt flats and of course camels. She looked at the photographs of the desert, which many of the tourists would never see. They came to Tunisia because it was different, a more exciting exotic holiday from the well-known European resorts, but only a few ventured far away from the coast to the desert. She pondered how different were the facets of this majestic and diverse country, from the deep sands of the Sahara a few hundred miles to the south, rough scrubland, olive and citrus groves, the ancient dusty beauty of Sousse and to the north, the cosmopolitan city of Tunis surrounded by hills blending into the majesty of the Atlas mountains.

She looked from one photograph to the next. There were ancient ruins scattered inland offering a complete contract to the coastal areas fringed by the clear white sands of the Mediterranean beaches. Some showed the neat lines of modern hotels which now infested Hammamet, Port El Kantaoui and other beach resorts.

Lucy was absorbed in the postcards. Many of the scenes she remembered having visited them with Farid in their little rental car. Most of all she loved the chotts. Amazing huge dry salt lakes in the south west. The beauty of the sunrise over the chotts she had never seen anywhere else. At one moment the flats were an insignificant dark or greyish white but with the sunrise they took on magical array of fiery red, deep pink and orange, the sunlight reflecting off the salt crystals as they sparkled like diamonds with the brilliance of the dawn sky like flames rising behind them.

She walked on down the promenade. There were a few people on the beach and one or two fishermen she could see in the distance. She noticed some of the beach bars were closed heralding the end of the main season and an assortment of white plastic chairs lay stacked up alongside the rows of sunbeds. The lonely clean white stretch of sand seemed at peace, enjoying respite from the marauding hoards until late Spring when a stream of pale bodies would descend once again to violate its tranquillity, swelling to a crescendo in July and August only to dwindle again towards the Autumn when the sands could slip quietly back into peaceful drowsiness until the whole embryonic saga would begin again.

She stopped and sat down on the low wall, lost in her own little world, her back to the road and dangled her feet over the edge looking out to sea. The horizon was an absolutely straight line across the bay where blue sky faded to a deep azure before meeting the gunmetal blue of the sea. Puffs of wispy clouds drifted aimlessly across the panorama, changing direction with the breeze as though searching in vain for something they would never find.

The vision of calm was rudely interrupted by the harsh clanging of a bell as the little train made its presence known. Affectionately known as Noddy trains they comprised of a crocodile of open sided wooden box coaches painted red, white or blue and run from the new resort to its older sister Hammamet. The driver stops if he sees a likely participant or if he is hailed. The red train drew up alongside Lucy, its driver wearing a broad grin under a thick bristling moustache. She shook her head, he shrugged and drove on still clanging his bell.

That looks fun, the kids will love that, she thought. She had heard that the train runs along the road and decided it was certainly a much more picturesque way of seeing the countryside, if considerably more uncomfortable and noisier than the numerous yellow taxis which prowl the curbs.

Lucy turned, went down onto the beach and took off her shoes, feeling the sand between her toes. She looked out to sea and watched the afternoon sun dappling the tiny waves in a mixture of every shade of gold. The horizon now blended into the darkness of the water. The breeze had all but disappeared and a heavy calm hung in the air. Lucy strolled along the beach carrying her sandals, her mind full of nothing but the panorama laid out before her. The sand was fine and white where no water save rain touched it and shifted with each step as her feet sank into its softness. Her legs started to ache a bit and she smiled to herself. *If I lived here I would have no need to go to a gym*, she thought. *I could just run on the beach.*

She came out from behind the line of low trees shielding that part of the beach from the road and turned towards the sea. She walked slowly until she felt the sand firm as she neared the glistening water. She stopped and peered up at the sun which had changed from hot white to a glorious deep orange as it dipped behind the line of buildings. It was getting late. She started back towards the road. Her eyes travelled lazily along the whiteness of the unbroken line of hotels to a gap between them where the road branched inland.

It was then that she saw it rising out of the scorched earth. Nestled deep into the purple hills its soft creamy walls tinted pink in the sunlight, gleaming white turrets luminous against the shadowy backdrop, a huge castle, the castle Alice had warned her about.

She dropped her sandals and gasped screwing up her face, her eyes tightly shut. She turned to run, where she couldn't care, just anywhere away from it. A searing pain shot through her ankle and she fell to her knees. She lay down in the sand curled up like a baby sobbing, her breath coming in huge tortured gasps until she felt she could not take another breath.

"Madame, are you alright?"

She heard a man's concerned voice and felt an arm under hers helping her to her feet. Still shaken, Lucy allowed herself to be lifted up and gratefully clung to him for support. He could feel she was shaking. He was a huge man and she looked up at into his kindly face, and managed a smile.

"Yes, thank you I just tripped. It was my own fault."

"Can you walk?" Lucy leaned heavily on him. "Your leg, it is okay?"

"Yes, I think so, I've just twisted my ankle." She put her injured foot forward and nearly fell again.

He put his arm around her waist. "With your permission, madame." She nodded. With little effort he picked her up and carried her back to the pavement. He lowered her gently onto the wall. She sat shivering, her eyes wide with fear and pain, her heart pounding so loudly she was sure he could hear it.

"You still look shaken. Here, come with me."

Half-hopping, half-carrying her the man helped her across the road to the café opposite.

"Thank you so much, I feel really stupid."

"Not at all madame, it is very easy to trip in the sand, near to the road there are many hidden plant roots from the bushes. You look as though you could do with a strong cup of English tea, as my wife would say."

"Please, I would love a drink but may I have a coffee?"

"Of course."

The waiter arrived. "Express, cappuccino and a bottle of water."

"Oh, no please, cappucin for me."

He looked at her quizzically. "You've been here before, I think."

She laughed, warming to the big man sitting opposite her. "Yes, I have, but I know most tourists prefer cappuccino."

The coffees arrived and he poured the two little phials of sugar into his and stirred it. Lucy sipped hers without bothering with the sugar.

The man looked at her closely, his eyes narrowed but he said nothing.

Lucy relaxed and smiled at him. "Your wife, she is English?"

"Yes, she came on holiday and I fell in love with her the moment I saw her! We have three children now. And you, you are married?"

"I was, but my husband died."

"I'm so sorry." He looked embarrassed.

"Oh please, it was many years ago."

"You have any children?"

"Yes, two boys and a girl."

"The same as me."

He laughed and then hesitated for a moment. "Madame, may I ask you, what frightened you on the beach?" Lucy looked at the table and flushed. "I am sorry, but I was watching you. You seemed to freeze and then turn to run as if something had scared you." He sounded genuinely concerned.

"That building, the castle, when was it built?"

"The Castille Hotel you mean. Last year. Is that what frightened you?" Lucy said nothing.

"No, I just wondered," she lied, "it's such a strange building for a place like this."

"You're not the first to say that. My wife says it's a monstrosity."

He struggled with the word and she laughed.

"Actually if I am being honest, it just shocked me. I felt as though I had seen it before, but I couldn't have done if it's only just been built."

"Rather a strange case of déjà vu, possibly?" *In the same way I am sure I have seen you before,* he thought.

"Possibly," Lucy smiled but shivered despite the heat, remembering Alice's words. "A castle not old but new."

She turned to look at it. It was actually rather beautiful.

"What are you thinking?"

Lucy giggled "I was thinking that the turrets look like a huge soufflé rising out of the dish when it first comes out of the oven."

They both laughed.

"That's a good description, I must remember it!"

"For how long are you here?"

"For a month, we arrived on Saturday."

The man's eyebrows lifted in surprise. "You stay so long, I think you like Tunisia." Lucy nodded.

"I think my wife would like to meet you, if of course you have time," he added "She loves Tunisia, but sometimes she gets sick for home and likes to talk with other English. Would you? We only live ten minutes' walk."

"Of course, I would love to."

"Where are you staying madame?" Lucy gave him the name of her hotel and he grinned.

"That's where I work, so we will see more of each other I think."

Lucy was surprised. "I haven't seen you there before. What do you do in the hotel?"

"I'm a reception manager." He noticed her apprehension and grinned. "I've been away this week which is why you haven't seen me."

" I'm sorry I didn't ask your name."

"Ali, and you, madame?"

"Lucy."

A strange expression passed momentarily across Ali's face and he smiled. "I think madame we have met before. You came to my wedding many years ago. I think you already know my wife, Ellen."

Lucy stared at him. "Ali? Ellen's Ali?" Her hands were shaking. Farid's childhood friend.

"The same." He held out a huge paw and Lucy took it.

Lucy spoke hurriedly trying to calm the thumping of her heart and her words tumbled out.

"Actually, I must confess something to you. I don't really know Ellen. I came to your wedding with one of Ellen's workmates from England. She didn't want to come here on her own and she asked Ellen it was all right to bring me along."

Ali nodded. "I remember, you wore a beautiful pink dress and all my friends fell in love with you and then you disappeared, like Cinderella." They both laughed, the tension broken.

"Cinderella?"

Ali flushed. "My daughter is now five years old and it is her favourite story. She makes me read it to her," he explained sheepishly.

Lucy grinned at him and lit a cigarette, tucking the lighter back inside the packet. She stirred her coffee and took a sip, savouring the thick strong liquid then picked up the glass of water and drank deeply.

Ali watched her. "May I ask you something?"

"Of course."

"Who taught you to drink coffee the Tunisian way and I notice you smoke our cigarettes? Most of the tourists remain with the brand they know."

Lucy's eyes widened and she felt the blood rush to her face as she stared at the packet.

She took a deep breath and gazed up at the kind face studying her. How she wanted to ask him about Farid, but then Farid had not been at the wedding so it was unlikely they had kept up their childhood friendship, so it would only serve to open up old wounds.

"Ali, before I came to your wedding I had been to Tunisia many times. I met a man. I fell in love. I knew him for over three years and I believe he loved me as much as I loved him. It was not part of the…" she hesitated.

Ali smiled. "I understand, go on, what happened, if I may ask?"

"It was many years ago and it just came to nothing. Don't misunderstand me please. Our worlds were just too far apart, I already had a child and he was a lot younger than me. I will always love him but things happened which were beyond my control. I behaved badly, I just never came back and there was so much left unsaid…" her voice trailed off and Ali noticed the buildup of tears.

"So you ran away."

Lucy nodded miserably. "And you kept on running until now, and now you have come back."

"Your man, what became of him? You never saw him again?"

"Ali, your wedding was the first time I had been back for almost seven years and yes, I did see him again in that week. I saw him in a café in Sousse just before I went back to England. He was there with his wife and baby and I ran away… again. He has forgotten his youthful crush so you see everything turned out right for him in the end."

"And for you, you have someone now?"

"No, I have no one, I could never love anyone else."

Ali was surprised by the pain in her face.

"For me, I have been very lucky. I met my Ellen and fell in love with her the moment I saw her, but I know there are many who have not been so lucky. I am truly sorry for you, Lucy."

He leaned across the table and took Lucy's hands in his own. "But why now have you come back?"

She looked at him like a cornered rabbit and he squeezed her hands encouragingly but he could see she was not going to say any more.

"I am sorry, I ask too many questions." She shook her head

"No Ali, it has been good to talk to you but now I must go now, or my children will think I have been abducted or something. Thank you for helping me and I hope we have a chance to talk more at the hotel."

"Goodbye… Lucy."

CHAPTER FIFTY-THREE

THE CHILDREN

Rose was not pleased. She was concerned her mother had got lost and was about to come and look for her. Ben was obviously sulking about something.

"What's the matter darling? I'm sorry I'm late. I slipped on the beach and I was lucky enough to be rescued by a nice man I used to know. He picked me up and bought me a coffee."

Ben glared at her. "Are you okay?"

"Yes, I'm fine, but what's the matter?"

Rose stifled a chuckle and Ben shot her a murderous glance.

"It's okay Mum, he's livid because he's been chatting up a couple of girls and they asked him if he wanted to go with them for the evening, and I told him he wasn't to go without asking you first."

"I'm not a baby."

Lucy smiled. "No darling you're not, but you are still only just sixteen."

"Mum, shut up." Ben looked around quickly.

Rose smirked. "It's okay bro, they've gone. Come on, I'm starving, let's eat."

"Can you can wait ten minutes and give me time to change quickly? I'll meet you in the bar."

"Okay Mum, don't be too long."

Lucy had a quick shower, changed into a pale turquoise dress, with thin straps. She brushed her hair and studied her reflection in the mirror. She looked like a ghost. Angrily she reached for her makeup bag. A few minutes later she stood back and took a second look in the mirror. She looked a little more human. As she went into the bar, Ben pretended to look astonished.

"Twenty minutes, well done Mum that must be a record." Lucy ignored him and sat down opposite them. Ben had a bottle of beer and Rose was sipping an evil looking blue concoction. She said nothing. Lucy told them about meeting Ali and said she was looking forward to meeting Ellen again. She sat back in her chair and watched them, a slight smile on her face as she sipped her drink. She looked around the bar but the weasel faced man was nowhere to be seen. She relaxed and looked at her daughter.

Rose smoothed her skirt and crossed her legs. She had on a white blouse and royal blue cotton skirt clinched in at the waist with a wide gold belt. Lucy thought how pretty she looked with her curls cascading down her back held in place with an Alice band. She noticed with amusement that Rose had painted her nails and her long lashes were enhanced with dark mascara which set off her golden eyes, which at that moment were firmly fixed on her mother.

"What?" she said defensively.

"Nothing sweetheart. I was just thinking how pretty you look." Rose beamed happily.

She looked at Ben. His glossy black hair was neatly combed and with his honey coloured skin here, even more than in England, his Arab heritage was obvious. He could easily have passed for a local. That evening he wore tight tailored black trousers and a short sleeved shirt. He already had a small shadow moustache over a firm mouth and strong masculine chin, which made him look a lot older than his years. Totally relaxed in his surroundings, he sat casually, one leg crossed over the other, one arm resting loosely on the arm of the chair. Like Farid. Her heart turned a somersault.

The following day they went to the old Medina in Hammamet on the little train. Ben was not at all sure, he said it made him feel like a tourist and Rose pointed out that is exactly what he was. Lucy was amused when she paid for their tickets the driver spoke to Ben in Arabic and Ben responded. The driver chatted to Ben until he realised he was not a local lad who had picked up a couple of tourists to take them to the Medina in return for a couple of dinar. He grinned sheepishly at Lucy and took a second look at Ben.

Lucy watched enchanted at the rows of hibiscus hedges, the brilliant scarlet trumpet flowers dotted amongst the leaves, their deep yellow stamens stretching out from the centre. At home she had only ever seen these plants growing as a small greenhouse shrubs, no more than knee height with a few solitary flowers lasting only a day or so. These hedges were used to border large houses, the thick lush green foliage shielding them from the road.

The little train trundled along, bouncing over the bumps in the road, Rose asked her if they could have one of the palm trees at home. Lucy explained that the huge trees only grew in hot countries. She pointed out their pineapple shaped trunks of overlapping layers of bark topped by tall fronds branching out from the centre in every direction waiving in the breeze as though inviting the sun's rays to their hearts. "You see my love, they need to be here in the sun to be truly happy." *As I do*, she thought.

A street café set almost on the road lay deserted save for two elderly men. The whole building was partly obscured by the tendrils of trailing bougainvillea and jasmine, in some places reaching almost to the ground. The plants intermingled into a riot of rich purple, fuchsia and white and the scent of jasmine wafted on the breeze. Lucy felt a lump in her throat.

As the train made its bumpy journey towards Hammamet the children chatted to each other. Lucy watched as the line of palms were replaced by thick bushes of oleander clothed in flowers of every colour. Lucy had an oleander bush at home in her garden but whereas these were thick and dense with long lance like leaves, hers was tall and spindly, bare at the base and appeared forlorn amongst the roses of England. She was happy if it produced half a dozen coloured bracts during the course of the whole summer. These bushes seemed to grow everywhere, on the edge of the roadside, in barren areas of dry earth and even in the middle of what appeared to be a deserted building site. She smiled to herself. Perhaps if I leave it alone instead of lovingly tending it the poor thing it might do better.

The little train pulled in beside the Medina. Streams of bright yellow taxis circled the roundabout before parking up in a line, their drivers sitting together or standing by their cabs calling out, "taxi, taxi, very cheap", at no-one in particular in the hope of picking up a fare. There were not a huge number of other cars but a vast array of motor scooters darting in and out of the cars. The air was hot and heavy and the clouds heralded rain but in the late summer months these were usually burned away by the sun before they had a chance to deposit their contents.

They stopped for a coffee at the large café overlooking the sea and the rocks which lined that part of the shore line. The children chattered and Lucy's mind drifted off as she stared over the wide bay and watched the sun dancing on the gentle ripples.

As they wandered under the archway which led from the café into the cobbled alleyways they were besieged by the numerous street sellers. After putting up with the barrage for a few moments Lucy heard Ben shout at one of the men. She suddenly realised it was rather useful that the stall holders now assumed Ben was their guide, particularly as he told them in no uncertain terms to leave the women alone to do their shopping in peace.

When they got back to the hotel Ben and Rose shot upstairs to change into their swimwear. Lucy sat down with a coffee and buried her nose in her book. She jumped as she felt the tap on her shoulder and turned.

"Alex! What on earth are you doing here?" She jumped up and hugged him.

"What do you think? After your call Sadie suggested it would be a good idea if I came over to make sure you were all okay. Seriously Mum you sounded scared on the phone."

Alex sat down and beckoned to the waiter with an authoritative wave. Lucy had never been so pleased to see her eldest boy.

"Right, tell me about this bloke."

"There's nothing much to tell except he followed me back to the hotel. I thought he would just walk on past but he came into the foyer and started talking to the reception clerk. They appeared to be checking the guest list and then he left, but I've also seen him sitting in the bar with another man. I don't know, one of them may even be a guest in the hotel."

"I don't like the sound of that at all. Are you sure that you didn't leave any unfinished business when you left, other than the obvious," he added, "no one who owed you a bad turn."

"Thank you for putting that so charmingly," she snapped.

"Mum, get off your high horse. I am only trying to help."

"I'm sorry, Alex, it is just that the incident has left me a bit jittery." She thought for a minute. "No, I can honestly say I cannot think of anyone who would wish to hurt me."

"Or Farid?"

Lucy stared at him. That had not crossed her mind. "Not that I know of." She hesitated. "Obviously I don't know Farid's life history, but very few people outside our own friends knew we were together. We rarely went out in the main town and kept ourselves to ourselves. Anyway this place wasn't even built when I was here before."

"But you said you thought you saw the same man following you in Sousse."

"That's true, and in fact that is probably why I think I might have known him. My mind is probably muddling everything up. I probably just remember him from Sousse. It may not even have been the same man but he has one of those nasty leering faces you can't easily forget."

"OK so long as you're okay that's all that matters. Look I've got to unpack and change. I am hot and dusty and desperately in need of a shower and a nap. The bloody plane arrived an hour late. Sure you'll be all right?"

"Stop worrying. I'm fine, go and get yourself sorted out." Lucy smiled broadly at him with a confidence that she didn't feel.

Shortly afterwards Lucy went upstairs to change. She showered and washed her hair luxuriating in the cool water. She left her hair loose to dry naturally. She felt relaxed as if the water had washed away not only the dust of the Medina but also the rest of her troubles. The evening promised to be warm and Lucy chose her favourite pale pink dress. The deep neckline just skimmed her breasts which had tanned to a pale honey. She applied her make up carefully and stood back and surveyed herself in the long mirror. She grinned at her reflection, *not too bad for an old bird,* she thought.

CHAPTER FIFTY-FOUR

ABDUCTION

Lucy sat with Rose in the cool reception area. Ali was now back on duty and she had managed a few words with him, but he had gone over to the sister hotel next door. She sat in her favourite spot reading her book, her back to the row of potted plants from where she could see the people coming and going. Lucy loved people watching. Rose had her nose buried in a glossy magazine. She looked particularly pretty in a white cotton dress with shoestring straps and a tight bodice which in Lucy's opinion showed rather too much of her fast developing bosom.

They waited for Ben who was taking his usual length of time to shower and change. She looked up searching for a waiter to order a drink. The weasel faced man and his companion were there and although the security guard glanced at them from time to time the reception clerk seemed unconcerned. Perhaps he was something to do with the hotel.

She watched as they walked up to side of the reception desk and sat down as though waiting for someone. She looked around for Ali but he hadn't come back. A third man came in whom she didn't recognise. He was expensively dressed, quite short, thick set and he wore several gold rings. He had probably been quite handsome in his young days but now his dark face was heavily lined and Lucy didn't at all care for the sinister expression. The three shook hands.

The weasel removed his sunglasses and Lucy realised with a shudder that she recognised him. It was the same slimy little man who had worked with Farid at the Palace years before, the one who had constantly annoyed her with his suggestive remarks.

The three men leaned towards each other deep in conversation. The third man glanced over at them, but quickly averted his eyes when he saw she was looking at him. From the way they were talking, Lucy doubted that whatever they were discussing was honourable. She glanced anxiously for Ben or Alex. When she looked back at the desk the third man had gone outside and was leaning on the wall smoking a cigarette.

She heard low voices speaking urgently in Arabic and glanced in the mirror. The weasel and the other man were standing behind the row of tall plants only a few feet away from her.

Although in the months before they came away Ben had attempted to teach Lucy some Arabic, she found it difficult and to start with much of what he had said had fallen on deaf ears. She could however understand more than she could speak. It was only when she heard Farid's surname that her senses sharpened and she strained to listen. She heard them mention the name Castille Hotel and was sure they were talking about drugs. She shuddered. She was terrified. A couple of other names came into the conversation and the name Hama was mentioned several times. She had obviously heard the name before and the shortened version of Mohammed was quite commonly used.

She thought hard and remembered that Farid had told her long ago about his sister's relationship with a man called Hama and how much he wanted to separate his sister from this person. She also remembered him saying that he was sure Hama was into drug trafficking and involved with prostitution amongst other things. He refused to elaborate further but from what he said he intended to make sure the man was locked up for a very long time. What if he had been successful in getting Hama arrested. There surely would be no love lost between Farid and Hama. It could not be a coincidence.

What frightened her was the linking of names Farid and Hama which sent a cold shiver down her spine. Surely Farid could not be mixed up in such a business. She felt sure she was being dragged into some awful plot which somehow involved Farid.

As she leaned forward to pick up her cigarettes, she knocked her lighter on the floor. The dark man turned around and looked at her.

She met his eyes and heard him swear quietly as he barked something at the weasel. She gathered that the one who had looked at her was concerned that she had understood their conversation. The weasel assured him that he was certain she spoke no Arabic.

Lucy was now very scared and there was still no sign of Ben. Thankfully she saw Ali walk past the reception and got up, but the dark man stood blocking her way.

Rose looked up from her magazine. "Mum?"

"Say absolutely nothing, please, Rose, just sit," she whispered.

"Madame, I understand that you are staying here with your children." He spoke in guttural French. She nodded mutely.

"Then you will please both now come with us. Do not shout or draw attention to yourself. If you do, you and your children will get hurt. If you do as I say you will not be harmed."

The weasel smirked and fixed his eyes on Rose's chest. Lucy felt very afraid for her daughter.

Rose sat rooted to her chair clutching the arms, her knuckles white. Lucy knew she had understood. She stood up, hoping her knees would not give way. To her dismay she saw Ben coming out of the lift. He was dressed as usual in dark trousers and white shirt, but he wore a tie and his hair was slicked back off his face and gleamed with gel. He was dressed to go out.

She opened her handbag, her mind working frantically. She spoke quietly to Rose. "Do not move and whatever happens say nothing, absolutely nothing."

She turned nervously to the man.

"Yes, we will come with you but you will excuse me if I first pay for my telephone calls."

He looked doubtful. "Please be quick, we must go."

Lucy raised her hand and hailed Ben, who looked surprised. She spoke quickly to him in French.

"Waiter, I would be grateful if you would please give this money to Ali, the reception manager, for my telephone calls." The expression on her face warned Ben to say nothing. He waited and Lucy continued, trying desperately to hide the shaking in her voice.

"You are new here, but you must know Ali, the very big man, would you please tell him…" she broke off as the man gripped her arm tightly.

"That's enough, come now," he muttered in her ear. Lucy turned to face him and spoke as calmly as she could.

"Actually, Ali is also a friend of mine who we are supposed to be having dinner with later on. I think it is much better if you want us to come with you that I offer Ali an explanation, otherwise he will start asking after us."

The man looked uncertain, but loosened his grip. Lucy turned back to her son. She knew the man was listening intently.

"Would you please tell Ali that I will be unable to make the soufflé tonight? I had forgotten we have to meet an old acquaintance to talk about Charlie. Please remember exactly what I have said. I hope he or his very tall English friend will understand."

As she spoke, Lucy look a single coin from a pocket in her handbag and pressed it hard into Ben's hand. "Please go and give the message to Ali and give him this money for my calls." She emphasised the word this. She remembered Cathy's remark that anyone who knew Farid would know Ben was his son. She remembered that Ali knew about the engraved coin, perhaps he would realise the coin was very old and look more closely at it. It was all hope against hope, but it was all she had.

Ben had no idea what she was talking about, but he nodded and replied formally "Yes, Madame, I will do so." He saw the fear in her face as her eyes implored him to do nothing until they had left.

The two men spoke openly to each other and Ben listened intently, memorising what was said. He watched his mother and sister as they walked towards the entrance doors, flanked by the weasel and the man who still held Lucy in a tight grip.

The dark man turned to Lucy. "What is this soufflé? What are you talking about? Explain to me."

Lucy held her breath, she had anticipated this. "Ali's wife is English, she asked us to dinner this evening and I promised to teach her how to make soufflé." The man grunted as he dismissed the female talk as insignificant rubbish.

They were met outside the doors by the thickset man with the sunglasses who linked his arm roughly through Lucy's. The weasel slipped his arm around Rose's waist, but the dark man shook him off angrily.

Ben was terrified. Her expression had told him not to interfere but to find Ali, who he recognised from his mother's description and knew he had to find as quickly as possible. He had seen Ali walk through reception a moment ago towards the restaurant and ran down the corridor.

As Alex came out of the lift he watched his mother and sister get into the car with the two men which pulled away towards the marina. He went quickly to reception and waited anxiously until the girl finished talking to another guest. He asked her if she had seen his brother. She stared blankly at him. Hastily Alex described Ben and the girl smiled and pointed to the corridor leading to the restaurant. He followed her direction.

Ben caught up with Ali and grabbed his arm. He spoke quickly in English

"Are you Ali? I must speak with you urgently." Ali took one look at the young man's face and drew him to one side.

"Right, my young friend. What's the matter?"

Ben tried to control the shaking in his voice.

"I have absolutely no idea what this means but I do know it is serious. My mother and sister have just left the hotel with two men and they didn't go willingly." Ben was babbling and Ali looked puzzled.

"I understand, but please speak slowly. Are you staying in the hotel, who is your mother and why do you come to me and not the director?"

"My mother says she knows you. She met you on the beach yesterday when you helped her after she fell."

Ali stared at him. "Lucy is your mother?"

"Yes, but please listen. My mother spoke to me in French as though I was a waiter and it was obvious she didn't want them to know I'm her son. She said to give you this money to pay for her telephone calls."

Ali took the coin and handed it back to Ben. "The calls, if she made any, would be charged to her room. What else did she say?"

Ben hesitated. "Quickly," said Ali impatiently. "Your mother is obviously trying to tell me something important. Tell me exactly what she said, word for word."

Alex appeared around the corner and Ben stared at him in amazement. "Alex! Thank God you are here." He was obviously very frightened.

Alex grabbed his arm. "What the hell is going on, and who the fuck are those men I've just seen getting into a car with Mum and Rose?"

Ben repeated what Lucy had said. Ali looked at the floor and pulled at his moustache. Ben stared at him.

"What was she talking about, a soufflé?"

Ali gave a bitter laugh. "When I helped your mother on the beach the other day, she asked me about the hotel in hills, the Castille, the one which looks like a castle. She said it reminded her of a huge soufflé so it follows that whatever this is about involves the hotel, but I still don't understand about an old acquaintance or to talk about Charlie. She said either you or your tall English friend would know. Does it make sense to you? Is there someone called Charlie she knows here?"

Ben thought for a moment and shook his head. Very tall English friend. Alex, could that be you?

Alex smiled grimly. "I may be able to answer that. Charlie is a slang expression in England for cocaine. Perhaps these men are into drugs, but I still don't understand how it involves my mother or little Rose."

Ali let off a stream of curses. Ben's eyebrows shot up. Ali glanced at him.

"My apologies. I did not know you spoke my language."

At Ali's obvious embarrassment Ben replied, "Yes but I admit some of the words were unfamiliar to me." He ran his hand through his hair and grinned broadly.

Ali stared at him as if he had seen a ghost. Suddenly everything Lucy said made sense as he stared into the face of his childhood friend.

Although he was away at the time, years later Farid had told him of the beautiful blonde English woman who had come back into his life and broken his heart when she disappeared, the same woman he himself had seen when they were playing football outside the café in Sousse years before, the woman who had been a guest at his own wedding, the woman he had helped on the beach. And now the reason why Lucy fled was standing next to him.

"Quick, give me that coin." Ben handed it to him.

"This is an old coin." He turned it over and muttered under his breath.

"I don't understand."

Ali handed the coin to Ben.

"Look, you see these initials 'F+L'?"

"Yes, what does it mean?"

"What it means is that your mother is in serious trouble. She would never have parted with this coin if she wasn't. There are only two coins with these initials on. One is your mother's and the other belongs to my friend Farid, who is your father, I think."

Ben felt the room swirling round his head and leant back against the wall. Ali shook him.

"Quickly, come with me. I'll explain on the way." All but dragging Ben with him, he hurried back down the corridor towards the car park. Alex followed and the three climbed into Ali's car.

As they drove he turned to Alex. "You must excuse me my English is not good enough. I will speak with your brother." He turned back to Ben.

"Right tell me everything you heard." Ben repeated the conversation as best he could.

Ali rubbed his chin. "Okay, let's try and make sense of this. Something is obviously happening at the Castille Hotel. Your mother and sister have been taken somewhere against their will. She said she can't meet me tonight so I think the message is that they will be at the Castille this evening and if as we suspect this is something to do with drugs, if I am not much mistaken the reference to an old acquaintance is a chap called Hama." Ben looked puzzled.

"Many years ago your father's younger sister was involved with this man. Your father knew that he was no good and found out that not only was he married already, but that he was deeply involved with a crime syndicate, drugs, prostitution, people trafficking and god knows what else." He turned to Ben.

"Can you describe the two men you saw inside the hotel with your mother?"

"They were middle aged, both Arabs. One was dark, very tall and strong looking but the other man was thin with lanky grey hair and a thin oily face and bad teeth. Oh and there was third man. He was waiting outside the hotel."

Ali shook his head. "Describe him, quickly…"

"He was stocky, very dark, sixty-ish, with a dark grey suit and he was wearing sunglasses and a lot of gold."

Ali felt the fear rise in his throat. "This is really bad. I saw the first two in here yesterday. The man on reception I do not trust and these two were with him looking at some hotel records. I was about to tell them to leave but they went of their own accord when they saw me. I think one is an Algerian who was mixed up in the same racket as Hama but was never caught. He has kept the business going while Hama has been away. The other I recognised as Mahmood whom Farid used to work with. From what your father told me, he wanted your mother for himself and was insanely jealous of Farid. Mahmood was the hotel contact for Hama's organisation but no one could prove it. I think it was Mahmood who must have recognised your mother, checked at reception and got word to Hama.

"The third man I think is Hama himself. He must have got out of prison somehow because the penalties for such activities here are very harsh and I doubt he would have been released. I had heard that he was back in the area, but they were only rumours. I am sure the police and the National Guard are looking for him. It must have been important for him to come to a public place like the hotel."

Ali looked at Ben's anxious face and in the mirror he saw Alex looked puzzled. He wondered whether to continue, but if they were to find the women he would need to explain. He spoke hesitantly in French.

"I must tell you this. Hama hates your father. I don't know the whole story but I do know that your father helped the police in putting him away. In truth, I don't think it is your mother Hama wants at all, I believe he may be using her to get to Farid."

He stopped and looked straight at Ben, "How old is your sister?"

"She's my twin, she's just sixteen."

Ali struggled to keep calm, but Alex noticed his face had gone ashen pale. He felt sick. Ali held his eyes and shook his head glancing at Ben.

Ben did not understand. "But my mother hasn't seen my father in years."

"Yes, but he knew about your mother and he would have been informed how she disappeared and of your father's attempts to find her. Hama's network is extensive and there is little which passes him by, even in prison. From what I know of Hama's character, I am sure he intends to somehow involve Farid and to get his revenge for what your father did to him. Your mother's appearance has given him the way to do it."

Ali glanced anxiously at Ben. "What worries me is that if Farid knows your mother is here and in trouble, he will be like a man possessed. He has never forgotten her and I am sure is still in love with her. I have no idea what he might do. I need to get to him before they do."

He reverted to Arabic. "Did you hear the two men say anything else? - please think, it is important."

Ben was struggling to take in everything Ali said. "I heard the thin man mention that they had to all meet somewhere in a place called Nabeul? I also heard them mention La Goulette."

"La Goulette, that is the port of Tunis. It makes sense. It must be where they intend to move whatever is being sold. There is a huge old house near Nabeul, which belongs to Hama's family, but it has been partly derelict for years. His younger brother, Jalal lived there for a short while with the old lady, his mother I think, but I thought the house had been empty again for some time. Yes, it starts to make sense."

Ben cut in quickly. "Jalal, yes, they did mention that name as well."

Ali looked worried. "If Hama and Jalal are back in business together you can be sure it is something big. They may be brothers, but there is intense rivalry between them. Jalal has always wanted what his brother has, whether it be money, power or a woman. Hama you cannot underestimate, but Jalal is not a man to make your enemy. With Hama you can sense the evil, but Jalal is cunning. Was there anything else you can remember - did they mention a time?"

"Yes! The thin man said they had to be at the hotel by midnight so the meeting could take place as arranged at 1a.m. The dark man seemed annoyed that the plans had been changed. Does this help?"

"Yes, I think I understand, but it may well mean more to my brother-in-law. My sister's husband is chief of police in this area. That will mean we can get the police involved immediately and if this deal is as big as I think it is it will involve areas outside the Nabeul district and I am sure he will bring in the National Guard. If Hama is indeed in the Hammamet area, the authorities would dearly love to get him behind bars again and round up the rest of his people they couldn't find before. Such dealings are rare in Tunisia and if we can indeed catch all the rats in one cage together it will rid this country of a scourge of which we are certainly not proud.

"I think it unlikely Hama usually attends these, shall we call them business meetings, but in this case if he has Lucy and believes he can draw Farid into this mess he will not be able to resist witnessing his revenge and we must pray that he does not realise your sister is Farid's daughter."

"What do we do? How do you propose to get my mother and sister back?" Ben's voice trembled.

Ali studied the boy. He looked just like his old friend at the same age. He smiled reassuringly.

"The first thing we do is take the two of you somewhere you won't be found. I'm quite sure your mother would not have gone with these men unless they had threatened her family."

Ben grabbed him. "You can't do that, I have to go with you."

"No that is exactly what you mustn't do."

"But what are you going to do?"

Ali smiled. "I will call your father and tell him to meet me around ten this evening. Whatever happens at the Castille will not happen until late. They could not risk it. This fits with what you say about midnight. Farid lives a little way from the town and my gut feeling is that Hama will send someone to his house, someone he knows.

"When I call Farid I will tell him to ignore what is said because it is a trap, but to play along with it and I will explain everything when I see him. Whoever they send will not offer to take him. If they are to incriminate Farid he will need to take his own car, as if he went of his own accord. I will tell him not to go to the Castille no matter what is said to him, but to come to the Sahara Oasis. I think it very unlikely Hama will have any contacts in that hotel. It is new, the best hotel we have and crawling with security, the type who are not in his pocket," he added grimly.

"Hama is going to want to get out of the country as soon as possible after he has completed his business. However flimsy the evidence against your father, Hama knows enough people to ensure he will be in serious trouble. We have to stop him. The only way any of you will be safe in the future is if that man is locked up for the rest of his life, or dead," he added darkly.

"And then?" Ben asked

"And then we wait for the rats to enter the trap."

Ben listened, his arms folded, his face still pale but flushed in anger. "With my mother and sister as bait."

"They will not be alone. Wherever they go we will be there, now we know where to look and when. We have the element of surprise. They will not know we have penetrated their filthy world."

"I don't understand a lot of this, but there is something I must ask you."

"Ask it."

"Does my father know that Rose and I exist?"

Ali hesitated. "No, in all sincerity, I truly believe that he has absolutely no idea."

He thought for a moment. "The men checked the hotel records so they would know your mother is here with her children, but you have an English name and they would not associate that with you. Did any of those men see you with your mother before she spoke to you in front of them?" He grinned at Ben. "You could pass for one of us, you know."

Ben smiled. "I am honoured. And no, I am sure they didn't see me with my mother and sister. The thin man may have seen me yesterday, but I was not sitting with them. I am sure he just thinks I am a waiter."

"Good. If by some chance they get to Farid before I do, he needs to have a clear head if this matter is to come to a successful conclusion without any of you getting hurt. I am sure they will say that Lucy is here which they know will make him come to Hammamet. I will tell him the whole thing is a set up. Whatever I say if there is any possibility, however remote, that Lucy could be in danger it will be bad enough, but if he learns of you and your sister it will be disastrous. I will make certain he never hears of it until this awful business is over."

Ali drove into the courtyard of a large white house set back off the road. He ran into the house, reappearing minutes later with a small woman and another man.

Ali said quickly "This is my sister, Sonia and her husband Mohamed. My sister will take you into her home and you will both wait there until you hear from me. Please do not leave or you may complicate matters further."

With that he turned to his brother in law. Ben listened as they spoke, interpreting quietly to Alex. Mohamed turned to him smiling.

"I see you speak our language, that is good. I will call you. Now please, go with my wife." The two men jumped into the car and drove quickly back towards the resort.

CHAPTER FIFTY-FIVE

THE OLD HOUSE

Lucy tried to remain calm because of Rose, who sat silently gripping her hand and was clearly terrified. Neither of them had been hurt, save that her arm ached where Hama had held her in vice grip. The driver glanced at her in the mirror. They drove quickly and in silence. She knew they were headed out of town on the main road towards Tunis. They passed the turn off to Hammamet and a little while later she saw the signpost to Nabeul. The car turned and after a short while stopped outside wide wrought iron gates. Hama spoke into the intercom, the gates opened and they pulled into a long dark driveway.

The house was huge, dark and menacing, hidden from the road by dense tall hedges and trees. It reminded Lucy of one of the sets of an old Hammer horror film and with Alice's words "there is evil in the house" did nothing to dispel her fears.

At first she thought it was deserted, but as they drew nearer she could see there were a few lights on which filtered through the heavy wooden shutters. The outline of the building was black against the early evening sky. As they drew up outside the house the driver got out and opened the door for Hama. He motioned for Lucy to get out of the car. She took Rose's hand and they waited. The dark man spoke to the driver who drove the car into one of the garages, pulling the metal door down after him, which closed with a loud bang. Rose jumped and Lucy winced as her daughter's nails bit into her hand.

Hama strode into the house leaving the dark man to follow holding Lucy tightly by the arm. She tripped on the hem of her dress and he put his arm out to steady her. His face was so close to hers she could smell the tobacco on his breath. He almost dragged her into a massive hallway lined with dark wood. The only furniture was a heavy wooden table in the centre and a bureau against the wall. The floor was the same dark wood, scattered with woven rugs. The room was lit only by one lamp and smelled of tobacco and damp.

They were led through the hallway into what appeared to be a meeting room, again lined with dark wood. There were several leather sofas, a couple of filing cabinets, a huge bookcase with a few books stacked at either end but little else. The windows were all shuttered and heavy maroon curtains were drawn across them. She noticed another curtain which covered part of the short wall. So far as she could see it served no purpose save decoration. At the far end of the room there was a large table, similar to the one in the hallway but much bigger. Around it were seated several men. As Lucy and Rose came into the room their talking stopped.

One of the men got up and walked towards them, his heavily lidded eyes half closed and a sly smile on his thick lips. The dark man barked something at him and Lucy caught the name Jalal. The man shrugged, looked again at Rose and sat down again.

Hama came back into the room. He walked towards the dark man. "Thank you Mahir. Your assistance is appreciated in this matter. Now I would ask you to go back to your people and we will meet again later, as we have arranged." He kissed Mahir on both cheeks and grasped his hand warmly.

Mahir nodded slightly. "As arranged," he replied and left the room.

Hama went upstairs and returned a short while later. He had shaved and seemed to Lucy to have added even more gold jewellery. He wore a smart pale grey suit which Lucy could see was good quality but sat badly on his stocky frame. He no longer wore his sunglasses and the little black eyes which watched the women were shrewd and hard but he spoke cordially in heavily accented English.

"Now Madame, you will come with me please." He offered her his arm, as though he was leading her into dinner. In any other circumstances Lucy would have found it amusing.

She ignored the arm and he smiled broadly, revealing one gold tooth. Lucy's knees buckled and Hama grabbed her arm to stop her falling. "An older man thick set who smiles with a flash of gold." Alice's words washed over her like a cold shower.

With Rose still clutching her hand she followed Hama into a smaller room in complete contrast to the other two rooms. There were no windows so the soft lighting in the room could not be seen from the outside. The walls were painted in cream and were hung with pictures and a large ornate mirror. Two tapestry sofas in shades of olive green, rust and cream faced each other. A large day bed lay against one wall. There was a small entertainment unit with a television and music system but she noticed there appeared to be no switch or remote control. It could obviously only be turned on from outside the room. She shuddered, he took no chances and she wondered if there had been other captives before them. She was surprised to see an English magazine on the low side table. Hama pointed to two chairs and told them to sit down.

An elderly woman came into the room, her black dress reaching almost to the floor, her iron grey hair was pulled back off her face which was mostly hidden under a black hijab She carried a small tray which she placed next to the magazine, on it one small cup of coffee, a bottle of mineral water and two glasses.

Lucy looked up at Hama. "This is correct I think?" She nodded mutely.

"And now you wait. We will be going soon." He left the room with the woman, turning the key in the lock behind him.

Lucy left the coffee. She was so frightened she didn't want to find that something had been put in her drink. She reached thankfully for the water and tested the seal to ensure it was unbroken. She picked up a glass, then changed her mind and drank directly from the bottle passing it to Rose who shook her head.

"Mum what is happening? Why are we here and who are these awful people?"

"Darling I can't answer any of those questions at the moment, but please say nothing and don't worry. I'm sure Ben will have got word to my friend and we will soon be out of this."

Lucy spoke with a confidence she did not feel, but she knew she had to appear calm for her child. She could hear the men talking but the walls were thick and the sound muffled.

Hama stood at the head of the table and spread his hands out in front of him, the thick pudgy fingers adorned with several thick gold rings. "Well, my friends, it would appear by tomorrow we will all be very rich and by good fortune I shall also be a very happy man." He grinned broadly and then the smile faded.

"Before we go any further, I must warn you the woman in the next room is mine. She is older than the ones I prefer but she has a special place in my heart and she will travel with me. The girl, who I assume is her daughter I am sure will prove a truly valuable addition to our enterprise." He turned to a large balding man seated at the far end.

"Khaled you will come with me into the Castille. We are not known there. I have reserved a suite and we will check in around nine. Youssef will drive us as usual, but remain in the car."

He focused his attention on the small elderly man next to him and beamed. "And you Massoud, you will be dropped at the marina. There is a boat there and the equipment is ready for you. You must ensure that the money is transferred. I hope for your sake you will get your sums right."

Massoud grinned back. "I have been doing this for many years."

"Let us hope you will long continue to do so."

Hama's expression was inscrutable and Massoud swallowed hard. He had worked in Hama's organisation for several years and knew that mistakes were not tolerated. He would still like to know what happened to the last money man who was with Hama before he was imprisoned. The money was short and the man had simply disappeared after Hama found out.

"May I ask a question?" Youssef spoke softly, but his voice had an edge Hama did not like. Hama acknowledged him. "Why have the plans changed? What reason is there for us to go to the Castille? Is this where the exchange will take place. We are all putting our heads in the noose and I don't like surprises and the women make me nervous."

His eyes held Hama's and the room was silent. There were usually no interruptions when Hama was speaking. Hama nodded his head and spread his fingers, studying the rings. Youssef was the one about whom he was unsure. He had come into his organisation only recently when his previous driver had been killed in a hit and run accident in Sicily. Youssef had come recommended and was available at a time he needed a driver. But he was cleverer than the others and Hama was nervous around anyone who thought too much.

"Circumstances in the last few days have come to light which will enable me to deal with two matters at the same time. One must be dealt with at the Castille. We must be here to meet Mahir at 1a.m. so we must be at the Castille by midnight."

"And the women…" Hama cut him short with an angry wave of his arm.

"As for the women, the girl is blonde, pale and I believe no more than fifteen, probably still a virgin and I trust will remain so whilst under the protection of this house. She will fetch an excellent price from the right man. I would not want my investment devalued."

He glared at each of the men in turn. "You, my brothers, will remain here to ensure this does not happen."

"The older woman will bring me the two things I require in addition to money. A body to abuse and revenge against the man who was instrumental in my incarceration."

The four men watched and waited. Without warning, Hama leaned forward and slammed his fists down on the table, his face puce with rage. His little black eyes darted around the room. The air was thick with silence. He straightened up and spoke softly but the menace in his voice was tangible. "Mistakes are unforgivable, but we are all guilty of under-estimating our enemy at some time in our lives. Those of us that learn from our mistake are those that will not make them again." He looked around the room at men. No one spoke.

"Many years ago I knew a girl. She was nothing special but she was young, she was willing and she fucked like a demon. I let my cock rule my brain as we men often do. But she had an older brother, and he was my one mistake."

He clenched his fists until his knuckles turned white. "This brother he asked questions about me, he delved into my business and learned things he should not have learned. He told people things he should not have told them and they took from me fifteen years of my life. They confiscated the half of my fortune they could find."

Hama reached for his drink and beamed, the gold tooth gleamed in the half-light. "And now I will take from him that which is most precious to him, his freedom… and his woman. He will know that whilst he lives in that hell hole they call prison, that I will be fucking the soul out of his woman and when I tire of her, she will simply disappear. He will know he will never see her again, after tonight."

"How do you know he will be at the Castille?" Youssef again. But this time Hama felt he was one ahead of him.

"I can hardly ask him to come here, can I? Mahmood tells me that his woman left him years ago but that he has never given up hope of finding her. I sent Amin to his house earlier this evening to tell him that she is staying at the Castille. I offered him money and Amin would sell his grandmother for money. Farid knows Amin and will believe him. Believe me also, he will come if there is even the slightest chance of finding the woman."

"And how do you know where he will go? Are we to watch every entrance to the hotel?" asked Youssef.

Hama regarded him as though he was an imbecile. "He will be told the woman is in the nightclub, which in the Castille is in the basement. The small storeroom next door leads directly onto the back entrance to the hotel where you will be waiting. Khaled will be in the nightclub. He will wait there for the arrival of our friend."

"And the woman, you are taking her with you?"

Hama took a deep breath. He was not used to having to explain himself. "Of course. She will sit in the nightclub with Khaled and Khaled I mean sit!" He glared at the bald man with look of contempt. "You will keep your hands to yourself. The woman is mine, you understand." The man scowled back at him, but dipped his head in acknowledgement.

"How do you know she will not shout or do something to attract attention?"

Hama was growing angry. "She is only a woman, but she is not stupid. I have been watching her through the mirror. She ignored the coffee and the glass and drank only from the unopened bottle of water."

Hama didn't see his brother smirk behind his hand, but the old lady seated in the shadows did.

"When we check into the hotel she will do nothing because she has already been told that if she acts in any way to draw attention to herself her children will get hurt. She will not cause any trouble but will sit quietly with Khaled." He bared his teeth in an evil smirk. "She does not know that she is to see her long lost love. What a reunion it will be."

Hama turned back to Youssef. "You see there is nothing to be concerned about, the only slight deviation from my plan are the women and a short diversion to the Castille to collect our friend. Now you see I have a scapegoat for our plans. When we leave he will remain. A call will be made to the police to tell them that there has been a lot of activity and many cars coming and going. When they arrive I will ensure that he will be high on cocaine and some of the merchandise will be left behind. It is known he came into a lot of money and what better or quicker way to make it than through trafficking. Whatever he tells them will not matter, he will not be believed. I have seen to that. Everything else is as I have arranged it."

Youssef thought quickly. This changed things. He had managed to make contact with Mohamed. He knew Hama would leave him in the car as the driver. He was no fool but neither was Hama. He also knew that Hama didn't trust him. He had been kept in the dark about when and where the deal was to take place. Until this evening all he knew was that it was to involve a major shipment and that it was to happen soon. Now he needed to get through again to Mohamed.

Hama used his people but he didn't trust any of them completely including his brother. He beamed benevolently. "Now I must ask you one favour."

The smile disappeared "Please hand to me your phones or any communication devices you may have. I would be most unhappy if anyone decided to have a chat with their friends today. They will be given back to you later."

Youssef was worried. He would now have no way of contacting Mohamed. The killing of the driver in Sicily had been easy and had succeeded in getting him in into Hama's inner circle, but up to now there had been no opportunity to bring the matter to a conclusion. Just as it seemed some headway was being made the women and Hama's insane desire for revenge could ruin everything.

The items were collected up and put into the filing cabinet which was then locked. Hama put the key in his pocket and beckoned his brother to follow him. The two men walked back into the small room where Lucy and Rose sat silently.

"Come, now we go." They stood up and Hama smiled at Rose. The gold tooth glinted and Lucy felt a shudder run down her back.

"You girl will stay here. I need only your mother at the moment. We will be back shortly. Please read your magazine and do not do anything stupid. My brother will sit with you."

Jalal smiled and his eyes shifted to Rose.

Rose started to cry and clung to her mother but Hama shook her off as he dragged Lucy out of the room. She was now petrified, not for herself but for her daughter. She knew well the look in the man's eyes when he looked at her daughter, but there was nothing she could do.

She made a last attempt. "My daughter is frightened. Would it not be better if she came with us?"

Hama smirked. "She will be well looked after. I understand your concern, but my brother is not a fool. He will do what is required of him and nothing more. We would not want the child walking off into the night, now would we?"

CHAPTER FIFTY-SIX

THE MESSENGER

Farid was surprised to receive Ali's call and particularly that Lucy's name was being used as a decoy, but as soon as he heard that Hama was involved he knew he had to do exactly as Ali said. It was a name he had hoped never to hear again. But regardless of what he was told, he would follow their plan to the letter. He knew of Hama's escape but thought it a rumour or that he had probably fled the country to start his sordid business activities elsewhere. It would seem he was wrong.

Amin was not at all sure Farid would accept the story. Although he had known him for many years they had never been close friends and he was not sure the promise of meeting a long lost girlfriend would be enough to bring him to the hotel. Hama had told him very little but he was under instruction to say only what Hama had told him to say, nothing more or less.

Amin drove up to the house. He knew where it was but had never been before. He was amazed at the pretty white house and grounds filled with flowers. It was not at all the house he imagined Farid would live in. He knocked and waited. Farid came to the door and to his surprise asked him to come in.

"Good evening, Amin. What brings you here?"

"I would have telephoned, but I did not have your number and I knew you would want to know what I have to say. I have information."

Farid was aware that he would be expected to pay for the information or Amin would not have bothered. He motioned to him to follow and led him into the sitting room. Amin sat uncomfortably on the low white settee and listened to the purring of the air conditioning. The air was thick with anticipation. Farid forced a smile and waited patiently.

"It is about your woman."

"My woman. I have no woman?"

"The one you lost many years ago. I am sure she is here in Tunisia."

The colour left Farid's cheeks and his eyes narrowed. He regarded Amin intently. If Hama was truly using Lucy as bait then he must really want him to bite.

"Go on."

Amin cringed at the steely softness in his voice. This was not the reaction he had expected.

"Look, Farid, I know we are not close friends but I too lost someone I loved."

This Farid acknowledged was the truth. He knew Amin's wife had died in childbirth. "Yes, I recall. I am sorry for your loss."

Amin smiled weakly. "So you see I understand loss. I remember the woman from many years ago, she is not one you can forget. I saw her walking into the Castille this afternoon. I thought I recognised her and asked at reception. Her name is Lucy Collins, I think?"

Farid nodded but said nothing. Amin noticed his hands gripped the edge of the chair. Farid thought quickly. If there were any truth in Amin's words he would not have expected Lucy's name would still be Collins. Had she not remarried? He remembered Ali's instructions. Take everything at face value and question nothing.

Amin was frightened. He just wanted to go. "Anyway, I just thought I would tell you that she is staying at the Castille. I must go now."

He got up to leave and waited. Farid handed him a note. He was surprised when the other man offered him his hand.

"Thank you for this, Amin. I will not forget it." His smile did not reach his eyes. Amin panicked, he had not said he would go to the hotel. This was not going as planned.

In desperation he asked "You will go to the hotel? I don't know how long she will be there."

"Of course, I will go. I will go this evening as soon when I have changed. If I am to see her again then I need to look my best."

The words sounded to him artificial, but Amin didn't seem to notice, he simply wanted to get out of the house and let Hama know his plan had worked.

Farid watched him as he disappeared down the drive. He checked his watch. 8p.m.

Amin telephoned Hama. "Yes, he took it all in. He didn't question me and he said he would come this evening. But what if he calls the Castille to check."

"I have already covered that. A blonde woman called Lucy Collins booked into the hotel this afternoon. Obviously not the right one, but they don't know that. Thank you. Amin, you have done well. Come to the house tomorrow and I will settle with you."

He smiled to himself as he replaced the phone in his pocket. By tomorrow he would be gone. Hama hated wasting money.

Amin put the phone back in his pocket and reached to start the car. He jumped at the knock on the window. An armed National Guardsman stood silently watching him. Amin tried to start the car and the man raised his gun. "Get out," he said simply. Amin complied.

"What have I done?"

"My orders are simply to detain you. Your phone please."

Amin handed over the phone. The armed guard carefully checked his pockets to ensure there was no second phone and no arms of any sort.

Farid watched as the Jeep drove away. He pulled out his phone and dialled the Castille.

"Castille Hotel. May I help you?"

"May I speak with Lucy Collins please?"

"One moment please."

After what seemed an eternity the pleasant female voice replied, "I am sorry sir, there is no reply from Mrs Collins' room. Do you wish to leave a message?"

"No, no message thank you."

Farid put the phone down. His hands were shaking as he lit the cigarette.

He called Ali. "Ali what the hell is going on? I've just phoned the Castille and they confirmed Lucy is staying there."

"Did you speak with her"

"No, there was no reply from the room."

"Farid, listen to me. Something really big is going down. Do you seriously think some guy who is not a particular friend of yours is going to recognise a woman he hasn't seen for years and drive half an hour just to tell you she's here? But you know Hama is no fool. If he is setting you up for this, he is going to cover every angle. Of course there is a Lucy Collins booked into the Castille. Hama knows the first thing you would do is to check. I told you they would use anything to get you to the hotel and what better way than that."

Farid acknowledged he was right. He was still shocked. He had hoped so much Lucy would answer the phone and he could hear her beloved voice again, but it was all a cruel trick.

"Farid, are you still there?"

"Yes. Ali, look I am sorry it was just a shock. And yes before you ask, they picked up Amin."

"Good, the instructions were to wait until he made his phone call, so he will have reported in and Hama will be none the wiser."

"What are they holding Amin for?"

"Absolutely nothing, he hasn't done anything. Mohamed said to simply take his phone and to search him. He will be stuck in a cell overnight and they will let him out tomorrow with some feeble explanation, no doubt. Enough of him, get to the Sahara Oasis, no later than ten. There is a lot to do."

CHAPTER FIFTY-SEVEN

THE STRATEGY

Although he was sure the tale Amin had told him was a lie and he knew Lucy was still out of his reach a little niggle of hope had remained. He showered, dressed and as he combed his hair and his moustache he smiled grimly. The white hairs had not been there before, but there were not too many of them, just the odd streak and a bit around the ears. He inspected his hairline and was pleased to note there was still no signs of receding which affected several of his friends but had so far passed him by. He wondered if her hair was still blonde then looked angrily at his reflection in the mirror. Damn Hama. Why had he reminded him of Lucy? Not that he could ever forget, the first thing he saw every morning was the photograph in his bedroom. A room which no other woman save for his sister Meriam had ever seen and never would.

He sat down on the bed his head in his hands. He checked his watch. There was still half an hour before he needed to leave. His mind flew back over the years.

Since he left the hotel management there had only been one woman who came close to him, one of Meriam's young friends. He had taken her out a few times and the last time he had brought her to the house, but as he watched her sitting on the settee where Lucy should be, he knew that he could not make love to another woman in Lucy's house. She had asked about the photographs on the wall and when he told her she too realised that she could never compete with this unknown woman and he drove her home shortly afterwards.

He gazed for a long time at the photographs and then locked up the house. He hesitated for a moment and then went back into the house, upstairs to the guest room. He pulled out the jacket, Lucy bought him the last time he saw her. He remembered their conversation as thought it had been yesterday.

"Lucy you are crazy. The price of this jacket is more than I can earn in a month."

He remembered her soft kiss on his cheek.

"I want you to have something which will last you a long time so you will remember me."

He had wondered about her words but thought it was because she would not be back for some months. He had been wearing it that New Year's Eve when he had spoken to her on the phone for the last time. He had not worn it again. Now he stroked the soft leather, closed his eyes and pulled on the jacket. It was a bit tighter than he remembered. He left it open.

The sleek white car purred down the driveway and into the unknown. Farid did as Ali had suggested and took the back road into the resort. He drove to the car park entrance and the security guard waved him through with a grin.

"Evening Farid. I saw Mr Ali heading for the bar about half an hour ago. Enjoy your evening."

Farid smiled to himself. How often had he himself greeted people with similar words from the little security box. He thought of Jane. Were it not for her and her amazing gift, he would probably still be doing the same thing. He pushed the reminiscence to the back of his mind, parked the car out of sight of the road and went into the hotel through the rear entrance.

Farid knew the Sahara Oasis well. Since he rekindled his friendship with Ali some years before they often met there for a drink. When the hotel was finished, the place had become their usual meeting place. The hotel was also one of his best customers, preferring the quality merchandise he could obtain to the inferior stuff which the more unscrupulous companies tried to sell them. The hotel was the best in the area, if not in Tunisia. The guests, mainly business men and their wives and colleagues, paid high prices and expected the best. It was Farid's job to ensure they got it and he was rewarded handsomely for his efforts.

Ali was seated at the back of the bar area and Farid was surprised to see two other men with him, both in casual clothes although he recognised Ali's brother in law, the chief of police.

The men got up and greeted him. Farid sat down in the fourth chair, lit a cigarette and waited.

"Farid, tell me what Amin said to you."

Farid repeated everything Amin had said. "Of course it threw me when he mentioned Lucy. Although I know it was a bloody great lie it still gave me a shock. What I don't understand is why it is so important I go to the Castille. Tell me, what exactly is going on?"

Ali regarded him anxiously. He had tried to work out the best way to tell Farid but whatever he said was going to upset his friend. He was glad Mohamed and Ahmed were with him.

"Farid, not everything Amin told you was a lie."

Farid's blood ran cold.

"Lucy is here in Hammamet or if she isn't she will be soon."

"Lucy is here! Where?" Farid jumped to his feet his eyes staring wildly. Ali stood up and put both hands on his shoulders.

"Farid, sit down and listen. Everything depends on how you deal with this. If you don't do exactly as Mohamed says, Lucy could get hurt and a probably a few other people as well."

Farid glared at him. "What d'you mean, get hurt. Is Lucy all right? Ali where is she? Ali what the fuck is going on?"

"Farid, you will listen to me and you will listen good."

Mohamed's voice was harsh and Farid turned on him. "How are you involved? Ali what the hell is happening and why is Lucy in danger? Tell me where she is."

At the sound of raised voices, one of two of the guests had turned to look at them. Ali put his hand on his friend's shoulder and forced him back into his seat.

"Hama has her," he said flatly. Farid went white and slumped back in his chair. Ali handed him a whisky and Farid downed the fiery liquid in one gulp.

"Oh dear God, anyone but him."

Mohamed's face softened. "Look, Farid, we have been aware for some time that Hama has been planning something big and we have a man on the inside, but until today our information was sketchy. We thought it was just drugs which would have been difficult to find, but we now have reason to believe he may be dealing in firearms as well which should be easier and possibly he's got back into the people trafficking as well. There's a lot of money involved in that trade. As I said we have suspected this for some time but we didn't know where or when until today. We now have it on good authority that the deal goes down tonight, which is why we haven't tried to pick him up yet."

Farid looked surprised. "I didn't know he was back into all that again."

Mohamed smiled grimly. "We don't advertise things like this. It hardly encourages either legitimate business or tourism does it? Since Hama was banged up we've had no major trouble, just the usual problems with small amounts of hashish every now and again.

"But back to the point. We are not sure where he is getting the stuff. If it's drugs I can only assume they've been bringing it in from Turkey by boat or to be frank it could be from anywhere. Unfortunately heroin is not perishable so it may have been coming in from Afghanistan for months. Also, there's been a lot of activity on the Libyan border recently which is why we think there may be other things as well as drugs, firearms perhaps.

"For the coke, they are probably using palm oil. With the total quantity of merchandise we believe is involved little boats would be useless. The rocks they will have to hide in some form of legal cargo and that takes up space. They could move it to Tangier then to Spain. The heroin they will probably take to Sicily and on by land. They can in a matter of weeks flood Europe with all manner of drugs. The hardware could be going anywhere. I believe they are selling the stuff or arranging to export it on one of the bulk cargo ships out of La Goulette. The port authority told me one arrived late last night. Thank God these big deals happen very rarely but it does mean that they manage to find new routes every time."

"How much are we talking about?"

"To be truthful, we have absolutely no idea, but we know it's big. By the people our man tells us are involved, it has to be. Farid I think we are talking in many many millions. Our source also said the

Algerians are involved and as I am sure you know there are links there to Al Qaeda. As for human trafficking, you know there is a disgusting trade in that, but if they are shipping girls they will need to get them on boats immediately. They couldn't risk travelling by road and I believe air travel would be impossible, No I am sure it would be by sea. Hama will not do this himself, he will sell the girls along with everything else. It will be the buyer's problem to get them out of the country."

"Okay, I can see your reasoning behind that side of it, but I still don't understand where I come in or how Lucy is involved?" Farid spoke quietly but Mohamed sensed his fear.

"Farid, you gave us the means to put Hama away, he knows it and he hates you for it. He does not like to be parted from his money or his liberty and you succeeded in arranging both. I am sure this deal has been planned for months, possibly years if he was cooking it up while banged up. Unfortunately there is little that happens that he doesn't know about and Lucy turning up has just given him the opportunity to add revenge against you. I am quite sure he now intends to involve you in this sordid business. Your success is based on your reputation."

He hesitated. "Think about it man, you left the hotel trade, it's common knowledge you disappeared from the area for a year or so and when you came back you had money. You are well known and well respected and you move freely between Europe and North Africa. You could have been involved in the business for years and what better cover than being the man who was instrumental in putting Hama inside. If he is successful in his plan you could go to prison for a very long time."

The more Farid thought about it the more convinced he became that Mohamed was right. Not even Ali knew of the depth of his involvement with Hama's arrest.

"What do you plan to do? I tell you now I will not go along with anything which would endanger Lucy." He swore loudly. "You don't think Hama will try to… to sell Lucy, do you?"

Mohamed smiled. "Farid, I understand your Lucy is a very beautiful woman, but she is a little older than the girls Hama needs for his business. No truly I doubt Lucy will be harmed. In fact the opposite. I think Hama's intense hatred of you will mean that he will ensure she is not harmed and he will make certain you are aware he intends to take Lucy with him, which he knows will cause you more pain even than the loss of your freedom."

Farid sat said nothing. The horror of what Hama would do to her was something he did not want to imagine.

"And Hama, what of him, and Lucy?"

"I am sure they will leave as quickly as possible. I don't think Hama will risk going to Tunis and if I were in his position, I would want to travel with only one or two people so as to attract as little attention as possible. I think more likely he will take a boat directly to Malta or Sicily and transfer from there to wherever he is going. He will probably use one of the yachts here in the marina. I already have men there. The frontier police are watching the harbour. Do not worry. I will call them once the deal has taken place and tell them to close the harbour entrance to all traffic in and out. I can't do it yet because I cannot risk alerting anyone by doing something out of the ordinary. Success depends on them being completely unaware that we know about their operation."

"What do you want me to do?"

Mohamed smiled. "From what my source said today, they intend to trap you at the Castille. I am certain the consignment, in whatever form it takes, will not be in the hotel. That is far too risky and with the amount we think is involved they could never store it without being found. It was again only today that we learned the meeting takes place at the old house in Nabeul around 1a.m. That is the only place where a large volume of merchandise could remain undiscovered. It was thought the house was deserted so no-one goes there. They could have been adding to their cache for some time. God only knows what they have got there."

Farid listened quietly and when he spoke his voice was cold.

"I understand everything you are saying, but let me get this quite straight, you want me to allow myself to be taken, but why? If you know the stuff is at the house why wait for Hama to go back there. If he is to lure me to the Castille, he must have Lucy with him. Could you not arrest him at the Castille and get your men to pick up the merchandise from the house at the same time?"

Mohamed had anticipated this question. He knew Farid was not stupid but he hoped to avoid any mention of Rose. He felt sure Hama would leave her at the house. There would be no reason for him to take Rose as well and it would prevent her mother from doing anything foolish. If his men were to storm the house at the wrong time she and whoever else might be in the house could easily be hurt or killed.

He chose his words carefully. "There are several reasons for that. On what grounds can we arrest Hama at the Castille? Attacking you is hardly a reason to put him away. Also if we do not get the timing absolutely right he could alert whoever is left at the house and people could be hurt. We want to catch the whole syndicate red handed, including the Algerians."

Farid watched him closely but Mohamed would not meet his eyes. He turned to his friend.

"Ali, what is he not telling me?"

Ali looked at Mohamed, who nodded wearily and turned back to Farid.

"When Lucy was taken she had a girl with her, I believe it is her daughter."

"Her daughter! Oh dear God, but why take a young child?"

Mohamed did not understand why Farid assumed the girl was a young child but said nothing.

Farid's head dropped forward and he sat back in his chair. So Lucy had another child. He remembered the boy he had seen. He was quite small then so must be about fourteen now. There had been no girl with her at the time so it seemed likely the girl arrived after she went back to her husband in England.

His lip curled in a sneer. "I suppose the bastard thinks that if he takes the kid, she will cooperate."

"Yes, I believe that is probably the reason and there would be no sense in taking the girl to the hotel."

Farid nodded. "I understand, then it seems I must allow myself to fall into this trap. I trust that you will be careful at the house. For myself, I do not care much, but be certain if I survive and either Lucy or her child do not, I will hold you totally responsible. What do you need me to do?"

"Just go along with everything until you reach the house. We will follow you from the hotel. If you can, make sure you or they take your car, it is much easier for us to follow."

Farid smiled. "I will do my best, and what happens when I get to the house, tell me now and hope that Hama does not simply decide to put a bullet in my head."

Ali patted his arm affectionately. "Farid, he wants you to suffer and to Hama that means to suffer as he did. He will want you locked up, not dead."

Farid took his friend by the hand. "I thank you for that, Ali, although I am not sure I feel any better!"

Mohamed spoke thoughtfully. "We need them all to be there and we know the time of the meeting. Hama is fanatical about being on time, this is a weakness of his and is well known. From what I remember of the house there are only three doors, the main door, the rear door and a small side door to the garage block. My men will cover all of them. The problem will be the rear door as it leads out onto an area of wasteland. If any of them manage to get out through there we will need a lot of men to round them up. The National Guard will have to deal with that."

Ali turned to Farid. "There is only the one road to the Castille, leading from Hammamet up to the hotel and back in a half-circle here. My guess is that they will come in through the main door, probably even booked into the hotel to avoid suspicion. They will go to the nightclub and when it is in full throttle around midnight, any activity in the adjacent storage room would not be heard. This is where I think they will hold you."

Farid smiled. "What am I to do when we reach the house?"

"Exactly what you are told to do, save that at some time after the exchange takes place, before any of them have a chance to leave the house you must find some way of causing as much confusion as you can inside the house to distract them and if humanly possible get someone to open the front door."

"This could all happen very quickly. What if we are wrong?"

"We are not. My source heard the whole discussion himself and one of my own men has also told me as much as he could. I was hoping he would contact me today but so far there has been no word. It was our source who told us where and when."

"Who is this source and how do you know you can trust him? If he knows so much could he not be one of Hama's own men spinning a story to put you off what is really happening."

Mohamed grinned. "Farid I can promise you this source is the most reliable I have ever used and for his own safety I cannot tell you anything about him."

Farid nodded. "I apologise, I shouldn't have asked."

"Time is actually on our side in this. The deal will have to take some time because the merchandise, whatever it is, will need to be checked. I am quite certain money will not change hands. Hama is not that stupid. He will have someone based elsewhere. Whoever it is will also need to get away fast so I am taking a chance that it will be one of the hotels near the marina or even a large boat. This will enable him to collect the information he needs to access the money. He will check to ensure the funds have been transferred directly to an account, or probably one of several, and until that person confirms to Hama that the transfer has been made, the goods will not change hands and he will not permit them to start loading."

"So what happens now?"

"Go to the hotel and ask at reception for Mrs Collins, who I am sure will conveniently have left a message as to where she can be found. You will be directed to the nightclub. Go there and wait. I have two of my people who will also be in there from about 11.30p.m. in case there is any last minute change of plan they will contact me. One is a man, the other a woman. They will be easy for you to recognise. She is very tall and slim and will be wearing a red dress and he has shoulder length grey hair will have on a yellow baseball cap. Do not approach them. They are there in case there are any hitches."

Farid smiled "Hitches, a good word. Let us hope that if there are any they will be small ones. Where will you be?"

"Ali will be in the hotel at reception to watch the front entrance. He will wait there until I contact him. He is often in the hotel and no-one will see anything unusual in his presence. Ahmed and I will wait at the end of the road where the hotel access joins the road to Nabeul." He looked at his watch. "It is time. Now we go."

CHAPTER FIFTY-EIGHT

ROSE

Lucy was desperately worried about leaving Rose. She had seen the way the one they called Jalal, had looked at her daughter and to leave her alone in a room with such a man petrified her. As they walked through the hallway she noticed the old lady followed them to the door and watched them leave. She seemed agitated.

Youssef drove at a leisurely pace towards the Castille. They wanted nothing to draw attention to themselves. Massoud sat in the front with him and Hama in the back with Lucy, one hand on her knee and tried to make conversation. She ignored him. They were approaching the turn of to the new resort when she heard Hama's phone ring. He answered it and she saw his expression change to one of total fury.

Rose was frightened at being left on her own with Jalal, who ignored her until the door closed behind his brother. When he heard the movement of the car tyres on the gravel he got up from the table and walked over to the fridge. He looked inside and pulled out a bottle of beer, turned to her and shrugged his shoulders. He offered her nothing but sat drinking his beer, a narrow smile on his face, his eyes never leaving her. She tried not to look at him.

Jalal told her to get up and sit on the day bed. She pretended not to understand until he raised his arm as though to strike her. She ran across and sat on the edge of the bed as far from him as she could get, but to her relief he sat in the chair on the other side of the room. He looked at his watch and called out to the old woman who shuffled back into the room. Jalal left and after a short while came back with a bottle of water, which he handed to Rose. He told the old woman to leave. She gave him an odd look but did as she was told.

Rose had refused the water earlier because she was too frightened to even think but now she was really thirsty. The room seemed terribly hot and her head was hurting. She desperately needed a drink. She looked at the bottle and remembered her mother had checked the seal. She did the same, it appeared unbroken. She picked it up and was relieved to hear the soft click as the seal broke.

Jalal held his breath as she took a long drink from the bottle. He opened another bottle of beer and drank from it, watching her, his black eyes gleaming.

She turned to look at him. He was younger than his brother, but to her still very old. They had the same thickset body, sinister expression and hard black eyes. She was frightened of him. She knew from what her mother had told her while they waited that Hama was a dangerous man but something told her this man was worse. She had been aware of his eyes roving over her body from the time he had first risen from the table when she arrived at the house.

She drank half the water and looked at him. His eyes were fixed on the tight bodice of her dress and he ran his tongue over his thick lips. He waited a few minutes, watching her intently. His hands were clasped tightly in front of him.

"Is the water to your liking?"

She looked up at him. "It's only water," she whispered.

"Is it?"

Rose's eyes widened and she stared at the bottle. "But it was unopened."

"Indeed, but you may find the label is a little loose my dear." Rose panicked and pulled at the label which came off easily. There was a small hole from which the water now seeped.

Jalal smirked and as he moved towards her she tried to stand up. Her mind screamed run but her body wouldn't move. He leaned towards her, brushing her hair back from her face and she tried to turn away. It was as though a rock rested on top of her head. She couldn't move. Gently he pushed her back so she rested on the cushions which were heaped at one end of the daybed. His eyes rested on the swell of her breasts.

"Oh my beauty, how much I have wanted to touch you and now there is no one to see what I am going to do to you. You will be powerless to stop me, you may even enjoy me."

Rose felt the bile rise in her throat but there was nothing she could do, her limbs would not obey her. She felt his fat lips against hers and smelt his hot breath as his tongue probed her mouth. She thought she was going to be sick. His hands roamed freely over her. He slid the straps from her shoulders and pulled her dress down to her waist and sat back and stared.

"How old are you, fifteen perhaps? Oh yes you are indeed very beautiful." He stroked her neck and traced his hand down to her breast massaging the nipple.

"With what my brother has planned for you I am sure that your future will be very interesting. Your blonde hair and soft pale skin will ensure that there will be many men who want to taste your sweetness, but I believe I will have the honour of being your first."

Rose did not fully understand, she only knew that he intended to rape her and felt the tears welling up and trickle down her cheek.

Jalal grinned and gently wiped them away. He turned his attention to her exposed body and eased himself down so that his face rested on her bosom. He took her breast in his hand and closed his lips over the nipple sucking greedily on it. She tried to scream.

He laughed. "Go on, little flower, call for help, but none will hear your silent screams."

Rose could hear nothing but the frantic beating of her own heart. She felt his hand travel down her body until it reached her knees. He sat back and pulled her dress up, exposing the thin wisp of material which was all that kept him from her. His hands shook as he raised her hips and gently eased off her knickers.

He took her limp hand and rubbed himself with it. She could feel the heat of him and the throbbing of his body. She retched. She tried to move her arm but couldn't. The beady black eyes held hers. With every ounce of strength she fought against him but he pushed her legs wide apart as though he was moving a feather. He eased his body down beside her and with a groan stroked her thighs until she felt his fingers invading her as he pushed his fat fingers inside her.

Rose gagged but was powerless to move. His belt buckle scratched her leg and she attempted to scream again but no sound came. He traced his free hand up and down her body, squeezing her breasts as he continued to probe.

After what seemed an eternity in hell, he stood up and leered down at her, her breasts bare and her legs apart. He could do anything he liked to her and there was nothing she could do to stop him.

"Oh my beauty, this is going to be much better than even I have dreamed of. When I am finished with you if you say one word to my brother or to anyone, then you have my word I will find a way to dispose of your mother and deliver you to a hell you could never in your worst nightmare imagine."

He moved her head so she was facing him. He undid his belt and pulled down his zip but took his time as though enjoying her agony. The trousers fell down round his ankles. Slowly he stepped out of them. She stared at the huge erection. He grinned and took her hand moving her fingers up and down as he forced her to stroke him. Then to her horror he knelt down over her and positioned himself between her legs, his face inches from her own. She clenched her eyes shut.

The door burst open. Hama stood in the doorway, taking in the scene before him. Jalal leapt up and made a grab for his trousers but Hama crossed the room with a speed that belied his build and with a vicious swipe sent his brother flying across the room. His furious screaming reverberated through the house.

"You filthy bastard. If you were not my brother I would kill you for this. I told you this girl is not to be touched and I trusted you, but our mother knows you cannot keep your cock in your trousers."

He stopped and looked at Rose's spread legs and back at his brother, his face contorted in rage and he screamed "You have not…"

Jalal shook his head in terror. Hama stared at him and then at Rose. He noticed redness around her nipples and the long scratch on her inner thigh. To her horror he thrust his hand between her legs, then he snorted and looked uncertainly at his brother.

"You are a lucky man my brother. If you had fucked this child I think I would have killed you, brother or not. Now go into the bathroom and toss yourself off, or whatever you need to do and get dressed. We have work to do and this time you will come with me."

He squared up to his brother. "But make no mistake Jalal, I will not forget this." Jalal scuttled out of the room and she heard his heavy feet on the stairs.

Hama turned back to Rose who lay motionless. With a curse he picked up the bottle of water, looked at the torn label and flung the bottle at the door.

He spoke softly, still with his back towards her. "I am angry with my brother, but he is a man. You pretty girl, if I had thought even for one moment you intended to give yourself to him, for whatever reason, you would not recognise your reflection ever again."

He turned to face her and hesitated, looking down at her with a slight smile his black eyes taking in her nakedness. She noticed a trickle of sweat run down his face.

"If I did not have other plans for you..." He bent down and stroked her breast. Rose gasped, surely he did not intend to finish what Jalal had started. He laughed harshly reading her thoughts. "Not yet my beauty, you have that pleasure to come, but not with me. You are worth too much money, I will make do with your mother. Now try and move. It should be wearing off by now."

He pulled her dress down roughly. She wanted to push him away and finally her arms moved. Hama pulled the cover off the day bed and handed it to her. With a huge effort she managed to clutch it round herself. A few moments later he pulled her to her feet. She fell against him and he chuckled holding her by her bottom before releasing her. She tried to control her trembling limbs and stood shakily as he watched her. The old lady came in with a coffee which she handed to Rose with a ghost of a smile. Rose sipped the harsh liquid and felt her strength returning.

"Once my would be fucker of a brother has finished we must go."

Jalal came back some minutes later fully clothed. He looked neither at Rose nor at Hama, but followed his brother to the car. The old lady closed the door behind them and then went back into the little room, where Rose sat clutching the rough material trying to bury herself in its folds. The woman stroked her hair murmuring in her own language. Rose cringed and was rewarded by a toothless smile.

To Rose's surprise she spoke softly in perfect French.

"I am sorry for what my son tried to do and in preventing him I have caused trouble between my sons."

"I don't understand. Why can't you just let me go?"

"This I cannot do."

"But what do they want with me?"

The old lady cackled. "You really have no idea, have you? It is better for you that you remain pure. The others are not so lucky they have already lost their value. A virgin brings much money. Hama will see to it that you are well cared for until you are handed over and then it will be up to you how you are treated."

Rose's eyes widened in shock as she realised she was to be sold. She started to scream.

"Yes, little one, better now than when they return. There is no one to hear you. I am sorry but it is the business you see."

She gave Rose a toothless grin, shrugged her shoulders and left the room locking the door behind her.

CHAPTER FIFTY-NINE

THE TRAP

Lucy did exactly as Hama had said and drew no attention to herself as they checked in. The clerk however noticed her eyes darted back and forth and she seemed frightened. Carrying only one small bag each the two men escorted her to the lift, Hama in front and he felt Jalal slide his arm around her waist. She resisted the urge to push him away.

In the room, Lucy sat silently on the settee and watched as her captors stood away from her talking quietly. She noticed Jalal looked at the floor and not at his brother. She heard Hama say he was going out to check on the arrangements for the evening. As he walked to the door he turned to his brother. "She will go with you. If you touch her, pray to Allah that you are not here when I return."

They walked in silence to the lift. Hama turned to his brother. "I am going to check with Youssef that everything is as it should be. You go now to the nightclub and remember, you just sit with her and that is all. I have sent Khaled also to the nightclub in case our friend is cleverer than we think."

Jalal nodded, his eyes still avoiding his brother's face. She wondered what had happened, what was the significance of the phone call and why had they gone back to the house. She had been left alone in the locked car for at least ten minutes while Hama went with the driver into the house. She gasped, had Jalal done something to Rose? Was this why Hama was so angry? Her head was swimming and she felt sick as images of what that brute might have done to her defenceless child.

As Hama had envisaged the nightclub was filling up. Lucy knew there was nothing she could say or do without endangering her children further. She sank gratefully into chair, Jalal rested his hand lightly on her leg and smirked at her. She wanted to rake her nails across that swarthy face. She wished with all her heart that he was dead.

Farid followed his instructions. He parked the car in the street as near to the fire exit as he could get without going onto the wasteland. Mohamed had explained to him that he must leave the car directly facing the road where they could reach it easily. Farid had the fastest car and if by chance there was a chase, he would be needed. He had given Ali the spare key in case, as Mohamed put it bluntly, he himself was unable to drive.

He walked quickly into the hotel through the main entrance, his heart beating until he thought it would burst. The reception area was full. He could see almost every table was taken. Couples and families, one or two with children, all blissfully unaware of the drama which was about to unfold below them. He knew Hama was ruthless and would not hesitate to use the pistol which Farid was certain he carried with him at all times.

He slowed his pace and walked to the reception desk. A young woman greeted him.

"Good evening, Mr Khalifa, can I help you?"

"Yes, I am supposed to be meeting Mrs Collins, but I'm afraid I am a little late. Has she left a message for me?"

The girl smiled at him. She had worked previously at the Sahara Oasis and knew Farid. She had always fancied him, but that he would notice her never crossed her mind. She had heard of his meteoric rise to riches, but she also knew he was rarely seen with a woman and then usually only with a business contact. She was a little surprised when he asked after the tourist, Mrs Collins. Karima's practised eye did not place her as the type she thought Farid would like. She was attractive enough, but her bottle blonde hair was frizzy, her clothes cheap and her voice hard. She looked as though her makeup had been applied with a palette knife.

Karima was embarrassed that he had read her thoughts as he held her eyes for a moment in his magnetic gaze and smiled at her.

"Mrs Collins?"

"Oh, yes I am sorry, she left a message that she would be in the nightclub if anyone asked after her."

"Thank you, Karima, I feel very guilty I am actually more than a little late and unfortunately I have never met Mrs Collins. She is the sister of a friend of mine. Can you help me?" Karima beamed back. He knew her name.

She chose her words carefully. "She is a blonde lady. When I saw her earlier she had on a purple blouse and black trousers. Have a good evening, Mr Khalifa. I am sure your friend will not mind you being a bit late."

She watched him walk to the stairs, his perfectly fitted trousers over slim hips moving enough to be sexy, his arms swinging loosely by his side in the expensive leather. She sighed. He was perfect. Whoever that Mrs Collins was she was a lucky woman.

She held out her hand and imagined a ring on her finger. As she did so her eye caught the hotel badge she wore. She chuckled, of course he knew her name.

Farid walked down the stairs, his mouth was dry. He knew the Mrs Collins described to him was not his Lucy. He knew she hated purple. He smiled to himself, he remembered things like that, even after so long. He looked around the nightclub and saw no one of that description. He noticed the man with the baseball cap and his companion. Then he saw Lucy. He hardly recognised her. Her hair was loose and untidy. Even in the dim lights of the nightclub he could see her face was ashen and she had dark circles under her eyes which were wide with fear, staring but not seeing. He knew instinctively Lucy would never have allowed herself to be seen in such a state unless by force. She sat with a thickset dark man whom he did not recognise. The man had his hand on her leg. Farid hesitated. It was then he felt the pressure on his lower back.

"Do not turn around. Back out slowly and walk quietly to the next room and go in. Believe me nothing would give me more pleasure than to use this thing."

Farid cursed himself, he should have expected something of this sort, but seeing Lucy everything else had suddenly become unimportant. He remembered what Mohamed had said about the girl left at the old house. He knew he had to obey. He opened the door. There was a small table on one side, several wooden chairs scattered about. He was pushed onto one of the chairs and heard the door close. The room was in darkness, the only light coming from the tiny window. He saw the outline of a man and as he turned towards him, the flash of teeth and light shining on a bald pate. The man hit Farid hard across the face and tied his hands behind him. Farid felt the blood trickle from the corner of his mouth. A few moments later the door opened again, two men walked in and the light was turned on. It was a single bare bulb and shed harsh shadows round the large room. Hama he recognised immediately. It was a face he would never forget.

Hama beamed at Farid. "Farid my friend, so good to see you again after so long. But, I believe there is someone you wish to see even more than me."

He nodded at Khaled who grinned and walked backed into the nightclub. A few moments later Jalal came into the room his arm tightly around Lucy. Hama glared at him and Jalal removed his arm. Farid stared at her. She was thinner than he remembered and her eyes huge in her white face, her dress was creased and he noticed the hem was dirty. Her hair was hair matted around her shoulders. Nausea filled his throat. What had they done to her?

Lucy stared back at him. She knew what she must look like and saw contempt in his face. Hama sneered at Farid, then walked over to Lucy and stroked her face. He pushed her gently onto one of the wooden chairs. His eyes never left Farid as he slowly ran his hand down her neck and slid his fingers inside her dress to cup her breast. Farid knew that if he ever got out of this chair Hama was a dead man, but his expression gave away nothing.

"What my friend, no word for your beloved?"

"What is there to say? - it appears she prefers the company of animals to that of men."

Whatever response Hama had expected this was not it. Lucy gasped in horror, her eyes fixed on Farid's face.

Hama glared at him. "Enough of this, now we wait. But I must admit my dear Farid, I never thought catching you would be this easy."

Mohamed drove slowly up to the hotel and turned off the lights. He motioned to Ahmed beside him to stay silent. He placed the car carefully where they could see the fire exit but where there were other vehicles parked so there would be no reason for anyone to think there was anyone still inside the car. The door to the fire exit was open and he could see the dim light where the door was ajar. He watched as Hama came out, pushing the door behind him, but it swung open and Mohamed could see at least four people in the room. He could not see Farid but he saw a woman seated with her back to the door. He was not surprised to see that Hama had surrounded himself with his henchmen. He never took chances but in coming to the hotel himself he had made a mistake. Hama glanced around quickly and then walked over to the large black saloon in which Youssef still sat. Mohamed heard the engine purr as the car moved away from the hotel to the edge of the roadway, positioned ready for an immediate departure.

The wide sweeping entrance to the hotel was lit with antique style black iron street lamps but beyond the narrow roads which led back to Hammamet and the resort were for the most part unlit and then only where there was a bend in the road. There were no turn-offs as the road circled from the town up to the hotel and then past it and down to the resort. It was impossible for anyone to turn off the road but if Hama got wind of their presence he had to be prepared for any eventuality.

His phone vibrated. "Yes, Ali."

"You were right. Two men checked into a suite this evening. They had a woman with them, a blonde woman. The night manager thought she was already a guest because a Mrs Collins had checked in during the day. He said she seemed agitated. Look Mohamed, I am sure you know what you are doing, but I am concerned about this. Do you have enough men?"

"Ali, I am the chief of this area. I have called in officers from all around and they have alerted the National Guard and the other areas police between here and Tunis. We will be stationed at different places, along the access road, at the back of the hotel, in the town, on the roads to Nabeul, Tunis and Sousse and at the frontier police in the marina are on alert."

"And the house?"

"Yes, we will cover the house. I cannot believe these men will go quietly and if as I expect firearms are used, we will deal with the situation. Our men will cover all exits from the house and the waste ground at the back. Once it runs out of our district others will take over. Ali, my friend, I do not intend to let this operation fail."

"I just hope you are all in time," Ali muttered.

Mohamed switched off his phone. "So do I," he muttered.

CHAPTER SIXTY

CAPTIVES

Hama pulled a chair into the middle of the room and sat down addressing Farid directly.

"Now we are all assembled, it is time to leave."

"Where are you taking us? Why involve Lucy? She has got me here, why do you need her?" It was futile and he knew it, but he needed to find out as much as he could about Hama's intentions.

Hama beamed at him. "I will explain later your part in my operation, but I can assure you that you will take centre stage. Your woman of course will not, as you say hers is but a bit part, the honey trap as they say. She will remain with me. When you are gone she will need a little male company, as you say."

Farid expression did not change and he shrugged his shoulders.

Hama was disappointed that he had not managed to coax Farid into anger. He stood up and motioned to Khaled. Farid felt the ropes which held him to the chair loosen but he knew he must not try to escape.

"Your car keys, please, where are they?"

"In my jacket pocket."

"Khaled you will drive his car. The woman will come with me. Follow us closely. I want nothing to go wrong."

He pulled Lucy to her feet and grasped her arm, leading her out of the fire exit door. Khaled followed with Farid and another man.

Lucy was bundled into the back of the black car and Massoud got back into the front seat. As Hama climbed into the back next to her, she stole a glance at the driver in the car mirror and his eyes met hers. She was surprised to see him wink at her. She was confused, could it be possible he was not really one of Hama's people. She brushed the thought away. From what she already knew of Hama it was very unlikely his key people would not be thoroughly investigated. No, it was yet another forlorn hope which meant nothing.

The black car moved slowly down the narrow road. Khaled followed, the white car bright in the moonlight, exactly as Mohamed had hoped.

He turned to Ali "Now it begins." The engine purred into life.

Youssef looked from side to side. He could see no-one, the white car was close behind him. He looked at Lucy in the mirror. He had tried to tell her to trust him, but had she read his sign or did she just think he was playing with her like the rest of the bastards. As he reached the junction he noticed an old black car parked at the side of the road. He could see a couple in the front seat, their arms around each other, the woman's face hidden behind her scarf. He smiled to himself. Sure enough when the two cars had passed, the could see the old car was following them at a distance.

Karim removed his headscarf and poked his companion in the ribs.

"Don't you ever do that again!" His companion grinned at him.

"Come on, Mohamed told us to look inconspicuous and you must admit your wife's new scarf does suit you!" Karim swore at him and flung the offending object on the back seat. "At least Mohamed was right, they did use the white car, thank God. Why the hell don't they light these roads? Anyway, just follow them, if Mohamed is correct when the reach the junction they will go straight on towards Nabeul."

He saw the roundabout approaching but to his dismay the car turned right towards the Marina

"Shit, what do we do now?"

"It's okay, I can see the other car waiting, they will take over, we just go straight on, as instructed and head up towards the house."

Hama had been watching the old car and was relieved when it carried straight on up the road. Although he had no reason to suspect he was being followed, he was taking no chances, there was too much at stake. Aymen pulled in behind the white car and picked up his phone. "Mohamed, they have turned off towards the marina."

"Yes, I thought that might happen. Stay close and see what happens, but do not stop. I have a car on the road by the Marina. Whatever happens do not allow him to suspect anything."

Youssef drove down the long straight road which runs down to the harbour and as instructed pulled into the kerb. Hama tapped Massoud on the shoulder. "Right, get out and head straight through on the main path to the larger boats. Draw no attention to yourself. The boat is called the Santa Esmerelda. It is moored at the far end near where the tourist pirate ships go from. You can't miss it. You are expected and you know what to do."

Massoud grinned and picked up his holdall. "I will await your call."

Aymen watched the little man scurry across the road and drove on. He called Mohamed.

"Good, now head up to the house. Park up at the back. Your job is to block any cars trying to head up towards Tunis. Others will join you later and we will close off the road after 1a.m."

Massoud was excited. He griped his bag tightly. All he had to do was make a couple of calls and relay a message to Hama, for which he was to be paid a lot of money. He need never work again. He was an old man, he had no family and had already decided he would go to France. His papers were in order and he was fed up with the summer heat and dusty roads of his native village far in the south of the country. The Riviera would suit him very nicely. Deep in thought he did not see the tall man walking silently behind him in the shadow of the building.

As Youssef made his way back down the long straight road to the roundabout he was worried. There was no-one behind him, then he saw a small motorbike pull out as he turned back onto the road towards Nabeul and Tunis. The rider waved at them as he zoomed past. "Bloody kids," exclaimed Hama angrily. Youssef took a deep breath. The man wore a yellow baseball cap, his grey hair flying out behind him and his passenger a bright red dress.

The road up to Nabeul was quite busy for the time of night and although Youssef was sure Mohamed had a car following, not even he could work out which one it was. He saw the signpost for Nabeul and turned. No one followed them.

Lucy felt her heartbeat speed up as the car pulled up in the driveway of the old house. She was desperate to see Rose. They got out and Hama barked out his instructions to Youssef. The driver turned the car around so it faced back down the driveway and parked it at the side of the house. Khaled parked Farid's car in front of it on the same side, again facing back towards the main road. Hama put out his hand and Khaled handed him the keys. Poised for flight, Lucy thought.

Once inside the house, Hama took her back through the hallway into the main room and pulled out a chair for her. She sat down and waited. There was no sign of her daughter. She looked at her watch and wondered what was going to happen.

Khaled dragged Farid into the room. She saw to her dismay his hands were bound, he had a bruise on his mouth and a gash below his right eye. She watched at Khaled sat him down against the wall, wrapping the straps around the back of the chair, his hands behind him.

Hama pulled out a chair, positioning it facing Farid. "Sit down my dear. You will not have long to wait now. Soon we will be together." He kissed her cheek and she turned away.

She sat down with her hands clasped watching Farid. Could he really have thought she wanted anything to do with these horrible people? Farid felt an evil jab in his ribs as Jalal adjusted the rope which held him prisoner, but Farid noticed his eyes were watching Lucy and he could feel the rope was looser than before. He started working his hands in an effort to free himself.

"Where is my daughter?"

Hama smiled at her. "Oh yes, I had almost forgotten the girl." He unlocked the door to the small room and Rose walked out. Lucy gasped in horror. Her daughter's huge frightened eyes looked out from a white face. She could see one side of her face was flushed. Her hair hung in knots around her shoulders and her white dress was crumpled and torn. One of the straps was broken. She ran sobbing to her mother.

"You fucking bastards!" Lucy screamed at Hama, who smirked.

"Actually no, and you may be surprised to know it is down to me that we are not, as you so sweetly say, fucking bastards. If it were not for my timely intervention my dear brother would unfortunately have abused our hospitality and your words would have a truer meaning."

Farid stared at the girl, a tiny image of her mother. She was not a child, she must be at least fifteen. He did not understand. He watched as Hama pulled Rose off her mother's lap where she crouched, her face buried in her mother's shoulder, her arms tightly around her neck. She screamed and Hama put his hand over her mouth.

"Shut up!" He cupped her chin in his hand and stared into the wide frightened eyes no more than inches from his own.

"Leave her alone." Farid shouted at him. Hama turned and looked around him as though wondering who had dared to speak. He pushed the girl onto the chair next to Lucy. She gripped her mother's arm and stared wildly around the room.

Hama walked slowly over to Farid and hit him hard across the cheek. Farid turned his head to his captor. The deep golden eyes blazed in anger and the hatred was tangible. Suddenly to the amazement of everyone in the room Hama burst in great guffaws of laughter. He stood with his hands on his hips rocking backwards and forwards.

"Oh, this is wonderful, this is quite wonderful!"

Jalal's mouth hung open. He looked at his brother as though he had lost his senses.

"Jalal, my brother, you do not realise what a lucky escape you truly had when I came back and stopped you from fucking this brat for now truly I would have killed you. I must be the first. You see I have changed my mind, she is not to be sold. The money is of no importance any more. I intend to keep her for myself, to break her body and her spirit. Each time I dig deep inside her young softness, I will feel an exhilaration that I had never dreamed of."

Rose started screaming hysterically.

"No!" Lucy leapt to her feet and ran towards him. Before anyone could stop her she raked her nails down his cheeks. Hama flung her to one side, his expression manic as his blood seeped out of the wounds.

He spun round to face Farid his lips peeled back into an evil sneer. "You imbecile. Do you not even recognise your own daughter?"

Rose stopped screaming. Complete silence hung in the air for a second and then Lucy started to weep. Her sobs filled the room. Hama lashed out at her with his foot.

Farid tried to stand up but Khaled pushed him back into his chair, a huge grin spreading across his face. Farid looked from the girl to Lucy. She met his gaze then clenched her eyes shut, her chin dropped forward and she lay on the floor sobbing. He knew it was the truth.

Rose stared at Farid and he smiled at her. It was though a great weight lifted from Rose's shoulders, she felt light headed, as though her body and mind had been transported away from this terrible place. Everything would be alright. Her father, her very own father, he would know what to do!

Mohamed felt Ahmed touch his sleeve and heard crunching in the gravel. Ahmed put a finger to his lips and pointed. He looked over as another car pulled in followed by a black van, both with Algerian plates. They drove slowly passed him and both went straight to the front of the house. Mohamed pulled back into his seat and waited. A few moments later, six or seven men disappeared through the front door closing it firmly behind them. That meant there must be a dozen people at least in the house, and those were only the ones he knew about.

Mohamed wondered how many people were actually involved. Hama trusted no one, and with the amount of merchandise involved it is likely that he would not have told any one person everything. He would not do what was expected of him. Each of the gang probably knew their own part to play but Hama would be the only one who could put the whole jigsaw together. Hama was well aware that the temptation of such a huge stockpile might prove too great. For the first time, Mohamed worried that there might not be enough of his own men to cope with the chaos which was sure to follow and he hoped the National Guard were already in position to catch those who might get away from the house and away from their province.

Hama sat down at the table with the others leaving Lucy, Rose and Farid facing each other. Farid heard the front door creak open. His mind was reeling with the impact of Hama's revelation. Hama stood up as several men walked into the room, all well-built and looking as though they could handle themselves he observed glumly.

Mahir walked over to Hama. He looked around the almost empty room and stared hard at the couple of boxes stacked up at the side of the room. He put his hand inside his jacket. "Is this some kind of a joke, where is it?"

Hama beamed and took a small key from his pocket. He went over to a large curtain which partly covered the wall and pulled it away. Behind there was a door which he unlocked and flung open in a theatrical gesture. Farid held his breath. The room was stacked with crates and boxes. Mohamed was right there must be millions in those containers. Even Mahir was silent.

Hama stood beaming like a benevolent father his arms outstretched. "I told you I would not disappoint you. The merchandise, it is all catalogued, each crate is marked with its destination. The ones on the left are for Tunis, those on the right for Sicily. The boxes, you know about those and the girls are upstairs."

Mahir recovered his composure and waved his hand towards his men. Two grinned at him and left the room following Khaled. Lucy heard their heavy tread on the stairs and offered silent thanks that her daughter was not with the other girls upstairs.

"Give me the list." Hama stood shifting his weight from side to side as Mahir checked the cost of the merchandise.

Hama grinned. "I just hope you have the money."

"We have as much as we need, we are well funded."

"Of that I am aware. Now do you wish to inspect."

Mahir glared at him and walked over to the crates, making a random selection. The chosen crates were moved into the middle of the room. Mahir took the wrench which was handed to him and opened two. He pulled out a selection of firearms, inspected and then replaced them. The crates were nailed back down. He motioned to one of the boxes, opened it and broke open one of the white packages inside. The second man stepped forward and tested the contents, nodding at Mahir.

"Now that one." Mahir pointed to one crate at the bottom of the heap.

Hama grunted impatiently. He was sweating profusely. "It's all there. I'm hardly likely to screw you, am I? I would like to survive to spend my money."

Mahir glanced at his companion. "Make the call."

Farid listened as the figure was given. No wonder Hama had worked for months on this deal. It was a huge amount of money.

The pain in his wrist was excruciating but he continued to work the straps, which he could feel was becoming looser. Now it was doubly essential he was free to protect not only Lucy, but his daughter.

On the boat, Massoud jumped as the ring of his phone broke the silence. "Yes, I understand. How much! Can you repeat that?" He wrote quickly on the pad beside him. "These are the details you require. Yes, yes I will call you when it is confirmed the transfer has taken place."

His hands were shaking and he felt sick. The phone was taken out of his hand and turned off. Massoud turned to face the policeman standing behind him, and felt the pressure of the gun firmly held against his ribs. "What do you want me to do now?" he stuttered.

"You will give me the account numbers where the money is to be transferred and then you will do as you are supposed to do. When the transfer has taken place, you will call and confirm it. Nothing more. You will of course then come with me to explain your part in this sordid affair. You will tell us everything you know."

Massoud gaped at him. "I can't do that. He will kill me, just like the other one. I can't please, I can't," he babbled.

The man shrugged. "As you wish."

Massoud started to cry and buried his head in his hands. The man ignored him.

CHAPTER SIXTY-ONE

JUSTICE

Farid could feel the blood trickling down from his wrists as he finally managed to free one hand. He knew he didn't have much time. About ten minutes passed. The atmosphere in the room was electric.

The phone rang. Hama almost dropped it. All eyes were on him, everything else forgotten. Farid knew enough time had passed for Mohamed's people to arrive, it was now a matter of getting Hama and his associates out of the house where they could be rounded up. He took a calculated risk. Suddenly to Lucy's surprise he smiled at her.

Hama put the phone back into his pocket. "Right it is done. Our Algerian friends have come good. We can start loading. Move the containers to the front door. Give us ten minutes and then back up the van."

Mohamed watched as the front door opened. A man came out and closed the door behind him. He climbed into the van. Mohamed picked up his phone speaking quickly. Every vehicle was in position. Now it was up to Farid.

Farid panicked. Somehow he had to cause a diversion, something which would mean the people inside the room were confused, and quickly. Something which would get them outside. Once the van was backed up it would offer them protection. He wanted them out in the open and whoever was left in the house would be less likely to get hurt. They were not anticipating trouble which gave the authorities the upper hand, but there was so much at stake and he knew that with Hama, anything could happen and he knew it was inevitable that firearms would be involved.

He looked at Lucy. She was staring at him her hands tightly clenched on her lap. He noticed she still wore his ring. An idea came to him, it was crazy but he could think of nothing else.

Hama looked over at Farid. His expression was pure evil.

Farid hesitated. "It seems you hold all the cards."

Hama smirked. "For once we are in agreement."

"May I have one minute with Lucy and… my daughter?"

Farid held his breath, everything depended on the reply.

Hama's smirk disappeared and he grinned broadly. "Why not, it is the last you will ever have." His voice was soft and gloating in his success.

He pushed Lucy and Rose roughly towards Farid. Lucy bent to kiss him, but he moved his head so his mouth rested by her ear. To her surprise he spoke in English.

"Give it a few moments and then cause as much noise trouble and chaos in any way you can, but please take no risks with your own safety. There is help outside."

To Lucy's surprise Rose bent towards her father her lips stretched in a strange smile and her eyes gleamed manically. "Yes, Father, I know how to do that." She kissed his cheek as he savoured the word father spoken to him for the first time in his life.

Lucy wondered what she meant. "Darling please do nothing, I could not bear it if you get hurt. Let me think, darling, please do nothing."

Rose looked at her mother, a strange distant smile playing on her lips.

"Elizabeth Taylor," she whispered.

Hama pulled them away viciously. "You have had your minute. And now my dear Farid I will leave you. You will remain here. With a body full of cocaine you will be found with enough stuff littered about and some nice little packages. A small price to pay for revenge. I will be gone in a matter of minutes and my whores with me."

Farid looked anxiously at Lucy. Her numb brain finally registered what he was telling her. Ben must have got his message to Ali. There were people outside to help them. He still loved her and it had all been a horrible act, but what was Rose talking about. Elizabeth Taylor, her favourite actress. Actress. Suddenly Lucy felt icy cold, and terribly afraid.

Hama put his arm around Lucy and drew her close to him. She could smell his aftershave which couldn't mask his bad breath and pushed him away angrily. He turned his attention to Rose.

To his surprise the girl smiled, but it was the smile of a demon. As she stepped back she grinned like madwoman and screamed in his face.

"You're loud and vulgar, dirty minded and a monster. You make me puke! You really are a hopped-up Arab slashing at everything, scaring up half the world, but let someone else try it, Oh no.

"Am I some trophy to be passed between you filthy lowlife? He wanted it, you want it, why not everybody have it?" With that she wrenched the straps from her shoulders and pulled her dress down at the front. She span around in a full circle so her skirt swirled out around her hips, She grinned manically moving from one person to the next. Lucy looked at her daughter in amazement.

Rose turned back to Hama, her face inches from his, her golden eyes blazing in frenzied hysteria. "Is it not enough that your revolting brother has fucked the living hell out me today…"

Whatever she was about to say was never heard as Hama's enraged scream and the sound of a chair hitting the wall filled the room.

"You lied to me you fucking prick, you did have her."

Jalal pressed himself back against the wall shaking his head vigorously.

"She is the one who lies," he squealed, his face contorted in terror.

Purple with fury Hama turned back to Rose. She stood, her eyes meeting his and her lips apart, her breasts exposed. He raised his hand to strike her.

She spoke softly, never taking her eyes from his. "Why should I lie? I am no longer a virgin. It might as well be you who fucks me, it no longer matters to me." She ran her tongue over her lips and slowly pulled up one strap in a sexy theatrical gesture.

She saw the indecision in his face and the anger of being cheated from his prize by his own brother's treachery. He hesitated, then span around to face his brother, pulled the gun from his belt and lunged at him. The gun went off, Jalal hurled himself towards the door and dashed outside into the darkness, followed closely by the two other men nearest the door.

Hama chased after him, dragging Rose by the arm. Khaled grabbed Lucy. She struggled and he hit her hard across the face and snarled "This is all your doing you bitch, you and that whore of a daughter." He ran towards the door pulling Lucy with him.

Farid struggled in vain with the rope but it was caught on the chair. As the front door opened Mohamed's men moved in. The rat-a-tat-tat of gunfire was everywhere. Men screamed. The noise split the silence of the night and echoed back off the dense trees. The Algerians and a girl a little older than Rose hurtled down the stairs. Her blouse had been ripped open and she was clearly petrified. Several other girls followed screaming in terror, one had her dress torn, another a gash across her face where she had been hit. Two wore nothing and clutched their clothes as they ran. The men ran to the back door nearly knocking over the old woman, who cowered in a corner her hands covering her face.

The first girl ran straight through the open front door. She stood rooted to the spot then squatted down on the ground holding her head in her hands rocking back and forth. Another girl ran past her and fell over a body lying on the gravel with a bullet hole through his head. She was violently sick and started screaming. The remainder crouched behind the door their arms around each other hiding their nakedness curled up like small animals.

On hearing the shot, Ali dashed down the driveway and into the house. Angrily he pushed one man out of his way with his huge paw and ran to Farid.

"Get me out of this fucking chair! Hama has taken them!" Ali yanked the ropes over the back of the chair and Farid leapt to his feet. He could not feel the pain in his wrists nor did he notice the blood which oozed out and ran down his hand as he ran for the door.

Rose pulled back against Hama as hard as she could, but she was light and but he was too strong. He had her arm in an iron grip. He pushed her into the back seat of the black car and she locked the door.

Youssef was standing next to the car, a pistol in his hand. "Open this door, get in and drive, you bloody fool," Hama screamed at him in fury. To Rose's surprise, Youssef ignored him and took a shot at one of the fleeing Algerians, who seemed to rise in the air before he fell motionless. Then he jumped into the car and drove off with Rose, leaving Hama shrieking obscenities at the disappearing vehicle.

Lucy watched the black car speeding away carrying her daughter to safety. She kicked out at Khaled's shin with us much force as she could muster. She was deafened by a single shot. She heard the whine of the bullet. Khaled fell, the blood spurting from his neck where the bullet passed through it. He dropped the pistol he carried and fell shaking to the ground.

Hama looked across the driveway, his face contorted in fury. "You will never be free of me," he screamed at her.

Lucy heard nothing. The noise around her faded into insignificance, her only conscious thought was of the hatred she felt for the man who had threatened her family and sought to destroy the brief happiness she had hoped for a moment would be hers. She watched as he ran towards Farid's white car. She bent down and picked up the pistol. She stroked the cold metal and smiled. A Browning, a little newer but familiar. She stood quietly in the midst of chaos, her legs slightly apart, her eyes never leaving the fleeing figure. She heard only the pounding of her own heart. Slowly she raised the gun, positioned her hands one behind the other as she had been taught, took aim and gently squeezed the trigger.

With a shriek, Hama crumpled to his knees. As he fell he turned to face her. She walked slowly towards him the gun still held in front of her, her finger still on the trigger. She stopped and gazed at her enemy. She could see the fear in his eyes, and the regret. Regret for the way he had lived his life and the people he had destroyed, or simply regret because he knew he was dying. She would never know.

Ahmed was stunned. He ran to her, tore the weapon from her outstretched hands and put another shot into Hama. She heard the dull thump of his head on the ground. As she stood motionless she felt a searing pain in her shoulder. The last thing she remembered was

Farid's anxious face as he held her in his arms. In the end blood was indeed thicker than water. Jalal, on seeing his brother fall, had shot her.

Farid was oblivious of the mayhem around him. He wrenched the keys from Hama's hand, gathered up the unconscious woman and carried her to his car. The white car screamed down the driveway and the tyres screeched as the car spun. Farid hauled on the wheel and set it back on the road towards Hammamet. He was shaking. To Farid the journey lasted a lifetime. He pulled up outside the clinic and carried her inside. Lucy was in deep shock. She moaned and whispered to herself but her arms clung around his neck like a vice and he felt her tears warm against his neck.

The wound was clean, the bullet had passed clean through the soft tissue missing the bone. Her shoulder was dressed and bandaged and she was in no danger. Farid refused to move and stayed with her as she slept, holding her hand.

She woke only once. "Rose, she is safe? she murmured.

"Rose is fine. That driver took her to the police. She is safe."

She smiled weakly at him and he kissed her gently as she drifted back into sleep.

Some of the Algerians made it to another car waiting behind the row of trees but were caught at the blockade on the road to Tunis. The two who had come downstairs with the girls got as far as the wasteland and a few miles down the road but were rounded up along with some of Hama's men by the National Guard. One tried to escape and was shot. The area was completely sealed off and the rest of them were caught as they boarded Hama's boat in the marina on their way to Sicily.

Mohamed waited until the officials arrived to remove the crates and boxes. When they had departed he drove back into town with Ahmed and Ali. They sat in the café at the back of the Sahara Oasis.

Ali looked anxiously from one to the other. "What are you going to do?"

Mohamed glanced at his brother in law. "What do you mean? It is over, there is nothing more to be done. Those that are not dead will be tried, convicted and locked up forever."

He got up and walked back into the café.

Ali stared at Ahmed. "What are you going to do?" he repeated, holding his breath.

The policeman smiled. "Absolutely nothing, no one will remember in all that chaos and if Jalal says anything it will be our word against his, that is if he can speak after the beating Farid gave him. As far as I am concerned I shot Hama, which is the truth."

Ali grinned, his relief obvious. "That's what I saw. You killed him. Mind you, off the record I would love to know where she learned to shoot like that!"

"Frankly all I care about is that the bastard is dead," muttered Ahmed.

Mohamed sat down inside the café and pulled his phone out of his pocket. He smiled to himself. That woman was something else. He could still see her as she raised the weapon, lined up her target, pulled the trigger and brought the man down with a single shot any one of his men would have been proud of. Justice had been done.

Ben grabbed the phone off the table before Sonia could get there. "Are my mother and Rosie okay? Was anyone hurt?"

"Your mother is fine, she has a bruised shoulder. Rose is in deep shock, but unharmed."

He omitted to tell him his mother had been shot, three of Hama's men had been killed, several had gunshot wounds and another had his brains almost knocked out of him by Farid, some of his own men had been wounded and a several young girls had been beaten, raped or both.

"And my father?"

"Your father is unharmed, other than a few cuts and bruises. Ben, we could not have done this without you. There could have been a very different outcome if you had not kept your head. We will not forget this."

Ben smiled weakly. "Thank you, Mohamed." He passed the phone to Sonia.

He felt sick with relief. He paced the room until Sonia made him sit down, saying he was making her giddy. Now he slumped onto the sofa next to Alex and buried his head in his brother's shoulder. "Alex, they are all okay." Alex put his arms around him and held him close as he wept.

A little later Ben turned to Sonia. "Can we go now? We need to see our mother and Rosie."

"Ben, they have been through a terrible ordeal. My husband says that your mother has at last gone to sleep. Ali says you are to stay here tonight. He is bringing Rose here and I will drive you to the hotel to meet up with your mother tomorrow."

"But we should be with her."

Alex smiled at him. "For once, Ben, do what you are told. Sonia is right, we can do nothing if Mum is asleep. Give her some peace and we can go tomorrow."

"Where is she?"

"She is in the clinic."

Ben glared at her. "I though she was unharmed."

"As my husband said, she has a bruised shoulder and she is in shock. They decided to keep her overnight so she could rest, and your father is with her."

Ben smiled. "Then I will leave them."

Sonia was worried. When Rose arrived she had said nothing that made any sense. She just kept smiling to herself as if in a dream of her own. She stared in front of her murmuring, "Elizabeth was I good, was I as good as you," over and over again.

Her brothers fussed over her until Sonia lost her temper. "Leave the poor girl alone. What she needs is sleep."

She tucked Rose up in bed and hugged her. To her dismay, Rose pushed her away. "Don't touch me, please don't hurt me." Sonia stepped back and Rose turned away from her dragging the covers round her tightly.

Sonia asked her husband what had happened to the girl. He said little, just that the child had been through a terrible experience. And now she had withdrawn from everyone and her speech was rambling. Who was the Elizabeth she kept talking to? She hoped sleep would lessen the incident and take away some of the pain, but she was not convinced that it would.

CHAPTER SIXTY-TWO

ROSE

Ellen arrived at the hospital in the morning. She was worried. She had spoken at length with Sonia about the child, who still seemed dazed and rambling incoherently. They agreed that neither Farid nor Lucy should be told. Hopefully the girl would recover but in any case it would serve no purpose burdening her parents at present. She was safe where she was.

Farid grabbed her arm. "Is my daughter all right? Where is she?"

"She is asleep and she is with Mohamed and Sonia."

Farid smiled. "Then I know she is safe. I will stay with Lucy."

Ellen was abrupt. "My dear Farid, you must try to put out of your mind forever what happened yesterday. If you want to renew your relationship with Lucy may I suggest you go home, get some sleep and then come back this afternoon. If I may be so bold as to suggest it, you could also do with a bath and I think Lucy would probably like to do the same."

Farid grinned. "A woman is always right, of course, but you must call me if there is any change."

"The only change will be if you do not go home and make yourself presentable and allow her to do the same, I think she might not want to see you."

Farid gave her a mock salute and disappeared out to his car. Half an hour later he walked into his room and picked up the photograph by his bed and studied it. How different was the dirty frightened woman whose hand he had held throughout the night from the young gentle girl who smiled at him from inside the frame.

He went into the bathroom and stared at his own reflection. His face was streaked with blood, his hair stood on end and his white shirt was torn and filthy where he had grappled with Jalal. He grimaced. It was unlikely that he had looked much like the man she remembered. He couldn't move the little finger on his right hand and his knuckles throbbed. He could see the deep purple bruises where his fist had hammered the other man's head into the rough gravel, the man who had shot Lucy, the man who by her own admission had "fucked the living hell" out of his daughter. He had every intention of killing Jalal and might well have succeeded had Ali not hauled him off.

His daughter. He repeated the words to himself and remembered her slender arms round his neck as she hugged him and called him father. He thought back to the last time he had seen Lucy, when he had told her of the child they would have, a boy dark like himself but with his mother's eyes. He laughed out loud. He had it completely wrong, he had a girl, she was pale like her mother but with his own eyes and he could not have been happier.

Now he understood the cause of her disappearance and with a maturity he did not have at the time he recognised the reasoning behind her decision, but he could still not accept it. Could they not have worked it out between them? It was something else he needed desperately to talk over with her.

His jacket lay on the bed. He was pleased the bald headed man had removed it before tying him up. At least it was undamaged. He stripped off his clothes and into the shower. He luxuriated as the hot water drenched him and he scrubbed at his body until the skin tingled. No matter how hard he scrubbed he knew he would never forget the memory of Hama's arm around Lucy and his fat hand on her breast, but Hama was dead, killed by the woman he had kidnapped and whose child his brother had abused. But Jalal was not dead.

He rubbed himself vigorously with the thick heavy towel and flung it on the floor as he climbed naked into bed and fell asleep.

He was woken by the sound of the phone. He glanced at the clock which read 14.00. Groggily he reached for the phone.

"Farid. Are you awake?" Ali's deep voice boomed over the stillness of the cool room.

"I am now."

"Sorry, I forgot, Ellen said you'd been at the clinic all night. Anyway, Lucy asked if you could come to the Sahara Oasis around four o'clock. Is that OK?"

"Of course it's all right. I'll be there as soon as I've got dressed."

"No, Farid, please. She wants time to sort herself out. Ellen said she only woke up half an hour ago and the words she said were 'Farid, oh what will he think of me?'."

"Sorry, Ali. I didn't think. I'll be there around four."

He rolled over in bed and lay on his back, staring at the ceiling his arms behind his head. He was scared. Yesterday all he had thought about was seeing Lucy again. Now he had time to think and everything was different. Would she still want him? Why had she come back? What about her husband. What had happened to her in the years since he last saw her? Above all, what had Hama and Jalal done to them? So many questions but how many of them could he ask her and how many would he leave to fester?

He showered again and dressed carefully. The weather was hot for the time of year and he decided not to wear a jacket. He chose a clean pair of dark trousers and short sleeved white shirt. In a vain gesture to turn back the clock he lightly gelled his hair and raised the front into small wiry peak, exactly as he had been when he had met Lucy as a man for the first time so many years ago.

Lucy was uneasy about seeing him again. She knew the time had come when she had to provide an explanation, the situation she had avoided for years. She rummaged through her wardrobe and pulled out a delicate pastel Georgette dress which she had never worn before. It was scooped over her bosom and fitted tightly around her body emphasising her tiny waist. The sleeves fell in soft tiers, hiding the bandage on her shoulder. The colours melted into each other and the feather light material seemed to float as she moved. It was a dress of dreams but would her dream come true. She laid the dress on the bed and turned to face the mirror. The shadows had almost gone after ten hours semi-conscious sleep but her skin was still ashen and her hair needed a good brushing.

Ellen laughed. "Lucy, will you stop it? He has seen you at your worst, here let me help you."

Lucy sat on the stool facing the mirror as Ellen brushed her hair. "You are very lucky you know, you seem to have missed the grey stage and the little white you have looks as though you've spent a considerable amount of money having highlights."

"Ellen, stop being kind. I feel like a middle aged clown. My face is drawn and old, my hands are bony and my boobs have drooped."

"Oh for Christ's sake woman. If I looked like you I'd be more than happy. Lucy, you are over fifty and you look about thirty-five. Here, stop mooching, pull yourself together and put your makeup on."

Half an hour later, Lucy studied her image in the long mirror. The little foundation she wore had brought the colour back into her face and her eyes shone. She blew a kiss at the mirror and turned to Ellen, smiling shyly.

Ellen grinned. "Put this on, a present from Ali and me." She handed Lucy a fine silver chain from which was suspended an oval pearl set in silver filigree.

"Ellen, it's beautiful, so delicate, thank you, but what have I done to deserve this?"

"You have rid the world of a scourge."

Lucy turned to her as the memory flooded back. "So Ali told you."

"Yes he did, but Lucy, please don't think you killed him. Ahmed shot him after he fell."

Lucy watched her intently. Her expression darkened. "Then I failed, I was sure I had killed him."

"So you wanted to kill him?"

"After everything he has done, oh yes, I swore to myself in that dreadful house that I would kill him, it seems I have been cheated."

Sonia gave a gentle smile. "Then no, Lucy, I can be truthful with you. You did not fail. Mohamed said Hama would have died anyway from your single shot. He also declared that your accuracy was something any of his men would have been proud to achieve, so you did not fail. Mohamed simply advised me not to tell you in case it added to your burden."

Lucy gave a bitter laugh. "It has taken away the burden. I have no regret in taking a man's life. Does that make me a bad person, I wonder."

Ellen snorted. "No, it makes you a saint."

"Ellen, he was still that old woman's son."

"That creature may have been born a man. He was a thing that resembled a human being but had forgotten how to be one. How many women's children do you think have been destroyed with his drugs and guns and how many girls forced into prostitution by him and his foul friends. Believe me Lucy, you don't know the half of what he has done. The world is free of a terrible evil, but there is something I must ask you."

"Go on."

"Where did you learn to shoot? Ali told me you handled the gun like a professional."

Lucy laughed. "I haven't fired a gun in years. In my teens I went out with a soldier. He was obsessed by small arms. We used to go to his club and he taught me not only how to target shoot but how to follow a moving target. We split up when he was posted to Germany and the only shooting I have done since then has been on the fairground. I suppose in the unreal situation of last night I just remembered everything he taught me."

"I wouldn't like to piss you off on a dark night." Ellen realised what she had said and they both giggled.

"Right, it's coming up to three thirty, let's go down and meet the boys and young Rose."

"Ellen, how is Rose? I admit once I saw Youssef drive off with her I realised she would be safe and all I could think about was Hama."

Ellen wondered what to say. Ali told her when the girl arrived at Sonia's house she just kept muttering to herself saying the same thing over and over again. Sonia was concerned she might still be in shock. The mind has a strange way of protecting itself. When she woke up she was rambling on in the same way. She chose her words carefully.

"I think she has had a terrible shock and it may take time for her mind to fully absorb what has happened and learn to put it behind her."

"I must go to her."

As they went into the lounge bar, Lucy saw Rose sitting on a settee next to Sonia. Sonia had persuaded her to shower and brushed her hair into a high ponytail. She wore a blue cotton dress and sandals and looked like any other young girl of her age. She gazed vacantly at her mother but made no move to leave her seat.

Sonia moved over and Lucy sat down next to her daughter and hugged her. "Darling you are such a brave girl."

Rose looked at her seriously. "Was I good? Was I as good as Elizabeth?" She dragged her eyes away from her mother and stared vacantly into space. "Elizabeth, will I ever be as good as you?"

Sonia touched Lucy's arm and spoke quietly. "This is what she was saying last night, she kept repeating it over and over again. Who was she talking to?"

Lucy smiled. "Elizabeth Taylor."

Sonia was astonished. "Your daughter knows Elizabeth Taylor, the actress Elizabeth Taylor?"

"No, but Rose has always been obsessed by her and becoming an actress. Last night it was Rose's acting which saved all of us."

"Mum. Was I as good as Elizabeth?"

Lucy cupped her daughter's face in her hands and kissed her cheek.

"My darling, you were as good as Elizabeth. You were wonderful. I was so proud of you and I know Elizabeth would have been proud of you too."

Rose flung her arms around her mother's neck sobbing, "Mum, I was so frightened, but I remembered the words from the film. I think I got it right, but then I had to add some of my own to make it work. I had to make that man believe me."

Lucy stared at her. "Rose, I believed you and so did everyone else."

She hesitated. She knew she had to ask but was scared to do so. She took a deep breath. "Darling I must ask you. How much of it was true?"

Rose gave a peculiar little smile. "Nothing. That awful Jalal, he did touch me though, all over. It was horrible. He gave me some water to drink but it wasn't just water and I couldn't move at all. Mum it wasn't my fault." Her words came in little gasps and she shuddered.

Lucy held her close. "I know it wasn't my love, so he didn't… hurt you then?"

"No, I know he was going to because he pulled his trousers down but his brother came in before he could… you know."

Lucy closed her eyes, she could only imagine the terror her child must have felt, alone, drugged and at the mercy of such a monster.

"Hama thought he had stopped him but after what I said he didn't know whether to believe me or his brother."

"And my darling, because you are such a wonderful actress, he believed you. And now I think you should try to forget both of them ever existed and when we get home we will have to see if we can get you some acting lessons, just like you asked."

Rose beamed and hugged her mother. "Mum, when will my father get here?"

"Soon my darling, but now why don't you go with Sonia and have some tea."

Sonia met Lucy's eyes over the top of the girls head.

"I think she is going to be alright," she murmured.

Lucy smiled back, but she wondered just how deeply rooted the experience would be in her daughter's subconscious mind and how long it would remain there.

CHAPTER SIXTY-THREE

FARID AND LUCY

Farid walked into the hotel reception and Karima greeted him happily. "Oh Farid, I am so pleased you are not hurt. What a terrible experience."

Farid smiled at her, amused by the use of his first name. News obviously travelled fast. Karima flushed to the roots of her hair. "I am so sorry, Mr Khalifa. That was very rude of me."

"No, Karima, it was very nice of you and please I think we have seen enough of each other for you to use my first name. Please, I would be happy if you did so in future."

Karima's blush deepened. "Thank you," she muttered, "but truly I am pleased you were not hurt. Mr Ali, he is waiting for you by the bar."

Farid walked across the wide reception area. There was the usual smattering of business clientèle but mostly tourists. He noticed the young man standing at the back looking out of the window, his attention fixed on a girl who had just climbed out of the pool and was standing drying herself with a towel. He smiled. Some things never changed. The man didn't look like a tourist, he was an Arab and smartly dressed. Farid thought he was probably the son of one of the wealthy families who used the hotel from time to time as a break from city life.

Ali walked over to him, his big face wreathed in smiles. "Farid, my friend, I see you are recovered."

"Where is she?"

Ali grinned "Look for yourself." Farid's eyes darted around the room and rested on the slim blonde woman seated alone on the far side of the bar. His hand reached instinctively to the chain he wore and felt the coin warm against his skin. He was once again the teenage boy gazing into a pair of soft green eyes, the same eyes that now met his own. In his mind he felt the softness of her cheek against his lips and the years fell away.

Ali was totally unprepared for what happened next. With no thought whatsoever of anyone else Farid ran towards her and lifted her out of the chair. Lucy forgot the pain in her shoulder as she breathed in the familiar scent of him and felt his arms around her and his lips on hers, a soft sweetness she believed she would never feel again. They stood arms around each other. He held her so tightly as though he feared she would evaporate before his eyes. Lucy felt warm tears on her cheek, his or hers she didn't know or care.

The director was astonished. Farid, the reserved sensible business man had gone mad. He started across the room but found his path blocked by the man mountain that was Ali.

"No, they have twenty years to find."

The director stared at him. "The coin?"

Ali grinned. "Yes, the coin."

The director smiled. He had known Farid for many years from when he had worked at the Palace. He knew there was a story somewhere particularly, as Farid was never seen without the chain around his neck. He remembered when Farid had first worn it and was told to remove the chain whilst at work and how he used to take the coin from his wallet at the end of his shift and fasten it back around his neck.

The director glanced around the room and saw that there were quite a few people watching the couple, some smiling but others looking distinctly uncomfortable.

"Ali, I do understand but please tell Farid that I cannot have this behaviour in the hotel."

Ali nodded and walked towards Lucy and Farid. "Farid, please, the director."

"Screw the director!"

"Farid, please." Ali took his arm. His friend laughed and sat down pulling Lucy down next to him., his arm around her shoulder. She winced.

"Oh my darling, I am so sorry."

She smiled. "It doesn't matter."

Her small face was upturned towards him and he kissed her gently. He didn't notice the crinkles at the corners of her eyes or the fine lines which ran across her forehead. He saw only the face that came unbidden into his dreams. He had to know.

"Why my darling, why?"

She shook her head mutely and raised her head, her eyes pleading with Ali.

"Farid, you asked me about the source of our information. I think it is time you met him. You don't need me to tell you that without his help the two of you might not be sitting here now"

He frowned at Ali. "Yes, of course you are right, I must thank him."

He watched as Ali walked towards the pool area and turned back to Lucy, waiting for an answer to his question.

Ben still had his back to them, watching the girl with the towel, and had missed the commotion his parents had caused. He turned at Ali's voice.

"Come there is someone I think you should meet."

He followed Ali to the far side of the bar.

Ali rested his hand lightly on his friend's shoulder. "Farid."

Farid rose to his feet and Ali stepped to one side. Farid stared in amazement at the young man who he had seen looking out over the pool and into the face he saw every morning in the mirror, save that the shocked eyes which now held his were Lucy's. The two men stood motionless. Slowly, Ben put out his hand and Farid took it. He looked at Lucy and back at the young man.

Ben who had rehearsed this moment a thousand times forgot everything, the questions, the recriminations were gone. He smiled and spoke in his father's language.

"I believe sir that you are my father."

Farid's knees gave way and he slumped back into his chair. He glanced wildly from Ben, to Lucy and to Ali, who wore a big stupid grin.

"My son?"

"Yes my friend, your son." The young man who listened to what was said to him and what he was not supposed to hear, who kept his head and came and told me everything. He was the source, the reason last night did not end up as a terrible disaster for us all.

Ben ran his hand through his hair and Farid smiled. Ali burst in great guffaws of laughter.

Farid got to his feet and engulfed Ben in a bear hug. "My son, my son," he repeated and the tears rolled down his cheeks. "I have a son and a daughter?"

"Yes, my love, we have twins."

Ali moved away quietly shaking his head and grinning from ear to ear.

Father, mother and son sat together. Lucy explained to Farid what had happened to her. Ben listened shocked, he hadn't realised exactly what his mother had been through. Farid remained silent, his expression set and only the muscle in his cheek twitching. He turned to Ben.

"Son, would you do something for me?" Ben nodded "Please go and ask Ali what happened to the others and Jalal. I must speak to your mother for a moment."

Ben got up and Farid turned to Lucy. "What my daughter said about Jalal." Lucy closed her eyes. She could never tell him what had happened to Rose, but she could tell him part of the truth.

"It is hard to explain. You said to cause as much trouble and chaos as we could and our clever daughter knew what to do. She has always wanted to be an actress and her idol is Elizabeth Taylor, you know, the actress."

Farid smiled. "Yes my darling, even I have heard of her, but how did this concern Rose?"

"Rose spends most of her time watching the actress's films. When she heard Hama say that he intended to keep her for himself she simply used the words from one of those films and added a bit of her own dialogue to convince Hama that Jalal had raped her. She had the sense to realise that if she could make Hama believed her would turn on his brother.

"The old lady called Hama when we were in the car, which is why we went back to the house. Hama must have known what his brother was like and he believed Rose."

"So he never…"

Lucy put her fingers to his lips. "No, he did not."

Farid stared at her. "And you…"

She shook her head. "No, they did not touch me, I swear it and I would ask you never to refer to it again. I do not lie."

Farid felt as though a rock had been lifted from his shoulders and held her close so her head rested on his chest and she could not see the relief in his face. Then he lifted her face to his own and kissed her gently.

Ben sat down beside them.

"Those that weren't dead were arrested this morning."

"Good, that saves me the trouble of killing anybody… and Jalal."

"Jalal will never recover. His back was smashed and his brain is damaged. He will be detained in a secure hospital, but he is unlikely to live long."

Farid gave a bitter smile. "Then there is no more to be done."

He turned towards Ben who had returned with an older man.

"I think you have met my brother once before." Farid smiled at the tall man in jeans and a baseball cap.

"Alex, you have grown since we last met."

"A lot of years have passed since then and I notice that we can now understand each other!"

Farid laughed. "Yes, as you say a lot of years have passed. I have learned English and I now have my own business and my own home."

Lucy frowned. "I didn't know you had your own house. But how, don't you work in the hotel anymore?"

Farid grinned. "Not exactly, I work for the hotel, lots of hotels in fact. My business is supplying hotels with quality merchandise. I travel a lot, gathering ideas and goods. Most of the things you see in this hotel came from my business."

Lucy's face was a picture of astonishment. "But how?" she repeated quietly.

"I think it is time we all went home and I will explain everything". He put his arm around Lucy's waist and they walked from the bar back through the reception to the front door. As they came out into the bright sunlight Lucy opened her bag for her sunglasses. Suddenly she stopped dead. How could she have forgotten his wife and child and now he wanted to take her to his home.

She pulled away from him. "We can't go with you, not to your home."

"Why not? - it is our home now."

"How can it be our home? What about your wife and child?" Her voice broke.

Farid was astonished. "What are you talking about? I have no wife. The only children I have are your children as well."

Ben looked at his father and then at Alex. "But Mum said you were married with a baby and that was years ago."

Farid turned to face Lucy and held both her hands in his. "Listen to me. I promise you, I have no wife, I have never been married. How could I marry another woman when I was still in love with you?" He hesitated. "And you, you did not marry again?" She shook her head, completely confused.

Lucy's hands shook as he held them firmly. "Lucy, please, just come with me now, you and the children and we can talk at home."

He led them to the sleek white car and Ben's face split into a wide grin.

"Wow, bloody hell."

Farid was worried. He had no idea what Lucy was talking about but he had to smile at Ben's youthful enthusiasm. His amusement grew when he noticed Alex staring into the narrow back seat.

"I'm sorry Alex, it is going to be a bit of a squash in the back, but I hadn't bargained on having so many children."

Alex clambered into the back and Ben after him. Somehow Rose managed to get in as well. Lucy sat quietly in the front as the car purred down the motorway. She was shocked. Her brain was whirling around in circles. He had never been married, but what she had heard, what she had seen with her own eyes, nothing made sense anymore. Her shoulder ached and now her head ached as well.

The car turned into the driveway. The white walls of the house were washed a pale salmon pink in the early evening light and the sun glistened on the movement of the water in the pool. Huge tubs of red and orange geraniums clashed happily with the deep pinks and purples of the bougainvillea and the air was heavy with scent of jasmine. Lucy stared at the house and burst into tears.

"Oh Farid, it's our house, the one we planned." Her aches and worries forgotten, she pushed open the car door and kicked off her shoes. She ran across the grass, trailing her arm against the swaying tendrils that clothed the walls and round to the back of the house. She gave a little shriek of delight.

"Farid, the jasmine. You remembered. Oh, it is the most beautiful place I have ever seen."

Ben looked at his father, his eyes shining. He had never seen his mother so happy. "It really is a beautiful house, did you honestly plan it together?"

"Yes, down to every detail. I had it built some years ago when I first came into the money, but that is another story for later on. Let's get your mother inside so she can inspect and tell me what I got wrong."

Alex smiled "Somehow I don't think she's going to find anything wrong."

He was absolutely right. Lucy sped from room to room, giving little gasps of pleasure. She came to the main bedroom and Farid followed her. He watched as she went to the wardrobe fitments and opened the door. His clothes were neatly arranged. She closed the door and turned to him. He waited. Slowly she opened the door on the other wide of the fitments. It was empty. She turned to him and her arms stole round his waist. "Oh Farid, you built this for me."

"I never gave up hope you would come back. No one has ever lived in this house but me. When the house was first completed, I couldn't bear to live here. My sister stayed with me for the first few weeks otherwise I think it would be empty today. No woman has slept in our house since then."

Rose sat silently on the settee gazing around the room. "Papa, is this really our house, this is not just some dream and I will have to wake up?"

Farid stroked her hair. "Yes, Rose, this is our house, it is not a dream and no-one will ever take it from us."

They went downstairs and ate a light supper of spicy cold chicken, salad, bread and wine. Lucy had not eaten all day and felt the wine going to her head.

They waited until the children went to bed and in the silence of the night sat in the cool room and talked.

She told him of her desperation when she found she was pregnant and why she had decided not to come back. The Farid of his youth would have been angry, but now he understood her reasoning, although he did not accept it. He realised the sacrifice she had made as she told him about the emptiness of her life where her only salvation had been her children.

"And you never married again."

"I have never had a relationship with a man where that could have occurred. As you said, how can you marry someone when you are in love with someone else?"

"You can't if you are true to yourself. I couldn't."

He told her about Sarra who had released him from his offer of marriage knowing he was in love with another woman.

"But I was told you were married."

"Who told you?"

"A girl I met at Ali's wedding. She said she knew you very well, extremely well as she was intent on impressing on me, but that you had gone and married someone else having let her down badly."

Farid thought for a moment when she mentioned the wedding and frowned. He spoke quietly.

"Was she a red-haired girl called Debbie, by any chance?"

"Yes" she answered simply, waiting for his reply.

Farid brought his fist down on the side of the table so hard she thought it would break. His English deserted him and he broke into a torrent of Arabic, spitting out the words. Lucy struggled to understand.

"Stop Farid, please explain to me so I can understand."

Farid was embarrassed. How could he have been so gullible to think even for a moment that Debbie had changed? She had told him Lucy was married so he would think her out of his reach. She had simply seen Lucy and thought by changing her clothes and losing the brash attitude that he would be interested in her.

He looked at Lucy. Her face had paled. "I understand though you did go out with her. How long for?"

"I never went out with her in that way."

"Are you sure?"

Farid watched here intently. Her face wore a mask of pale calm, but her eyes were filled with fear and reproach.

She knows!, he thought helplessly, *but how*?

He said nothing. "Please, Farid, there must be no secrets between us."

He took a deep breath, surely he could not now lose her again, but he must tell her the truth. His mouth was dry and he struggled to find the words.

"The first time I had a drink with her, she was already partly drunk. I walked with her and she pushed herself at me, kissed me and fondled me through my trousers. Lucy, there had been no one for a year. I asked her if she wanted sex and she said yes."

"And did you give her what she wanted?"

"Lucy, she was rubbing herself against me. I thought I was going to explode. No, I did not go to bed with her as she wanted, I simply took her against the wall. She struggled but I was beyond caring. I closed my eyes and it lasted only seconds. She told me as I came I called your name."

"I know, Cathy saw you."

Farid stared at her in horror.

"Oh dear God, no. That anyone should have witnessed that. It is the one thing I have done in my life that I truly regret and I had hoped I should never have to relive that awful time."

"And did you see her again?"

He told her everything, how he had spurned the girl but she kept coming back.

"She told me you were married and that you had children and no longer loved your Tunisian boyfriend."

Lucy was shocked. She could not believe that someone so young could be so vicious, so calculating.

"What a bitch, I suppose she felt that if she could not have you, then I couldn't either. So did you resume your relationship?" Her voice was cold.

"No, my darling, she asked me to go for coffee and because I wanted to find out if she knew anything about you, I agreed. Then I took her money to pay for our drinks and told the waiter to keep the change." Lucy smiled.

"There were others?"

Farid blushed. "Lucy I was a man in my twenties when you left me. You have been gone seventeen years. Yes, there were others, but I never went with a woman more than once or twice. She never had what I wanted, what I was waiting for, you my darling. No-one touched my heart, not even the outermost part of it."

He looked at her, wondering whether to ask.

"And you, there were others?"

"Just one."

He waited. "Who was the man?"

"His name was Yassine. It was just after that girl had told me you were married. We met at the hotel, he was a guest. He told me I looked sad and I told him you no longer wanted me. He said you were a stupid man."

"He was most certainly very wise," Farid muttered.

"We both needed someone at the same time. He was kind and gentle and held me when I desperately needed to be held. It was once only and I never spoke to or saw him again."

He took her clenched hands in his own and gave a wry smile.

"The strange thing is my love, that it is partly down to that awful Debbie and a revolting woman who accused me of attacking her, that my life changed. I moved to a different hotel and it was there where I met this amazing old lady." He told her about Jane and how he had come to care for her and the incredible legacy she had given him.

"You see, it was because of Jane that I now have everything I have ever dreamed of, but wait stay there for a moment. I have something to show you."

He came back a few minutes later and handed her a small blue envelope. Lucy read the letter Jane had written and her eyes filled with tears. "What a wonderful woman."

He looked away. "Yes, she was. She told me that if it was meant to be then I would find you again and never to lose faith."

"Many years ago another old lady once told me that same thing."

She told him about Alice and they sat silently for a moment in mutual understanding. Farid kissed the tip of her nose. "It seems the old are indeed much wiser that we were."

"Farid, I must ask you. Why were you not at Ali's wedding?"

"I lost touch with him for a while. I knew about there was a wedding, but my uncle died so I was in mourning. When I was told he had married a pretty English girl I am not sure I would have gone anyway. Too many memories."

Lucy dropped her eyes and spoke in a low whisper. "After that horrible girl told me you were married I saw you in Sousse. Who was the woman with the baby?"

"I knew it was you! There couldn't be two women with hair of sunlight and eyes so green a man could dive in and lose his soul." He kissed her eyelids. Lucy blushed and a tingle ran down her spine.

"Who was the woman?"

He grinned wickedly. "That was number one wife and child."

He felt her stiffen and cupped her face in his hand. "You little idiot, that was my sister and her baby. She persuaded me to walk with her, she was very close to my uncle and still upset about his death. I couldn't refuse her."

Lucy stared at him in amazement. "But why the café?"

"I had no option, Meriam was tired, a combination of the heat, our uncle and her husband being away. She saw the café and asked to sit down, I couldn't say no, could I? Lucy, I never go to the café save on one day of each year, the day we met. I spend an hour there alone with nothing but my memories of the most beautiful girl I have ever known, my lady, my Lucy."

He reached inside his shirt "And I kiss the most precious gift I have ever received."

He kissed the old coin, the metal worn so thin over the years that it was little more than a shiny disc. He took her hand and placed her palm flat against warm coin. She felt the heat from his body and a familiar shaft of desire flashed from her to him.

"The most precious gift I have ever received, until now. Now not only have you come back to me but you have given me my children."

Mindful that her children slept next door, their love making was tender and gentle and when he asked her for the second time in her life to marry him, Lucy had no need to answer him with words.

A short while before their wedding, Farid again visited the jeweller in the Medina and chose for his bride a narrow chain link gold bracelet. On it he placed one charm, a small white enamel jasmine flower set in a simple heart shaped gold setting. Lucy was enchanted. He kissed the charm as he placed the bracelet around her wrist. "And there will be another each year so you will never forget me."

"I will first forget how to breathe," she replied.

CHAPTER SIXTY-FOUR

TOGETHER

Once the arrangements were made, Lucy called Marie.

"Hello, M. It's me. I'm getting married!"

M nearly dropped the phone.

"But how, I thought you said he was married, or have they changed the law out there?"

"Idiot, of course they haven't and no he isn't married and never has been. I'll explain it all when you get here, you will come won't you?" she added uncertainly.

"Don't be daft. If you hadn't told me I promise you I would never have spoken to you again."

"Look, you can stay with us, there's no need to book into a hotel."

"How can I stay with you? I thought he worked in a hotel. Lucy what the hell is going on?"

"No he doesn't work in a hotel anymore and he built me a house! Look M, it's too complicated but I'll explain everything when I see you. Get the afternoon flight on the 20th and we'll collect you from the airport. Is that okay?"

"Yes, of course it is."

"Good, I'd hoped you'd say that. Alex will contact you in the next day or so and you can come over with him. See you then, and oh you'll need something light. There is a heat wave at the moment. Bye."

Marie put the phone back in her pocket and sat down. The cat jumped on her lap and she stroked the soft fur absently. She was stunned. It seemed only a matter of weeks since her friend had sat with her on the sofa with tears in her eyes before she had gone off on her wild goose chase.

And now she was getting married. She shoved the cat off her lap and was rewarded by an angry wail and a rosette of sharp claws in her leg. She went into the kitchen and turned on the kettle, then changed her mind and with a grin reached for the wine bottle. This called for something stronger.

The same evening the phone rang again and she was surprised to hear Ben's excited voice.

"Look, M, Mum doesn't know I'm calling you. She thinks she's going to get away with a quiet wedding, but I think she's crazy." M was fascinated as the young man told her exactly who to contact and to make sure they all arrived together. As they talked she found herself drawn to Ben's enthusiasm and volunteered one or two names of her own.

When Farid drove Lucy to the airport to collect M, Alex and his family, Lucy was astonished to see her friend, her face wreathed in smiles, followed by Jackie and Ewan, John and Hana Clark and with them Amal. She stared in disbelief as Jonathan appeared with Robin Bartholomew and his wife, and at least a half a dozen other people from her past life.

The chairman enveloped Lucy in a bear hug.

"I had to come didn't I? I mean after that amazing scene in my garden, now I have a chance to meet the cause of the chatter which seriously slowed down production in my firm for a whole week afterwards."

Lucy looked embarrassed and muttered an apology. Peggy Bartholomew laughed, her eyes twinkling. "My dear girl, don't apologise, Robin has dined out on that story so many times, you wouldn't believe it."

She looked past Lucy to where Farid waited, a little smile curving his lips as he watched Lucy's obvious delight at seeing her friends. "And now I understand," she added softly.

The quiet wedding turned into three days of joyous celebration, a mixture of young and old, English and Tunisian and it was past midnight on the last day when the last of their guests departed. M and the children remained in the guest house leaving Mr and Mrs Khalifa to the sanctuary of their own home.

It all happened so quickly. Lucy had been swept along on the tide of meeting her beloved man again and the preparations for the wedding. She had little time to reflect on the past years and there was still the niggle in her mind that after everything that had happened to them would it at last be their time for each other. They lay beside each other in the big bed and she felt his warmth next to her. He ran his finger down her neck and stroked her breast and his mouth was soft on her own. All reservation left her. This was the man she loved. Her body arched towards him and his lips took hers with a ferocity which left her shaking. She melted into him as his hands roamed freely over her until there was no part left he had not rediscovered.

Her breasts were swollen and ached for him to touch her but he tormented her with little kisses until at last his lips fastened on her nipple and she felt the waves of heat pulsing through her. He held her hips tightly and sank himself into her so deeply she cried out.

A feral groan escaped him as he pulled even deeper into her. As he moved the blood rushed through her like a fever, an exquisite lasting heat which radiated to her fingertips. Farid felt her spasms as she climaxed and held her close with a strength that took her breath away. He luxuriated in the pulsing of his own body by which he finally made her his wife.

They lay together neither wanting to break the spell.

"So you no longer want me?"

Farid growled and rolled her on top of him.

"My darling, you do not escape so easily. I have waited too long for this day."

Lucy's eyes widened as he pulled her down onto himself until he was completely buried inside her. She held him tightly, her head sank to his chest and he raised her face to his, tasting the sweetness of her mouth. Afterwards he cradled her and his last thought as he sank into sleep was the scent of jasmine in her hair and the softness of her breasts cupped in his hands.

Farid awoke concentrating on taming his impatient body. Gradually he took control. He moved Lucy onto her back as she slept and gazed at her. His wife. Her eyes were closed, the long lashes resting on her flushed cheeks, her hair was spread in a tangled cloud across the pillow. "What have you done to me, woman?" he whispered.

He stood naked looking out of the window and she studied him. His bottom was still firm and his legs strong, but she noticed his waistline had thickened a little. The muscles of his shoulders rippled as he stretched his arms towards the sky. She crept up behind him and her arms stole around his waist. She pressed herself to him and kissed his shoulder. He smiled and reached back so he held her and they stood moulded together. Her hands stroked his belly and sneaked downwards to touch him.

Abruptly Farid turned to face her, holding her eyes in a stern gaze.

"I spent my night giving you pleasure and you are still not satisfied my little whore."

Lucy looked meekly at his feet, a little smile playing on her lips.

"I am sorry master, I beg your forgiveness."

She sank to her knees, her arms around his hips and rubbed her face against him. He ran his fingers through her hair and she turned her face up to him mischievously.

"And now my master, I must pay for my wrongdoing."

She stroked him her hand moving back and forth. She felt him grow and she released him and sat back, a little smile on her face "Am I forgiven master?"

"No you are not," he growled, his eyes glittering. Lucy flicked her tongue over the most sensitive part of him and muttering an oath he pulled her towards him. Her lips opened and he slid into the warmth of her mouth. Her tongue caressed him and his fingers wound around her hair held her in an iron grip as he shuddered and she tasted the salty sweetness of him. "*Mon ange ou demon.* Now you are forgiven."

Lucy stood up and he held her close. A knock on the door was followed by a cheery woman's voice

"Are you decent?"

Farid looked wildly about him. His legs felt like jelly and he grabbed the nearest thing he could see, the bath towel flung on the end of the bed. He wrapped it around them both as best he could. The door opened and M stood gaping at them, a tray of tea and croissants in her hands. It was obvious the two were naked, Farid was barely covered and despite herself, M couldn't help appraising his broad shoulder and muscular chest, still damp with sweat.

"Oh shit," she muttered. "The rabbits are at it again!"

Lucy giggled, "M you are incorrigible."

M smirked at her, "Not me, my dear, you!"

She put the tray down and made as dignified an exit as she could but they heard her stifled laughter as she went downstairs. Farid glared at Lucy, painfully embarrassed.

"That is the nearest thing to naked any woman has seen me that I was not about to fuck," he complained angrily. Lucy giggled again and he smacked her bottom. "Have you no shame woman?"

"None with you my love."

She noticed that later when they went downstairs he refused to look at M, or she at him. Lucy looked from one to the other and burst into peals of laughter. She took his hand.

"Farid, this is my best friend, Marie. Marie meet Farid." She forced Farid to hold out his hand. M took it and blushed.

"Marie, I hope during your stay you two will see more of each other," she added wickedly.

Farid dropped M's hand as if it were a hot coal. M flushed to the roots of her hair and mouthed "Bitch" at Lucy.

Farid's icy glare went from one woman to the other. "I know your friend and I think she has already seen enough of me," he snapped as he strode into the garden, reaching for his cigarettes and muttering to himself "Crazy English."

Lucy watched as he sat puffing furiously, but she was sure she saw a tell-tale little smile.

M was speechless for a moment. "Lucy that was utterly unfair."

Lucy nodded. "But pretty good, wasn't it! Come on time to cool off I think."

Neither woman needed to be ashamed of their bodies, but both agreed that the time for bikinis ended around forty. M wore a neat black swimsuit trimmed with white which set off perfectly her tiny frame and soft tan. Lucy's suit was deep turquoise and the frill around the neckline partly hid the still plainly visible scar on her shoulder, her one physical reminder of the recent trauma and like the memory would never complete go away but with time it would fade.

Farid was a strong swimmer and Lucy watched him as he swept lazily up and down the length of the pool, a powerful brown shape gliding noiselessly through the ripples. He pulled himself out of the water, the sun shining on the droplets as they fell. His shorts had slipped down round his hips and with a broad grin he pulled them up and ran his hand back through his hair in a gesture so familiar it made her heart skip a beat. She never tired of looking at him.

To her amusement, M was also watching him over the top of her sunglasses. Lucy nudged her. "Penny for them."

M regarded her seriously.

"He's one of the few men I know who I'd recommend wore briefs!"

Lucy choked on her drink and immediately Farid had his arm round her, patting her back. "You are all right my love?" M flashed her a warning look.

"I'm fine darling, it was just the drink going down the wrong way."

Farid looked puzzled as the two women burst into giggles.

A whoop of laughter sounded from the house and Rose rushed out with Ben in hot pursuit.

"You little bitch," he shrieked as he lunged at her.

He missed as Rose sidestepped and dived into the pool. Ben lost his balance and tumbled in after her. Being by far the stronger however he soon caught her and Rose was soon held under the water, her arms flailing as he held her. He released her and she surfaced gasping for breath as she pummelled ineffectively against his chest.

Farid stood watching them, his legs apart and his hands resting loosely on his hips. A wide smile lit his face. "What has she done now?" Rose's laughter bubbled up.

"I caught him trimming what he is hopelessly trying to pass for a moustache, so I nudged him and he cut a bit off by mistake." Farid tried not to laugh.

"Rose that was unkind. A man's moustache is very important to him."

"But Daddy, your moustache is beautiful, Ben's is just bum-fluff."

Ben grabbed her outraged. "You're a rotten skinny little cow," he yelled and hauled her back under the water by her hair. He turned back to Farid, who had disappeared. Ben looked around him and felt Rose slither out of his grasp as his own legs were swept from under him.

Father and son surfaced together, Ben spluttering in indignation and Farid grinning from ear to ear.

"The first lesson I teach you my son is never to insult a woman in front of her father unless you keep him well within your sights."

Ben looked crestfallen but Farid placed his hand on the younger man's shoulder. "And the second lesson I teach you is how to treat your moustache and keep her safe from marauding females. Come, we will deal with that now."

Ben smirked at Rose and took his father's outstretched hand.

Half an hour later, Rose looked up. She touched her mother's arm. "Mum, look."

Lucy's hand flew to her mouth with a little gasp. Father and son were both dressed in jeans and white t-shirts. Farid had coaxed Ben's blossoming moustache into a neat replica of his own and lightly gelled the front of his hair in the same way he wore his. The likeness was uncanny. Both men smiled at her and she felt the tears pricking the back of her eyes as she remembered the first day of Ben's life and the words she had said to him.

"Now there are two beaux Tunisians," she whispered to herself.

A few days later, having waved goodbye to their English visitors, the couple sat together on the same beach where they had sat so many years before, in the relative cool of early evening, leaning against the stack of sun loungers packed up for the night, as before away from inquisitive eyes. They talked of things which had happened since they first met and of those their lives had touched, many of whom had come and gone. They spoke of their dreams and fears in the past, happiness and despair but always of hope. They were not wrapped around each other as they had been as new lovers. There was no desperation, no frantic illicit lovemaking. Her head rested gently on his shoulder, his inclined so his cheek rested on the softness of her hair. Theirs was a peace which comes of unshakeable love.

The sun dipped below the horizon and Lucy watched enthralled as the sky was flooded with brilliant colours. The spectacle lasted only a few minutes as the colours bled into the smoke grey clouds lining each with a soft pink lining. He raised his head and gazed enraptured at his woman, her face turned towards the setting sun. He took in the contour of her still beautiful face, he didn't see the lines only her sweet smile - the picture which had burned itself into his mind it seemed for his entire life.

"I love you my lady, as I have always done and will forever," he murmured in Arabic.

She smiled and her mind travelled back to a hot sunny day in Sousse so long ago.

"I don't know what you said, but it sounded beautiful," she murmured.

He smiled at her. She entwined her fingers with his.

"My love and at last my husband."

His fingers felt the new gold band on her left hand as he nuzzled her ear and smelled the familiar perfume. He kissed her deeply and she felt his arms steal around her waist as she leaned against him. Alice had been right. She was at last completely happy.

CHAPTER SIXTY-FIVE

ROSE AND WASSIF

It was many months later that Farid informed Lucy, Jalal had died of his injuries. Although they knew he could never pursue them, it was still a relief to know he had followed his brother into whatever afterlife awaited him.

The matter was never discussed with their children. Ben preferred to forget and the only reference he ever made was that although it had been a terrible experience it was that which had brought his parents back together.

Rose kept her feelings to herself but Lucy noticed that she had lost her sparkle and the childlike innocence had gone forever. She was comfortable with men, but only in the company of her own family. Lucy was worried about her. She had told Rose that Jalal had died but she knew the memory of the terror she had suffered at his hands would unfortunately not die with him.

"I can only hope that when she is alone with a man for the first time she will be able to cope with it," she confided to Farid.

"Sweetheart, in a way it is a good thing because it means she will have to trust and love her man before she gives herself to him." Lucy felt that sometimes her husband knew her daughter better than she did herself.

But she hoped with all her heart that her experience had not scarred Rose irrevocably. She knew her daughter avoided being alone with a man and declined all invitations. She rarely even went out, unless in a group. Meriam and Rose had become close and Lucy had confided in Meriam her fears about her daughter. Meriam put her arm around sister-in-law. "Then we need to introduce her gradually to people of our own family and friends that she can learn to trust."

One day in late summer, Meriam came with her family to the house. She brought with her their cousin and his children. The elder boy, Wassif was a handsome young man, twenty years old. He was tall and athletic, his colour the same soft honey as Ben. Lucy noticed his soft brown eyes rarely left her daughter, and worried at the obvious attention her was lavishing on her. Farid told her not to interfere.

"Wassif is a good man, she will come to no harm with him and he will help her learn to trust again."

To Lucy's surprise, Rose seemed content to talk to him, even without the protection of her family. They walked through the garden talking together and Lucy was happy to see her daughter's young face light up in a smile as Wassif bent his head and whispered something to her.

She could not help but notice Ben's undisguised annoyance at Wassif monopolising his sister and hoped there would not be words between the two.

Farid watched her. "My darling, Ben will have to learn that one day both he and his sister will make their own lives and that another man and girl will be part of those lives."

"But Farid, she is still so young and after everything…" her voice trailed off.

"She will come to terms with that in time, when she feels the embrace of a man who loves her. Remember I fell in love at fourteen… and became a man at sixteen," he added wickedly. "Our daughter is now seventeen years old."

She kissed his cheek. "It isn't quite the same, you are a randy Arab man. Our daughter is a good English girl."

He grinned. "Wrong my sweetheart, Rose is half English but the other half is me, she has the Arab passion in her blood."

Lucy slapped his leg. "Don't worry me even more," she laughed, but she could see that Rose, whether consciously or not, was flirting with Wassif and even allowed him to kiss her cheek when he left with the family that evening.

Each time Meriam came to visit, Wassif was with her and Lucy was relieved to see that her daughter seemed to accept his presence. He was no threat to her, and in fact treated her simply as one of the family although it was obvious to her parents that he would like to know her better.

One evening he arrived at the house on his own and asked Rose to go with him for a coffee. She hung back but with Lucy's encouragement shyly agreed. They left the house in Wassif's little Renault but Lucy noticed she watched her mother at the door until the car turned onto the main road.

Rose was not frightened of Wassif, in fact quite the opposite, but nervous of how she would respond should he make any move towards her whilst they were alone. They drove towards the resort and Rose was concerned when he did not turn at the roundabout into town centre. "Where are we going?"

"I thought we would have coffee at home if that's okay with you."

She stared at him and immediately he was conscious of her anxiety. He grinned "Don't worry, I'd just like you meet my friends."

Rose blushed, embarrassed at her own irrational fear, but lacking the words to explain. "I'm sorry, I didn't mean anything but…" Her voice tailed off and she clasped her hands tightly on her lap.

"Rose, I know something happened to you a year or so ago, because I heard my parents talking about it."

He heard her gasp and was dismayed to see her face was wet with tears. He pulled the car to the side of the road and turned off the engine.

She turned her pale face to him. "I'm sorry, Wassif, I'm just not ready to talk about it to anyone, not yet."

"I understand, but if ever you do, if I can help, I will."

Very gently he put his hand on hers but she curled up against the car door and he removed it. "Rosie, I'll never put any pressure on you, but please don't think everyone is the same. We don't know each other very well, but please believe me, you can trust me." She saw the hurt in his face and placed her hand over his.

"Wassif, this is something I must deal with myself." She took a deep breath and her smile was bright and artificial. "Now shall we go and see your friends?"

"Are you sure, but they don't bite you know!"

He put his hand under her chin and forced her to look at him. His expression was serious with no trace of amusement or mockery and gently he ran his finger down her cheek and across her lips. Rose felt a little flutter of excitement at his touch. He smiled and restarted the car.

They drove in silence past the marina onto the main road and he turned into a narrow dirt track just wide enough for the car.

"I'm afraid my home is not very impressive. It's about as different from yours as you can get. I'm sorry but you'll have to rough it for an hour or so. As you know my family live on the far side of Sousse and as I work in Hammamet I share a place with three others." He laughed. "My sister tells me it will do me good, having to wait on myself instead of her doing it."

He parked the car in a small square surrounded by small sandy single-storey buildings. There was a garden area in the centre with a tree and a couple of old plastic chairs. A few young men sat together smoking and drinking beer. Rose noticed all the houses were similar, with one large window at the front under which grew a tangled mass of bright red geraniums, straggling untended along the ground. Each window had open wooden shutters and wrought iron work, which was both decorative and practical as it prevented unwanted visitors gaining entry.

Wassif called to a small dark man in a yellow vest who waved back at him. "That is my friend Mourad. He works in the Medina."

He led her in through the open door. There was one large white room, sparsely furnished with just one large flat seat which ran the length of one wall, a table and a couple of armchairs. On the far wall was a battered table, covered with cigarette packets, bottles and an assortment of bits and pieces. The room was still hot from the day and the two men sitting on the long seat were dressed in short trousers and vests.

Rose smiled to herself. He was right, it was certainly very different from the cool elegance of her home. Wassif pulled forward one of the armchairs and quickly picked up a screwed up T-shirt and towel which he chucked on the seat. He looked at her apologetically. "I did warn you."

Rose grinned and sat down. "All I want at the moment is a drink and not coffee."

"That I can manage." He walked over to the fridge set into the wall in the corridor to the back of the house. "Beer, water or wine?"

"Whatever you're having." He took out a bottle of wine.

"Rosé for Rose," he quipped. She giggled.

One of the men stood up and offered her a cigarette. She hesitated for a moment and took one. Wassif's eyes narrowed but he said nothing. Rose sipped the cool wine and looked around the room.

She started as another man and girl walked in, but they acknowledged her with a smile accepting her being there and started chatting. Rose relaxed, whether because of the presence of another woman or simply because she was amongst people of her own age who offered no threat, she didn't know, but when Wassif drove her home she knew she could truthfully say she had really enjoyed herself away from the protection of her own family for the first time in almost two years.

When he stopped outside the house, a little way down the driveway he turned to her and to his surprise she slipped her arm around his neck and kissed him gently on the lips. "Do you have a minute?" she whispered. He nodded without speaking and waited.
"You know about the business the year before last, when several men were killed in a police raid up near Nabeul?"

"Yes, I heard about it, something to do with firearms and drug trafficking." He stared at her. "Oh, Rose, you weren't involved in that were you? God, how awful."

Rose looked at him. "Yes, my mother and I were taken by those men. The man who was killed hated my father. I don't want to go into what happened but the police came and none of us were badly hurt." She hesitated. "Wassif, one of the old men tried to rape me."

Wassif swore. "Rosie, as long as I live, no one will ever hurt you again."

Rose crumpled into his arms. He held her to his chest, his arms holding her tightly. She buried her head in his shoulder and the tears which had for so long been held back now fell until her breath came in harsh strangled sobs. He kissed her swollen eyes, her nose, her neck and she felt the gentleness of his lips on hers. She clung to him and returned his kiss. He made no move to touch her and she lay curled in his arms like a baby.

Many times over the next few months Wassif's little car carried Rose off to one café or another, to the homes of his friends, to the security of his arms, but Rose was always back home before the night owls came out, which Wassif seemed to accept. Rose was almost back to the carefree girl she had been. Lucy noticed the change in her daughter and wondered whether she had told Wassif anything of her experience but never raised the subject. She knew her daughter would confide in her when she was ready.

One evening, Rose returned after midnight, her long hair tangled and her face flushed with a glow that Lucy recognised only too well.

"Where the hell have you been?" she snapped, more with worry than anger.

"Oh Mum, I'm so sorry, I just forgot the time. I went with Wassif to a barbecue, there were lots of other people there," she added hurriedly. "And where was this barbecue?"

"On the beach just outside Hammamet."

"Yes, I can see you have been on the beach, your back is covered in sand!"

Rose went red. "Oh Mum, he's so wonderful. I think I'm in love with him." She hesitated "How do you know when that happens?"

Lucy laughed at her child's upturned face, flushed with happiness and she guessed a lot more besides. "My darling, only you will know that."

Rose's face took on a dreamy look. "You know when I look into his eyes, it is like looking into soft dark melted chocolate. I feel I could just dive straight in and lose myself forever. He is so handsome, his lips are soft and when he tells me he loves me, it makes me tingle. I feel so safe with him as though nothing in the world could ever hurt me again."

"Sweetheart, I think you have answered your own question, but give it time you are still very young."

Rose regarded her seriously. "Yes, that is exactly what Wassif says. He believes we should wait. He needs to complete his apprenticeship and I have told him I will be expensive to keep."

"So you are a high maintenance girl!"

"Absolutely, Mum, and I will settle for nothing less than the happiness that you and Dad have."

Lucy's expression was guarded. "Rose, your father and I had many hurdles to cross and at times they seemed like mountains. But if you love him and it is supposed to be, then I hope with all my heart that you will be as happy as we are."

It was to be another three years before Rose and Wassif were married, but their parents knew she had found the right man.

CHAPTER SIXTY-SIX

BEN

It has been some years since my father retired. My mother had joined him in the business and he told me often how thrilled he was to see how hard she worked and with such enthusiasm. He says she brought a different perspective to the goods he supplied, as she put it, a woman's viewpoint. She charmed guests and customers alike. Few people were aware of their terrible experience and none spoke of it.

The events leading up to the revolution in our country were not unexpected. There had been political unrest for some long time in protest against blatant corruption, repression, unemployment and dreadful living conditions under the Ben Ali administration. But the spark which lit the fire was indeed terrible. In the middle of December in the small town of Sidi Bouzid a young man set himself alight in the town centre in protest against the corrupt regime. Some said he had been drinking and did it by accident, but it was a terrible thing to happen. Huge demonstrations followed and the country was in turmoil. The young man died at the beginning of January and ten days later on the 14th of January Ben Ali resigned. Within days he and his family had fled abroad taking with them a vast amount of money, valuables and other ill-gotten gains.

Although there was a natural backlash in that tourism suffered and the hotels for several years were no longer full during the season as they had been previously, our business was largely unaffected. As a respected businessman my father was approached by the caretaker government to take a senior position within the governerate of Gabes and an active role in rebuilding the country. Although he no longer took a hands-on part in the business it was based in Hammamet and to accept would have meant leaving his home, so my mother became upset. He assured her that he had learned to his cost that involvement in politics and matters of national security was ill advised so he declined, kept his counsel and waited for matters to calm down.

Retirement had been my father's idea. He said he wanted to spend more time with his wife. He had handed over the running of the business to Sami who had been with him from the start. At my own request I had completed a hotel management course, at the same college that my father had attended, but when I expressed an interest in the business after some consideration my parents agreed. Between them they trained me, as they put it, to know their way of doing things.

My mother says I grow more like my father in every way, including picking up some of his bad habits. I know my father wants eventually to hand over the business to me and my mother tells me that Sami thinks it is right. I am honoured to know that Sami considers me capable and would be happy to work with me. He told my father that the business will be safe with me. I will not disappoint either of them.

My parents spend much of their time travelling, but always return home for their anniversary. It is understood amongst our family that they spend that day together, just the two of them. They swim in the morning, spend some time at their café in Sousse and then go to the small jewellers shop in the Medina. Since their wedding, each year my father buys my mother another charm for her bracelet, always the same one, a white enamel jasmine flower set in gold. Later they sit on the beach before joining us for dinner.

For me, it was many years before I married. My parents' act was a hard one to follow. I was sure if I waited there must be a girl somewhere in the world that I would love in the same way my father loved my mother. I found her in Elise, half English and half French, blonde like my mother. We have been blessed with twins, who, to their grandparents' delight we named Farid and Lucy. We spend most of our time here in Tunisia but travel often to England to see Elise's family.

Last year when my parents celebrated their wedding anniversary we decided it was time everyone got together. It was a wonderful evening, Elise and I, Rose and Wassif, as well as Alex, Sadie and their children came from England with my mother's friend M. My aunt Meriam was there with her family and my uncle Saleem with his tiny little wife and three children. I was happy to see that Ellen and Ali, Cathy and Sami all came with their families. It was a happy noisy affair and although it was clear my parents really had eyes only for each other, they sat hand in hand indulgently watching as three generations of friends and family honoured them.

It was not long afterwards when my mother said she felt a bit peculiar, as she put it. A few days later she suffered a stroke and was taken into hospital. Alex and Marie both flew over the next day. My father never left her side. She could only speak a little but made it clear she would not be parted from him and she just wanted to go home. As she was in a private room my father slept next to her, stretched out on the couch beside her. The doctor confided in me that he was concerned not only for his patient but for her husband.

"He doesn't eat unless she does and although he seems to sleep it is as though he sleeps with one ear open in case she should need him."

"Is she going to be alright?" I asked him.

The doctor looked at me gravely.

"If you mean, will she recover I can only be truthful and say just that I hope so. Her speech may be limited, although it has become clearer over the last few days. She should improve to a certain level but how far I don't know at this stage and to start with she will be unable to take care of herself and will need help eating and drinking."

My father frowned. "Can she come home?"

The doctor regarded him thoughtfully. "I don't think it is a good idea. A stroke is unpredictable and at least for the near future she will need constant attention. Do you think you can honestly provide that, would she not be better here?"

My father looked at him as though he was from another planet. "I will take care of her, I will always be there for her."

I was shocked at his appearance. He was unshaven, his face had an unhealthy grey tinge and the eyes which glared at the doctor were manically bright. I doubted he could even look after himself, without the burden of providing day and night care for my mother.

M put her arm around my father's shoulder. "Farid, I have no ties in England, I will stay if you will permit me. I have known Lucy almost as long as you have and I think sometimes she might like the company of a woman as well as a doting husband. Anyway," she added, "if you carry on like this I will end up looking after you as well, and that I am not prepared to do. I have no experience of looking after a man and I am too old to start now."

She peered over her spectacles at him and my father looked at her gratefully.

"Your offer is accepted, M and I would not dream of asking you to look after me, your strict regime would drive me quite mad!"

M grinned back, conscious that for the first time he had used Lucy's pet name for her. She nodded and he kissed her on both cheeks. I noticed she wiped away a tear when she thought no one was looking.

My father went back into my mother's room and we followed him. He sat on the bed holding her hand. She tried to say something and he bent his face close, his cheek resting against hers as he listened. Her white face pleaded with him and he sat back as he spoke, looking around at us.

"It is settled. My wife says she wants to go home."

That afternoon he drove my mother home to their beautiful white house. The evening air was warm and still, heavy with the scent of jasmine and he tucked her up in the chair so she could look out over her beloved garden. They spent most of their time outside although as the summer drew to a close the days were getting shorter and cooler and they were forced to retreat into the comfort of their home. She was much improved but her speech was still limited.

Alex had returned to England but came back as often as he could for the weekends. In October he said he was going to bring the family with him. My mother was adamant she would look her best. She vehemently refused the nurse's suggestion that if she cut her hair it would be much easier to manage. My father was horrified at the suggestion and roughly informed the nurse that it was his job, nor hers, to look after my mother's appearance and that included her hair. He loved nothing as much as gently combing through the soft waves until they lay around her shoulders like a shawl of pale gold, although now liberally laced with silver.

We left my mother with M and Rose when we went to the airport to meet Alex and his family. We were gone just over an hour. When we returned my mother was still where we had left her on the settee. Rose stood behind her smiling, her hands resting lightly on my mother's shoulders. M stood next to her, her arms folded, grinning like the Cheshire cat. My father stopped dead and stared at his wife.

She wore a deep red gypsy skirt and white frilled blouse which draped loosely and fell into soft tiers to her wrists. Marie had arranged her hair as my father liked it. Rose had skilfully made up her ashen face and painted her nails. My mother's eyes shone with happiness and her face was radiant.

My father walked slowly over to her and cupped her face in his hands as he kissed her.

"My darling, I have never seen you look more beautiful."

My mother look a deep breath and spoke slowly but clearly.

"I love you so much, Farid. I have always loved you and I always will."

He stood back, hesitated a moment and scooped her up in his arms. His laughter filled the room. He turned to Alex.

"Quick, your camera!"

He placed my mother gently back onto the settee and sat down beside her. He turned her face a little towards him, put his arm round her shoulder and cuddled her, his head resting lightly against hers.

Alex took the photograph and we all changed places for our photographs to be taken with them. My mother never stopped smiling.

It was a good week but I could see she was tired and I was secretly pleased when we took Alex and his family back to the airport.

I shook hands with my brother. He hesitated. "You will tell me if…"

"If there is any change I will call you."

Alex nodded and hugged me. "Take care of her Ben."

I laughed "If my father lets me."

Alex smiled, but I could see he was worried.

During the months that followed my mother improved a little. She could now speak and take care of her own needs, but we knew she would never walk again without a stick. She hated it but hated her lack of independence more and grudgingly agreed to use the offending object so they could leave the house. He drove her to all the places they loved. Their café permitted him to park alongside the tables and he would carry her to their table so she did not have to use the stick

M returned to England but made me a promise that if my mother needed her she would be on the first plane back. She accompanied Alex several times when he came to visit my mother and could not get over how much improved her friend appeared to be.

CHAPTER SIXTY-SEVEN

LUCY

It was the late the following summer when my mother suffered the second stroke and was again taken to hospital. This time the doctor's grim face told us what we had dreaded. My father was distraught. He sat talking to her but she couldn't hear him. She had been there about three days when she opened her eyes. My father was overjoyed, now she was going to get better again. He would not listen to anyone who told him otherwise.

"Is she getting better?" I asked the doctor.

He frowned. "In all honesty, no. The drugs may help temporarily but there is too much damage. Although her speech seems no worse, there has been no physical reaction to any stimulus down the whole of her left side. My opinion is that her body will not be able to cope and her heart will give out. Ben, I think you need to prepare for the worst."

Alex and Sadie travelled over immediately with M. I told them what the doctor had said, but I said nothing to my father. The doctor spoke to him alone. He refused to accept it. My mother was surrounded by machines and wires and looked so tiny, her pale face almost the colour of the single sprig of white jasmine my father had placed in the bud vase beside her bed.

We went into to see her one by one. Alex went first. When he came out he put his arms round me.

"It doesn't seem to have affected her speech like before and she is trying so hard, but Ben... Oh Christ, I know she is going and there is nothing I can do. I feel so helpless."

I put my arms round him. There was nothing to be said.

Rose and our father had grown even closer over the past year since my mother became ill. She and Wassif moved into the house and between them they had cared for my mother and father, the house and themselves. Now Rose refused to leave our mother's bedside. I saw them whispering together and my mother stroked her thick curls. It was only at my father's insistence that she lay down on the truckle bed in the corner of the room and went to sleep.

As I sat down beside my mother, one arm flopped down beside her and I gently tucked it back under the sheet.

She gave me a weak smile. "My children and my husband, I have been so blessed. I love you all so much."

I rested my head on her shoulder and her good hand stroked my arm. I felt like a little boy as I started to cry.

"No my darling you must be strong, you will soon have a little daughter. Oh Ben, I am so sorry I will never see the baby."

"Mum don't speak like that of course you will."

She smiled at me and raised her eyebrows. "I don't think so," she whispered. "What are you going to call her?"

I looked up at her. "Jasmine."

I noticed her eyes filled with tears and she breathed deeply taking in the scent of the flowers beside her bed.

"My darling, take care of your father and Rosie. You will need each other… and I will watch over you."

The light is very bright. The old ache in my shoulder is back, but along with it I have a strange numbness down my side. My head feels heavy as though it belongs to someone else but my mind is clear. There is a glorious sweet smell coming from the delicate flowers beside my bed. It is so familiar and reminds me of my home. I can feel someone holding my hand and his head rests on my chest. My arm feels like lead but I raise my other hand and stroke his thick black hair. He raises his face to me, his beautiful eyes bright with tears. I feel his lips touch mine and his cheek is wet. I want to comfort him but the words will not come. My head refuses to move but at least my eyes obey me. He sees me looking at the calendar on the wall. The tears stream down his face.

"It is the 7th of September," he whispers as he kisses me again. I can taste the salt and my lips are dry as I take the taste of his tears into my mouth. I manage a smile.

"My Lucy, stay with me my darling. I love you so much," I hear him say, his voice quivering.

"And I love you," I whisper back. Whether the words came from my mouth I don't know. I can hear them in my head and he smiles so I think he hears me.

I think back over our lives. I was an ordinary girl from an ordinary English family. An only child with ordinary aspirations of meeting Mr Right and producing my own ordinary children and living happily ever after. And then I came to Tunisia and on the 7th of September so many years ago my life changed forever when a boy smiled at me.

I think of our first meeting and the love that grew when we met again which I thought could never end. And then the wasted years when our own ignorance and stupidity and the prejudice and jealousy of others kept us apart and our last years when we have been as we should always have been, together.

His arms hold me close and I snuggle in to him feeling the warmth of him and the beating of his heart. My eyes are heavy. How tired I feel, I think I will sleep now.

CHAPTER SIXTY-EIGHT

THE PARTING

"Ben… Ben." I hear my sister's voice but I do not recall much of the rest of the day. We sat mutely in her room, my father lay on the bed, cradling her in his arms, whispering to her. Occasionally a tiny smile flickered on her face and she whispered back to him and then with a soft sigh she closed her eyes for the last time. The tears streamed down my father's face and eventually he had to be taken out of the room. He sat mutely on the chair his head in his hands murmuring to himself.

I drove him back to the house and still he said nothing. Elise and I stayed in the blue room which had always been mine, and Rose and Wassif in her room. Alex and Sadie had the last room. My parents had built the guesthouse in the grounds to accommodate their growing family but Alex was not happy about M staying there overnight.

"Ben, I think it would be better if Sadie and I stayed in the guesthouse. I am worried about your father. Marie is probably the only one of us who can talk any sense into him at the moment and I really think she should be on hand. Frankly I am not sure what he is likely to do, but if he does break down, Rose will probably join him and you and I are not going to be much use."

I thought about this and it made sense so M stayed in the house. My father refused food or water and curled up on the settee in the foetal position with his back to us. He refused to go upstairs and stayed on the settee throughout the night. When I came downstairs in the morning the room was completely silent. My father lay sleeping. The picture of my mother had gone from the wall and was clasped tightly to his chest. The sunlight filtered through the shutters, another beautiful day, mocking the misery of those inside the house.

M followed me into the room and walked out again into the kitchen taking me with her.

"Leave this to me, there are things which must be done and it is your father's responsibility, not his children's. Alex told me that Lucy is to have a Christian burial, am I right?"

I nodded. "Yes she respected my father's beliefs but she never converted, said it wouldn't be right to do so because they were his beliefs not hers. It was something they agreed on, so yes, it will be a Christian burial, which of course means we can all be there."

M smiled sadly. "I remember Lucy saying quite forcibly she didn't agree with the tradition of funerals being a men only thing, as if men alone had the right to say goodbye. She was very indignant about that."

"What about my father?"

She gave me a funny little look. "Let me deal with him."

She walked back into the living room and opened the shutters. The light streamed into the room and my father swore loudly. She ignored the outburst and faced him, her hands on her hips.

"Farid, is this what Lucy would have wanted? Lucy loved you, all of you. You were her life. If you believe that she is watching you, do you want her to be miserable, seeing you in the state you are in and she unable to comfort you? You have your family, you must live now for them, as she has always done for you. You have lost your wife, but her children have lost their mother. And now you have things to do, so get up."

I watched as my father sat up and angrily brushed his hair back from his face. His expression would have turned most people to stone. M was not one of those people. He stood up slowly until he towered over her. I held my breath. To my surprise he bent down and hugged her.

"M, Lucy always said you were a bossy cow!" She grinned at him.

"Get off me, you wretch." My father released her and stepped back his arms raised in mock defence.

"No worry, you're not my type."

Their eyes locked and M slowly put her arms round his waist and he held her close, his head resting on hers.

"So what now? I shall need some help from you, I'm afraid I'm a bit out of my depth with this."

"I know," she said gently patting his head like a child.

M made the calls to England. Jackie and Ewan, John and Hana Clark and Ruby James amongst them. My father said afterwards he was humbled to see how many of Lucy's friends from England had come over. "I never realised how many people she left behind her when she came here to me and gave up her life at home, she never spoke of it."

M muttered gruffly. "She loved you. That is all that mattered to her. She had a lot of years with us, the rest of her life she wanted to spend with you."

The day of the funeral was hot and the sun shone from a cloudless sky. Farid looked up at the sky. "She loved the sun," he whispered to no-one in particular. He said little but I was pleased to see that he nibbled a croissant which M banged down in front of him, followed by two cups of coffee. He looked up at her and she acknowledged him with a nod.

My mother was buried in a long white skirt and a lacy rose coloured blouse. Her hair was arranged in loose waves, framing her face. My father had insisted upon it. I asked him why. He smiled weakly at me. "It was the last thing she said to me. She wanted to be just as I first saw her."

The coffin was pale wood. My own posy of red roses, Alex's pink roses and Rose's freesia lay on top of an abundance of white jasmine. Their scent filled the quiet room. The service was short. M said Lucy was not one for long drawn out speeches. She said a few words about her friend and even that she had disapproved of my father on first acquaintance, but how for one of the few times in her life she had to admit she was completely wrong.

I knew my father dreaded having to speak. Alex, Rose and I sat in the front row watching him. Rose's hand gripped mine and she was crying. My father looked out over the sea of people, his hands resting lightly on the narrow shelf in front of him. He was dressed in a dark suit. His black hair streaked with silver was immaculate but his magnetic eyes were dull and lifeless. I could see his lip tremble but he spoke clearly in English. I was immensely proud of him.

"I fell in love with my wife the first day I saw her. I was almost fifteen years old."

I noticed with a smile that there were a few raised eyebrows, even those who thought they knew my mother well were unaware of that fact. He held his breath for a moment. "I knew then that this was the only woman I would ever love and I can say truthfully that this is still the same today."

He spoke briefly and I could see the strain telling as he turned to look at us. "My wife gave me three children. Two of my own blood and one I have been privileged to regard as my own. I have my family around me, I have grandchildren. I am an old man, but one who has been blessed with a love in my life that many will only dream about. I have my Lucy to thank for that and for that I can never repay her. She was my life, she is my life and she will always be my life."

No one could doubt the depth of feeling emanating from this man, standing alone speaking to so many people, many of whom he had never met. Rose was sobbing and he smiled sadly at her. Without shame, the tears trickled down his own cheeks as he turned and looked at the coffin. He held his head high as he walked back to his seat as the haunting melody of Simon and Garfunkel filled the room. It had been her choice "the music that brought me back to you" she told him.

He gripped my arm and whispered. "Ben, please get me out of here. I don't know how much longer I can hold on."

We stood beside the grave. The scent of the flowers was intense. My father's face was ashen and his mouth a hard line under his moustache. He knelt down and placed one arm across the coffin, resting his head near hers. Finally he kissed the hard wood which separated him from his beloved wife and I listened as he spoke to her in his own language, then he broke off a small piece of the jasmine which covered the coffin and put it in his pocket.

He stood up and turned to Elise and me, his face wet with tears. "I will always love her," he said simply.

There was nothing I could say. I put my arms around him and he held me close for a moment. I could smell the scent of the flowers on his jacket.

Elise kissed him on the cheek. "Do you mind me asking, what did you say to Lucy?"

My father smiled. "Why, sweetheart, just the same thing I said to her on the day I first saw her, almost fifty years ago."

Then he turned, took one last long look at the grave and walked away, his eyes fixed in front of him. He didn't look back.

Elise turned her puzzled face to mine. "Ben, tell me what he said."

I looked down at her and smiled. He said, "My name is Farid. Remember it beautiful lady and wait for me, for I love you and one day we will meet again, Insh'allah."